READER'S DIGEST CONDENSED BOOKS

Dogwood   *by William A. Bake*

READER'S DIGEST CONDENSED BOOKS

Volume 2
1990

THE READER'S DIGEST ASSOCIATION, INC.
Pleasantville, New York

CONTENTS

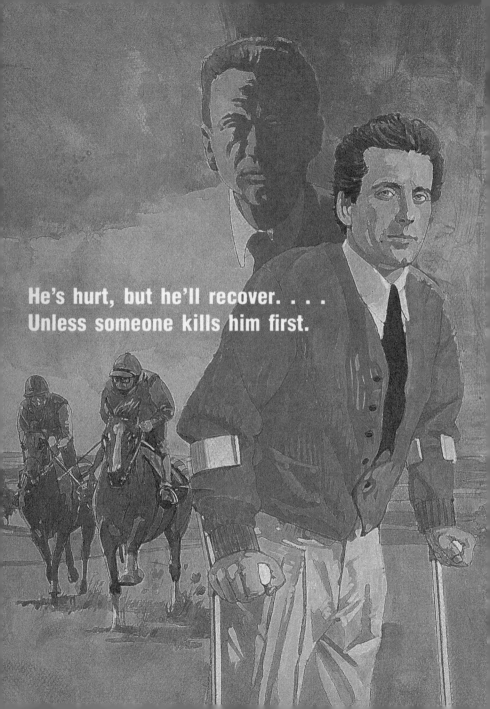

He's hurt, but he'll recover. . . .
Unless someone kills him first.

DICK FRANCIS
STRAIGHT

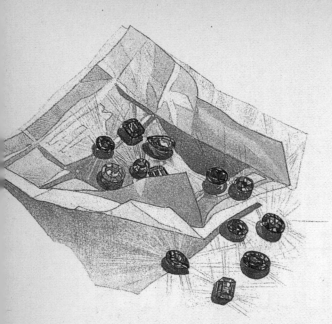

Derek Franklin is a champion jockey—
no stranger to hazards. He's already
hobbling around on a broken ankle from a
racing fall. But when his brother, Greville,
dies and bequeaths him a wealth
of assets—including a stunning
array of gemstones—Derek finds he's in
a very different, very deadly sort of contest.

Because someone is on his tail.
Someone who wants the fortune Derek
is only now discovering. And this dangerous,
unknown foe is determined that Derek
will not reach the finish line.

CHAPTER 1

I INHERITED my brother's life. Inherited his desk, his business, his gadgets, his enemies, his horses and his mistress. I inherited my brother's life, and it nearly killed me.

I was thirty-four at the time and walking about on elbow crutches owing to a serious disagreement with the last fence in a steeple-chase at Cheltenham. If you've never felt your ankle explode, don't try it. As usual, it hadn't been the high-speed tumble that had done the damage but the half ton of one of the other runners coming over the fence after me, his forefoot landing squarely on my boot on the baked earth of an Indian summer. The hoof mark was imprinted on the leather. The doctor who cut the boot off handed it to me as a souvenir. Medical minds have a macabre sense of humor.

Two days after this, while I was reluctantly coming to terms with the fact that I was going to miss at least six weeks of the season and with them possibly my last chance of making it to champion again (the middle thirties being the beginning of the end for jump jockeys), I answered the telephone for about the tenth time that morning and found it was not, as I'd expected, another friend ringing to commiserate.

"Could I speak," a female voice asked, "to Derek Franklin?"

"I'm Derek Franklin," I said.

"Right." She was both brisk and hesitant. "We have you

9

listed," she said to me, "as your brother Greville's next of kin."

Those three words, I thought with an accelerating heart, must be among the most ominous in the language.

"I'm speaking from St. Catherine's Hospital, Ipswich," she went on. "Your brother is here, in the intensive care unit. . . ."

At least he was alive, I thought numbly.

"And the doctors think you should be told."

I said slowly, not wanting to know, "What happened?"

"He was involved in a serious accident," she said. "He has multiple injuries and is on life support."

"I'll come," I said. I thanked her, not knowing what for, and put down the receiver, taking the shock physically in light-headedness and a constricted throat. He would be all right, I told myself. Intensive care meant simply that he was being carefully looked after. He would recover, of course.

I shut out the anxiety to concentrate on the mundane practicalities of traveling about a hundred and fifty miles across country— from Hungerford, in Berkshire, where I lived, to Ipswich, in Suffolk—with a crunched ankle. It was fortunately the left ankle, but on that particular day even with painkillers and ice packs the ankle was hot, swollen and throbbing. I couldn't move it without holding my breath, and that was partly my own fault.

Owing to my phobia about the damaging immobility of plaster of paris, I had spent a good deal of the previous day persuading a long-suffering orthopedic surgeon to give me a plain crepe bandage instead of a cast. He was himself a plate-and-screw man by preference and had grumbled at my request. A bandage might be better for one's muscles, he had reminded me, but it gave no protection against knocks, and it would be more painful.

"It's time you stop breaking your bones," he said with a sigh, winding the crepe on. "At least I haven't had to pin anything this time. Now go home and rest it. Give those ligaments a chance."

The ligaments took their chance in the back seat of my car while Brad, taciturn and obstinate, drove me to Ipswich. Brad made a scratchy living doing odd jobs in our neighborhood for anyone willing to endure his moods. As I much preferred his long silences to his infrequent conversation, we got along fine. He looked forty, hadn't reached thirty, and lived with his mother.

He found St. Catherine's Hospital without much trouble and helped me out and handed me the crutches, saying he would park and wait in the reception area. I knew that he would wait for hours, expressing neither impatience nor sympathy, as he had waited outside the doctor's office the day before.

The intensive care unit proved to be guarded by brisk nurses who looked at the crutches and said I'd come to the wrong department. But once I'd identified myself, they kitted me sympathetically with a mask and gown and let me in to see Greville. In the room the light was dim, the atmosphere peaceful, the noise level just above silence.

Greville lay on a high bed, with wires and tubes all over the place. He was naked except for a sheet lying loosely across his loins, and they had shaved half the hair off his head. Other evidences of surgery marched like centipede tracks across his abdomen and down one thigh, and darkening bruises were everywhere.

Behind his bed a bank of screens showed blank rectangular faces as the information from the electrodes fed into other screens in a room directly outside. He didn't need, they said, an attendant constantly beside him, but they kept an eye on his reactions all the time.

He was unconscious, his face pale and calm, his head turned slightly toward the door, as if expecting visitors. Part of his skull rested on a large, pillowlike dressing.

Greville Saxony Franklin, my brother. Nineteen years my senior: not expected to live. It had to be faced. To be accepted.

"Hi, guy," I said.

It was an Americanism he himself used often, but it produced no response. I touched his hand, which was warm and relaxed. He had a pulse; his heart beat by electric stimulus. Air went in and out of his lungs mechanically through a tube in his throat. Yet inside his head the synapses were shutting down. Where was his soul? Where was the intelligent, persistent, energetic spirit?

I didn't want just to leave him. No one should die alone.

I went outside and said as much to a doctor in a green overall, who replied that when all the remaining brain activity had ceased, they would ask my consent before switching off the machines. I was welcome to be with my brother at that crisis point as well as before. He paused. "There is a waiting room along the hall, with coffee and things," he said.

Bathos and drama, I thought; his everyday life. I crutched all the way down to reception, gave Brad an update, and told him I might be a long time. All night, perhaps.

I went back upstairs and found the waiting room occupied by a very young couple engulfed in grief, whose baby was hanging on to life by threads not much stronger than Greville's.

I listened to the mother's sobs and thought of the misery that soaked daily into those walls. Life has a way of kicking one along like a football, I've found. Fate had never dealt me a particularly easy time, but that was normal. Most people, it seemed to me, took their turn to be football. Most survived. Some didn't.

Greville had simply been in the wrong place at the wrong time. I gleaned from the hospital that he had been walking down Ipswich High Street when some dismantled scaffolding had fallen on him from a considerable height. One construction worker had been killed; a second had broken a leg.

I had been given my brother's clinical details. One metal bar had pierced his stomach; another had torn into his leg; something heavy had fallen on his head and caused massive brain damage. It had happened late the previous afternoon. He had been unconscious from the moment of impact and hadn't been identified until workmen clearing the rubble in the morning had found his diary and given it to the police.

"Wallet?" I asked.

No, just the diary, with, neatly filled in on the first page, "Next of Kin: Derek Franklin, brother." Telephone number supplied.

The afternoon stretched out, strange and unreal, a time-warped limbo. I spent more time with Greville, but he lay unmoving, oblivious in his dwindling twilight, already not himself. I thought of him as he had been and of our lives as brothers.

We had never lived together in a family unit. When I was born, he was away at university; by the time I was six, he had married; by the time I was ten, he'd divorced. For years he was a semi-stranger whom I met briefly at family gatherings which grew less and less frequent as our parents aged and died, and which stopped altogether when the two sisters between Greville and me both immigrated, one to Australia and one to Japan.

It wasn't until I'd reached twenty-eight myself that—after a long Christmas-and-birthday-card politeness—we'd met unexpectedly on a railway platform and during the journey ahead had become friends: not close, but enough to telephone each other sporadically, exchange restaurant dinners, and feel good about it.

We had been brought up in different environments, Greville in a Regency London house when our father managed a great landowning estate, I in the comfortable country cottage of his retirement. Greville had been taken to museums, art galleries and the theater; I had been given ponies. Greville best remembered our parents' vigorous years; I'd been with them through their illnesses and deaths.

We didn't even look alike. Greville was six feet tall, I three inches shorter. Greville's hair, now graying, had been light brown and straight, mine darker brown and curly. But we had both inherited amber eyes from our mother and leanness from our father.

Standing next to Greville's bed, I shifted uncomfortably on the crutches and thought of asking for a chair. Greville's stillness was absolute. I wouldn't see him smile again, I thought—not the lightening of the eyes and the gleam of teeth, the quick appreciation of the black humor of life, the awareness of his own power.

He was a magistrate, a justice of the peace, and he imported and sold semiprecious stones. Beyond these bare facts I knew few details of his day-to-day existence, as he always seemed more interested in my doings than in his own. He had himself owned horses from the day he telephoned to ask my opinion. Someone who owed him money had offered a racehorse to settle the debt. What did I think? I looked up the horse, thought it was a bargain, and told Greville to go ahead if he felt like it.

The horse had won handsomely and given him a taste for ownership, though he never went to see his horses run, which wasn't particularly unusual in an owner, but was always to me mystifying. He refused absolutely to own jumpers on the grounds

13

that he might buy something that would kill me. I was too big for flat races, so he'd felt safe with those. I couldn't persuade him that I would like to ride for him, and in the end I stopped trying. When Greville made up his mind, he was unshakable.

A NURSE came quietly into the room, checked that all the electrodes and tubes were still in order, and went away. I watched the pulse that flickered in my brother's throat, thinking how thin were the ties that linked us. When he was gone, I knew, I would go back to my own life, remembering this night with overall sorrow, but no more.

After a couple more hours I went along to the waiting room to rest my legs. The desperate young parents were still there, hollow-eyed and entwined, but presently a somber nurse came to fetch them, and in the distance, shortly after, I heard the rising wail of the mother's agonized loss. I felt my own tears prickle for her, a stranger. A dead baby, a dying brother. I grieved for Greville most intensely then, because of the death of the child, and realized I had been wrong. I would miss him very much.

I put my ankle up on a chair and fitfully dozed, and sometime before daybreak a nurse came to fetch me in my turn.

I followed her along the passage and into Greville's room. They had switched on the bank of monitoring screens behind the bed. Pale greenish lines moved across them, some in regular spasms, some uncompromisingly straight. The straight lines, of course, were the sum of the activity in Greville's brain. None at all.

There was no private good-bye. I was there, and that was enough. They asked for and received my agreement to the disconnection of the machines, and presently the pulsing lines straightened out also, and whatever had been in the quiet body was there no longer.

IT TOOK a long time to get any arrangements made in the morning, because it turned out to be Sunday.

I thought back, having lost count of time. Thursday I broke my ankle; Friday the scaffolding fell on Greville; Saturday Brad drove me to Ipswich. It all seemed a cosmos away.

Trying to make decisions, I realized I didn't know what Greville would want. Maybe he'd left a will somewhere with instructions. Maybe no one but myself, I thought with a jolt, actually knew he was dead. And I didn't know who to notify.

Presently I was given everything my brother had had with him: his diary, keys, watch, handkerchief, signet ring, a small amount of change, shoes, jacket. The rest of his clothes had been incinerated. Everything had been tipped out of a large brown plastic bag that said ST. CATHERINE'S HOSPITAL in white on the sides. I put the shoes, handkerchief and jacket back into the bag; then I shoveled the large bunch of keys into my trouser pocket, along with the watch, the ring and the money, and finally consulted the diary.

On the front page Greville had entered his name, his London home telephone number and his office number, but no addresses. Near the bottom, in a space headed "In case of accident please notify," he had written, "Derek Franklin, brother, next of kin." The diary itself was a racing diary I had sent him at Christmas, and that he should have chosen to use it I found unexpectedly moving. That he had put my name in it made me wonder what he had really thought of me—whether there was much we might have been to each other and had missed.

With regret I put the diary into my other trouser pocket. The next morning, I supposed, I would have to telephone his office with the dire news. I couldn't forewarn anyone, as I didn't know the people who worked for him. Indeed, I'd need his home address from them, as he had moved recently.

When I'd signed for everything I was taking, I looped the plastic bag strings around my wrist and crutched down to the reception area. Brad saw me, came over, and said, "Shall I fetch the car, then?" and when I nodded, he wheeled away. I followed slowly in his wake. I didn't seem to be thinking fast in any way.

Outside, the early October morning was bright and warm. I breathed the sweet air and patiently waited. I was totally unprepared to be savagely mugged.

One moment I was upright, leaning on the crutches, the next I received a battering-ram shove in the back and went sprawling face forward onto the hard black surface of the entrance drive. I put my left foot down instinctively, and it twisted excruciatingly beneath me. In a haze I fell flat on my stomach and hardly cared when someone tugged at the bag round my wrist.

He—it had to be a he, I thought, from the speed and strength—thumped on my back, yanked my arm up, and cut through the plastic with a slash that took some skin with it. I scarcely felt it. Messages from my ankle obliterated all else.

A voice approached, saying, "Hey! Hey!" urgently, and my attacker lifted himself off me and sped away.

It was Brad who had come to my rescue. On that Sunday morning no one else seemed to be around to notice a thing.

"Friggin' hell," he said from above me. "Your hand's bleeding." He helped me to my feet, adding, "We'd better go back into the hospital." As I didn't feel like arguing, that's what we did.

The woman behind the reception window was horrified. "Someone stole your plastic bag," she said, round-eyed. "Everyone around here knows what those bags are for. I mean, everyone knows they can contain valuables, but I've never heard of one being snatched. You'd better report it to the police."

The futility of it shook me with weariness. Some punk had taken a chance that the dead man's effects would be worth the risk, and the police would chalk it up as another unsolved mugging. I on my crutches had been a pushover, literally.

I shuffled painfully into the washroom and ran cold water over my bleeding hand, and found that the cut could sensibly be classified as a scratch. What a bloody stupid postscript, I thought, to the accident that had taken my brother.

Outside, Brad said with anxiety, "You going to the police?"

"Not unless you can give them a detailed description."

He shook his head, and when I asked him again on the way home, all he said was, "He had jeans on, and one of them woolly hats. And he had a knife. I didn't see his face—he sort of had his back turned my way—but the sun flashed on the knife, see? It all went down so fast. I did think you were a goner."

Brad, having contributed what was for him a long speech, relapsed into silence, and I wondered what the mugger would think of the worthless haul. Whatever of value Greville had set out with would have been in his wallet, which had fallen to an earlier predator.

I then began to wonder what Greville had been doing in Ipswich. Wondered if he had parked his car somewhere and, if so, how I would find it. I wasn't even sure if he still had a Porsche. Someone else would know, I thought, easily. His office, his local garage, a friend. It wasn't really my worry.

By the time we reached my home in Hungerford three hours later, Brad said that if I wanted him to go on driving me during the following week, he would be willing.

"Seven thirty tomorrow morning?" I suggested, reflecting, and he said, "Yerss," on a growl, which I took to mean assent.

He drove me to my door, helped me out, handed me the crutches, locked the car, and put the keys into my hand.

"Thanks," I said.

He ducked his head, not meeting my eyes, and turned and shambled off on foot toward his mother's house. I watched him go—a shy, difficult man with no social skills who had possibly that morning saved my life.

CHAPTER 2

I HAD for three years rented the ground floor of an old house in the ancient country town. There was a bedroom and bath facing the street and the sunrise, and a large room to the rear, into which the sun flooded. Beyond that, a small garden, which I shared with the owners of the house, an octogenarian couple upstairs.

Brad's mother had cooked and cleaned for them for years; Brad mended, painted, and chopped when he felt like it. Soon after I'd moved in, both had casually extended their services to me, which suited me well. It was all in all an easy, uncluttered existence. But if home was where the heart was, I really lived out on the raucous racetracks where I worked.

I let myself in and sat with ice packs, watching the sun go down. I should have stayed in the Ipswich hospital, as my left leg hurt abominably, and it was clear that falling had intensified Thursday's damage disastrously. In the end I took another Distalgesic.

At midnight I telephoned to Tokyo and Sydney, where it was already morning, and by good luck reached both of my sisters. There was a little long-distance grief. "Poor Greville," Susan and Miranda said sadly, and, "Do whatever you think best." "Send some flowers for us." "Let us know how it goes."

I would, I said. Poor Greville, they repeated, meaning it, and said they would love to see me, whenever. Their husbands were fine. Was I fine? Poor, poor Greville.

In the morning I dressed slowly, with a shoe on the right foot, sock alone on the left. Brad arrived five minutes early.

"We're going to London," I said. "Here's a map with the place marked. Do you think you can find it?"

"Reckon so." He helped me inch into the back seat and drove seventy miles through the heavy morning traffic. Then he zigged-zagged across Holborn and drew up with a jerk in a busy street around the corner from Hatton Garden.

"That's it," he said, pointing. "Number Fifty-six."

He helped me out, gave me the crutches, and came with me to hold open the heavy glass entrance door. Inside was a security guard who asked me forbiddingly what floor I wanted.

"Saxony Franklin," I said.

"Name?"

"Franklin."

"Your name, I mean."

I explained who I was. He raised his eyebrows, picked up a telephone, and said, "A Mr. Franklin is on his way up."

Brad was told he could park the car in a yard round the back. He would wait for me, he said. No hurry.

The office building, which was modern, rubbed shoulders to the sixth floor with Victorian curlicued neighbors, soaring free to the tenth with a severe lot of glass. Saxony Franklin was on the eighth floor. I elbowed my way through some heavy double doors into a lobby furnished with a reception desk, several armchairs and two policemen.

Behind them was a middle-aged woman who looked flustered.

I thought immediately that news of Greville's death had already arrived, but it seemed the force was there for a different reason.

The woman gave me a blank stare and said, "That's not Mr. Franklin."

I repeated that I was Greville Franklin's brother.

"Oh," said the woman. "Yes, he does have a brother." They all swept their gaze over my comparative immobility. "Mr. Franklin isn't here yet," the woman told me.

"Er . . . what's going on?" They looked disinclined to explain. I said to her, "I'm afraid I don't know your name."

"Adams," she said distractedly. "Annette Adams. I'm your brother's personal assistant."

"I'm sorry," I said slowly, "but my brother won't be coming at all today. He was involved in an accident."

Annette Adams heard the bad news in my voice. She put a hand over her heart. "What sort of accident? A car crash? Is he hurt?"

She saw the answer in my expression, and with her free hand felt for one of the armchairs, buckling into it with shock.

"He died in hospital yesterday morning," I said to her and to the policemen, "after some scaffolding fell on him last Friday."

One of the policemen pointed at my dangling foot. "You were injured at the same time, sir?"

"No. This was different. But I was with him in the hospital."

The two policemen consulted each other's eyes and decided after all to say why they were there. "These offices were broken into during the weekend, sir. Mrs. Adams here discovered it when she arrived for work. There's a good deal of mess, but we don't know what's been stolen. We were waiting for your brother."

"Oh dear, oh dear," said Annette, gulping. "What does it matter? It doesn't matter now."

"Is there anyone else here?" I asked her. "Someone who could get you a cup of tea?" Before you faint, I thought.

She nodded, glancing at a door behind the desk, but when I swung over and tried to open it, the knob wouldn't turn.

"It's electronic," Annette said weakly. "I can't remember today's numbers." She and the policemen had apparently come through and let it swing shut behind them.

One of the policemen pounded on the door, which had the desired effect. Without finesse he told the young woman who opened it that her boss was dead and that Mrs. Adams was about to pass out and was needing some strong, hot, sweet tea, love.

Wild-eyed, the young woman retreated to spread more consternation behind the scenes, and the policeman nullified the firm's defenses by wedging the electronic door open with a chair.

I took in more of the surroundings: the light greenish gray carpet, armchairs in charcoal and the desk in matte black unpolished wood. The walls, palest gray, were hung with black-framed geological maps, the doors painted the same gray. The total effect, lit by recessed lights, looked both straightforward and immensely sophisticated, a true representation of my brother.

Mrs. Adams, still flaccid from too many surprises on a Monday morning, wore a cream shirt, a gray skirt and a string of pearls. She was dark-haired, in her late forties, perhaps, and just beginning to realize that the present upheaval would be permanent.

The younger woman returned with a steaming scarlet mug, and Annette Adams sipped from it obediently, listening to the policemen tell me that the intruder had come up a lift at the rear to the tenth floor, climbed some service stairs to the roof, and by some means had come down outside the building to the eighth floor, where he had smashed a window to let himself in.

"What sort of means?" I asked.

"We don't know, sir. We've had only a quick look around. See, we don't want to waste our time for nothing. Hatton Garden is packed with the jewel trade. We get break-ins all the time."

The other policeman said, "Mrs. Adams says nothing seems to be missing from the stockrooms. And only Mr. Franklin has a key to the vault, which is still shut."

Mr. Franklin had no keys at all. They were in my own pocket. There was no harm, I supposed, in producing them.

But the sight of what must have been a familiar bunch brought tears to Annette Adams' eyes. She put down the mug, searched around for a tissue, and cried, "He really is dead, then," as if she hadn't thoroughly believed it before.

When she'd recovered a little, I asked her to point out the vault key, and we all left the reception area through the propped-open door and walked down a corridor with spacious offices to either side. Shocked faces looked out at us. We stopped at an ordinary-looking door that might have been mistaken for a cupboard.

"That's it," Annette insisted, so I slid the narrow key into the ordinary keyhole. The thick, heavy door swung inward, and a light came on automatically, shining in a large walk-in cupboard with rows of white cardboard boxes on shelves stretching away along the left-hand wall. Nothing seemed to have been disturbed.

"Who knows what should be in the boxes?" I asked, and got the expected answer: my brother.

I took the lid off one of the nearest boxes, which bore a label saying $MgAl_2O_4$, BURMA. Inside, there were about a dozen glossy white envelopes. I lifted one out to open it.

"Be careful!" Annette Adams exclaimed. "The packets unfold."

Clumsily balanced on the crutches, I handed it to her, and she unfolded it carefully. Inside, cushioned by white tissue, lay two large red translucent stones, cut and polished, oblong in shape, almost pulsing with intense color under the lights.

"Are they rubies?" I asked, impressed.

She smiled indulgently. "No, spinel. Very fine specimens."

"Any diamonds in here?" one of the policemen asked.

"No. We don't deal in diamonds."

I asked her to look into some of the other boxes, which she did, first carefully restoring the two red stones to their right place. There were clearly no dismaying surprises, and finally she said that nothing at all was missing as far as she could see.

If nothing was missing, the policemen had other burglaries to look into. They would put in a report but good-bye for now.

When they'd gone, Annette Adams and I looked at each other. "What do I do?" she said. "Are we still in business?"

I hadn't the foggiest. I said, "Did Greville have an office?"

"That's where most of the mess is," she said, leading me back to a large corner room near the entrance lobby. "In here."

I saw what she meant about mess. The contents of every drawer seemed to be out on the floor, most of it paper. Pictures had been removed from the walls and dropped. One filing cabinet lay on its side like a fallen soldier. The desk top was a shambles. I looked around. "How many people work here altogether?"

"Six of us. And Mr. Franklin, of course. . . . Oh dear."

"Is there anywhere I can meet everyone?"

She nodded mutely and led the way into another large office where the staff were already gathered, wide-eyed and rudderless— four women and two men, all uncertain and looking to me for decisions. Greville, I perceived, hadn't chosen potential leaders to work around him.

I introduced myself and described what had happened.

They had liked Greville; tears were shed on his behalf. I said I needed their help to notify people about his death—his solicitor and his accountant, for instance, and his closest friends, because I didn't know who they were. Annette went to fetch Greville's address book from his office but returned in frustration: in all the mess she couldn't find it.

"There must be other records," I said, sitting beside one of the desks. I pointed across the room. "What about in that computer?"

The girl who had brought the tea brightened a good deal and informed me that this was the stock-control computer, but there was another computer used for letters. She was out the door by the end of the sentence, and Annette remarked that June was a whirlwind always.

June, blond, long-legged, flat-chested, came back with a fast printout of Greville's ten most frequent correspondents (ignoring customers), which included not only the lawyers and the accountants but also the bank, a stockbroker and an insurance company.

"Terrific," I said. "Can you now get through to the big credit card companies and see if Greville was a customer of theirs? Say his cards have been stolen and that he's . . . deceased." I then asked if any of them knew Greville's car. They all did: a ten-year-old Rover 3500—without radio or cassette player, because his Porsche had been broken into twice and finally stolen.

"That old Rover's bursting with gadgets, though," the younger of the two men said, "but now he keeps them all locked in the boot." The young man had rows of badges attached to a black leather jacket, and orange spiky hair set with gel. A need to prove he existed, I supposed.

Greville had always been a sucker for gadgets, full of enthusiasm for the latest fidgety way of performing an ordinary task. When we'd met, he'd told me more about those toys of his than about his own human relationships.

The telephone rang on the desk beside me, and Annette picked up the receiver. She listened with a worried expression and then, covering the mouthpiece, asked me, "What shall I do? It's a customer who wants to give an order."

I said instinctively, "Just take the order."

She seemed glad of the direction and wrote down the list, and when she'd disconnected, I suggested that they should all take and send out orders in the normal way, and that if asked, say Mr. Franklin was out of the office and couldn't be reached. We wouldn't start telling people he was dead until after I'd found out our legal position. They were relieved, and agreed without demur. I sent everyone back to work.

I had a feeling of being sucked feetfirst into quicksand. All I knew about the jewelry business was where to find two red stones in a box marked $MgAl_2O_4$, BURMA. With office procedure beginning to tick again around me, I put a call through to the lawyers.

They were grave and sympathetic; they were at my service. I asked if Greville had made a will, if he had left any burial instructions. They looked up his files and found that indeed they had drawn up a will for him three years earlier. He had expressed no preference as to the disposal of his remains.

"Shall I just . . . go ahead, then?"

"Certainly," they said. "You are in fact named as your brother's sole executor. It is your duty to make the decisions."

Hell, I thought, and I asked for a list of the beneficiaries so I could notify them of the death and invite them to the funeral.

After a pause they said they didn't normally give out that information on the telephone, but they supposed there was no harm in my knowing. Greville's will was extremely simple; he had left everything to Derek Saxony Franklin, his brother. To my good self, in fact.

"What?" I said stupidly. "He can't have."

He had written his will in a hurry, they said, because he had been flying off to a dangerous country to buy stones. I felt the quicksand rising above my knees.

"Is it legal," I asked, "for this business to go on running?"

They saw no impediment in law. Subject to probate, the business would be mine.

I asked how long the probate would take.

Anything between six months or two years was the answer, depending on the complexity of Greville's affairs, the accountants and the inland revenue. Meanwhile, good luck.

Two years! I put the receiver down in sinking dismay. This business, like any other, might run on its own impetus for two weeks, maybe four, but after that . . . After that I would be back on horses.

Annette Adams asked anxiously if it would be all right to begin clearing up Mr. Franklin's office, and I said yes, thinking that her lack of drive could sink the ship.

Please would someone, I asked, mind telling the man in my car that I wouldn't be leaving for two or three hours, and June with her bright face whisked out and soon returned to relate that he would wait for me. Then she asked if I would like her to bring me a sandwich when she went out for lunch, and surprised and grateful, I accepted.

"Your foot hurts, doesn't it?" she said judiciously.

"Mm."

"You should put it up on a chair." She fetched one without ado and watched with a motherly air of approval as I placed my leg on it. She must have been all of twenty, I thought.

A telephone rang, and she went to answer it.

"Yes, sir, we have everything in stock. Yes, sir. What size and how many? A hundred twelve-by-ten-millimeter ovals. Yes. Yes." She tapped the lengthy order rapidly straight into the computer. "Yes, sir, they will go off today. Usual terms, sir, of course."

She hung up, printed the order, and laid it in a shallow tray. A fax machine simultaneously clicked on and whined away and switched off, and she tore the emergent sheet off and tapped its information also into the computer, making a printout and putting it into the tray.

"Do you fill all the orders the day they come in?" I asked.

"Oh sure. Within twenty-four hours without fail. Mr. Franklin says speed is the essence of good business."

She remembered with a rush that he would never come back. Tears welled in her uncontrollably, and she stared at me through them, which made her blue eyes look huge.

"You couldn't help liking him," she said. "Working with him, I mean."

I felt almost jealous that she'd known Greville better than I had, yet I could have known him better if I'd tried. Regret stabbed me again, a needle of grief.

Annette came to announce that Mr. Franklin's room was partially clear, so I transferred myself to Greville's luxurious black leather swiveling chair. As I smoothed a hand over the grainy black expanse of the oversized desk I felt like a jockey, not a tycoon.

Annette had retrieved some of Greville's army of gadgets, assembling them at one end of the desk, most of them matte black and small. Easily identifiable at a glance were battery-operated things like a pencil sharpener, a hand-held copier, and a printing calculator, but most needed investigation. I picked up one, a casing with a dial face plus a head like a microphone on a lead.

"What's this?" I asked Annette, who was picking up papers from the far reaches of the floor. "Some sort of meter?"

She flashed a look at it. "A Geiger counter," she said matter-of-factly.

I flipped the switch to ON, but nothing happened.

"A lot of stones change color for the better under radiation," Annette said. "They're not radioactive afterward, but Mr. Franklin was once accidentally sent a batch of irradiated topaz from Brazil that bordered on dangerous. It had come in without a radioactivity import license. He got the Geiger counter then." She paused. "He has an amazing flair for stones, you know."

Her face crumpled, and she blinked her eyes rapidly, turning away from me and making a great fuss among the papers. Finally, with a sniff or two, she said indistinctly, "Here's his desk diary,"

25

and then, more slowly, "That's odd—October's missing."

She stood up and brought me the diary, which proved to be a largish appointments calendar. The month on display was November, with only a few of the daily squares filled in. I flipped back the page and came to September.

"Has the address book turned up?" I asked.

"No." She was puzzled. "It hasn't."

It seemed bizarre that anyone should risk breaking in via the roof simply to steal an address book and some pages from a desk diary. Something else had to be missing.

I went along to the packing room and saw the efficient hole that had been smashed in the six-by-four-foot window. All the glass that must have been scattered over every surface had been collected and swept into a pile of dagger-sharp, glittering triangles, and a chill little breeze ruffled papers in clipboards.

You don't break glass this quality by tapping it with a fingernail, I thought.

WHILE glaziers fixed the window I watched the most senior of Greville's employees take transparent bags of beads from one cardboard box, insert them into bubble-plastic sleeves, and stack them in another cardboard box. The man, a white-haired grandfatherly figure in storemen's brown overalls, put a list of contents on top, crossed the flaps, and taped up the whole box.

"Where do the beads come from?" I asked.

"Taiwan, I daresay," he said, affixing a large address label.

"No. . . . I meant, where do you keep them here?"

He looked at me in pitying astonishment. "In the stockrooms, of course. Down the hall."

"Of course." I went back to Greville's office and asked Annette to show me the stockrooms. Her heavy face lightened with pleasure, and she led the way to the far end of the corridor.

"In here," she said with obvious pride, passing through a doorway into a small inner lobby. "There are four rooms." She pointed through open doorways. "In there, mineral cabochons, oval and round; beads; oddities; and in there, organics."

"What are organics?" I asked.

She beckoned me forward, and I walked into a windowless space lined from floor to shoulder height with columns of narrow gray metal drawers, each with an identifying label.

"Organics are things that grow," Annette said patiently. "Coral, for instance." She pulled open a drawer and showed me the contents: clear plastic bags, each packed with many strings of bright red twiglets. "The best coral comes from the Mediterranean." She closed that drawer, walked a few paces, pulled open another. "Abalone, from abalone shells." Another: "Ivory. We still have a little, but we can't sell it now." Another: "Mother-of-pearl. We sell tons of it. . . . Pink mussel. . . . Freshwater pearls."

She smiled at my bemused expression and led me next door.

Floor-to-shoulder-height metal drawers, as before, not only lined the walls but filled the center space with aisles.

Amethyst to turquoise via garnet, jade, lapis lazuli and onyx, with dozens of others I'd only half heard of. "Semiprecious," Annette said briefly. "All genuine. Mr. Franklin doesn't touch glass or plastic." She stopped. "Didn't," she said lamely.

His presence was there strongly, I felt. It was almost as if he would walk through the door, all energy, saying, "Hello, Derek, what brings you here?"

In the third stockroom a woman named Lily was pushing a brown cardboard box around on a trolley, collecting bags of beads and checking them against a list. With her center-parted hair drawn back at her neck, her small pale mouth and rounded cheeks, Lily looked like a Charlotte Brontë governess. She raised downcast eyes briefly to my face and, at Annette's prompting, told me she was putting together a consignment of rhodonite, jasper, aventurine and tiger-eye for a large jewelry manufacturer.

"We import the stones," Annette said. "We're wholesalers. We sell to about three thousand jewelers, maybe more. We're at the top of the semiprecious trade." She swallowed. "People trust us."

Greville, I knew, had traveled the world to buy the stones, but he'd never told me more than the destinations. I at last understood what he'd been doing. He couldn't easily be replaced.

Depressed, I went to telephone his insurance company and his bank.

They were shocked and they were helpful, impressively so. The bank manager said Saxony Franklin, as a limited company, could go straight on functioning. To the insurance company, also, my brother's death seemed scarcely a hiccup. I said I would like to claim for a smashed window. No problem.

After that I telephoned the Ipswich undertakers and arranged that Greville should be cremated. They said in a hushed, obsequious voice that they had "a slot" at two o'clock on Friday. Would that do? "Yes," I said, sighing. "I'll be there." I wondered what it must be like to do business always with the bereaved. Happier by far to sell glittering baubles or ride jump-racing horses at thirty miles an hour—win, lose, or break your bones.

I made yet another phone call, this time to my orthopedic surgeon. I said I'd fallen on my ankle and twisted it and I was running out of Distalgesic. "Be here at five," his receptionist said.

I said gratefully that I could, and reckoned I'd have to leave soon after two thirty to be sure of making it back home to Hungerford. I told Annette, and asked what they did about locking up.

"Well, the front double doors bolt on the inside. All the other doors have electronic bolts. Mr. Franklin changes—changed— the numbers at least every week." She paused. "The electronic locks are very simple, really. You only have to remember three digits. Mr. Franklin and I both have a key, though, if we need to unlock them manually."

"And the vault," I said. "Does that have any electronics?"

"No, but it has an intricate locking system in that heavy door. Mr. Franklin always locked the vault before he left. When he went away on long trips, he gave me the key."

We stared briefly at each other, and she lifted a face heavy with loss. "What will happen without Mr. Franklin?"

"I don't know yet," I said awkwardly, "but for now we keep to all the old routines and practices. Except you will arrive first and leave last, if you don't mind."

"That's all right. I always do when Mr. Franklin's away."

Back in Greville's office, I wrote down for her my own address and telephone number. "I'll come back here tomorrow after I've seen the bank manager. Will you be all right till then?"

She nodded shakily. "What do we call you? We can't call you Mr. Franklin. It wouldn't seem right."

"How about Derek?"

"Oh no. Would you mind, say, Mr. Derek?"

"If you prefer it." It sounded quaintly old-fashioned to me, but she was happy with it and said she would tell the others.

"About the others," I said. "Sort them out for me."

"June works the computers and the stock control," she said. "Lily fills the orders. Tina, she's a general assistant. She helps Lily and does some secretarial work. So does June. So do I. We all do what's needed, really, except Alfie just packs up orders."

"And that younger guy with the spiky orange halo?"

"Jason? Don't worry about the hair. He's harmless. He's our muscles. The stones are very heavy in bulk, you know. Jason shifts boxes, fills the stockroom, does odd jobs, and hoovers the carpets. But like I said, we all do anything."

Collective responsibility, I thought. From the look of the place, it worked, and I bowed to my brother's wisdom.

On my way out I closed and locked the vault door, gave Annette what I hoped was a reassuring smile, and rode down in the lift to find Brad.

Hell, I thought wearily, why did Greville have to die?

CHAPTER 3

THE orthopod—as I called him—x-rayed and unwrapped my ankle and tut-tutted. From toes to shin it looked hard, black and swollen, the skin almost shiny from the stretching.

"My brother died. . . ." I explained about the mugging and also about having to see to Greville's affairs.

He listened carefully, a strong, sensible man with prematurely white hair. I didn't know a jockey who didn't trust him. He said, "You've now completely ripped the lateral ligament, which normally binds the ankle together. The whole joint is insecure and coming apart inside."

"So how long will it take to heal?" I said.

He smiled briefly. "In a crepe bandage you could be back on a horse three weeks from now. Another three weeks after that, the ankle might be strong enough for racing. But don't fall on it again in the next month, or you'll be back to square one."

"I'll try not to," I said.

He bandaged it all tight again, from below the knee down to my toes and back, and gave me another prescription for Distalgesic, saying, "Remember—no alcohol with this." Then he thoughtfully went over to a cabinet that held packets and bottles of drugs. He came back with a small envelope, which he held out to me.

"I'm giving you three of something known as DF 118s. They are serious painkillers, not to be used unless something like yesterday happens again."

"Okay," I said, putting the envelope into my pocket. "Thanks."

"If you take one, you won't feel a thing." He smiled. "If you take two at once, you'll be high as a kite. If you take all three at once, you'll be unconscious, so be warned. They are a last resort."

"I won't forget," I said, "and I truly am grateful."

BRAD drove to a chemist's, got my prescription, and finished the ten miles home. Outside my door, I said, "Same time tomorrow morning," then let myself into the house.

I refueled with sardines on toast, then telephoned to the man in Newmarket who trained Greville's two present racehorses.

He picked up the receiver as if he'd been waiting for it to ring.

"Yes?" he said. "What are they offering?"

"I've no idea," I said. "Is that Nicholas Loder?"

"What? Who are you?" he said brusquely. Then, with more honey, "I beg your pardon, I was expecting someone else. I'm Loder, yes. Who am I talking to?"

"Greville Franklin's brother."

It meant nothing to him immediately. From what I knew of him, Loder was a big, light-haired man in his forties, with enormous presence and self-esteem. He was a good-to-great trainer but could be overbearing and condescending to his owners, I'd heard. Greville kept his horses with him because the original horse had been in that stable. Loder had bought Greville all his subsequent horses and done notably well with them, and Greville had assured me he got on well with the man.

I explained that Greville had died, and after the first sympathetic exclamations of dismay Loder reacted on a practical level.

"It won't affect the running of his horses," he said. "They're owned by Saxony Franklin, not by Greville himself. I have the company's authority to act. There should be no problem."

"I'm afraid there may be," I began.

"No, no. Dozen Roses runs on Saturday at York. In with a great chance. I informed Greville only a few days ago."

"The problem is," I said, "about my being his brother. He has left the Saxony Franklin company to me."

The size of the problem suddenly revealed itself to him forcibly. "You're not his brother *Derek* Franklin? The jockey?"

"Yes. So could you find out from Weatherby's whether the horses can still run while the estate is subject to probate?"

"My God," he said weakly. Professional jockeys, as we both knew well, were not allowed to own runners in races. "Dozen Roses should trot up on Saturday."

Dozen Roses was currently the better of Greville's two horses. A triple winner as a three-year-old, he had been disappointing at four, but currently, as a five-year-old, he had regained his old form and had scored three times in the past few weeks. A trot-up—a win—on Saturday was a reasonable expectation.

Loder said, "If Weatherby's give the thumbs-down, will you sell the horse? I'll find a buyer by Saturday."

Loder sounded a lot more fussed than seemed normal. "I don't know," I said cautiously. I realized that I didn't totally trust him, and it wasn't a doubt I'd have felt before the phone call. He was one of the top five flat-race trainers in the country, reliable because of his success.

"Greville's funeral is on Friday at Ipswich," I said. "What if I call in at Newmarket that day, as I'll be over your way, to see the horses and complete any necessary paperwork?"

"No," he said instantly. "I always discourage owners from visiting. They disrupt the stable routine. Greville and I only spoke by phone. If I need you to sign anything, I'll arrange it."

"All right," I agreed mildly, not crowding him into corners. "I'll wait to hear from you about what Weatherby's decide."

He said he would get in touch, and abruptly disconnected.

Perhaps I had been imagining things. But I knew I hadn't.

SHELVING the enigma of Loder's behavior, I pondered the persisting difficulty of informing Greville's friends.

He'd lived alone, as I did. He'd told me nothing about any love life. He'd said merely, "Bad luck" when three years earlier I'd remarked that my live-in girlfriend had gone to live in somewhere else. I'd asked him once about his long-divorced wife. "She remarried. Haven't seen her since," was all he'd said.

All I could do was tell his world—the semiprecious stone fraternity. I remembered I had his pocket diary then, even if his desk diary had lost October, so I went and fetched it from my bedroom. I turned the pages of the slim brown book, seeing only short entries like "R arrives from Brazil" and "B in Paris" and "Buy citrine for P."

In March I was brought up short. Because it was a racing diary, the race meetings were listed under the day's date. I came to Thursday, March 16, which listed "Cheltenham." The word Cheltenham was ringed in pen, and Greville had written "Gold Cup" in the day's space, then the words "Derek won it!"

It brought me to sudden tears. I couldn't help it.

I longed for him to be alive so I could get to know him better. I wept for the lost opportunities, the time wasted. I longed to know the brother who had cared what I did, who had noted in his almost empty diary that I'd won one of the top races of the year.

THERE was only one telephone number in the address section at the back, identified merely by the initials NL. Nicholas Loder.

I looked again at what few entries Greville had made. He had noted the days his horses had run, again only with initials. DR, Dozen Roses, appeared most, each time with a number following, like 300 at 8s, which I took to mean the amounts he'd wagered at what odds. Greville's second horse, Gemstones, or G, had run six times, winning only once but profitably—500 at 100/6.

Out of curiosity I flicked through the book and came across a lot of doodling and then a list of numbers. The doodling was the sort one does while listening on the telephone, a lot of haphazard boxes and zigzags. On the page facing, there was an equation: $CZ = C \times 1.7$. I supposed it had been of sparkling clarity to Greville, but it was of no use to me. The numbers overleaf were the sort I kept in my own diary: passport, bank account, national insurance. Down the page, in small capital letters, was the single word DEREK. Another jolt, seeing it again in his writing.

I wondered briefly if Greville had used my name as some sort of mnemonic. There was no way to tell. Sighing, I riffled back through the pages and came to an entry for the day before his death.

"Koningin Beatrix?" he had written. I wondered idly if it was the name of a horse. Then I thought that perhaps he'd written the last name first, and that he'd been going to Ipswich to meet a Beatrix Koningin, but directory enquiries told me that no Koningin lived anywhere around there.

I returned to the horse theory and got through to Milo Shandy, the trainer I'd ridden most for the past three seasons. He inquired breezily about the ankle and said would I please waste no time in coming back.

"I could ride out in a couple of weeks," I said, and then asked about Koningin Beatrix, spelling it out.

"Don't know of any horse called that, but I can find out. By the way, I heard your brother died. Bad luck."

"Yes. . . . How did you know?"

"Nicholas Loder just rang me, explaining your dilemma and wanting me to persuade you to lease him Dozen Roses."

"But that's crazy. His ringing you, I mean."

He chuckled. "I told him I could bend you like a block of teak. Anyway, leasing wouldn't solve anything. Jockeys can't own racing horses, period. If you lease a horse, you still own it."

"Loder bets, doesn't he?" I asked. "In large amounts?"

"So I've heard." Milo told me to get some massage for my ankle, then added, "Well, take care."

I put down the phone, smiling at his farewell. Jump jockeys were paid not to take care. Milo would be horrified if I obeyed him.

IN THE MORNING BRAD DROVE me to Saxony Franklin's bank to see the manager, who was young and bright and spoke with deliberate slowness, as if waiting for his clients' intelligence to catch up. He told me Greville had borrowed a sizable chunk of money, and he would be looking to me to repay it. "One point five million United States dollars. In cash."

"One point five million dollars," I repeated. *"What for?"*

"For buying diamonds. Diamonds from the DTC of the CSO are, of course, normally paid for in cash, in dollars." Bank managers around Hatton Garden, it seemed, saw nothing extraordinary in such an exercise.

"He doesn't . . . didn't deal in diamonds," I protested.

"He had decided to expand, and of course we made the funds available. Your brother was a careful and conscientious businessman. A valued client. We have always been repaid punctiliously." He cleared his throat. "The present loan, taken out three months ago, is due over five years, and as the loan was made to the company, the terms are unchanged by his death."

"Do you hold security for the loan?" I asked.

"We lent the money against the stock of Saxony Franklin."

"All the stones?"

"As many as would satisfy the debt."

He produced papers for me to sign. He didn't ask what experience I'd had in running a business. Instead, he wished me luck.

I rose to my crutches and shook his hand, thinking of the things I hadn't said. I hadn't told him I was a jockey. And I hadn't told him that if Greville had bought one and a half million dollars' worth of diamonds, I didn't know where they were.

"DIAMONDS?" Annette said. "No. I told you. We never deal in diamonds."

We were in Greville's office, I in his swivel chair, Annette sorting yesterday's roughly heaped papers back into the drawers.

"The bank manager believes Greville bought some recently," I said to her. "From something called the DTC of the CSO."

"That's the De Beers Central Selling Organization. The DTC is their Diamond Trading Company. But he can't have done."

"Well, has your stock increased in the last three months?"

"It usually does," she said. "Mr. Franklin comes back from world trips with new stones all the time. He can't resist them. He sells the special ones to a jewelry designer who has several boutiques—Knightsbridge, Bond Street. Gorgeous costume jewelry but with real stones. One-offs, designed for a single stone."

"Who is the designer?"

"Prospero Jenks," she said impressively.

I hadn't heard of him, but I nodded all the same. "Does he use diamonds?"

"Sometimes. But he doesn't buy those from us."

"You don't think Greville would ever have kept diamonds in this actual office, do you?" I asked.

"Certainly not." The idea shocked her.

June, with her incongruous motherliness, brought in a chair for my foot. I asked if her stock-control computer kept day-to-day tabs on the number and value of all the stones.

"Goodness, yes," she said with amusement. "You name it, the computer will tell you what we've got and what it's worth."

"But no diamonds?"

"No. We don't deal in them." She gave me a bright, incurious smile and swiftly departed, saying over her shoulder that they'd been bombarded by Christmas rush fax orders overnight.

"Who reorders what you sell?" I asked Annette.

"I do, for ordinary stock. June tells me what we need. Mr. Franklin ordered the faceted stones and anything unusual."

She went on sorting the papers, basically unconcerned. Solid but not large, she had a settled, well-groomed, middle-aged air.

The telephone rang, and I answered it. A male voice said, "I want to speak to Mr. Franklin, please."

"Er . . . could I help? I'm his brother."

"This is the clerk of the West London Magistrates Court. Your brother was due here twenty minutes ago, and it is unlike him to be late. Could you tell me when to expect him?"

"Just a minute." I put my hand over the mouthpiece and told Annette what I'd just heard.

Her eyes widened in horrified memory. "It's his day for the

35

bench! He sits on alternate Tuesdays. I'd clean forgotten."
I returned to the phone and explained the situation.

"Oh. Oh. How dreadfully upsetting." He did indeed sound upset, but also a shade impatient. He said good-bye gloomily, and I sighed to Annette that we had better begin telling everyone else as soon as possible, but the trade was to expect business as usual.

We began with a notice in *The Times*. I wrote out a brief paragraph that ended with "Cremation, Ipswich, Friday, two p.m."

"Have you any idea," I asked Annette, "what he could have been doing in Ipswich?"

She shook her head. "I've never heard him mention the place. But then he used to say that the best security was a still tongue. He asked us not to talk about our jobs to strangers. People in the trade are security mad, and the diamantaires can be paranoid."

"What are diamantaires?"

"Not what, who," she said. "They're dealers in rough diamonds. They get the stones cut and polished and sell them to manufacturing jewelers." She paused. "I'm sure the bank manager must be wrong. Mr. Franklin would never have bought diamonds."

If he hadn't bought diamonds, I thought, what the hell had he done with one point five million dollars in cash?

The telephone rang again, and this time Annette answered it.

"Saxony Franklin. . . . I'm very sorry, you won't be able to talk to Mr. Franklin. . . . Could I have your name, please?" She listened. "Well, Mrs. Williams, we must most unhappily inform you that Mr. Franklin died as a result of an accident over the weekend. We are, however, continuing in business. Can I help you?"

She listened in increasing puzzlement, then said, "Mrs. Williams?" She put the receiver down, frowning. "She hung up. I don't know her, but she has a voice you don't forget."

"Why not?"

"Cut glass," she said succinctly. "Like Mr. Franklin."

I was amused, though I wondered briefly about the cut-glass Mrs. Williams who hadn't asked where, or how, or when Greville died.

My ankle heavily ached—the result, I daresay, of general depression as much as aggrieved bones and muscle. I was worried. I'd never before handled finances bigger than my own bank balance, and the only business I knew was training racehorses. In Greville's world I could be taken for a ride and never know it.

Greville's great black desk stretched away, flanked by twin stacks of drawers. I began desultorily to investigate the nearest on the left. I first found the toys—the small black gadgets now tidied away into serried ranks. I picked out a small black contraption about the size of a paperback book.

"That's an electric measurer," June said, breezing into the office with her hands full of paper. "It'll tell you how far it is from the desk to the ceiling. Mr. Franklin got it when he was redesigning the stockrooms."

"You like computers, don't you?" I said.

She laughed. "Love them. All shapes, all sizes. Mr. Franklin was always buying the tiny ones." She picked out one the size of a pack of cards. "This little dilly is a travel guide. It tells you things like phone numbers for taxis, airlines, tourist information." She demonstrated, pushing buttons happily.

"Where did he get all these things from?" I asked.

"Mail-order catalogues, mostly." Then she looked at me curiously. "Alfie says," she said slowly, "that there's a steeplechase jockey called Derek Franklin." She looked at my foot as if with new understanding. "Champion jockey one year, he said. Always in the top five. Is that . . . you?"

I said neutrally, "Yes."

"I *had* to ask you," she said. "Annette said Mr. Franklin never mentioned anything about you being a jockey. She only knew he had a brother he saw a few times a year." She paused. "But yesterday, after you'd gone, Alfie said—they all said—they didn't see how a jockey could run this business. If you were one, that is."

I was faintly surprised. "You tell Alfie and the others that if the jockey doesn't run this business, their jobs will be down the tubes and they'll be out in the cold before the week's over."

Her blue eyes widened. "You sound just like Mr. Franklin!"

"And you don't need to mention my profession to the customers, in case I get the same vote of no confidence."

Her lips silently shaped the word wow. She disappeared fast from the room and presently returned, followed by all the others, who were only too clearly in a renewed state of anxiety.

I said to them, "You all look as if the ship's been wrecked. Well, we've lost the captain, and I agree we're in trouble. My job is with horses, but this business is going to stay open and thrive. One way or another I'll see that it does. I'm not my brother, but I'm not a fool either. So just let's get on with the orders and, er, cheer up."

Lily said meekly, "We don't really doubt your ability—"

"Of course we do," interrupted Jason. He stared at me with a snigger. "Give us a tip for the three thirty, then."

I listened to the street-smart bravado that went with the spiky orange hair. He thought me easy game.

"When you are personally able to ride the winner of any three thirty," I said, "you'll be entitled to your jeer. Until then, work or leave. It's up to you."

There was a resounding silence. Alfie and Tina almost smiled. Jason looked merely sullen. Annette took a deep breath, and June's eyes were shining with laughter.

They all drifted away silently, and I listened to the echo of my own voice saying I wasn't a fool. Until the diamonds were found or I'd lost all hope of finding them, I thought it more essential than ever that Saxony Franklin Ltd. should stay afloat. All hands, I thought, to the pumps.

June came back and said tentatively, "The pep talk seems to be working. Alfie gave Jason a proper ticking off, and Jason's staying. What can I do to help?"

I looked at her thin, alert face and realized that without her the save-the-firm enterprise would be a nonstarter.

"How long have you worked here?" I asked.

"Three years. And I love the job. What can I do?"

"Look up diamonds in your stock computer's memory."

She was briefly impatient. "I told you, we don't deal in diamonds." But she shrugged and was gone. I got to my feet—foot— and followed her, and watched while she expertly tapped her keys.

"Nothing at all under diamonds," she said finally.

"Do you happen to know the chemical formula for diamonds?"

"Yes," she said instantly. "It's C. Diamonds are pure carbon."

"Could you try again, then, under C?"

She tried. There was no file for C.

I pondered, staring at the blank, unhelpful screen. "Are there," I asked eventually, "any secret files in this?"

She stared. "We never use secret files."

"But if there were, would you know that they were there?"

She nodded briefly. "I could find out. But what do I look for?"

"Diamonds. My brother said he was going to buy them, and I need to know if he did. If he made a private file, I need to find it."

She shook her head but tapped away obligingly. Finally, frowning, she found something that gave her pause. The screen was showing the word password.

"I don't understand," she said. "We gave this computer a general password, which is Saxony, but you can put in any password you like on any particular document, to supersede Saxony. This entry—Pearl—was made only a month ago. The date is on the menu. But whoever made it didn't use Saxony as the password. The password could be anything, literally."

I said, "By document you mean file?"

"Yes, file. Every document has a name—say, Oriental Cultured Pearls. If I load that name onto the screen, I can review our whole stock of those pearls. But this document with an unknown password is listed under Pearl, singular, and I didn't put it there."

"Have another try to guess the password."

June tried Franklin and Greville, without result. "It could be *anything*," she said helplessly.

"Try Dozen Roses—Greville owned a racehorse with that name. And another one called Gemstones."

"Really? He never said." She tried Dozen Roses and then Gemstones. Nothing, except another demand for the password.

"Why would he enter something under Pearl?" I asked. "What is a pearl? Does it have a formula?"

"Oh." She suddenly sat up straight. "It's one of the birthstones for the month of June," she said. "I could try it, anyway."

She typed June, and the screen flashed up its secrets.

We hadn't found the diamonds. But the screen said:

June, if you are reading this, come straight into my office for a raise. You are worth your weight in your birthstone, but I'll only increase your salary by twenty percent. Regards,

Greville Franklin.

"Explain," I said as June sat transfixed.

"One morning . . . " She stopped, her mouth screwing up in an effort not to cry. "One morning he told me he'd invented a little puzzle, and he would give me six months to solve it. Then it would self-destruct. I looked everywhere, even in the computer, but I just never thought it would be filed as a secret. My eyes just slid over the word Pearl, as I see it so often. Silly of me."

"I don't think so, and I'll honor my brother's promise."

She gave me a swift look of pleasure but shook her head. "You found it." She hesitated. "How about ten percent?"

"Twenty," I said firmly. "I'm going to need your help. And if Annette is personal assistant, as it says on her door, you can be deputy personal assistant, with a new salary."

She blushed, pressed a few buttons, and the screen went blank.

I asked her if she would print out first a list of everything currently in the vault, and then as many things as she thought would help me understand the business better, like the volume and value of a week's sales and which items were most popular, which least.

She began tapping keys. "I'll print you a crash course."

"Thanks." I smiled and waited while the printer spat out a gargantuan mouthful of glittering facets. Then I took the list and asked Annette to give me a quick canter round the vault.

"You don't seem like a jockey," she said faintly.

"On the whole," I said mildly, "jockeys are like anyone else. And you're stuck with me. Twist of fate. Do your best for the poor fellow."

She involuntarily smiled a genuine smile. "All right."

In the vault, she showed me that besides its chemical formula, each label bore a number. If I looked at that number on my list, I would see the formulas and the names of the stones, with colors, shapes and sizes and country of origin.

"Why did he label them like this?" I asked Annette. "It just makes it difficult to find things."

"I believe that was his purpose," she answered. She smiled and pointed to a row of boxes. I looked at the labels and read $CuAl_6(PO_4) 4 (OH)_8.4-5(H_2O)$ on each of them.

"Enough to put anyone off for life," I said.

"Exactly. Mr. Franklin could read formulas as easily as words, and I've got used to them myself now. No one but he and I handle these stones in here. We pack them and seal them ourselves before they go to Alfie for dispatch." She did her best to educate me. "We sell these stones at so much per carat. A carat weighs two hundred milligrams, which means five carats to a gram, a hundred and forty-two carats to an ounce, and five thousand—"

"Stop right there," I begged. "Give me a day or two on this."

She nodded and said she had better get on with the ledgers.

Ledgers, I thought, wilting internally. I hadn't even started on those.

It was by that time four o'clock in the afternoon of what had seemed a very long day. I went back to Greville's office and dialed Nicholas Loder's number. He came on the line with almost none of the previous evening's agitation.

"Weatherby's told me there's no problem," he said easily. "Before probate the horses belong to Saxony Franklin Limited, and they will not bar them from racing."

"Good," I said.

"They say, of course, that the company has to appoint at least one registered agent to be responsible for the horses, and as your brother appointed both himself and myself, I can now act for the company on my own."

"Ah," I said.

"So," Loder said happily, "Dozen Roses runs at York."

"And trots up?" As he chuckled confidently I added, "I'd be grateful if you could let Saxony Franklin know whenever the horses are due to run in the future."

He sounded reluctant, but I read out the office phone number.

"Don't forget, though," he said, "that there's only a month left of the flat season. They'll probably run only once more each.

41

Then I'll sell them for you; that would be best. Leave it to me."

He was right, logically, but I still disliked his haste.

"As executor I'd have to approve any sale," I said, hoping I was right. "In advance."

"Yes, yes, of course." Reassuring heartiness. "Well, good-bye, then." He put down the receiver in great good humor and left me wondering what I'd missed.

A call then came in from a man who introduced himself as Elliot Trelawney. He was a colleague of Greville's from the West London Magistrates Court and had heard about Greville's death. He asked if I could meet him for a drink the next evening.

I thought a bit, agreed, then hung up and asked Annette if she would mind phoning Prospero Jenks in the morning. "Tell him about Greville and ask if I can go to see him to discuss the future. Just say I'm Greville's brother, nothing else."

She grinned and said she would make the call.

I levered myself upright and said I'd see her tomorrow.

Going down the passage, I stopped to look in on Alfie, whose day's work stood in columns of loaded cardboard boxes waiting to be entrusted to the post.

"How many do you send out every day?" I asked him.

He looked up briefly from stretching sticky tape round yet another parcel. "About twenty, twenty-five regular, but more from August to Christmas. Twenty-eight so far today."

"Do you bet, Alfie?" I asked. "Read the racing papers?"

He glanced at me defiantly. "I *knew* you was him," he said.

"You know Dozen Roses too?"

A tinge of craftiness took over in his expression. "Started winning again, didn't he? I've had a little tickle since."

"He runs Saturday at York. Nicholas Loder says he'll trot up."

Alfie knew who Nicholas Loder was; didn't need to ask. He must have been well into his sixties, I thought, with deep lines in his face. His dark-veined hands were nimble and strong, however. A tough old customer, and essentially more in touch with street awareness than the exaggerated Jason.

"Wouldn't put my shirt on it. Mr. Franklin's horses run in and out," he said pointedly. "As a jock you'd know about that."

Before I could decide whether or not he was intentionally insulting me, Annette came hurrying down the passage, calling my name.

"Derek? Oh, there you are. Phone call for you." I followed her back to Greville's office, noticing she'd dropped the mister from my name now that I was established as a jockey.

I picked up the receiver. "Hello? Derek Franklin speaking."

A familiar voice said, "Thank God for that."

It was Milo Shandy, calling from Lambourn.

"I've a crisis on my hands," he bellowed urgently. "The Ostermeyers have flown over from Pittsburgh, and I told them Datepalm is for sale, and if they buy him, I can keep him here. And they want you here first lot tomorrow when they see him work on the downs. So for God's sake, *come*."

Interpreting the agitation was easy. Datepalm was the seven-year-old horse on which I'd won the Gold Cup. Its owner was leaving England, and if Milo could sell Datepalm to one of his other owners, she wouldn't send it to public auction. Milo had been in a panic since then because none of his other owners had thought the horse worth the astronomical asking price. But he and I thought Datepalm better than his press.

"Calm down," I assured him. "I'll be there."

"Thanks, Derek." His voice dropped to normal decibels. "Oh, by the way, there's no horse called Koningin Beatrix. Weatherby's say it means Queen Beatrix, as in Queen of the Netherlands. They frown on naming racehorses after royalty."

"Oh," I said. "Well, thanks for finding out."

"Anytime. See you in the morning. Don't be late."

"What I need," I said to Annette, putting down the receiver, "is an appointments book."

She began looking through the drawerful of gadgets, but without result. "Mr. Franklin had an electric memory thing you could use," she said. "I'll ask June where it is."

She went away busily, and I thought about how to convince the Ostermeyers, who could afford anything they set their hearts on, that Datepalm would bring them glory, if not necessarily bucks.

An alarm like a digital-watch alarm sounded faintly, muffled. I

43

opened the gadget drawer to investigate, but it stopped. Shrugging, I closed the drawer again, and Annette came back.

"June doesn't know where the Wizard is," she said.

"What's the Wizard?" I asked.

"A baby computer. It's about the size of a paperback book and it was Mr. Franklin's favorite object. He took it everywhere."

"Maybe it was stolen in the break-in," I said.

She stared at me. "But the thief would have to have known what it was. It folds up flat. You can't see any buttons."

"All the gadgets were out on the floor, weren't they?"

"Yes." It troubled her. "Why the address book? Why the engagements for October? Why the Wizard?"

Because of diamonds, I thought instinctively.

"I'll get here a couple of hours late tomorrow," I said to Annette. "If you reach Prospero Jenks, arrange for me to see him soon. Write off Friday because of the funeral."

Greville had died only the day before yesterday, I thought. It already seemed half a lifetime.

I RODE down in the service lift and swung across to Brad in the car. He hopped out of the front seat and shoveled me into the back, tucking the crutches in beside me.

"Home?" he said.

"No. We'll stop in Kensington for a while, if you don't mind."

He gave the tiniest of nods. I'd provided him in the morning with a map of West London to work out where Greville had lived.

We neared the area, and Brad drew up so confidently outside Greville's address that I wondered if he had reconnoitered earlier. He handed me the crutches, opened the gate of the small front garden, and said loquaciously, "I'll wait in the car."

"I might be an hour or more," I told him. "Would you mind having a quick recce round here to see if you can find an old Rover with this number?" I gave him a card. "My brother's car," I said.

He headed off, and I looked up at the tall town house Greville had moved into three months ago. It was creamy gray, gracefully proportioned, with balustraded steps leading up to the black front door, and businesslike but decorative grilles behind every window.

There were three locks on the door. Cursing slightly, I yanked out Greville's half ton of keys and by trial and error found the way into his fortress.

Late afternoon sun slanted yellowly into a long drawing room on the left of the entrance hall. The walls, pale salmon, were adorned with vivid paintings of stained-glass windows, and the furniture was covered in a confusing dark brown and white herringbone. The drawing room was dustless and tidy, unlived in.

I returned to the front hall and went through a door at the rear. This opened into a much smaller room filled with a homely clutter of books, newspapers, magazines, black leather chairs, a tray of booze, framed medieval brass rubbings on deep green walls. This room was all Greville, I thought. This was home.

I left it for the front hall again and hopped downstairs to the semibasement, where a decorator-style dining room looked out to a rear garden, a narrow, spotless kitchen alongside.

Fixed to the fridge by a magnetic strawberry was a note:

Dear Mr. Franklin,

I didn't know you'd be away this weekend. I brought in all the papers, they're in the back room. You didn't leave your laundry out, so I haven't taken it. Thanks for the money. I'll be back next Tuesday as usual.

Mrs. P.

I found a ballpoint, pulled the note, and wrote on the back, asking Mrs. P. to call Saxony Franklin and speak to Derek or Annette. I put it back under the strawberry, a sorry message in waiting.

Then I hauled myself up to the hall again and went on upstairs, where there was a bedroom and bathroom suite in self-conscious black and white. Greville had slept there. He had been sparing in his possessions, leaving in the built-in cupboard a single row of shoes, several white shirts on hangers, six assorted suits and a rack of silk ties.

There was little else to see. The bedside table drawer revealed indigestion tablets and a paperback. No gadgets, no treasure maps. Anything interesting seemed likely to be found in the small back sitting room, so it was to there that I returned.

I sat for a while in the chair that was clearly Greville's favorite. Places that people had left forever should be seen through their eyes, I thought. Greville's presence was strong in that room. Beside the chair was a small table with a telephone and an answering machine. A red message light was on, so I pressed REWIND and then PLAY.

A woman's voice spoke without preamble. "Darling, where are you? Do ring me."

There was a series of between-message clicks, then the same voice again, this time packed with anxiety.

"Darling, please, please ring. I'm very worried. Where are you, darling? *Please* ring. I love you."

Again the clicks, but no more messages. Poor lady, I thought. Grief and tears waiting in the wings.

I got up and explored the room more fully. Two drawers in a table beside the window contained two baffling small black gadgets, which I stowed in my pockets, and a tray containing a rather nice collection of small bears, polished and carved from shaded pink, brown and charcoal stone. I laid the tray on the table next to a box made of greenish stone, also polished, and, true to Greville's habit, firmly locked. I brought out the bunch of keys again and began to try the smallest in it.

I was balancing on one foot and leaning a thigh against the table, my arms out of the crutches, intent on what I was doing and disastrously unheeding. The first I knew of anyone else in the house was a muffled exclamation behind me, and I turned to see a dark-haired woman coming fast toward me through the doorway, her wild glance rigidly fixed on the green stone box. She was pulling out of a pocket a black object like a long, fat cigar.

I opened my mouth to speak, but she brought her hand round in a strong, swinging arc, and the short black cylinder doubled its length into a silvery flexible stick that crashed with shattering force against my left upper arm. It was enough to stop a heavy-weight in round one.

CHAPTER 4

MY FINGERS went numb and dropped the box. Swaying, I toppled in a spitting fury from the force of the impact, thinking sharply that I mustn't this time put my foot on the ground.

The woman gave me a baleful glare and picked up the telephone, pressing three fast buttons. "Police," she said. "I want to report a burglary. I've caught a burglar."

"I'm Greville's brother," I said thickly, from the floor.

It didn't seem to reach her. "What?" she said vaguely.

"*I'm Greville's brother.* Are you deaf? I'm not a burglar." I gingerly sat up and found no strength anywhere.

She put the phone down. "Why didn't you say so?"

She held at the ready the fearsome thing she'd hit me with, looking as if she thought I'd attack her in my turn, which I certainly felt like. In the last six days I'd been crunched by a horse, a mugger and a woman. All I needed was a toddler to amble up with a *coup de grâce*.

I struggled up off the floor and sat on a chair. "Who are you?" I said. But I knew who she was: the woman on the answering machine. The cut-crystal accent. *Darling, where are you? I love you.*

"Did you ring his office?" I said. "Are you Mrs. Williams?"

She seemed to crumple inwardly. "Is he really dead?"

"Yes."

She was forty, perhaps more. My height. In no way tiny or delicate. A woman of decision and power, sorely troubled.

She wore a leather-belted raincoat and plain court shoes. Her thick, dark hair, expertly cut, was combed smoothly back to curl under on her collar, giving her a cool, groomed look.

"How?" she said eventually.

I had a strong impulse to deny her the information, to punish her for her precipitous attack. But I knew there was no point in it, so I explained about the scaffolding. "He died on Sunday."

She looked at me directly. "Are you Derek?"

"Yes."

"I'm Clarissa Williams. I came to fetch some things of mine." She hesitated. "A few letters, that's all."

"I played the phone messages," I said.

"Oh God." She looked agonized. "I want to wipe them off." Tentatively, as if asking my forbearance, she walked to the answering machine, rewound the tape, and recorded silence over what had gone before.

"Do you want a drink?" she said abruptly, going over to the tray of bottles.

"Yes. Soda water," I said. "Make it a double."

She tightened her mouth and poured soda into a glass for me and vodka and tonic into her own. Then she set my glass on the table beside me, next to the little stone bears, and drank deeply from her own. Alcohol, the world's first anesthetic, I thought. I could have done with some myself.

"Where are your letters?" I asked. The on-creeping dusk in the garden deepened abruptly toward night. I wished she would hurry, because I wanted to go home.

She switched on a table light and went over to the bookshelves. "In a book, I think. Some of these books are hollow."

Oh Greville, I thought. How would I ever find anything he had hidden? I liked straight paths. He'd had a mind like a labyrinth.

She began pulling out books from the lower shelves and opening the front covers. After a while, on her knees, she found a hollow one, which she laid open on the floor.

The interior of the book was in effect a red velvet box with a close-fitting lid that could be pulled out by a tab. When she pulled the lid out, an envelope was revealed.

She looked at it. "It's not my letters. Not my writing paper."

I said, "Greville made a will leaving everything he possessed to me."

She didn't seem to find it extraordinary, although I still did. "You'd better see what's in here, then," she said calmly.

The envelope contained an ornate key, about four inches long. I asked her if she knew what it unlocked. She shook her head.

"I haven't seen it before. He was a man of secrets."

I listened to her wistfulness. A man of secrets . . . Greville had apparently not opened his mind to her much more than to me.

I put the key back into its envelope and handed it across.

"It had better stay in the book for now," I said, "until I find a keyhole it fits."

She returned it to the shelves and shortly afterward found her letters, not a great many but carefully kept. She put them into a plain black leather handbag that lay beside her on the carpet.

I collected the crutches and stood up. Clarissa Williams watched me go to Greville's chair with a touch of awkwardness.

"Look," she said, "when I came in, I didn't notice the crutches."

She still ought to have asked questions before waging war.

I went over to the telephone table and picked up the brutal little man tamer where she'd left it. The heavy knurled handle, a black cigar-shaped cylinder, was about seven inches long. Protruding was a thick, chromium-plated, closely coiled spring, with a narrower spring extending beyond that—the whole flexible, shining, horrific, tipped with a black metal knob. Fifteen or sixteen inches overall, with a kick as hard as a horse.

"What is this?" I said, holding it, feeling its weight.

"Greville gave it to me. He said the streets aren't safe. As a magistrate he heard so much about women being attacked. He said one blow would render the toughest man helpless."

My dear brother, I thought. Thank you very much. Wordlessly, I closed the thing up and offered it to her.

"It's called a kiyoga," she said, putting it familiarly into her raincoat pocket. Then she looked unhappily and uncertainly at my face. "I suppose I can't ask you to forget I came here?"

"Impossible." Another time I suppose I might have liked her. She had generous eyes that would look better smiling, and a basic good humor despite her jumbling emotions.

She swallowed. "Greville told me about you. I guess I'll have to trust to his judgment." She brought out from her other pocket a plain key ring with three keys on it. "You'd better have these. I won't be using them anymore." In her eyes I saw the shininess of sudden tears.

"He died in Ipswich," I said. "He'll be cremated there on Friday afternoon. Two o'clock."

She nodded speechlessly, went past me down the hall, and closed the front door with a quiet finality.

With a sigh I looked around the room. The book box that had contained her letters still lay open on the floor, and I restored it to the shelves. I wondered just how many books were hollow. I'd look tomorrow. Meanwhile, I picked up the fallen green stone box and put in on the table. A whole load of no progress, I thought moodily.

There was a polished cupboard that I hadn't investigated, and I bent down and pulled one of the doors open. A video machine with two shelves of videotapes below slid outward as a unit. I pulled a tape out at random and was stunned to see the label stuck to its front, RACE VIDEO CLUB, and underneath, in typing, JULY 7TH, SANDOWN PARK, DOZEN ROSES.

The Race Video Club sold tapes of races to anyone interested. Greville, I thought in growing amazement, must have given them a standing order: every race his horses had run in for the past two years was there.

The front doorbell rang, jarring and unexpected. I went and looked through a small peephole and found Brad standing on the doorstep, blinded by two spotlights shining on his face.

I opened the door. "Hello. Are you all right?"

"Turn the lights off. Can't see."

I looked for a switch beside the front door, found several, and by pressing them all upward indiscriminately, put out the blaze.

"Was coming to see you were okay," Brad explained. "Then those lights just went on."

Another manifestation of Greville's security, no doubt. Anyone who came here after dark would get illuminated for his pains.

"Sorry I've been so long," I said. "Now you're here, would you carry a few things?"

In the small sitting room he obligingly picked up about ten recent tapes, balancing the green stone box on top.

Before leaving the house, I pressed all the switches beside the front door downward. The spotlights didn't go on, but a dog started barking noisily behind us.

"Strewth," Brad said, whirling round. There was no dog.

But there was a loudspeaker on a hall table emitting the deep-throated growls and barks of a determined Alsatian.

"Let's go," I said in amusement, and Brad could hardly wait.

DURING the evening I failed both to open the green stone box and to understand the two gadgets from Greville's sitting room.

Sighing, I fed Greville's tapes into my video machine and watched the races. Brad had picked up the six most recent outings of Dozen Roses', interspersed by four of Gemstones'. I played all six of Dozen Roses' first, starting with the earliest, back in May. On the screen, there were shots of the runners going down to the start, with Greville's pink-and-orange colors bright and easy to see.

Down at the start, there was some sort of fracas involving Dozen Roses. I rewound the tape and played it through in slow motion and couldn't help laughing. Dozen Roses, his mind far from racing, had been showing unseemly interest in a mare.

I remembered Greville saying once that he thought it a shame and unfair to curb a colt's enthusiasm: no horse of his would ever be gelded. Trainers didn't normally run mares that had come into season, but sometimes one couldn't tell early on. Horses knew, though, and Dozen Roses had been aroused.

The mare was loaded into the stalls in a hurry. After that, Dozen Roses had run without sparkle and finished midfield.

Too bad, I thought, smiling, and watched Dozen Roses' next attempt three weeks later. No distracting attractions this time. The horse performed quietly. The next race was much the same, and if I'd been Greville, I would have decided it was time to sell.

Greville, it seemed, had had more faith. After seven weeks' rest Dozen Roses had raced full of zest and zoomed over the finishing line in front, netting fourteen to one. He had next produced two further copybook performances of stamina and determination, which brought us up to date. I could see why Loder expected another trot-up on Saturday.

Gemstones' tapes weren't as interesting. Despite his name he wasn't of much value, and the one race he'd won looked like a fluke. I would sell them both, I decided, as Loder wanted.

Early on Wednesday, Brad drove me to Lambourn, not far from where I lived in Hungerford. The ankle was sore but less of a constant drag. Clarissa Williams' attentions had worn off, except for a little stiffness and a blackening bruise. That didn't matter. For much of the year I had bruises somewhere or other from falls in steeplechasing. I healed fast—bones, skin and optimism.

Milo Shandy, striding about in his stable yard, came over to my car as it rolled to a stop, and yanked open the door. "A chauffeur, by God. Coddling yourself, aren't you?"

Brad got out of the car, gave Milo a Neanderthal look, and handed me the crutches as usual.

Milo, dark, short and squarely built, watched the proceedings with disgust. "I want you to ride Datepalm," he said.

"Well, I can't."

"Do you want to keep the horse here or don't you?"

I did.

Milo Shandy was pugnacious, dynamic and outspoken, and produced winners by the dozen. I'd been outraged by the way he'd spoken to me when I first rode for him, but one day when I yelled back at him he burst out laughing, and we got along just fine after that.

The Ostermeyers arrived at that point, with *their* chauffeur, which Milo took for granted. His bullishness at once disappeared, replaced by the jocular charm that had owners, including the Ostermeyers, regularly mesmerized.

They were not so delighted about my crutches.

"Oh dear," Martha Ostermeyer exclaimed in dismay. "What have you done? Don't say you can't ride Datepalm. If we're going to buy him, we want to see him with his real jockey up."

Harley Ostermeyer nodded in agreement, benignly.

Not really my week, I thought.

The Ostermeyers were all sweetness and light while people were pleasing them, and I'd never had any trouble liking them. Harley Ostermeyer was the boss of a giant supermarket chain. Martha Ostermeyer was also rich, a fourth-generation multi-millionaire in banking. I'd ridden for them in the past and been well rewarded, as generosity was their pleasure.

Milo drove us up to the downs, where Datepalm and the other horses were already circling. The day was bright and chilly, the downs rolling away to the horizon, the sky clear, the horses' coats glossy in the sun. A perfect day for buying a champion 'chaser.

Milo had brought a spare helmet with us, and with an inward sigh I put it on. The enterprise was stupid, really, as my leg wasn't strong enough. And if anything wild happened to upset Datepalm, he might get loose and injure himself.

"When you give me a leg up," I said quietly to Milo, "put both hands round my knee, and don't twist my foot."

"You're such a wimp," he said.

Nevertheless, I landed in the saddle with little trouble.

Datepalm looked good. A handsome bay with black points, excellent head and short, sturdy legs, he filled the eye.

He and I and two others presently trotted to the far end of the gallop. I stood in the stirrups with all my weight on my right foot while cursing Milo imaginatively for the sensations in my left. Datepalm, who knew he should not be ridden lopsided like this, did a good deal of head and tail shaking, but otherwise seemed willing. He and I knew each other well, as I'd ridden him in all his races for the past three years. We had a definite rapport.

At the far end the two lads and I and our three horses set off at a working gallop back toward Milo and the Ostermeyers, and Datepalm put up one of his smoothest performances, coming away alone and then sweeping collectedly past the Ostermeyers with fluid power. If the jockey found it an acutely stabbing discomfort all the way, it was a fair price for the result. Even before I'd pulled up, the Ostermeyers had shaken hands on the deal.

"Subject to a veterinarian's report, of course," Harley was saying as I walked Datepalm back to join them. "He's superb."

Milo's smile looked as if it would split his face.

Afterward we all went to Milo's house for breakfast, and over coffee, toast and eggs Milo and the Ostermeyers planned Datepalm's future program, including all the top races, with, of course, another crack at the Gold Cup. After a dozen repetitions of the horse's virtues Milo told the Ostermeyers the saga of Dozen Roses, and they invited me to the York races on Saturday.

"Our dear friends Lord and Lady Knightwood have asked us to lunch," Harley said. "Why don't we give Derek a ride up there to see his horse run?"

Milo was looking at me anxiously: pleasing the Ostermeyers was still an absolute priority. I said I'd be glad to accept.

BRAD and I went on to London, traveling in silent harmony.

I took the two baffling little gadgets from Greville's sitting room upstairs to his office and showed them to June.

"That one," she said immediately, pointing to the thumb-size gadget with the whine, "is a device to discourage mosquitoes." She laughed. "He said every man should have one."

She picked up the other gadget and frowned at it.

"Oh yes." She pulled it out to its full extent. "He used to have a transmitter that started his car from a distance. This one doesn't do so much—I think it only switches the lights on, or makes the car whistle so you can find it in a dark car park. I haven't seen it for ages. I think he'd got tired of carrying all his gadgets about."

"You just earned your twenty percent all over again," I said.

"What?" Then she said suddenly, "You're going to take this to Ipswich, aren't you? To find his car? Isn't that what you mean?"

I nodded. "Let's hope it works. It's quite a big town, and the car could be anywhere." I looked at her bright, intelligent face. "June," I added slowly, "don't tell anyone else about this carfinder gadget."

"Whyever not?"

"Because," I said, "someone broke into this office looking for something and we don't know if they found it. If it is in the car, I don't want anyone to realize that the car is still lost."

I hadn't needed to tell her about the mugger who had stolen Greville's bag of clothes, which was looking less and less a random hit and more and more a shot at a target. Someone must have known Greville was dying, I thought.

The useless thoughts squirreled around and got me nowhere.

Annette came into the office then, carrying a fistful of papers that had come in the morning post and needed to be dealt with: letters from insurance people, fund-raisers, dissatisfied customers, gemology forecasters, and a cable from a supplier in Hong Kong.

"Incidentally," she said, "I did reach Prospero Jenks. He'll be in his Knightsbridge shop at two thirty today, if you want him."

I smiled. "Fine."

She took the letters off to answer them, and I went from department to department on a trip to the vault—two thirds of which I still had to check—watching everyone at work, all of them capable and beginning to settle obligingly into the change of regime. I asked June to go down and tell Brad I'd need him at two; she went and returned like a boomerang.

I unlocked the vault and started on topaz: thousands of brilliant, translucent, slippery stones in a rainbow of colors, some bigger than acorns, some like peas. After that, garnet, which could be yellow, green and red, I found, and then boxes of citrine—two and a half hours of unfolding and folding glossy white packets, and no diamonds.

After lunch I went down to the car and gave Prospero Jenks' address to Brad. "It's somewhere near Harrods," I said, climbing in.

He nodded, drove through the traffic, and found the shop.

"Great," I said. "Now if the car phone rings, you'll have to answer it, because there's nowhere to park."

He shook his head. He had resisted the suggestion several times before.

"It's very easy. When it rings, pick it up and press this button, and you'll be able to hear me. Okay? I'll ring when I'm ready to leave; then you just come back here and pick me up."

He looked at the telephone as if it were a cobra. I put it ready on the passenger seat beside him and hoped for the best.

Prospero Jenks' shopwindow sparkled, but the lettering of his name over the window was neat and plain, as if ostentation there would have been superfluous. I looked at the window with a curiosity I would never have felt a week earlier, and found it filled not with conventional rings and watches but with joyous toys: model cars, airplanes, yachts, horses, all gold and enamel and shining with gems. Almost every passerby paused to look.

Pushing awkwardly through the heavy glass front door, I stepped into the little shop.

"Can I help you?" a voice said. A neutral middle-aged man in a black suit was coming from a doorway at the rear.

"My name's Franklin," I said. "Came to see Prospero Jenks."

"A minute." He retreated, returned with a half-smile, and invited me through to the privacies beyond. A much longer space doubled as office and workroom, containing several tiers of drawers like the ones in Saxony Franklin. On one wall a large framed sign read NEVER TURN YOUR BACK TO CUSTOMERS. ALWAYS WATCH THEIR HANDS. A fine statement of no trust, I thought in amusement.

Sitting on a stool by a workbench, a jeweler's lens screwed into one eye, was a man in striped shirt sleeves, fiddling intently with a small gold object fixed into a vise. He put down his tool and rose to his feet, turning to inspect me with growing surprise.

He was maybe fifty but looked younger in a Peter Pan sort of way—a boyish face with intense bright blue eyes and a lot of lines across the forehead. Fairish hair, no beard, no personal display. I had expected someone fancier, more temperamental.

"Grev's brother?" he said. "What a turnup. There I was, thinking you'd be his age, his height." He narrowed the eyes. "I'll tell you, unless you know as much as he did, I'm in trouble."

His voice was a long way from cut glass—more like East End London tidied up for West. Jenks was the sort that came from nowhere and made it to the top from sheer, undeniable talent.

"I'm just learning the business," I said cautiously. "I'll do what I can."

"Grev was a genius with stones," he said explosively. "He'd bring me one-offs from all over the world, and I've made pieces . . ." He stopped and spread his arms out. "They're in palaces and museums, and mansions in Palm Beach too. By the way, Grev said he had some decent spinel. Have you still got it?"

"Er," I said, "red?"

"Red," he affirmed. "I'll take all you've got."

"We'll send it tomorrow."

"By messenger. And a slab of rock crystal—like the Eiger. Grev showed me a photo. I've got a commission for a fantasy."

"All right," I said, and hid my doubts. I hadn't seen any slab of rock crystal, but Annette would know, I thought.

57

He said casually, "What about the diamonds?"

I let my breath out consciously. "What about them?"

"Grev told me he'd got them and in fact sent a batch off to be cut. Are they back yet?"

"Er, not yet," I said, hoping I wasn't croaking. "Are those the diamonds he bought a couple of months ago?"

"Sure. I asked him to. I'm setting some of my stuff now with bigger diamonds, and I wanted Grev to get them, because I trust him. Trust is like gold dust in this business, even though diamonds weren't his thing, really. So he bought a share of a sight from a sight holder, and he's having them cut in Antwerp as I require them, as I expect you know."

I nodded. I knew, only because he'd just told me.

"I'm going to make stars of some of them—to shine from the rock crystal. And I'm making a mobile, with teardrop diamonds on gold trembler wires that move in the lightest air." He gave a self-deprecating smile. "Diamonds are ravishing in sunlight."

I had never thought about diamonds in sunlight before, though I suppose I would in future. "I haven't caught up with everything yet," I said, which was the understatement of the century. "How many diamonds are involved?"

"About a hundred."

"Do you happen to know the name of the Antwerp cutter?"

"I don't know who Grev knew there, exactly. He never said a word he didn't have to. I'd talk; he listened. We got on fine. He understood what I do better than anybody."

The sadness of his voice was my brother's universal accolade, I thought. He'd been liked, trusted. He would be missed.

I stood up and said, "Thank you, Mr. Jenks."

"Call me Pross," he said easily. "Everyone does."

"My name's Derek."

"Right," he said, smiling. "Now, I'll keep on dealing with you, but I'm going to have to find me another traveler like Grev, with an eye like his. He's been supplying me ever since I started on my own. He gave me credit when the banks wouldn't; he had faith in what I could do. . . ." He clicked his mouth. "I do go on a bit."

"I like to hear it," I said.

I borrowed Prospero's telephone to get Brad, but although I could hear the ringing tone, he didn't answer. Cursing slightly, I asked Pross for a second call and got Annette.

"Please keep on trying this number," I said. "When Brad answers, tell him I'm ready to go. We're off to Kensington."

I thanked Pross for the calls, stood on the pavement, and wondered pessimistically how long it would take Brad to answer the telephone, but he surprised me by arriving within a very few minutes. When I opened the car door, the phone was ringing.

"Why don't you answer it?" I asked, wriggling my way in.

"Forgot which button."

I answered it myself and talked to Annette. "Brad apparently reckoned that if the phone rang, it meant I was ready, so he saw no need to answer it," I said.

He gave a silent nod.

"Annette, what's a sight holder, and what's a sight?"

"You're back to diamonds again!" she exclaimed. "A sight holder is someone who is permitted to buy rough diamonds from the CSO. There are only about a hundred and fifty sight holders worldwide, I think. They sell the diamonds then to other people. A sight is a sale the CSO hold every five weeks."

"Is a sight holder the same as a diamantaire?" I asked.

"All sight holders are diamantaires, but all diamantaires are not sight holders. Diamantaires buy from the sight holders, or share in a sight, or buy somewhere else, not from De Beers."

Ask a simple question, I thought. I switched off the telephone, feeling absolutely swamped.

Brad miraculously found a parking space right outside Greville's house, at five o'clock. "Twenty past, for the pub?"

He was referring to the Rook and Castle, round the corner from Greville's, where I'd blankly agreed to meet with Elliot Trelawney, Greville's colleague.

"If you wouldn't mind."

He ducked his head in assent, and I maneuvered up to the front door. No floodlights came on; no dog barked. It was daylight. I opened the three locks and pushed the door.

The house was still. No movements of air. I propped the door

59

open and went down the passage to the small sitting room. No intruders. No mess. No amazons waving riot sticks.

I started taking all of the books off the shelves methodically, riffling the pages and putting each back.

There were ten hollow books altogether, with titles like *Tales of the Outback* and *With a Mule in Patagonia*. Five were empty, including the one that had held Clarissa Williams' letters. One held the big ornate key.

Two of the remaining boxes contained large keys, and one a leaflet on how to set a safe in concrete. The last revealed two very small plastic cases containing microcassette tapes, all of two inches long. Nowhere among Greville's tidy belongings had I found a microcassette player. I left the tiny tapes in the book.

With the scintillating titles and their secrets all back on the shelves, I stared at them gloomily. Not a diamond in the lot.

Instructions for concrete nests were all very well, but where was the safe? Tapes were okay, but where was the player? Keys were fine, but where were the keyholes? Frustrated, I began opening the mail that had accumulated in the letter box.

I kept telling myself it was necessary, but I felt as if I were trespassing. There were bills, a bank statement, a gemology magazine and two invitations. No letters from Antwerp. I put the letters into a large envelope to take home to Hungerford later, reflecting ruefully that I loathed paperwork.

CHAPTER 5

Brad whisked me round to the Rook and Castle at five thirty. The pub was old-fashioned, a lot of dark wood and Tiffany lampshades, with no jukebox. I paused inside the door.

Judging Elliot Trelawney absent, I ordered some Perrier at the bar and swallowed a Distalgesic. The morning's gallop had done no good to the ankle department.

A bulky man of about fifty soon came in and looked purposefully around, coming without hesitation to the bar.

"Mr. Franklin?" He knew me by the crutches I'd told him of. I shook his offered hand.

"What are you drinking?" he said briskly, eyeing my glass.

"Perrier."

He smiled swiftly, showing white teeth. "You won't mind if I have a Glenlivet? Greville and I drank many together here. I'm going to miss him abominably. Tell me what happened."

I told him. He listened intently, then suggested we sit down. And without more ado he picked up our glasses and carried them over to a small table by the wall.

"That's better," he said, eyeing me over his glass. "So you're the brother he talked about so proudly. You're Derek."

"Yes, I'm Derek," I said, surprised.

Elliot Trelawney was almost bald, with half-moon glasses, and a face with thin lips and laugh lines around his eyes. On a snap judgment he seemed a realist with a sense of humor.

"By God, I'll miss him," he said. His voice was deep. "We were friends for twenty years."

I envied him. I wanted intolerably what it was too late to have, and the more I listened to people remembering Greville, the worse it got.

"Are you a magistrate?" I asked.

He nodded. "We often sat together. Greville introduced me to it, but I've never had quite his gift. He seemed to know the truth of things by instinct. He said goodness was visible."

"What sort of cases did . . . do you try?"

"All sorts." He smiled again briefly. "Shoplifters. Vagrants. Possession of drugs. Sex offenders. Motoring offenses, speeding and so on." He took a sip. "But we don't sit every day, only twice a month in Greville's and my cases, plus a little committee work. And that's really why I called you. I'd like the notes Greville was making on the licensing of a new gaming club. He said he'd learned disturbing allegations against one of the organizers and he was going to advise turning down the application."

"I'm afraid that I haven't so far found any notes like that."

"Damn. . . . Where would he have put them?"

"I don't know. I'll keep my eyes open, though."

Elliot Trelawney reached into an inner jacket pocket and brought out a black notebook.

"This was Greville's," he said. "I brought it for you. He left it after a committee meeting last week. Dammit," he finished explosively. "Why should such a futile thing happen?"

No answer was possible. I regretfully picked up the black notebook and opened it at random. " 'The bad scorn the good,' " I read aloud, " 'and the crooked despise the straight.' "

"The thoughts of Chairman Mao," Trelawney said dryly. "I used to tease Greville—he said he'd learned to clarify his thoughts by writing them down." He smiled. "You'll find parts of that notebook especially interesting."

I stowed the notebook in a pocket, considering. "Do you make enemies much, because of the court?" I asked.

He shrugged. "We get cursed at now and then. But usually not. The only real enemy Greville might have had is the gambling-club organizer who's not going to get his license. Name's Vaccaro. A drug baron, Greville called him, a man suspected of murder, but not tried, through lack of evidence. He appeared before the committee and seemed perfectly straightfoward. And then someone contacted Greville and uncovered the muck."

"Does Koningin Beatrix mean anything to you?" I asked now. "Or CZ equals C times one point seven?" C, I thought, stood for diamond.

"Nothing," Elliot Trelawney said.

We talked a while longer and parted eventually on friendly terms.

"Look," he said, "keep in touch now and then, would you? And let me know when you find those notes."

"Sure," I said.

When he'd gone, I used the pub's telephone to ring the car, and after five unanswered brr-brrs, disconnected and went outside, where Brad, with almost a grin, reappeared to pick me up.

"Home," I said, and he said, "Yerss," and that was that.

On the way, I read bits of Greville's notebook, pausing to digest the passing thoughts that had clearly been chiefly prompted by the flotsam drifting through the West London Magistrates Court:

Goodness is sickening to the evil, as evil is sickening to the good. Both the evil and the good may be complacent.

Crime to many is not a crime but simply a way of life. If laws are inconvenient, ignore them, they don't apply to you.

Infinite sadness is not to trust an old friend.

I stopped reading and stared out at the autumn countryside, which was darkening now. I flicked over one more page and came to an entry so private and impassioned that I felt my mouth go dry. Alone on the page were three brief lines:

> May I deal with honor.
> May I act with courage.
> May I achieve humility.

I felt as if I shouldn't have read it; knew he hadn't meant it to be read. May I achieve humility. . . . That prayer was for saints.

WHEN we reached my house, I told Brad we would go to London tomorrow, Ipswich on Friday. He loped off into the night, tongue-tied as usual.

Everything was quiet in the house, everything orderly. I ate a microwaved chicken pie and made an unenthusiastic start on Greville's letters, closing his accounts, declining his invitations, saying sorry, very sorry. After that I read right through Greville's notebook, looking for diamonds. There were pearls of wisdom, but no instructions like turn right at the fourth apple tree, walk five paces, and dig.

I did, however, find the answer to one small mystery:

> The green soapstone box pleases me as an exercise in misdirection and deviousness. The keyhole has no key because it has no lock. It's impossible to unlock men's minds with keys, but guile and pressure will do it, as with the box.

Even with the plain instruction to be guileful and devious, it took me ages to find the secret. I tried pressing the hinges, the lock, everything with the box upside down. The green stone stayed stubbornly shut.

Misdirection, I thought. If the keyhole wasn't a lock, maybe the hinges weren't hinges. Maybe the lid wasn't a lid.

I tried the box upside down again and pushed, and as if with a sigh for my stupidity, the bottom slid out halfway and stopped.

With great curiosity I brought out two well-worn chamois leather jewelers' pouches with drawstrings, the name of the jeweler indistinctly stamped on the front. Both of the pouches were empty, to my great disappointment, but the faded lettering said JACOB VAN EKEREN, PELIKAANSTRAAT 70, ANTWERP.

There had to be, I thought, about ten thousand jewelers in Antwerp. All the same, better find out.

In the morning I took one of the pouches to London, and through telephone inquiries found Jacob van Ekeren's number.

The voice that answered spoke either Dutch or Flemish, so I tried French. I waited, and was rewarded with a courteous, non-committal and extremely English voice asking if he could help.

I said I was from Saxony Franklin, London gemstone importers. "Do you," I said baldly, "cut and polish rough diamonds?"

"Yes, of course," he answered. "But before we do business with any new client, we need introductions and references."

"Um, would Saxony Franklin Limited be a client of yours already? Or Greville Saxony Franklin? It's important."

He paused, took my name, and said he would call back.

I put down the phone and asked Annette and June to find Jacob van Ekeren in Greville's files. They had no records of any Jacob van Ekeren. It wasn't exactly surprising.

I went along and opened the vault, telling Annette about Prospero Jenks' wanting all the spinel. "And a piece of rock crystal like the Eiger."

"Ah." She chose a heavy box from the bottom shelf. "This is it," she said, humping it onto the shelf and opening it. "Beautiful."

The crystal, filling the box, was lying on its side, but given diamond stars and the Jenks sunlight treatment, it could make a fantasy worthy of his name. "Do we have a price for it?" I asked.

"Double what it cost," she said cheerfully. "Plus Jason always takes the stuff over in a taxi. I'll see to it. Oh, and the pearls that came yesterday."

I moved down to where I'd given up the day before, and while Annette counted and stored the new intake of pearls I checked my way through the old. Boxes of all sizes. No diamonds.

"Does CZ mean anything to you?" I asked Annette idly.

"Cubic zirconia," she said promptly. "We sell a fair amount."

"Isn't that, um, imitation diamond?"

"It's a manufactured crystal very like diamond, but many times cheaper. If it's in a ring, you can't tell the difference."

"Can't anyone?" I asked. "They must do."

"Mr. Franklin said that most jewelers can't at a glance. But they'd take the stones out of their setting and weigh them. Cubic zirconia's much heavier than diamond, so one carat of cubic zirconia is smaller than a one-carat diamond."

"CZ equals C times one point seven," I said slowly.

"That's right," she said, surprised. "How did you know?"

From noon on, I sat in Greville's office reading June's printout of a crash course in business studies, beginning to see the pattern of a cash flow that ended on the side of the angels. There wasn't a trace of diamonds in the spreadsheets or the ledgers. Annette, who had been banking the receipts daily, produced a sheaf of checks for me to sign, which I did, feeling it was the wrong name, and she brought the day's post for decisions, which I strugglingly made.

Several people in the jewelry business telephoned in response to the notice in the papers of Greville's death. Annette, reassuring them that the show would go on, sounded more confident than she looked. "They all say Ipswich is too far for them to come, but they'll be there in spirit," she reported.

The small, insistent digital alarm went off again, muffled inside the desk. Twenty past four, my watch said. I reached over and pulled open the drawer, and the alarm stopped, as it had before.

Jason with his orange hair appeared then, and without any trace of insolence told me he'd taken the stuff to Prospero Jenks and brought back a check, which he'd given to Annette. "She said to tell you." An amazing improvement, I thought.

I stayed behind that evening after they'd all left, and went slowly round Greville's domain looking for hiding places that were guileful and devious and full of misdirection. I concluded he wouldn't have used the stockrooms to store diamonds, because the others might easily have found what they weren't meant to. That was the trouble with the whole place, I decided. All of Greville's staff seemed to pop in and out of his office familiarly whenever the need arose.

Hovering always was the uncomfortable thought that any pointer Greville left to the diamonds' whereabouts vanished with the break-in artist, leaving nothing for me to find. Indeed, I found nothing. After a fruitless hour I went home.

THE day of Greville's funeral dawned cold and clear, and we were heading east when the sun came up. The run to Ipswich taking three hours altogether, we came into the town with generous time to search for Greville's car.

I explained the car finder to Brad, producing a street map to go with it. "You drive, and I'll press, okay?"

He nodded, seeming amused, and we began in the town center, near to where Greville had died, very slowly rolling up and down the streets, checking them off on the map. Nowhere did we get a whistle or turn lights on. None of the Rovers we saw was Greville's. Disappointment settled heavily as lunchtime dragged toward two o'clock.

The crematorium was set in a garden with neatly planted rose trees. Brad dropped me at the door, and I was met by two black-suited men who introduced themselves as the undertaker I'd engaged and one of the crematorium's officials. A lot of flowers had arrived, they said.

The official indicated two long rows of bright bouquets blazing with colorful life in that place of death. "They've been arriving all morning. Which do you want on the coffin?"

"I sent some from myself and our sisters," I said doubtfully. "The card has Susan, Miranda and Derek on it. I'll have that."

They took pity on the crutches and helped me find the right flowers, and I came first not to my card but to another. "I think of you every day at four twenty. Love, C."

The flowers were velvety red roses; twelve sweet-smelling blooms. Dozen Roses, I thought. Heavens above.

"I've found them," the undertaker called, picking up a large display of pink and bronze chrysanthemums. "Here you are."

"Great. We'll have these roses as well, and this all-white wreath from the staff in his office."

I asked the official where the other flowers had come from. Businesses, he said; he would give the cards to me afterward.

During the very quiet half hour that followed, the clergyman read the whole service, though I was the only mourner; it was fitting. I half listened, half watched the way the sunshine fell onto the flowers on the coffin from the high windows, and I thought of Greville, not as he'd been alive but what he had become to me during the past week.

His life had settled on my shoulders like a mantle. Through Monday, Tuesday, Wednesday and Thursday I'd learned enough of his business never to forget it. People who'd relied on him had transferred their reliance onto me, including Clarissa Williams, who had sent her flowers knowing I would see them. Nicholas Loder aimed to manipulate me for his own ends. Prospero Jenks was asking for the diamonds, and the bank loan hung like a thundercloud in my mind.

Greville, cold in the coffin, hadn't meant it to happen.

A man of honor, I thought. I mentally repeated his own prayer. *May I deal with honor. May I act with courage. May I achieve humility.* I didn't know if he'd managed the last one; I couldn't.

The clergyman droned to a halt. The official removed the flowers from the coffin, and with a loud whirring and creaking of machinery the coffin slid away out of sight, heading for fire.

Good-bye, pal, I said silently. Good-bye, except you are with me now more than ever.

I went out into the fresh air, thanked everyone, and arranged for the flowers to go to St. Catherine's Hospital. The official gave me the cards—I saw one from Elliot Trelawney—and I waited for a while for Brad to return, which he did, sporting a grin.

"I found it," he said. "Your brother's wheels."

"You didn't! Where?"

He wouldn't say. He drove us off in triumph to the center of town, barely three hundred yards from where the scaffolding had fallen. Then he drove through the forecourt of a used-car business, where rows of cars stood under fluttering pennants.

We found ourselves outside the wide-open doors of a garage. Brad held the car finder out of his window, pressed the red button, and somewhere in the depths of the garage a pair of headlights began flashing on and off and a piercing whistle shrieked.

A cross-looking mechanic in oily overalls came hurrying out. He told me he was the foreman in charge and he'd be glad to see the back of the Rover 3500. I owed him a week's parking, besides the cleaning of the spark plugs, plus a surcharge for inconvenience.

"Here," said the foreman, handing me the account and the keys. "The boot won't open. Some fancy lock. Damn nuisance."

I mollifyingly gave him a credit card in settlement and swung over to the Rover.

I looked at it. "Can you drive that?" I asked Brad.

"Yerss," he said gloomily.

I smiled and pulled Greville's keys out of my pocket to see if any of them would unlock the boot, and one did, to my relief. The treasure so well guarded included a large brown envelope, an overnight bag, a portable telephone, a personal computer, a portable fax and a polished wooden box containing a beautiful set of brass scales with featherlight weights. No diamonds.

I locked the boot again, which seemed a very Greville-like thing to do, and took a quick look round inside the car. From the driver's door pocket I picked out a road map of East Anglia, the route from London to Ipswich drawn heavily in black. The marked route, I saw, didn't stop at Ipswich but went on to Harwich.

Harwich, on the North Sea, was a historic ferry port. Harwich to the Hook of Holland. I didn't know if the Harwich ferries still ran.

I said abruptly to the foreman, who was back, impatient for my signature, "Is there a travel agent near here?"

"Three doors along," he said, pointing.

I signed the slip and left Brad with the cars while I peg legged to the travel agent's.

To my inquiries about ferries an obliging girl replied, "The *Prince Henry* goes over to Holland every morning, and the *Koningin Beatrix* every night."

I must have looked as stunned as I felt.

"What's the matter?" she said.

I closed my open mouth. "Nothing. Thank you very much."

I shunted back to the garage with my chunk of new knowledge, which solved one little conundrum but posed another: What was Greville doing with Queen Beatrix—not a horse but a boat?

BRAD drove the Rover to London and I followed in my own car, the pace throughout enough to make a snail weep. Whatever the Ipswich garage had done to Greville's plugs hadn't cured them. Resting my left foot on the floor sent frequent jabs up my leg, but in comparison with the ride home from Ipswich five days earlier it was chicken feed.

We reached Greville's road eventually. I told Brad that I would sleep in London that night to be handy for going to York with the Ostermeyers the next day, and if Brad would go to Hungerford in my car, I would return there by train. Greville's car, ruin that it was, could decorate the street. I stood on my crutches as Brad transferred all the gear from Greville's boot into the back of my car.

Sitting in Greville's chair later, once I'd switched the dog off, I opened the big brown envelope and read all about Vaccaro, the gambling-club organizer Elliot Trelawney had told me about.

He had been a very bad boy indeed. Most of the envelope's contents were a copy of Vaccaro's detailed application, but on an attached sheet Greville had handwritten:

Ramon Vaccaro, wanted for drug-running, Florida, USA. Suspected of several murders, victims mostly pilots wanting out from flying drug crates. My info from scared-to-death pilot's widow. She won't come to committee meeting.

Vaccaro seduced private pilots with big payoffs until they

69

finally got rich enough to have cold feet. Widow says her husband scared stiff but left it too late. She's remarried, lives in London, couldn't believe it when she saw newspaper snippet— Vaccaro's Family Gaming—with his photo. Family!

We don't have to find Vaccaro guilty—just don't give him a gaming license. Widow says he's dangerous and vengeful, but how can he silence a whole committee? The Florida police might like to know his whereabouts. Extradition?

I telephoned Elliot Trelawney at home and read the red-hot notes to him, which brought forth a whistle and a groan.

"But Vaccaro didn't kill Greville," I said.

"No." He sighed. "I'm sorry I couldn't get to the funeral. How did it go?"

"It was fine," I said. "Thank you for your flowers."

I said I would send the Vaccaro notes by messenger on Monday to the Magistrates Court.

IN THE morning, after a dream-filled night in Greville's black-and-white bed, I met the Ostermeyers at their hotel as we'd arranged.

They were in very good form, Martha resplendent in a red wool dress with a mink jacket, Harley with a new English hat over his easy grin, binoculars and racing paper ready. Both of them seemed determined to enjoy whatever the day brought forth.

Their mustached chauffeur, Simms, brought a huge Daimler to the front door exactly on time, and the Ostermeyers arranged themselves on the rear seat, while I sat in front, my crutches stowed in the boot.

"Is that foot still bothering you?" Martha said, frowning.

"It's much better," I said truthfully.

"Good. As long as it doesn't stop you riding Datepalm."

Harley said, "Milo says Datepalm might go for the Charisma Chase at Kempton next Saturday. What do you think?"

"A good race for him," I said calmly. I would kill Milo, I thought. A gallop was one thing, but no medic on earth was going to sign my card in *one week* to say I was fit to race. Half a ton of horse over jumps at thirty plus miles an hour was no puffball matter. "Milo might prefer to save him for the Mackeson at Cheltenham next month," I said judiciously, sowing the idea. "Or, of course, for the Hennessy Cognac Gold Cup." I'd definitely be fit for the Hennessy, six weeks ahead.

Martha sighed ecstatically. "It's all so exciting."

Harley said as the car sped north toward York, "You're expected at lunch with us, Derek. I talked with Lord Knightwood yesterday evening, and he said right away to have you join us. They're giving their name to a race. It'll be a big party."

"Which race?" I asked. Knightwood wasn't a name I knew.

Harley rustled the racing newspaper. "The University of York Trophy. Lord Knightwood is some kind of figurehead at the university. A Yorkshire VIP. Anyway, you're expected."

I thanked him. There wasn't much else to do.

Harley returned to his paper, and soon we arrived at the club, the driver dropping us neatly at the entrance. One could get addicted to chauffeurs, I thought, accepting the crutches gravely offered.

The first trainer we saw was Nicholas Loder. He looked truly furious and, I thought in surprise, alarmed to see us.

"What are *you* doing here?" he demanded brusquely.

"Do you know the Ostermeyers?" I asked politely, introducing them. "They've bought Datepalm. I'm their guest today."

He simply glared; then he marched off without another word.

"Well!" Martha said, outraged.

I didn't understand Loder's reaction. If he wanted a favor from me, which was that I'd let him sell Dozen Roses and Gemstones to his other owners, he should at least have shown me some politeness. And if Dozen Roses had been cleared to run, why was Loder scared that I was there to watch it? Crazy.

The York University lunch was to be held at one end of the club members' dining room, so I showed the way there, reflecting that it was lucky I'd decided on a decent suit for that day. There was already a small crowd of people, glasses in hand, chatting away inside a temporary white-lattice-fenced area, a long buffet set out behind them with tables and chairs.

71

"There are the Knightwoods," said the Ostermeyers, clucking contentedly, and I found myself being introduced presently to a tall, white-haired, kindly-looking man, perhaps seventy, who had benevolence shining from every wrinkle. He shook my hand amicably as a friend of the Ostermeyers'.

"Have you met my wife?" Lord Knightwood said vaguely. "My dear"—he touched the arm of a woman with her back to us—"you remember Harley and Martha Ostermeyer? And this is their friend Derek Franklin that I told you about."

She turned and warmly greeted the Ostermeyers, and held out a hand to me, saying, "How do you do. So glad you could come."

"How do you do, Lady Knightwood," I said politely.

She gave me a very small smile, in command of herself.

Clarissa Williams was Lord Knightwood's wife.

CHAPTER 6

SHE had known I would be there, it was clear, and if she hadn't wanted me to find her out, she could easily have developed a strategic illness.

She was saying graciously, "Didn't I see you on television winning the Gold Cup?" and I thought of that frightful kiyoga and the tumult of her feelings last Tuesday.

Lord Knightwood was introducing us to a professor of physics who with twinkles eagerly asked what I fancied for the races, and the said lord moved off with his wife and the Ostermeyers.

Clarissa, by accident or design, remained out of talking distance throughout lunch, and I didn't try to approach her. The party broke up during the first race, although everyone was invited to return for tea, and I spent the afternoon, as I'd spent so many others, watching horses stretch and surge and run as their individual natures dictated. The will to win was born and bred in them all, but it was those with the impulse to lead a wild herd who fought hardest and oftenest won. Datepalm and I both, on the same primitive plane, wanted to win.

"What are you thinking?" someone asked at my shoulder.

I would have known her voice anywhere, I thought. I turned to see her half-calm, half-anxious expression, the Lady Knightwood social poise explicit in the smooth hair and the tailored clothes, the passionate woman merely a hint in the eyes.

"Thinking about horses," I said.

"I suppose you're wondering why I came today when I knew you'd be here. . . ." She stopped, sounding uncertain.

"I'm not Greville," I said. "Don't think of me as Greville."

Her eyelids flickered. "You're too damned perceptive. But yes, I wanted to be near you. It's a sort of comfort."

We were standing by the rails of the parade ring, watching the runners for the next race walk round, led by their lads. There were crowd noises all around and the clip-clop of horses walking by, and we could speak quietly, as in an oasis of private space, without being overheard.

"Are you still angry with me for hitting you?" she asked a shade bitterly, as I'd made no comment after her last remark.

I half smiled. "No."

She sighed. "Greville said if I ever had to use the kiyoga in earnest, to escape at once and not worry what I'd done to my attacker."

"I'm surprised he gave you a weapon like that," I said mildly. "Aren't they illegal? And him a magistrate."

"I'm a magistrate too," she said unexpectedly. "That's how we met—at a magistrates' conference. I've not inquired into the legality of kiyogas."

"Where did he get it?" I asked curiously.

"America."

"Do you have it with you here?"

She nodded and touched her handbag. "It's second nature."

She must have been thirty years younger than her husband, I thought inconsequently. I didn't know whether or not I liked her, but I did recognize that there was a weird sort of intimacy between us and that I didn't resent it.

The jockeys came out and stood around with the owners in little groups. Nicholas Loder was there with a thickset, powerful-looking man, the pink club badge fluttering from his lapel.

"Dozen Roses," I said. "Was he named for you?"

"Oh God," Clarissa said, disconcerted. "However—"

"I put your roses on the coffin for the service."

"Oh . . ." she murmured with difficulty, her throat closing, her mouth twisting. "I . . . I can't . . ."

"Tell me how York University came to put its name to a race." I made it sound conversational, to give her composure time.

She swallowed, fighting for control. "I'm sorry. It's just that I can't mourn for him except inside—can't let it show to anyone except you, and it sweeps over me." She paused and answered my unimportant question. "The clerk of the course wanted to involve the city, and Henry persuaded the university bigwigs to

74

join in. He and I come here to meetings now and then."

"Your husband doesn't actually lecture at the university?"

"Oh no. He's chairman of a few things here. A public figure."

Vulnerable to scandal, I thought, as she was herself, and Greville also. She and he must have been unwaveringly discreet.

"How long since you first met Greville?" I asked.

"Four years." She paused. "Four marvelous years. Not enough. Whenever we could be together, he bought twelve red roses. It just . . . well . . ." She stopped, swallowing again.

The jockeys swung up onto the horses and moved to the course. Loder and his owner went to the stands. And Clarissa and I watched the race side by side on the grass in front of the grandstand.

Nicholas Loder's two-year-old won the sprint at a convincing clip, and I caught a glimpse of the owner afterward looking grimly satisfied. Clarissa went off then to join her husband for the university race, and I went with my crutches in search of Dozen Roses, who was being led around in the pre-parade ring before being taken into a stall to have his saddle put on.

Dozen Roses looked docile to dozy. An unremarkable bay, he was a good performer, I knew, but he didn't give an impression of going to be a trot-up within half an hour. Was this the colt that had won his last three races full of verve? Was this the young buck who had tried to mount a filly back in May?

No, I saw, he was not. I peered under his belly more closely. He had been gelded.

Stunned, I unfolded my race card, and there, sure enough, against his name stood not *c* for colt or *h* for horse, but *g* for gelding.

It explained so much—the loss of form when he had his mind on procreation rather than racing, and the return to speed once the temptation was removed. Horses very often did better after the operation.

Nicholas Loder's voice, vibrating with fury, came from behind me. "That horse is not your horse. Keep away from him."

I turned. Loder was advancing fast with Dozen Roses' saddle over his arm, the heavily unjoyful owner still in tow.

"Mine or not, I'm entitled to look at him," I said. "And either he is not Dozen Roses, or you have gelded him against my brother's express wishes."

Loder's mouth opened and snapped shut. He said to me vehemently, "You can't do anything about it. I have an authority to act. I am the registered agent for this horse, and what I decide is none of your business."

"You knew my brother refused to have his horses gelded. But you were sure he wouldn't find out, as he never went to the races."

He glared at me. He was aware that if I lodged a formal complaint, he would be in a good deal of trouble. Even if I only talked about it, it could do him damage. The hungry racing press would pounce on it, and the owners of all the princely colts in his prestigious stable would worry. He had understood all that, I thought, when I'd first told him I was inheriting Dozen Roses.

"How much do you want, then?" he demanded roughly. "Name your price, and get out of my way."

My own turn, I thought, to gape like a fish. "It's not a matter of money." I glanced at the attendant owner, who might repeat this conversation, said merely, "We'll discuss it later, okay?" and hitched myself away.

Behind me the owner was saying, "What was that all about, Nick?" and Loder replied, "Nothing, Rollo. Don't worry about it." When I looked back, both of them were stalking off toward the saddling boxes, followed by Dozen Roses and his lad.

Despite Nicholas Loder's anxious rage, or maybe because of it, I came down on the side of amusement. I would myself have had the horse gelded; Greville had been pigheaded on the subject.

Harley and Martha Ostermeyer, coming to see the horses saddled, were full of beaming anticipation. They had backed the winner of the University Trophy and had wagered all the proceeds on Dozen Roses.

"You won't get much return," I warned them. "It's favorite."

"We know that, dear," Martha said happily. "Where is he?"

"He's inside that box"—I pointed—"being saddled."

"Now, Harley and I have had a marvelous idea," she said sweetly. "We want you to dine with us when we get back to London. London on weekends is a graveyard."

With an inward grin I accepted my role as graveyard alleviator and, in the good cause of cementing Ostermeyer-Shandy-Franklin relations, said I would be pleased to stay to dinner.

Dozen Roses emerged saddled from his box and was led to the parade ring. He walked well, I thought, his good, straight hocks encouraging lengthy strides. He also seemed to have woken up a good deal, now that the excitement was at hand.

In the horse's wake hurried Nicholas Loder and his friend Rollo. Perhaps because they were crowding him, Dozen Roses pulled backward on his leading rein, buffeting the Rollo man and knocking him to his knees.

Martha with instinctive kindness rushed forward to help him as he floundered to his feet. She bent and picked up a thing like a blue rubber ball that had fallen out of his jacket, and held it toward him, saying, "You dropped this, I think."

He snatched it from her with a fierce stare and hurried into the parade ring after Nicholas Loder.

"What a perfectly horrid man," Martha said, making a face. She was brushing dust off her gloves, as if getting rid of contamination. Harley had meanwhile picked something else up off the grass.

"Oh," Martha said with recognition, "that's the other half of the baster. You'd better have it, Derek, if you want to give it back."

I frowned at what Harley gave me, which was a rigid plastic tube, semitransparent, about an inch in diameter, nine inches long, narrowing to half the width at one end.

"A baster," Martha said again. "For basting meat when it's roasting. What an extraordinary thing to take to the races."

"Mm," I agreed. I tucked the plastic tube into an inside jacket pocket, and we went up to the stands to watch Dozen Roses race.

The stable money was definitely on the horse, I thought, watching the forecast odds on the information board. When a gambling stable didn't put its money up front, the whisper went around and the price eased dramatically. The whisper where it mattered that day had to be saying that Loder was in earnest about the trot-up.

Perhaps as a result of his year-by-year successes Loder's stable had always attracted serious gamblers as owners. That wasn't the truism it seemed, because in steeplechasing most owners realistically expected to have to pay for their pleasure.

Wondering if the Rollo man was one of the big Loder gamblers, I looked up his name in the race card beside the horse of his that had won the sprint. "Owner, Mr. T. Rollway," the card read. Rollo for short to his friends. Never heard of him, I thought.

Dozen Roses cantered down to the start with at least as much energy and enthusiasm as any of the other seven runners and was fed into the stalls without fuss. He'd been striding out well, an old hand at the game by now—as I was also, I thought dryly.

I'd ridden in several flat races in my teens as an amateur, learning that the hardest and most surprising thing about the unrelenting flat-race crouch over the withers was the way it cramped one's lungs and affected one's breathing. A long time ago, I thought, watching the distant gates fly open and the colors spill out—long ago, when I was young and it all lay ahead.

If I could find Greville's diamonds, I thought, I would in due course be able to buy a yard in Lambourn and start training on a decent scale. I had no longer any doubt that when my body packed up mending fast, I would be content with the new life, even though the consuming passion I still felt for race riding couldn't be replaced. If I didn't find the diamonds, I would just scrape together whatever I could and borrow the rest.

Dozen Roses and the others swung left-handed into the long bend around the far end of the track, the bunch coming apart as the curve hit them.

Turning into the straight, five furlongs from the winning post, Dozen Roses was in fourth place and making not much progress. I wanted him quite suddenly to win, and was surprised by the strength of the feeling. I wanted him to win for Greville, and perhaps also for Clarissa. Sentimental fool, I told myself. Anyway, when the crowd started yelling home their fancy, I yelled for mine also, and I'd never done that, as far as I could remember.

There was not going to be a trot-up. Dozen Roses was visibly struggling as he took second place at a searing speed. He wouldn't have got the race at all if the horse in front hadn't veered at the last moment and bumped into him.

"Oh dear!" Martha exclaimed sadly. "Second. Well, never mind."

"He'll get the race on an objection," I said. "Your winnings are safe."

Sure enough, almost immediately the loudspeakers were announcing, "Stewards' inquiry."

The three of us descended to the area outside the weighing room, where Dozen Roses, steam flowing from his skin, was moving about restlessly, his lad holding tight to the reins.

"He didn't give up," I said to Martha. "That's what matters."

"Result of the stewards' inquiry," said the loudspeakers. "Placing of first and second reversed." Nicholas Loder came out of the weighing room and saw me standing with the Ostermeyers, but before I could utter even a 'well done,' he gave me a sick look and hurried off.

Martha, Harley and I returned to the luncheon room for the university's tea, where Clarissa, seeing me, developed renewed trouble with the tear glands. I drifted across to her side.

"So silly," she said crossly, blinking hard as she offered me a sandwich. "But wasn't he great?"

"He was."

"I wish . . ." She stopped. I wished it too. No need at all to put it into words. But Greville never went to the races.

"I go to London fairly often," she said then. "May I phone you when I'm there?"

"Yes, if you like." I wrote my home number on her race card. "I live in Berkshire, though, not in Greville's house."

She met my eyes, hers full of confusion.

"I'm not Greville," I said.

"My dear chap," said her husband boomingly, coming to a halt beside us, "delighted your horse finally won. And the professor says you tipped him three winners."

"A miracle."

He was shrewd enough, I thought, looking at the intelligent eyes amid the bonhomie. Not easy to fool. I wondered if he'd ever suspected his wife had a lover, even if he hadn't known who.

Martha Ostermeyer gushed up to say how marvelous the whole day had been, my cue to say good-bye. I shook Clarissa's outstretched hand in farewell, and also her husband's, who stood beside her. They looked good together.

Harley, Martha and I then left the racecourse and climbed into the Daimler, Simms stowing the crutches.

"And now," Martha said happily as we set off south toward London, "Harley and I have had another marvelous idea." She laughed. "We think we'll buy Dozen Roses and send him to Milo to train for jumping. If your brother's executor will sell him."

"Martha!" My brother's executor was dumbstruck.

"There," she said. "What do you say? Will you sell?"

"I certainly will."

"Then let's use the car phone to call Milo." She was full of high spirits, but when she reached Milo, she handed the phone to me with a frown, saying, "He wants to talk to you."

"That horse is an entire," Milo said. "They don't jump well."

"He's a gelding," I assured him. "Loder did it without permission. Anyway, the horse got the race today on a stewards' inquiry, but he ran gamely, and he's fit."

"All right, then."

"Milo, why," I asked, "would one of Nicholas Loder's owners carry a baster about at the races? It's really for cooking. You've got one. You used it as a nebulizer."

He used it, I reflected, when it was the best way to give medication to a horse. One dissolved the medicine in water and filled the rubber bulb. Then one fitted the tube on, slid it up the horse's nostril, and squeezed the bulb sharply. One could puff out dry powder with the same result. It was the fastest way of getting some drugs to act.

"At the races?" Milo was saying. "An owner?"

"That's right. His horse won the five-furlong sprint."

"He'd have to be mad. They dope-test two horses every race."

"He had a baster with him, that's all."

Milo said, "Oh, I almost forgot. There was a phone message for you. Something about your brother's diamonds." He sounded doubtful. "Is that right?"

"Yes. What about them?"

He must have heard the urgency in my voice, because he said, "It's nothing much. Just that someone had been trying to ring you last night and today, but I said you'd slept in London and gone to York. He—or she—will phone your brother's house tonight."

"Who was it?"

"I'm not a message service," he said testily. "Why don't you switch on your answer phone like everyone else?"

I switched the phone off with a smile and passed on Milo's approval of Dozen Roses, wondering who'd been trying to reach me. It had to be someone who knew Greville had bought diamonds. Maybe Annette?

As soon as we got back to London, the three of us ate dinner together, during which Martha announced yet another marvelous idea. She and Harley would get Simms to drive us all down to Lambourn the next day to take Milo out to lunch, so that they could see Datepalm again before they went back to the States on Tuesday.

When we phoned Milo, he told me again he'd do practically anything to please the Ostermeyers, including Sunday lunch. He also said that my informant had rung again and he had told him-her that I'd got the message.

"Thanks," I said. "See you tomorrow."

I thanked the Ostermeyers inadequately for everything and went to Greville's house by taxi. I did think of asking the taxi driver to stay until I'd reconnoitered, but I thought he would think me a fool or a coward or both, so I paid him off and, fishing out the keys, opened the gate and crutched up the path until the lights blazed on and the dog started barking.

Everyone can make mistakes.

I DIDN'T get as far as the front-door steps. A dark figure, dimly glimpsed in the floodlights' glare, came launching itself at me in a cannonball rugger tackle, and when I reached the ground, something very hard hit my head.

I had no sensation of blacking out or of time passing. I woke up on the grass in the dark. I was in Greville's front garden. Alive.

Groaning slightly, I rolled onto my knees and groped about for the crutches. Without thinking, I got up and started toward Greville's front door, and of course the lights flashed on again and the dog started barking.

I stood rooted to the spot, swaying unsteadily on the crutches, absolutely dim and pathetic. The door was ajar, I saw, the hall lights on, and while I stood dithering, it opened wide and the cannonball figure shot out.

The cannonball was a motorcycle helmet, shiny and black, its visor pulled down. There was an impression of jeans, denim jacket, gloves, black running shoes, all moving fast. He vaulted the gate and set off at a run down the street.

When my head cleared, I went up to the door. The keys were still in the lowest lock—Clarissa's small bunch of three that I'd been using instead of Greville's larger bunch. I'd made things simple for the intruder, I thought, by having them ready in my hand.

I switched off the floodlights and the dog, and in the sudden silence closed the front door. Greville's small sitting room, when I reached it, looked like the path of a hurricane. I surveyed the mess in fury rather than horror and picked the tumbled phone off the floor and called the police. A burglary, I said.

Then I sat in Greville's chair with my head in my hands, swore aloud with heartfelt rage, and gingerly felt the bump swelling on my scalp. A bloody pushover, I thought. Like last Sunday. Too like last Sunday to be a coincidence: the cannonball had known both times that I would be an easy target.

I looked wearily around the room. The pictures were off the walls, the glass smashed. The drawers had been yanked out of overturned tables. The video recorder had been torn from its unit, and the videocassettes of the races lay in yards of ruined tape.

Two policemen arrived eventually. They'd seen a great many break-ins, and took down without emotion an account of the assault.

"Well, sir," they said, not caring much about Greville's wrecked room, "what's been stolen?"

Nothing large, I said, because the burglar had had both hands free when he vaulted the gate. We went on a tour of the house and found the tornado had blown through all of it.

Upstairs, we found that the black-and-white bedroom had also been ransacked. Clothes were scattered everywhere. In the bathroom, pills lay on the floor. A toothpaste tube had been squeezed flat by a shoe, and a can of shaving cream lay in the washbasin, the contents squirted on the mirror.

We all descended to the kitchen, where the mess again was indescribable. Every packet of cereal had been poured out, sugar and flour sieved in a strainer. Half of the floor of carpet tiles had been pulled up from the concrete beneath. The policemen went phlegmatically around, looking at things but touching little.

"How long was I out?" I said. "He did all this. . . ."

"Twenty minutes, I'd say," one said, and the other nodded. "He was working fast, you can see. I'd say he was pulling up these tiles, looking for a floor safe when you set the alarms off again."

I explained about the Saxony Franklin office being broken into. "We weren't sure what had been stolen, apart from an address book. In view of this"—I gestured to the shambles—"probably nothing was."

They looked around in the garden on the way out and found half a brick lying on the grass near where I had woken up. Robbery with violence, that made it.

I thanked them for coming, and they said they'd be putting in a report. Then I shut the front door, switched on the alarms again, and, feeling depressed and stupid, went slowly to the kitchen to turn the lights off.

Whoever had come had come because the diamonds were still somewhere to be found. I supposed I should be grateful for that information. But could I find them if I looked harder?

I hadn't noticed on my first trip downstairs that the kitchen's red carpet was in fact warm, washable carpet tiles. They weren't stuck to the hard surface beneath, and the intruder had had no trouble in lifting them up.

I drew the curtains and pulled up several red tiles, thinking about Greville's security complex. It would be just like him to build a safe into the solid base of the house.

The last tile sat under a serving table. Under that carpet square, when I'd moved the table, I found a metal circle flush with the hard base floor, a recessed ring in it for lifting.

Amazed and suddenly unbearably hopeful, I pulled the ring up and tugged, and the metal circle came away, revealing another layer of metal beneath: a solid-looking dinner-size plate in which there was a keyhole and another handle for lifting. I tried all of Greville's keys in the keyhole, but none of them fit.

There were keys in the hollow book, I remembered wearily. I shifted upstairs and dug out *With a Mule in Patagonia* and the others, rediscovering the two businesslike keys and also the decorative one. True to Greville's mind, however, it was that very flamboyant one which slid easily into the keyhole and under pressure turned the mechanism inside.

I lifted the lid triumphantly. The space below was big enough to hold a case of champagne, but to my acute disappointment it contained no nest egg, only a clutch of businesslike brown envelopes. Sighing deeply, I took out the top two. The first contained the deeds to the house and the second the paperwork for the mortgage. Another contained a copy of his will, and another his birth certificate and insurance policy.

Hell and damnation, I thought. If I couldn't find the damned diamonds, I'd be failing Greville as much as myself.

I stuffed the envelopes back, replaced both metal plates, and laid a carpet tile on top. I couldn't imagine why Greville hadn't used the hiding place for jewels.

Feeling defeated, I climbed at length to the bedroom. By the time I'd swallowed a Distalgesic, brushed my teeth, and swept the crunching underfoot junk to one side, I had used up that day's ration of stamina pretty thoroughly.

In Greville's bed, I just lay still and let the hours pass, thinking of bad and good and of why things happened, and by morning felt calm and much better.

By hopping and holding on to things, I took a long, luxurious shower, rewrapped my still swollen ankle, and dressed, borrowing one of Greville's white shirts. Down in the forlorn little sitting room, I telephoned to Nicholas Loder.

He didn't sound pleased to hear my voice.

"Well done with Dozen Roses," I said. "And to solve the question of who owns him," I continued, "I've found a buyer."

"Now, look here!" he began angrily. "I—"

"Yes, I know," I interrupted. "You'd like to sell him to one of your own owners and keep him in your yard. I sympathize with that, but Mr. and Mrs. Ostermeyer, the people I was with yesterday at York, would like the horse themselves. They want to send him to Milo Shandy to be trained for jumping."

"I strongly protest. You owe it to me to leave him here. Four wins in a row . . . It's downright dishonorable to take him away."

"He's suitable for jumping now that he's been gelded." Into Loder's silence I added, "If you find a buyer for Gemstones, though, I'll give my approval."

He grunted, which I took to mean assent, but he also said grittily, "Don't expect any favors from me, ever."

"I've done one for you," I pointed out, "in not lodging a complaint. Anyway, the Ostermeyers will do the paperwork today, so Milo should be collecting Dozen Roses sometime this week."

"Rot you," he said. He slammed down the phone and left me feeling perplexed as much as anything by his constant rudeness.

I picked up my overnight bag and felt vaguely guilty at leaving so much chaos in the house. I'd done minimum tidying upstairs, but the rest was physically difficult and would have to wait.

I went by taxi to the Ostermeyers' hotel and again found them in champagne spirits, and it was again Simms who chauffeured us. We arrived without delay in Lambourn, at Milo's door, where Milo himself greeted me with the news that Nicholas Loder wanted me to phone him at once.

"It sounded to me," Milo said, "like a great deal of agitation pretending to be casual. He doesn't want me to have Dozen Roses, for some reason. Derek, get it over with while we go and look at Datepalm." Milo bore the Ostermeyers away with twinkling charm, and I phoned Nicholas Loder.

"Look," he said forcefully, "I've an owner who'll offer double what your Ostermeyers are offering. You'll make a good, clear profit this way."

"Please tell your owner I'm sorry," I said, "but no. Loyalty to the Ostermeyers comes first."

"Think it over. Everyone can be bought," he said, and slammed the receiver down again.

I had no appetite for chronic feuds. I went out into the yard, where, seeing me, Milo broke away from the Ostermeyers, who were feasting their eyes on Datepalm.

"What did Loder want?" Milo demanded, coming toward me.

"He offered double whatever I was asking the Ostermeyers to pay for Dozen Roses."

Milo stared. "Double? Without knowing what it was? If you've accepted, I'll flatten you."

I laughed. Too many people that past week had flattened me already. "I told him to stuff it."

"Good." He looked at me attentively. "Are you all right?" he asked suddenly. "You don't look too well."

I told him briefly about being knocked out in Greville's garden.

"Those phone calls you took," I said, "were designed to make sure I turned up in the right place at the right time. So I walked straight into an ambush. I feel a fool."

"Derek!" He was dumbfounded, but also of course practical. "It's not going to delay your getting back on a horse?"

"No. And I won't bother the Ostermeyers with it, of course."

He nodded in complete understanding. To Martha and to Harley, proprietorship in the jockey was as important as in the horse. I'd never undervalued that feeling. They were the best owners to ride for, even if often the most demanding, and I would never jeopardize my place on Datepalm for a profit on Dozen Roses.

When they had finished admiring Datepalm, we all returned to the house, where we telephoned to the bloodstock agent for an opinion about Dozen Roses and then agreed on a price. Milo beamed. Martha clapped her hands with pleasure. Harley wrote a check carefully to Saxony Franklin, subject to a vet's certificate.

Martha and Harley and I all signed change-of-ownership forms, and business concluded, Milo drove us all to lunch at a restaurant that was crammed with Lambourn people. Martha and Harley held court as the new owners of Dozen Roses and were pink with gratification over the compliments on their purchase. I watched their stimulated faces, hers rounded and still pretty under the blond-rinsed gray hair, his heavily handsome. Both now looking sixty, their enthusiasms and enjoyments were almost childlike in their simplicity—which did no harm in the weary old world.

All we needed now was for Datepalm and Dozen Roses to carry on winning.

Milo took us back to the Daimler, and we drove out of the yard, with Martha settling back into her seat with murmurs and soft remarks of pleasure. I told Simms the way to Hungerford so that he could drop me off there, and the big car purred along with Sunday-afternoon somnolence.

Martha said something I didn't catch, and I turned my face back between the headrests, looking toward her and asking her to

87

repeat it. I saw a flash of raw horror begin on Harley's face, and then with a crash and a bang the car rocketed out of control across the road toward a wall. There was blood and shredded glass everywhere, and we careened off the wall, back onto the road and into the path of a fifty-seater touring coach, which had been behind us and was now bearing down on us like a runaway cliff.

CHAPTER 7

IN THE split second before the front of the bus hit my side of the car I totally believed I would be mangled to pulp within a breath.

There was no time for any emotion. The bus plunged into the Daimler, turned it again forward, and both vehicles screeched along the road together, monstrously joined wheel to wheel, the noise and buffeting and speed of everything truly terrifying.

The two vehicles, dragging slower, were blocking the whole road. Toward us, around a bend, came a family car traveling fast. The driver, in a frenzy, braked so hard that his rear end swung round and hit the front of the Daimler broadside with a sickening jolt.

Against all probability I was still alive, and that seemed enough. After the first stunned moments of silence, there were voices shouting and screaming, and a sharp smell of raw petrol.

The whole thing was going to burn, I thought. Explode. Fireballs coming. The heat of the dead engine filled the cracked-open body of the car. There was dread and despair and a vision of hell.

I couldn't escape. Part of the doorframe had bent across my chest, pinning me deep against the seat. At most, I was breathing.

Martha too was alive. I could hear her whimpering behind me, a small moaning. Simms and Harley were silent. I thought wretchedly that Martha was dying, but in a quavery, small voice she said, "Derek?"

"Yes." My voice croaked.

"I'm frightened."

So was I, by God. I said futilely, "Don't worry."

She was saying, "Harley? Harley, honey?" in awakening anguish. "Oh God, get us out, please, someone."

My side of the car was jammed tight against the bus. In time people tried to open the doors on Simms' side, but they were immovably buckled. Dazed people emerged from the family car in front, the children weeping. People from the coach spread along the roadside, all of them elderly.

Then a man was presently yelling through the window to Martha that he was going to smash the rear window and she should cover her face in case of flying glass.

Martha hid her face against Harley's chest, weeping, and the rear window gave way to determination and a metal bar.

Strong arms hauled Martha out bodily. Almost at once her rescuer was himself inside the car, this best of British workmen lifting the still unconscious Harley far enough to be raised by other hands outside. Then he took a look at me and Simms.

"Lord," he said. He was smallish, with a mustache and bright brown eyes. "They'll have to cut you out." He wrinkled his nose at the petrol smell and retreated through the rear window, and Simms and I sat on in our silent immobility.

It was odd, I thought, that for all the risks I took, I very seldom felt any fear of death. I thought about physical pain and remembered things I'd endured. I swallowed and felt lonely, and hoped that if the imagined pain of burning came, it would be quick.

There were sirens at length in the distance, and the best sight in the world, as far as I was concerned, was the red fire engine forcing its way forward through the scattering spectator cars to either side of the road. Behind the fire engine I could see the flashing lights of a police car and an ambulance.

Figures in uniforms appeared, the best being in flameproof suits lugging a hose. One of them shouted to me, "There's petrol running from these vehicles. We're going to spray the road underneath you. Shut your eyes and cover your mouth and nose."

I managed to shield my face in the neck of my jersey. I listened to the long whooshing of the spray and thought no sound could be sweeter. I wiped blood and sweat off my face and felt shaky.

After a while some of the firemen brought up metal-cutting

gear and tore out the door next to where Harley had sat. Into this new entrance edged a policeman, who took a look at Simms and then perched on the rear seat, where he could see my head. I glimpsed a serious face, about my age and full of strain.

"A doctor's coming," he said. Then he drew out a notebook. "Did you see what caused all this?"

"No," I said. "I was looking back at Mr. and Mrs. Ostermeyer when the car just seemed to go out of control." I thought back. "I think Harley—Mr. Ostermeyer—may have seen something. For a second he looked horrified. Then we hit the wall and rebounded into the path of the bus."

He made a note. "Mr. Ostermeyer is now conscious." He sounded carefully noncommittal. "He says you were shot."

"We were *what?*"

"Shot. Not all of you. You—personally."

"No." I was bewildered. "Of course not."

"Mr. Ostermeyer is quite clear he saw a gun. He says the chauffeur had just pulled out to pass a gray car in front of you, and the driver of that car was pointing a gun out the window at you, and you were shot. Twice. He saw the spurts of flame."

I looked at Simms and at the solidly scarlet, congealed mess below his jaw. "No," I protested, not wanting to believe it. "I'm not bleeding. It's Simms' blood that's on me."

"Well, sir, we are treating this as a possible murder inquiry. I'm afraid the firemen say it may be some time before they can get you loose. They need more gear. Can you be patient?"

I nodded. I could be patient for hours if I didn't burn.

He slithered out of the car and left me thinking. The bullet that had torn into Simms would have gone through my own neck or head if I hadn't turned round to talk to Martha.

A good many people arrived, looking official with measuring tapes and cameras, taking photographs of Simms, and consulting in low tones. A police surgeon solemnly put a stethoscope to Simms' chest and declared him dead, and, without bothering with the stethoscope, declared me alive. How bad was the compression, he wanted to know.

"Uncomfortable," I said, adding that my toes, fingers and lungs were okay and that I had cramps in my legs, and the instrument panel was inhibiting the digestion of a good Sunday lunch.

He allowed himself a small smile and wriggled his way out. Simms and I went on sitting for what seemed several more ages, but finally the extra gear appeared in the form of winches, cranes and a laser saw.

Once large mechanics pulled Simms' stiffening body out, they decided to cut off the back of Simms' seat to give themselves more room to work. They yanked padding out from behind me and then with a hacksaw took the back of the seat off. Finally, with one of them supporting my shoulders, another pulled out handfuls of springs and seat innards, and the bear-hug pressure on my abdomen and arm and legs was relieved, and I had only blessed pins and needles instead. My rescuers hooked their arms under my armpits and at last retracted me from the car's crushing embrace like a breached calf from a cow.

Relief was an inadequate word. Sitting each side of me, they gave me a minute's rest on the back seat, all of us breathing deeply.

"Thanks," I said briefly.

"Think nothing of it."

One by one we edged out onto the road, and I was astonished to find a crowd waiting around, both officials and assorted bystanders. There was a small cheer as I stood up free, and I smiled in both embarrassment and thanksgiving.

I was offered a stretcher but said I'd much rather have the crutches that might still be in the boot, and someone brought them out unharmed, about the only thing still unbent in the whole mess. I stood for a bit with their support, simply looking at all the intertwined wreckage—at the bus and the family car, and above all at the Daimler, mangled and compressed like a stamped-on toy. I thought it incredible that I'd sat where I'd sat, and lived. I reckoned that I'd used up a lifetime's luck.

THE Ostermeyers had been taken to Swindon Hospital and treated for shock, bruises and concussion. From there, recovering, they had telephoned Milo and told him what had happened, and he had said they must stay with him for the night and had come to collect them. All three were on the point of leaving when I in my turn arrived.

There was a predictable amount of fussing from Martha, and Milo pressed me to come to his place later. But soon they all bustled off, and I went through the hospital routines, got discharged, and was invited to give a more detailed statement to the police. Some of their questions were disturbing.

How long had the gunman's gray car been in front of us?

I couldn't remember—hadn't noticed.

Could anyone have known we would be on that road then?

I stared at the policeman. Anyone in the restaurant for lunch. Anyone there could have followed us back to Milo's house, perhaps, and waited for us to leave, and passed us, allowing us then to pass again. But why?

Mr. Ostermeyer said the gun was pointing at you, sir.

With all due respect, one couldn't be certain.

Could I think of any reason why anyone should want to kill me? Me, personally?

No . . . I couldn't.

They pounced on the hesitation, and I told them I'd been attacked the previous evening. I explained about Greville's death. I told them he had been dealing in precious stones and I thought my attacker had been trying to steal part of the stock. But I had no idea why the would-be thief should want to shoot me today when he could have bashed my head in yesterday.

They wrote it down without comment. Had I any idea who had attacked me the previous evening?

No, I hadn't.

They didn't say so, but they thought anyone attacked twice in two days *had* to know who was after him. I would have liked very much to be able to tell them. I'd better find out soon, I thought.

I'd better not find out too late.

I STAYED that night in an anonymous hotel in Swindon, where unknown enemies wouldn't find me. From the hotel I phoned Milo to ask how Martha and Harley were doing.

"They're quavery. Martha keeps crying. She's terribly upset about Simms, and she thought you were dying too."

"Persuade them to sleep. I'll come in the morning and pick them up and take them back to their hotel in London."

"All right, then. See you at breakfast."

I put down the receiver and got through to Brad at home.

"Cor," he said. "You were in that crash."

"How did you hear about it?" I asked, surprised.

"Down the pub. It's shook everyone up."

"Have you still got my car?" I said.

"Yerss." He sounded anxious. "You said keep it here."

"Yes. Do you still want to go on driving?"

"Yerss." Very positive.

I explained where I was and said I would meet him at eight a.m. outside the hotel. We would be going to London. "Okay?"

"Yerss," he said again, signing off, and it sounded like a cat purring over the resumption of milk.

I ran a bath, took off my clothes and the bandage round my ankle, and lay gratefully in hot water, letting it soak away the fatigue. Then, my overnight bag having survived unharmed along with the crutches, I scrubbed my teeth, put on sleeping shorts, rewrapped the ankle, and was asleep by nine. I dreamed of crashes and fire and hovering, unidentified threats.

BRAD came on the dot in the morning, and we went first to my place, still quiet and unransacked, in a necessary quest for clean clothes. His mum, Brad agreed, would wash the things I'd worn in the crash. I changed, and repacked my traveling bag, and we drove in good order to Lambourn.

Martha and Harley were still shaking over breakfast, the coffee cups trembling against their lips. I looked at them with affection, their surrogate son–nephew, and hoped it wouldn't be long before their habitual preference for enjoyment resurfaced.

"The only good thing about yesterday," Martha said with a sigh, "was buying Dozen Roses. I'm sure he'll be brilliant."

Milo offered more coffee, but they were ready to leave, and in a short while we were on the road to London. No one passed us and slowed, no one ambushed or shot us, and Brad drew up with a flourish outside their hotel, at least the equal of Simms. Martha with a shine of tears kissed my cheek, and Harley gruffly shook my hand. They would come back soon, they said, but they were sure glad to be going home. I watched them go shakily away and hoped Datepalm would cover himself with glory for them, and Dozen Roses also, once he could jump.

"Office?" I suggested to Brad, and he nodded, and made the now familiar turns toward Hatton Garden.

Little in Saxony Franklin appeared to have changed. It seemed extraordinary that it was only a week since I'd walked in there for the first time, so familiar did it feel going back. The staff said, "Good morning, Derek" as if they'd been used to me for years.

"How was the funeral?" Annette asked sadly, laying out letters from Friday on the desk.

A thousand light-years ago, I thought. "Quiet," I said. "Good. Your flowers were good. They were on top of his coffin."

She looked pleased. "It didn't seem right, not being at his funeral. We had a minute's silence here at two o'clock."

I was moved, and let her see it. She smiled sweetly in her heavy way and went off, leaving me floundering in the old treacle of deciding things on a basis of no knowledge.

June whisked in, looking happy, and told me we were low in blue lace agate chips, snowflake obsidian and amazonite beads.

"Order some more, same as before."

"Yes, right."

She was on her way out again when I asked her if there was an alarm clock among all the gadgets. I pulled open the deep drawer.

"An alarm clock?" She peered at the assorted black objects. "Telescopes, dictionaries, Geiger counter, calculators . . ."

I brought out all the gadgets and stood them on the desk. None of them, as far as I could see, had an alarm function.

"I've an alarm clock in my room. Would you like that?"

"Um . . . yes, perhaps. Could you set it to four fifteen?"

"Sure, anything you like."

She vanished and returned, fiddling with a tiny black clock the size of a credit card. "There you are," she said. "Four fifteen—

p.m., I suppose you mean." She put the clock on the desk.

"This afternoon, yes. There's an alarm somewhere here that goes off every day at four twenty. I want to find it."

Her eyes widened. "Oh, but that's Mr. Franklin's watch. It's a computer itself, a calendar and a compass."

That watch, I reflected, was beside my bed in Hungerford.

"I think," I said, "that he may have had more than one alarm set to four twenty."

The fair eyebrows lifted. "I did sometimes wonder," she said. "I mean, why four twenty? If he was in the stockroom and his watch alarm went off, he would stop whatever he was doing for a few moments. I asked him once, but he just said it was a convenient time for communication or something. I didn't understand."

She spoke without resentment. I thought that Greville must have enjoyed having June around him as much as I did.

"What's this one?" I asked, picking up a small gray contraption with black ear sponges on a headband with a cord.

"A sound enhancer. It's for deaf people, really. Put the earphones on. You can hear everything said anywhere in the office."

I put on the earphones and pressed the ON switch, and sure enough, I could straightaway hear Annette across the hallway talking to Lily about asking Derek for time off for the dentist.

I removed the earphones and looked at June.

"It's uncanny!" Some of Greville's toys, I thought, were decidedly unfriendly.

June left for lunch, and I tried to apply myself to answering the tricky letters when the telephone rang.

It was Elliot Trelawney, asking about the Vaccaro notes, as they had a committee meeting at two o'clock. "You said you would send them this morning," he said with a tinge of civilized reproach. "Do you remember?"

"Yes." I did, vaguely. They were in Greville's sitting room. Somewhere in all the mess, unless the thief had taken them.

I apologized. I didn't actually say I'd come near to being killed twice since I'd last spoken to him, just that things had cropped up. I would get them to the court by two.

"Vaccaro is first on the committee's agenda," he said. "It's

95

frightfully important that we turn this application down."

"Yes, I know," I replied. "I'll get them to you."

I went down to the yard to find Brad, gave him the small ring of keys to Greville's house, and explained about the upheaval he would find and the Vaccaro notes.

"Can you make the journey?" I asked a shade doubtfully.

"Yerss." Seeming slighted by my tone, he took the address from me with brusqueness and drove out of the yard.

Upstairs, Annette said there had just been a call from Antwerp, and there was a number for me to ring back.

Antwerp. With an effort I thought back to Thursday's distant conversation. Jacob van Ekeren.

I got through and was rewarded with the smooth bilingual voice of Hans van Ekeren, Jacob's nephew. "My uncle says he knew your brother for a long time, and about six months ago your brother telephoned for advice about a sight holder. He was considering buying diamonds, and trusted my uncle's judgment."

"Ah," I said hopefully. "Who did your uncle recommend?"

"Three or four possible names. My uncle said they were all trustworthy. One of them was certainly Guy Servi, here in Antwerp, but my uncle can't remember the others and doesn't know which one your brother decided on—or if he did business at all."

"Well, thank you, anyway. You've been very kind."

He disconnected with politeness, having dictated to me the address and telephone number of Guy Servi. I dialed the number and eventually reached someone who spoke English.

Mr. Greville Saxony Franklin, now deceased, had been my brother? Again the rigmarole: they would consult their files and call me back. Finally, after a long hour, they did so.

What was my problem, they wanted to know.

"My problem is that our offices were ransacked, a lot of paperwork is missing, and I'm trying to sort out Greville's affairs. Was it your firm who bought diamonds for him?"

"Yes," the voice said matter-of-factly, "we did."

Wow, I thought. "Could you, er, give me the details?" I asked.

"Certainly. We purchased a sight box of color-H diamonds of average weight—three point two carats—at the July sight at the

CSO in London, and we delivered one hundred stones, total weight three hundred and twenty carats, to your brother."

"He, er, paid for them in advance, didn't he?"

"One point five million United States dollars in cash."

"Thank you," I said. "Um . . . when you delivered them, did you send any sort of, er, packing note?"

It seemed he found the plebeian words packing note faintly shocking. "We sent the diamonds by personal messenger," he said austerely, "to your brother at his London residence. Your brother inspected the merchandise and weighed it, and when he was satisfied, he signed a release certificate. He has the carbon copy of that release. There was no other, uh, packing note."

"I don't doubt you," I said hastily. "It's just that I can't find the carbon copy." I thought a bit and asked, "You don't happen to know who he was getting to cut and polish them?"

"I understood they were to be cut for one special client who had his own requirements, but no, he didn't say."

I sighed. "Well, thank you, anyway."

"We'll be happy to send you copies of the paperwork."

"Yes, please," I said. "It would be most helpful."

I put the receiver down slowly. I straightened my neck and back and eased a few of the muscles that had developed small aches since the crash. Then I called June in.

"I want a list of diamond cutters and polishers, starting with Antwerp. After Antwerp, the other main centers—New York, Tel Aviv and Bombay, isn't that right?"

"But we don't deal—"

"Don't say it," I said. "We do. Greville bought some for Prospero Jenks, who wants them cut to suit his sculptures."

"Oh." She looked first blank and then interested. "Yes, all right. I'm sure I can do that. Straightaway."

I watched her back view disappear. Gray skirt, white shirt. Blond hair. Long legs. Flat shoes. Exit June.

THE day wore on. I assembled three orders in the vault by myself and then made a slow tour of the whole place, calling in to see Alfie pack his parcels, watching Lily with her squashed-governess air collecting orders, seeing Jason manhandle heavy boxes of newly arrived stock, stopping for a moment beside strong-looking Tina, whom I knew least, as she checked the new intake against the packing list and sorted it into trays.

None of them paid attention. I was already wallpaper.

By four o'clock June had produced a long list of Antwerp cutters and a shorter one so far for New York. Tel Aviv was coming, and she had nothing for Bombay.

At the rate all the cautious diamond dealers worked, I thought, it would take a week just to get answers from the Antwerp list. But it would be worth trying. I was down to straws.

June's tiny alarm clock suddenly began bleeping. She returned through my doorway at high speed and paid all the other gadgets vivid attention. She checked the drawers and peered into filing cabinets, leaving everything open, as I asked.

The minutes ticked away, and at four twenty the little alarm duly sounded, very distantly. June looked wildly at the assembled gadgets and put her ear down to them.

I think of you every day at four twenty.

Clarissa had written it on her funeral card. Greville had apparently done it every day in the office. It had been their own private language, a long way from diamonds. I acknowledged with regret that I would learn nothing from it.

The muffled alarm stopped. June raised her head, frowning. "The sound was still inside the desk." She was mystified. "But I've taken everything out."

"There must be another drawer."

She called in Annette, who said with a worried frown that she knew nothing about another drawer. The three of us looked at the enormous three-inch slab of black, grainy wood that formed the top surface. I thought back to the green stone box, to the keyhole that wasn't a keyhole, to the sliding base.

To the astonishment of Annette and June I lowered myself to the floor and looked up under the kneehole part. In the center, three inches in from the front, there was a sliding switch. With satisfaction I regained the chair, felt under the desk top, and pressed back the switch. Nothing happened.

Something had to have happened, I reasoned. Nothing about Greville was for nothing. I banged my fist with frustration down on the desk top, and a section of the front edge fell off in my lap.

Annette and June gasped. The piece was like a strip of veneer with metal fastening clips. Behind it was more wood, but with a keyhole. Watched breathlessly by Annette and June, I brought out Greville's bunch of keys and tried those that looked the right size, and one of them turned obligingly. I pulled it toward me, and like silk, a wide, shallow drawer slid out.

We all looked at the contents. Passport. Little flat black gadgets, four or five of them. No diamonds.

June was delighted. "That's the Wizard," she said.

She pointed at a small black rectangle and opened it like a book on the desk. The right-hand panel was covered with buttons and looked like an ultra-versatile calculator; the left-hand side had a small screen at the top, and a touch panel at the bottom with headings like EXPENSE RECORD and TIME ACCOUNTING.

"It does everything," June said. "It's a diary, a phone directory, a memo pad, an appointments calendar, an accounts keeper. . . ."

"And does it have an alarm set to four twenty?"

She switched the thing on, pressed three keys, and showed me the screen. "Daily alarm," it announced, "4:20 p.m., set."

For Annette the excitement seemed to be over. She went back to work, and June began to tidy away all the gadgets while I investigated further the secret drawer. I frowned over the passport, having assumed that in going to Harwich, Greville had meant to catch the ferry. Perhaps he'd been going to *meet* the *Koningin Beatrix*. But meet whom?

I looked at his photograph, which, like all passport photographs, wasn't very good, but good enough to bring him vividly back into the office—his office, where I sat in his chair.

I put the passport back with regret and took out a flat, square object, like the Wizard, with a curl of paper coming out of it.

"That's the printer," June said, "for the Wizard."

She plugged the printer's short cord into a slot in the side of the Wizard and dexterously pressed a few keys. With a whir the tiny machine began printing out a strip of telephone numbers.

"Lovely, isn't it?" June said, pressing a STOP button. "When he was away, Mr. Franklin would enter all his expenses on here, and we would print them out when he got home. . . . Oh dear." She smothered the uprush of emotion.

"Is there an instruction manual?" I asked.

"Of course. All the instruction manuals are in this file."

I laid the manuals on top of the desk next to the Wizard and the printer and took a third black object out of the drawer. This was the microcassette recorder that went with the tiny tapes I'd found in the hollow books.

"That's voice activated," June said, looking at it.

I brought out the last gadget, a gray hand-size thing that had an ON/OFF switch, but no obvious purpose.

"That's to frighten dogs away." June smiled. "Mr. Franklin didn't like dogs. I think he was ashamed of it."

I hadn't known Greville didn't like dogs. I fiercely wanted him back, if only to tease him about it. The real trouble with death was what it left unsaid, and knowing that that thought was universal made it no less sharp.

I put the dog frightener back beside the passport, closed and locked the shallow drawer, and fitted the veneer in place with a click. The vast top again looked wholly solid.

The telephone rang. I picked up the receiver and said, "Saxony Franklin," out of newly acquired habit.

"Derek? Is that you?"

"Yes, Milo, it is."

"I'm not satisfied with this horse Dozen Roses." He sounded aggressive, which wasn't unusual, and also apologetic, which was. "The damn thing arrived half asleep today. I'm getting the vet round at once, and I'll want urine and blood tests. Get down here, will you? Take a look at him."

"In a couple of hours," I said, and put down the receiver with an inward groan. I did not want to go belting down to Lambourn to a crisis. I wanted my aches to unwind.

I telephoned the car, but Brad, as usual, didn't answer. After saying good night to everyone and collecting the gadgets, I went down to the yard and found Brad there waiting.

"Did you find those papers okay?" I asked, climbing in.

"Yerss," he said. "And delivered them."

"Thanks. Great. And now, please, to Lambourn," I said as we turned out of the yard. "But on the way, back to my brother's house to collect something else. Okay?"

Just before we reached the house, he pointed to Greville's car, still standing by the curb. "It's been broken into," he said.

He found a parking place, and we went back to look. The boot had been jimmied open and now wouldn't close again.

"Good job we put the things in my car," I said.

He shook his head. "In our house, under the stairs. Our mum said to do it, what with your car outside our door all night."

"Very thoughtful," I said.

He nodded. "Smart, our mum."

He came with me into the house—daylight: no floods, no dog— and waited in the hall while I collected the tapes from the forlorn little sitting room. On the way out I placed a note prominently on the lowest step of the staircase:

Dear Mrs. P.,
   I'm afraid there is bad news for you. Don't clean up the house. Telephone Saxony Franklin Ltd. instead.

I added the number. I would have to warn Annette to go gently with anyone ringing. Nothing else I could do to cushion the shock.

IN THE yard Milo was striding about. He yanked my door open and scowled at me as I reached for the crutches and stood up.

He said crossly, "The damned horse wouldn't give a sample."

I chuckled. It sounded so simple to take a regulation urine sample from two horses after every race. In practice it meant waiting around for the horses to oblige.

"Come away," I said. "He'll do it in the end."

He followed me reluctantly, and we went into the kitchen. A few minutes later a car scrunched into the yard, and Phil Urquhart, veterinary surgeon, came breezing in, asking if there were any results. He read Milo's scowl aright, and laughed.

He was small and sandy-haired, about thirty, the grandson of a three-generation family practice, and to my mind the best of them.

"What will you test Dozen Roses for?" I asked him.

He raised his eyebrows. "Barbiturates, in this case."

"At York," I said thoughtfully, "one of Nicholas Loder's owners was walking around with a nebulizer. A kitchen baster, to be precise."

"An owner?" Phil asked, surprised.

"Yes. He owned the winner of the five-furlong sprint. He was also in the saddling box with Dozen Roses."

Phil frowned. "What are you implying?"

"Nothing. Merely observing. The stable money was definitely on. They wanted to win, and they knew if the horse won, he'd be tested. So the only question is, What could you give a horse that wouldn't disqualify it?"

"Nothing that would make it go faster. They test for stimulants," Phil said.

"What if you gave it, say, Adrenalin?"

"Straight into the mucous membranes. . . . Well, I suppose it's possible. And there'd be no trace." He paused and considered me with friendly professional eyes. "You do realize you're saying that if anything was done, Nicholas Loder condoned it?"

"Doesn't seem likely, does it?" I said.

A commotion in the darkening yard heralded the success of the urine mission.

"Right," Phil said. "I'll be off now. Take care."

He loaded the sample and his gear into his car and scrunched away. I soon followed with Brad, but decided again not to go home.

"Tonight let's try the Chequers Hotel, in Newbury," I said.

"Yerss," he said, understanding.

"Thanks," I said, and meant it wholeheartedly.

I booked in at the Chequers, Brad drove himself home, and I spent the evening in an armchair learning my way round the Wizard.

CHAPTER 8

COMPUTERS weren't my natural habitat as they had been Greville's, so it probably took me longer to get results.

But it soon became clear that Greville had used the gadget extensively. There were three telephone and address lists, a daily appointments calendar, a prompt for anniversaries and an information file. After a few false starts I ended with long printed lists of everything, and read them with growing frustration. None of it seemed to have anything to do with Antwerp or with diamonds.

Then I thought of my question to June the day she'd found her way to Pearl: What if it were all stored in secret?

According to the Wizard's two-hundred-page manual, entries marked secret could only be retrieved by knowing the password, which could be any combination of up to seven numbers and letters. Forgetting the password meant farewell to the entries.

I tried every combination of letters and numbers I thought Greville might have used, but got nowhere. Clarissa was too long, 12roses should have been right, but wasn't. In the end I was ready to throw the confounded Wizard across the room.

I finally played the tiny tapes instead—a lot of office chat. I couldn't think why Greville hid them. The only interesting thing was his voice. The only way I would ever hear him again.

"Going out to lunch," he was saying. "Back by two."

Annette's voice said, "Yes, Mr. Franklin." Then a click.

Almost immediately, because the time lapse had been cut, a different voice said, "I'm in his office now, and I can't find them. He hides everything. He's security mad, you know that." Click. "I can't ask him. I don't think he trusts me." Click. "Annette'd never tell me anything." Click. "I'll have to go; he doesn't like me using this phone. He'll be back from lunch any second." Click.

End of tape.

Bloody hell, I thought. I knew the voice, as Greville must have done. My brother had left the recorder on, I guessed by mistake, and he'd come back and listened—with, I supposed, sadness—to treachery. It opened up a whole new world of questions, and I went slowly to bed, groping toward answers.

Hours later I woke, and thinking of Greville, it occurred to me that there was one password I hadn't tried.

Impelled by curiosity, I switched the Wizard on and typed the word Greville had written on the last page of his racing diary, below the numbers of his passport and national insurance: Derek.

I pressed ENTER, and the Wizard let me into its data.

I BEGAN printing out everything in the secret files, the baby printer clicking away line by line and not very fast.

From the memo section came a long list of days and dates: "Monday, Jan. 30, Wednesday, March 8 . . ." Mystified, I watched the sequence lengthen, noticing only that the dates were five or six weeks apart. The list ended five weeks before Greville's death. It began, I thought blankly, four years earlier. Four years ago—when he first met Clarissa.

I felt unbearable sadness for him. He'd fallen in love with a woman who wouldn't leave home for him, whom he hadn't wanted to compromise. He'd kept a record, I was certain, of every snatched day they'd spent together, and hidden it away as he had hidden so much else. A whole lot of roses, I thought.

The schedule section contained appointments not hinted at earlier, including the delivery of the diamonds to his London house. For the day of his death there were two entries: "Ipswich. Orwell Hotel, P. 3:30 p.m." and "Meet *Koningin Beatrix* 6:30 p.m., Harwich." For the following Monday he had noted, "Meet C King's Cross 12:10. Lunch Luigi's."

But he hadn't. Poor Clarissa. Tuesday she learned he was dead.

The printer produced another entry for the Saturday after. "C and Dozen Roses both at York! Could I go? Not wise. Check TV." Then it stopped, as Greville's life had. No more appointments.

Next I printed the telephone sections—private and business overseas. Private contained only Knightwood, but from business overseas I watched with widening eyes the emergence of five numbers and addresses in Antwerp. One was van Ekeren, one was Guy Servi; three were so far unknown to me. I breathed almost painfully with exultation.

I printed the expense manager's section last, as it looked the least promising, but the first item to emerge was galvanic:

Antwerp says 5 of the first batch of rough are CZ.
Don't want to believe it.
Infinite sadness.
Priority 1: Arrange meetings. Ipswich?
Undecided. Damnation!

I wished he'd been more explicit, but it was actually surprising he'd entered these feelings at all. No other entries afterward held any comment, but were short records of courier expenses with a firm called Euro-Securo. There was nothing else disturbing.

THE next morning at Saxony Franklin I asked Annette whether my brother had had a gadget that warned you if someone was listening to your conversation on an extension.

"No, he didn't," she said, troubled. "Are you implying that we listened in on him?"

"Not you," I assured her quickly, "but yes, I'd think it happened. Anyway, at some point this morning I want to make sure of not being overheard, so when my call comes through, perhaps you'll all go into the stockroom and sing 'Rule Britannia.' "

Annette never made jokes. I had to explain I didn't mean sing literally. She rather huffily agreed that when I wanted it, she would go round the extensions checking against eavesdroppers.

"If Mr. Franklin wanted to be private," she added, "he went down to the yard and telephoned from his car."

There, I supposed, he would have been safe. He had been conscious of betrayal—that was for sure.

I sat at Greville's desk, the door closed, and matched the unknown Antwerp names from the Wizard with three on June's list.

The first and second produced no results, but from the third, once I explained who I was, I got a voice on the far end cautious to the point of repression.

"We at Maarten-Pagnier cannot discuss anything at all with you, monsieur. Monsieur Franklin gave express orders that we were not to communicate with anyone in his office except himself."

"My brother is dead," I said. "Will you please telephone to his lawyers and get their assurance that he's dead and that I am now managing his business?"

After a pause the voice said austerely, "Very well, monsieur."

I gave him the name and number and waited for ages, during which time I received a frantic call from a nearly incoherent woman who wanted to speak to Mr. Franklin urgently.

"Mrs. P.?" I asked tentatively.

Mrs. Patterson, she said. I gave her the abysmal news and listened to her telling me what a fine, nice gentleman my brother had been, and oh dear, had I seen the mess in the house?

"Just leave it," I said. "I'll clean it up later. Then if you could come after that to hoover and dust, I'd be very grateful."

Calming a little, she gave me her phone number. "Oh dear."

Finally the Antwerp voice returned, and begging him to hold on, I hopped over to the door and told Annette to secure the defenses. She looked disapproving as I again closed the door.

Back in Greville's chair, I said, "Please, monsieur, tell me if my brother had any dealings with you. He has left few records."

"He asked us particularly not to send any records to his office. He said he could not trust everyone there as he would like. If you ask his accountants, you may find the records there."

"Good grief. I didn't think of asking them," I said blankly.

"He said for tax purposes . . ."

"Yes, I see." I hesitated. "Did he," I asked a shade breathlessly, "send you a hundred diamonds, color H, average uncut weight three point two carats, to be cut and polished?"

"No, monsieur. He sent twenty-five stones, but five of them were not diamonds."

"Cubic zirconia," I said, enlightened.

"Yes, monsieur. We told Monsieur Franklin as soon as we discovered it. He was extremely upset. He had himself measured and weighed the stones when they were delivered to his London house. He sent them to us in a sealed Euro-Securo courier package. We assured him that the mistake could not have been made here by us, and it was soon after that he asked us not to send or give any information to anyone in his—your—office." He paused. "He made arrangements to receive the finished stones from us, but he didn't meet our messenger."

"Your messenger?"

"One of our partners, to be accurate. It was agreed he should cross to Harwich by boat and return the same way. When Monsieur Franklin failed to meet him, he brought the diamonds back here. We have been waiting for fresh instructions, as Monsieur Franklin had forbidden us to reach him at his office. We are very sorry to hear of his death. It explains everything, of course."

I said, "Did your partner travel on the *Koningin Beatrix?*"

"That's right, monsieur."

I took a deep breath. Twenty of the diamonds at least were safe. Five were missing. Seventy-five were unaccounted for.

The Antwerp voice said, "The stones cut very well. Twelve teardrops of great brilliance and eight stars. What shall we do with them, monsieur?"

"I'll let you know."

"Very good, monsieur. At your service, monsieur."

I put the receiver down slowly, richer by twelve glittering teardrops destined to hang and flash in sunlight, and by eight handsome stars that might twinkle in a fantasy of rock crystal. Better than nothing, but not enough to save the firm.

Using the crutches, I went to Annette and asked her if she would please find Prospero Jenks and make another appointment for me, that afternoon if possible. Then I went down to the yard, taking a tip from Greville, and on the car phone called his accountants. Brad, reading a golfing magazine, paid no attention.

The accountants helpfully confirmed that they were holding unopened envelopes from both my brother and Antwerp, pending further instructions.

"Please tell me who the letters from Antwerp are from," I said.

The letters were all either from Guy Servi, the sight holder, or from Maarten-Pagnier, the cutters. No other firms.

I thanked them, and thought about disloyalty and the decay of friendship. It was restful in the car, I decided. Brad went on reading. I thought of robbery with violence and violence without robbery, of being laid out with a brick and watching Simms die of a bullet from a gray car meant for me, and I wondered whether, if I were dead, anyone could find what I was looking for—or whether they reckoned they now couldn't find it if I was alive.

I stirred and fished in a pocket and gave Brad a check I'd written out for him upstairs.

"What's this?" he said, peering at it.

I explained I hadn't enough for what I owed him. "When we get to the bank, I'll swap it for cash. Otherwise you could bring it back here. It's a company check. They'd see you got cash for it."

He gave me a long look. "Is this because of guns and such?"

I shrugged. "You might say so."

He folded the check deliberately and stowed it away, then picked up the magazine and stared blindly at a page. I was grateful for the absence of comment and said that I was going upstairs for a bit, and why didn't he get some lunch.

Upstairs, Annette said Prospero Jenks would be expecting me in the Knightsbridge shop any time between three and six.

"Great."

She frowned. "Mr. Jenks wanted to know if you were bringing him the goods Mr. Franklin bought for him. I asked what he meant about goods, and he said you would know."

"He's talking about diamonds," I said.

"But we haven't—" She stopped and then said desperately, "I *wish* Mr. Franklin was here." She gave me a look full of her insecurity and doubt of my ability. As she plodded off, I thought that with what lay ahead I'd have preferred a vote of confidence; and I, too, with all my heart, wished Greville back.

Phil Urquhart telephoned, given my number by Milo's secretary, to tell me that Dozen Roses had tested clean for barbiturates and he would give a certificate of soundness for the sale.

"Fine," I said.

"I've been to examine the horse again this morning. He's still very docile. It seems to be his natural state."

"Mm. He's excited enough every time cantering to the start."

"Natural adrenaline," Phil said. "But look, do you want me to get different tests done, for things not usually looked for? I mean, if you really think the horse was given something . . ."

"Yes," I said. "Nicholas Loder was afraid."

"Oh." He was briefly silent. "I could get the tests done anonymously."

"Get them done, then. I don't want to sell the Ostermeyers a lemon. If Dozen Roses can't win on his own merits, I'll talk them out of the idea of owning him."

"I hear the Ostermeyers are coming back to England to see Datepalm run in the Hennessy. How's your ankle?"

"Good as new by then."

I could hear his smile. He disconnected and left me thinking that there still were good things in the world, like riding Datepalm in the Hennessy, and I stood up and put my left foot flat on the floor for a progress report.

It wasn't so bad if I didn't put any weight on it, but there were still jabbingly painful protests against attempts to walk. Oh well, give it a day or two, I thought. It hadn't exactly had a therapeutic week and was no doubt doing its best against odds. On Thursday, I thought, I would get rid of the crutches. By Friday, definitely. Any day after that I'd be running. Ever optimistic.

The ever busy telephone rang again, and I answered it.

"Derek?"

"Yes," I said.

Clarissa's unmistakable voice said, "I'm in London. Could we meet?"

I hadn't expected her so soon, I thought. I said, "Yes, of course. Where?"

"I thought perhaps . . . Luigi's bar and restaurant? It's in Swallow Street, near Piccadilly Circus. Would you mind coming at seven, for a drink?"

"And dinner?" I said.

"Well. . . ." I heard her sigh, "Yes. All right," as she disconnected, and I was left with a vivid understanding of both her compulsion to put me where she had been going to meet Greville and her awareness that perhaps she ought not to.

I could have said no, I thought, but hadn't, and a little intro-spection revealed ambiguities in my own response, like did I want to give comfort or to take it?

AT FOUR Brad took me to Prospero Jenks' shop in Knightsbridge. Prospero Jenks was where I'd found him before, sitting in shirt sleeves at his workbench. He stood up with a smile on his young-old Peter Pan face and offered me a chair.

"Glad to see you," he said, sitting down again. "Have you brought my diamonds?"

"No. Afraid not."

He was disappointed. "I thought that's why you were coming."

"No, not really."

I looked at his long, efficient workroom with its little drawers full of unset stones and thought of the marvels he produced. The big notice on the wall still read NEVER TURN YOUR BACK TO CUSTOM-ERS. ALWAYS WATCH THEIR HANDS.

I said, "Greville sent twenty-five rough stones to Antwerp to be cut for you."

"That's right."

"Five of them were cubic zirconia. Did you," I asked neutrally, "swap them over?"

The half-smile died out of his face, which grew stiff and expres-sionless, and the bright blue eyes stared at me.

"That's rubbish. I'd never do anything stupid like that."

I didn't say anything, and it seemed to give him force.

"You can't come in here making wild accusations. Go on, get out. You'd better leave." He half rose to his feet.

I said, not moving, "When the cutters told Greville five of the stones were cubic zirconia, he was devastated. Very upset. He used to write his thoughts in a notebook, and in there, it says, 'Infinite sadness is not to trust an old friend.'"

He sat back on the stool. "So what?"

"Since Greville died, someone has been trying to steal his diamonds from me. That someone had to know they were there to be found. Greville didn't tell even his staff he'd bought them—for security reasons. But of course you yourself knew."

He said again, "So what?"

"If you remember," I said, still conversationally, "someone broke into Greville's office after he died and stole an address book and an appointments diary. I began to think the thief had also stolen other papers that might lead to the diamonds, but I know now there weren't any, because Greville was full of distrust from the day the Antwerp cutters told him about the five stones."

Pross, Greville's friend, said nothing.

"Greville bought the diamonds," I went on, "from a sight holder in Antwerp, who sent them by messenger to his London house. There he measured them, weighed them, and signed for them. Then it would be reasonable to suppose that he showed them to you, his customer. He sent twenty-five back to Antwerp by Euro-Securo. Five diamonds had mysteriously become cubic zirconia, and yes, it was an entirely stupid thing to do, because the substitution was bound to be discovered almost at once. You knew it would be. I think you reckoned Greville would never believe it of you, but would swear the five stones had to have been swapped by the couriers or the cutters."

"You can't prove it," he said flatly.

"No, I can't. But Greville was full of sorrow and distrust. Why—if he thought his stones had been taken by strangers?"

I looked with some of Greville's own sadness at Prospero Jenks. A likable, entertaining genius.

"I'd think," I said, "that after your long friendship, all the treasures he'd brought you, your tremendous success, that he could hardly bear your treachery."

"Stop it," he said sharply. "It's bad enough. . . ." He shut his mouth tight and seemed to sag internally. "I wished I hadn't done it almost from the beginning," he explained wretchedly. "It was just an impulse. He left the diamonds here while he did a bit of shopping, and I happened to have some rough CZ the right size, and I just . . . exchanged them. I didn't think he'd lose by it."

"He knew, though," I said. "He knew you, and he knew a lot about thieves, being a magistrate."

"Stop it. Stop it. He forgave me."

"When?"

"In Ipswich. I went to meet him there."

"Ipswich. Orwell Hotel, P. three thirty p.m.," I said.

"What? Yes." He seemed unsurprised that I should know. He seemed to be looking inward to an unendurable landscape.

"I saw him die," he said. "I saw the scaffolding fall on him." He'd stunned me to silence.

"We talked in the hotel. In the lounge there. Then we walked down the street to my car. We said good-bye. He crossed the road and walked on, and I watched him. I wanted him to look back and wave . . . but he didn't."

Forgiveness was one thing, I thought, but friendship had gone. What did he expect? Absolution and comfort? Perhaps Greville in time would have given those too, but I couldn't.

Prospero Jenks with painful memory said, "There wasn't any warning. Just a clanging noise and metal falling and men with it. It buried Grev. I ran across the road to pull him out, and there were bodies, and he . . . I try to forget, but I see it all the time."

I waited, and in a while he went on.

"I didn't move him. Couldn't. There was so much blood . . . and a man lying over his legs. . . . People came running. . . ."

He stopped again, and I said bleakly, "When the police came, why didn't you stay with Greville and help him?"

"You know how it is." He gave me a little-boy shamefaced look, much the same as when he'd admitted to changing the stones. "Don't get involved. I didn't want to be dragged in. The police took endless statements. I sat in my car till they let us drive out. They'd taken Grev off in an ambulance before that. His head was dented . . . and bleeding. . . . I thought he was dead."

Dead men don't bleed, I thought, but didn't say it. Prospero Jenks looked about to throw up.

I said, "In the Orwell, did he accuse you of changing the stones?"

"Yes." He swallowed. "And I apologized. He was sad more than angry. I said I would give his diamonds back, of course. And he forgave me. I asked if we could go on trading together. I mean, no one was as good as Grev at finding marvelous stones. And he always loved the things I made."

"Did Greville agree?" I asked.

"Yes. He said he had the diamonds with him, but he had arrangements to make. He didn't say what. He said he would bring them here to the shop at the beginning of the week, and I would give him his five stones and pay for the teardrops and stars. He wanted cash for them, as he couldn't trust me."

Greville certainly hadn't trusted him.

"If I give you those diamonds now, then will that be the end of it?" he said. "I mean, you won't make a fuss, will you? Not the police . . . Grev wouldn't have wanted that, you know."

I didn't answer. Greville would have to have balanced his betrayed old friendship against his respect for the law, and I supposed he wouldn't have had him prosecuted.

Prospero Jenks gave my silence a hopeful look, rose from his stool, and crossed to the ranks of little drawers. He pulled one open and felt deep inside. Then he brought out a twist of white gauze fastened with a band of sticky tape and held it out to me.

"Five diamonds," he said. "Yours."

I took the unimpressive little parcel and said we would weigh them right there and he would write out the weight and sign it.

"Come on, Derek." He was cajoling. "Grev didn't."

But I was not Greville. "Weigh them," I said.

With a sigh he cut open the little bag when I handed it back to him, and on small, fine scales weighed the contents.

It was the first time I'd actually seen what I'd been searching for, and they were unimposing—five dull-looking grayish pieces of crystal the size of large, misshapen peas, without a hint of the fire waiting within. I took them off the scales and rewrapped them.

"Satisfied?" he said with a touch of sarcasm, watching me stow the packet in my trousers pocket.

"No. Not really."

"They're genuine," he protested. He signed the paper on which he'd written their weight, and gave it to me. "I wouldn't make that mistake again." He studied me. "You're harder than Grev."

"I've reason to be."

"What reason?"

I sighed slightly. "Greville hid the letters and invoices dealing with the diamonds because he distrusted someone in his office.

115

Someone that he guessed was running to you with little snippets of information. Someone who would spy for you."

"Nonsense." His mouth seemed dry, however.

I pulled out of a pocket the microcassette recorder and laid it on his workbench.

"This is voice activated," I said. "Greville left it switched on one day when he went to lunch, and this is what he found on the tape when he returned."

I pressed the switch, and the voice familiar to both of us spoke. "I'm in his office now, and I can't find them. He hides everything. He's security mad, you know that. I can't ask him. I don't think he trusts me. . . ."

Jason's voice, full of the cocky, street-smart aggression that went with the orange spiky hair, clicked off into silence.

"Jason was the regular messenger between you and Greville," I said to Prospero Jenks. "I sent him round here myself last week. He wouldn't take much seducing to bring you information along with the merchandise. But Greville found out."

Jenks made a gesture of half-suppressed fury.

"I don't know how you know all this," he said.

It had taken nine days and a lot of searching and a good deal of guessing at possibilities and probabilities, but the pattern was now a reliable path through at least part of the maze.

I said, "So what did he say about Jason when you and he were talking in the Orwell?"

Prospero Jenks capitulated. "He said Jason would have to leave Saxony Franklin. It was a condition of us doing business again."

"But you didn't tell Jason that," I said. "Because when Greville died, you decided to try to steal not only five stones but the lot."

The blue eyes almost smiled. "Seemed logical, didn't it?" he said. "Grev wouldn't know. The insurance would pay. No one would lose."

Except the underwriters, I thought. But I said, "The diamonds weren't insured. You were stealing them directly from Greville."

He was almost astounded, but not quite.

"Greville told you that in the Orwell, didn't he?" I guessed. Again the little-boy shame. "Well, yes, he did."

"Pross," I said, "did you ever grow up?"

"You don't know what growing up is. Growing up is being ahead of the game. You have to make what you can. The day I understood all customers are suckers was the day I grew up."

I said, "I'll bet you never said that to Greville."

"Grev was a saint—the only truly good person I've ever known. I wish I hadn't cheated him. I regret it something rotten."

I heard the sincerity in his voice, but his remorse was barely skin-deep. Nowhere had it altered his soul.

"Jason," I said, "knocked me down outside St. Catherine's Hospital and stole the bag containing Greville's clothes. I thought at the time it was an ordinary mugging. The attacker was quick and strong. I didn't bother to report it to the police, because there was nothing of value in the bag."

"So how can you say it was Jason?"

I answered him obliquely. "When I went to Greville's firm and discovered he had bought diamonds, I began looking for them. Everyone in the office knew I was looking; they also discovered I was a jockey. I asked them not to tell the customers that they were now trading with a jockey, not a gemologist, but I'm certain that Jason told you."

"What makes you think that?"

"You couldn't get into Greville's house to search it," I said, "because it's a fortress. And I had the keys. So you set it up through the trainer I ride for to get me there."

"But I never went to Greville's house," he said.

"No, not you—Jason. Strong and fast in the motorcycle helmet that covered his orange hair, butting me over again just like old times, and vaulting the gate. That couldn't have been you. He turned the house upside down, but I'm sure he didn't find what he was looking for."

"Why not?" he asked, and then said, "That's to say—"

"Did you mean Jason to kill me?" I asked flatly. "You can kill people," I added, "hitting them with bricks."

"No! He said . . ." Jenks stopped dead. He gave a hopeless little sigh. "He said it depended on where he hit you."

Callous and irresponsible, I thought, and unforgivable, really.

"Jason knew which office window to break," I said, "and he came down from the roof." I paused. "Were you with him?"

He gave me a shattered look. Eventually, without shame, he said, "We both went. That Sunday. Late afternoon. After he brought Grev's things back from Ipswich and they were a waste of time. And after Jason told me that Grev's brother had turned up, some frail creature on crutches, and it was good because he'd be an easy mark . . . which you were."

"Yes."

He shrugged. "Well, I thought it was worth looking in Grev's office, but that too was a waste of time. In the end we simply gave up. Grev had been too careful. I got resigned to not having the diamonds unless I paid for them. Then Jason said you were hunting high and low, and I got interested again. You can't blame me."

I could and did, but I didn't want to interrupt.

"Then," he said, "like you guessed, I inveigled you into Grev's garden, and Jason had been waiting ages there, and let his anger out on the house. Then you set the alarms off, and Jason wasn't going to wait around for handcuffs. So Grev had beaten us again."

"When did Jason break into Greville's car?"

"Last Saturday, when he finally found it in Greville's road. I'd looked for it at the hotel and round about in Ipswich, but Grev must have hired a car to drive there."

"Why Ipswich?" I said. "Why did he want you to go there?"

"No idea," he said blankly. "He'd often ask me to meet him in odd places. It was usually because he'd found some heirloom or other and wanted to know if the stones would be of use to me."

I was shaken with the pity of it. So much soaring, priceless imagination and such grubby, perfidious greed.

I thought of all Pross had told me, and was struck by one unexplored and dreadful possibility.

"When the scaffolding fell," I said slowly, "when you found Greville lying there bleeding, did you steal his wallet?"

Pross's little-boy face crumpled, and he put his hands up to cover it. I couldn't bear him any longer. I stood up to go.

"You thought he might have diamonds in his wallet," I said bitterly. "Even when he was dying, you were ready to rob him."

He said nothing. He in no way denied it.

I felt such anger on Greville's behalf that I wanted suddenly to hurt the man before me with a ferocity I wouldn't have expected in myself, and I stood there trembling with the self-knowledge and the essential self-restraint. I took three steps, then used the crutches to make my way back into the shop and out onto the pavement, and I wanted to yell and scream at the bloody injustice of Greville's death and the wickedness of the world and call down the rage of angels.

CHAPTER 9

I STOOD blindly on the pavement, oblivious to the passersby finding me an obstacle in their way. The swamping tidal wave of fury and desolation swelled and broke and gradually ebbed, leaving me still shaking from its force, a tornado in the spirit.

I took a few sketchy breaths and telephoned Brad, who picked me up in five minutes. I shoved the crutches into the back and climbed wearily in beside him, and he said, "Where to?" giving me grandmotherly solicitude in his face, if not his words.

"Uh," I said. "I don't know."

I had intended to go to Greville's house to change into my suit, which was hanging in his wardrobe, before meeting Clarissa at seven, and it still seemed the best thing to do, even if my energy for the project had evaporated.

Accordingly, we made our way there. "I think I'll sleep here tonight," I said. "You can go on to Hungerford now, if you like."

He didn't look as if he liked, but all he said was, "Tomorrow?"

"Yes, please, to the office."

He nodded. He got my overnight bag and came in with me to see that the house was empty of murderers. When he'd departed, I checked the alarms and went to change.

I borrowed another of Greville's shirts and a navy silk tie, and shaved with his electric razor, and thought with an odd frisson that all these things were mine now, that I was in his house, in his room, in his clothes . . . in his life.

I put on my own suit and came across the baster tube, still in an inner pocket. Leaving it on the chest of drawers, I checked in the looking glass that Franklin, Mark II, wouldn't entirely disgrace Franklin, Mark I. He had looked in that mirror every day for three months, I supposed. Now his reflection was mine, and the man that was both of us had dark marks under the eyes and a taut thinness in the cheeks, and looked as if he could do with a week's lying in the sun. I gave him a rueful smile and phoned for a taxi, which took me to Luigi's with ten minutes to spare.

SHE was there before me, sitting at a small table in the bar area, with an emptyish glass in front of her. She stood up when I went in, and offered me a cool cheek for greeting, but battling, I thought, with an undercurrent of diffidence.

She called the waiter and said, "Double water?" to me with a small smile and, when I nodded, ordered Perrier with ice and fresh lime juice for both of us.

I was now down to only two or three Distalgesics a day. I wondered which would have made me feel better, a damper I'd just taken for the ankle or a large Scotch for everywhere else.

Clarissa was wearing a blue silk dress with a double-strand pearl necklace, pearl-sapphire-and-diamond earrings and a sapphire-and-diamond ring. I wouldn't have noticed in the simple old jockey days. Her hair curved smoothly in the expensive cut, and she looked a polished, well-bred woman of forty or so, nearly beautiful, slender, with generous eyes.

"What have you been doing since Saturday?" she asked.

"Peering into the jaws of death. What have you?"

"We went to—" She broke off. "What did you say?"

"The Ostermeyers and I were in a car crash on Sunday."

"Heavens. I didn't like to comment, but you look . . ."

"Frazzled?" I suggested.

"Smooth." She smiled. "Frazzled underneath."

The waiter came to ask if we would be having dinner, and I said yes, and we read the menus.

Luigi's was a comfortable place, the fare chiefly Italian, with few diners yet. It was not, I was interested to note, a habitual rendezvous for Clarissa and Greville: she was not treated as a regular. I asked her about it, and startled, she said they'd been there only two or three times, always for lunch.

Then she gave me a slightly embarrassed look. "Do you disapprove of me and Greville?"

"No," I said. "You gave him joy."

"Oh." She was comforted and pleased. She said with a certain shyness, "It was the first time I'd fallen in love. I suppose you'll think that silly. It was the first time for him too, he said. We were . . . as if twenty years younger. I don't know—laughing. Lit up."

"As far as I can see," I said, "the thunderbolt strikes at any age. You don't have to be teenagers."

"Has it . . . struck you?"

"Not since I was seventeen and fell like a ton of bricks for a trainer's daughter."

"What happened?"

"Nothing much. We laughed a lot. Slept together. She married an old man of twenty-eight. I went to college."

"I met Henry when I was eighteen. He fell in love with me. I was flattered. And he was so good-looking. And kind. He'd already inherited his title. I married him, and we had a son and daughter, both grown now. It hasn't been a bad life, just . . . incomplete."

"A better life than most," I said, aiming to comfort.

"You're very like Greville," she said unexpectedly. "You look at things straight. You've got his sense of proportion."

"We had realistic parents."

"He didn't speak about them much. He lived in the present, and he looked outward, not inward, and I loved him to distraction and in a way I didn't know him." She stopped and swallowed. "I do miss him," she said.

"What will you eat?" I asked, reading the menu.

She gave me a flick of a look and said, "You decide."

"Did Greville?"

"Yes."

"If I order fried zucchini as a starter, then fillet steak in pepper sauce with linguine tossed in olive oil, will that do?"

"I like it. Unusual. Nice."

We transferred to the dining room and ate the proposed program. As it was early, I asked if she had a train to catch.

"No, I'm down here for two nights. Tomorrow I'm going to an old friend's wedding, then back to York on Thursday morning." She concentrated on twirling linguine onto her fork.

There was a long stretch between now and then.

I said, "Every five weeks or so, Greville met you at King's Cross, isn't that right, and took you to lunch?"

She said in surprise, "Did he tell you?"

"Not face to face. Did you ever see that gadget of his—the Wizard?"

"Yes, but . . . he surely didn't put me in it?"

"Not by name. Only under a secret password. You're safe."

She ate the forkful of linguine, her eyes down.

"After lunch," she said with pauses, "if I had appointments, I'd keep them, or do some shopping. I'd register at a hotel and change, and go to Greville's house. We'd have drinks, talk. Go to dinner early, then back to his house." Her voice stopped.

I said, "Do you want to go to his house now? I'm sleeping there tonight, but that's not a factor."

After a while she said, "I don't know."

I said to her, "Come if you like, just to be near him, to lie on his bed, weep for him. I'll wait for you downstairs . . . and take you safely to your hotel before the fairy coach changes to a pumpkin."

"Oh!" She turned what was going to be a sob into almost a laugh. "Can I really? Thank you. Yes."

I warned her what a mess the house was, but when we'd left the restaurant and arrived at Greville's, she was inconsolable.

"He would have hated this. I'm so glad he didn't see it."

We went into the small sitting room, and she went round picking up the stone bears, restoring them to their tray.

"I gave him these," she said. "He loved them. They're rhodonite, he said."

"Take them," I said. "To remember him by."

She paused, holding the last bear. "You're very kind to me."

"It's not difficult. And he'd have been furious with me if I weren't."

"I think," she said with diffidence, "I'll go upstairs now."

I nodded.

"Come with me," she said.

I looked at her. Her eyes were wide and troubled, but not committed, not hungry. Undecided. Like myself.

"All right," I said.

She went upstairs ahead of me, and I heard her moan at the desecration of the bedroom. When I joined her, she was standing forlornly, looking around, and with naturalness she turned to me and put her arms loosely round my waist, laying her head on my shoulder. I shed the confounded crutches and hugged her tight, in grief for her and for Greville, and we stood there for a long minute in mutual and much needed comfort.

She let her arms fall away and went over to sit on the bed, smoothing the black-and-white checkerboard counterpane.

"He was going to change this room," she said. "All this drama . . . He wanted me to choose something softer, that I would like. But this is how I'll always remember it."

Then she lay down flat, her head on the pillows, watching me with big eyes. I half hopped across the room and sat beside her.

"Do . . . you want this?" she asked.

"Yes," I said. "But I'm not Greville."

She sat up fast and put her arms round my neck in a sort of released compulsion.

"I do want this," she said. "I've been telling myself I shouldn't, but I do. I know you're not Greville, but this is the only way I can love him. Can you understand it, if it's him I love?"

I understood it, and smiled. "Just don't *call* me Greville."

She looked me in the eyes. "Derek," she said, "make love to me. Please."

"Don't beg," I said.

I put my mouth on hers and took my brother's place.

THE catharsis was over, and her tears. Clarissa looked younger and sweeter, having purged her grief, and I was seeing, I knew, what Greville had loved. He had been a lucky man.

"Tomorrow," she said, "can I come here again?" She put her

fingers lightly on my mouth to stop me answering at once. "This time was for him. Tomorrow for us. Then I'll go home."

"Forever?"

"Yes. I think so. What I had with Greville was unforgettable and unrepeatable. . . . I decided that whatever happened with you, or didn't happen, I would do my best with Henry."

I knew she was right. I kissed her lightly.

"Tomorrow for us," I agreed. "Then good-bye."

When I went into the office in the morning, Annette told me crossly that Jason simply hadn't turned up for work.

"He won't be coming back," I said to her astonishment.

June came zooming into Greville's office, waving a tabloid newspaper and looking at me with wide, incredulous eyes.

"Did you know you're in the paper? Lucky to be alive, it says here. You didn't say anything about it!"

She laid the *Daily Sensation* open on the black desk. There was a picture of the smash, in which one could more or less see my head inside the Daimler. The headline read Driver Shot, Jockey Lives.

"It happened on Sunday," June exclaimed, "and you came here on Monday! No wonder you looked knackered."

"June!" Annette disapproved of her slang.

"Well, he did. Still does." She gave me a critical, kindly, motherly-sisterly inspection. "He could have been killed, and then what would we all have done here?"

The dismay in Annette's face was a measure, I supposed, of the degree to which I had taken over. The place no longer felt like a quicksand to me either. But I hadn't forgotten there was racing at Cheltenham that day. I turned the pages of the newspaper and came to the runners and riders. That was where my name belonged, not on Saxony Franklin checks. June looked over my shoulder and understood at least something of my sense of exile.

"When you go back," she said, "what will we do here?"

They looked apprehensive, but I smiled to reassure them.

"What we'll do is this. Annette will be office manager. She'll run things generally, and keep the keys."

Annette didn't look displeased, repeating office manager, as if trying it on for size.

I nodded. "Then I'll look for a business expert, a finance manager, to try to keep us afloat. Because it's going to be a struggle."

They both looked shocked and disbelieving.

"Greville did buy diamonds," I said regretfully, "and so far we've only found a quarter of them. They cost one and a half million dollars, and we'll still owe the bank for three quarters of that when we've sold what diamonds we have."

Their mouths opened in unhappy unison.

"We have to persuade the bank that we'll climb out of the hole," I said. "So we'll want this finance manager, and we'll pay him out of Greville's salary."

They began to understand the mechanics, and nodded.

"Then," I said, "we need a gemologist who has a feeling for stones and what the customers like. We'll create the post of merchandise manager, and that"—I looked at June—"will be you."

She blushed a fiery red.

"You know what sells," I told her. "You and the finance manager will work together. You'll still work the computer, and teach Lily or Tina how to use it for when you're away."

"Tina," she said. "She's quicker. But what about you?"

"I'll be general manager. I'll come twice a week. Everyone will tell me what's going on, and we will all decide what is best to be done, though if there's a disagreement, I'll have the casting vote."

Annette said, "Surely you will need Mr. Franklin's salary."

I shook my head. "I earn enough riding horses. Until we're solvent here, we need to save every penny."

"It's an adventure!" June said, enraptured.

"Well," I said, bringing out Pross's twist of gauze, "we have here five uncut diamonds that cost about seventy-five thousand dollars altogether. How do we sell them?"

They more or less gasped. After a pause Annette said, "Interest a diamantaire."

"Do you know how to do that?"

After another moment's hesitation she nodded, but fearfully.

The telephone rang, and Annette answered it.

"A packet for you down at the front desk," she said, and was out the door on the words, returning shortly with a brown Jiffy bag. I opened it and shook out two objects and one envelope.

One of the objects was the microcassette recorder I'd left on Prospero Jenks' workbench in my haste to be gone. The other was a long black leather wallet with gold initials G.S.F. in one corner and Prospero Jenks' business card inside.

"That wallet is Mr. Franklin's," Annette said blankly. "Where did Mr. Jenks get it from?"

"He found it," I said.

The wallet contained a Saxony Franklin checkbook, credit cards, business cards and a small pack of bank notes, which I guessed were fewer in number now.

Annette and June went off to tell the others the present and future state of the nation, and I was alone when I opened the envelope.

Pross had sent me a letter and a certified bank draft: instantly cashable money. I blinked at the numbers on the check and reread them very carefully. Then I read the letter:

Derek,
    This is a plea for a bargain. The check is for the sum I agreed with Grev for the twelve teardrops and eight stars. I know you need the money, and I need those stones.
    Jason won't be troubling you again.
    Grev wouldn't have forgiven the brick on your head, though he might his own wallet. For you it's the other way round. You're very like him. I wish he hadn't died.

                                                                Pross

What a mess, I thought. I did need the money, yet if I accepted it, I was implicitly agreeing not to take any action against him.

Would Greville want me to extend his forgiveness, or at least suspend revenge, or to rise up in wrath and tear up the check?

In the midst of this the phone rang, and I answered it.

"Elliot Trelawney here," the voice said.

"Oh, hello."

He asked me how things were going, and I said that life was

proving to be full of dilemmas. Ever so, he said with a chuckle.

"I was ringing to thank you for sending the Vaccaro notes," Trelawney said. "We turned down Vaccaro's application, and now we find we needn't have bothered, because on Saturday night he was arrested and charged with importing illegal substances. He's still in custody and about to be extradited to Florida on murder charges. And we nearly gave him a gambling license! Funny old world."

"Hilarious," I said, wondering who it was who had taken a shot at me. Vaccaro had been in jail, and I didn't believe it was Pross.

"How about a drink in the Rook and Castle?" he suggested. "Shall I ring you one evening next week?"

"Okay."

I put the phone down and picked up Pross's huge check. It would solve all immediate problems—pay the interest already due, the cost of cutting the diamonds, and more than a fifth of the capital debt. If I didn't take it, we would no doubt have to sell the diamonds later, but they might not easily fit necklaces and rings.

A plea. A bargain. A chance that the remorse was at least half real. Or was he taking me again for a sucker?

I computed some sums and asked Annette what she thought. "Is that the sort of profit margin Greville would have asked?"

Setting prices was something she well understood. "Yes," she said. "It looks about right. Not overgenerous, but Mr. Franklin would have seen this as a service for commission."

"Prospero Jenks says this is what he and Greville agreed on."

"Well, then," she said, relieved, "he wouldn't cheat you."

I smiled with irony. "We'd better bank this before it evaporates."

"I'll do it at once," she declared. "With a loan as big as you said, every minute costs us money."

She put on her coat and took an umbrella to go out with, as the day had started off raining.

The ever demanding telephone rang, this time with Nicholas Loder on the other end, spluttering with rage.

"Milo says you had the confounded cheek," he said, "to have Dozen Roses dope-tested."

"For barbiturates, yes. He seemed very sleepy. Our vet said

he'd be happier to know the horse hadn't been tranquilized for the journey before he gave him an all-clear certificate."

"I'd never give a horse tranquilizers," he declared. "It's shabby of you. Offensive. I expect an apology."

"I apologize," I said sincerely enough, and thought guiltily of the further checks going on at that moment. Weigh the merchandise, I thought.

"You've behaved disgustingly," Loder grumbled. "I've got a buyer for Gemstones, I think, though you don't deserve it. Where will you be this evening, if he makes a definite offer?"

"In Greville's house, perhaps."

"Right, I have the number. And I want a written apology from you about those tests. I'm so angry I can hardly be civil to you."

He hardly was, but I was pleased enough about Gemstones. And I still held the Ostermeyers' check for Dozen Roses, waiting for Phil Urquhart's final clearance. The horses would make up for a few of the missing diamonds.

June, out of habit, brought me a sandwich for lunch. She was walking with an extra bounce, with unashamed excitement.

Way down the line, I thought, if we made it through the crisis, what then? Would I simply sell Saxony Franklin as I'd meant to do, or borrow against it to finance a stable? I'd learned a good deal in the last ten days. I had also—though I found it surprising—grown fond of Greville's firm.

AGAIN the telephone interrupted, with a long order for cabochons. I hopped to the door and yelled for June to pick up the call, and Alfie came along to complain we were running out of binding tape and to ask why we'd ever needed Jason. Tina did his work in half the time without the swearwords. Annette almost with gaiety hoovered everywhere, and Lily came to ask meekly if she could have the title of stockroom manager.

"Done!" I said with sincere pleasure, and before the day was out, we had a shipment manager (Alfie) and an enabling manager (Tina). It seemed to me that such a spirit had been released there that the enterprise was now flying. Whether the euphoria would last or not was next week's problem.

I telephoned Maarten-Pagnier in Antwerp and discussed the transit of twelve teardrops, eight stars and five fakes. I asked if he would insure them for the journey and send them by Euro-Securo. I said we did not dispute that five of the stones had been cubic zirconia. The real stones had been returned.

"I rejoice for you, monsieur. We are at your service."

After that I asked Annette if she could ring Prospero Jenks to tell him his diamonds would be coming. She soon appeared in my doorway, saying he wanted to speak to me personally.

With inner reluctance I picked up. "Hello, Pross."

"Truce, then?" he asked.

"We've banked the check. You'll get the diamonds Friday."

"Thanks." He sounded fervently pleased. Then he said with hesitation, "You've got some light blue topaz, emerald cut—five or six big stones, Grev said. Can I have them?"

"Give it time," I said. And thought, What unholy nerve.

"Yes, well, but you and I need each other," he protested.

It had done Greville no harm in the trade to be known as the chief supplier of Prospero Jenks. Could I afford pride?

"If you try to steal from me one more time," I said, "I not only stop trading with you, I make sure everyone knows why."

"Derek!" The threat was a dire one.

"You can have the topaz. We have a new gemologist who's not Greville, grant you, but knows what you buy. We'll take it step by step."

"I thought you wouldn't!" He sounded extremely relieved. "I thought you'd never forgive me the wallet. Your face—"

"I don't forgive it. Or forget. But after wars, enemies trade. We'll see how we go."

Disconnecting, I ruefully smiled. I'd made the same compromise that Greville had—to do business with the treacherous child, but not to trust him.

At four o'clock I answered the telephone yet again, and found myself talking to Phil Urquhart, whose voice sounded strained.

"I've just phoned the lab for the results of Dozen Roses' tests." He paused. "I don't think I believe this."

"What's the matter?" I asked.

"Do you know what a metabolite is?"

"Vaguely. The result of metabolism, isn't it?"

"Yes," he said. "It's what's left after some substance has broken down in the body, the way viruses produce antibodies. So if you find a particular metabolite in the urine, it means a particular substance was earlier present in the body. Well, the lab found a metabolite in Dozen Roses' urine." He paused.

"Go on," I urged. "What is it the metabolite *of?*"

"Cocaine," he said.

I sat in stunned, disbelieving silence.

"Racehorses aren't routinely tested for cocaine, because it isn't a stimulant," Phil continued. "Normally, a racehorse could be full of cocaine and no one would know."

"If it isn't a stimulant," I said, "why give it to them?"

"It potentiates adrenaline. I particularly asked the lab to test for all such drugs because of what you said about adrenaline yourself. With a normal adrenaline surge an enzyme comes along to control it. Cocaine blocks out that enzyme, so the adrenaline goes roaring round the body for much longer."

"My God," I said blankly. "Loder must have known."

"Almost certainly. You'd have to administer the cocaine very soon before the race, because its effect is short lived. In humans the rush from cocaine is fast. In horses it would probably induce skittishness at once. It wouldn't make the horse go faster, but just make the adrenaline push last longer."

"Why don't they test horses for cocaine?" I asked.

"Heaven knows. Perhaps because enough to wind up a horse would cost more than winning a bet. But cocaine's getting cheaper, I'm told. There's more and more of it around."

"I don't know much about drugs," I said. "Not my scene."

"Do you know what they'd call you in America?" he said to me.

"What?"

"Straight," he said. "You're straight through and through."

I thought for a moment about Dozen Roses taking cocaine into his bloodstream. Between the saddling box and starting gate at York, he'd certainly woken up dramatically.

"Phil," I said, "I still have the baster from York, but it's clean."

"It might look clean," he said slowly, "but if cocaine was blown up it in powder form, there may be particles clinging."

I sighed. "If I send the tube to you by tomorrow morning, can you get it tested anonymously?"

"Sure. Like the urine. I'll get the lab to do another rush job. We might get a result late tomorrow. Friday at the latest."

"Good. And, er, don't mention it to Milo."

"You may be sure," Phil said seriously.

It was the worst dilemma of all, I thought, replacing the receiver. Was cocaine a stimulant or was it not? The racing authorities didn't think so. And if I believed it didn't affect speed, then it was all right to sell Dozen Roses to the Ostermeyers. Saxony Franklin needed that money. But if he'd won all his four races as high as a kite, then it wasn't all right.

If I disclosed the cocaine, would Dozen Roses be disqualified for his last win? Would Nicholas Loder lose his license to train?

If I caused so much trouble, I would be finished in racing. Whistle-blowers were regularly fired from their jobs.

My thoughts made me sweat.

CHAPTER 10

BRAD drove me to Greville's house and came in with me while I went upstairs and put the baster tube into an envelope and addressed it to Phil Urquhart.

Downstairs again, I said to Brad, "The Euro-Securo main office is in Oxford Street. This is the address." I gave it to him. "They're expecting this. You don't need to pay; just get a receipt."

"Yerss."

"Then pick up a friend of mine from the Selfridge Hotel and bring her here—she'll phone you in the car. Then go on home, if you like." I'd suggested all this to Clarissa the previous night.

Brad gave me a glowering look. "Same time tomorrow?"

"If you're not bored."

He gave me a totally unexpected grin. "Best time o' my life," he said, and departed.

In bemusement I went along to the little sitting room and tidied up a bit more of the mess. If Brad enjoyed waiting around for hours, it was all right by me.

By that evening, there was a big improvement in the ankle. I laid one crutch aside and used the other like a walking stick, putting my left toe down for balance. Distalgesic, I decided, was a thing of the past. I'd drink wine for dinner with Clarissa.

The front doorbell rang, which surprised me. It was too early to be Brad dropping off Clarissa. I hopped along to the door with one crutch, looked through the peephole, and was astounded to see Nicholas Loder on the doorstep. Behind him stood his friend Rollo, looking in boredom at the small garden.

In dismay I opened the door, and Nicholas Loder immediately said, "Oh, good. You're in. We happened to be dining in London, so I thought we'd come round to discuss Gemstones rather than negotiate on the telephone."

"But I haven't named a price," I said.

"Never mind. We can discuss that. Can we come in?"

"Well, yes," I said, looking at my watch. "But not for long. I have another appointment pretty soon."

"So have we," he assured me. "Come on, Rollo."

I turned to lead the way, ostentatiously not closing the front door behind them as a big hint not to stay long.

"The room's in a mess," I warned them over my shoulder. "We had a burglar."

"We?" Nicholas Loder said.

"Greville and I."

"Oh."

Rollway blinked around in an uninterested fashion. At close quarters he wasn't any more attractive than at a distance—a dull, dark lump of a man, thickset, middle-aged and humorless.

"This is Thomas Rollway," Loder said, making belated introductions. "One of my owners. He's interested in buying Gemstones."

Rollway didn't look very interested in anything.

Nicholas Loder sat in Greville's armchair, and Rollway perched on the arm of the other armchair. I sat on the edge of a hard chair, wanting them to hurry, laying the second crutch aside.

I looked at Loder—big, light-haired, with brownish eyes, full of ability. And not angry with me. I thought guiltily of the cocaine analyses going on behind his back. If he'd been this normal from the beginning, I'd have seen no reason to have had the tests done.

"Gemstones," he said. "What do you want for him?"

I'd seen in the Saxony Franklin ledgers what Gemstones had cost as a yearling two years ago. He was no bright star. I doubled his cost and asked for that.

Nicholas Loder laughed with irony. "Come on, Derek. Half."

"Half is what he cost Greville originally," I said.

"So we've been doing our homework." He actually smiled. "I've promised Rollo a reasonable horse at a reasonable price. Gemstones is no world-beater. His cost price is perfectly fair."

"Meet me halfway," I said, "and he's yours."

Nicholas raised his eyebrows at his friend. "Rollo?"

"I don't want Gemstones at any price," Rollo said flatly, and they were the first words he'd uttered since arriving.

Loder protested, "But it was your idea to come here!"

Thomas Rollway, as if absentmindedly, stood and picked up my abandoned crutch, holding it by the stick end. Then he swung it round forcefully a bare four inches above the carpet.

It was so totally unexpected that I wasn't quick enough to avoid it. The elbow rest and cuff crashed into my left ankle, and Rollway came after it like a bull, kicking, knocking me down.

I was flabbergasted more than frightened, and then furious. It seemed senseless, without reason, out of any sane proportion.

I glimpsed Nicholas Loder looking dumbfounded, his mouth and eyes stretched open. As I struggled to get up, Thomas Rollway reached inside his jacket and produced a handgun with a silencer on the end.

"Keep still," he said to me, pointing the barrel at my chest.

A gun. Simms. The gray car. I began dimly to understand and to despair pretty deeply.

Nicholas Loder was shoving himself out of his chair. "What are you doing?" His voice was high with panic.

"Sit down, Nick," his friend said. "Don't get up." And such was the grindingly heavy tone of his unemotional voice that Loder subsided, looking overthrown, not believing what was happening.

"But you came to buy his horse," he said weakly.

"I came to kill him." Rollway said it dispassionately, as if it were nothing. His eyes coldly considered me as I half sat, half lay on the floor, propped on my elbow and without any weapon within reach. Then, again with no warning, he stamped hard on my ankle and for good measure pressed down on it.

I swore at him, unable to move, and thought idiotically, feeling things give way inside, that it would take me a lot longer now to get fit.

Rollo, standing determinedly on my ankle, said to me, "You picked up a piece of my property at York races. An official told me you'd put it in your pocket. I want it back."

I said nothing. Damn the official, I thought. So helpful. So deadly. I hadn't even noticed one watching.

Nicholas Loder, bewildered, said, "What piece of property?"

"The tube part of the nebulizer," Rollway told him.

"But what does it matter?"

Rollway pointed his gun at me and answered without taking his gaze from my face.

"You yourself, Nick," he informed him, "told me you were worried about Franklin. He was observant and too bright."

"But that was because I'd gelded Dozen Roses."

"So when I found he had the nebulizer, I asked one or two other people about him, and they all said the same. Brainy. Intelligent. Bright." He paused. "I don't believe in waiting for trouble. And dead men can't make accusations." Rollway stared at me. "Where's the tube?"

I didn't answer. If I told him I'd sent it to Phil Urquhart, I could be sentencing Phil to death too. Besides, if I opened my mouth at all, what might come out would be something between a yell and a groan.

"But he would never have suspected," Loder feebly said.

"Of course he did. Why has he had that bodyguard glued to him? Why has he been dodging about and not going home? And he had the horse's urine taken for testing. I'm not going to jail."

"But you wouldn't."

"Be your age, Nick. I import the stuff. I take the risks. And I get rid of trouble as soon as I see it."

Nicholas Loder said in wailing protest, "I told you it wasn't necessary to give it to horses. It doesn't make them go faster."

"Rubbish. You can't tell. *Where's the tube?*" he finished.

If not telling him would keep me alive a bit longer, I wasn't going to try telling him I'd thrown it away.

"You can't just shoot him," Nicholas Loder said despairingly. "Not with me watching."

"You're no danger to me, Nick," Rollway said flatly. "Where would you go for your little habit? One squeak from you, I'd see you went down for possession. And for conniving with me to drug horses. They'd take your license away. You'll keep quiet."

The threats, uttered in a measured, unexcited monotone, made my hair bristle. He wouldn't wait much longer, I thought, for me to tell him where the tube was.

With the strength of desperation I rolled my body and with my right foot kicked hard at Rollway's leg. He grunted and took his weight off my ankle. I pulled away from him, shuffling backward to reach the chair I'd been sitting on. I saw him recover his balance and straighten his arm, aiming along the barrel. That stance was going to be the last thing I would see, and my last emotion the blazing fury of dying for so pointless a cause.

Nicholas Loder sprang with horror from the armchair and grabbed at Rollway, shouting, "No, no, Rollo. No, don't do it!"

I took the last opportunity to grab something. A crutch.

"I won't let you," Loder frantically persisted.

Rollo shook him off and swung his gun back to me.

"No." Loder was terribly disturbed, almost frenzied. "It's wrong." He put his body against Rollway's to push him away.

Rollway simply shrugged him off, all bull muscle and undeterrable. Then, very fast, he pointed the gun straight at Nicholas Loder's chest and without pausing pulled the trigger twice.

I heard the rapid *phut, phut.* Saw Nicholas Loder fall.

There was no time to waste on terror, though I felt it. I gripped the crutch and swung at Rollway's right hand, landing a blow fierce enough to make him drop the gun.

135

It fell out of my reach.

I scrambled for it, but he was much faster, and he picked it up with a tight look of fury as hot as my own.

He began to lift the gun at me again, and again I hit him with the crutch. He didn't drop the gun that time, but the gun barrel wavered. When he pulled the trigger, the flame spat out and the bullet missed me.

He was still between me and the door. I had to get up, smash him out of the way, and run, run . . . run into the street. I stood up on my right foot. Put down the left. It buckled. It needed the crutch. And I needed the crutch to fight until I was dead.

A figure appeared abruptly in the doorway behind Rollway. Clarissa. I'd forgotten I'd left the front door open.

"Run," I shouted agonizedly. "Get away."

Rollway sneered, seeming to think the instructions were for him. I lunged at his gun, making his aim swing wide again. Flame. *Phut*. The bullet zipped over my shoulder and hit the wall.

"Run," I yelled again with fearful urgency. "Oh, be quick."

Clarissa didn't run. She brought her hand out of her raincoat pocket, holding a thing like a black cigar, and she swung her arm in a powerful arc, like an avenging fury. Out of the black tube sprang the fearsome silvery springs with a knob on the end, and the kiyoga smashed against the side of Rollway's skull.

He fell forward, cannoning me backward. I ended on the floor, sitting, his inert form stomach down over my shins.

Clarissa came down on her knees beside me, trembling violently. I was breathless, shattered, trembling too. Neither of us was able to speak. When she could, it was a whisper, low and distressed.

"Derek . . ."

"Thanks," I said jerkily, "for saving my life."

I glanced over at Nicholas Loder, and Clarissa seemed to see him for the first time. He was on his back, unmoving.

"Dear God," she said faintly. "Who's that?"

I introduced her posthumously to Nicholas Loder, racehorse trainer, and then to Thomas Rollway, drug baron. They'd squirted cocaine into Dozen Roses, I said, struggling for lightness. I'd found them out. Rollway wanted me out of the way.

I could feel Rollway's breathing on my legs. A pity, on the whole.

I touched Clarissa's hand, brushing my fingers over hers, grateful beyond expression for her courage. I took the kiyoga gently out of her grasp and laid it down.

"Phone my car," I said, "quickly. Brad'll take you back."

"I can't just . . . leave you."

"How would you explain being here to the police?"

She looked at me in dismay and obstinacy. "I can't."

"You must. What do you think Greville would want?"

"Oh." It was a sigh of grief, both for my brother and, I thought, for the evening together that she and I would not now have.

"Derek . . ."

"Go and do it, my dear love."

She got blindly to her feet, dialed Brad, and let it ring. With luck he would reckon the calls spelled emergency.

She handed me the phone then, and I rang the police.

"Push the telephone table over," I said. "If the police find me sitting here, they'll take the scene for granted."

"Derek! I can't leave you." Her eyes were strained, and she was still trembling, but her composure was on the way back.

I picked up the kiyoga, and she took it out of my hands, twisted it, banged the knob on the carpet, and expertly returned it closed to her pocket.

"I'll think of you, and thank you," I said, "every day that I live."

"At four twenty," she said as if automatically. She knelt down again and kissed me, then rose reluctantly and went to the doorway. Lady Knightwood, I thought, a valiant deliverer with not a hair out of place.

She went quietly down the passage, but wasn't gone long. Brad himself came bursting into the room with Clarissa behind him. "Gray Volvo," he said. "Parked round the corner." He almost skidded to a halt, the prospect before him enough to shock even the garrulous to silence.

"Strewth," he said economically.

"As you say," I replied. "Take my friend back to the Selfridge," I added. "Forget she was here. Forget you were here. Go home."

"Can't leave you," he said. "I'll come back."

"The police will be here. Go home; the danger's over."

He considered it. Then he said hopefully, "Same time tomorrow?"

I moved my head in amused assent. "Why not?"

He seemed satisfied in a profound way, and he and Clarissa went over to the doorway, pausing there and looking back.

"Brad," I said finally, "don't shut the front door behind you. I want the police to walk in here nice and easy."

Then I gave them a brief wave, and they waved back before going. They were both, incredibly, smiling.

CHAPTER 11

IT WAS a long, dreary evening.

I sat quietly in Greville's chair, largely ignored, while relays of people measured, photographed, took fingerprints, and dug bullets out of walls.

I had faced a barrage of preliminary questions, which ended with Rollway groaning his way back to consciousness. At my mild suggestion they handcuffed him before he was fully awake, which was just as well, as his bullish violence was the first trait to surface. He was on his feet, threshing about, before he knew where he was.

The police phlegmatically arrested him, told him his rights, and I watched him stumble away.

While the investigating activity went on around me I wondered how drug runners came so easily to murder. Like Vaccaro gunning down his renegade pilots. People like Rollway and Vaccaro, I thought, held other peoples' lives cheap because they aimed anyway at destroying them. They made addiction and corruption their business, willfully profiting from the collapse of countless lives, deliberately enticing young people onto a one-way misery trail. Their greed had filthy feet.

I wondered how people grew to be like them. They weren't happy-go-lucky dishonest, like Pross. They were uncaring and cold. If I ever added to Greville's notebook, I thought, it would be something like "The ways of the crooked are mysterious to the straight," or even "What makes the crooked crooked and the straight straight?"

I thought about Martha and Harley and the cocaine in Dozen Roses. I would ask them to keep the horse and race him, and if he never did any good, I would give them their money back. What the racing press would have to say about the whole mess boggled the mind. We'd probably have to lose the York race.

I thought of Clarissa in the Selfridge Hotel. I hoped she would ring up her Henry, reach back to solid ground, mourn Greville peacefully, be glad she'd saved his brother. I would leave the Wizard's alarm set to four twenty p.m. and remember them both when I heard it. It was sentimental, and I endorsed it.

At some point in the evening a senior plainclothes policeman arrived and introduced himself as Superintendent Ingold. He invited a detailed statement from me. He was short, piercing and very businesslike. He was also, usefully, a man who liked racing—who sorrowed over Nicholas Loder and knew of me.

I told him pretty plainly most of what had happened, omitting only Clarissa's presence, and making that hopeless fight a rapid knockout.

"The crutches?" he inquired. "What are they for?"

"A spot of trouble with an ankle at Cheltenham nearly two weeks ago."

He merely nodded. The crutch handles were heavy enough for clobbering villains, and he sought no other explanation.

Then I told him about the car crash near Hungerford. I said I thought it possible that it had been Rollway who shot Simms, that of course they would compare the bullets the Hungerford police had taken from the Daimler with those from Greville's walls and no doubt Nicholas Loder's silent form. I wondered innocently what sort of car Rollway drove. The Hungerford police, I told him, were looking for a gray car. There was a gray Volvo outside.

A policeman was dispatched to search the street. He came back wide-eyed and was told to cordon off the car.

It was dark by then, and every time the police came into the house, the mechanical dog started barking and the lights blazed on. I thought it amusing, but it wore the police nerves.

"Flip up all the switches beside the front door," I said eventually, which they did, and got peace.

"Who made all the mess?" the superintendent asked.

"Burglars. Last Saturday. Two of your men came round."

"Are you ill?" he said abruptly.

"No. Shaken."

Eventually they took poor Nicholas Loder away. The superintendent handed me the crutches and asked where I would be going.

"Upstairs to bed," I said.

"Here?" He was surprised. "In this house?"

"This house," I said, "is a fortress. Until one lowers the drawbridge, that is."

THEY sealed the sitting room, then let themselves out and left me alone in the newly quiet hallway.

I sat on the stairs and felt awful. Cold. Shivery. Old and gray.

As happened in many sorts of battle, it wasn't the moment of injury that was worst, but the time a couple of hours later when the body's immediate natural anesthetics subsided. At the moment of maximum adrenaline, fight or flight, I'd believed I could run on that ankle. Two hours later the idea of even standing on it was impossible. Movement alone became breathtaking.

There was no more pretending. I knew the damage to bones and ligaments was about as bad as before. Rollway had cracked them apart again. Back to square one, and the Hennessy only four and a half weeks away. I was bloody well going to ride Datepalm in it. I'd get physiotherapy. . . . It could be done. Piece of cake.

Meanwhile, there were the stairs.

Up in Greville's bathroom, in a zipped bag with my washing things, I would find the envelope containing three small white tablets: the DF 118s my surgeon had given me. Only as a last resort, he had said. Tonight, I reckoned, qualified.

I went up the stairs slowly, backward, sitting down, hooking the crutches up with me. It was pretty fair hell. I reminded myself astringently that people had crawled down mountains with much worse broken bones. Eventually I sat on the top step with the crutches beside me.

I made it to the bathroom, opened the door of the medicine cabinet, and pulled out my bag.

One tablet, no pain, I thought. Two tablets, spaced out. Three tablets, unconscious.

I swallowed one with a glassful of hot water and waited there at the basin for miracles.

The miracle that actually happened was extraordinary, but had nothing to do with the pills.

I stared at my gray face in the looking glass over the basin, then looked vaguely at the objects in the medicine cupboard. Talc. Deodorant. Shaving cream. Shaving cream. Most of one can of shaving cream had been squirted all over the mirror by Jason. A pale blue and gray can. UNSCENTED, it said.

The damn pill wasn't working.

I looked at the second one longingly. Wait a bit—think about something else.

I picked up the second can of shaving cream, which was scarlet and orange and said REGULAR FRAGRANCE. I shook the can and took off the cover and tried to squirt foam onto the mirror.

Nothing happened. I shook it. Tried again. Nothing at all.

Guile and misdirection, I thought. Hollow books and green stone boxes with keyholes, but no keys. Safes in concrete, secret drawers in desks. Take nothing at face value. Greville's mind was a maze . . . *and he wouldn't have used scented shaving cream.*

I twisted the shaving cream can this way and that, and the bottom ring moved and began to turn in my hand. I caught my breath. Didn't really believe it. I went on turning . . . unscrewing.

It would be another empty hiding place, I told myself. Get a grip on hope. I unscrewed the whole bottom off the can, and from a cotton nest a chamois leather pouch fell out into my hand.

Well, all right, I thought, but it wouldn't be diamonds.

With the help of the crutches I took the pouch into the bedroom and sat on Greville's bed and poured onto the counterpane a little stream of dullish-looking pea-size lumps of carbon.

I almost stopped breathing. Time stood still. I couldn't believe it. Not after everything . . .

With shaking fingers I counted them. Ten . . . fifteen . . . twenty . . . twenty-five.

Half of what Greville had bought. With half, Saxony Franklin would be safe. I offered heart-bursting thanks to the fates. I came dangerously near to crying.

Then, with a sense of revelation, I knew where the rest were. Where they had to be. Greville really had taken them with him to Ipswich, as he'd told Pross, maybe to give them to the Maarten-Pagnier partner to take back to Antwerp for cutting.

I'd searched through the things in his car, and I'd held his diamonds in my hand and not known it.

They were—they had to be—in another scarlet-and-orange can, inside his overnight bag, safe as Fort Knox, now under the stairs of Brad's mum's house in Hungerford. She'd taken them off the street to keep them safe in a dodgy neighborhood.

Smart, our mum. . . .

The DF 118 was at last taking the edge off the worst.

I rolled the twenty-five precious pebbles around under my fingers with indescribable joy and thought how relieved Greville would have been. Sleep easy, pal, I told him, uncontrollably smiling. I've finally found them.

He'd left me his business, his desk, his gadgets, his enemies, his horses, his mistress. Left me Saxony Franklin, the Wizard, the shaving cream cans, Prospero Jenks and Nicholas Loder, Dozen Roses, Clarissa.

I'd inherited his life and laid him to rest, and at that moment, though I might hurt and I might throb, I didn't think I had ever been happier.

There seems to be no stopping Dick Francis. Since 1962 Britain's former champion steeplechase jockey has written a book a year, gaining new fans all the time. Nearly all of his novels—and they now number twenty-eight—have centered around his first love, horse racing. But his works have also opened doors to other fascinating fields. "People seem to enjoy my books," Francis says, "because they learn something about a trade they know little or nothing about."

*Dick and Mary Francis
at home in Florida*

In *Straight* that trade is gems and precious stones. His research, however, did not begin in a city such as Antwerp, famous for its gem industry, but quite literally next door to his condominium, in Florida. During a morning swim one day the author learned that his closest neighbors were among the top gem importers in the United States. "They were most helpful," Francis acknowledges. "They read the manuscript before it went to the publisher, and found only one small mistake."

But most research for a Dick Francis novel is a family affair. His principal researcher is his wife. "I couldn't work without her," he says. "It's very happy for us both. Mary loves researching a new subject." Among the areas she's explored are photography (for *Reflex*), merchant banking (for *Banker*), and wines (for *Proof*).

Their two sons often help with research as well. Merrick, their elder son, is a racehorse trainer back in Lambourn, England, and their younger son, Felix, is head of the physics department in a large English school and is also a skilled marksman. "He is very helpful in research for physics and armaments," states the proud father.

Looking ahead to future Francis novels, will other family members help out with research? Most likely. Dick and Mary Francis have five grandchildren—the youngest of whom is three years old.

No Roof
But Heaven
Jeanne Williams

Kansas, 1875: a lonely sweep of prairie that is no place for a decent woman. Certainly it is no place for Susanna Alden, a gently bred young schoolmistress from Ohio. Susanna has come here—to a dirt-floored soddy— to teach children whose families have been torn apart by the Civil War. Families who still suffer from that bitter conflict.

But here, too, Susanna will learn her own valuable lessons. Especially about independence, about courage, and about love.

One

BUCKBOARD was a fitting name for this—this vehicle! Susanna gripped the splintery board seat of the wagon, which truly did buck, and cast a desperate glance at her trunk. Would Grandmother Alden's teapot and two remaining eggshell-thin cups survive this last part of the journey from Ohio to Kansas? Susanna had carefully swaddled them among her garments and lilac-scented bedding, and the trunk was jammed among tools, sacks, and boxes so that it didn't slide around. But the dried mud of the rutted tracks kept everything in the wagon jouncing and vibrating, including Susanna.

The man who gripped the reins in one expert hand didn't jounce, and she couldn't imagine him vibrating, though the thought made her want to chuckle for the first time since leaving Pleasant Grove, Ohio, this September of 1875. The station agent back in Dodge City had called the spare dark-haired young man Doc, but Susanna would never have dared. In spite of the hot day, he wore a coat. His straight mouth curved down, and his grooved, sun-browned skin etched at the corners of eyes that had a disturbing luminescence, like gray clouds lit by wintry sun. Along his square jaw, carelessly trimmed sideburns struggled to curl, black like the hair that fell across his right temple.

He had frowned as the agent explained Susanna's plight. "This here's the new Mason-Dixon schoolmarm, Doc. Henry Morton

147

was supposed to meet her, but he ain't back yet from Topeka."

The scrawny little man had waved a hand at the broad street of false-fronted, flimsy buildings, which were mostly saloons and dance halls. Leaving or entering them were painted women, raffish men, and what had to be cowboys—leathery young men, with jingling spurs fastened to high-heeled boots, bright necker-chiefs, and big hats. Sprung from a soddy erected only three years ago, beside a lone cottonwood tree marking the ford of the Arkan-sas River, Buffalo City had changed its name to Dodge City as the rails approached.

"When it was a hide hunters' town," the agent went on, "this place was hides, bones, dust, and hell. Since the stockyards and loading chutes were built last winter, now it's cows, cowboys, dust, and hell! Won't be much out of your way, Doc, to set Miss Alden down at Ase McCanless's ranch."

The man introduced as Matt Rawdon had given an impatient shrug. "All right, Clem, I guess I'll have to haul her out there. Give me a hand with the trunk."

Haul! As if she were a sack of potatoes! Even though she was twenty-seven and painfully aware that she was becoming one of Pleasant Grove's numerous old maids, Susanna wasn't used to being treated as a nuisance by men. Beautiful she wasn't, but she had swift rippling laughter, and lots of curly brown hair that sparked with red glints in the sun, though it was now demurely rolled into a French knot hidden by her brown bonnet. Her eyes varied from gold to brown, with sometimes a hint of green, de-pending on light and mood. And her severely cut brown dress brought out the smooth creaminess of her skin and molded the slender, still youthful blooming of her figure. Stung by Rawdon's ungracious manner, Susanna said in her coolest tone, "I'll pay for my transportation, sir."

"Save your money for your ticket home, miss."

Bewildered by his hostility, Susanna had placed her satchel under the seat and set her foot on the narrow iron step attached to the wagon bed. But she hadn't scrambled up soon enough to please Rawdon, for with an extraordinarily strong arm the tall man had hoisted her almost bodily onto the bare plank seat. As he did so, she had glimpsed his other hand, ridged with scars and hanging as if he had little use of it.

What a misfortune for a doctor! Susanna's face must have shown her dismayed sympathy. Rawdon had let go of her as if burned, and strode to the other side. Leaping up easily, he had settled his long legs and given her a harsh, challenging grin, as if prepared to enjoy her discomfort. "Well, Miss Alden, let's see how you like a buckboard. Don't ask me to drive slower. After I drop you off, I have to get to my claim in time to milk the cows."

"I haven't asked you to drive slow, sir, and I won't." Folding her hands in her lap, Susanna sat primly, determined not to complain if she died for it. She didn't complain, but she quickly unfolded her hands and held to the seat as the deeper bounces threatened to tumble her off her perch. Now she braced her feet and scanned the plains in vain search for a tree, hill, or habitation.

Reaching to infinity, a cloudless dazzling sky bowed at last to the prairie rim. As far as the eye could search, coppery grass with fringed leaf tops bent before the wind, and then swept back, darker, like a mussed pile of velvet rubbed the wrong way. Another kind of yellowing grass had crescent seed heads; some taller clumps flaunted golden plumes, and subtle hues of black, gray, silver, crimson, and white threaded stands of dun and reddish brown. Asters dipped purple heads, and other flowers—yellow, orange, and white—spangled the tapestry.

So there was beauty here, something besides the lonely sweep of plains and sky that could be home only to winged creatures, like the hawk lazily skimming circles till it suddenly plunged. Susanna's heart contracted, and she felt the terror of whatever small, furry creature was now gripped in those talons.

"Hawks and eagles have wonderful vision, but they miss more often than not," Rawdon said, raising his voice to be heard above the rattling and clanking.

He wore a battered gray hat. Could he have been in the Confederate army? Even though the war was ten years over, Susanna tensed. The man she would have married had died in that war; and her father had returned so crippled and pain-ridden that it took more and more whiskey to ease him. She still felt terrible

149

guilt for the relief that overcame her when she'd taken him his breakfast one morning six months ago and found that his sleep had deepened into death. For ten years, except for the four hours daily that she taught literature and composition at her aunt's school for young ladies, Susanna had taken care of her father. His death freed her, but at the same time, she'd felt suddenly useless, deprived of her reason for existing.

Now she had a choice of what to do, a choice of what was left to a woman of a generation bereft of so many of its best young men, like her Richard. She had to accept that there might never be another man for her, not simply because Richard—fair, reckless, and laughing—had been so dearly loved, but because in her small Ohio town there wasn't a man she could even consider. Aunt Mollie had invited her to move in with her and Uncle Frank and teach full time, but to Susanna that had seemed like losing any chance to really live. These reflections were shattered by a distant booming from the west. It sounded like a battle.

Indians? Comanche, Kiowa, Cheyenne, Arapaho—the names flashed through her head like flaming arrows. She knew that the southern Plains Indians were supposed to live on reservations in Indian Territory, which was situated between Kansas and Texas, but only the summer before there had been raids in western Kansas that took the lives of twenty-seven whites.

"Buffalo hunters," Rawdon said with a jerk of his head. "Not many shaggies left around here. But when I first came three years ago, the big kill was just starting. When word spread that there was a big market for buffalo hides, several thousand hunters swarmed over the prairies. An expert shot could kill seventy-five to a hundred in a day." As Susanna gasped he added, "One old hunter told me he guesses over three million buffalo were killed on the southern plains, and that didn't count well over a million killed in those three years by Indians."

"Don't the Indians need them?"

"Sure. For food, shelter, clothing, everything. Killing off the herds forced the horse Indians onto the reservations a lot faster than soldiers. A simple matter of might makes right, as the North taught the South."

"Right? You call slavery right?"

He brushed away the question with a flick of his hand. "I never owned a man or woman and I never thought it just. But if you're to teach history, ma'am, do get your facts straight. The war was fought over whether states have the right to secede. I still maintain they have the right, but they don't have the power. That's all that counts."

"If you think I'll teach children such cynical views—"

"No need. They'll find out soon enough. Just as you'll learn why your prospective school is called Mason-Dixon."

"I suppose that the name means the district has some former Unionists and some former Confederates."

"For that brilliant deduction, Miss Alden, you get a big red A plus, with a gold star."

If this was a sample of how southern gentlemen behaved, she doubted that she could keep her equanimity and be an effective teacher. Whirling on him, she demanded, "Why are you so—so rude? Because I'm from Ohio, because I'm a woman, or did your teacher switch you as much as you probably deserved?"

He cast her a startled look before he laughed. That relaxed the stern set of his features and made him seem younger and less formidable, though from the lines at his eyes and mouth she judged him to be in his early thirties.

"You'd love to thrash me, wouldn't you?" he taunted. "Very well. I beg your pardon. But I didn't wish for your company, and since you bring it up, I don't much care for Yankees, women, or teachers. Nothing personal, I assure you."

"Nothing personal! Let me remind you, sir, that the North suffered, too, not that it'll do much good, since you admit to being a bigoted, jaundiced misogynist." Swallowing hard, she fixed her eyes on the horizon.

Just then the wheels struck an especially bad rut. Susanna's teeth were jarred. Looking back, she was reassured to see her trunk was still there. Strange that almost everything she had in the world was in it. The lamentable truth was that her father had been a physician, not a businessman. Charles Alden had lived with zest and loving-kindness, though he had never married again after childbed fever stole his adored wife, Serena. When he had died that spring, nearly everyone in the little town attended the funeral.

The pretty little white house where he and Susanna had lived brought enough with its simple furnishings to pay for his burial, outstanding debts, and Susanna's passage west. The fifty dollars that remained after she had bought her ticket was prudently lodged in a pocket Aunt Mollie had sewn to the inside of her bodice.

Over the puzzled and somewhat indignant objections of her aunt and uncle, she had insisted on leaving Pleasant Grove. "In a few years you could take over as headmistress of the school," plump, rosy Aunt Mollie had said tearfully.

"I can't. I want to go somewhere new, someplace different, where my teaching can really be important."

Thinking of her aunt and uncle brought a wave of homesickness, and Susanna's eyes blurred.

"Save your tears till you meet the school trustees," Rawdon advised. "Then you'll really have something to cry about."

"I'm not crying! Whatever the trustees are like, they can't be as horrid as you!"

"And bigoted, jaundiced, and misogynic?" he supplied.

"I hope you don't have children in my school, and I feel mightily sorry for your wife, if you've got one."

His face closed. "I don't, and the chance of my ever having children in your school is slim as a whisker."

As if they had reached some kind of stalemate, they were both silent. Up ahead Susanna saw the first sign of human existence since leaving Dodge City—a house of mud bricks, roofed with sod.

Rawdon said, "Pete Townsend hauls freight while he's proving up on his claim—has to live on it five years, build a house, and do some planting before he gets title."

"Are you homesteading?"

"I bought out a couple of settlers who were tired of drought, hail, blizzards, tornadoes, and grasshoppers."

"If western Kansas is so dreadful, why did you settle here?"

"I can't be much of a doctor with only one useful hand, and I didn't choose to set up practice in Dallas, as my sister urged, although I owe Amanda a lot. We were orphaned when I was ten and she was only sixteen. She kept me in school while she worked, and arranged for me to work my way through medical school, where I became fascinated with surgery. Amanda had meanwhile nursed a well-to-do widower through a serious illness. He was much older, but there was true affection between them. He died during the war, leaving her his big house. Amanda hoped I would share it. But I left Texas in search of cheap land with good grass. I farm a little, but mostly I'm raising horses."

Susanna frowned. She knew she should mind her own business, yet it seemed such a waste for this man not to use his talent and training. "Why can't you be a doctor? I'd think there'd be lots you could do with one hand."

"Not surgery."

"But in a region like this where you're surely needed, it seems almost wicked not to practice your profession."

"Make the best of things?" His eyes bored into her. "Is that what you're doing, Miss Alden?"

"I'm doing just that, sir, and I'm not ashamed of it."

This time the silence lasted till they passed a mud house with a partially destroyed roof. The door was gone and a hide flapped at one small window. Susanna repressed a shudder. This vast plain made her feel as if—as if the roof and walls of a comfortable house had suddenly blown off and she were left with no roof but heaven, no floor but the grass, no neighbor but the wind.

She shivered, but there was something spacious and wonderfully free about this prairie, something that whispered there was all the room in the world to grow, to be what you couldn't be inside walls. Her head ached from the pins that held her hair in place. How good it would feel to pull off the sedate bonnet and let the wind blow her hair!

After her one brief moment of shock at the audacity of unpinning her hair in front of a strange man, she pulled the ribbon, and as Rawdon shot her an amazed look she loosed her hair and threw back her head into the western breeze.

To her surprise Rawdon chuckled. "Till you did that, I figured you for the perfect schoolmarm."

"Who never lets down her hair?"

His eyes touched her only for a moment, but their curious light seemed to pierce her and see deep inside. But there was something more—a flash of danger and a heady, intoxicating feeling she had never had before. Startled at the way Rawdon's glance sent her pulse racing, she looked away.

"You bet she doesn't let down her hair, Miss Alden." His tone now was almost contemptuous. "She's careful of her clothes, her money, and her reputation."

"Any woman has to guard her reputation," Susanna said defensively.

"Then you'd better twist that pretty hair back into a knot, because the dust and smoke looks like a branding crew up ahead and Ase McCanless may be there. He's chairman of the board of trustees."

As they approached the pall of dust, Susanna could hear shouts and the angry, frightened bawling of cattle. A distance from the track, some mounted men roped calves and hauled them to a fire, where long irons glowed red. When a calf was wrestled down by two more men, a third applied one of the irons. The man with the iron called one of the herders, gave him the iron, and appropriating his horse, rode over to the buckboard.

Sweeping off a soiled wide-brimmed hat, the big stranger gave a curt nod to Rawdon before he stared at Susanna. "You the new schoolmarm, lady?" Lean and tough, and dark as the leather of his saddle, he had blue eyes and sandy brown hair. About Rawdon's age, she guessed him. "No offense," he continued in a lazy drawl, "but you don't look old enough to be traveling around by yourself."

"That's flattering, sir, but I'm twenty-seven and I've been teaching for years."

Eyeing her with caution, he sighed. "Henry said you're from Ohio. Too bad we couldn't get a southern lady, but I reckon their menfolk won't let 'em go gadding around the country."

"My fiancé was killed in the war," Susanna said. "And my father recently died. When the county superintendent of schools invited me to come, he knew I'm what you doubtless call a Yankee."

"Now don't go flyin' off the handle, ma'am. Two of the board want you because you *are* from the North, like them." He set his hat firmly back on his head. "I'm Ase McCanless, ma'am, owner of Ace High ranch. And I reckon you're Miss Susanna Alden. I got to get back to work, but Rawdon, just take her on to the house, and much obliged."

As he started up the team Rawdon said to Susanna, "I'm . . . sorry about your father and fiancé."

That had taken an effort. Moved to honesty, she said, "I'm sorry about your hand."

His face went red, then pale. He spoke in a tight, hard tone. "My hand, Miss Alden, is absolutely none of your concern."

Stung and bewildered, Susanna could think of no good answer. They drove along, the silence heavy, till what must be McCanless's home came into view, a wide-porched white frame house dominating a sprawl of sod buildings and corrals.

"Here you are." Rawdon got down, hitched the team to a post, and impatiently helped her alight. He greeted an old man who limped out of a shed and came to help with the trunk as the door flew open and a plump elderly lady hurried out.

"Come in, dear," the woman greeted. "Your room's ready. Johnny'll fill a tub for you, and I'll bring you some nice soup. I'm Betty Flynn, Mr. McCanless's housekeeper."

She bore Susanna into a carpeted hall and motioned up the stairs. "First door on your right, dear."

Susanna started up the stairs. Rawdon met her on the landing.

"Thank you," she said to him with cool civility, and opened her satchel. "I want to pay you for bringing you out of your way."

The landing was dim, but that made his eyes more disconcertingly brilliant than ever. "Yankees think they can pay for everything, don't they? I don't want your money, Miss Alden."

He gave her a curt nod and was down the stairs before she could move. Dreadful nasty bigoted jaundiced misogynist rebel! Whatever the Mason-Dixon school board was like, it couldn't be made up of more difficult men than Matt Rawdon!

FEELING grimy and bedraggled after three days on the train and the hot, dusty trip from Dodge City, Susanna made grateful use of the water brought up by Johnny. When she'd demurred at the

155

grizzled lame man's carrying buckets, his faded blue eyes twinkled and he grinned.

"I been rolled on by one bronc too many, ma'am. But the doggone leg don't hurt; it's just unreliable. Doc Rawdon rigged me a brace that helps a lot. So don't fret about me, but enjoy yourself. Nothin' like a good bath after comin' in off a long trail."

Not only had he filled the round tin tub, but he had left two extra buckets. Susanna washed and rinsed her hair in these, and eased into the tub with a blissful sigh. Weariness and miles soaked gently away. She was close to drowsing when a thunderous slam somewhere in the house made her jump. Hastily scrubbing herself, she stepped out, toweled, and pulled on a nightgown.

There was a rap at the door. "I've brought your soup, dear," Betty Flynn called.

Hurrying into a wrapper, Susanna opened the door. The housekeeper came in and set a tray on a small marble-topped table, which stood beside an armchair upholstered in rose satin to match the elegant satin coverlet and rose wool rug.

"This is a beautiful room," Susanna said.

"Ase left furnishing the house up to me. Wanted it nice for his daughter, Jenny—not that Jenny gives a hoot. All she wants to do is tag her daddy and tear around on her pony like a wild Indian. That was her just banged the door fit to break windows."

Betty's full bosom lifted and fell in a sigh. "When Ase was just getting started down in Texas, Jenny's mother got dragged to death by a bolting horse when she was helping herd cattle. Jenny was just a baby. Ase can't get over it. So he wants Jenny to have everything her mother didn't. And all Jenny wants is to be with her daddy and do everything he does. They're both mule-stubborn, and I hate to think what'll happen if they keep on wrangling."

"I suppose you've talked with Mr. McCanless."

"I have, but you might as well waste breath on a rock. He needs a wife who could be a mother to Jenny and sort of stand in between them. If somebody loved Ase . . ."

"You do."

"He's the son I never had." Betty's hazel eyes softened. "We were neighbors in Texas. After my man died, he asked me to move in and look after Jenny." Betty clapped her hand over her mouth. "Here I am, rattling on while your supper gets cold! Enjoy it, dear, and get a good rest."

Betty Flynn shut the door behind her, and Susanna sat down to her tray. The cream of tomato soup was delicious, with moist corn muffins still hot enough to melt butter, and a glass of cold buttermilk. Susanna relished each bite, but this luxuriating was ruined by her conscience when Johnny knocked and began to carry out her bathwater. When he descended with the buckets, Susanna dragged the tub out into the hall on the round braided rug it sat on.

"Hold it right there, ma'am!" An outraged Johnny hurried from the porch, clanking the buckets. "That's my job!"

"It makes me feel so lazy," Susanna pleaded. "Won't you let me help you carry this down?"

"I sure won't! Why, Ase would skin me alive—"

"I'll help." The door at the end of the hall opened, and a tanned girl, perhaps eleven, with a thick braid of yellow hair, raced to the stair and grasped one handle of the tub.

With a defiant laugh that showed white teeth and several dimples, the girl gave Susanna a challenging stare from eyes such a deep blue that in the shadowy hall they looked almost black. "Grab hold, lady, if you really mean what you said."

Growling, Johnny held to the banister as if needing support while Susanna and the child, who could only be Jenny, went down the stairs with the tub, carefully, in order not to splash.

"We'll dump it on the trees," Jenny said. "Not enough soap to hurt 'em." Susanna held the hems of her white gown and wrapper out of the gritty dust of the bare yard and helped pour out the water. Turning the tub upside down on a bench beside the house that held several others, Jenny stared directly at Susanna.

"Betty says you're going to start a school."

"That's why I came."

"I don't want to go."

"Whether or not you go is between you and your father," Susanna said coolly. "Whether you learn is your choice."

"You won't try to make me study?"

"I'll give you the grades you earn." Susanna started up the

steps to the side porch. Jenny ran ahead and turned to confront her from the step above.

A jaw, firm in spite of childish contours, dropped a little. "Daddy won't like that."

"Again, that's between the two of you."

"If you can't teach me, you won't keep the school." Recovering her confidence, Jenny spoke boastfully. "The only reason Daddy helped with it was because he hopes I'll learn more that way than I did from those silly women he hired. Governesses! They didn't govern me. None of them lasted a month."

Smothering a retort, Susanna continued up the stairs to her room. "Thank you, Jenny, for helping me empty the water. Good night."

Entering, Susanna closed the door. There was the sound of pelting steps, and then, down the hall, a door slammed even more loudly than it had the first time. To Susanna's surprise she found that she was trembling. Never had she encountered a child like this. No wonder the governesses had fled. She won't be my only pupil, Susanna comforted herself. Some will want to study, be hungry to learn.

Or would they? Maybe youngsters out here were different. And these pupils were bound to share the animosities of their parents, former Unionists and Confederates. Panic flooded her.

Susanna walked to the window and leaned on the sill, welcoming a breeze that at the gathering of twilight was somewhat cooler. Blue-gray prairie merged with a sky that was lighter at the horizon, darker above, showing the first stars. Why, that was the Big Dipper, the Great Bear! It was heartening to see the familiar heavenly lights.

Swept with longing for her father as he had been before the war, Susanna gripped the window ledge and blinked back tears. She gazed at the stars and whispered into the night, "Daddy, let me know it's well with you."

As if he'd been waiting, she felt him near, heard him in her mind, though there were no audible words: It's very well. Where I am there's endless day, my darling, perfect peace and perfect joy.

The awareness faded, but she was comforted. Maybe it was all a trick of her senses, conjured up from fatigue and feeling so apprehensive and alone in this strange place. However it came, it was the best medicine her physician father had ever given her. Anytime she saw the stars they'd watched together, she could remember him, and happily. His death had given him back to her.

She lit the rose hobnail lamp, and after burrowing in the trunk, she found a worn volume, the *Meditations* of Marcus Aurelius, her father's book. She sat down near the lamp, opening the pages to the ribbon that marked her father's favorite passage: "Art thou unwilling to do the work of a human being? And why then dost thou not make haste to do that which is according to thy nature?"

The work of a human being. That meant more than simply work, carrying out one's allotted tasks. It meant to fulfill the duties and obligations of the mortal state, live with as much grace, kindness, and fortitude as possible. Only by trying for the best could she hope to shape a life that would count for something.

Again she thanked her father, and again she felt him close. She braided her hair, blew out the lamp, and fell into the deepest sleep she'd had since her father had died, but not before she wished she could see Matt Rawdon's mouth tender and happy, without that twist of bitterness.

Two

$\mathcal{A}$s SHE started to dress next morning, Susanna, with her usual reluctance, picked up her corset. She started to hook it up, but then paused. Betty didn't lace. Probably none of the homestead and ranch women out here did, except for special occasions. She tossed the corset on her trunk. This was her new life. Why shouldn't she get rid of hampering relics of fuss and vanity?

In her coolest dress—a dark green tarlatan—Susanna went downstairs. She found Betty making buckwheat cakes, which Johnny, seated at a red-checkered-oilcloth–covered table, devoured with such speed that he seemed to breathe them in. He paused to grin appreciatively at Susanna as he got up and limped around to seat her. She smiled and thanked him as Betty set a stack of hotcakes before her and poured coffee. Betty dropped two more cakes onto Johnny's plate before sitting down to her own.

"Where is Jenny?"

"In her room, I expect," said Betty.

Johnny gave a sad shake of his gray head. "If Ase don't loosen his reins, she'll prob'ly run off with some cowboy when she's fifteen or so. He can gentle a filly 'thout breakin' her spirit, but he don't know how to do that with his daughter." He gave Susanna a look. "How'd you and Jenny get along?"

"Not too well," Susanna had to admit.

"Can't expect you to believe it, but at heart she's a good kid." Johnny finished his coffee and pushed back his chair. "Want I should take you to see the school, ma'am?"

"Is it far?"

"Not more'n a mile. Ase built it close so you and Jenny wouldn't have to go far. It's on his land."

"Did he deed the building and site to the school district?"

Betty and Johnny looked at each other and burst into laughter. "Ase McCanless give up control of his land?" Johnny said.

"I haven't been hired yet," said Susanna, suddenly queasy and losing her appetite. "But I can't teach in a privately owned school that sets on private land. I won't teach in a school controlled by one patron. I can't think of anything more detrimental to education, especially in a divided community like this."

"Is that so?"

They all whirled toward the open door. Absorbed in their talk, they hadn't heard Ase McCanless approach. Pushing sweaty sand-brown hair off his forehead, he sloshed coffee into a blue enameled mug, took a long swallow, and stared at Susanna.

"Miss Alden, I guess you're balkin' at the school bein' on my place." Thick bleached brows almost met above his rather flat, pugnacious nose.

"Not just balking, sir. Your owning the school puts you in a position to wield improper influence."

A slow smile eased the grim line of his mouth. "Improper influence, ma'am? Sounds like it might be fun. But I sure don't aim to tell you what to teach any more'n any trustee has a right to."

"Mr. McCanless, let me make it clear right now that I won't take the school unless it's understood that I'm in charge of it. If the trustees and patrons don't approve of the results, they can refuse to offer me another contract." Taut with anxiety at the prospect of having to give up this school, Susanna tried to keep her features expressionless. Her muscles went slack with relief when McCanless threw back his head and laughed.

"I'll make you a deal, Miss Alden, fair and square. Have a look at my school, think about what else is around, and I won't buck your decision. What's fairer than that?"

"It *sounds* fair," she agreed doubtfully.

His laughter rumbled again, and he swung a chair to the table. "Betty, reckon I could tuck away some of your good hotcakes. And I'll call Jenny down. Her nose is all out of joint because I sent her home yesterday. But ridin' along with us ought to sweeten up her disposition." He shouted her name.

"What do you want?" called Jenny's faint, truculent voice.

"Eat your breakfast and you can ride Scout over to the school with the teacher and me."

There was a silence. "Can I use a real saddle?"

McCanless smothered a groan. "Just this mornin', on account of Miss Alden'll need your sidesaddle."

Susanna excused herself and hurried upstairs to put on her fullest skirt, since she had no riding habit. As a child, she'd ridden bareback on a gentle old mare who'd pulled Charles Alden's phaeton, but she was sure a ranch horse would be far different. If only she didn't fall off and disgrace herself!

Even if she did, she wasn't changing her mind about Ase McCanless's school.

JENNY, in Levi's, swung astride a proud-headed spotted pony, who danced while Susanna helplessly studied the sidesaddle cinched to a sorrel mare Johnny held by the reins.

"Her name's Cindy, ma'am, in case you have to holler at her," said Johnny reassuringly. "Want I should give you a hand up?"

"She needs a lot more than that." Jenny's tone was derisive. "She's not got the faintest notion of how to sit on that thing."

Susanna was almost grateful to have her embarrassing secret laid bare. Catching her breath, she laughed. "You're absolutely

161

right, Jenny. I don't know where to put my knee or foot or—"

The unmentionable part of her anatomy was perched on the saddle seat before she could protest McCanless's lifting her bodily by the waist and tossing her up as if her weight were nothing. "There, ma'am," McCanless said. "Cindy'll stay with us, so you can just settle back and enjoy the scenery."

At first Susanna sat stiffly. Gradually, though, her body adapted to the mare's easy pace. Relaxing, she began almost to enjoy the outing, though she wondered if she'd ever get used to this vastness—the burnished, cloudless sky curving to a rolling sea of grass. The awesome expanse made her uncomfortable, but the boundlessness also invited her. If the eye could encompass so much, couldn't the spirit also reach and perceptions sharpen? Till yesterday she'd never thought of grass as more than the lush green of meadows and lawns; this grass was different—individual, tough, and colorful as the people she was meeting.

McCanless reined back. "Everybody on the board of trustees is pretty busy right now, Miss Alden—cattlemen with branding and farmers with harvest. I've sent word to the others, though, and we'll try to meet at the school this Sunday. That gives Henry Morton four days to get out here. If he don't make it, we'll vote about hiring you anyway." His slow grin was probably meant to be reassuring. Then he said in a tone of pride, "There it is, ma'am."

Except for Ase's home, it was the first decent-looking building she'd seen in all western Kansas—a simple oblong frame structure, painted white, with a roof of shingles split from logs.

"I'll bet it's the best Kansas school west of Wichita," Ase said. He sprang down from his chestnut horse. Jenny did the same. "Come. Have a look." Without waiting for Susanna's consent, he swept her from the saddle and started to usher her inside.

Susanna balked, withdrawing her elbow from his hand. "Your school is worlds better than anything I expected. But I won't teach here unless you deed it to the school district."

The sun-whitened eyebrows jerked together before Ase bit back whatever he'd started to say and gave a shrug. "Scout around the building, ma'am, and then you can have your final say."

If men weren't exasperatingly stubborn before they came here, the place must make them so. Scowling at him, Susanna lifted her skirt enough to climb the single step. Whitewashed walls added to the light from the sparkling windows. A potbellied iron stove in the back of the room and a bin in the corner were providently full of yellow-brown disks that had to be the dried products of cattle or buffalo, which, Susanna knew, were used for fuel in this almost treeless region. Long plank desks faced a blackboard and a real oak teacher's desk with a barrel-backed chair.

Susanna turned and stepped out into the wind. "This is a wonderful school, Mr. McCanless. I wish I could teach in it. But I can't."

He slammed one big fist into an open palm. "Of all the confounded stiff-necked persnickety Yankee schoolmarms, why did we have to get one who's crazy to boot?"

Seared by his anger, Susanna left him and marched toward Cindy. Too hurt and furious to be nervous of the mare, she snatched up the reins, looped them over the mare's neck, and set her foot in the stirrup. But before she could clamber up, McCanless lifted her to the saddle. By the time she hooked her knee over the horn, he was mounted and riding ahead with Jenny.

No one spoke till they neared the house. Then Ase said to Susanna, "I'm going to the brandin'. I'll sure be interested to hear what you tell the trustees about turnin' up your nose at the best schoolhouse in Ford County."

Susanna caught her breath. "You mean you want me to wait and see the trustees?"

He gave a harsh laugh. "Miss Alden, we've tried for three years to get a teacher. The few who've applied weren't fit to teach hogs how to stick their feet in a trough." He lifted the reins.

"Wait!" cried Susanna. "I don't know what other buildings might be used for a school."

He shrugged. "You better make your pick of the places on abandoned claims. Jenny can show you where they are." Touching the brim of his hat, he trotted south.

"How far are these buildings?" Susanna asked Jenny.

Jenny jerked her head northward, so that her thick yellow plait bounced. "There's a soddy maybe three miles that way and another one a mile and a half southeast of Dad's school."

"Could we go see the north soddy now and look at the other one this afternoon?" Susanna asked.

"You may be too stiff to ride this afternoon."

"I'll ride."

"We'll see," said Jenny. Bending over the spotted pony's neck, she let out a wild yell and was off, the pony's hoofs seeming to skim the grass rather than touch it. Susanna followed horse and rider into the red-brown ocean of grass.

Before long Jenny looped back to her as Susanna reined up at the soddy and stared at earthen walls crumbling where the roof had fallen in on one side. She shook her head decisively.

"This won't do."

"You won't like any soddy, let alone a dugout," Jenny said, turning her horse, Scout, so that Cindy followed. Her lip curled. "You may decide to use Dad's school after all."

DINNER was beans; corn bread, deliciously crusty on top; cool buttermilk; and plump wedges of gold-glazed dried-apple pie. While Susanna was freshening up, Jenny must have told Johnny and Betty about Susanna's rejection of Ase's school, for afterward Betty said, "One thing you'd best consider, dear, is how far a place is from the patron families. The kiddies have to get back and forth, and of course you will, too, boarding around."

"Boarding around? Isn't there a house for the teacher?"

"Land's sake, no, child. It's different in towns, I suppose, but out here teachers take turns staying with their patrons." Betty gave a delicate cough. "I know Ase figgered the teacher could just stay with us, since we're the closest to the building."

And then he really would have the teacher in his pocket, wouldn't he? Susanna thought. Jenny was all ears and eyes; only that kept Susanna from blurting that thought aloud.

"That would be extremely kind and generous of Mr. McCanless," Susanna said. "However, living in any patron's home seems prejudicial to discipline, and I frankly abhor the thought of shifting myself and my belongings every month or so."

"But Susanna, that's how it's done out here," Betty wailed.

"Then it's fortunate I haven't accepted the position. I want a place of my own—however small and crude—that might provide both a school and home. If the trustees won't find me something, I'll refuse the school." A sudden hope glimmered. "That soddy we're going to this afternoon, Jenny. Does it have more than one room?"

"I've never been close enough to tell," Jenny said.

"That was the Madsen place," Betty said, frowning. "Let me think. Yes, there's two rooms—one good-sized and a smaller bedroom."

"Maybe the bedroom could serve as my quarters. I'm willing to pay for any supplies needed to fix up the room, and if I boarded with families, they'd have to feed me. So why can't they just give me the same amount of food?"

"Sounds fair," Johnny said with a nod.

Betty glared at him. "And what about tornadoes? Prairie fires? Blizzards? What's fair got to do with a young lady living miles from the closest neighbor?"

"Miles?" Susanna echoed faintly.

In her revolt against staying with patrons, she'd forgotten she wasn't living in a town. There'd be no close neighbors. All the same, she couldn't live in Ase's house, and boarding around was unthinkable. Summoning a laugh, she said, "Betty, it's sweet of you to care about me, but I'm more concerned about my living conditions than possible catastrophes."

Betty shook her head. "It makes me sick to think of that pretty room setting empty while you try to get along in a soddy."

"Most people can, and I will, too." Susanna softened her words with a quick smile. "That's the best corn bread I ever tasted, Betty, and the pie was delicious. I ate so much Cindy may not want to carry me."

Jenny shoved a last large bite into her mouth and sprang up, wiping her hands on her Levi's. "Ready to go?"

"As soon as we do the dishes."

Jenny stared. "Betty never asks me to do the dishes."

"Perhaps not, but I am. Betty cooked our meal."

Jenny scowled, glanced rather shamefacedly toward Betty, and after a moment grudged, "I'll dry if you wash."

The task was quickly done with hot water from the side of the stove. She wouldn't have a stove, Susanna knew. Did that mean she'd have to cook in a fireplace? With cow chips?

Well, she thought, hadn't she come out here to be a pioneer?

THE good things about the soddy were that it had two rooms, a roof, probably in place because the roots of flowers and grass had knit together to hold it to the rafter poles, and it commanded, from a gentle slope, a pleasant view of the bend in a creek fringed by cottonwoods. The bad things started with the dirt floor, the mud walls, and the frightening hairy-legged creature that dropped from the ceiling in front of Susanna.

Susanna screamed and stepped back, bumping Jenny, who burst out laughing. "It's only a tarantula. They won't sting unless you really pester them. A black widow or some kinds of scorpion can hurt you a lot worse."

Susanna was glad when the four-inch-long tarantula disappeared in the weeds by the door.

Braced for whatever else might happen, Susanna inspected the sod fireplace, built in the wall between the two rooms so that it could heat both. The chimney needed repair, but otherwise it looked serviceable, and the center wall helped support the rafters. The thick sod made it cool inside, and that would be a blessing in hot weather. It also made it dark as a cave. The main room was lit by two small paneless windows, which sent shafts of light to the floor, and the bedroom had one window.

Susanna turned to Jenny. "How long a walk will it be for the children?"

Squinting in concentration, Jenny counted off on her fingers. "Prades live across the creek, about three miles away. The Taylor girls are only two miles south. Hardy kids live across the creek a couple of miles. Browns ranch southwest of us, but Freck and Dottie have horses, so they won't mind six miles." She hesitated, then burst out, "Will you let a breed come to school?"

"A *what?*"

"You know, a half-breed. Part Indian, part white."

Instead of chiding Jenny for the offensive term, Susanna said, "Any child in the district is supposed to come to school."

Jenny almost smiled. "I hope Ridge will come. But he's mighty proud. Daddy reckons a breed can get along fine in an Indian village, but he'll always have trouble around whites."

"It might help if they weren't called breeds," Susanna suggested as gently as she could.

Jenny's eyes widened. "Why, that's what they are! People say someone's a full-breed or a half-breed."

"Do they say someone's a full-breed white man?"

"No, but . . ." Jenny considered. "I'll bet Daddy never thought about that. He likes Luke Tarrant—that's Ridge's father—and Daddy says Luke's wife is a lot better woman than most white ones. Prettier, too. Luke calls her Millie, since that's pretty close to her Indian name. Luke was a bullwhacker on the Santa Fe Trail when the train he was with found Millie. Her camp had been attacked by Kiowas and her parents killed. She was only ten. Luke put her in a wagon, took care of her all the way to Santa Fe, and left her with a nice Mexican lady. He'd go see her when he came to town, and when she was thirteen, she followed the train back to Missouri. Luke put her in a convent school in St. Louis, but she ran off again to track him. So he finally promised to marry her when she was sixteen if she'd stay in the school until then."

"After all that, I hope they've been happy."

"Oh, they are!" Jenny's eyes shone. "Why, you wouldn't even think they were married. They're like—like sweethearts."

With a pang Susanna thought of Richard. Pushing away such a thought, she said briskly, "This is about as central a location as possible, then, for our school."

Jenny peered in the bedroom with its single window. "You really want to live here instead of at our house?"

Susanna didn't try to hold back the ripple of laughter. "Of course I like that beautiful rose room a lot better. But this is where I should be, Jenny, and so, yes, I do want to live here."

"Spoken like a rock-ribbed Yankee puritan," came a voice from outside. Ducking, Matt Rawdon entered. He must have been working, for his gray shirt, open at the throat and with sleeves rolled up, clung to him, and he had a good pungent male odor. He had bared his head, and the thick mass of hair curved damply in a wave where it touched his face. Surveying the interior, he regarded Susanna. "Can I believe my ears? You're planning to live in this hovel?"

Susanna's cheeks burned. "I can't see that it's any of your business, Dr. Rawdon. You don't have children in school."

"My dear young woman, you have so much to learn about this kind of community if you don't know that everything is everybody's business. And my land's across the creek. I was virtuously scything hay when I saw riders stop here and linger inside so long that I came to investigate."

In this dimmed room his eyes were more luminous than ever. He looked brown and fit and handsome. The hand ruined for surgery was well able to grip a scythe. Or hold a woman? The unbidden image deepened the blush on Susanna's face. "Your place borders the creek?"

"Don't sound so dismayed, Miss Alden. My soddy, such as it is, sets on a section of my land that's a good four miles east." His eyes searched her. "How come you're not tickled with Ase's new school?"

"Because it is his, and it sets on his land."

"You told Ase this and he didn't yell loud enough to blast you straight back to Ohio?"

"He didn't like it." Susanna had to smile before the doubts that had been gathering suddenly settled on her like a weight. "I know it's dangerous for a school to be the property of one patron, but it's so light and clean and this is so—so—"

"Dark and dirty?"

"Yes. It'll be so much more uncomfortable for the children. I feel as if I'm wronging them—"

She broke off, turning away. To her amazement, his tone was almost sympathetic. "Don't trim your sails, Miss Alden. Remember, Ase can always make the school over to the district, and the trustees don't have to hire you."

"Of course they don't!" Why had she forgotten that, taken the whole load of responsibility on herself? Heart lifting, Susanna took a deep breath, laughed, and caught Rawdon's hand.

It was an instinctive gesture of thanks. She hadn't thought

about his maiming, but when her fingertips touched ridged scars, she glanced down. Rawdon snatched his hand away.

"I wish you luck with the trustees, Miss Alden, though your best luck would be for them to reject you, so that you could find a school where you could enjoy both a decent building and your principles." He backed out the door. "Good-bye, Miss Alden."

He strode down the slope. If the trustees wouldn't hire her, this would be her last glimpse of him. Why had he snatched his hand away as if she'd deliberately tried to shame him? He was terribly sensitive about those scarred fingers. Had he loved a woman who recoiled from him? Taking her gaze from him, Susanna said, "Thanks for bringing me, Jenny. There's nothing more I can do till I meet with the board."

As they rode, Susanna was busy thinking up ways to improve the soddy, and wondering whether to be glad or sorry if she stayed. Because from time to time when he worked the neighboring part of his land, she was bound to see Matt Rawdon.

Three

$\mathcal{F}$OUR days later, at two o'clock in the afternoon, the board of the Mason-Dixon School met at Ase McCanless's school. As they rode to the meeting Ase told Susanna something about each trustee. "Your Yankees," he said, "are Will Taylor, from Missouri, who has a passel of little gals; and Saul Prade, from Illinois, who's kind of a strange duck. Got four kids, and a wife who'd be a beauty if she didn't look so tired." Ase frowned a moment before he went on. "Luke Tarrant used to be a freight hauler. Married a pretty Cheyenne girl young enough to be his daughter, but they sure seem happy, even if Luke did come home from the war with a bad limp. Kermit Brown was a Texas Ranger, who helped me chouse cows out of the brush after the war and decided to trail up here when I did. He married a real nice gal, Hettie, from San Antonio, red-haired like him, and the kids take after 'em. Cash Hardy's too lazy to scratch fleas, which goes to show that hailin' from Iowa won't necessarily mean a body's not shiftless. He and his missus have three boys and a gal."

The school came in sight. As they neared enough to see tethered horses and a number of men, Susanna's heart leaped into her
throat and pounded hard.

What would the trustees be like? What would they ask? For all
her resolve not to board around or teach at Ase's school, she
wanted desperately to win this contract!

McCanless swung Susanna down. A gangling man in a dark
coat doffed his hat to reveal wispy fluffs of brown hair that con-
trasted with his pink bald head. He beamed at her and enthusiastically pumped her hand.

"So here you are, Miss Alden! I'm Henry Morton. Let me ac-
quaint you with the board of trustees, and then we'll move inside."

As Mr. Morton introduced each board member Susanna offered
her hand. Heavyset red-haired Kermit Brown took her fingers as if
afraid of breaking them. "Proud to meet you, ma'am," he drawled,

and his blue eyes were friendly, even if he was a southerner.

Will Taylor, lanky and rawboned, with a kinky black beard and hair, barely touched her hand and mumbled something. Limping forward, Luke Tarrant enclosed her hand in both of his. He was gray-haired, of average height, and compactly muscled, and his hazel eyes beamed at her in a fatherly way. "Glad you're here, Miss Alden, and we hope you'll be glad, too."

"She's not hired yet, Tarrant." The most striking man of all confronted Susanna, arms crossed, while cold green eyes inspected her. Tall as Ase, he was gracefully built, and his features were almost too perfect. He inclined his golden head. "I'm Saul Prade."

That was all. No pleasantries. He was a Union man, Susanna remembered. He should have been her ally, but somehow she knew he would not be. As if sensing her uneasiness, Henry Morton said, "Come on in, folks. Cash Hardy won't be joining us. Said he was down in the back."

Getting the teacher's chair, Ase placed it for Susanna before facing the other trustees, who had taken seats on the largest bench while Morton hovered nervously in the rear.

"Before we start askin' Miss Alden questions," Ase said, "maybe she should tell us a little about herself." He paused and glanced at her. "Could be some things we'd better know right off."

Rising, Susanna thanked him and gave the briefest facts of her life, before drawing in a deep breath and plunging ahead.

"I've already told Mr. McCanless that I cannot teach in this excellent school building, because it's his private property. This would give the appearance, if not the reality, of his having undue influence on the school." There was a buzz at this.

They might as well have it all at once, Susanna thought, and spoke loud enough to be heard over the commotion. "I hope the soddy to the south of here can be fixed for a school, and I wish to live in the bedroom instead of boarding with patrons."

The trustees stared at Susanna, then at one another, and back to her. "Board's part of your salary." Will Taylor rubbed a floppy earlobe. "How much more money would you want?"

"None, if you'll make the bedroom habitable, give me food to cook, and supply fuel."

"Do you think you're too good to live with us?" Prade demanded. "How'll we get to know you?"

"I can't see why we need to know each other that well," Susanna said, and was confused when everyone laughed except Prade, who watched her with narrowed eyes.

Kermit Brown shifted a wad of tobacco in his cheek and leaned forward. "Guess what I want to know, ma'am, is what you're goin' to teach about the war, you bein' from Ohio, and all."

Susanna's nape tingled. "I'll teach the truth, as best I can find it—that the South was agricultural and the North industrialized, that though the South used slaves, New England ships brought them to this country and made fortunes selling the slaves to plantations in the South."

"I never heard that before," said Will Taylor, frowning. "But even if it's so, you can't get around the fact that the rebs tried to wreck the Union."

"We weren't rebelling, Taylor," cut in Ase. "We were doin' what we damned well had a right to—break free of the North and have our own government."

"And keep your slaves," added Prade, giving a jeering laugh.

"Hell, I never had a slave and neither did most folks," Ase shot back. "But most owners treated their slaves a heap better than Yank factory owners treat the women and kids *they* work to a nub."

There was a silence as northerners and southerners warily eyed one another. Ase held up his hands. "Anyone got more questions for Miss Alden?"

"What subjects kin she teach?" asked Taylor.

"The usual curriculum, Mr. Taylor," Susanna answered. "I would teach reading, penmanship, spelling, grammar, composition, mental and written arithmetic, history and geography—"

"Joggerphy!" Taylor stiffened his gangling frame and crossed his arms. "I've got three sweet little girls, gentlemen. I don't want their minds putrified with learnin' about a lot of heathen places across the ocean."

"Mr. Taylor," Susanna said, "an important part of education is to help us understand people who aren't like us and develop a view of our country as one of many nations that have to share the world."

Kermit Brown turned toward Ase. "Miss Alden suits me right down to the ground. You can tell by listenin' to her that she's got more book learnin' than the whole bunch of us. I say let's give her a contract for six months, Henry."

The superintendent said, "Considering Miss Alden's superior qualifications, thirty dollars a month, with fuel and food, seems reasonable."

"That agreeable to you, ma'am?" inquired Ase.

Susanna nodded.

"If you'll step outside with me, ma'am, while the board votes," said Henry Morton. As they moved a little way around the building, keeping in its shade, he added, "If this cantankerous bunch don't hire you or if they're too ornery to get along with, you just let me know, ma'am, and I'll find you a school someplace else."

As THE trustees took their leave Saul Prade came noiselessly up beside Susanna. Prade's sculpted mouth curved in a bleak smile. "They voted for you, but I didn't." He carried a few supple willow branches, perhaps four feet long, and now offered them to Susanna. "These have enough play in them to raise welts, and that's what you'll have to do to conquer your students."

Susanna shrank away. It was broad day, but this man terrified her. "I don't want to conquer the children, Mr. Prade."

He still offered the switches. She knew she was making a dangerous enemy, but outrage drove her to take the slender limbs and hurl them to the ground. They stared at each other. What gazed out from behind those chilling eyes? Something cruel. Something evil. He swung away from her, mounted, and rode east.

Shaken by the exchange, Susanna was left with Ase, who helped her mount and cast a brooding glance at the soddy. "It beats me how you can be so all-fired stubborn."

"You must have voted for me."

"Sure, I did. You're the only one who applied. And any fool can tell you're a good teacher. The trustees will get the soddy ready and a barn raised next week so's you can start up the first week in October." He cleared his throat. "Reckon I might ask you a question that's none of my business, ma'am?"

"If I don't wish to answer, I'll say so."

"How come a woman as pretty as you are isn't married?"

"My fiancé was killed in the war."

"I'm plumb sorry for that. But the war's over ten years."

"I was nursing my father till he died this spring."

He rubbed his blunt chin. "Well, here's another none-of-my-business question, ma'am. A man's got a free hand to swing a rope at you, don't he? You're not moonin' around over somebody?"

Matt Rawdon's lean face rose from the back of her mind, but she told the rancher, "My affections aren't engaged, sir. However, though I'm not wearing black, I couldn't, from respect for my father, keep company with a gentleman till a year after his death. Further, I feel it would be a grave breach of propriety for a teacher to—to become involved with a patron."

After some moments of glum silence, Ase swung toward her. "School's out the end of March. You won't be an employee then. Meanwhile, we'll move the desks and benches and such to the soddy. No use makin' the kids suffer for *your* principles, ma'am."

That was a relief. She had her contract and at least the tentative approval of most of the trustees. Now she had to prove that she could teach their children.

THE next day two Ace High ranch hands helped haul furnishings from Ase's school over to the soddy and transplanted the frame privies on either side of a nearby sandhill plum thicket.

While Susanna tacked cheesecloth to the rafters to prevent at least some spiders, bugs, roots, and dirt from falling to the floor, Kermit Brown repaired the chimney. Ase's men helped Luke Tarrant plaster the walls, starting with the bedroom, where Ase, as soon as the door was finished, started making a bunk.

The Tarrants had donated a small table and a leather-bottomed chair for Susanna's quarters. Mrs. Brown supplied a dresser with a mirror, and when Susanna came in, Ase was through with the bunk and was hammering the last nails into shelves against the wall next to the fireplace. Mrs. Prade, who owned a sewing machine, had sent a ticking mattress filled with corn husks. Susanna covered it with sheets embroidered with her initials. Out of her trunk she took her own down pillow and her favorite quilt—wreaths of roses appliquéd on calico. She spread it on the bunk.

Amazing how much the quilt improved the little room. Carefully unwrapping her grandmother's teapot and the two fragile cups and saucers, Susanna sighed happily to find them intact, and arranged them on the top shelf. Her brush, comb, and silver mirror that had been a gift from her father went on the dresser, along with the Marcus Aurelius book. She placed her other books on the shelves, each loved and often read: Dickens, Tennyson, the Brontë sisters, Whitman, as well as an assortment of textbooks.

By then it was noon, and the men were outside eating. Susanna continued to work. Undergarments and shawls in the dresser, shoes neatly arranged beneath it; dresses and cloak spread on the bunk to go on pegs, as soon as the plaster dried; Dutch oven, skillet, water kettle, and cooking pot ranged on the clay hearth near the fireplace, with a broom and ash shovel and bucket in the corner. Ase had supplied a wood box with a tight-fitting lid, which held flour, cornmeal, rice, and dried corn from the Tarrants. For sweetening, she'd use the sorghum molasses contributed by the Prades. Under the bunk were stored a bushel of potatoes, onions, and a box of beans from the Browns, as well as a keg of sauerkraut brought by Will Taylor, who had also supplied some bacon. Ase was responsible for the tin of Arbuckle's coffee, cans of tomatoes and peaches, and raisins, dried apples, and prunes in jars to protect them from mice. A leather bag, suspended from a rafter, held jerked beef prepared by Millie Tarrant. Salt, pepper, baking soda, and a can of lard completed the supplies.

Surveying her home with satisfaction, Susanna noticed the bare window. At night any passerby could peer right in at her; curtains for at least this window were a must. Susanna remembered a tablecloth embroidered with yellow pansies in the trunk. She measured it to the window, and moving the chair so she could see through the window to the creek, she hemmed till her neck and shoulder hurt. Then, stretching, she went to look at the classroom.

Bless Ase! He had brought over the blackboard and teacher's desk and chair, as well as the students' desks, which were arranged to get as much light as possible. The recitation bench was close to the fireplace, facing the teacher's desk, and the blackboard was attached to the wall, which had dried to a creamy pale brown. To make the room seem really hers, Susanna got out her handbell and clock and set them on her desk. A large, carefully folded world map added color to the wall by the blackboard. Getting out a small flag rolled around its rod in the bottom of the trunk, she thrust it securely in a crack where the corners joined.

Susanna took a last sweeping glance around, gathered up the curtains to finish later, and went out to thank the trustees and say that in the next few days she'd come to visit their families.

STRANGE. Ten days ago, Susanna had been nervous of gentle old Cindy and deathly afraid of falling beneath her hoofs. Now she no longer rode filled with anxiety. Nor was she troubled about riding by herself across the prairie. Leaving Ace High, she followed Johnny's directions. All she need do to find the Hardys' was to cross the creek beneath its bend near the school and follow the stream south a few miles. To reach Taylors', she'd leave Hardys', tracing wagon tracks across Matt Rawdon's property, and travel north till she struck the Missouri family's homestead. After that, the rutted way led to the Prades'.

Margaret Hardy was glad to have a woman visitor, though she was embarrassed to be caught barefoot and hastily laced on worn black boots. She was only five or six years older than Susanna, but exposure to sun and wind had grooved lines at the corners of her brown eyes. Still, she was a pretty woman, with a dimpled chin and a mass of curling yellow-brown hair.

"It's dark inside," she said with an apologetic glance at the half dugout burrowed into the side of a slope. Two windows were covered with scraped, oiled hides, and the leather-hinged door hung open. "Why don't we sit out here and I'll bring you a glass of beverage? Rosie, fetch the chair for Miss Alden."

Rosie, with bouncing pigtails, dragged out a cane-bottomed chair, bobbed her head shyly at Susanna's thanks, and brought out a wooden box. Digging the bare toes of one foot beneath the instep of the other, she held out the skirt of her green plaid gingham dress, much too big for her, and confided, "Aunt Madge sent this and two other nice dresses my cousin Marilyn outgrew. It's a shame she doesn't have some boys so she could send my brothers things."

"Rosie! I declare, honey, your tongue's fastened in the middle and wags at both ends."

Margaret Hardy gave Susanna a glass of faintly tinted fluid that Susanna decided was water flavored with vinegar. She settled on the box and positioned her daughter in front of her. "I hope you don't mind my altering the dress while we talk, Miss Alden, but she's set on wearing it the first day of school. Now, just let me tell you how glad I am you're going to have a school! Dave's fifteen and Ethan's twelve, and they got some schooling before we left Iowa four years ago, but Rosie and Georgie haven't had any. Rosie is ten and Georgie's only seven." Her eyes grew wistful. "My sister Madge and her husband wanted Dave to stay with them and finish his education, but with Cash not able to do much heavy work because of getting his back hurt in the war, we just had to bring Dave along." She brightened. "If he can finish eighth grade, Miss Alden, can't he go to the teachers' summer institute, take the examination, and get his teaching certificate?"

"I don't know the Kansas regulations, but that sounds very likely, Mrs. Hardy."

Susanna's sympathetic tone led her hostess to glance around as if to make sure the audacity wasn't overheard. "Davie dreams about going on to further learning. But I don't see how he ever could."

"Why not?" The instant the question was out, Susanna would have recalled it if possible. The answer was all too evident in the glassless windows and a veritable cave, instead of the comparative comfort of a soddy. Dave would be needed at home, at the very least till his brothers and sister were grown. Still, Susanna couldn't accept this. "If that's what he wants to do, Mrs. Hardy, don't you think we should encourage him?"

"He—he's such a good boy." The mother's lips trembled. "I'd hate for him to be disappointed."

"Isn't it better to be disappointed in trying for what you want than just giving it up?"

"Who's to say?" Bitterness for the first time edged into the other woman's voice. "Cash worked on the river docks before the war, but he couldn't do that with his bad back. We thought homesteading was the answer." Her words muted. "Turned out that plowing hurt Cash's back. I washed and baked for Jem Howe, who lives east of here, though, and he broke enough sod with his oxen that first year so we could plant corn. We had beautiful corn and wheat a year ago, but in July the grasshoppers came. Lots of settlers gave up and we would have, too, only we didn't have anywhere to go." Margaret paused. "Doc Rawdon's done all he can for Cash—brings him medicine and won't take a cent. When Georgie broke his arm last year, Doc set it, and when Rosie had pneumonia, he sat up with her three nights to let me rest. Jem Howe's been mighty good to us, too. I certainly shouldn't complain."

"Sometimes it helps to talk," Susanna said.

This visit starkly underlined the isolation of these prairie women, the hunger for another woman to talk with. Though Susanna had planned to wait till her pupils could make a good showing before setting plans in motion to bring the families together, she decided not to delay. "Every Friday afternoon parents are invited to come to school," she said. "We'll have spelling bees and ciphering matches, and perhaps some of the children will want to give poems they've memorized."

"That's wonderful! Cash might even come."

"I hope so." Susanna had sipped all her beverage and rose with a smile. "Thank you. I have to be going."

Rising, Margaret gave Susanna a shy, swift embrace. "Good luck to you, dear, and if you ever have a speck of trouble with any of my children, let me know and I'll talk it out with them."

"I'll look for you next Friday," Susanna promised. As she rode over the slope she waved back at Margaret Hardy, who stood and flourished her apron till Susanna was out of sight.

RIDING through Matt Rawdon's hayfield, Susanna wondered what he would think when he learned that she wasn't, as he'd so condescendingly predicted, retreating to Ohio. But why should it matter to her what he thought?

It did matter, though. She fought away a sudden recollection of those strangely luminous eyes. She was years past the age when she should have felt the sort of magnetism that coursed between her and Rawdon. That must be why it affected her so. Thank goodness she'd be too busy teaching to think much about him.

Ahead now, she saw what must be the Taylor house, sheltered from at least some of the wind by a gentle knoll. A saddled, clean-limbed gray horse waited in front. The Taylors had a visitor.

As Susanna approached she heard voices, one high-pitched and querulous, the other a deep masculine tone that she recognized even before Matt Rawdon appeared at the door. "I think it would be wise," he was saying, "in view of your heart palpitations, to limit yourself to one cup of coffee a day."

"It's the one thing I enjoy, Dr. Rawdon," said the woman with pale blond hair, so aggrieved that she didn't notice Susanna. "I had hoped you could give some real help."

"I'm sorry, Mrs. Taylor, but no one can give you health, like a pill." His gaze moved to Susanna. "You have a visitor, ma'am. Good morning, Miss Alden."

"Good morning, sir." Susanna smiled at him, but his nod was barely polite. He fastened his medical bag behind the saddle, swung up, and rode down the track.

Mrs. Taylor, pouting, turned to Susanna. Three girlish faces peered around her. "You must be the new teacher." The woman had classic features, fair skin, and cool blue eyes. She wore a pretty black wrapper, with a floral design, and kid slippers. "Do come in."

Dismounting, Susanna followed her hostess inside. The interior was dim, but the floor was wood and the room was graced by a piano, a chaise longue, and several polished chairs. Sinking down on the chaise, the woman said, "Please do sit down, Miss Alden. I'm Delia Taylor, and these are my daughters, Charlotte, Berenice, and Helen. Charlotte, love, bring us some coffee."

Charlotte had her mother's eyes and hair and looked about thirteen. Berenice, perhaps eleven, had dark brown eyes and her father's long face. Helen was about six.

"If you're not feeling well, Mrs. Taylor, I can call another day," Susanna said.

"Oh, it's chronic." Delia Taylor lowered her voice. "In town, near my doctor, I might have recovered in time, but Mr. Taylor was set on coming out here. Oh, serve the teacher first," she instructed Charlotte, who offered a tray with coffee in delicate china cups. "If only my fiancé had lived," Delia Taylor went on. "But he gave his life for his country that first awful summer of the war. Mr. Taylor, who served with him, was wounded in the same battle and sent home to recover. He brought the sad news." Mrs. Taylor blotted a tear. "I visited Mr. Taylor while he was recuperating, and we married before he went back to the front."

Her tragic glance left it to Susanna to picture the martyrdom of a refined woman mismatched with a crude farmer. But what Susanna also saw was that Charlotte didn't look a bit like Will. Threatened with disgrace, Delia might well have preferred marriage with an otherwise unacceptable suitor.

They talked a bit about the children and school. Then, rising, Susanna thanked Delia for the coffee and said that Friday afternoon would be visiting time for parents.

"I doubt that I can come." The woman sighed. "Jolting along in the wagon puts me in agony. I'm sure Mr. Taylor'll come, though. He dotes on the girls."

Delia Taylor rose and walked with Susanna to the door. "My girls have been well brought up, Miss Alden. I trust that you'll watch Charlotte carefully." She lowered her voice. "Charlotte's thirteen, and those older boys . . . Well, I'm sure you understand what I'm worried about."

"While the children are at school they're my responsibility, and if you have any problems, please let me know."

Delia Taylor didn't return the offer.

Saul Prade's personality seemed to permeate his sod house, which, like the Taylors', had two rooms, with the bedroom separated by curtains. Unlike the Taylors', it had a sod roof, but the windows were glass and the inside was comfortable and attractive, with braided rag rugs, curtains, and bright quilts. On the scrubbed wood table a blue glass vase held a bouquet of grasses and wildflowers. In spite of all this, though, Susanna's gaze fixed immediately on the heavy braided whip, coiled like a rattlesnake, as it hung from a peg above a massive homemade chair draped with a buffalo robe. Small, dainty Laura Prade would be lost in that chair, and Susanna was sure that when Saul was enthroned there, his wife didn't sing as she had when Susanna rode up.

Singing and sewing. Laura's treasure was the Singer sewing machine, placed where it caught the best light from one of the two living-room windows. "I'm getting the children ready for school," she explained. Bending, she put an arm around a boy and a girl who looked a little older than Georgie Hardy and who had their mother's violet eyes and hair of pale silver. "These are the twins, Paul and Pauline. Sarah, their big sister, has got them through her *Second Reader,* and they can do easy sums. Children, go to the well house and tell Sarah to bring Miss Alden a glass of cool buttermilk."

Their mother smiled after them; then something shadowed her eyes. "Sarah's thirteen and a wonderful help to me. She's churning out in the well house because it's cooler there and she's at that age when she needs to get away sometimes from her brothers and sister. Frank's helping his father cut cane." There was a darkening again of those clear, lovely eyes. Did Laura know that side of her husband which Susanna feared and shrank from? "Frank's fourteen. He can read through the *Fourth Reader.* It's hard for him. He—" Laura broke off, as a girl as tall as she was came into the house. "Thank you, dear," said the mother as her daughter handed Susanna a cup of buttermilk. "Why don't you sit with us awhile?"

Laura introduced them, and Susanna, taking Sarah's firm hand, fairly ached at the girl's beauty. She had her father's golden hair and green eyes. She also had Laura's mouth, gentle voice, and hesitant smile.

"We proved up on our claim last year," Laura said. "Of course, when the grasshoppers ate our crops into the ground, we weren't so sure our homestead was any great prize."

Susanna nodded. "It must be terrible to see fields wither or be devoured by grasshoppers. But it must also be wonderful to harvest the grain and know it grew from a tiny seed you planted."

181

"It is for me, but I grew up on a farm. It's different for my husband. He grew up on army posts and ran away when he was fourteen because his father was . . . severe. When the war broke out, he enlisted. I met him when he came home on leave with my brother, who was in his company. We were married that spring of 1862." Laura paused. That shadow was in her eyes again. "After the war, there was an unfortunate partnership. We lost everything. Saul freighted supplies to Fort Dodge till we saved enough to"—here flashed laughter—"grow broke homesteading."

How did Laura see her husband? Was it possible that even now she didn't know him all that well? Had Susanna misjudged him? She would have been glad to think so, but remembering how he had looked when he held out the switches, she knew in her bones that the evil she had sensed in him truly existed.

Just as instinctively she felt Laura's goodness. Her gaze involuntarily going to the bullwhip, Susanna thought of the boy out in the field with his father. Was he like that father?

More disquieted than she'd been at either Hardys' or Taylors', Susanna stayed only a short while before inviting Laura to the Friday afternoon activities and taking her leave.

Laura's eyes lit. "It'll be fun to have an outing."

Cautioning Susanna to watch out for rattlers and gopher holes, Laura stood in the door with Sarah, and Susanna was waved out of sight. Following directions, she soon encountered the trail looping back to the Ace High.

She'd met the homesteader women and most of her pupils. Tomorrow, Saturday, she'd visit the ranchers—an all-day undertaking, since the Browns lived three miles from the Ace High and the Tarrants were at least eight miles southeast of them.

That left Sunday. She decided that she'd move over to the soddy then and spend the day accustoming herself to the place while it was light and she could investigate any suspicious sounds. And the curtains! Before night fell, they had to be in place.

Thinking of what might prowl around the soddy sent a flood of panic through her. But there was no retreat from her resolve to live at the school, so the sooner she gritted her teeth, laughed at her own nonsense, and got used to it, the better.

Four

$\mathcal{A}$se and Jenny escorted Susanna to the soddy early Sunday morning. Tied behind three saddles or tucked into saddlebags were the rest of Susanna's belongings and Betty's contributions— fresh-baked wheat bread, cinnamon rolls and pie, butter, cottage cheese, and a carefully wrapped jar of sourdough starter.

Jenny had accompanied Susanna to the Browns' and the Tarrants'. When thirteen-year-old Freck Brown had muttered that he was only coming to school to look after Dottie, his nine-year-old sister, Jenny had pointed out that he'd get to see Ridge Tarrant nearly every day instead of once in a coon's age.

She'd used the same argument on deer-lithe Ridge, a handsome thirteen-year-old, who had his father's hazel eyes and his mother's black hair. Jenny's importunity may have weighed a little with Ridge, but from the way he looked into his parents' hopeful eyes and sighed, Susanna knew it was their wish that moved the boy on a path he would not choose of his own will.

At the soddy Susanna's things were quickly unloaded. Then, to Jenny's mutinous groan, Ase switched the sidesaddle to the pinto pony and swung his daughter up before he walked a little way back toward the school with Susanna. He cleared his throat. "You can move back to the rose room anytime. Betty's going to miss you."

"She says she's coming to the Friday afternoon exercises," Susanna said. "Will you?"

He grinned. "Why, ma'am, I wouldn't miss it for worlds."

He mounted in an easy swing, lifted his hat, and rode off beside his daughter. Watching them out of sight would make her feel more alone and deserted, so Susanna went inside.

She put away the things she'd brought and then set to work finishing the window curtain, with paper and pencil close at hand so she could jot down ideas about her students and curriculum.

She knew which readers some of them should be able to get through. Except for the first graders, Ridge Tarrant seemed the only one who couldn't read at all. How was she going to handle that without humiliating a sensitive boy who didn't want to be in school in the first place? There'd be a wide range of knowledge of arithmetic. All the children would need lots of drill in spelling and penmanship, and except for the oldest children, who might remember something from earlier schools, history, geography, and grammar would start from scratch. She might have almost as many classes as there were pupils.

North and South, cattleman and homesteader aside, this was going to be hard, Susanna thought. Marcus Aurelius! I'm willing to do the work of a human being, but this would scare even you, I'll bet!

She shook out the curtains, wide enough to fall in pretty gathers, and hung them from a branch used as a curtain rod.

Using dry grass and weeds as a starter, Susanna built her first fire with the cow chips plainsfolk called prairie coal. They smoked more than wood, but she knew from watching Betty cook that their worst drawback was constant need of replenishment.

It was past noon when she set beans on to cook and went outside to enjoy a raisin-studded cinnamon roll. Then, going into the schoolroom, she arranged all her texts between bookends in a row across the front of the desk—the full set of McGuffey's readers, Webster's spellers, Clark's grammar, Ray's *Mental Arithmetic*, Monteith and McNally's geographies, and several histories. She made up an attendance chart, writing in the names of the students, and roughed out a plan for the next day. Toward the back of her ledger she wrote each child's name on a separate page with spaces for grades. She paused over Frank Prade's name. He was the only one of her pupils she hadn't met. What would he be like?

Susanna took long, even breaths. She gazed out at the big, medium, and small desks and benches, picturing the room full of eager, laughing children, the future of this country. She glanced at the flag hanging from a staff planted in the crack between sod bricks and hoped that in this little room North and South would gradually come to be simply American.

Light slanting through the western window was so orange-gold now that Susanna looked and saw the sun touching the horizon. She got up quickly to bring what she considered an ample supply of prairie coal into her quarters before shutting and bolting the door. She decided she needed a curtain to screen off her room from the schoolroom, and would rig up a sheet right now to serve till she could get suitable cloth.

She lit the lamp, pulled her window curtains, and got a sheet from her trunk. Then she drove the stoutest pegs she could find onto either side of the opening, strung cord across, and draped the sheet over it.

Having stoked the sulky fire, she washed her hands, mashed a cup of cooked beans, and mixed them in the kettle for thickening. Then, following Betty's directions, she mixed a sort of spoon bread with cornmeal and poured it into the frying pan to bake.

How aggravating! What she'd considered an abundance of fuel was nearly consumed. If she wanted water at the boil for her tea, she'd have to venture out to the shed. And now it was dark.

She couldn't, wouldn't give in to such absurd fears! Picking up her fuel basket, she slipped past the sheet and unbarred the door. The stars shone for their own splendor, not to light distant humans, and there was no moon. She set the basket down and, reaching gingerly into the shed, began to fill it.

"Good evening, ma'am."

Susanna jumped almost out of her skin. She hadn't heard a sound, but as she gasped, whirling, she saw a large shape blacker than the night.

After that first heart-stopped second, she'd known Matt Rawdon's voice and gone limp with relief, but now anger flared up.

"What do you mean, sir, sneaking up like that?"

"I didn't sneak," he said equably. "You were just making so much noise that you didn't hear me." He finished filling the basket, lifted it, and said, "Aren't you going to invite me in?"

"Why didn't you come in the daytime?"

"I didn't know you'd moved in till night fell and I saw light."

"You can see it from your place?"

He laughed softly. "After dark in this country, light shines a long way. I could say the same for a pretty woman."

Did he think she was pretty?

Annoyed at the way she felt herself beginning to melt at the caressing note that crept into his voice, she opened the door.

"Since you're here, you may as well come in, though for propriety's sake you surely understand that—that—"

"I understand perfectly, Miss Alden. Following the cardinal precept of schoolmarms, you're guarding your reputation."

He stepped inside and Susanna closed the door. With one long stride he reached the fireplace and set the basket down. He bullied the fire into showing a little spirit, and added some chips.

Then in the dim light she could see that he was grinning at the sheet that separated the rooms. Flushing, she snatched it down, breaking the pegs. He made her too angry to care.

"Nice curtains," he said, looking around. "Hard to see through."

"That's why they're up," she retorted, stung past caring what he thought. "And why I hung the sheet, and a good thing, too! If I hadn't, you might have—"

"Looked in your windows?"

"You sneaked up behind me!"

An exasperated breath ripped from him. "You couldn't have heard a tornado the way you were rooting around in those chips." Crossing his arms on his chest, he stared at her. "And if I had seen you feeding the fire, do you think it would so enflame my senses that I'd break down your door?"

She silently watched him till he reddened.

"I beg your pardon, Miss Alden."

"Let's cry quits. Have you eaten supper?"

"Hours ago, but if that teapot's out for a reason . . ."

Maddening as he could be, she was strangely glad that he'd be the first person in this new life to drink from her grandmother's china, to take hospitality. "I'm making tea and you're welcome. Do have the chair. I can sit on the trunk."

"So can I, but first I'll fetch in what I brought you." He raised a hand as she started to protest. "It's not personal. It's something for the school."

"But you don't have any children."

"No, but I am—was—a doctor. I doubt if it's occurred to you that you're far from help and will probably have to treat all kinds of cuts and sprains and the other things youngsters do to themselves and each other."

He was right. She hadn't thought of it at all. A whole alarming new problem yawned before her, and she appealed, "You will come, won't you, if there's an accident or something serious?"

He hesitated, then gave a shrug. "I will if I can be found, but it's close to four miles to my house, Miss Alden. Many injuries need immediate treatment." Again he hesitated, and when he spoke, she wasn't sure whether he was grudging or diffident. "It might be a good idea for me to give you some advice."

He went out and came back with a wooden case, which he set on the table and opened.

The teakettle was boiling. Susanna tipped a little water into the teapot to heat it, dumped that water into her washbasin, and then poured steaming water over tea leaves.

"Eat your supper, Miss Alden, and I'll explain what's here."

Susanna poured tea for both of them and then served herself beans and spoon bread.

"You'll have one of Betty's cinnamon rolls?" she asked.

He said heartily, "No need to ask a man who's living alone a question like that."

She brought him one. There was something delightfully intimate about sitting at the table and sipping from the teacups that had been in her family for so many, many years.

Their eyes met. Flame—sweet, wild, and intoxicating—leaped through her. It's what comes of being an old maid, she scolded herself, and wrenched her gaze from his.

Willing her hand not to tremble, she poured more tea for him and said in her most dry, deliberate tone, "Please, Dr. Rawdon. Will you show me what you've brought and how to use it?"

BANDAGES, including a triangular one that Rawdon showed Susanna how to tie for a sling to support a broken arm; a muslin-padded splint; adhesive plaster; tincture of iodine—these were her armory against the host of accidents that might befall.

"The body's its own best healer," Rawdon said. "If a wound bleeds freely, it'll cleanse itself. So don't wash a cut unless it's dirty. Then use warm water and soap. Don't bandage unless necessary to keep the wound clean or hold its edges together." When she

187

nodded her understanding, Rawdon produced from his coat two small jars filled with packets. "Administer these only if the child's in serious condition and I can't be found. The Dover's powders are ipecac and opium, for dysentery or pain. The calomel and quinine are for ague. I've written instructions on the bottles. But any child sick enough to need these should be sent home immediately."

In time he shut the case and got to his feet. "Good night, Miss Alden. Thanks for the refreshment."

"Thank you for the kit," Susanna said. "I hope I don't have to use it often, but it makes me feel better to have it." She added, "It's a comfort to know I can send for you in real need."

"Make sure it's real," he warned with a bitter laugh. "I can almost hear your mind whirring, Miss Alden, trying to salvage me for the benefit of my neighbors and my own recalcitrant soul."

"It—it seems such a waste." Of a man and his power to live, not only of a doctor, she thought.

He hesitated, then burst out, "Do you know what I really hoped to specialize in? Abdominal surgery—repairing hemorrhaging organs, suturing perforated intestines." He held up his scarred hand, the fingers ridged. "Would you like to have this clumsy hand use a scalpel near your arteries, try to manipulate forceps or probe in your delicate innards?"

She flinched at his words, not at his scars, but he misinterpreted. With a jeering, cruel laugh he raised his hand and brushed those fingers across her face.

Outside the soddy a horse suddenly whinnied and was answered. Rawdon froze.

"More company," he said, scowling. "Expecting someone?"

"No more than I was expecting you."

A loud knock came at the door. "Who is it?" Susanna called. "Saul Prade."

Grateful that Matt was there in spite of gossip, Susanna unbarred the door to this second visitor. "What brings you this way, Mr. Prade?" she asked him.

"I was over at Hardys' and thought I'd drop by to make sure you were settled in." Prade slanted a male smile at Rawdon before he looked down at Susanna. "There's nothing in your contract about callers, Miss Alden, but you know how folks talk. I'd suggest you entertain during the day."

"I brought Miss Alden a medicine chest," Matt said. "If there's any talk, Prade, I'll know where it started."

Susanna spoke decisively. "It's not my intention, sir, to have gentlemen stopping by at night, though when there's a reason like Dr. Rawdon's kind errand, I trust there'll be no colorful speculation. Let me also make it clear that trustees are no more welcome after dark than any other man of the district."

"Ma'am," said Rawdon swiftly, "far be it from me to tarnish your reputation! And so you won't, Prade, let's leave together."

"I have some questions for Miss Alden."

"I'll wait."

Prade glanced around the darkly shadowed room, his hair the only brightness, and primeval dread chilled Susanna's spine. "How do you intend to enforce discipline, Miss Alden?"

"I won't, sir. I'll send home pupils who don't want to learn."

"Want to learn!" he echoed. "It's your job to teach them."

"I'm not a jailer."

"Or much of a teacher, from your birdbrained notions. Children—especially boys—are young animals who only learn through their hides. My sincere best advice to you is to take the first student who gets out of line and thrash him till be begs."

Susanna had to swallow before she could trust her voice, and then it was frayed. "Kindly give me a chance to teach, Mr. Prade, before deciding my ways won't work."

"You'll learn. This school isn't like your young ladies' academy." Turning, Prade ducked his head to pass through the door.

"Good night, ma'am." It must have been an accident, but Rawdon's hand lightly brushed her hair. Bending his head close to hers, he whispered, "Give 'em hell!" and was gone.

As Susanna barred the door her heart contracted at the thought of how badly Prade's visit would have shaken her had Matt not been there. Matt's had shaken her, too, but in a different way.

Her private room, as she hung up the sheet again, was filled with his presence. Here he'd built up the fire, now winking embers. There he'd lounged on the trunk while she made tea.

189

There was the cup his lips had touched, and beside it the chest—his gift to her and the children.

Turning back the quilt and sheet, she examined her bed for creepers and crawlers. As she lay down, her tired body gratefully relaxed until she was too drowsy to summon up the willpower to banish the memory of Matt Rawdon's deep voice. Snuggling deeper into her pillow, she melted into sleep.

Five

Susanna slept sound till dawn glowed through the curtains, dressed quickly, built the fire, set on the coffeepot, and made her bed. When the aroma of coffee filled the soddy, she opened a can of Borden's milk. Liberally pouring it into a mug of coffee, she took the last cinnamon roll and went outside to breakfast to the call of meadowlarks and the high, faint hailing of a migrating squadron of sandhill cranes. What a beautiful sparkling day! It felt wonderful just to be alive.

She heard distant shouts and laughter. Goodness! It was almost time for school. Hurrying inside, she made a tour of the soddy, peering into dark corners. A gray spider was starting a web under the water bench. She scooped it up on a piece of paper and was depositing it outside when a spotted pony streaked past—yellow-braided rider crouched low—and swept to circle back at a trot to Dottie and Freck Brown, who were mounted on buckskin mares.

"Scout won!" yelled Jenny.

"Wouldn't have if I'd let Dusty run," growled Freck. "But you know doggone well, Jenny, that Dottie cries if I get ahead of her."

"Mama says not to race," choked Dottie. "And so does your dad, Jenny!"

Jenny stuck out her tongue and led Scout closer to the creek, having managed not to look at Susanna or greet her.

"Mornin', Miss Alden." Freck swept off his old hat in a surprisingly courtly gesture and helped his sister down. At nine she rode astride, and unlike bareheaded Jenny, she wore a pink sunbonnet that didn't go very well with her yellow calico dress.

Rummaging in his saddlebag, Freck produced two tin lunch

pails, a geography book, a tattered McGuffey primer, and a speller.

"Take care of these," he charged his sister, "while I look after the horses." Vaulting to the saddle, he led the old mare toward where Jenny was hobbling Scout.

The Hardy youngsters were walking up from the creek. They had two lunch pails between the four of them, several books, and Rosie, in her green plaid gingham, carried a small parcel.

With a sinking heart Susanna saw that though his younger brothers and Rosie wore shoes, Dave was barefoot. All the brothers wore bib overalls—clumsy, baggy garments, especially compared with the faded Levi's fastened around Freck's waist with a wide silver-buckled belt. The three Taylor sisters came from the northeast, walking with Sarah Prade, who was shepherding the twins. All the girls wore sunbonnets, and the Taylors' matched their dresses. Some distance behind trudged a strongly built boy with silvery hair. Frank Prade? And the rider on the black horse trotting from the south must be Ridge Tarrant.

A tug at Susanna's skirt brought her gaze down to Rosie, who handed her a small basket in which seven eggs nestled in dried grass. "Mama sent you these, Teacher."

"Thank you, dear," Susanna said. "They'll be delicious."

Rosie watched as Susanna went inside and put the eggs on the shelf near the kitchen side of the fireplace. Nodding satisfaction, the taffy-haired child went to admire the flag and the map.

Time to begin. Though she'd been teaching for years, it hadn't been like this. Susanna's mouth felt dry as she picked up the handbell, walked to the door, and rang it in a welcome.

TEN minutes later they were all inside, with lunch pails lined up on the water bench. The pupils were seated at desks according to size—older boys directly in front of Susanna, younger children at the low desk to the side, the bigger girls behind them. Though she was grateful there were desks at all, Susanna wished each pupil had one, preferably that fitted. Dave and Frank, close to man-size, were cramped at the desk that was high for Ethan, though it suited Ridge and Freck physically. Ridge was like a tethered hawk, one moccasined foot in the aisle as if poised to bolt.

Fifteen pairs of young eyes were fixed on Susanna. "Good morning," she said, trying to meet each child's gaze, reading in various faces trepidation, excitement, curiosity, or suspicion.

Frank Prade's expression was masklike. He had his father's brilliant green eyes, and Susanna felt as if he watched the world from behind an invisible wall, a different remoteness from Ridge's, which was more that of a confined wild creature.

"We'll start each day with a few songs," she said. While planning the schedule, she'd hit on the idea of working in history with music, stressing common roots. "I think all of us have ancestors who came here from England or Scotland and brought their songs with them. Do you know 'Weevily Wheat'?" Most of the girls' hands went up, so Susanna launched into the song.

> *"I don't want your weevily wheat*
> *And I don't want your barley,*
> *I need some flour in half an hour*
> *To bake a cake for Charlie.*
> *Charlie, he's a fine young man*
> *And Charlie, he's a dandy . . ."*

By the time they finished, the littlest children were lustily coming in on the chorus. Ridge and Frank abstained. "That song's about Bonnie Prince Charlie," Susanna said. "His Highlanders were crushed by the English at Culloden in 1746. That broke the Scottish clans, and after that more and more Scots came or were sent to Australia, Canada, and the Colonies—remember, at that time there was no United States. Charles Stuart died in exile, but we still have the song."

"Daddy's great-grandfather fought at Culloden," put in Jenny. "I reckon those redcoats were almost mean as the Yankees."

"My mama's great-grandfather fought there, too," retorted Sarah. "But I guess the British couldn't have treated folks crueler than the Confederates did."

Clamor broke out. "My father . . ." "My uncle . . ." "Grandpa . . ."

Susanna rang the bell. "Children, we're going to study the war and talk about it, but not till we've gone back to the beginnings of our country. Remember, all of our forebears helped make this country. Perhaps a good thing to do each morning would be for one of you to tell something about your ancestors."

"Do we have to?" Frank Prade grimaced.

"No," said Susanna pleasantly. "And you don't have to sing." She paused. "I do expect you to get your lessons, hold up your hand and wait till I call your name to speak. Get your drinks and take care of private needs at recess and lunch hour. Once we get your classes sorted out, I'll write assignments for the day on the blackboard so you can prepare in between recitations. I don't mind if you talk about your studies and help each other while I'm hearing another class, but please be as quiet and courteous as possible.

"Berenice, will you give the devotion tomorrow?" Susanna went on. "And on Wednesday, Jenny, would you tell us something about your ancestors, pointing out their countries on the map? Now, which of you older students will help Georgie and Helen with their primers while I hear the rest of you read?"

Sarah and Dave volunteered. Jenny tugged at Susanna's skirt. "Miss Alden," she said under her breath. "Will you let me help Ridge? I've brought all my schoolbooks, so I've got a primer."

Teaching Ridge might inspire Jenny more than anything. "All right. You may sit in Freck's place for a while."

By noon Susanna had heard all but the primer students. Dottie, Rosie, the Prade twins, and Jenny were in the *Second Reader*. At thirteen Charlotte almost cried at being placed in the *Third Reader*, but sulked less when she learned that Freck would share her recitation period. To her he was a dashing figure.

Berenice easily read in the book her older sister had yet to master and went into the *Fourth Reader* with Ethan. Dave, Sarah, and Frank were in the *Sixth Reader*. Ringing the bell, Susanna said, "Line up to wash your hands and get your lunch pails. Stay close to the school. When you've eaten, you may play till I ring the bell."

She felt as if the morning had lasted a week.

THE easiest way to supervise the playground was to play, so Susanna, after a hasty snack of bread and preserves, caught Helen and Berenice by the hands and cried, "Let's play drop the handkerchief! Georgie, you can be it to start with."

"That's for little kids," scoffed Frank, and gave the older ones a challenging smile. "Who's not scared to play crack the whip?"

Dave, Freck, Ethan, and Ridge apparently felt they had to prove themselves and formed a chain with tight-clasped hands. Jenny scrambled into the dangerous position of last in line.

Frank, at the head, ran across the field—surprisingly quick in his heavy work shoes—dragging Freck, whose cowboy boots weren't suited to a sprint. Then, when momentum was carrying them all along, Frank veered abruptly to one side, halted, and cracked the whip, by giving Freck a yank that almost jerked him off his feet. Dave, next in line, held tight, as did Ridge and Ethan, but Jenny was snapped loose and tumbled headfirst into the dry grass. Dave and Ridge hurried to help her, but she was up and laughing.

"Let's do it again!"

Dave shouted, "Teacher! Let's play blindman's buff now. Everyone can do that."

Everyone did except Frank, who disappeared in the direction of the creek. After a time Dave, too, slipped away, but Susanna didn't know how he'd spent the rest of his free time till she came in to ring the bell and found that he had refilled the water buckets and heaped the fuel basket high.

She thanked him quietly, and that afternoon while ascertaining that he knew his multiplication tables and could do long division, she said, "David, I could use someone to help clean the school and do chores. If you will, I'll give you a dollar a month." His eyes lit and Susanna followed up. "I want to pay you in advance each month, and you have to promise me something."

His brow furrowed. "What's that, ma'am?"

"That your first money goes to buy you some shoes."

He winced and went crimson, but nodded eagerly.

"After school I'll pay you for the month," Susanna said.

Dave returned to his seat with a buoyant tread.

LATE that afternoon Ase McCanless appeared as the children exploded from the soddy and pelted off in all directions. "Well, Teacher, looks like you made it through the first day."

"I guess I did." Susanna couldn't restrain a long sigh, but

smiled at the end of it. Remembering that he was, after all, the head of the board of trustees, she gave him a brief report.

Ase nodded satisfaction. "Got everything you need?" he asked. "Got enough books?"

"They're mixed up, but we can manage. When we start penmanship, we'll need pens with steel nibs, ink, and ruled paper."

He nodded. "Need anything for yourself?"

"If Betty could spare some old material—anything—for a curtain to hang between my quarters and the schoolroom, I'd really appreciate it. Otherwise, I'm quite comfortable. Thank you."

He frowned. "I still don't like your bein' out here alone."

Susanna chuckled. "Actually, I had rather a lot of company yesterday evening." She told about Rawdon's gift of the medical chest and passed lightly over Prade's visit.

"By grannies," complained Ase. "If I'd have known you were entertainin' the whole district, I'd have come, too."

"Come on, Daddy!" Jenny shouted, loping up.

"So long, then, Miss Alden," he said, touching the brim of his hat. "If you have any problems, let me know." He swung easily into the saddle and waved as he rode after his daughter.

Susanna turned to find that Dave, having washed the blackboard, was sweeping the floor. "I filled your own water bucket, Miss Alden. Anything else I can do?"

"You've thought of everything." She smiled. Going to her room, she took a dollar from the top dresser drawer. "Remember, Dave, this is for shoes," she said as she handed it to him.

"Yes, ma'am!" He glanced longingly at the books on her desk. "Miss Alden, could—may I borrow the geography?"

"That's what the books are there for."

Smiling after him as he went off, Susanna thought what a pleasure her work would be if all students were as eager to learn. On the other hand, the not so eager were certainly a challenge. To capture wayward Jenny, restless Freck, and stoic Ridge—that would take all of a teacher's skill, fortitude, humor, and ingenuity.

Frank's problem was by far the most alarming. He had an excellent intelligence, but his nature was warped. He'd taken real delight in snapping Jenny off the end of the column. It wasn't his

195

mind that needed education, but his heart. Saul Prade had possessed his son for fourteen years, and something there was very wrong.

Sitting at the desk, Susanna opened her ledger, and beside each name, where she'd already recorded the pupil's position in various subjects, she added anything she'd observed that day that might help her deal better with that child. Tomorrow each class would write the week's spelling words, and she'd start the little ones at printing. The middle and older students would have geography two days a week and history for three, with grammar every day. She also wanted to work in nature study. Oh, there was so much to teach, and not enough time to do it!

As she closed the ledger, the slanting evening sun called to her, to tensed nerves and muscles aching from the day. A walk would do her good. Shutting the door behind her, she moved toward the creek. In the fine sand at the crossing she could see the tracks of the Hardy children and a whole museum of damp hieroglyphs.

The doglike ones were doubtless coyote, and those three- and four-pronged ones must be birds, but what were those graceful loose spirals? And these like tiny hands with pointed nail tips?

Here was perfect nature study—if she could find a teacher. Since Ridge was part Cheyenne, she immediately wondered if he might not be their track expert.

Intrigued, Susanna followed some curious tracks through the sand. There was a small irregular round print and above it, slightly to the side, five tiny marks. Then, descending from the bank, were shoe tracks, and then—

Susanna stopped, freezing. A beautifully patterned yellow-green shell was caved in, the bloody pulp buzzing with flies and insects. But the turtle hadn't died quickly by an accident. The legs had been torn off, and the head, tossed under some willows, looked as if it had been yanked off the body.

Frank had been off in this direction most of the noon hour, Susanna thought as she whirled to run away from the horrible sight. Retching, she leaned against a cottonwood tree, unable to believe what her eyes had seen. Clammy face pressed against the rough bark, she wept. How could anyone be so cruel? She was still sobbing when she heard the rumble of a wagon.

Who could that be? Making her way through the willows, she reached the crossing as Matt Rawdon's buckboard rattled down the opposite bank and splashed across.

"Been having a wade?" he asked, staring at her draggled skirts. Then his gaze came to her face. "What on earth?"

Reaching over, he swung her up on the seat beside him. She was instantly welcomed by a wagging plumy tail and fervent licks from a red tongue, both belonging to a large black dog with cinnamon trim on face and feathery forelegs, a white patch on his chest like an old-time courtier's neckcloth, tulip ears, and a broad forehead. "This is Hank," Rawdon said. "I thought he'd be better protection than curtains, and lots better company. But what's the matter? Were the little devils that bad?"

She shook her head, unable to speak. When they moved up the bank and reached the soddy, he hitched the team to one of the posts supporting the well windlass. Susanna scrambled down, followed by the dog. Rawdon barred the way in front of Susanna while the wagon was at her back.

"All right, Teacher. If it's not the kids, what is it?"

It was a relief to let the turtle's plight pour out. "Why would Frank do it?" Her voice broke. "Why? There was absolutely no reason. It was just to torture something."

"So there's your why. Can you talk to his parents?"

Susanna shivered. "I'd hate for his mother to know. And Saul Prade—he'd cut me some more switches."

Rawdon watched her with a strange expression. Susanna broke the spell by moving past him and looking at the dog, who was investigating the surroundings—ruff, tail, and forelegs' fringes giving him a jaunty, gallant air that reminded her of a cavalier, all frothy lace and plumes.

"Are you really giving him to me?"

"If you want him."

"He's wonderful! But I can't take your dog."

"He hasn't been mine long. He belonged to an old lady who died a few months ago. She asked me to take care of him, but I don't need him; I'm not afraid of things that go bump in the night." Rawdon laughed. Going to the wagon, he tossed a rug off an object and lifted it out. "Mrs. Slade, Hank's mistress, didn't have any close kin, and since I sort of took care of her, she left me her belongings. I don't need this rocking chair or hooked rug."

"You don't need a dog. You don't need a chair. You don't need a rug." Susanna shook her head. "Is that a point of honor with you? Not to be human like the rest of us and need or want?"

"Take the confounded chair or I'll use it for kindling."

After a moment his mouth curved down as if he were trying not to grin, and Susanna argued no further. She got the rug and followed Rawdon as he carried the rocker into her room. Hank had come after them. When Susanna spread the thick, cushiony rug by the bed, the dog lay down, nose between his paws, and thumped his tail.

"He approves of the arrangement," Rawdon said.

Because he thinks you're staying, too, Susanna thought.

Their eyes met. Her heart caught, stopped.

"Let's go outside." His voice was rough, husky. "I want to hear how the first day went, but God knows we'd better not be inside if one of your trustees comes snooping around."

Hank padded after them. Absently stroking the dog, Rawdon stared at where the sun was lost in streamers of red, gold, and purple clouds that blazed across the whole western horizon, painting the grass a ruddy bronze. "Tell me. No battles between North and South? How did you fare with the redoubtable Jenny?"

She told him about how gamely Jenny'd been the tail of the whip. Then, since he seemed truly interested, she told him about the rest of the day's perplexities and small triumphs.

She gave him a challenging smile. "I may not need my fare back to Ohio."

"Too soon to guess about that," he warned. The sun disappeared, colors flaming in a last wild glory before they began to ebb. "I've got to get along and do my chores. You don't have to worry much about feeding Hank. When he's hungry, he'll hunt up a rabbit. Good night, Miss Alden."

Unhitching the reins, he climbed up. Hank, with a regretful glance at Susanna, prepared to jump into the wagon.

"No, boy," Rawdon said. Reaching down, he patted the black

head. "You're to stay with the lady. Stay." He said the last word emphatically and started the team.

As the wagon swung around, the dog watched, head atilt, ears up, tail drooped. Susanna bent to hug him. "If you miss him too much, I'll send you back to him. But I'm so glad to have you, Hank—that's an awful name. Would you mind if I called you Cavalier? Cav, for short?"

Suddenly cold in the gathering twilight, Susanna stroked her new companion, scratched him behind the ears, and started for the soddy. "Come, boy!" she invited. "Come, Cavalier!"

He followed, head and tail lowered dejectedly, and at once took up his place on the rug, pointing his nose between his cinnamon paws. His eyes, mournful now, watched Susanna as she built the fire and put the teakettle and her supper on to heat. Even if Cav was self-supporting, she wanted to feed him something. "How about some spoon bread and milk, Cav?"

That brought a tail thump. She filled one of her two serving bowls and set it down, calling him. He wolfed it and waited.

"That's all for now, boy." Recognizing finality in her voice, he resumed his usual pose, but later, after Susanna had eaten and done the dishes and pulled the rocker near the lamp so she could prepare next day's lessons, he forsook the rug and came to lie at her feet, crossing his paws and resting his muzzle on them.

What a difference his presence made! As she worked Susanna talked to him, and he gave her a consoling look or let his tail thud in agreement. When she went to bed, he lay on the rug.

It was a blessed mercy that he was there. It helped, too, knowing that Matt Rawdon, for all his cynicism, had wanted her to feel safer and not be alone.

Six

WHEN school took up, Cav settled himself as guardian of the door, near enough the water buckets for children to give him a quick pat as they went for drinks. That morning they sang songs of the gold rush—"Sweet Betsy from Pike" and "Oh, Susanna!"— which gave an opening to talk about how the nation had spread westward, not only in quest of riches as in 1849, but just as their parents had, in a steadier, quieter search for homes.

After Berenice gave the devotion, the Twenty-third Psalm, Susanna heard the large *Second Reader* class. The twins, Dottie, and Rosie had obviously studied, and read their paragraphs without a bobble, but Jenny floundered through, snagging on a number of words and not knowing how to sound them out.

The morning flew. Susanna flashed multiplication cards, showed little hands how to shape the lines and circles that comprised printed letters, heard reading classes, gave out spelling words, and began Ethan and Berenice in division. But Frank's cold-eyed, watchful presence tormented Susanna. Should she confront him? She decided against that, since she had no hope of shaming him or making him sorry.

At noon Susanna rang the bell for attention. "Most of you prepared your lessons and have done very well this morning," she said. "Remember, your parents are invited Friday afternoon, and though they won't expect a lot this first week, wouldn't it be fun to surprise them?"

Jenny scowled, Frank looked superior, and Ridge looked long-suffering, but the rest of the students cheered and clapped.

As they rose to file to the washbasin before lunch, Susanna said, "I'm responsible for you during school hours. No one is to leave the school ground. That means to stay in plain sight." Frank stared at her, a taunting glint in his eyes.

At four, as she saw the children off and Dave went about his tasks, Frank loitered behind. When Susanna was alone, he strode back to her.

"Teacher." His tone, though soft, was just on the edge of impudence. "May I ask you something?"

"Of course, Frank."

"Did you take a walk along the creek yesterday?"

"I did. And I think you know what I found."

He smiled and shrugged. "Thought you must have, the way you told us to stay where you could watch us."

Too horrified to refrain, she caught his shoulders and barely kept herself from giving him a shake. "Why did you do it?"

Her intensity took him aback. "It was just a turtle."

"It was alive! And you killed it, tortured it, for no reason! How could you do it, Frank?"

He pulled free of her. "You want to see something messy, Teacher, come over next month when we butcher a hog." As she stared at him, wordless, he turned away. "Good-bye, Teacher."

Susanna stood as if rooted. She told herself she must not be afraid of one of her pupils. But she was. Of him, and for him.

THAT Friday afternoon Susanna was playing fox and geese with the children when the first wagon appeared. "Hurry, children!" she called. "Tidy up, and let's be ready for our visitors."

The Taylors rolled up first, in a buckboard, Delia's side cushioned with pillows. When Will helped his wife down, she put her hand to her back and by way of greeting said accusingly to Susanna, "That jarring and jolting will give my back miseries for days, but the girls begged so hard that I had to come."

"I'll have Dave bring my rocker for you," Susanna said, then hurried to embrace Betty, entering ahead of Ase. Next came the

Prades—Laura in a violet dress that matched her shining eyes, Saul filling the door, his eyes fixing on Susanna with the vigilance of an eagle. Margaret Hardy, in a faded green dress, introduced the man with her as their neighbor, Jem Howe.

"Cash isn't feeling good," she said. "Jem was interested, and Dave thought it'd be all right for him to come."

"Everyone's welcome." Susanna at once liked this older man with gray eyes. The Browns arrived just then, Hettie patting her bonnet-mussed brownish red hair into place, and Kermit speaking courteously to Susanna. Luke Tarrant limped in with Millie, whose proud head wore no bonnet. Her lustrous black hair was drawn back in a coiled loop, secured by silver ornaments.

Susanna introduced the Cheyenne woman to the homesteaders' wives. Millie bowed and spoke with civility, and Luke ushered his wife along to sit by Ase, who rose to greet her. Though the women were chatting, the cattlemen and farmers conversed with their own kind—ranchers about cattle, homesteaders about crops.

Going to stand by her desk, Susanna smiled around at the visitors, who hastily took seats if they hadn't already. They were divided—ranchfolk on the recitation bench, homesteaders on water bench, rocker, and teacher's chair.

"Welcome to our school, and thank you for coming. These Friday afternoons are a review of some of the week's work, along with a little fun. To begin with, we'll have the week's devotions and the songs we've sung. If you know the words, please join in."

Freck began the singing by strumming his guitar as he sang a song that had plenty of Texas geography in it, for it named most of the rivers. That warmed everyone up for the songs they all knew, and for twenty minutes the soddy was filled with voices that didn't blend too well, but to Susanna's ears sounded sweeter than any choir she'd ever heard. If the Mason-Dixon School patrons could sing together, it was a start.

Next, the children who'd talked about family origins that week went to the map in turn to point to the countries their forebears had hailed from. All had at least one ancestor from Scotland, Ireland, England, or Wales, but Sarah and the twins pointed also to France, while the Taylors added Holland and Denmark. Jenny touched Sweden, as well as Orkney and Scotland, and Freck and Dottie had a Hessian soldier in their ancestry.

Spelling followed, the students standing in a line while Susanna gave each one a word till every pupil had spelled five. The primer class—dark little Helen Taylor, ebullient Georgie, and Ridge—had learned the alphabet, and were spelling easy words like cat and dog. Looking ahead to this performance, Susanna had asked Ridge if he wouldn't like to learn some harder words.

"Like eagle?" he had asked, sudden interest lighting those hazel eyes, so startling in his brown face. "Hawk? Warrior?"

"You tell me words you want to learn. I'll print them, and I'm sure Dave will help you practice." So now Ridge stood between Ethan and Frank and, to his parents' evident astonishment and delight, spelled words suitable to his age.

Charlotte, flighty and excited, missed words she'd spelled that morning. Freck and Jenny also did poorly—Freck because he had trouble, as he put it, bending his mind to books, and Jenny because she simply wouldn't study. But Berenice Taylor's plain little face glowed, and so did Will's, as the girl spelled the hardest fourth-grade words.

At five to four, Susanna told the last spellers to take their seats. "Why don't we close with a song?" she asked the assembly.

"Let's sing a Kansas song," Will Taylor said, grinning. "Bet most everyone except the teacher knows 'Kansas Land.'"

Freck strummed, and Will, in a rich tenor, led a song that was indeed new to Susanna but familiar to the others.

> *"Oh Kansas land, sweet Kansas land,*
> *As on your burning sands I stand,*
> *I look away across the plains*
> *And wonder why it never rains,*
> *We do not live, but only stay,*
> *We are too poor to move away!"*

"Next time," said Ase good-naturedly, "we're going to sing 'Git Along, Little Dogies' and 'Chisholm Trail.'" He rose. "Thanks for havin' us, Miss Alden." He glanced around at the other visitors. "Think we hired the right lady?"

Saul Prade did not join in the applause that followed, nor had he sung with the others. Delia Taylor on her way out gave Susanna an aggrieved look. "Some children, like my Charlotte, are high-strung and sensitive, Miss Alden. I don't think they should be forced to perform in front of a lot of strangers."

Will, coming in from hitching up the wagon, took his wife's arm and gently but firmly steered her toward their wagon.

Margaret Hardy then clasped Susanna's hand, amber eyes sparkling. "I'm just so proud of my young ones," she said.

"It was lovely, dear!" cried Betty, hugging her. "It did my heart good to see all those children showing what they'd learned." She chuckled at the sight of Jenny tucking books into her saddlebag. "Our young lady didn't like havin' her daddy see that everybody in her class can outspell her."

"No," said Ase, between chagrin and hope. "I watched her when Ridge spelled all those words. My guess is she'll figger if he can study, she can, too. But I'm mighty glad we hired you."

As Ase's buckboard creaked off and Betty kept turning to wave, Susanna waved back, feeling that on the whole the afternoon had been a success. "At least," she said, bending to hug Cavalier, "no one got into a fight or an argument, and they sang together."

All except for Saul Prade.

On Monday morning Ridge said he would like to tell about his forebears. Standing by the map and addressing the class, the darkly handsome youth began, "Long ago many Cheyenne wandered the plains east of the Rocky Mountains. Sometimes they fought Comanche and Kiowa. My mother's uncle, Mouse's Road, was one of a party that set out to steal horses from the Comanche and Kiowa, who were camped on the South Platte. The Cheyenne passed through the camp by night, took fifty or sixty of the best horses, and quietly drove them away. Next day the Kiowa and Comanche caught up with them. The Cheyenne fought bravely, but at last all were killed except my mother's uncle. His bow was broken and he was on foot, but he killed many chiefs with only his knife. Two Kiowa with guns got off their horses and waited. When he was close enough, they fired. He fell with a ball in his

hip, and all the others swarmed in. Someone cut off his head."
Ridge's voice dropped. "When they did that, Mouse's Road sat
upright, blood spurting from his neck. The enemy jumped on
their horses and raced to camp, afraid he would follow them.
They and their women fled, leaving their lodges standing."

"That's a lie!" Frank Prade sneered. "Except for your uncle
being a horse thief."

Ridge sucked in his breath and started for Frank, who jumped
up and raised his fists. Dave got between the two. Susanna caught
Frank's arm. "Frank, we don't talk like that here. Apologize."

"I won't," hissed Frank, wrenching free of her. "It's bad
enough going to school with a gut-eater, but . . ."

Rising, Sarah stood with Dave between the two furious boys.
"Stop it, Frank!" she cried. "Stop it right now."

"Apologize, Frank, or go home," Susanna said. Wondering
what she could do if he refused to leave, for he was stronger than
she, Susanna was relieved when he turned, face set in a snarl, and
started for the door. Sarah caught Susanna's hand.

"Oh, Miss Alden, please don't make him go home!"

Green eyes, the same color as the girl's father's and brother's,
watched Susanna with distress. Susanna winced, but she couldn't
let Frank get away with such behavior.

"Frank may stay if he apologizes, Sarah."

Sarah ran after her brother. Her voice could be heard pleading.
After a while she came back, and put her head down on her desk
and wept silently, shoulders heaving. Susanna touched the bright
hair. "I'm sorry, dear."

Susanna was haunted all that day by Frank's scared but defiant
face. Laura Prade might not know how severely her husband
punished their son, but Sarah evidently did.

Susanna passed a restless night and rose early, unable to sleep.
She was eating breakfast the next morning when she heard the
grate of the door pushing open. She had unbarred it to let Cav out
and, since dawn was breaking, hadn't barred it again. She sprang
to her feet as Saul Prade ducked his raw-gold head to enter,
shoving Frank in front of him. He unbuckled a broad leather belt
and thrust it toward Susanna. "You've got a choice, woman. Lay

on good and hard, till the blood runs if need be, or I'll whip him for you right here."

"Get out of here, Mr. Prade!"

Shrugging, he yanked Frank's shirt open and peeled it from his shoulders. Susanna gasped. Faded weals and some still healing scarred the boy's back and shoulders. Prade raised the belt.

She threw herself in front of Prade, blocking him, her arms around Frank. A convulsion ran through Frank's body. "I'll apologize," he choked. Turning, he set her aside and faced his father. "I'll mind the teacher, Dad."

Saul's eyes were green fire. "And beg that dirty Indian's pardon?" He struck his son so hard the boy staggered. "That's for getting yourself in a spot where you have to eat dirt!"

He stalked out with a crack of the belt. Dazed, Susanna turned to meet a gaze that was at once fierce and anguished.

"Why didn't you let him whip me?" Frank cried.

"Frank, you wish I'd let him beat you—the way he has before?" The horror of what she'd seen overwhelmed her, and she blurted, "How can your mother let him do that?"

His face closed. "Mother doesn't know."

"Doesn't know?"

"Dad whips me in the barn or in the field. Bandages me up if there's blood." He shrugged. "She mustn't ever know. If she did . . . Well, Teacher, what could she do?"

Dave's whistle floated up from the creek. Frank gulped. "About apologizing. Can I say it just to Ridge?"

Susanna resisted the impulse to let him off easy. "Where did you insult him?"

Frank sighed. "All right. Let me do it first thing and get it over with." He went out, and Susanna sat down to finish her cold coffee. Suddenly overcome, she buried her face in her hands and sobbed as if her heart must break. Should she tell Laura? How could she not? Prade was taunting her, compelling her to know his cruelty, gambling that she wouldn't tell his wife.

And he was right. Doing that would break faith with Frank. He was back in school and had chosen to obey her. She must take comfort and hope in that. Susanna decided to hold her peace.

Seven

Rain doesn't pitter, patter, pound, or drum on a sod roof. It beats. What doesn't sluice off soaks in, seeks crevices, and begins to drip. "Fortunately, it doesn't exactly rain inside," Susanna wrote Aunt Mollie and Uncle Frank, casting a rueful glance around the room where muddy trickles, after three days of wind and bright sunshine, continued to splash in every vessel she could use. "But I can see why women who live in soddies say what they do—that it rains one day outside and four more inside."

The rains abated by the end of October, and the first week of November brought a frost that browned the gold of the cottonwoods, bleached side oats dropseed white, and painted the various bluestems rich tones of red and purple. Thanksgiving was

207

approaching, and on Saturday, Susanna took her bowl of corn bread crumbled into beans outside to eat, enjoying the sun while she pondered whether to celebrate the holiday with a program for the community. President Lincoln had proclaimed it a national holiday in 1863, which made many southerners feel it was a Yankee occasion, but its official origin went back to the days of the New England Puritans. Tracing the day's history could also sketch in the country's. She'd bring it up to the trustees, who were meeting at the school tomorrow afternoon.

Cav gave a soft bark, ears pricked toward the crossing, and Susanna looked that way to see riders coming up the bank. Two jolted up and down on workhorses. A third was mounted on a small white mule. And the fourth was Matt Rawdon on his gray gelding, Saladin. Cav, with a joyful bark, bolted for his former master.

Even before Matt introduced the three strangers, she was sure they were foreigners. They wore cloth caps, long vests buttoned to the throat over full-sleeved shirts, and as they dismounted, Susanna saw that their trousers had ample gathers. All wore a kind of sturdy sandal. Holding their caps in their hands, they gazed hopefully at Susanna.

Matt said, "My new neighbors have school-age children, so they've come to talk to you. This is Frederick Krause." A solid man in his forties, with a dark brown beard and hair, inclined his head. "Peter Krause is his brother." At his name the older man with graying hair and keen gray eyes smiled and nodded. Matt turned last to the big yellow-haired, blue-eyed stranger. "Jacob Reighard is betrothed to Frederick's eldest daughter. He worked on a Pennsylvania farm for a year, so he speaks a lot of English."

"Good day, miss," said Jacob bashfully. "Is it possible that to you the children come to learn? Only German-speaking are they, though I have taught them a few words."

"Since they live in the district, they're welcome," Susanna said, though she wasn't sure what the trustees would say and expected trouble, at least from Prade. "You are from Germany?"

"From Holland a long time ago. Then a hundred years ago from Prussia." Jacob smiled. "Catherine the Great—German she was—knew Mennonites for good farmers, and invited them to the

Russian steppes and the Crimea." He went on to explain that Catherine had offered the settlers the right to practice their religion and freedom from military conscription, knowing their religion prohibited bearing arms.

In 1871, however, the czar determined to make them Russians. It was proclaimed that in ten years those special privileges would be revoked. Some Mennonites chose to stay, said Jacob. But most, fearing that they would be forced into military service, traveled to the United States to look for land. He and the Krauses were the only emigrants from their village.

"They bought two homesteads north of me," Matt said. "Moved in three weeks ago, and they've already plowed and planted a sort of hard red winter wheat they brought from Russia. It can usually be harvested before drought blasts it."

"Welcome to Kansas," Susanna said. "The children may start school Monday. It would be good if you could make a desk and bench for them. If they ride, you'll need to put hay in the barn."

Jacob explained, "Freddie and Magdalena, the youngest, will ride the little mule. Cobie and Valentine, walk they will."

Susanna invited them to look around the schoolroom. Then, thanking her, the Mennonites departed. Matt stayed behind, playing with Cav.

"How could you give him away?" Susanna asked as he knelt to ruffle the dog's ears and hold his muzzle between his hands.

Matt rose. "You need him. I don't."

The arrogant words roweled Susanna. "Are you proud of that?" she demanded. "Are you glad you can get along without anyone or anything to love or love you?" Bowing her head, she whispered, "I'm afraid of the dark and snakes and scorpions and a lot of things, Matt Rawdon, but that's better than being afraid of life."

He gave a harsh, startled laugh. "You think I am?"

"Aren't you? Hiding away out here by yourself, refusing to use your gift of healing because you can't do fancy surgery?" She looked up at him and cried in a voice that trembled, "I'd rather be afraid of all the things I am than be afraid to live!"

The blaze of his eyes flashed through her. Transfixed, she could do nothing as he caught her in his arms, swept her against him, and took her mouth with a bruising kiss till his lips softened and moved sweetly on hers. His hand found the nape of her neck and fitted her even more closely to him. When at last he drew away, Susanna would have staggered if he hadn't steadied her.

"Shall we go to your bed, Miss Alden? Or would you prefer an elemental tumble in the grass?"

Hurt and humiliated, Susanna clenched her hands. "I don't think I've done anything to provoke such an insult."

"What's insulting about being considered a healthy woman with healthy needs?" he said with a shrug. "Come now, Miss Alden. How can you say you're not afraid to live when you shy away from what has to be one of the most pleasurable, well-nigh necessary, parts of living?"

"I can't believe a man with any pretensions to decency would make such an offer," she said when she could control herself. "I suppose I should slap you or swoon away or cry." Her cheeks flamed at the enormity of it, not only that he would speak so to a woman with no male protectors, but that she was actually tempted, wished it were possible.

"Forgive me that I don't know your southern idea of how a woman should answer such an insult," Susanna went on. "I'll concede that I might yield to love—I'm human and I do have feelings. But my comfort is my work and Cav and books—just being alive. And I am alive, Matt Rawdon, whatever you may think!"

The twist of his lips faded, and he was suddenly haggard. For a moment pain was almost palpable between them. He inclined his head. When he raised his eyes to hers, he was masked again. "All true, Miss Alden, and commendable. As a male, though, I deplore the waste of a lovely woman." With a last caress for Cavalier he started for his horse, then turned with a wicked chuckle. "Let me congratulate you on discarding your corset, even if the stays are still laced tight around your formidable Yankee rectitude."

He was in the saddle and away without a backward glance.

No MATTER how sternly she applied herself to grading compositions, Susanna's treacherous body kept melting as it had in Matt's arms. Richard's boyish kisses had done nothing to ready her for a man's embrace, not that anyone at all could have prepared her for the—the ravishing of Matt Rawdon's kiss.

But now she wondered. What if he hadn't meant the kiss except as humiliating punishment? She writhed inwardly at that thought, yet she was glad that at least once—however slightingly he intended it—the man she now realized she loved had held her, set his mouth to hers. A taste of honey to mock Susanna, who would ache for him. Trying as tomorrow's board meeting threatened to be, she was glad she wouldn't have to get through Sunday by herself.

ASE and Saul Prade arrived early. Deciding to get it over with, Susanna told them about the Mennonite children.

"You said they could come?" Prade demanded. "I don't want my kids going to school with a pack of dirty little Dutchies! I'll go over there after this meeting and tell them you had no business agreeing to let them come."

"Hold on, Prade." Ase, brow furrowed, spoke for the first time. "That's for the whole board to decide."

Will Taylor's Missouri twang came from outside, and Kermit Brown's lazy Texas drawl. Susanna turned to greet the trustees, who, having all arrived, now entered the school. Northerners Will Taylor and Saul Prade slid into the big boys' desk; southerners Ase, Kermit Brown and Luke Tarrant occupied the recitation bench. Susanna sat near the blackboard, hands folded in her lap, knees pressed together to keep from fidgeting.

Ase called the meeting to order. Susanna asked what they thought about holding a Thanksgiving program, presenting it tactfully as a holiday going back to Colonial times before Washington, a Virginian, made it a national celebration.

"Well, if Washington thought it was all right, I guess it is," said Kermit grudgingly.

Ase shrugged. "Reckon it won't hurt."

Luke Tarrant nodded as did Will Taylor, but Saul Prade stood up. "Before we talk about what happens the last Thursday of the month, we need to talk about tomorrow and something that's been going on that I'm dead against. Taylor, did you know you've got a bunch of dirty Dutchies east of you?"

Will's dark eyes widened. "Can't say's I did know. They Mennonites like those around Newton?"

"Yes," said Prade. "And these should've stayed with the rest of their kind. We can't keep them from buying land, but we sure don't have to let them come to our school."

"We're pretty mixed up as it is," said Kermit. "From what I hear, those folks are honest and don't cause any trouble."

Prade looked at Will. "How'd you like one of your girls to marry one of them?"

"Well . . ." began the lanky Missourian.

Luke Tarrant's hazel stare fixed on Prade. "They're in the district. Can't see why we even have to talk about it."

"*You* wouldn't," Prade said angrily.

"You're slurrin' my wife." Tarrant was on his feet in one continuous motion. "Looks like you haven't got a gun. Would you know how to use one if Ase loans you his?"

Ase got to his feet. "Men, we agreed to have a school. We don't have to like each other, but we got to get along. And Prade, that means you don't bemean Luke's wife and son—or the Mennonite folks, either, on account of everyone but you says to let 'em come. You give your word you won't make any more of this kind of trouble, or we'll throw you off the board right now."

Slowly glancing around, Prade saw agreement on every face. After a tense silence he sat down. "Guess I don't have much choice." He sat like stone through the rest of the meeting.

BECAUSE of the Mennonites' origin, Susanna had expected flaxen-haired little strangers to appear on Monday. Instead, the only child with yellow hair was six-year-old Magdalena; her red-haired cousin, seven-year-old Frederick, had already become Freddie to the younger Hardys, with whom they had joined forces. Similarly, Magdalena's twelve-year-old brother, Valentine, slim and dark-haired, had received the name of Val. Cobie, whose black hair peeked from beneath the triangular kerchief tied snugly under her chin, was ten years old. She and Freddie were the youngest of Peter Krause's brood.

Val swept off his brown cap. "Good morning, our teacher."

"Good morning." Susanna smiled. As the day passed she found they understood her better than she could them. With their bits of English and what they puzzled out of her schoolgirl German and many gestures, they were able to sound out words and copy their spelling.

Till the Krauses delivered a new desk and bench, the new pupils had to crowd in with the older. Fortunately, Magdalena and Freddie had sufficient room with the four younger children.

Cobie did have to squeeze, for there were already six big girls, but Rosie and Sarah made room for her between them. Ridge got up to motion Val to a place between him and Freck. Dave worked with the younger boy that day, but it was aloof, reserved Ridge who took Val in hand. Here was someone more different than he, someone he could teach and protect.

Frank simply ignored the newcomers. Increasingly withdrawn, he worried Susanna more than he had before, but her attempts to bring him into discussions failed. Susanna could only hope that time would bring him out of his apathy, and she prayed that his father wasn't beating him.

The overcrowding lasted only until Wednesday morning, when Jacob Reighard drove up behind the Krauses' white mule, Flora, with a desk and a bench. Susanna asked Jacob to tell the elder Krauses about the Thanksgiving program.

"They will come. To meet the teacher they are eager." Jacob's tanned brow furrowed. "Except for Grandfather Anselm. The father of Peter and Frederick, he fears the children will forget their religion. To ourselves he thinks we should live."

Much time went into the Thanksgiving program. The children decided to tell a little about the countries their people had come from. They would trace the holiday from Colonial times and conclude with songs. Arriving early for that Friday's exercises, the women united in asking Susanna if they couldn't all bring food and begin the celebration with a shared meal.

"Do you suppose Jem Howe could come?" inquired Margaret.

"Several bachelors live north of us," put in Laura Prade.

"Let's bring plenty of food and invite the whole dang shootin' match," urged Hettie Brown, her warm eyes sparkling.

This was the first fragile shoot of community spirit extending beyond the school. With trepidation and delight Susanna slipped out the door and rang the bell to call the children in.

IT SNOWED the week before Thanksgiving. The snow soon melted and disappeared, so that the school ground wasn't muddy on the holiday, when shortly before noon, horses and wagons brought everyone Susanna knew in that region and a number of people that she didn't. Matt Rawdon was introducing the Krauses to their neighbors as Susanna hastened to welcome them, shaking their hands as she carefully avoided Rawdon's eyes. Cav, joyful at seeing his master, frisked like a puppy.

Anna, Frederick Krause's wife, and her daughter Catherine, Jacob's betrothed, both had clear blue eyes fringed with long dark lashes. Beneath a plain, close-fitting black cap Anna's hair was light brown. Catherine wore a black kerchief that revealed the bright hair shared with Magdalena, her little sister. Peter's buxom wife, Freda, had red cheeks, graying black hair, and the almond-shaped green eyes she'd bequeathed to Cobie.

There were other strangers to Susanna, and with a smile of temporary farewell to the Krauses she hastened to meet the group clustered around Margaret Hardy. Could the lanky man with tobacco-colored eyes be—at last—Cash Hardy?

He bobbed his head as Margaret happily presented him. "Sure appreciate havin' you here, ma'am. Sorry this durned back keeps me from pullin' my weight for the school district, but I reckon Dave does his best to make up for it."

"Indeed he does," Susanna said.

Turning to welcome two strange men who were talking with Will Taylor, Susanna spotted Matt Rawdon. He was watching her. As their gazes met, his mouth curved down in an ironic smile. Blood rushed to her face as she remembered his indecent proposal. How dare he behave as if nothing had happened? She turned her back on him and thought she heard soft, mocking laughter as Will Taylor introduced her to two bachelors with claims north of the Prades'.

Ase and Kermit had started laying planks across the wagon

beds, and the other men joined in this chore while women hurried to arrange the food. No boards were spread across the Tarrant buckboard, for two huge iron kettles sat at the rear—one holding stewed antelope, the other beef in a thick gravy.

Ase and the Browns set out great pans of roast beef, though the rest of the food ran to corn prepared in every way desperation and ingenuity could devise. There were pots of beans, bowls of turnips and cabbage, and hoarded white flour had gone to make crusts for an array of pies—rhubarb, sandhill plum, elderberry, and mince. When Anna, Freda, and Catherine Krause fetched their crocks and platters, they flushed with pleasure at the unmistakable enthusiasm manifested at the sight of balls and rounds of cheese, several kinds of sausages, and large seed-sprinkled loaves of bread. Everything was ready, but Susanna had forgotten to ask someone to say the blessing.

As head of the school board, Ase was the logical person. Susanna rang the bell, and glanced around the gathering as talk faded away and all faces turned to her. These were her children, her people. This was home, as Ohio could never be, for she had chosen this place and it was here she carried out her work as a human being, the teaching that was according to her nature.

"Mr. McCanless, will you please say the blessing?"

Ase jumped as if he'd been shot. He swept off his hat, ducked his head, and cleared his throat. "God bless the grass. Amen."

That was all. Will Taylor said, "No offense, Ase. That may be enough of a prayer for a cattleman, but I reckon us homesteaders need a little more."

Will thanked God for everything bad that hadn't happened, as well as the good things that had, and wound up with, "Most of all, on this day, Lord, we thank You for our school and this good teacher You sent us."

There was a chorus of amens.

Everyone had utensils, plates, and cups, mostly of tin. Susanna urged the Krauses into line. No one else needed coaxing. Soon women were perched on the desks and benches that had been carried out. The children sat on the grass, and men hunkered on their heels or stood.

Susanna moved from group to group, chatting and complimenting the women on whatever it was each had brought. When she stopped with the Krause women, who sat with Margaret Hardy, Susanna praised the nutty flavor of the bread.

"From red turkey wheat our flour is made," said Jacob. "If God grants to us a good harvest, gladly will we give seed wheat to our neighbors."

"It'll be a cold day in July before I need some foreigner telling me how to farm," Saul Prade remarked, keeping his back turned to Jacob.

The young man blushed. To Susanna's relief Matt Rawdon said carelessly, "I'm sure going to ask them how, Prade. This red turkey sounds like it's worth a try."

When, amazingly, most of the food had disappeared, Susanna rang the bell. Seats and desks were carried in and occupied by the women and younger children. Everyone else stood.

The history of Thanksgiving was traced from 1621 in Massachusetts to Abraham Lincoln's setting it on the last Thursday in November. Only northerners clapped at the Lincoln part, but at least there were no catcalls. Each group of children was applauded as they told about their ancestors' countries and what brought them over the ocean. The momentary silence following Ridge's account of the Cheyenne migration turned into clapping led by Ase.

The program finished with singing, and after a few old favorites shared by North and South, everyone moved outside. While the children played their own games their elders formed a double circle for "Jolly Is the Miller Boy." Though Susanna didn't know these play-party numbers, she was about to let herself be pulled into the circle when she saw the Krauses moving toward their wagons. She called their names, and as they turned, Jacob, blushing, said, "Dancing is against our religion."

"I'm sorry."

He smiled. "Do not be. Expect others to be like us we do not."

Peter spoke, and the others nodded. Then Jacob said, "A wonderful day this is for all of us. To hear the children speak well the English and tell of our journey was very good. I wish there were a school for us, too, the grown ones."

Susanna's thoughts were racing. "If you wish and can spare the time, I would be happy to come to your homes when the weather's good and hold a class either Saturday mornings or afternoons." It was four miles each way, but she enjoyed walking.

"You would?" Jacob grinned. "Too good you are!" Jacob spoke to the Krauses and turned back to Susanna.

"If willing you are, we invite you to have dinner on any Saturday, and then we will have school. If you send word by the children on Friday, one of us will call for you with a wagon."

"Supposing I walk over? That way, if the weather or something changes, you won't have a trip for nothing. Then I'll be very glad to be driven home. I'll try to come this Saturday."

She waved them off and turned to find Saul Prade watching her. "We're not paying you to teach Dutchies, Miss Alden."

"Indeed you're not. What I do on Saturday is my own affair."

His lips thinned. "You can't deny that the time you spend on those squarehead brats is stolen from ours."

Susanna trembled with indignation. "The other trustees agree the Krause children belong."

He laughed fleetingly. "They'd agree with anything you said. I'll be glad when they see what comes of this softheaded slush you're teaching. Let in an Indian and look what happens!"

"To Millie and Ridge we're the foreigners," Susanna retorted.

"Well, you be damned sure that breed doesn't make up to my daughter. If he ever does, I know how to fix him so he won't be a problem to any white woman—any woman, for that matter."

Susanna stared at him. "What's made you like this?" she whispered.

"My father taught me early the truth about people and the world. What he didn't show me, the war did. You're a fool, woman, and I'll see the day when these other fools want to get rid of you as much as I do."

Ase McCanless was striding toward them, and Prade lounged off. "What's he saying to you?" Ase demanded.

"Nothing important."

"If he causes any trouble, you let me know. Promise?"

Almost overwhelmingly tempted to confide in Ase, tell him

217

about Prade's savage treatment of his son, Susanna forced back the poisonous facts it would have been a relief to share.

"I'll tell you if Mr. Prade makes problems at school," she said, and then explained her arrangement with the Krauses.

Ase whistled. "Mighty nice of you, ma'am. But I came over to tell you Betty won't hear of you stayin' in this dark old soddy by yourself for the Christmas holidays, and neither will I."

"I'll be delighted to stay at the Ace High," Susanna said demurely. "It would be lonely to pass Christmas by myself."

Ase's eyes held hers. "So you're human like the rest of us," he said. "Sometimes I've wondered." Grinning boyishly, he took her arm. "Well, while your Yankee starch is a mite wilted let's get in on some of this Presbyterian waltzin'! Sure looks like a Virginia reel to me, but if it makes everybody happy to call it a singin' game, that's fine with me!"

It was fine with Susanna, too. This was the happiest, proudest day of her whole life.

Eight

*T*HE first Saturday in December dawned bright and chill. Putting on her warmest dress, the gray wool grenadine, over both her red flannel petticoats and two cambric ones, Susanna had breakfast standing near the fireplace for warmth. She wrapped a wool scarf around her head, tossing the ends over her shoulders.

The Krause children had taken home a speller, a primer, and an American history book that Jacob was reading to them, so Susanna needed to carry no books. Finally, pulling on her mantle and mittens, Susanna unbarred the door, laughing at Cav's joy that she'd be walking with him. The track ran past Hardys' and forked at their east boundary, the left road traveling past Matt Rawdon's and on to the Krauses. She would almost certainly see Rawdon, and no matter how she chided herself, that filled her with anticipation.

To bridge the creek, shortly after school started, Dave had felled a dead cottonwood across the water. Susanna, skirt and petticoats swaying, found it difficult enough. Cav had dashed ahead, glancing back encouragingly.

"It's fine for you," she grumbled, catching a breath of relief as she stepped onto the bank. "You've got four feet."

As several sod barns and a sod house with a shingled roof came in sight Susanna's heart beat faster, and she strained to see everything she could about this place where Matt lived.

Perhaps a score of horses grazed—among them gray Saladin—and a number of leggy half-grown colts raced off at her approach.

Averting her eyes from the house, Susanna was somewhat past it when she heard the creak of a door. Matt called her name, catching up with her in a few loose strides.

"When I saw you coming, I thought you'd decided to accept my proposal," he said. "Alas, you marched right past my abode. But I noticed that you paused to admire my horses."

"They, sir, deserve admiration."

"And I don't?" He shrugged and chuckled. "Too true, I'm afraid. But where are you going?"

When she explained she was going to the Krauses to teach the adults English, he said almost angrily, "You can't walk that far in the middle of winter. I never heard such nonsense!"

Her toes were so numb she was prone to agree, but she said defensively, "If it looks threatening, I won't leave home, and if it clouds up while I'm at the Krauses', I'm sure they'd want me to spend the night. Besides, if a storm did catch me, I could shelter at Hardys'—or even at your place, if things were bad."

"Thank you, ma'am." He bowed. "Salutary as it might be to see you grovel up through snowdrifts to my door, I can't say I'd care to find you frozen stiff a few feet from it, and believe me, in a blizzard that can happen."

"I'll be careful," she said.

He groaned with exasperation. "Go your way, most dutiful of teachers, who seems to think it's your calling to educate everybody in sight." He turned serious. "If a storm does loom when you're near my house, make yourself at home if I'm not there. If I am, I promise to behave." His eyes laughed. "At least till the storm's over and you can run away if you feel so inclined."

"That's kind of you—I think." Tucking her scarf over her nose, she said in muffled tones, "Good day, Dr. Rawdon."

He pulled his tousled forelock in mock obeisance. "Farewell, pretty lady." Their eyes caught, held as if locked. Lightning swept between them. Susanna's body felt weighted, heavy.

With a smothered sound he swung away. Cav started after him. "Go, Hank!" Matt said roughly, not looking back.

Wordlessly, Susanna bent to give the dog a hug, brushed away tears that were icy fire on her cheeks. "He doesn't need you, Cav, and he certainly doesn't need me!"

AFTER three hours of spelling and reading in English, the Krauses all gathered around the big table in Peter's house. The patriarch, Anselm, whose weathered face made his white hair and beard look even snowier, intoned a very long and heartfelt prayer.

There was no levity at the table, but voices were calm and amiable as twelve people applied themselves to tureens of steaming soup—borscht, Jacob explained—crusty wheaten bread, and succulent dumplings stuffed with white cheese.

Susanna looked around this largest room, which was kitchen, dining, and living room. Table and chairs were plain and hand-made, probably here, but a tall carved cupboard of golden oak looked as if it had been lovingly polished by many generations. The floor was packed earth, but though the Krauses had come late in the year, the sod roofs had been replaced with shingles, and each house boasted an ingenious brick stove built into the wall. Jacob told her that in the fall they planned to build frame houses, incorporating the brick stoves and reusing the shingles.

"For Catherine and me, there will also be a house," he said with shy pride. "Then we marry in winter."

A clock, with its revolving sun, moon, and stars, was striking a sonorous two in the afternoon when Susanna prepared to leave.

A basket covered with a linen towel was pressed upon her, and smiling, Freda lifted the towel to reveal a wood firkin of butter, a ball of cheese, and two loaves of the good-smelling bread.

"It's too much," Susanna protested.

But Jacob said, "We are grateful. Let us show it."

Except for Anselm, everyone stepped out to wave good-bye as Jacob helped her into his shiny green wagon. Val, who'd been holding the horses, handed Jacob the reins, and they were off.

As they rumbled along they passed the Rawdon place, and Matt seemed to be training a rambunctious sorrel colt to obey the lead of a halter. Touching the edge of his cloth cap, Jacob gave a rueful smile. "Our Valentine, to Mr. Rawdon he is always coming, when he is not at home, so that he can help train the horses. Always horses he has loved. With our workhorses Val is good, but his heart is with the fleet ones."

Susanna spent one more Saturday morning with the Krauses before Christmas. As she approached, Cav at her heels, Val was out by one of the barns on a clean-limbed blue-gray mare.

The mare was so beautiful that even though she knew little about horses, Susanna halted in admiration. When she was ready to leave that night, Jacob grinned and said, "Please to come out and see Valentine's surprise."

Thin face aglow, Val held the bridle of the mare. "Please, our teacher," he said proudly. "This Schatzie is."

"Mr. Rawdon has given to Valentine the mare in return for his helping train the horses." Jacob laughed.

"Now, our teacher," cried Val joyfully. "You—to us you need not be walking! You will ride. On my horse, *mein* Schatz."

My sweetheart. Confound Matt Rawdon! Of all the sneaky tricks! How could she possibly dash that proud delight from the boy's face? Suddenly Susanna had at least a partial solution.

"Val," she said. "I will be glad to ride Schatzie back and forth to your home, but during the week I have no time to ride or spend with her. It would be best if you rode her home on Mondays and then on Friday left her with me."

His eyes shone. "You are sure?"

"Very sure."

Val thought a moment. "The saddle, when I tell—told Mr. Rawdon what I do, he loan it." As Jacob helped Susanna mount, Val caressed the mare's neck and whispered, "Monday, little horse. I will see you then."

As the assembly waved her off, Susanna sat a little stiffly, but by the time they had gone a mile, she relaxed and began to enjoy the swinging pace. She intended to give Matt Rawdon a piece of her mind, though she was touched at his concern. When they neared his place, she looked for him, but he was not to be seen.

As Susanna neared her soddy the mare lifted her head and nickered. A gray horse was in the schoolyard. It whinnied, and Matt Rawdon came forward, grinning, not a whit afraid to face her.

"Fine horse you've got there, ma'am."

Susanna didn't try to restrain a snort. "A lot of good she'd do Val if I kept her all the time! Well, at least he can pick her up on Mondays and have her till Friday."

"Clever lady!" Matt twinkled.

Deflated as she wondered if he'd expected that, too, she said, "May I ask why you're here?"

"Can you dismount, Miss Alden?"

"I—I don't know."

"Ride over by this stump and try. Weight on the stirrup foot, knee easy off that hook, and foot on the stump—that's the way."

Standing on the stump, Susanna looked straight into his eyes. That was so disconcerting that she scrambled down. "Now lead your horse to the barn and let's see you take care of her."

He had come to make sure his horse was properly tended. A bit piqued but glad that he had that much concern for animals, Susanna led Schatzie inside. Matt produced a piece of old blanket and a currycomb. "Now you rub her down, and I'll show you how to groom her." He squinted at Susanna. "Better take off that mantle, or you'll soon need a currycomb yourself."

When Susanna had finally done everything to his satisfaction, he cleaned the brush and hung it on a peg. "Reckon you'll manage. After all, it's only Sunday that Val won't be checking her."

"I didn't ask for your horse," Susanna snapped, brushing without much success at the hairs embedded in her wool dress. "Take her home if you're so worried. Tell Val I'm too pigeon-brained to be trusted with a horse, even if most people seem to think I can look after their children."

His startled expression broadened to a grin. "Surely you're going to offer me a cup of tea."

She evaded, "I'd have to build up the fire and boil the water."

"I took the liberty of stoking your fire and setting the kettle on," he said. "One cup of tea and I'll be on my way."

She took that as a promise. "Come in, then."

It was pleasant to be greeted by a fire instead of a dark, chill interior. Matt fed the flame and perched on the trunk as Susanna got out some of Anna Krause's ginger cake, and when the water boiled, she poured it into Grandmother Alden's teapot.

As the fire warmed the room Matt's presence made her glow inside. It was such happiness to be with him that she desperately wished they could just spend time like this, even if he could never learn to trust her enough to love her. She would rather have his company than have everything—children, marriage, a shared life—with anybody else. Then, as she handed him his tea their hands brushed, and sweet, dizzying flame leaped between them. She retreated to the rocking chair and her tea.

Silence deepened. Indicating a magazine on the table, she swallowed and said, "This *Atlantic* my aunt sent me has a most diverting account of a Welsh governess who was employed to teach the children of the King of Siam—"

"Hang the King of Siam!" Rising abruptly, Rawdon loomed over her a moment before he reached the door in a single stride. "There you sit sipping your tea while— Never mind!" His tone gentled. "I'm sorry, Susanna. It's not your fault. I should know myself better." He patted Cav, but when the dog started to follow him, he said sternly, "Stay here, Hank."

"His name's Cavalier!" Susanna fought back tears. "Now go ahead, Matt Rawdon!"

Matt's eyes plunged into hers. He took a step forward. Susanna closed her eyes. There was a harsh intake of breath; she heard quick steps moving away, and then the door shut hard.

Susanna stood smoothing Cav's head, and then the tears came.

THE Friday afternoon Christmas program was a great success, but when feathery snowflakes began to float by the schoolroom windows, the carol singing was cut short. Amid holiday wishes people bundled up and started home.

"Don't forget our Christmas ball," Hettie Brown called. "The fiddler's coming and we'll dance all night!" She ignored Delia Taylor's sniff of disapproval. "Ase, mind you bring Miss Alden."

"You bet I will," he said.

Jenny rode ahead with the Browns, who promised not to let her take the fork to the Ace High if there was any question of its being safe. Meanwhile Ase hitched up the team, and Betty helped Susanna set things in order for her absence.

"What a lot of sweet presents the young uns brought you," Betty said, admiring gifts heaped on Susanna's desk, including embroidered handkerchiefs from Sarah, molasses candy from the Taylors, beaded moccasins from Ridge, and from Val a pencil sketch of Schatzie, mane and tail flying. "That child's a proper artist," Betty said in awe.

"Yes." Susanna put on her wraps and picked up her satchel. "I'm afraid the Krauses don't quite know what to do with him." Cav rose up from beside the door, shaking off the snow, as they stepped outside and shut the door tight.

"Honey," blurted the older woman as Ase drove up with the buckboard. "I'm sorry Jenny didn't bring you something. I tried to get her to, but. . . Well, you know how she is."

"I know."

No point in distressing Betty further by saying that Jenny had left on her desk, unopened, the small gift she'd been able to give each child, thanks to Jem Howe's shopping in Dodge for hair ribbons for the girls and pocket combs for the boys.

It hurt more that Jenny had disdained the gift than that the girl hadn't brought her some remembrance. In class Jenny was as sullen as she dared be. Susanna could only hope that she wouldn't be so rude to her in front of Ase that he'd punish her and ruin the holiday.

SNOW stopped falling before Christmas morning and wasn't deep enough to keep people from attending the ball that had been planned at the Browns' that night. So Ase's young cowhands, Tom Chadron and Bert Mulroy, were full of high spirits when they joined the family for a holiday breakfast Betty had prepared. After Johnny had stoked the stove, Jenny handed out the presents—new Stetsons for the hands, a gown of misty gray satin for Betty, gifts of fruitcakes and handkerchiefs from Susanna. Jenny retired to the heap of gifts her father had bought her. Ase stepped into the hall and came back with a beautiful big globe in a brass floor stand. "This is for you and the school, ma'am," he said, and turned the sphere slowly. "Here's the mountain ranges all wrinkled up, and the deserts sand-colored, with green for the jungles."

"It's the best, easiest-to-read one I've ever seen!" said Susanna, delighted. "The children will love it!"

Ase glanced at Johnny. "If you want to ride the buckboard to the Browns', we better leave around three."

"Sure hope there's some girls," Tom said, and blushed as Bert kicked him. "Beg pardon, ma'am," he stammered. "You're purtier'n any girl, but—" Bert kicked him even harder.

"No need to apologize, Tom." Susanna laughed. She couldn't resist a sober-faced tease. "If you'll wait four or five years, Sarah and Charlotte will be courting age."

Jenny, holding up a coral necklace, said importantly, "In four or five years I'll be grown up, but I'm going to marry Ridge."

"In five years, young lady, you'll still be a damned long sight from marryin' anybody," Ase said grimly.

Jenny sprang up, eyes flashing stormily. "You—you think I'm a baby. But you make me use that awful old sidesaddle and horrid nasty skirts!" Her venom switched to Susanna. "And her . . . She's mean and hateful and gives me bad grades!"

"Jenny!" Ase thundered, but she had already bolted through the door.

Dumbstruck, they all stared at one another. Bert and Tom hustled out. Johnny decided the stove needed stoking. Betty picked up her dress, murmuring something about trying it on. Mortified, Susanna fought back tears, but Ase's broad, honest face was so distressed that she felt sorrier for him than for herself. "Look, ma'am, don't let a contrary little filly ruin your Christmas. Shucks, you handle nineteen kids five days a week. You can't let one throw you." He smiled. "Come on, Miss Alden. Let's get this globe up to your room."

WHEN THEY PULLED UP TO THE Browns' spacious shingled soddy, Johnny helped Susanna, Betty, and Jenny down and handed them the boxes of pies and baskets of bread that Betty had packed, climbing out himself with a great enameled kettle of beans. Ase drove off to unhitch and put his team in one of the long sod barns. Hettie, brown eyes dancing, embraced them at the door and led them into the living room, warmed on one end by a stove and the other by a fireplace. Susanna saw that the company overflowed into the three bedrooms. Apparently not many people shared the Prades', Taylors', and Krauses' conviction that dancing to a fiddler was wicked; or if they did, they'd decided to risk it.

Susanna didn't realize she was searching for Matt Rawdon till she felt bitter disappointment that he wasn't there—a disappointment that grew deeper with each new arrival. She must have been the only person in the house who had no appetite, even though the food was delicious. As dishes were cleared away Seth Riley, a gnarled little man with a wild mop of kinky gray hair, climbed up on a high stool. His bow struck the strings, and the men swarmed to capture the women, who were in short supply. As what looked like a mass of eager males bore down on her Susanna fled into a bedroom, but Ase followed.

"Case you don't know it, ma'am, you're supposed to partner first with the man who brought you."

"I can't dance with anyone, Mr. McCanless." Her hand went defensively to the throat of her black silk, and his eyes widened.

"Beg pardon, ma'am. I plumb forgot." He started for the door, but changing his mind, marched back. "Listen, Miss Alden, you looked after your daddy since you were what—seventeen?"

"Yes, but I don't see what—"

"Just this. I reckon you mourned your daddy then. Mourned him every day. Seems to me you've mourned him enough."

She gasped at this startling view, and he continued. "If you won't dance, I'm just goin' to stay right here and talk to you." He moved toward her. "Miss Susanna, though I don't see Christmas dancin' as a slight to your daddy, I respect your waitin' for a year before you let anyone come a-callin'. I just want you to carry this in your mind, though, when you're usin' that globe." Slow and deliberate, he dropped each word. "If you'll have it, I want to give you my world." Moving aside from the door, he chuckled. "Miss Alden, ma'am, you'd be safer dancing."

He held out his arm, and on impulse she slipped her hand through it. He was right. She had done her mourning.

Above the cry of the fiddle, Seth was shouting, "Come on now, prance lively! Swing your lady, swing her sweet! Paw dirt, doggies, stomp your feet!"

Polkas, reels, waltzes—Susanna danced till she collapsed. During brief interludes, when Seth had to stop to soothe his throat, Kermit would sing while Freck strummed his guitar.

The song that brought the most applause and a couple of rebel yells was one that had, Kermit boasted, been sung by the Duchess of Manchester for Queen Victoria and the Prince of Wales.

"I'm glad I fought the Yankees,
I only wisht we'd won,
An' I don't want no pardon
For anything I've done. . . .

"Three hundred thousand Yankees
Lay dead in southern dust,
We got three hundred thousand
Afore they conquered us. . . ."

Susanna's breath constricted. One of those three hundred thousand Yankees was Richard, her Richard, dead at twenty!

Several noticed when Susanna had leaped up. She made her way to the center of the room.

"Aw, Miss Alden," Kermit began, crimsoning. "I plumb forgot!"

"One good song deserves another, Mr. Brown," she said, looking at the Hardys and other northerners. "Mr. Hardy, I'd think you know 'The Battle Hymn of the Republic.' "

"Bet your life I do. Every single verse."

"Let's sing it."

The homesteaders did, and the southerners, all ranchers and cowboys, endured it, but when the last marching chorus ended, Kermit said dryly, "If you're goin' to holler 'Glory, hallelujah!' for the Union, ma'am, I reckon we're entitled to 'Bonnie Blue Flag.' "

Susanna smiled at him. "Better sing than fight, Mr. Brown. I think we've just stumbled on the way to teach the war."

She laughed with a happiness that made him blink in puzzlement. With singing that song, honoring her dead in the midst of former enemies, her mourning was over.

SUSANNA had dreaded teaching the war—to her, there was really only one—in her American history class. But now, purged by the songs sung at the Christmas ball, she was at peace enough with her own feelings to think she could arrange a fair presentation. There was no way to teach a war so recently over, but she believed that singing the songs of both sides would bring festering bitterness into healing openness. When school reopened after the holidays, she sent notes home to the men who had fought, asking them if on the next Friday visitors' afternoon they'd tell the children as much as they deemed fitting of their memories of the war—and come prepared to sing.

When the day came, Prade was the only one whose eyes glittered as he spoke of killing. The others spoke huskily of comrades wounded or slain; of grief and shock over men they had killed; of hunger, filth, terror; of battles that were horrible whether won or lost; of the relief at finally coming home, even—as the southerners did—to defeat and vengeful Reconstruction.

Except for Prade, the men, whether Union or Confederate, choked up and blinked back tears. When Will Taylor, the last one to speak, stammered to a finish, Ase said, "You know, if it wasn't for the way we talk, wouldn't be a way to tell who fought on which side."

"That's the gospel truth." Will nodded.

Glancing from Will to Cash and Jem Howe, Ase said, "I guess the ones of us who fought have a lot more in common than them as didn't." And then they sang.

WHEN she rode to the Krauses next day, Susanna didn't see Matt, and no smoke rose from his chimney. The place looked so abandoned that Susanna felt a surge of panic, before she reminded herself that the horses were around. Matt might be gone for a time, but as long as the horses were there, he'd be back.

The Krauses explained that the day before he'd asked Val to keep an eye out for his horses while he made a trip to Texas.

Texas! Susanna felt as if a giant hand had crushed her chest. What if he'd gone to make arrangements for moving back? What if he'd gone to see a woman? Susanna was sure there had to be one.

Oh, what was the use in guessing? Susanna only knew he was gone, and that made her feel as if the sun had left the sky.

Nine

*M*ONDAY morning was unusually mild, but by noon the sky was overcast, and a piercing wind howled out of the north. It had happened so quickly that Susanna was afraid to send the children home. At the frigid onslaught, the horses had refuged in the barn. Susanna sent the older boys out to fill the mangers, secure guide ropes from the barn to the school, and shut the heavy barn door. The other children brought in fuel, which they heaped along the walls, and filled all the buckets and a tub with water.

By the time these chores were finished, razor-edged sleet cut into exposed faces, and Susanna hustled the children inside.

She kept classes going till four thirty. By then the windows were totally covered with wind-packed sleet, which had forced itself through the cracks. Susanna served ginger cake and tea.

While she stirred lots of raisins into a kettle of creamy rice, she pondered sleeping arrangements. The children, of course, would sleep in their clothing and coats, removing only shoes. The ten girls might be able to snuggle together, lying across the bed, with a bench for the feet and legs of the taller ones. Desks could be cleared from in front of the fire, and the recitation bench, water bench, and three remaining seat benches could be aligned to make a bed for the boys. It could be padded with magazines, the rug, and the divider curtain. Susanna would sit in the rocker, wrapped in her mantle and shawl, and keep the fire going.

Mustering all her dishes and pans, Susanna, with the help of the older girls, served beans and chunks of delicious wheaten bread, and then the children had their fill of sweet rice pudding.

Sarah washed dishes and Cobie and Rosie dried, while Susanna sat in the rocker, cradling a sleepy Magdalena in one arm and Helen in the other. Georgie and Freddie sat on the rug at her feet and used Cav for their pillow, and the rest of the children pulled benches near the fireplace, where they could hear Susanna as she told all the fairy tales she knew.

At midnight Susanna sent them all to bed. The wind keened like a pack of wolves, but amazingly she did sleep until about six o'clock, when Val got up and whispered that he was going to follow the rope to the barn and see about the horses. Dave and Ridge silently joined Val. After they had returned twenty minutes later, reporting that sleet had sifted in several inches deep but that the animals were getting moisture from it and were fine, Dave shoveled from door to shed, and Val brought in more fuel.

By then the other children were getting up, yawning and rubbing their eyes. Susanna had put on a big kettle of mush, which, lavished with diluted Borden's and molasses, disappeared to the last scraping. Sarah presided over the gingerly washing of faces and hands, while Dave, Ridge, and Val helped tie shoes, comb hair, and encourage the little boys to scurry outside before they burst. Desks and benches were restored to their proper places. While the storm raged, Susanna rang the bell for classes.

TURNING recitations over to Dave and Sarah, Susanna put corn bread to bake in the Dutch oven, then noticed that Jenny was in a surly mood. As Sarah patiently corrected her mispronunciations in the reading lessons, Jenny imitated her in a sneer. Susanna was about to call out a reprimand when she heard Ridge say in a tone of quiet disgust, "Jenny, be ashamed."

"She's not the teacher and neither are you!" cried Jenny in a voice quivering with outraged hurt. "What do I care if a half-breed likes nesters and Dutchies better than me?"

"Jenny!" Susanna had to exert every ounce of willpower not to shake the girl till her teeth rattled. "You can apologize to Ridge and Sarah or come sit in my room by yourself."

"I won't apologize!" Jenny screamed. "I—I'd rather die!"

"Bring your reader and speller and sit in here," Susanna ordered. All the time spent trying to win this spiteful girl boiled up and exploded. Susanna said, "I'm going to tell your father that he'd better send you away. You won't let me teach you, Jenny, and I'm sick and tired of trying."

Jenny paled, got her books, and stalked into the bedroom, pulling Susanna's desk chair into a corner. She refused to eat at noon, and Susanna, feeling herself an abysmal failure, didn't coax her.

Sometime during the noon hour Jenny disappeared, evidently darting out when someone went for fuel. It wasn't till Susanna rang the bell and watched the students take their seats that she noticed Jenny wasn't in hers, and glanced at the corner.

There sat the chair, but not Jenny. "Jenny!" Susanna called. She swallowed and asked the youngsters, "Have you seen Jenny?"

As the schoolroom erupted Susanna fought for control. "Sit down, children! Sarah and Dave, you take charge and keep everybody inside. Maybe she's hiding in the barn." Dave caught Susanna's arm as she started for the door.

"Let Ridge and Val and me look, ma'am."

Susanna scarcely breathed during the eternity before the boys returned. "She's not there," Dave said heavily. "Her horse is. She's not in the shed. We used the rope from the barn and headed for where we reckoned the privies were. Stumbled into them. She's not there." He made a helpless gesture. "She—she just isn't anywhere but out in that storm."

Susanna felt as if she were slipping into blackness. Death was in that blizzard.

"What we must do," said Ridge, "is knot the ropes together and go out as far as they'll stretch, moving in a half circle. Freck and I have ropes on our saddles. They can be added on."

Each moment was agony as Dave and Ridge battled their way to the barn, returning with the ropes. When Freck and Val had tied the ropes together, the combined lengths made a line about a hundred and twenty feet long.

"We'll space ourselves out along the line," Dave said, taking hold of the end. "That way, if Jenny's down, we're more likely to run into her."

Frank, without a word, picked up the rope. Ridge came next, then Val, Freck, and Ethan. Susanna took hold of the rope about twenty feet from where it was tied to the door.

"Miss Alden, you stay inside," urged Dave.

"I can't." Susanna looked at the boys who were ready to brave that ferocious gale of pulverized ice.

"I'll head for the barn," Dave said, knit cap pulled down to his eyebrows. "When I get as far as the ropes stretch, I'll start the sweep south; that'll put the wind to our backs. I don't think we can hear, so if you find Jenny, give the line three tugs. And if your fingers start numbin', get back down the ropes to the school. Before we go out, pull your scarf over your nose and lower face."

He opened the door. The boys and Susanna ran out, shutting the door behind them. The cold blasting wind and stinging, blinding particles stopped Susanna's breath, even through the wool scarf, but then she bowed her head and inched forward.

I'd rather die! Tormented, she again heard Jenny's words. Jenny loved her horse and might not have wanted to risk him. Or she may have stolen out with that bitter childish cry in her heart, They'll be sorry when I'm dead.

Cav had come out after Susanna. She felt him by her skirts and prayed that he wouldn't stray off and be lost.

The line tautened, then began to tug at an angle away from the wind. Turning laboriously, Susanna followed. What if they swept the whole circle and found nothing? Susanna was determined that none of these boys should freeze or lose hands and feet. If they made the circle, she'd make them go in. But she herself couldn't take shelter while Jenny was out here.

Lashed by gusts that drove her repeatedly to her knees, she existed in a blind, eerie world of wailing shrieks. Her feet were clumsy blocks with no feeling, each step a labored push into the drifts. The rope. She had to hold it. Where was Cav? Was that him barking above the wind? She strained to hear, but it was useless. Cav, though, was no longer plunging along beside her.

And then he was, gripping her mantle, trying to drag her backward. Whatever Cav wanted her to come to was probably beyond the stretch of the rope. She wouldn't risk the boys. She had to trust that Cav could lead her back to the school, that he could lead her now, pray God, to Jenny.

She drew in a searing breath, and let go of the rope.

Now she was in that slashing, piercing void, forcing through the frigid mounds, Cav hauling at her.

He stopped. Susanna tripped against something. Bending down, thrusting her deadened hands through several inches of ice particles, she found a bundle, heaved it up against her, and knew she held Jenny, who didn't respond to Susanna's calling her name.

Wresting the body from the drift, Susanna bent almost double, dragging the child as Cav tugged them along.

It seemed forever. Then she staggered against something, someone—Val—just reaching the soddy door. Somehow, still dragging Jenny, Susanna stumbled in and was caught and supported.

Sarah wavered before her as her frozen eyelashes unmeshed, and she gazed around to count the muffled, blanched faces of the boys. All of them were safe. Dave scooped up Jenny while Sarah brushed powdery ice from her. Bending close, Susanna felt faint breath. "We've got to get her warm. Sarah, you and Rosie and Berenice take off your dresses and shoes and we'll tuck Jenny in amongst you."

"We'll be just like hot-water bottles," Sarah told the younger girls as she swept them into the bedroom, where Dave was gently taking off Jenny's shoes.

Susanna and Sarah undressed Jenny to her chemise as Dave went back to take charge of the other youngsters.

Susanna laid her palm against Jenny's pale face; it was resilient. Nesting the girl against Rosie and Berenice, Susanna held the covers while Sarah slipped in and gathered Jenny in her arms, so that the child was completely surrounded by her schoolmates.

Next Susanna made tea and gave several cups to each of the boys shivering by the fire. Hovering over Jenny, she lifted the quilts enough to peer at her face. She was less pallid, and the lips were pinker. "Jenny," Susanna said. "Jenny, can you hear me?"

Golden eyelashes fluttered. The girl whimpered; then the dark blue eyes opened slowly. It was a moment before they focused on Susanna. "It—it was you. You found me."

"Cav found you," Susanna said, smoothing the yellow hair.

"It was you."

"No. It was all of us." Susanna explained how Ridge had thought of tying the ropes together and how the boys had spaced themselves to make the circle.

Jenny sat up, and her gaze wandered around her schoolmates, who were all crowding at the foot and sides of the bed. "You— you cared about me," she whispered. Tears glistened in her eyes. "I was so nasty—especially to you, Val, and you, Ridge!"

Ridge said gravely, "You ought to know, Jenny, that Miss Alden let go of the rope to find you."

Color rushed to Jenny's face. She lifted her chin and looked at Susanna. "When I sneaked out, I was so mad at you that I just wanted to make you sorry and cause a lot of trouble. But after I was in the storm a while, I knew I didn't want to die. I yelled and tried to come back, but I couldn't find the way." She gulped. Tears spilled over and ran down her cheeks. "I'm sorry—really sorry. If—if you don't want me in your school, Miss Alden, I'll let Daddy send me away."

Susanna sank down and took Jenny in her arms. "We want you, honey. We all want you here."

A few hours later the storm slackened, but the drifts were too high for safe travel, and Susanna and the children passed the night as they had the one before. Seizing a moment by the water bucket, Susanna said to Frank, "It was brave and good of you to help look for Jenny."

He shrugged. "Didn't want anyone to think I was scared to go out." Before she could say anything else, he moved off.

Next day the sun rose in a burst of fiery brilliance. At noon the children made a family of snow people. Jenny didn't go out, but stayed close to the fire, a most subdued little girl.

Most of the fathers appeared early in the afternoon, beginning with Ase McCanless. "I knew you'd keep the kids corralled inside and that you had plenty of fuel and food," he said to Susanna, glancing up in some surprise from Jenny's fervent hug. "Hold on, sweetheart. What's got into you?"

"Oh, Daddy! I—I've been so bad, and I'd be froze to death out there if Susanna hadn't let go the rope—"

Ase glanced from her to Susanna. "What's this?"

Jenny blurted out her story, Ase kneeling to let her sob against his shoulder. When she quieted, he rose and looked over at Dave.

"Thank you, son," said Ase. "And you, Frank, and you, Val. Freck, Ridge, I'm most mightily obliged." Shaking his head at Susanna, he muttered, "Can't think how I'll ever settle with you, Miss Alden. But you must know how I feel."

"I know." Her own eyes were misty. "I'm just so thankful the storm's over and everyone's all right."

Will Taylor and Saul Prade drove up almost at the same time, just as Luke Tarrant rode along the slope. Kermit Brown brought his horse through mounded snow. Jacob rode up on a plow horse.

"We live so close that Dad didn't bother to come" was Dave's offhand comment on Cash's conspicuous absence.

Next morning the Hardy children didn't come to school, but Jem Howe rode into the yard as Susanna was ringing the bell. Dismounting, his gray eyes full of trouble, he said that Cash had left for town the day of the blizzard. He hadn't come home. After riding to the Hardys' to check on the family yesterday morning, Jem had gone to search for Cash.

He found him late last evening on the prairie, hand protruding from a drift, while the horse nibbled grass where it was free of the snow. The storm had found its victim after all.

MORNING and evening, as the days lengthened and January yielded to February, Susanna heard the low fluting notes of prairie cocks. As the ground thawed, farmers started breaking sod with their ox teams. The great horned owls began their nests, and still Matt Rawdon had not returned.

It was on the last Saturday of February, the last day that the Krauses could spare for study, that she rode out on Schatzie and saw smoke lifting from his chimney. She approached with mingled joy and trepidation. Had he come alone? What had happened in Texas? She was wrestling with whether she should stop when the door opened and he came toward her, black head atilt.

"Well, Miss Alden," he said, after bending to play-tussle Cav, who had streaked to meet him. "I hear you've tamed the terrible-tempered Jenny and become a heroine."

Hurt by his mocking tone, Susanna said stiffly, "I keep telling everyone it was Cav who found Jenny."

"All the same, I reckon she'd welcome you now as her stepmother."

"As to that, Dr. Rawdon, I cannot say."

His smile flashed. "Am I to take it, then, that Ase McCanless hasn't taken advantage of Jenny's tractability to press his suit?"

"Perhaps you've forgotten, sir, but women in mourning do not entertain proposals."

"Well then, since it seems I don't immediately have to find you a wedding gift, I'll let you get on to your Saturday pupils."

"Wait!" she called as he started to turn away. "Why are you so concerned about whether Mr. McCanless has proposed to me?"

He took a long stride back to her before he said, "I wondered if you might be more amenable to that suggestion I made last winter."

How dare he? Swallowing wrathful tears, Susanna brought her heel against Schatzie's flank—something she had never done before—and had to grab for the front of the saddle as Schatzie soared into a lope.

Vexed as she was at Matt's arrogance, she was filled with a dizzying flood of thanksgiving. He hadn't returned with a woman.

SCHOOL would end the last of March, and in addition to attending a summer course for teachers at the institute in Dodge City, Susanna intended to make a visit to Ohio.

That might give her a better perspective on Matt. The board, with Prade voting against it, had already offered her a contract for the next school year. She wanted to teach these children she had come to care about so deeply. But in a way that was folly, for she couldn't imagine getting interested in another man so long as she was where she'd even occasionally have a glimpse of Matt.

Considered from that light, when school ended, she should pack all her things and look for a school a long way from the Mason-Dixon district. And yet . . . a year. She could surely manage one more year. This stretch of prairie, these people, had become hers. If only she hadn't had to love a man so bitter about the past that he wouldn't reach for the present.

FOR the last few weeks Susanna integrated study around preparation for the school year's grand finale, the closing-day program. The whole community would arrive midmorning to attend it.

Sarah and Berenice wrote a play, a simplified *Midsummer Night's Dream*, with parts for all the children. With the older girls' help Susanna assembled costumes of cheesecloth tunics for the girls, and for the boys there were cloaks dyed a greenish tan. Betty contributed gilt paper for fairy diadems and wands. Ridge created a hollow donkey's head, maned with real horsehair, from rawhide stretched over a willow frame and padded with grass.

On the great day, as horses and wagons began arriving, benches were carried outside for the spectators, and the play was presented with the soddy used as backstage.

Freck, in the donkey's head, brought roars of laughter, and Charlotte took the role of Titania. Jenny and Val burlesqued the mixed-up lovers, while Athenians and fairies played their roles. Shakespeare wouldn't have recognized the dialogue, but the production was ringingly applauded.

In conclusion, Susanna handed written reports to each child and thanked the parents for their cooperation and understanding.

Planks spread across wagons sagged with food, and when everyone had eaten, Freck got out his guitar and they finished with the Kansas rivers song.

The children, parents, and friends began to depart, and Matt Rawdon, mounted on Saladin, reined in beside Susanna as she waved good-bye to them.

"Well done, Miss Alden." Attuned to sarcasm in his tone, she was surprised to detect none. "A most satisfactory last day of school. I hear that you're departing soon for Ohio."

"As soon as I catch up on my records, Dr. Rawdon."

"May I take you to your train?" he asked.

"It's not your responsibility, sir. I'm sure one of the trustees will offer."

"No doubt. But will you let me? Cav can ride along and see you off. I presume you planned to leave him with me."

"I was going to ask."

"Fine. When shall I call for you? Four days? A week?"

"A week, if you're sure . . ."

"I'm sure." He touched his hat and cantered off.

Johnny had driven Betty home in the buckboard, while Jenny raced with Freck and Dottie, so Ase was the last person at the school. His broad, weathered face had a determined set as he said, "School's out, Miss Alden, ma'am. You're not the teacher. I'm not the head of the board." He surveyed her dark green tarlatan. "And you're not in mourning."

The blue eyes searched her in a way that made her blush, but didn't find what they looked for. He gave a shrug. "I hope you'll let me take you to town when you leave for Ohio."

Her blush deepened. "That's kind of you, very kind, but Dr. Rawdon's taking me." Ase's gaze probed deep till she could endure it no longer and looked away. He shook his head.

"Doc's a fine man, but from piecin' things together, folks reckon he came up here because the woman he was engaged to took a horror of his hand. It sure has soured his notions of females. He might love you, Miss Alden. But he'll never trust you."

Burning with humiliation, she bent all her will to keep from crying. But Ase's tone was understanding and genuinely concerned, and her tears spilled over as she blindly spun away. He took her in his arms.

"It's rotten damned luck, honey. But look, it's not the end of the world. Hearts are tough things. When my wife died, I thought I'd never care about another woman. But here you are!"

She sobbed harder at that, regretting for both their sakes that she didn't love him. He held her till she began to sniff and pull away in embarrassment. Then, grasping her shoulders, he held her at arm's length, and though those deep blue eyes were serious, they also held merriment.

"If you'll give me a chance, Susanna, I reckon I can make you love me. But if you won't . . . when I see it's no use for good and all, well, honey, I'll shine up my boots, slick down my hair, and find me somebody who can love me back."

Removing herself from his hands, she straightened her hair. "A laudably practical decision, Mr. McCanless."

His grin broadened. He fumbled in an inner vest pocket and produced what looked like a railway ticket. "The trustees figured you have a bonus comin'. If we've got to import a teacher, least we can do is pay her fare back and forth."

That seemed equitable. After considering, Susanna thanked him and took the ticket with a smile. Striding toward his horse, Ase called over his shoulder, "If you want me to collect you in Dodge, just drop me a line." He turned to wave, then sent the horse into his pace.

Susanna moved into the soddy and for the first time noticed a ruffled calico-covered box on her desk. A neat card was fastened to it. "To our Dearest Miss Susanna Alden, From all of us!"

As she took off the lid, folded papers spilled out. On a piece of cardboard Val had drawn Susanna standing by the globe. There were notes or letters from all the children—some several pages long, some, like Frank's, very brief. "You are a good teacher. I hope you come back." And Rosie wrote, "I love Mama and Dave and Ethan and Georgie, and I love God and Miss Alden."

Susanna laughed till, overwhelmed, she cried. Six months till school began again. It seemed too long a time.

Ten

$\mathcal{M}$ATT, arriving shortly after sunrise a week after closing day, frowned at her satchel and one large bundle. "You must be forgetting a trunk or valise, Miss Susanna."

"No." She took a final look around both rooms. Turning to Matt, she found him watching her in a way that sent her pulse racing. She hurried outside and said a little breathlessly, "I have a lot of things to shop for." She had close to all her wages saved, and that was fortunate, because she was sick of her drab garments. "Besides, I hate my clothes and I'm going to get some new ones."

He whistled Cav into the buckboard, then lifted Susanna up. For a moment their faces were perilously close, and she went faint, remembering that one harshly sweet kiss. His eyes touched her mouth. He moved around to climb up beside her.

"Will you do something for me?"

She said with forced lightness, "That depends on what it is."

"Get yourself a dress the color of the sky on a clear, fine day like this—something with a little flow and grace. Just as easy to wear pretty clothes as dowdy ones."

"So I'm dowdy?"

"Aren't you?"

That was exactly how she'd been feeling, but she choked at this matter-of-fact indictment. Before she could think of a withering retort, he scowled at her brown bonnet. "And for Pete's sake, take that thing off. It makes you look like a missionary."

"Dr. Rawdon, if you're going to criticize me all the way to Dodge, kindly drop me off at the Tarrants', and I'll ask Mr. Tarrant if he'll drive me in."

"You took off your bonnet the day I fetched you from Dodge," he said softly. "That was when I decided there was more to you than a prim, proper Yankee schoolmarm who was careful of her—"

"Clothes, money, and reputation!" Susanna finished.

"Just so," he said, chuckling.

She was undone. After all, why not let the wind finger her hair this last day? She untied the ribbons, loosed the coiled hair, threw back her head, and laughed. To be with Matt, wheeling across the prairie, filled her with joy.

"You have a sweet laugh, Susanna. I haven't heard it much."

"That," she shot back in good humor, "is because you're forever telling me what to do, fussing at me for being a Yankee, or tricking me into keeping Cav or using Schatzie. I've learned, Dr. Rawdon, that I have to be on guard around you."

It was meant playfully, but he stiffened. "Just for the trip, Susanna, let's drive a bargain. I won't transgress, so you can safely relax, and you won't bedevil me to practice medicine. Agreed?"

"Agreed." She hesitated then. "May I ask you something?"

"So long as it's not why I'm not patching up my fellowman."

"Did you have a good trip to Texas?"

His mouth jerked down. "The trip was fine," he said. "I'll tell you about it while we're having dinner at the Dodge House, before I put you on your train." Before she could argue, he gave her a challenging smile. "May I ask you something?"

"You may ask. But maybe I won't answer."

"Fair enough." He turned enough to watch her closely. "Has Ase proposed to you?"

Her blush answered, so she nodded. His hands tightened. In an elaborately casual tone he asked, "What did you tell him?"

Susanna's heart pounded. "I—I told him no."

The hands gripping the reins loosened. "Knowing Ase, I don't reckon that's the last time you'll get asked."

Susanna tried to turn it into a joke. "He let me know if I don't wake up to my good fortune in whatever he considers a reasonable time, he's going to find somebody else. I don't really think it's me so much as just that he's tired of being single."

"It's you."

Matt gave her such a glance that her heart skipped. Time, more than time, to talk of something else. "Is Val too busy with farm work to help now with the horses?"

"He's breaking sod. The men all are, except for old Anselm. These folks don't farm by season. They farm by the decade, even by the century. That's why they'll last."

The rest of the way to town they talked about neighbors, Matt's horses, and the children, holding dangerous topics at bay.

Six months before, Dodge City had looked makeshift with its false-front buildings. But Susanna hadn't set foot in any kind of settlement since then, and now it seemed a hub of activity.

Stopping in front of the Dodge House, Matt hitched the team and helped her down. They entered the hotel and were seated in the dining room, which seemed opulent with its chandelier, white tablecloths, and gleaming silver plate. In her whole life Susanna had dined out only a few times. This was a treat, but bracing for what Matt had to tell her had robbed her of appetite. She looked helplessly at the bill of fare.

"The lady will have the Welsh rarebit," Matt told the waitress when she appeared. "Saratoga chips, Russian salad, lemon tart, and . . ." He raised an eyebrow at Susanna. "My dear, would you prefer sauterne or champagne wine? Coffee, tea, or chocolate?"

My dear—as if they were married. It would be ungracious to argue in front of the waitress, so Susanna contented herself by saying, "Oh, please, dear, do finish making up my mind for me."

Not in the least chastened, he said, "The lady will have sauterne and French coffee. I'll have the same."

The middle-aged woman whisked away, and Matt leaned forward. "Susanna, can we just enjoy our meal and each other's company before I tell you what I need to?"

"No!" She started to tremble.

"Oh, Susanna! Oh, my sweet . . ."

He looked so stricken and remorseful that she wove her fingers together beneath the starched tablecloth and swallowed hard. "Tell me this." She was past pretending. "Are you going back to Texas? Is your—your fiancée coming here?"

"Neither."

The pressure on her lungs and heart slackened. With a sigh of reprieve she said, "All right. Let's eat, drink, and be merry."

ASSURED that neither of the things she had most dreaded was going to happen, Susanna found that she was indeed hungry. The tangy rarebit whetted her appetite for the salad and the thickly sliced potatoes fried to a golden brown. Matt beguiled her with amusing stories from his childhood. The sauterne made everything sparkle, and feeling slightly dizzy, she allowed herself to imagine that when night fell, Matt would take her in his arms again.

She glanced up to find his eyes dwelling on her, blushed from head to toe, and thought distractedly that she shouldn't have had that second glass of sauterne. But oh, she felt so deliciously happy, so light and floating.

Matt said something beneath his breath, reached across the table, and took her hand in his. "Susanna, what I have to tell is quickly said. My sister, Amanda, implored me to come to Dallas for a visit. She thinks I'm at the ends of the earth and should come back and start a practice among 'our own kind.' I tried to set her mind at rest, but my real mission was to ask my former sweetheart to explain to me frankly how she felt about my hand."

Susanna started to speak, but he motioned her to silence. "Melanie wept. She said she still loved me, though she's married and has two children. She'd been ashamed of her shrinking from me and tried to conceal it when I first returned, but when I touched her, she flinched. She could close her eyes, she said, and try not to look at my ruined fingers. But when she felt them on her, it was . . . Her very descriptive phrase was 'like being gripped by a corpse hand.' "

"Matt, I don't feel that way!"

"How do you know how you'd feel when I touched you?" Shock made her catch in her breath. Before she could speak, he said roughly, "I'd rather die, Susanna, than have you shrink from my touch or, even worse, endure it with gritted teeth."

"I love you," she said swiftly.

She hadn't spoken those words to a man since Richard left for his regiment twelve years ago. It was like breaking tight bonds, and this time she spoke softly and slowly. "I love you, Matt."

Reaching beneath the table, she dared to take his hand in both of hers, but he snatched it away, shaking his head. "You can nerve yourself to touch my scars, but that's a far cry, my darling, from feeling them on your body."

"I don't understand," she pleaded. "Once you asked me to . . ."

"That was when I was trying to convince myself that I couldn't be falling in love with you."

"What if I'd said yes?"

"I was sure you'd recoil, just as Melanie did." His voice dropped. "But it was too late. I think it's been too late since the minute you took down your hair and gave it to the wind and laughed."

"It's wicked, Matt Rawdon! To not even give me a chance . . ."

He said harshly, "I'm giving you the best chance I can. To marry someone like Ase McCanless."

"I'm not going to marry Ase."

"You might. If I went away."

"Don't talk like that! You've got your homestead and horses. People need you." She swallowed hard. "I'm leaving after this coming year. Till then . . . Oh, Matt, I want to see you sometimes—the way we have this year—even if it hurts."

The lights in his eyes were now twin fires. "My love, I'll do my best." He got abruptly to his feet and drew back her chair. "Come along. We'd better head for the depot."

Their day was ending—this sweet, terrible day she would never forget, when she had known for certain she was loved.

Matt helped Susanna locate a seat on the train. Having stowed her baggage beneath the seat, he straightened. Tears blurred Susanna's eyes, and as she blinked, one ran down her cheek. Matt caught in his breath. Then suddenly, devilishly, he embraced her, kissed her astonished mouth, drew back, and patted her cheek.

"Have a good visit with your aunt, my love," he said loudly enough to be heard by the men at the back of the car. "I'll take good care of the children." He dropped another kiss on her forehead and went down the aisle before she could think of words to chastise him without betraying to the interested onlookers that there were no children and he was not her husband.

In spite of the desolation she felt at leaving him, she had to smile at his roguishness, which had let him kiss her good-bye. She settled into her seat and turned to look out the window. Matt came in sight, Cav at his heels. He'd brought him to see her off. The train groaned into motion. Between tears and laughter Susanna waved back at man and dog as long as she could see them, and wished that instead of chugging toward Ohio, she could go back with them to a prairie home where they could be together.

In Topeka she changed lines and had a sleeping car for the rest of her journey, though she got little enough sleep. It was worth it, though, to be hugged and petted by her aunt and uncle, who were waiting at the station.

"Well, child, you've thinned a bit and your complexion's got a touch of sun, but it becomes you." Aunt Mollie's quick hazel eyes appraised Susanna, and she smiled. "Come along now. Dinner'll be ready by the time you've had a bath and changed."

After months of living in a dirt-floored soddy and being responsible for nineteen children, it was as delicious as Aunt Mollie's cooking to be cosseted and live in a real house, with waxed oak floors, a sound roof, and plenty of windows.

Susanna's days passed quickly. She took over the housekeeping, and shopping took up considerable time, as did delving into stored belongings for those she wanted to take back to Kansas.

The trunk in her room filled by the day: fitted pencil boxes for each child, and for each at Christmas a carefully chosen book. For Catherine and Jacob's wedding gift Susanna found a ruby cutglass creamer-and-sugar set in a trunk of her stored things. When pads and pastels for Val had been tucked away, she spent pleasant hours deliberating with her aunt over styles pictured in *Harper's Bazaar,* and more time choosing material for two new dresses. One would be of olive sateen and the other—the one she had promised Matt—of sky-blue bengaline, a corded cotton-and-wool fabric. One of Susanna's trunks yielded a sprigged muslin and a daffodil poplin that she'd folded away when her father died. Since a sod schoolhouse was no place for elaborate poufs, the dresses would be simple. Susanna conserved her dwindling funds by using her aunt's sewing machine and making the gowns herself.

In this house full of old memories and so far removed from things that would remind her of Matt, Susanna sometimes succeeded in going for an hour or more without explicitly thinking of him, though his presence was always at the back of her mind.

Would he haunt her, she wondered, all the rest of her life? And yet, could she have banished him, she would not have done it; remembering him was painful, but it was her deepest pleasure.

THE luxuriant green of early April prairie grass had paled to August's soft yellows and browns as Susanna watched from the train with the eagerness of homecoming.

She had written Henry Morton that she'd be arriving the day

before the institute began, and he was at the train to meet her and convey her with her baggage to the Dodge House. "Mr. McCanless will be in to take you out to the Mason-Dixon School after the institute." Morton gave her a benevolent side-glance. "Downright set on it, he was."

The institute was absorbing, the two-day session taught by professors from the state normal school and the state university. Perhaps the main benefit was talking with other teachers about their problems and solutions. Now she knew she had allies in the battle to educate children under adverse conditions.

Susanna came down to the hotel dining room the morning after the institute ended to find Ase McCanless drinking coffee and watching the door.

"Here you are!" Rising, he reached her in two long strides, taking both her hands in his. She wore her daffodil dress, ruffled at wrists and yoke, and he gave a soft whistle. "Doggoned if you haven't got purtier'n ever. Light and have your breakfast." He escorted her to the table and pulled out her chair.

After Susanna had ordered apple fritters and coffee, Ase gave her the news. Everyone was fine, he said. The Krauses' red turkey wheat had been cut early in July. They'd given a bushel of seed wheat to anyone who wanted it, and that proved to be everyone except Saul Prade. The regular wheat and corn and cane had grown well, but were now beginning to wither from drought.

Though he must know she was burning to hear about Matt, Ase did not mention him, and there was something in Ase's manner that made Susanna sure he was concealing something.

Sipping her coffee, she stared at Ase. "Mr. McCanless, you've been fidgeting. What is it you haven't told me?"

He looked sheepish. "I—well . . . Oh hell, Miss Susanna! Beg your pardon. But Doc Rawdon's sister, Miss Amanda, she's come to keep house for him, though I reckon what she's really after is to herd him back to Texas." Ase sighed. "She's a nice lady, but she sure is . . . determined."

The cup had almost dropped from Susanna's fingers. She set it down with care, unable to breathe for a moment. It struck her that in spite of Matt's resolve not to make love to her, she had been unconsciously hoping that something would happen to give her a chance to prove to him that his infirmity didn't matter.

Commanding her voice not to shake, Susanna said, "Having a woman to look after him should be a welcome change for the doctor. But I should think she won't like the soddy."

Ase grinned. "That's not the half of it. She's building a house. She hired carpenters, had lumber freighted in, and the house is about finished. Jem Howe says when she turned up with her maid, cook, and housekeeper, Doc moved out to the barn and let her have the soddy."

The thought of a southern lady crowding into a soddy with three servants struck Susanna as so ludicrous that she laughed. It was ludicrous, too, for her to be jealous of this sister, but she was.

As SHE had before in times of grief or distress, Susanna found relief in the dailiness of life. The Ace High had been her first home here, and it was good, during the three weeks she visited, to share tasks and chat with Betty, listen to Johnny's yarns, and ride with Jenny. Ase was busy with roundup, so she didn't see him often, but on the evening that she said she must get to the soddy next day and start preparing for school, he said, "You haven't changed your mind about the school? Or . . . anything else?"

Why couldn't she love him when she liked him so much? It was no use, though. Longing for a home and a family would certainly have induced her to accept Ase if she hadn't met and loved Matt.

Meeting Ase's wistful eyes, she said regretfully but firmly, "No, Mr. McCanless. I haven't changed my mind."

"I won't pester you again, Miss Susanna," Ase said. "In fact, I'm going to St. Louis and start huntin'."

"Good luck," she said.

No SUNFLOWERS or grass swayed on top of the soddy, and it took her a stunned moment to believe her eyes. "The soddy. It's got a shingled roof. A real roof!"

Ase chuckled at her delight as he helped her out of the buckboard. "Didn't want you and the kids gettin' rained on again. Makes it lighter inside, too."

It did, though after her months away and the drive in the blazing sunlight the soddy seemed murkily dark as she stepped inside. As her eyes grew accustomed to the dimness she saw that the floors were freshly swept and the fuel basket was full.

When she turned to thank Ase, he shook his head. "Dave helped with the shingling as much as he could. I told him about when you'd be coming. Guess all you need's a bucket of water."

He got that while Susanna lightened the trunk of books, handing them to Jenny, who had ridden along on her pony. With help from the two of them Ase got the trunk inside and brought in the provisions Betty had amassed for the first month.

"I smell chocolate cream pie," Ase said.

"Let's all have a piece," Susanna said, laughing, and that was her homecoming.

SUSANNA missed Cav as she made her bed, put away books, and hung up her dresses. There was a sound outside, and then, as if the thought had conjured him, Cav thrust his head under her hand and pressed against her with rapturous tail waggings.

"Oh, Cav!" Bending, she hugged him. "Cavalier!"

"His name's Hank." Matt stood just beyond the door. "How are you, Susanna?"

Feeling as if her bones had dissolved and she might crumple like a rag doll, Susanna straightened slowly. "I'm well."

He cleared his throat. "I suppose you've heard my sister's come. Allegedly, she's seeing that I don't live in male squalor. What she really wants is to plague me into setting up shop in Dallas and prescribing tonics and sleeping potions to her high-strung friends."

"If that's so, it's strange she'd build a fine house here."

"Amanda's generous with her money and contributes to many worthy causes, but she hasn't the slightest nostalgia for hardship." He made a rueful grimace. "She's gone to all this trouble, so I can't refuse to live in her home, but she can't stick this out too long. The winter should do it."

By then I'll be leaving, Susanna thought. "Matt," she began. "Please, can't we—"

He raised his scarred hand, held it between them. "Susanna,

249

my love, my darling, I know I must seem a coward to you, but I don't dare risk marrying you. I simply don't dare."

"You—you don't have to."

His eyes went almost black. "Do you think I'd take from you what some men deem the most important thing about a bride and then not give you the protection of my name?"

"But I love you. I'm asking you. You'll owe me nothing."

He turned away. "You're so much braver than I am that you make me ashamed. Let's not talk about it again. This is the last time I'll call you my love. I dare not even kiss you."

He moved away like an old man. She huddled down by Cavalier, held him tight, and wept.

ON THE following day Susanna visited Margaret Hardy.

"Dave and Ethan are planting that red turkey wheat the Krauses gave us," she said. "They've worked like men, and of course Dave almost is—turned sixteen in July. The wheat'll be ready for cutting soon." Her cheeks pinkened. "Jem will help. He doesn't want the boys to miss school."

To a woman with a farm and children that was the kind of wooing that counted. Susanna thought that Margaret would marry soon. She was glad for her. After hard years with a feckless man she deserved someone who'd try to give her a good life.

Susanna on different days walked to visit the Taylors, the Krauses, and the Prades. At Prades', she found Laura's silvery blond head bent over her sewing machine while Sarah mended. The twins were gathering wild plums, and Frank, of course, was in the fields with his father.

Fourteen now, Sarah was tall as Susanna, and with her golden hair, caught back by a ribbon, and her dark-lashed green eyes she was startling. Laura greeted Susanna warmly, but there was a shadow in the violet eyes. She spoke of the promising wheat crop with hope and fear.

"Now that Mr. Prade's heard the Krauses are building frame houses this fall, he's bound we must have one. This crop means so much to him that it—well . . ." She smiled uneasily. "It seems like tempting fate."

When Susanna took her leave, Sarah asked if she might walk a little way with her, and both older women consented.

"I got through *Seventh Reader* this summer," she told Susanna as they walked along. "And I've been studying algebra with Frank."

Susanna said, "That's wonderful, Sarah. You may be able to do eighth-grade work and finish school next spring."

"Oh, do you think I can? I want to get a certificate next summer and find a school."

She would be neither the first nor last fifteen-year-old to teach at a frontier school, but Susanna was disturbed by the desperation in her voice. "Why, dear?"

Drooping her head, Sarah whispered, "You know Father beats Frank. Mother knows Frank gets punished, but she doesn't know how—and we don't ever want her to." Tears formed in her eyes. "I have to get Frank away! He acts like he's dead inside. And that drives Father wild. I'm afraid something awful will happen."

Tears were running down Sarah's face, and Susanna took her in her arms. "Have you tried to talk to your father?"

"Yes," the girl said, drawing away. "His eyes get so strange. I'm scared of him. I can't try again, not even for Frank."

"We'll get you through school," Susanna said, clasping Sarah's hand. "But remember this, dear. If anything happens, come to me. Will you promise?"

Some of the tension eased out of Sarah's body. She gave her word, and turned back with a lighter step.

Susanna went the heavier. If anything happened to either child, she'd never forgive herself. But what could she do?

Eleven

*T*HE next day Susanna was working on lesson plans at her desk when Cav ran in, whining, and tugged at her skirt.

"What is it, boy?" The wind carried a scorched odor. Hurrying outside, Susanna stopped in her tracks. The whole southeastern sky swelled with a roiling cloud of coppery brown across the plains. From miles away the gusting wind brought the acrid smell of burning grass.

Prairie fire. Terror drenched Susanna with cold sweat, but her mind recalled with sharp clarity all she'd ever heard about this scourge of the grasslands. People in soddies or dugouts should be fairly safe. Since the men were in the fields, they'd see the conflagration in time to take shelter with their animals, possibly even plow fireguards around their homes—sets of furrows with a space in between where the fire would have nothing to devour. The unharvested crops would be consumed. There was no time to plow fireguards around acres of grain.

It was out of the question to run. She and Cav would be as safe in the soddy or the barn as anywhere the fire reached. Her gaze fixed on the shingled roof. That would burn. On the realization she ran inside, seized the water bucket, and dashed bucket after bucket upon the low slanted roof. In order to have water ready for dousing flames, she filled the washtubs. With tears streaming from smoke and cinders, she brought up a final bucket of water and dashed for the house as the smoke hid sky and sun.

Panting, Cav at her heels, she barred the door—as if that would keep out this invader! Keeping up a flow of encouragement to the frightened dog that helped calm her as well, Susanna put the china and her favorite books in the trunk. The smoke was thick and strangling. She wet a handkerchief and held it over her eyes and nose. In spite of the thick sod walls, the room began to heat. Bucket at hand, Susanna knelt on the rug beside Cav, breathed through the cloth, and waited.

Were her ears playing tricks or had the fury hurtled past? Susanna crept into the other room, where she reached the window, held her breath, and peered out. Squinting, she could faintly make out the barn, and she could *see* the wind, for it was charged with blackened ash.

Choking, she sank down on the earth again, blessing the sod that had been her refuge. She wouldn't breathe freely, even in clean air, till she knew Matt was safe. She thought of hurrying to see if the Hardys were all right, but the black wind was blinding. Besides, if anyone came looking for her and she was gone, it might set off a frenzied search—the last thing the community needed.

Skimming charred dust off the water in the bucket, Susanna

filled Cav's water bowl and drank some water herself before she began to clean off the food supplies. Anxiety grew in her as she worked, but she knew she'd have to endure it. The men would be fighting the fire, and till it died or was defeated, she wasn't likely to hear anything. She found a relatively clean washcloth and was washing her begrimed face when a rap sounded on the door.

Hurrying to unbar it, she pushed it open. She knew Matt by his eyes, not his blackened face, and went limp. "Oh, Matt!"

They were in each other's arms, clinging as if to make sure they were really there. They held each other a long time; then he kissed her gently and stepped back.

"Hardys are fine—Jem's with them now. We stopped the fire at the bend of the creek beyond Prades', though it burned Ase's school to the ground."

"Is everyone all right?"

"Seem to be."

"Your horses?"

"I got them all in the barn or soddy. Krauses also plowed a fireguard so wide it stopped the fire on that side."

"The crops?"

"Burned. Except at Krauses'. They'd made fireguards around all their fields."

Susanna shook her head. "I wish Saul Prade had saved his crops."

"He's lucky to be alive and have his family and stock safe."

"I'm afraid he won't see it that way. He's already jealous of Krauses. Since they saved their grain, he'll hate them."

Matt shrugged. "Krauses said they'll share their grain with whoever needs it and give seed wheat to anyone who wants to plant this fall. Ase is giving half a beef to every family that lost its crops. No one's going to have to give up."

"Are you hungry?" Susanna asked him.

"I guess I am. Didn't think about it."

"Come in. Wash your face and hands." She stoked the fire, and while the water heated for tea she opened a can of peaches. While he started on that she mixed corn fritters and dropped them into the frying pan. He was ravenous, so it pleased her to set food before him. She was spooning more fritters onto his plate when someone knocked.

It was Ase, blackened as Matt had been. "Wanted to be sure you're all right." His gaze went past her to Matt, who raised a hand.

"Come in and wash up," Susanna said. "Have some fritters and peaches. I'll put on coffee."

"Obliged, but I better get home."

"Sit down, Ase," Matt urged. "You must be as starved as I was."

Susanna put her hand on his shirt. "Please, Mr. McCanless."

His cindery face widened in a smile. "Well, how can I do anything but what you want when you talk nice like that, Miss Susanna? I'll wash outside."

While Ase finished a can of peaches and the remaining fritters, Susanna made more. But when Matt rose to go, Ase jumped up, too. They departed at the same time, riding off in opposite directions into the same stinging haze that thickened what was now really twilight.

Susanna did the dishes and began wiping off the furniture. Black dust would be settling in the house for days, but she had to make a start.

GREETINGS and laughter filled the October air as the children met again after months when most of them had been too busy to visit one another and play.

When the youngsters trooped in and spied the pencil boxes at each place, there was fresh delight. Seeing that most were too excited to settle down at once, Susanna let them stand and sing the Kansas rivers song before she read from Walt Whitman.

"The spelling assignments are on the board," she then told them. "The rest of you study those while I hear seventh-grade reading."

As she had suspected, Sarah, Dave, and Frank could read the last part of the *Seventh Reader* without a mistake. And from the determination in Sarah's and Dave's faces, she knew they'd conquer the eighth-grade work along with seventh. As for Frank, who could tell?

As she heard each child read, Susanna was pleased to find that most of them had gone through their old or next readers during the summer. She was able to do some regrouping, advancing Ridge to *Third Reader* to join Jenny. Comparing the ease of beginning studies this year with last year's confusion, Susanna wondered with a pang who would ring the bell for her children next October. Who would guide them into their next books and watch them grow up?

FALL rains washed away some of the charred prairie stubble and encouraged fresh green growth, like a second spring, before frosts covered the grassland. With a sound roof over her head Susanna enjoyed the rain, but with a tinge of sadness. By next spring, she'd be gone.

Fortunately, teaching left her little time to brood. Berenice and Ethan took up Sarah and Dave's tutoring of younger children. Susanna was able to spend considerable time with Dave, Sarah, and Frank, and it was a joy to encourage such good students.

Susanna's pleasure in her students was marred by only one thing—Saul Prade. When he stopped by the first time, she wasn't concerned. She'd invited parents to visit outside the regular Friday afternoons. But she grew nervous as he began to drop in three times a week and silently observe for fifteen or twenty minutes.

What was his intention? If it had been any other homesteader, she'd have thought he was simply passing time, idled by the loss of the crops. He was the only settler who hadn't planted the Krauses' red turkey seed wheat in his burned fields, so he had little in the way of occupation.

Early in December he came one morning before recess and watched quietly till Susanna dismissed the children. When she started to follow them out, he stepped in front of her.

Fear shot through her. It took all her will not to fall back, but when he spoke, his tone was civil enough. "Seems to me you're spending a lot of time on the older kids, miss."

"I'm trying to make up for last year," she explained. "Because some of the pupils had never been in school before and so many were just starting to read, I tended to let Sarah and Dave study on their own more than I would have if I'd had more time."

He gave her a wintry smile. "Sounds like you're admitting taking on those Dutchies robbed our kids of schooling."

"Every child passed last year. In fact, most did extremely well. If you have any complaints, Mr. Prade, please take them to the trustees. If you'll excuse me . . ."

He stepped aside. "I'll be watching. And someday you'll make a mistake even McCanless can't shrug off."

Susanna drew herself up. "You're a trustee, Mr. Prade, but in future, kindly visit only on Friday afternoons."

Casting her a glance full of hatred, he turned and strode off. Shaken, Susanna steadied herself against the door. Picking up the bell, she rang the children in.

Autumn snow fell, cloaking the ravaged plain. Prade ceased his unnerving visits. Margaret Hardy married Jem Howe. Cobie and Val reported excitedly on the progress of their new homes, and the house where Jacob and Catherine would live was nearing completion.

Susanna had dismissed school one afternoon about a week before Christmas when she heard the rumble of a wagon. All the children were gone except the Prade youngsters, who were waiting while Sarah asked about a complicated geometry problem.

"Just a minute, Sarah." Susanna went outside and found Jacob pulling up with a load of hay.

"The hay in the barn I will put," he said. "But I am come to invite you to our wedding, mine and Catherine's. Two days before Christmas we will be married. To Ase McCanless I have already been. He will stop for you with his buckboard."

"That's wonderful, Jacob. I'll look forward to it." Susanna reached up her hand to shake his. He clucked to the horses, and she returned to help Sarah solve several examples.

When they were finished, she stepped outside with the children to see Saul Prade lash Jacob with a doubled horsehair rope.

"Stop!" Susanna shouted. Sarah cried out, too, and they both ran forward.

Jacob was as big as Prade and much younger, but he didn't try to take the rope away or attack Prade. Advancing, Prade redoubled the rope, slashing at Jacob till the young man reeled.

"Dirty damned Dutchie!" hissed Prade. "You set that fire! Wanted to burn the rest of us out—turn us into your hired men!"

Susanna frantically glanced around for a weapon, found none, and did the only thing she could think of—moved in front of Jacob, protecting him with her body.

Prade checked a moment, arm raised, then with a laughing snarl drew his arm back further and swung the rope. The looped ends wrapped stingingly around Susanna's throat and upper body. With a cry Jacob dragged her away. In the same instant Frank seized his father's wrist. Prade knocked him aside.

Frank went down and got the full force of a mighty swing of the rope. "Raise your hand to me, you whelp?" panted Saul. He kicked the boy, and while Frank doubled up on the ground, gasping, his father swung back the rope.

Susanna knelt over Frank, shielding him, braced for the lashing. It never came.

The glazed look faded from the man's eyes. Breathing heavily, Prade twisted the rope, flung it away. "You're no son of mine," he said to Frank in a choking voice. "I won't have you under my roof! Come on, Sarah, you and the twins."

Sarah hesitated. Frank had managed to get up, though his face was ashen. "Go on, Sarah. I—I'll be all right," he said.

The man stalked off with Sarah. Paul and Pauline trailed behind. "Are you all right?" Susanna asked Frank.

"I—I hurt pretty bad."

Susanna said, "Frank, it probably is a good idea for you to see Dr. Rawdon. Jacob, you'd better let the doctor examine those slashes." She added, "Please, both of you, don't tell anyone that Mr. Prade hit me. It could start a lot more grief than we've already had." When they both nodded assent, she said, "Jacob, I'll ride along with you as far as Howes'. More than likely Jem or Dave will bring Frank back to their place after the doctor sees him."

They arrived at the Howes', and Margaret responded as Susanna was sure she would. "Of course the lad can stay with us." She shook her head. "Poor Laura! What's she going to do? Her man's plain daft, it seems."

Susanna was in fact more worried about Laura and Sarah than

Frank. He was out of Prade's way. But how could Laura live with what her husband had done?

After bidding good-bye to Margaret, Susanna stepped out into the twilight and headed for home. Tomorrow was Friday. She'd have to keep a scarf looped high around her throat and wear one at the wedding, too, which was Saturday. She hoped Jacob knew no one else shared Prade's wild notion that the Mennonites had started the disastrous prairie fire.

Did Prade believe it himself? Was he truly insane? If he was, what would he do next? Was she endangering other people by trying to keep his behavior at least partly secret?

Susanna had crossed the creek and was halfway to the soddy when she heard a horse coming. In a moment a rider loomed against the lighter, lower rim of the sky that met the dark horizon.

"Susanna?"

It was Matt. A rush of warm gladness filled her. "Is Frank all right?" she asked.

"He will be. Dave's taking him home."

"Jacob?"

"His face'll be bruised and puffed up awhile. Nothing serious." They had reached the school. He swung down from Saladin. "Come in, Susanna. I'm having a look at you."

"They said they wouldn't tell!"

"They didn't tell. But Jacob, don't forget, can't tell a lie. When I asked point-blank if Prade had hurt you, he could only mumble that he couldn't answer that. Come here."

She moved reluctantly forward and obeyed his motion to sit down near the lamp. He tilted her head back. The black pupils swelled over the gray of his eyes as he peered and touched, but his tone was professionally detached. "Can you swallow?"

"I haven't tried."

He filled a glass with water and handed it to her. "Try it."

Her throat knotted and ached throbbingly, but the water went down. "Now your chest and shoulders."

She slipped down the bodice. Like his voice, his examining hands were cool and disciplined.

"Nothing but bruising and contusions," he said, helping her

slip her arms back down the sleeves. "He could have killed you, though, with that blow across your trachea."

The cold rage in his voice terrified her. "Matt, you—you won't do anything?"

"What I would do, were it not for Laura Prade and four nice youngsters, is put a bullet in his head." Matt strode to the door and turned. "What I will do is ride over and tell that murderous lunatic that if I hear he's troubled you again, I'll kill him as if he were a rabid dog."

"But Laura . . ."

"I have compassion for her, Susanna, but if that man were dead, she'd surely find a better one. She couldn't find worse."

His hand was on the door. Seeing her fright, his gaunt face softened. "So you won't worry, I'll ride past on my way home. I won't come in, just call a good-night."

She caught in a relieved breath. "Thank you."

Matt not only called a good-night several hours later, but shouted through the door, "Prade knows he's earned a hanging. I think he'll be damned careful from now on."

It was a long time since Susanna'd had night terrors, but now she did, wave after wave of images. At last she lit the lamp, and found refuge in a book until morning.

BEFORE class next day Sarah hurried to Susanna and whispered, "How are you, Miss Alden?"

"Fine. I suppose Dr. Rawdon told you that Frank will be all right."

"Yes." Sarah kept her beautiful eyes lowered as if in shame. "Daddy told Mother Jacob caused a fight and Frank came in on Jacob's side. When Mother wanted to go to Frank, he told her if she did, not to come back. I got her away, and I told her Frank and I are going away next spring. She—she cried and held me, but finally she said maybe that was best." Sarah's voice broke. "I'm so ashamed of what happened! And I'm so worried for Mother."

"She has you and that's a lot."

Green eyes somber, the girl said, "She won't have me long."

For that Susanna had no answer.

259

Twelve

SNOW fell softly all Friday night, but the day of Catherine and Jacob's wedding dawned bright and radiant. The service would be at noon, conducted by Anselm, who was both the elder and the minister of the small Mennonite congregation, and the feast would follow.

Peter and Frederick Krause, Val, and Jacob met guests as they arrived, and showed them where to leave their vehicles. The barns had roofed storage shelters in between them, and within this protected area several large stacks of hay had been heaped up so the guests' animals could feed.

A way had been cleared from the barns to the middle one of the three identical square white houses trimmed in green. This was the home of Anna and Frederick, Catherine's parents. The Krause women, including Cobie, and a glowing Catherine in her white bride's dress, made their neighbors welcome, accepting the gifts everyone had brought with gracious thanks. Susanna handed Catherine the wrapped ruby cut-glass creamer-and-sugar set.

Benches, chairs, and tables had been carried in from the other houses. The tables, spread with snowy cloths, held platters of cheese, sausages and ham, all manner of pickles and preserves, and mounds of bread, cakes, rice pudding, and dozens of pies. Guests were offered tea or coffee, and then stood visiting.

Matt Rawdon came in with his sister. Few of the gathering had met her, and Amanda was instantly the focus of attention. She shrugged her velvet cloak into Matt's hands, accepted a cup of tea from Catherine, and wished her joy on her wedding day.

Sipping her tea, Amanda studied the furnishings of the room, very much the fairy-tale dowager queen, in iridescent deep green taffeta. Golden hair was swept up and secured with a large lace-and-taffeta bow. The elegant gown whispered Paris or London, and Susanna was painfully conscious that the blue dress she'd been so proud of had been stitched by her inexpert hands.

Matt presented his sister to the women. She acknowledged them all with perfect courtesy, but she looked astonished when

Hettie Brown seized her hand and gave it a vigorous pumping.

Then Anselm appeared for the first time, and Jacob addressed the crowd. "Dear neighbors, glad we are you have come. Elder Krause, our minister, will perform the service in German, but we will tell you in English when it is time to feast!"

The ripple of laughter quieted as Anselm spoke with loving seriousness to his granddaughter and her bridegroom. He then pronounced them man and wife. There was a long, reverent moment. Jacob, his bride's hand in his, turned, and the weals and bruises on his face couldn't obscure his joy.

"Please." He spread his hand toward the laden tables. "You are welcome, good neighbors and friends!"

As a close friend, Susanna was invited to sit with Jacob and Catherine, her parents, and Anselm. Tempting as the food was, she had no appetite, but talked with Anna and the beatific Catherine. It was a relief to her when Freda served final cups of coffee and the honored guests could blend into the crowd. Susanna was joining the ladies, who were clustering by the stove, when Anselm addressed her in German.

"Professorin! Will you please to come with me? Get your mantle, for we must go to the barn."

Puzzled, Susanna excused herself and, wrapped in her mantle, went out with the elder, who marched down to the last barn, which was across the courtyard from the new houses. Motioning her around behind the manger, Anselm pointed at the back of it. "Look. This is what the boy does when he should be working!"

The broad expanse was a mural done in pastels. Obviously Val hadn't expected anyone else to go behind the mangers, since it would be his task to fill them. He had drawn horses, some caught in motion, with tails and manes flying. At the far end was Michelangelo's Creator God, white beard and hair flowing, as in the Sistine painting Susanna had shown Val.

"See?" Anselm tried to scowl, but pride shone through. "He has drawn me, Professorin! Is it not a likeness?"

"Indeed it is, Elder Krause." Susanna wasn't about to tell him about the model. "Valentine has a rare gift."

"But Mennonites—we farm the land." Anselm tugged at his

beard. "Artists loaf and drink. We'll have none of that among us."

"God has surely given Valentine this talent," Susanna reasoned in her most persuasive tone. "I don't think you have to worry about Valentine turning into a wastrel. Some artists—"

A tall figure rose from behind the manger and, at the same instant, clubbed the unsuspecting Anselm from the back with a shovel. Susanna's scream, as she turned to run, was stifled by Prade's hands clamping her throat in an iron grip. He smelled strongly of kerosene. What had he been doing? she wondered.

She clawed for his eyes, but he squeezed till the world spun black. He hurled her down, and she knew dimly that he was gagging her and knotting ropes around her wrists and ankles.

Through flashing explosions his face wavered before her. "I'll be back and set you afire with the hay," he said. "Think about burning, you devil bitch, you who set my son against me! Stay there and think about it while I burn those new frame houses. I'll teach those Dutchies to fire my wheat." He laughed eerily, caught Anselm under the arms, and hauled the limp body outside.

Still giddy from strangulation, Susanna struggled with the ropes, but they gave not a fraction, so tightly was she lashed. Some way to give a warning . . . some way to stop Prade . . .

Struggling to her knees, she advanced. She couldn't walk; she couldn't use her hands. The knees supporting her gave the answer. She would crawl. It was the only chance.

Susanna struggled forward on elbows and knees, using her weight to thrust herself along. Prade hadn't thought it necessary to bar the door. It yielded at a push from her shoulder.

Blinded by light, Susanna lurched onto the cleared frozen ground. If only someone would step outside or glance through a window! It was all too likely, though, that it would be Prade who'd see her as he ran from lighting one house across to the other. Anselm lay crumpled before her. She couldn't see his face, but his breathing was quick and stertorous.

Susanna inched along. The houses seemed an infinite distance away. In a grotesque race she forced herself on, past the second soddy barn, past the first new house, sobbing for breath. She smelled kerosene strongly now.

"Damn you!" Prade sprang out of the door of the house at the end, flames leaping behind him, a torch in his hand.

With frenzied strength Susanna heaved to her knees and slammed her bound hands into the lowest windowpane. Glass shattered. The laughter stopped. Then Prade seized her wrists and dragged her toward the nearest haystack. He bent to grip her and toss her into the center. With all her might she threw her body sideways against him, knocking him backward, the torch still in his hand. When the fire touched the dry hay, it fairly exploded as it engulfed Prade. Susanna rolled toward the snow surrounding the stack.

The flames and Matt reached her at the same time. Her hair and clothing blazed, but he buried her in the snow as the stack flared into a withering inferno. Men threw snow on the blaze, but nothing could stop it, so they ran to battle the fire in the end house. The flames were nearly vanquished by the time it took Matt to determine Susanna's hurts, cut the ropes from her bleeding wrists and ankles, and carry her into the house, where a bed was readied.

So dazed that she scarcely knew what was happening, except that Anselm had been found and was being supported into the house by his sons, Susanna clung to Matt as he lowered her to the pillows. "It's all right, my love," he told her very softly. Gently disengaging her, he said, "I'm going to see how Anselm is."

Betty and Margaret took off Susanna's mantle and worked off her dress. Her garments had protected her, though her knees and elbows were abraded. They shooed her into bed, pulling up the covers, then went out. Matt returned.

She pulled the quilt to her chin. "How is Elder Krause?"

"He'll just have a headache for a day or two." He studied her with an expert eye. "In my experience the best treatment for minor burns is immersion in cold water, and I've asked Catherine and her mother to bring several basins."

Matt arranged the pillows so that Susanna could lower her face to the one basin and rest her hands in the other.

Cobie ran in with the news that the fire in the house was out and the haystack blaze was flickering its last. Susanna went sick at the thought of vestiges of what had been Saul Prade charred to blackened bones.

She raised her head at Ase McCanless's voice, demanding of Matt how she was. "I'm all right," she answered for herself.

"Is she, Doc?"

Matt nodded. "I don't think the burns will leave scars, except maybe on her right hand. It got the worst of it."

"You think she can travel? I can take her to my place."

"I'd better see to her." As Ase hesitated Matt added, "Don't worry. She won't be left alone as long as she needs me."

That would be forever, Susanna thought. A warm glow filled her at the way Matt was taking charge of her.

Guests taking their leave poked their heads into the bedroom to inquire after Susanna. Amanda stepped in, shook her head, and commiserated with Susanna before turning to Matt.

"Have you done all you can for Miss Alden?" A nice way of saying she wanted him to take her home.

"If you're in a hurry, ride with the Howes," he suggested. "I'm taking Miss Alden home."

Amanda raised her eyebrows. "Are you indeed?"

"We'll be glad to drop you off, ma'am," offered Ase.

Amanda gave Susanna a long, considering look. "You were very brave, Miss Alden. But for you, some of us would surely have perished. Thank you for what you did."

Astounded at this handsome speech, Susanna said faintly, "Anyone would have done it."

"Fiddlesticks!" Amanda turned to her brother. "Take good care of her, Matthew, and send if I can do anything." She took Ase's arm and swept out in an opulent rustle.

Matt and Susanna exchanged startled glances. Then he studied her hands and face. "Do the burns still hurt?"

"Not much."

"I think we'll get along, then, and have you in your own bed before dark. Doctor's orders."

Jacob and Catherine bundled Susanna into Matt's carriage in soft feather beds.

Anselm, head bandaged, said in German, "God protect you,

264

gracious lady. With his help you were the instrument of our salvation." He smiled at Val. "If I had not taken you to see the work of this artist of ours . . . Yes, the hand of our Lord is surely in it."

"Just settle back and rest," Matt advised her.

Reveling in the bliss of being looked after, Susanna sighed and closed her eyes. She woke to Cav's joyful barking. Dashing from the barn, where he napped on the rare occasions when she went somewhere without him, he danced along as Matt lifted Susanna, feather beds and all, and carried her into the house.

"Stay in those till the place warms up," he commanded, depositing her on the bed and building up the fire from the few remaining banked coals. "I'll take care of the team and be right back."

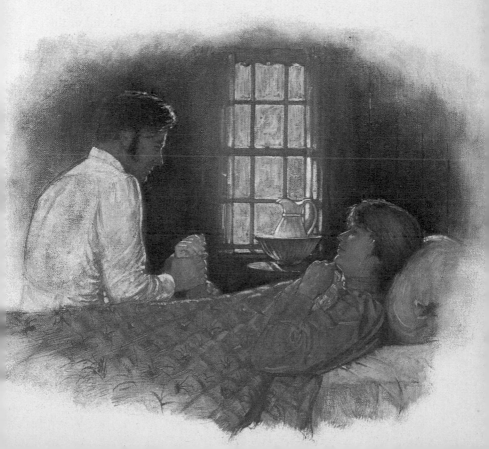

When he returned, he put more fuel on the fire, lit the lamp, and pulled the curtains on the twilight.

Susanna watched him with a mixture of dismay and pleasure. He behaved so exactly as if he were at home! If only he were. He asked prosaically, "Anything we can heat up for supper?"

"How about potato-and-onion soup?" Susanna asked. "It's in the kettle just inside the schoolroom."

"Another feast." He grinned. "I recommend that you put on your nightgown while I step into the other room."

He went into the schoolroom, followed by Cav. Susanna made haste to extract her nightgown and climb under her own quilts.

"Ready?" called Matt.

She made a noncommittal sound. What was he going to do?

He sat on the edge of the bed and took her hand, careful of the burns. "Susanna, you deserve better . . . but will you have me?"

"You—you mean—"

"I mean, will you marry me?"

"Oh, Matt! Are you sure?"

"Before I knew how badly you were burned, while I thought your face might be permanently changed, I knew it wouldn't matter to me. I love *you*—what's under the skin. You're a lot better and kinder and wiser than I am, Susanna. If I felt that way, I had to believe you did."

At first they embraced like survivors after a disaster, but after a time he shifted to seek her mouth. Susanna slipped free of the quilts to mold closer to him. With a groan he wrested his mouth from hers and held her against his shoulder.

"Now I have to be as careful of your reputation as I once accused Yankee schoolmarms of being," he murmured against her ear. "It'll be hard, but we can wait because, my love, my beloved Yankee, we're going to have our whole life long together."

He finished with a kiss. "That's our ration for the evening," he said, rising. "We're going to eat, and then I'm tucking you in." At the question in her eyes, he said, "As your doctor, it's my opinion that you shouldn't be alone tonight. I'll put benches together in the schoolroom and repair to them with the feather beds."

Matt brought her soup on a tray and carefully poured tea into

Grandmother Alden's cups. Lifting his to her, he said in a voice that reached and warmed her heart, "Here's to our life, Susanna. Here's to our love."

AFTER a Christmas morning kiss Matt went to see to his horses while Susanna dressed, and together they made breakfast. She had made no present for him, but before they started their meal, he took something out of a compartment in his wallet. It was a broad gold band etched with leaves and flowers.

"My mother's wedding ring," he explained. "I know you can't wear it on your finger yet, but maybe you'll wear it on a ribbon or chain around your neck."

Susanna looked up from the golden band and smiled at Matt. "It's the most beautiful ring in the world." She took his scarred hand, pressed it to her breast, and then to her lips.

ON THE last day of Christmas vacation Matt came by with a pretty bay mare saddled for Susanna. It was so wonderful to be riding with Matt that in spite of dreading what lay ahead, Susanna's spirits rose, and rose even more when he told her Amanda was preparing to move back to Dallas.

"She'll stay for our wedding, though," he said. "And she wants to give us the house for a wedding present. It seems big and formal now, but some children should take care of that."

Susanna shook her head in wonderment. "Is it true? We're going to have a house? We're going to have children?"

"We're going to have a home," he said, and rode close, kissing her thoroughly.

They bantered, and Susanna told him that among other neighbors, Ase had stopped by to say that Frank was a changed boy, taking his place as man of the family. After an interval Catherine and Jacob would visit Laura, but except for Delia, the other neighbors had already called and shown their wish to help.

"I doubt if that would have happened if folks hadn't gotten to know each other on your visitors' afternoons," Matt said. "This wasn't a community till you came, Susanna. You made us one."

Overcome at such praise, Susanna said, "I've only done my job."

Chuckling tenderly at her, Matt mercifully changed the subject. "Say, isn't that Ase's horse out in front of Prades'?"

It was. Laura and Sarah had been mending by the fire while Frank, in his father's big chair, read *Gulliver's Travels* to the twins, who perched on either side. The coiled bullwhip was gone. Ase, who was standing by the fire with a cup of coffee, seemed a bit flustered, but he smiled at Susanna in a warm fond way that told her they would always be friends. She remembered that he'd always admired Laura. Who knew? Ase might not have to go to St. Louis to look for a bride.

"Good to see you out, Miss Alden, ma'am. Don't forget. The board of trustees is meetin' at the school this afternoon." Draining his cup, Ase picked up his hat, and Laura saw him to the door. Then, with a look at Susanna that asked her to follow, she went into a bedroom. The two women looked at each other a moment. Then they were in each other's arms, weeping.

At last, straightening, Laura said, "It sounds terrible, but it's a relief to have it over. I've known Saul was changing, and after the wheat burned . . . Well, he got the way his father was before he went insane and killed himself." She stared out the window at the plains. "Do you think I ought to leave, Miss Alden? Take the children where no one will know?"

"I think you belong here. Now more than ever."

Laura gave her a slight swift smile of thanks, and they returned to the others.

AFTER a quick bowl of soup and some slow kisses Matt had to go. She watched him ride off, glowingly aware of the ring suspended on the chain between her breasts. Very soon now she would wear it on her finger. She had written to Aunt Mollie and Uncle Frank, asking them to come to Kansas for the wedding. Even with mail's vagaries, she hoped to have an answer back in time to marry late in January or early the next month.

Closing the door, she dusted the desks and polished the globe stand. The trustees would meet at two, so she put on fresh coffee.

At the rumble of a wagon, she looked out to find Ase assisting Betty from the buckboard while Johnny clambered down and

Jenny unsaddled Scout. Susanna had scarcely exchanged hugs with Betty when the Howes pulled up, the whole Brown clan came riding across the prairie, and the Tarrants appeared from the south. Here came the Taylors from the north, and behold, three small green Mennonite wagons were splashing across the creek.

"Ase McCanless," Susanna demanded, "what's going on?"

His eyes danced. "Hold your horses, Miss Alden, ma'am. Soon's everybody gets here, you'll know all about it." Susanna hurried to greet the newcomers, all of whom carried food, as Matt drove up with Amanda, helped her out, and grinned at Susanna.

While he drove toward the barn and unhitched the horses, Amanda came in, advanced on Susanna, and took both her hands. "I'm glad to see you recovered from your ordeal, my dear." She lowered her voice. "I regret, of course, that Matthew won't be coming back to Dallas, but I can see that he's made a place for himself here, just as you have. I do wish you happiness."

"Thank you." Susanna looked into her future sister-in-law's eyes and thought that in time they might become fond of each other. "You're very dear to Matt, you know. It's kind and generous to give us your lovely house. I hope that you'll often come to visit us."

"I will," Amanda promised, "but I won't wear out my welcome." As Matt entered, an air of expectancy filled the room.

Ase stepped to the door and bellowed, "Hey, you kids! We're ready!"

The youngsters hurried in and gathered around Freck, who had his guitar. They launched into "Kansas Land." Then to Susanna's surprise, for these songs had never been sung in the school, the children—northerners, southerners, and Mennonites—sang "Dixie" and "The Battle Hymn of the Republic."

Unable to believe her ears, and then believing, seeming to see her father's smile and hear him say, Well done, my daughter, she was overcome and bowed her head. Tears ran down her cheeks. Matt gave her a handkerchief, and as the voices stilled she saw that his eyes were suspiciously bright.

Looking at her students, knowing and loving each face, Susanna couldn't speak on her first effort. But she swallowed hard and managed to say, "Thank you so very very much."

"Just one more thing before we eat," Ase said. He stepped out and returned in a moment with a large varnished cedar sign.

They held it up. Flowers and birds were carved all around the border. In the middle, large letters read SUSANNA SCHOOL.

"Guess Mason-Dixon don't fit us anymore," Ase said. "Now, folks, soon as we hang that sign over the door, Elder Krause's goin' to bless us, and we'll set down to dinner."

The children flocked around Susanna. "We practiced at noon and recess," Freck explained proudly. "Did you like it, ma'am?"

She shook her head. "Oh, Freck, I can't tell you how much I liked it. This—this must be the happiest day of all my life." She kissed him and he colored over his freckles. Dave looked eager, so she kissed him, too, and by the time she'd hugged and kissed all of them, the sign was pronounced satisfactorily hung. The crowd hushed as Elder Krause gave a blessing in German—and then, incredibly, prayed in English.

As guest of honor, Susanna was compelled to go first to fill her plate, but as she was hustled forward she glanced up at Matt. "I— I'm so happy I don't think I can stand it!"

"Wait," he promised. "You're going to be happier."

The light in his eyes and her own heart made her believe him.

"I believe teaching is the most important job in the world," says Jeanne Williams. "It affects our children, and they are our future. And I think that the profession is underappreciated. A true teacher has a definite talent. She's always there—we just don't hear about what she does. That's what I wanted to show in *No Roof But Heaven*."

Jeanne Williams

This prolific author of fifty-two books also believes that the frontier backdrop of the Kansas prairie, with its beauty and unpredictability, makes the experiences of her heroine, Susanna Alden, all the more vivid. In fact, Kansas is a favorite locale for her. A previous novel set in the Sunflower State, *Lady of No Man's Land,* was a Condensed Books selection in 1988.

Not surprisingly, Jeanne Williams was born in Elkhart, Kansas, and raised by grandparents who were homesteaders and a father who was a cowboy. In her teens she attended a one-room schoolhouse not much different from the one in *No Roof But Heaven*. "It had a potbelly stove," the author recalls, "and we carried water and used two privies. It was very similar to the old, old days!"

The late nineteenth century, when her heroine arrives at the Mason-Dixon School, is also a significant time in Kansas history, the author adds. "Southern ranchers spread up from Texas while Union soldiers were coming in and homesteading at the same time."

For her next novel Jeanne Williams has moved even farther west, to the Arizona Territory in the 1880s. The book is set in a region she knows well, for it is where she and her husband live today. The heroine is a young woman who is "pretty independent." Adds the author, "To me, women actually *were* the frontier. Until they came, there were no communities. The women wanted a school and a church, and they needed stores. And that is what really changed the West."

THE EVENING
NEWS

ARTHUR HAILEY

They are the stars of a national
television news show: Crawford Sloane,
the polished, assured anchorman; and
Harry Partridge, Sloane's colleague since
their days as Vietnam War correspondents.
Off-camera these men share one other
thing: an intense love for the same
woman—Jessica, Crawford Sloane's wife.
And when, abruptly, Jessica becomes
a pawn in a terrorist's game, both men
find themselves in a brutal, fearsome
world, a world where power is all
and life is cheap.

A drama as fast-breaking as
tonight's news, bristling with the
authenticity that is the trademark
of this premier storyteller.

PART ONE

Chapter 1

AT CBA Television News headquarters in New York the initial report of a stricken Airbus A300, on fire and approaching Dallas–Fort Worth International Airport, came only minutes before the network's first feed of the *National Evening News*.

It was six twenty-one p.m. eastern daylight time when CBA's bureau chief at Dallas told a producer on the New York Horseshoe through a speakerphone, "We're expecting a big aircraft crash at DFW any moment. There's been a midair collision—a small plane and an airbus with a full passenger load. The small plane went down. The airbus is on fire and trying to make it in. The police and ambulance radios are going wild."

"Jeez!" another Horseshoe producer said. "What's our chance of getting pictures?"

The Horseshoe, an outsized desk with seating for twelve people, was where the network's flagship news broadcast was planned and nurtured from early each weekday morning until the last second of airtime every night. Over at rival CBS they called it the Fishbowl, at ABC the Rim, at NBC the Desk. But whatever name was used, the meaning was the same.

Here, reputedly, were the network's best brains when it came to making judgments and decisions about news: executive producer, anchorman, senior producers, director, editors, writers, graphics chief and their ranking aides. There were also half a dozen computer terminals, wire service printers, a phalanx of state-of-the-art telephones, and TV monitors on which could be called up instantly anything from unedited tape, to a prepared news segment ready for broadcast, to competitors' transmissions.

The Horseshoe was on the fourth floor of the CBA News building in a central open area, with offices on one side for senior staff members. Presiding at the head of the often frenzied Horseshoe was Chuck Insen, executive producer. Lean and peppery, he was a veteran newsman at age fifty-two, and elderly by TV standards, though he showed no sign of diminished energy even after four years in a job that often burned people out in two. Chuck Insen could be curt and often was; he never suffered fools or small talk. One reason: under the pressures of his job there wasn't time.

At this moment—it was a Wednesday in mid-September— pressures were at maximum intensity. Since early morning the lineup of subjects for the *National Evening News* had been reviewed, debated, amended and decided. Correspondents and producers around the world had contributed ideas and received instructions. In the process the day's news had been whittled down to eight reports averaging two minutes each, plus two voice-overs and four tell stories. A voice-over was the anchorman speaking over pictures; a tell story, the anchorman without pictures. For both, the average was twenty seconds.

Now, suddenly, because of the breaking story from Dallas, it had become necessary to reshape the entire news lineup. Though no one knew how much more information would come in or if pictures would be available, at least one item had to be dropped, others shortened, and the sequence of stories changed. The broadcast would start while rearrangement was continuing. It often happened that way.

"We'll go with Dallas at the top." The crisp order came from Insen. "Crawf will do a tell story. Do we have wire copy yet?"

"AP just in. I have it." The answer was from Crawford Sloane, the anchorman. He was reading an Associated Press bulletin handed to him moments earlier.

Sloane, whose familiar craggy features, gray-flecked hair, jutting jaw and authoritative yet reassuring manner were watched by some seventeen million people every weeknight, was in his usual privileged seat on the executive producer's right. He, too, was a news veteran and had climbed the promotion ladder steadily, especially after exposure as a CBA correspondent in Vietnam. Now, after three years in the nightly anchor slot, he was a national institution, one of the media elite.

In a few minutes Sloane would leave for the broadcast studio one floor below. Meanwhile, for his tell story he would draw on what had already come from Dallas plus some additional facts in the AP report. He would compose it himself. Not every anchor wrote his own material, but Sloane liked to do it when possible. Right now he had to do it fast.

Insen's raised voice could be heard again. He was telling one of his three senior producers, "Kill Saudi Arabia. Take fifteen seconds out of Nicaragua."

Sloane maneuvered his swivel chair backward to confront a computer keyboard. Concentrating, mentally shutting out the commotion around him, he tapped out the opening sentences of tonight's broadcast.

From Dallas–Fort Worth. This word just in on what may be a tragedy in the making. Minutes ago there was a midair collision between two passenger planes over the town of Gainesville, Texas, north of Dallas. One was a heavily loaded airbus of Muskegon Airlines. The other plane—a small one, it's believed— went down. There is no word on its fate or of casualties. The airbus is still in the air but on fire as its pilots attempt to reach Dallas–Fort Worth Airport for a landing. On the ground, fire fighters and ambulance crews are standing by. . . .

Sloane added a sentence telling viewers to stay tuned for further developments, then hit a key for printout. By the time he reached the broadcast studio, the tell story would be ready for him to read from the TelePrompTer screen.

As Sloane headed for the stairs, Insen was demanding of a senior producer, "Damn it, what about pictures from DFW?"

"Chuck, it doesn't look good." The producer, a phone cradled in his shoulder, was talking to the national editor. "The burning airplane is nearing the airport, but our camera crew is twenty miles away. They won't make it in time."

Insen swore in frustration.

The executive producer had a philosophy about those millions out there who watched the evening news. What they wanted, Insen believed, were the answers to three questions: Is the world safe? Are my home and family safe? Did anything interesting happen today? Above all else, he tried to ensure that the news each evening supplied those answers.

Right now he was tight-lipped and unsmiling. The question of the moment was, Will there or won't there be a story soon, with pictures, from DFW?

IF MEDALS were awarded for dangerous service in the field of television, Ernie LaSalle, the national editor, would have had a chestful. A small, energetic man of only twenty-nine, he had served with distinction as a CBA field producer in Lebanon, Iran, Angola, Nicaragua and other messy places. Nowadays LaSalle viewed the domestic American scene, which could be equally messy at times, from a comfortable chair in a glass-paneled office that looked out on the main newsroom.

As national editor, LaSalle's responsibilities were large. He was one of two senior functionaries in the newsroom; the other was the foreign editor. Both had newsroom desks, which they occupied when any particular story became hot.

The newsroom was one floor below the Horseshoe, next to the broadcast studio, which used the bustling newsroom as its visual backdrop. Viewers had the illusion that the anchorman was in, and part of, the newsroom. But, in fact, there was thick sound-proof glass between the two so that no newsroom noises intruded. A control room, where a director put the technical components together, was in the news-building basement.

It was now seven minutes since the Dallas bureau chief had first reported the wounded airbus approaching DFW. LaSalle slammed down one phone and picked up another, at the same time reading a computer screen on which a new AP report had just appeared. He would continue to cover the story and keep the

Horseshoe advised of developments. From his newsroom desk he could see the usual prebroadcast action in the brightly lit studio as Crawford Sloane came in. The time was six twenty-eight p.m., two minutes before first-feed air.

As SLOANE slipped into the anchor-desk chair, facing the center camera of three, a makeup girl moved in. Sloane had had makeup applied ten minutes ago, but since then he had been sweating. Now the girl mopped his forehead, dabbed on powder, ran a comb through his hair, and applied a touch of hair spray.

Sloane murmured, "Thanks, Nina," then glanced over his papers, checking that the opening words of his tell story on top corresponded with those displayed in large letters on the Tele-PrompTer in front of him, from which he would read while appearing to look directly at viewers. The papers, which newsreaders were often seen to shuffle, were a precaution, for use only if the TelePrompTer failed.

The studio floor manager called out loudly, "One minute!"

IN THE newsroom Ernie LaSalle suddenly sat up straight, attentive, startled. What the Dallas bureau chief was reporting on the phone caused him to smile broadly.

LaSalle picked up a red reporting telephone that connected him through amplified speakers to every section of the news operation. "National desk. LaSalle. Good news. We now have immediate coverage at DFW Airport. Partridge, Abrams and Canh are on to the story and running. Abrams just reported to the Dallas bureau. More: A mobile satellite van has abandoned another assignment and is en route to DFW, expected soonest. We expect pictures in time for the first-feed news."

A muffled cheer drifted down the open stairway from the Horseshoe above. Crawford Sloane, in the studio, swung around and gave LaSalle a cheerful thumbs-up.

An aide put a paper in front of the national editor, who glanced at it, then continued on the speakerphone, "Also from Abrams, this report about the passengers . . ."

When LaSalle finished reading, he thought, Everything that

had come from Dallas in the past few minutes was totally professional. But then it was not surprising, since the team of Abrams, Partridge and Canh was one of the crack combinations of CBA News. Rita Abrams, once a correspondent and now a senior field producer, was noted for her quick assessment of situations and a resourcefulness in getting stories back. Harry Partridge was one of the best correspondents in the business. He normally specialized in war stories and, like Crawford Sloane, had reported from Vietnam, but he could be relied on to do an exceptional job in any situation. And cameraman Minh Van Canh, a Vietnamese who was now an American citizen, was noted for his fine pictures, sometimes shot in dangerous situations with disregard for his own safety.

By now it was a minute past the half hour, and the *National Evening News* had begun. Reaching for a control beside his desk, LaSalle turned up the audio of an overhead monitor and heard Crawford Sloane doing the top-of-the-news tell story about DFW. On-camera a hand slipped a paper in front of him—the report LaSalle had just dictated. Glancing down and ad-libbing, Sloane incorporated it into his prepared text. It was the kind of thing the anchorman did superbly.

UPSTAIRS at the Horseshoe the mood had changed. Now, though pressure and urgency remained, there was cheerful optimism that the Dallas situation was well in hand. Chuck Insen and others were huddled, watching monitors, arguing, making decisions, squeezing out seconds, doing still more cutting and rearranging to leave the needed space. There was a sense of everyone doing what he did best—coping in a time-confined, exigent situation.

Swift exchanges, jargon loaded, flowed back and forth.

"This piece is picture poor."

"Make that copy shorter, pithy."

"The last fifteen seconds of that piece is deadly. Drop it."

"First segment just finished. Have gone to commercial. We're forty seconds heavy."

"Take out that sequence. It does nothing."

An observer unfamiliar with the scene might wonder, Are these people human? Don't they care? Have they no feelings of involvement, not an ounce of grief? Have any of them spared a thought for the nearly three hundred terrified souls on that airplane who may shortly die?

And someone knowledgeable about news would answer, Yes, they will care, maybe right after the broadcast. Or, when some have reached home, the horror of it all will touch them, and depending on how it all turns out, a few may weep. At this moment, though, no one has the time. These are newspeople. Their job is to record the passing parade, the bad with the good, and to do it swiftly, efficiently and plainly.

FOR the group of four journalists at Dallas–Fort Worth Airport the day had begun in predawn darkness, when they had left El Salvador and flown to Mexico City; then they had traveled onward to DFW.

The four were Harry Partridge, Rita Abrams, Minh Van Canh and Ken O'Hara, the CBA crew's sound man. All were weary from two months of rough and dangerous living while reporting on several nasty wars in Latin America. Now, in a bar in terminal 2E, they were awaiting flight connections to different destinations.

Partridge, a tall and lanky figure, had an untidy shock of fair hair that made him look boyish, despite his forty-odd years and the fact that his hair was graying. At this moment he was relaxed and expecting to leave, a few minutes from now, on an American Airlines flight to Toronto. He had ahead of him three weeks of sorely needed rest.

Rita Abrams' connecting flight would be to Minneapolis–St. Paul, from where she was headed for a holiday on a friend's farm in Minnesota. A tough woman who was as demanding of herself as of those she worked with, she had a weekend rendezvous planned there with a married senior CBA official, a piece of information she was keeping to herself. Minh Van Canh and Ken O'Hara were going home to New York. Canh was a quiet, sturdy figure, not much more than five feet tall, with wide brown eyes that looked out impassively from his dark pockmarked face. The trio of Partridge, Abrams and Canh was a frequent working combination. On their most recent trip O'Hara had been with them, as sound recordist, for the first time. He was young, pale and pencil thin. Around them all lay the cameras and equipment on which the CBA logo was prominent.

Rita was forty-three, and six years ago was still appearing on-camera as a news correspondent, though far less often than when she was younger and more glamorous. Everyone knew it was a rotten, unfair system that allowed men to continue facing the camera as they grew older, whereas women were shunted aside. A few women had tried to beat the system, but Rita, instead of starting a fight she knew she wouldn't win, had switched to producing, and had been triumphantly successful. Along the way she'd gotten some tough foreign assignments. Now she was sent automatically—along with Harry—to where the fighting was fiercest and the living hardest.

Partridge became aware of some activity nearby. Two of the airport's department of public safety officers had walked into the bar casually but had suddenly become attentive. They were listening to an announcement over their walkie-talkies. Partridge caught the words "midair collision . . . approaching runway one seven left. . . . All DPS personnel report . . . ." Abruptly, hurrying, the officers left.

The others in the group had heard too. Rita jumped up. "I'll find out what's happening." She left the bar hurriedly, and Canh and O'Hara began to gather their cameras and sound gear.

One of the DPS officers was still in sight. Rita caught up with him. "I'm from CBA News." She showed her network press card. "What's going on? It's urgent, isn't it?"

The officer hesitated. "You're supposed to call the public information office—"

Rita said impatiently, "I'll do that later. Tell me."

"Muskegon Airlines is in trouble. One of their airbuses had a midair. It's coming in on fire. We're on Alert Two, which means all the emergency stuff is rolling, heading hard for runway one seven left." His voice was serious. "Looks pretty bad."

"I want my camera crew out there. Now and fast." Rita knew

they would not get far without an escort. She pointed to the officer's walkie-talkie. "Can you call public information?"

"I could."

"Do it. *Please!*"

Her persuasion worked. The officer called and was answered. He explained her request, but Rita gestured to the walkie-talkie. "Let me speak."

The DPS officer pressed a TRANSMIT button and held the radio out. Rita spoke urgently into the mike. "We're network. We'll do any paperwork you want afterward. But please, *please*, get us to the scene now."

"Stand by." A pause, then a new voice with crisp authority. "Okay, get to gate nineteen fast. Look for a station wagon with flashing lights. I'm on my way to you."

Rita squeezed the officer's arm. "Thanks, pal!"

She hurried back to Partridge and the others. Briskly she related what she had learned. "This could be big. Go out on the airfield. I'll do some phoning, then come to find you." She glanced at her watch: five twenty, six twenty p.m. in New York. "If we're fast, we can make the first feed."

Partridge nodded, accepting Rita's orders. Officially, a field producer such as Rita Abrams was in charge of an entire crew, including the correspondent. However, in the case of a "big foot" senior correspondent like Harry Partridge, the official pecking order sometimes got turned around, with the correspondent taking charge. But when Partridge and Rita worked together, neither gave a damn about status. They simply wanted to send back the best reports they could.

While Rita hurried to a pay phone, Partridge, Canh and O'Hara moved quickly toward gate 19, looking for an exit to the air-traffic ramp below. Near the gate was a doorway marked RESTRICTED AREA, and beneath that, EMERGENCY EXIT ONLY—ALARM WILL SOUND.

Without hesitation Partridge pushed through, the others following. As they clattered down a stairway an alarm bell sounded behind them. They ignored it and emerged onto the ramp.

It was crowded with aircraft and airline vehicles. Suddenly a station wagon appeared, traveling fast, with roof lights flashing. Its tires screeched as it halted at gate 19.

Canh, who was nearest, opened a door and jumped inside. The others piled in after him. The driver, a slim young black man, pulled swiftly away. Without looking back, he said, "Hiya, guys! I'm Vernon—public info."

Partridge introduced himself and the others.

From the ramp area they crossed two taxiways and traveled east on a parallel access road. Two runways were on their right. Alongside the farther one, emergency vehicles were assembling.

RITA Abrams, in the terminal, was talking on a pay phone with CBA's Dallas bureau. The bureau chief, she discovered, had been trying to get a local CBA crew to the scene. He learned with delight of the presence of Rita and the others.

She told him to advise New York, then asked, "What's our satellite feed situation?"

"Good. A mobile satellite van is on the way from Arlington."

The news excited and elated her. Arlington, she learned, was only thirteen miles away. There was now a good possibility of getting a story and pictures to New York via satellite in time for the first-feed *National Evening News.*

THE station wagon carrying the CBA trio was nearing runway 17L. It halted on a taxiway from where the incoming aircraft's approach and landing would be seen. "This will be the on-site command post," Vernon said to them.

Emergency vehicles were arriving. From the airport's fire-fighting force were four mammoth Oshkosh M15 foam vehicles, an aerial ladder truck and two smaller Rapid Intervention Vehicles. Half a dozen police cruisers disgorged officers, who pulled out silver fire suits and climbed into them. Ambulances from nearby communities were streaming into the airport and assembling nearby, but clear of the runway area.

Partridge had been the first to jump from the station wagon and, standing beside it, was scribbling notes. Minh Van Canh had clambered onto the car's roof and now, standing, his camera ready, was scanning the sky to the north. Behind him was Ken O'Hara, trailing wires and a sound recorder.

Almost at once the stricken inbound flight was visible, about five miles out, with heavy black smoke behind it. Canh raised his camera, holding it steady, one eye tight against the viewfinder.

As he filmed, the shape of the approaching airbus was becoming clearer in the viewfinder. Also clearer was a halo of bright flame on the right side. To Canh it seemed amazing that the entire airplane had not yet been engulfed.

Inside the station wagon Vernon had switched on an aviation band radio. The calm voice of an air-traffic controller could be heard speaking with the airbus pilots. "You are slightly below glide path . . . drifting left of centerline. . . . Now on glide path, on centerline . . ."

The pilots were clearly having trouble holding altitude and an even course. At moments the plane's nose veered away; then, as if from urgent efforts in the cockpit, it swung back toward the runway. Those on the ground were asking themselves, Will the airbus make it all the way in?

Canh, fondling a zoom lens, had his camera running. The airbus was over the airport boundary. . . . Then it was closer in, barely a quarter mile from the runway. But the fire was growing more intense, and two of the four right-side tires of the landing gear were burning. There was a flash as a tire exploded.

Now the burning airbus was over the runway, its landing speed a hundred and fifty mph. As it passed the waiting emergency vehicles they swung onto the runway, following at top speed. The airplane's landing gear made contact with the ground, and another tire exploded, then another. Suddenly all the right tires disintegrated; the wheels were down to their rims. Simultaneously there was a banshee screech of metal, a shower of sparks and a cloud of cement dust in the air. Somehow, miraculously, the pilots managed to hold the airbus on the runway. And as it stopped, the fire flared up.

The fire trucks closed in, within seconds pumping foam. Gigantic whorls of it piled up, like mountains of shaving cream.

On the airplane the two forward doors were opening, escape

slides tumbling out. On the left side, away from the fire, a mid-fuselage door was open. Some passengers were already coming down the slides. But at the rear neither of the two escape doors had so far opened.

Through the three open doors, smoke from the airplane was pouring out. Passengers emerged, coughing and gasping for air.

Firemen from the RIVs had swiftly rigged ladders to the unopened rear doors. As they opened the doors more smoke poured out. The firemen hurried inside, intent on extinguishing any interior fire and helping passengers to leave.

Noticeably the outward flow of passengers slowed. Harry Partridge made a quick estimate that nearly two hundred people had emerged of the two hundred and ninety-seven reportedly aboard. Firemen began to carry some who appeared badly burned—among them two female flight attendants.

Minh Van Canh continued to videotape the action around him, thinking only professionally, aware he was the only cameraman on the scene and that in his camera he had something special and unique. Probably not since the Hindenburg airship disaster had a major air crash been recorded visually in such detail.

Ambulances had arrived at the on-site command post. Within minutes the crash victims would be on their way to area hospitals. With the arrival of a helicopter bringing doctors and nurses, the command post was becoming an improvised field hospital.

The flight deck crew now emerged from the airbus, pointedly declining help. The captain, a grizzled four-striper, already knowing that many were dead, was openly crying. Canh held the captain's grief-stricken face in close-up. It proved to be the final shot as Rita's voice called, "Harry! Minh! Ken! Hurry! Bring what you've got. We're feeding to New York by satellite."

Rita had arrived on a public information shuttle bus. In the distance the promised mobile satellite van could be seen. Its folding satellite dish was being opened and aimed skyward.

Canh lowered his camera. Two other TV crews had arrived on the same shuttle bus as Rita, along with print press reporters and photographers. They and others would carry the story on. But only Canh had the real thing, the crash exclusive pictures. And he knew with inward pride that today and in days to come his pictures would be seen around the world and become a piece of history.

ON THE way to the satellite van Partridge began drafting the words he would shortly speak. Rita told him, "As soon as you're ready, cut a sound track, do a closing stand-up. Meanwhile, I'll feed quick and dirty to New York."

As Partridge nodded acknowledgment Rita glanced at her watch: five forty-three p.m., six forty-three in New York. For the first-feed *National Evening News* there was barely fifteen minutes left of broadcast time.

Partridge continued to write, mouthing words silently. Canh handed two tape cassettes to Rita, then put a fresh cassette in the camera, ready for Partridge's audio track and stand-up close.

Inside the satellite van, in a small control room, a technician was aligning the van's uplink transmitter with a satellite more than twenty-two thousand miles above them. Whatever they transmitted would go on the satellite, then instantly by downlink to New York to be rerecorded.

Rita expertly ran Canh's tapes through an editing machine, viewing them on a TV monitor. Not surprisingly, she thought, the pictures were superb. On normal assignments a producer and videotape editor together would select portions of the tapes. Then, over a sound track of a correspondent's comments, they would put all components together as a fully edited piece. But today there wasn't time. So, making fast decisions, Rita chose several of the most dramatic scenes, which the technician transmitted as they were—in TV jargon, quick and dirty.

Outside the satellite van Partridge completed his script and, after conferring briefly with Canh and O'Hara, recorded a sound track. Allowing for the anchorman's introduction in New York, he began:

"Pilots in a long-ago war called it comin' in on a wing and a prayer. There was a song with that name.... It's unlikely anyone will write a song about today.

"The Muskegon Airlines airbus was sixty miles from Dallas–Fort Worth . . . with a near full passenger load . . . having come from Chicago . . . when the midair collision happened. . . ."

The best news writing, as this correspondent knew, was not in neat sentences and paragraphs. Fragments of sentences worked better. Facts must be taut, verbs strong and active; a script should crackle. Finally, by manner and intonation the correspondent should convey a meaning too. Yes, he or she had to be an excellent reporter, but an actor as well.

Partridge concluded with a stand-up—himself, head and shoulders, speaking directly to the camera. Behind him activity was continuing around the wrecked airbus.

"There is more of this story to come . . . tragic details, the toll of dead and injured. But what is clear, even now, is that collision dangers are multiplying . . . on the airways, in our crowded skies. . . . Harry Partridge, CBA News, Dallas–Fort Worth."

The cassette, with the narration and stand-up, was passed to Rita inside the van. Still trusting Partridge, knowing him too well to waste precious time checking, she ordered it transmitted to New York.

THE CBA News headquarters building in New York was a plain and unimpressive eight-story brownstone on the east side of upper Manhattan. Formerly a furniture factory, it now had only the shell of the original structure remaining, the interior having been remodeled to house a sultan's fortune in electronic wizardry. And here, two floors below street level, was a vital department with a prosaic name—the One-inch-tape Room.

All news reports from CBA crews around the world came into the One-inch-tape Room. From there, too, all taped recordings of finished news went out to viewers. Endemic to the One-inch-tape Room were enormous pressures, taut nerves, instant decision making and urgent commands, especially just before and during broadcasts of the *National Evening News*. At such times, to the uninitiated the scene might give an impression of bedlam.

But, in fact, the operation functioned smoothly and quickly. Mistakes could be disastrous. They rarely happened.

Half a dozen sophisticated reel-to-reel tape machines, using one-inch magnetic tape and built into consoles with TV monitors above, dominated the activity. At each console sat a skilled operator receiving, editing and transmitting tapes swiftly.

An hour or so before *National Evening News* broadcast time a senior producer moved down five floors from the Horseshoe to preside over the One-inch-tape Room. There, shouting instructions while semaphoring with his arms, he viewed incoming material for that night's news, ordered further editing if necessary, and kept the Horseshoe informed of which expected items were now in-house and how they looked.

The senior producer most often in charge was Will Kazazis, Brooklyn born of an excitable Greek family. Despite his inherited excitability, he never lost control. It was Kazazis who received Rita Abrams' satellite transmission from DFW—first Minh Van Canh's pictures, sent quick and dirty, then Harry Partridge's audio track and stand-up tape.

The time was six forty-eight—ten minutes of news remained. A commercial break had just begun. Kazazis told the tape operator who had taken the feed, "Slap it together fast. Use all of Partridge's track. Put the best pictures over it. Now move, move, move!"

Through an aide Kazazis had already let the Horseshoe know that the Dallas tape was coming in. Now, by phone, Chuck Insen, who was in the broadcast control room, demanded, "How is it?"

Kazazis told the executive producer, "Fantastic! Beautiful!"

Knowing there wasn't time to view the piece himself, Insen ordered, "We go after this commercial. Stand by."

With less than a minute to go, the tape operator was continuing to edit, hurriedly combining pictures, commentary and sound.

INSEN's command was repeated to the anchorman and a writer seated near him. A lead-in had already been prepared by the writer and was passed to Crawford Sloane, who skimmed it, quickly changed a word or two, and nodded thanks. A moment later the anchor's TelePrompTer switched over to the DFW story. In the broadcast studio, as the commercial break neared its conclusion, the floor manager called, "Ten seconds . . . five . . . four . . ."

At a hand signal Sloane began:

"Earlier in this broadcast we reported a midair collision near Dallas between a Muskegon Airlines airbus and a private plane. The private plane crashed. There are no survivors. The airbus, on fire, crash-landed at Dallas–Fort Worth Airport a few minutes ago, and there are heavy casualties. On the scene is CBA News correspondent Harry Partridge, who has just filed this report."

Only seconds before had the frantic editing in the One-inch-tape Room been completed. Now, on millions of TV sets across much of the United States and Canada, a dramatic picture of an approaching burning airbus filled the screen, and Partridge's voice began. The exclusive report and pictures had made the first-feed *National Evening News*.

There would be a second feed immediately after the first. There always was, and it would be broadcast in the East by affiliate stations that did not take the first feed, widely in the Midwest, and most western stations would record the second feed for broadcast later.

The Partridge report from DFW would, of course, lead the second feed. CBA's while-it-happened pictures were a world exclusive and would be repeated many times in the days to follow.

Chapter 2

IT WAS seven forty p.m. when Crawford Sloane, driving a CBA News Buick Somerset, left the garage at headquarters. A few minutes later, as he turned onto Fifty-ninth Street from Third Avenue, heading east toward the FDR Drive, he thought about the broadcast just concluded and about Harry Partridge.

For Partridge, Sloane recognized, the reporting job from Dallas had been one more solid performance in an outstanding professional career. Through DFW's airport paging system Sloane had been able to reach Partridge by phone and congratulate him and his crew. From an anchorman that kind of thing was expected. Where Partridge was concerned, though, the conversation had a touch of awkwardness.

Within the car, in a moment of silent, private honesty, Sloane asked himself, How do I feel about Harry Partridge? The answer, with equal honesty, came back: He makes me feel insecure.

The two of them had known each other for more than twenty years, the same length of time each had been with CBA News. They were successful professionally, yet opposites in personality.

Sloane was precise, fastidious in dress and speech. He could be slightly distant with people he did not know well, though in any human contact there was almost nothing his sharp mind missed.

Partridge, in contrast, was casual in behavior, his appearance rumpled; he favored old tweed jackets. He had an easygoing manner that made people feel comfortable. Sometimes he gave the impression of not caring much about anything, but only because he had learned early, as a journalist, that he could discover more by concealing his keen intelligence.

They had differences in background too. Crawford Sloane, from a middle-class Cleveland family, had done his early television training in that city. Harry Partridge, Canadian born, had served his TV-news apprenticeship with the Canadian Broadcasting Corporation and before that had worked as an announcer-newscaster-weatherman for small stations in Alberta, where his father was a farmer.

Sloane had a degree from Columbia University. Partridge hadn't even finished high school, but in the working world of news his de facto education expanded rapidly.

For a long time at CBA their careers were parallel; as a result, they came to be looked on as competitors. In late 1967 the network sent them both to Vietnam, supposedly to work as a team. Sloane, though, viewed the war as a golden opportunity to advance his own career; even then he had the anchor desk in his sights. One essential, he knew, was to appear on the evening news as often as possible. Therefore, soon after arriving in Saigon, he decided it was important not to stray too far from Pentagon East—headquarters of the Military Assistance Command for Vietnam, outside Saigon.

Harry Partridge had remarked, "Crawf, you'll never get to understand this war by attending the Saigon Follies or hanging around the Caravelle." The first was the name the press corps gave to military briefings; the second, a hotel that was a popular watering hole with the press, senior military and U.S. embassy civilians.

"If you're talking about risks," Sloane had answered huffily, "I'm willing to take as many as you are."

"Forget risks. I'm talking about coverage in depth."

No one could ever say about his time in Vietnam that Sloane didn't work hard. And he also took risks. On occasion he went along on missions to where the Vietcong were operating. But he was seldom away more than twenty-four hours and was usually available in Saigon for military and diplomatic briefings.

His shrewd ploy worked. He had always been impressive on camera and was even more so in Vietnam. He became a favorite with the New York Horseshoe producers, was frequently on the evening news and had built up a following.

Harry Partridge, on the other hand, sought out deeper stories, which required longer investigation and which took him, with a cameraman, to distant parts of Vietnam. Some of his reports contradicted official military statements in Saigon; others confirmed them. It was that second kind of reporting—fairness to the U.S. military—that separated him and a handful of others from the majority of Vietnam correspondents. An example was Partridge's report that U.S. forces during the enemy's Tet offensive were doing much better than they were being given credit for. The media proclaimed Tet as a smashing communist victory, a claim that calmer research two decades later showed to be untrue.

Partridge's excursions into areas of heavy fighting usually kept him away from Saigon for a week, sometimes longer. Once, when he went underground into Cambodia, he was out of touch for nearly a month.

Every time, though, he returned with a strong story, and after the war some were still remembered for their insights.

Unfortunately, because his reports were less frequent than Crawford Sloane's, Partridge didn't get noticed as much.

Something else in Vietnam affected the future of Partridge and Sloane: Jessica Castillo.

CRAWFORD Sloane swung onto the northbound ramp of the FDR Drive. Moments later, alongside the East River, his speed increased. His home in Larchmont, New York, north of the city, on Long Island Sound, was half an hour away.

Behind him, a blue Ford Tempo increased its speed also.

Sloane was relaxed, as he usually was at this time of day. And as his thoughts drifted they returned to Jessica, who in Saigon had been Harry Partridge's girlfriend. But in the end she had married Crawford Sloane.

In those days she had been twenty-six, slim, with long brown hair, a lively mind and, on occasion, a sharp tongue. She took no nonsense from the journalists with whom she dealt as a junior information officer at the United States Information Service.

Members of the press went to the agency sometimes more than they needed, bringing queries that might allow them time with Jessica. She played along with the attention, but when Sloane first knew her, Harry Partridge was firmly number one in her affections.

Even now, Sloane thought, there were areas of that early relationship between Partridge and Jessica of which he had no knowledge, some things he had never asked about and would never know. But he would never stop wondering about the details and intimacies of those times.

JESSICA Castillo and Harry Partridge were drawn to each other the first time they met—even though the meeting was antagonistic. Partridge had gone to USIS seeking information that he knew existed but that had been refused him by the U.S. military. It concerned the widespread drug addiction of American troops in Vietnam.

Partridge had seen plenty of evidence of heroin addiction during his travels, and the New York Horseshoe had given him a green light to pursue the story. But when he entered Jessica's office and broached the subject, she clammed up tight. "I can't talk about that."

Her attitude offended him, and he said accusingly, "You mean you *won't* talk? This problem needs a public airing so something can be done, lady. So other green kids coming out here can be warned and maybe saved. You call yourself an information officer. I call you a concealment officer."

Jessica flushed. She was unused to being talked to that way, and her eyes blazed with anger, her fingers clenching around a glass paperweight. Then, noticeably, the anger diminished, and she asked quietly, "What is it you want to know?"

Partridge moderated his tone to match hers. "Statistics mostly. I know someone has them, that records have been kept, surveys taken."

She tossed back her brown hair in a gesture he would later become used to and love. "Do you know Rex Talbot?"

"Yes." Talbot was a young American vice-consul at the embassy, on Thong Nhut Street, a few blocks away.

"I suggest you ask him to tell you about the reports he has on file. There's no need to have him know I sent you. You could let him think you know . . ."

He finished the sentence. ". . . a little more than I really do. It's an old journalist's trick."

"The kind of trick you use all the time."

Partridge smiled. "You're not as soulless as I thought. How about exploring this subject some more over dinner tonight?"

To her own surprise, Jessica accepted.

It turned out to be the first of many such meetings, for later they discovered how much they enjoyed each other's company. They dined together often at the Caravelle, afterward moving into the hotel garden, an oasis of quiet amid the discord of Saigon. Inevitably they found the same delight in each other physically as they had in other ways, and Jessica told Harry, "Oh, I love you so!" Partridge would remember that time as one of those rare and magic moments when all problems and concerns—Vietnam, the war's ugliness, future uncertainties—seemed so far away; all that mattered was the present and themselves. Long after, he could never remember if he had told her that he truly loved her, but he knew he had and always would.

In any other time and place they might have married quickly. Jessica wanted to be married; she also wanted children. But Partridge, for reasons he afterward regretted, held back. In Canada he had had one failed marriage and knew that marriages of TV newsmen so often were disastrous. TV-news correspondents led peripatetic lives, could be away from home two hundred days a year or more, were unused to family responsibilities, and encountered temptations on the road that few could permanently resist. Coupled with that was Vietnam. Partridge's life was at risk each time he left Saigon, and though luck had been with him so far, the odds were against that luck's enduring. So it wasn't fair, he reasoned, to burden Jessica with the likelihood of heartbreak later on.

He confided some of this to her early one morning after they had spent the night together. Jessica was shocked and jolted by what she perceived as a puerile cop-out by a man to whom she had already given her heart and body. She told him coldly that their relationship was at an end.

Partridge left Saigon a few hours afterward, and was away a month.

Crawford Sloane had met Jessica several times while she was in Harry's company, and saw her occasionally in the USIS offices when his work took him there. He was strongly attracted to her and longed to know her better, but recognizing she was Partridge's girl, he had never asked her for a date. But when Sloane learned that she and Partridge had split up, he promptly asked her to dine with him. She agreed, and they went on seeing each other. Two weeks later Sloane proposed marriage.

Jessica, taken by surprise, asked for time to think. Her love for Harry had been passionate and all consuming. And she still loved him; she was sure of that. If he had come back and asked her to marry him, she would probably have said yes. But, clearly, Harry wasn't going to ask.

On the other hand, there was Crawf. Jessica felt a strong affection for him. He was kind and gentle, loving, intelligent. And he possessed a stability that Harry, while an exciting person, sometimes lacked. But for a lifetime, which was more important— excitement or stability? After weighing everything as best she could, Jessica accepted Crawford Sloane's proposal.

Sloane was ecstatically happy. They were married at once, in the U.S. embassy by an army chaplain. Partridge did not learn of the marriage until his return to Saigon and only then did it dawn on him, with overpowering sadness, how much he had lost.

If Jessica shared some of Partridge's feelings, she kept them to herself and also put them behind her. She had made her choice and was determined to be a good wife, which she was. Now— incredibly, it seemed—Jessica and Crawford's silver wedding anniversary was less than five years distant.

AT THE wheel of the Buick Somerset, Sloane was midpoint in his journey home. The same Ford Tempo that had followed him from CBA News headquarters was still behind.

It was not surprising that he had failed to notice the other car either tonight or during the past several weeks when it had followed him. Its driver—a young, thin-lipped, cold-eyed Colombian, code-named Carlos—was an expert at stalking any quarry.

Carlos, who had entered the United States two months ago on a forged passport, shared this stealthy surveillance with six others— five men and a woman. Like Carlos, the others were identified only by fictitious first names. Until their present task began, they were unknown to one another. Only Miguel, the leader, who tonight was several miles away, was aware of real identities.

In the fast-moving expressway traffic Carlos allowed three other cars to move up between himself and Sloane. Beside Carlos another man noted the time and made an entry in a log. This was Julio—swarthy, bad-tempered, with an ugly facial scar from a knifing. Behind them, in the back seat, was a mobile cellular phone, one of six that linked vehicles and a hidden temporary headquarters.

As the Buick entered the streets of Larchmont the Ford Tempo followed discreetly, stopping well short of the Sloane house, which was located on Park Avenue, facing Long Island Sound. The house, befitting someone with Sloane's substantial income, was large and imposing. Sloane used a remote control in the car to open the door of a three-car garage, then drove in, the door closing behind him.

SLOANE could hear voices and laughter as he walked through the enclosed corridor between the garage and the house. He opened a door to the carpeted hallway and heard Jessica call out from the living room, "Is that you, Crawf?"

He made a standard response. "If it isn't, you're in trouble."

Her melodious laugh came back. "Welcome, whoever you are! Be with you in a minute!"

He heard a clink of glasses and knew that Jessica was mixing martinis, her nightly homecoming ritual to help him unwind from whatever the day had brought.

"Hi, Dad!" the Sloanes' eleven-year-old son, Nicholas, shouted from the stairway. Nicky was tall for his age and slim, with curly brown hair. His intelligent eyes lit up as he ran to hug his father.

Sloane returned the embrace. It was the kind of greeting he appreciated, and he had Jessica to thank for that. Almost from the time Nicky was born, she had taught him that love should be expressed in tactile ways. Jessica would have none of Crawf's built-in reserve. "When you're married, darling, barriers come down. It's why we were 'joined together'—remember those words? So for the rest of our lives you and I are going to say to each other exactly what we feel—and sometimes show it too," she'd told him.

With other people his reserve lived on. Sloane couldn't remember when he had last hugged his own father, uncertain how old Angus—stiff, even rigid in his personal behavior—might react.

"Hello, darling!" Jessica appeared wearing a soft green dress, a color he always liked. They embraced warmly, then went into the living room. Nicky came in for a while, as he usually did; he had eaten dinner earlier and would go to bed soon.

Sloane asked his son, "How are things in the music world?"

"Great, Dad. I'm practicing Gershwin."

Neither Sloane nor Jessica could remember exactly how old Nicky had been when he began to exhibit an interest in music, but it was in his very early years, and now music was his dominant interest. He played often on their grand piano.

Nicky took lessons from a former concert pianist living nearby. A few weeks ago the tutor had told Jessica, "Your son already has a mastery of music unusual for his age. Later he may follow one of several paths—as a performer or composer. Music will, I predict, be the mainstream of his life."

Now Jessica glanced at her watch. "Nicky, it's getting late."

"Ah, Mom, let me stay up. Tomorrow's a school holiday."

"And your day will be as full as any other. The answer is no." Jessica was the family disciplinarian, and after affectionate good nights, Nicky left. Soon after, they could hear him playing a portable electronic keyboard in his bedroom.

In the softly lit living room Jessica returned to the martinis she had been mixing. Watching her, Sloane thought, How lucky can you get? It was a feeling he often had about Jessica and the way she looked after more than twenty years of marriage. She no longer wore her hair long and didn't bother to conceal streaks of gray. There were also lines around her eyes. But her figure was slim and shapely, and he still felt proud to enter a room with her beside him.

As she handed him a glass she commented, "A rough day?"

"It was. You saw the airplane story on the news?"

"Yes. Those poor passengers—what a terrible way to die! They just had to sit there, waiting."

"What did you think of Harry?"

"He was good."

"He was better than good. He did it like that." Sloane snapped his fingers. "With hardly any time. Rita and Minh also came through. We beat the pants off the other networks." The martini was relaxing him, as it always did.

"You're feeling good tonight," Jessica said, "and you have another reason to." She handed him an envelope, already opened, a normal procedure since she handled most of their private business. "It's a letter from your publisher and a royalty statement."

Sloane took the papers out and studied them, his face lighting up with a smile.

Crawford Sloane's book, *The Camera and the Truth,* had been published several months earlier. In terms of sales it got off to a slow start. But as weeks passed, certain comments in it gained attention in news columns—the best publicity a book can have. In a chapter about terrorism Sloane had written bluntly:

> No politician anywhere has the guts to say it, but hostages, including American hostages, should be regarded as expendable. Pleas from hostages' families should be heard sympathetically, but should not sway government policy.
>
> The only way to deal with terrorists is by counterterrorism, which means whenever possible seeking out and covertly destroying them—the only language they understand. It includes not striking bargains with terrorists or paying ransom, directly or indirectly, ever!
>
> We who live in the United States will not remain free from terrorism in our own backyard much longer. But neither are we prepared for this pervasive, ruthless kind of warfare.

Sloane put aside the impressive royalty accounting.

"You deserve what's happened, and I'm proud of you," Jessica said. "Especially because it isn't like you to take chances in being controversial." She paused. "Oh, your father phoned. He's arriving early tomorrow and would like to stay a week."

Sloane grimaced. "That's pretty soon after the last time."

"He's lonely and getting old. Maybe if you're that way someday, you'll have a favorite daughter-in-law you'll want to be with."

They both laughed, knowing how fond Angus Sloane was of Jessica and vice versa. In some ways the two were closer than the father and son. Since the death of Crawford's mother several years ago, Angus had been living alone in Florida.

"I enjoy having him around," Jessica said. "So does Nicky."

"Okay, then, that's fine."

Talk between Sloane and Jessica continued over dinner, always a favorite time. Sloane said thoughtfully, "I know what you meant earlier, that it isn't like me to venture out on limbs. I guess in my life I haven't taken chances as often as I might. But I felt strongly about some things in the book. Still do."

"The terrorism part?"

He nodded. "Since the book was written I've done some thinking about how terrorism could affect you and me. It's why I've taken some special precautions. Until now I haven't told you, but you ought to know."

While Jessica regarded him curiously, he went on. "Have you ever thought that someone like me could be kidnapped, become a hostage?"

"I have when you've been overseas."

He shook his head. "It could happen here. Like some others in television, I work in a goldfish bowl. If terrorists begin operating in the U.S.—and I believe they soon will—people like me will be attractive bait because anything we do, or is done to us, gets noticed in a big way."

"What about families? Could they be targets too?"

He shook his head. "That's highly unlikely. Terrorists would be after a name. Someone everybody knows."

Jessica said uneasily, "You spoke of precautions. What kind?"

"The kind that would be effective *after* I'd been taken hostage, if it happened."

"I don't like this conversation," Jessica said. "You're making me nervous. And what good are precautions after it happens?"

"Before it happens," he said, "I have to trust the network to provide security protection. But afterward I wouldn't want any ransom to be paid by the network or anyone else. So I've made a solemn declaration—it's all in legal form—to that effect. After that declaration was made public, I'd like to think you wouldn't go some other route."

Jessica protested, "You'd rob me of the right to make a decision!"

He said gently, "No, dearest. I'd relieve you of a terrible responsibility and a dilemma."

"But supposing the network were willing to pay a ransom?"

"I doubt they would be, but certainly not against my wishes, which are on record."

"You said the network is giving you some kind of security

protection. It's the first I've heard of it. Just what kind?"

"When there are telephoned threats, or screwball letters which sound a certain way, or a rumor of some kind of possible attack—it happens at all networks and especially to anchor people—then private security men are called in. They hang around the CBA News building, wherever I'm working, doing whatever security people are supposed to."

"You've never told me," Jessica said. There was an edge to her voice, though clearly she had not made up her mind whether to be angry or just anxious.

Sloane told his wife, "When someone is kidnapped, nowadays it's a certainty they will make, or be compelled to make, video-tape recordings. Then those recordings are sometimes played on television. If there's a prearrangement of signals, a hostage has a good chance of getting a message back."

"If this weren't so serious, it would sound like a spy novel," Jessica said. "So what kind of signals have you arranged?"

"Licking my lips, which is something anyone might do, would mean, 'I am doing this against my will. Do not believe anything I am saying.' Scratching or touching my right earlobe would mean, 'My captors are well organized and strongly armed.' Touching my left earlobe would mean, 'Security here is sometimes lax; an attack from outside might succeed.' There are some others, but we'll leave it for now. I don't want all this to distress you."

"Well, it does distress me," Jessica said. She wondered, *Could it happen? Could Crawf be kidnapped and spirited away?* It seemed unbelievable, but almost every day unbelievable things happened.

That night, still troubled by what had passed between them, Jessica found it difficult to sleep.

Outside, the occupants of the Ford Tempo watched as one by one the lights in the house went off. Then they made a report by cellular phone and, ending that day's vigil, drove away.

SHORTLY after six thirty a.m. the surveillance of the house resumed. A Chevrolet Celebrity was being used this morning, and slouched down in the front seats were Carlos and Julio.

301

At seven thirty an unforeseen event occurred when a taxi arrived at the Sloane house. From it an elderly man emerged, carrying a suitcase. He went into the house and remained there. The newcomer's unexpected presence prompted a call to the watchers' temporary headquarters, some twenty miles away.

Their efficient communications and ample transport typified an operation on which expense had not been spared. The organizers were associates of Colombia's Medellín cartel, a coalition of vicious, criminal, fabulously wealthy drug lords. In the present instance, while operating undercover in the United States, Medellín was working not for itself but for the Peruvian Maoist terrorist organization Sendero Luminoso, or Shining Path. Recently in Peru, Sendero Luminoso had grown more powerful, while the official government had become increasingly inept and weak. Drug money contributed heavily to Sendero finances.

Now, in the surveillance Chevrolet, the two Colombian hoodlums were searching through a collection of Polaroid photos.

Julio, on the telephone, spoke in code phrases. "A blue package has arrived. Delivery number two. The package is in storage. We cannot trace the order." Translated: A man has arrived by taxi. He has gone into the house. We do not know who he is.

The sharp-edged voice of Miguel, the project's leader, snapped back, "What is the docket number?" Translated: What age is he?

Julio looked to Carlos for help. *"Un viejo.* How old?"

"Tell him, Docket seventy-five."

Julio did, producing another terse question. "Is anything special about the blue package?"

Abandoning code, Julio lapsed into plain language. "He carried a suitcase in. Looks like he plans to stay."

SOUTH of Hackensack, New Jersey, in a dilapidated rented house, the man whose code name was Miguel silently cursed Julio's carelessness. Those idiots he was forced to work with! He had warned all of them over and over that on radiophones anyone could be listening. *Estúpidos!* The success of their mission, plus their lives and freedom, were at stake.

Miguel himself had always been obsessively cautious. It was

why he had never been arrested, even though he was on most-wanted lists of police forces in North and South America and some in Europe, too, including Interpol's.

In his late thirties, he was physically unremarkable; anyone passing him on a street might think he was a bank clerk. This ordinariness had been Miguel's great good fortune, as was the fact that he did not radiate authority. His power of command remained hidden, except to those on whom he exercised it, and then it was unmistakable.

Although Colombian, Miguel could also appear American. In the late 1960s and early '70s he had attended the University of California at Berkeley, majoring in English and learning to speak it without an accent. In those days he was using his real name, Ulises Rodríguez.

Miguel's father, a well-to-do Bogotá neurosurgeon, hoped his only son would follow him into medicine. Instead, as the 1970s neared, the son foresaw opportunities for himself in Colombia, a country that was changing from a prosperous democracy to a lawless, rich mobsters' haven ruled through dictatorship, savagery and fear.

After Berkeley, back home in Colombia, Miguel flirted with the developing alliance of mad-dog drug lords. He had a pilot's license and made several flights conveying coca paste from Peru to Colombia for processing into cocaine. Then came the infamous Medellín drug cartel, with its brutal murders. Miguel participated in all the major killings, many minor ones, and had long since lost count of the corpses in his wake. Killing did not trouble him at all. He became a gun-for-hire terrorist who was, because of his icy calm and efficiency, constantly in demand.

It was this life of danger, risk and action he enjoyed that had brought him, on a fake passport, to the United States a month and a half ago.

In New York, Miguel had gone immediately to "Little Colombia," a sizable Colombian community in Jackson Heights, Queens. A thriving narcotics center, it was one of New York's most dangerous high-crime areas. There, in a safe house arranged by a Medellín cartel agent, Miguel began his planning, drew on money made secretly available, and assembled the small force he would lead. That force's seven members, including Miguel, had been selected in Bogotá.

Julio, at this moment on surveillance duty, and Socorro, the woman in the group, were Colombians. Several years ago both were sent to the United States by Medellín, their only instructions to establish themselves and wait until their services were needed. That time had now arrived.

Julio was a communications specialist. Socorro, during her waiting period, had trained and qualified as a nurse's aide. She had an additional affiliation. Through friends in Peru she had become a member of the revolutionary Sendero Luminoso.

The other Colombians in the group were Rafael, Luís and Carlos. Rafael, heavily built, was a mechanic and general handyman. Luís had been chosen for his driving skills—he was expert at eluding pursuit. Carlos was young, quick-witted and had organized the surveillance of the past four weeks. All three spoke English fluently.

The final member was an American, code-named Baudelio. Miguel mistrusted him totally, yet Baudelio's knowledge and skills were essential to the mission's success.

Now, in Hackensack, at the group's temporary operating center, Miguel considered his response to the surveillance report from Larchmont.

Before leaving Bogotá, Miguel had received a dossier on the Sloane family. Crawford Sloane had a father who fitted the description of the new arrival. Well, Miguel reasoned, if the old man had come to visit his son, it constituted a nuisance but nothing more. The father would almost certainly have to be killed later today, but that presented no problem.

Depressing the telephone transmitter, Miguel ordered, "Take no action about the blue package. Report new billing only." New billing meant "if the situation changes."

"Roger," Julio acknowledged curtly.

Replacing the cellular phone, Miguel glanced at his watch. Almost seven forty-five a.m. In two hours all seven members of the group would be in place and ready for action. Everything to follow had been carefully planned, with problems anticipated, precautions taken. There could be no postponement. Outside the United States other movements, dovetailing with their own, were already in motion.

Chapter 3

Angus Sloane put down his coffee cup and patted his silver-gray mustache with a napkin. "No better breakfast," he declared, "has been served this morning in all of New York State."

"And none with higher cholesterol either," his son said from behind an opened *New York Times* across the table. "Don't you know all those fried eggs are bad for your heart?"

"Who's counting?" Jessica said. "Besides, you can afford the eggs, Crawf. Angus, would you like another?"

"No, thank you, my dear." Angus, sprightly and cherubic—he had just turned seventy-three—smiled benevolently at Jessica and gave a contented sigh.

They were all seated in the bright and cheerful breakfast annex, where Jessica had prepared for Angus his favorite bacon and eggs. He had arrived half an hour earlier, embracing his daughter-in-law and grandson warmly and shaking hands more formally with Crawford.

"About my heart and eggs," Angus said. "I figure if my ticker's lasted this long, I shouldn't worry about cholesterol. My heart and I have been in some tight spots and come through them. I could tell you about a few that happened during my war. That's World War Two to you, Nicky."

"Weren't you on the first B-17 bombing raid to Schweinfurt, Dad?" Sloane asked.

"Yes." Then to Nicholas, "That was deep in Germany, Nicky. At the time, not a nice place to go." The old man's face became creased by memory and pain. He went on, his voice quavering, "At Schweinfurt we lost fifty B-17s. There were ten people in a crew. That's five hundred fliers lost that single day. They were good men. So many good men. So many of my friends."

"Gramps," Nicky said. He had been listening intently. "When you were in the war, were you frightened very much?"

"Frightened? I was terrified! But let me tell you, Nicky, there's nothing wrong with being scared. It can happen to the best. What counts is hanging on, somehow staying in control and doing what you know you should."

"I hear you, Gramps."

Sloane glanced at his watch. It was time to leave. He rose from the breakfast table, put on his suit jacket, and said good-bye to Jessica and Nicky. Then he approached his father. Moving close to Angus, he put his arms around him and kissed him on both cheeks.

The old man seemed flustered. "Hey, hey! What's all this?"

Looking him directly in the eye, Crawford said, "I love you, you old coot."

At the doorway he glanced back. On Angus' face was a small, seraphic smile.

WHEN the surveillance duo of Carlos and Julio saw Crawford Sloane leave his home, they reported immediately by code to Miguel.

By now Miguel had left the Hackensack operating center and, with others, was crossing the George Washington Bridge from New Jersey to New York in a Nissan van.

Miguel issued, also in code, the order that prearranged plans were now in effect. He reasoned confidently that what they were about to do was the totally unexpected.

AT ABOUT the same time Crawford Sloane left his Larchmont home to drive to CBA News headquarters, Harry Partridge awakened in Port Credit, near Toronto. He had arrived last night on a delayed flight from Dallas and had slept deeply. He spent the first few moments of the new day taking in the familiar landmarks of his apartment's bedroom.

The nomadic nature of his work meant that Partridge got to the apartment for only a few brief periods each year. And even though he stored his few possessions here, the apartment was not registered in his name. The official tenant was V. Williams—the V for Vivien—who resided here permanently.

Every month, from wherever in the world Partridge happened to be, he sent Vivien a check for the rent, and in return she lived here and kept it as his haven. The arrangement—which had other conveniences, including occasional lovemaking—suited them both.

Vivien was a nurse who worked in the Queensway Hospital nearby, and he could hear her now, moving around in the kitchen. In all probability she was making tea, which she knew he liked each morning, and would bring it to him soon. She was in her mid-forties, with angular, strong features and straight black hair, now streaked with gray. Warm, easygoing and generous, she had been widowed before Partridge knew her, and had one child, a daughter, in Vancouver.

Partridge was fond of Vivien though not in love with her, and aware he never would be. He suspected that she was in love with him and would love him more if he encouraged it. But as it was, she accepted the relationship they had.

Vivien came into the bedroom carrying a tray with morning tea. While he sipped it she regarded him quizzically. His face showed lines of strain and tiredness; his unruly shock of fair hair was in need of trimming.

Aware of her appraisal, Partridge asked, "What's the verdict?"

Vivien shook her head in mock despair. "Just look at you! I send you off healthy and fit. Two and a half months later you come back looking tired, pale and underfed."

"I know, Viv." He grimaced. "It's the life I lead. There's too much pressure, lousy hours and junk food." Then, with a smile, "So here I am, a mess as usual. What can you do for me?"

She said with a mixture of affection and firmness, "First I'll give you a good, healthful breakfast. I'll bring it to you in bed. After that, I'm going to trim your hair. Later I'm taking you for a sauna and massage—I've already made the appointment."

Partridge lay back and threw up his hands. "I love it!"

Vivien went on, "Tomorrow I figured you'll want to see your old cronies at the CBC—you usually do. But in the evening I have tickets for an all-Mozart concert in Toronto. You can let the music wash over you. I know you like that. Apart from all that, you'll rest or do whatever you wish." She shrugged. "Maybe in between those other things you'll feel like making love."

For a moment Partridge felt more gratitude for Vivien than he had ever felt before. She was rock solid, a refuge. He asked, "Don't you have to work?"

"I've arranged to take some vacation, starting today."

He told her, "Viv, you're one in a million."

When Vivien had gone and he could hear her preparing breakfast, Partridge's thoughts returned to yesterday. There had been that congratulatory call—they had paged him for it in the DFW terminal—from Crawford Sloane.

Crawf had sounded awkward, as he often did when they talked. There were times when Partridge wanted to say, "Look, Crawf, if you think I have any grudge against you—about Jessica or your job or *anything*—forget it! I haven't and I never did." But he knew that kind of remark would strain their relationship even more, and probably Crawf would never believe it anyway.

Inevitably when thinking in a personal way about Sloane, there was always the memory of Jessica, though it was never more than memory, because there was nothing between them now, not even occasional communication, and they seldom met socially. Nor had Partridge ever blamed Sloane for his loss of Jessica, having recognized that his own foolish judgment was the cause. When he could have married her, Partridge had decided not to, so Sloane had simply stepped in, proving himself the wiser of the two, with a better sense of values at that time.

Vivien reappeared, bringing breakfast in stages. It was, as she had promised, a healthful meal: freshly squeezed orange juice, thick hot porridge with brown sugar and milk, followed by poached eggs on whole wheat toast, strong black coffee, the beans freshly ground, and finally more toast and Alberta honey. He was grateful once more to Vivien for her thoughtfulness.

JESSICA went shopping every Thursday morning, and she intended to follow her usual routine today. When Angus learned this, he volunteered to accompany her, and Nicky, who had a school holiday, asked to go too so he could be with his grandfather.

The three of them left the house in Jessica's Volvo station wagon shortly before eleven a.m. It was a beautiful fall morning, with sunlight glistening off Long Island Sound.

The Sloanes' day maid, Florence, was in the house and through a window watched the trio leave. She also saw a car parked across the street start up and follow in the same direction as the Volvo. She gave no thought to the second vehicle.

Jessica's first stop was the Grand Union supermarket in the central business area of Larchmont. She parked in the store lot, then, accompanied by Angus and Nicky, went inside.

The Colombians Julio and Carlos had trailed the station wagon. Carlos, who had reported the departure from the house, now made another cellular phone call, announcing that the "three packages are in container number one."

This time Julio was driving. Following Miguel's instructions, Carlos left the Chevrolet Celebrity and moved on foot to a position near the store. Unlike other days when he had been casually dressed, today he was wearing a neat brown suit. When he was in place, Julio drove the Chevy away to the safe seclusion of the Hackensack operating center.

THE phone messages reached Miguel in the Nissan van, parked near Larchmont's railroad station. With him were Luís, Rafael and Baudelio, though all four were out of sight because of dark, thin plastic sheets covering the van's windows. Luís was at the wheel.

When they heard that three people had left the house, Rafael exclaimed, "Ay! That means the viejo's along."

Miguel was still considering the complication of the third person. Their long-standing plan had involved only the Sloane woman and the boy. All along they—not the newsman Crawford Sloane—had been the Sendero Luminoso–Medellín objective. The two were to be seized and held as hostages for as yet unspecified demands.

When Carlos' second message came, indicating that all three were inside the supermarket, Miguel nodded to Luís. "Roll!"

The next stop, just half a dozen blocks away, would be the store parking lot. While they were moving, Miguel turned to look at Baudelio, the American in the Medellín group, who continued to be a source of worry.

Baudelio was in his mid-fifties but looked twenty years older. Gaunt, lantern-jawed, with sallow skin and a droopy gray mustache, he had the appearance of a walking ghost. He had once been a doctor, a specialist in anesthesiology practicing in Boston, and a drunk. When left to his own devices, he was still a drunk. But he was no longer a doctor, at least not officially; his license to practice had been revoked.

With no future in the United States he had decided to go to Colombia, a place where he could use his considerable medical skills without arousing any questions. He was in no position to be particular and took whatever came his way. By reading medical journals, he managed to stay up to date in his specialty. All of this background had been made known to Miguel, with a warning that while this assignment lasted, Baudelio was to be deprived of any alcohol. Also Miguel decided not to trust him with a firearm. Thus he was the only one in the group not armed.

The Grand Union supermarket was now directly ahead. Carlos saw the Nissan passenger van arrive. The parking lot was not crowded, and the Nissan entered a conveniently vacant slot alongside Jessica's Volvo. When Carlos had observed this, he turned into the store.

JESSICA gestured to her partly filled shopping cart and told Angus, "If there's something you especially like, just drop it in."

Nicky said, "Gramps likes caviar."

"I should have remembered," Jessica said. "Let's get some." They moved to the gourmet section, Angus inspecting prices.

It was at that moment that Jessica noticed a young man, slightly built and well dressed, approaching a woman shopper nearby. He appeared to ask a question. The woman shook her head. Mildly curious, Jessica watched the young man as he approached her.

"Excuse me, ma'am," Carlos said. "I'm trying to locate someone." Jessica noticed a Spanish accent, though that was not unusual in New York. She also thought the speaker had cold, hard eyes. "It's a Mrs. Crawford Sloane."

Jessica was startled. "Oh? I'm Mrs. Sloane."

"Ma'am, I have some bad news." Carlos' expression was serious. "Your husband has been in an accident. He's badly injured. The ambulance took him to Doctors Hospital in Manhattan. I was sent to take you there. Your maid said you'd be here."

Jessica gasped and turned deathly pale. Nicky, who had heard only the last few words, looked stunned.

Angus, though equally shocked, was the first to recover and take charge. "Jessie, let's go."

"It's Dad, isn't it?" Nicky said.

Jessica put her arm around Nicky. "Yes, dear. We're going to him now." Still dazed by the shattering news, they went quickly with the young man toward the store's main door. Angus followed. Something was bothering him; what, he wasn't sure.

Outside, in the parking lot, Carlos led them toward the Nissan van. He said to Jessica, "We'll go in this vehicle, ma'am. It will be—"

"No, no!" Tense and anxious, she was groping in her purse for car keys. "I'll take my car. I know where Doctors Hospital—"

Carlos interposed himself between the Volvo and Jessica. Grasping her arm, he said, "Ma'am, we'd rather you—"

Jessica attempted to withdraw her arm; as she did, Carlos held her more firmly and pushed her forward. She said indignantly, "Stop that! What is this?"

A few feet behind, Angus now realized what had been troubling him. The strange young man had said, "The ambulance took him to Doctors Hospital." But Doctors Hospital doesn't take emergencies, he thought. Last year Angus had visited a patient there and gotten to know the hospital well. Emergencies were sent to New York Hospital, a few blocks south.

So the young man was lying! Two men—Angus didn't like their looks at all—had just appeared from around the back of the van and were forcing Jessica inside. Angus shouted, "Jessica, don't go! Nicky, run! Get—"

The sentence was never finished. A pistol butt crashed down

on Angus' head, and he fell, uncon-
scious. Luís had jumped out of the van and attacked him
from behind. In almost the same motion Luís grabbed Nicholas.

Jessica began screaming, "Help! Someone . . . please help!"

The burly Rafael, who had joined Carlos in seizing Jessica, now
clamped a massive hand across her mouth and flung her inside
the van. Then, jumping in himself, he continued to hold her
while she struggled. Jessica's eyes were wild.

From a medical bag Baudelio produced a gauze pad soaked in
chloroform. He slapped the pad over Jessica's nose and mouth
and held it there. Instantly her eyes closed, her body sagged, and
she became unconscious. Nicholas, struggling too, was hauled
inside and given the same treatment.

The former doctor knew the effect of chloroform would not last long. Working quickly, he used scissors to cut the sleeve of Jessica's dress, then injected a strong sedative into her upper arm. He gave the boy a similar injection.

Miguel had dragged the unconscious Angus over to the van. To Miguel's amazement, no one seemed to have witnessed what had happened. He now ordered Rafael, "Help me get him in."

It was accomplished in seconds. Then, as he entered the van himself, Miguel saw he had been wrong. An elderly woman, white-haired and leaning on a cane, was watching from some twenty yards away. She appeared uncertain and puzzled.

As Luís moved the van forward Miguel called in a cheerful voice, "Don't be alarmed. It's just part of a film we're making."

He saw relief on the woman's face. Then they left the parking lot and, soon after, Larchmont. Within five minutes they were on the New England Thruway, heading south and moving fast.

313

Chapter 4

PRISCILLA Rhea had been a schoolteacher in Larchmont who had pounded into several generations of area youngsters the fundamentals of square roots and quadratic equations. She had also urged them to have a sense of civic responsibility and never to shirk their duty. But all of that was prior to her retirement fifteen years earlier, before age and illness had slowed her body, then her mind.

Nevertheless, she was exercising her thought processes now. Her natural anxiety at seeing three people taken into a van, apparently against their will, was relieved by the shout that it was all part of a film show. That made sense. Film and television crews seemed to be everywhere nowadays, photographing against real backgrounds. But then the moment the van had gone, Priscilla looked around for the cameras and film crew, and for the life of her she couldn't find any.

The sensible thing, she told herself, was to mind her own business. Just the same, there was her lifelong credo of not shirking responsibility, and perhaps she shouldn't even now.

She walked slowly, using her cane, over to the still empty parking slot next to Jessica's station wagon. Her attention was caught by small pools of liquid on the ground. Curious, she leaned down to touch one. Seconds later she looked with horror at her fingers. They were covered in what was unmistakably blood.

OFFICER Jensen, from the Larchmont Police Department, stood by his patrol car outside the Grand Union and listened skeptically to what Priscilla Rhea had to say.

She remembered details: the color of the van—a light tan—and the fact that it had dark windows. No, she had not noticed a license number, but when she told him about some splotches on the parking lot that looked like blood, his interest began to mount. He walked over to inspect. By this time most of the liquid had dried, though there was enough that was moist to reveal it as red to the touch.

Hurrying back to where he had left Priscilla, he found her talking with several others curious about what was going on.

One man volunteered, "Officer, I was inside and saw four people leave in a hurry—two men, a woman and a boy."

"I saw them too," a woman said. "That was Mrs. Sloane, the TV anchorman's wife. She often shops here. When she left, she looked upset—like something bad happened."

The officer asked, "Did anyone see a van, color light tan?"

"Yes, I saw that," the first man said. "It pulled into the lot as I was walking to the store. It was a Nissan passenger van with New Jersey plates. Oh, one other thing. It had dark windows."

"Hold it," the officer said, addressing the growing crowd. "Any of you who have information, please stay." He jumped into the white police cruiser and grabbed the radio mike. "Car four twenty-three to headquarters. Possible kidnap at Grand Union parking lot. Request help."

Sirens from other cruisers were soon heard responding to the request.

SOME eight miles away the Nissan van was about to leave the New England Thruway and enter a maze of streets in the New York City borough of the Bronx. Both Luís and Miguel had been looking behind for signs of any pursuit. There were none.

Just the same, Miguel urged Luís, "Move it!"

Since leaving Larchmont, Baudelio had several times checked the vital signs of their two sedated captives, and all appeared to be well. The old man was now stirring, slight moans escaping him. Anticipating trouble, Baudelio prepared another hypodermic of sedative and injected it. The stirring and moans subsided.

Rafael now produced three brown blankets, and he and Carlos, with Baudelio watching, wrapped the prisoners in them. Each blanket was left folded at the top so it could cover the face when the three were removed from the van. Carlos tied each rolled bundle with cord around the middle.

Conner Street in the Bronx, which they had reached, was desolate, gray and depressing. Luís turned right into a deserted industrial area and halted the van. As he did, a truck from the opposite side of the street pulled across and stopped ahead of the Nissan. The truck was a white GMC with a painted sign SUPERBREAD on either side.

There was no such product as Superbread. The truck was one of six vehicles obtained by Miguel. Like all his other vehicles, it had been repainted several times. Today the truck was being driven by the woman, Socorro, who jumped out and went around to open the rear doors. At the same time the door of the van was opened, and the bundles, the faces covered, were quickly transferred to the GMC truck.

Miguel and Luís were busy removing identifying features from the Nissan van. Miguel peeled off the dark, thin plastic sheets from the windows, while Luís replaced the van's New Jersey plates with New York plates.

Luís then took over the wheel of the GMC truck, which now contained the unconscious Jessica, Nicholas and Angus, as well as Miguel, Rafael, Baudelio and Socorro. After a swift U-turn they headed back to the thruway and, within ten minutes after leaving it, were back on it in the new vehicle, continuing south.

Carlos, now driving the empty Nissan van, also made a U-turn. He, too, went to the interstate, but headed north.

After three miles he left the thruway, then continued north on secondary roads as far as White Plains. There he drove to a public parking garage adjoining an indoor shopping complex—Center City Mall.

Parking on the third level, Carlos moved with apparent casualness through his next activities. From a locker in the van's interior he withdrew a Styrofoam container. It contained a formidable quantity of plastic explosive plus a small detonator unit with a release pin, two lengths of pliant wire and a roll of adhesive tape. He taped the explosive and detonator out of sight behind the front seats, then ran wires from the release pin to the inside handles of each front door. Getting out of a side door, he carefully locked all doors. Now, opening either front door would pull the release pin from the detonator.

Carlos left the parking garage through the mall, then used public transport to Hackensack, where he would rejoin the others.

BERT FISHER LIVED AND WORKED in a tiny apartment in Larchmont. He was sixty-eight and a widower. His business cards described him as a news reporter, though in the parlance of journalism he was more realistically a stringer.

Like other stringers, Bert was the local representative of several news organizations. He submitted information or written copy and got paid for what was used. Though age had slowed him a little, journalism was still in his bloodstream, and he kept several scanner radios switched on, thus hearing communications of local police, fire departments and other public services.

That was how Bert heard Officer Jensen's transmission alerting Larchmont police headquarters to a possible kidnap. At the word kidnap Bert sat up straight and reached for copy paper to make notes.

By the time the transmission was finished, Bert knew he needed to call New York City television station WCBA.

AT WCBA-TV an assistant news director took Bert Fisher's call. A wholly owned affiliate of the CBA network, WCBA was a local station serving the New York City area. In a bustling, noise-filled newsroom the assistant news director listened while Bert Fisher described the police radio message and his intention to go to the Larchmont scene.

"All right, Fisher, get going!"

Hanging up, the assistant news director walked over to the newsroom desk where the station's news director presided and told her about the call.

After hearing him out, she confirmed his decision. But afterward a thought occurred to her. She picked up a telephone that connected her directly to CBA network news and spoke to Ernie LaSalle, the national editor. Repeating what she had just heard, she added, "I know Larchmont is where Crawford Sloane lives. So I thought you'd want to tell him."

"Thanks," LaSalle said. "Call if there's anything more."

When he hung up, Ernie LaSalle momentarily weighed the information. On instinct and impulse he picked up the red reporting phone. "National desk. LaSalle. We are advised that at

317

Larchmont, New York, the local police radio reports a possible kidnapping. No other details. Our friends at WCBA are following up and will inform us."

As always, the national editor's words were carried throughout the CBA News headquarters. One floor above the newsroom, senior producers at the Horseshoe paused to listen. One of them, pointing to Crawford Sloane, who could be seen through the closed glass door of his private office, observed, "If there's a kidnapping, let's be thankful it's someone else in Larchmont. Unless that's Crawf's double in there." The others laughed.

Sloane heard LaSalle's announcement through his desk speaker. His interest quickened at the mention of Larchmont. Curious for more information, he headed for the newsroom.

AFTER telephoning WCBA-TV, Bert Fisher hurried out of his apartment to his battered twenty-year-old Volkswagen bug. He kept a scanner radio in the car and set it to the Larchmont police frequency as he headed downtown to the Grand Union. Partway there some more radio exchanges caused him to change direction.

"Car four twenty-three to headquarters. Proceeding to house of possible victims of incident. Address, Sixty-six Park Avenue. Request a detective."

"Headquarters to four twenty-three. Ten four."

A brief pause, then, "Headquarters to car four twenty-six. Proceed urgently to Sixty-six Park Avenue. Investigate officer's report, car four twenty-three."

Clearly the action was heating up. Now, heading for Park Avenue, Bert felt excited about that address—66. He wasn't sure, but if the house belonged to the person he thought it did, this was really a big story.

OFFICER Jensen had just entered the driveway of 66 Park Avenue when a second police car pulled in behind him. Detective Ed York, an old-timer on the force, stepped out. York and Jensen conferred briefly, then walked to the house together. The policemen identified themselves to Florence, the Sloanes' day maid, and, surprised, she let them in.

"There's a possibility," York informed her, "that something may have happened to Mrs. Sloane." He began asking questions, which Florence answered, her concern mounting as she did.

Yes, she had been in the house when Mrs. Sloane, Nicky and Mr. Sloane's father left to go shopping. That was about eleven o'clock. Mr. Sloane had left for work just as Florence arrived, which was nine thirty. No, there had been nothing unusual when Mrs. Sloane and the others drove away. Except, well . . .

"What do you mean by 'except, well'?" the detective asked.

"Well, when they were leaving, I saw a car parked on the other side of the street. When Mrs. Sloane drove away, all of a sudden the car went the same way she did. I didn't think about it then."

"Can you describe the car?" Jensen asked.

"It was dark brown, I think. Sort of medium size."

"Did you recognize the make?"

Florence shook her head. "They all look the same to me."

The detective and Jensen returned outside. As they did, two more police cruisers arrived. One brought a sergeant, another the Larchmont chief of police. The chief was tall and rangy, with a deceptively low-key manner. After a hasty conference the chief asked Detective York, "You think this is for real—a kidnap?"

"At this moment," York said, "everything points that way."

The chief mused. "If it *is* a kidnap and they cross a state line, it becomes the FBI's jurisdiction. That's the Lindbergh law." He added decisively, "I'm calling in the FBI now."

He returned to his car and picked up the radio mike. A minute or two later, rejoining the others, the chief ordered York to go back to the house and stay inside. The sergeant and Jensen were instructed to remain on duty outside.

Knowing that Larchmont's most famous resident was involved, the chief said sourly, "Soon there'll be more people here than flies around a garbage truck. Let no one past the front gate except the FBI. When the press get here with their questions, direct them to headquarters."

At that moment they heard the sound of a noisy approaching car. Their heads turned. It was a battered Volkswagen bug, and the chief said glumly, "Here's the first."

319

Bert Fisher stopped his VW at the curb and climbed out, then hurried forward. "Chief, can you make a statement?"

"A statement about what?"

"Oh, come on, Chief! I've heard all the radio buzz, including your instruction just now to call in the FBI." Bert looked around him, realizing his hunch was right. "This is Crawford Sloane's home, isn't it? And is it Mrs. Sloane who's been kidnapped?"

The chief hesitated, then said, "Well, if you heard all the messages, you'll know we aren't certain of anything yet. But yes, we do think Mrs. Sloane may have been abducted, along with the Sloanes' son, Nicholas, and Mr. Sloane's father."

Bert, scribbling as the chief spoke, knew this was the most important story of his life. "Do you have any idea who might have done this?" he asked.

"No. Oh, just one thing. Mr. Sloane has not been informed, and we're trying to get in touch with him. So before you start sounding off, for God's sake give us time to do that."

The chief turned away, and Bert dived for his VW. Despite the chief's caveat, he had no intention of waiting for anything. As he turned out of Park Avenue he saw another car turning in and recognized the local stringer for WNBC-TV.

So the competition was on to the story. Now if Bert was to stay ahead, he had to move fast.

Not far away, on Boston Post Road, he found a pay phone. He punched out the numbers of WCBA-TV, his hand trembling.

AT ELEVEN twenty a.m. in the pressure-driven newsroom of WCBA-TV, tension was rising, as it always did during the hour preceding the local New York station's *News at Noon*. Today, especially, there was a heavy budget of news, with several developing stories competing for the lead position.

Amid a scene of near bedlam Bert Fisher's phone call was routed to the same assistant news director as before. On hearing who was calling, the assistant snapped, "We're swamped here. Make it short and quick!"

Bert did, at which the young newsman said incredulously, "You're sure? Absolutely sure?"

"I have confirmation from the chief of police," Bert said proudly. "He gave me an exclusive statement."

The assistant was already on his feet, shouting urgently to the news director, "Line four!" He told an assignment editor beside him, "We need a camera crew in Larchmont fast."

The news director listened to Bert Fisher, making notes of the essentials. "Stay on the line," she told him. Then to a writer at a desk nearby, "Take line four. It's Fisher, Larchmont. Get everything he has; then write it as our noon lead."

She picked up a telephone connecting her to the network. Ernie LaSalle answered, and she told him, "The kidnap in Larchmont is confirmed. Half an hour ago unknown persons violently seized Crawford's wife, his son and Crawford's father."

"Good God!" The national editor's shock and incredulity came down the line. "Has Crawf been told?"

"I don't think so."

"Are the police involved?"

"Very much so, and they've called in the FBI." She added, "We've heard that WNBC is on to the story, though a tad behind us. Look, we'll go with this at noon, and I'm considering breaking into programming now. But I thought, since this is family—"

LaSalle snapped, "Don't do a damn thing. The brass will be in on this. And if anybody breaks it, we will."

TAKING seconds only, Ernie LaSalle debated his options. He had several.

One was to take time to contact Crawford Sloane and gently convey to him the frightening information. A second was to pick up the red reporting phone and announce to the entire news division the kidnapping of the Sloane family, after which urgent action to make an on-air report would undoubtedly begin. The third was to issue an order to interrupt network programming with a special bulletin. In LaSalle's judgment the news just received was not only preeminent but of immense public interest.

He opted for the second choice. He knew that another New York station, WNBC-TV—owned by NBC network—was on the scene. Therefore, there wasn't time for humane niceties.

I'm sorry as hell to do this to you, Crawf, LaSalle thought, then picked up the red reporting phone.

"National desk. LaSalle. The earlier reported kidnapping at Larchmont, New York, has been confirmed by the local chief of police. The reported victims are Mrs. Crawford Sloane, young Nicholas Sloane and"—despite his resolve and professionalism, LaSalle found his voice breaking—"Crawford's father, who were violently seized and driven away by unknown persons. WCBA has reliable on-scene coverage. National desk recommends taking network air immediately."

Horror and consternation swept through the news division like a tidal wave. Everyone stopped working. Many looked at one another, asking silently, Did I really hear that?

Senior staffers at the Horseshoe were equally appalled, though their shock lasted only moments. After it, out of habit and discipline, they were galvanized to action. Chuck Insen, as senior producer in the building, left his office on the run for the broadcast control room, four floors below.

Impatiently awaiting an elevator, Insen was overflowing with sympathy for Sloane. He must have heard the hot-line call. Which raised a question. When urgent breaking news was deemed significant enough to interrupt programming, it was the evening-news anchorman—in CBA's case, Crawford Sloane—who faced the cameras. But there was absolutely no way Sloane could be expected to handle this harrowing news about his own family.

At that moment an elevator arrived, and the business correspondent of CBA News, Don Kettering, prepared to step out. Kettering, middle-aged, with a thin mustache, looked like a well-to-do businessman himself. Before he could leave the elevator, Insen shoved him back inside. The elevator doors closed.

Insen said, "You heard the speakerphone just now?"

"Yes. I'm damn sorry. I was going to tell Crawf—"

"Where you're going," Insen said, "is on the air. Get to the flash studio and take the hot seat. Crawf can't do this. You're available. I'll talk to you from the control room."

Kettering, a quick thinker and an experienced general reporter, nodded. "Do I get some briefing?"

"We'll give you all we have. You'll get a minute to do a quick study, then ad-lib. More will be fed to you as it comes in."

"Right."

As Insen left the elevator Kettering pressed a button that would take him up to the broadcast floor.

Elsewhere, other activity was in high gear. In the newsroom the northeast assignment editor was rounding up two network camera crews and correspondents. They were to proceed posthaste to Larchmont and obtain pictures of the kidnap scene as well as interview police and any witnesses. A mobile transmitting van would follow.

In a small research department adjoining the Horseshoe half a dozen people were hastily assembling the few known facts about Crawford Sloane's family—few because Jessica Sloane had always insisted on privacy for herself and Nicholas. Main research, though, had acquired a photograph of Jessica, which was coming through on a fax machine, and a graphics editor was waiting to convert it to a slide. Printing out from a computer was the war record of Angus Sloane. There would be a photo of him too.

A research assistant grabbed all the material and ran down a flight of stairs to the flash facility studio, where Don Kettering had just arrived. Right behind, a messenger from the national desk brought a printout of Bert Fisher's report, received from WCBA-TV. Kettering sat down at the studio's central desk and immersed himself in reading. Around him technicians were arriving, lights coming on. Someone clipped a microphone onto Kettering's jacket. A cameraman framed Kettering in his lens.

The flash facility was the smallest studio in the building, no bigger than a modest living room. It had a single camera, and the studio could be activated and ready in moments.

Meanwhile, in the darkened control room where Chuck Insen was now established, a director slid into her seat facing a bank of TV monitors, an assistant beside her. Operators and technicians were taking their places, a stream of orders flowing.

"Stand by, camera one. Mike check."

"Bill, this will be a live announce. 'We interrupt this programming' open and a 'resume programming' close. Okay?"

"Okay. Got it."

"Do we have a script yet?"

"Negative. Don may go ad lib."

"Bring the video up ten units."

"Camera one, let's see Kettering."

More monitors were coming alight, among them one from the flash facility. The face of Don Kettering filled the screen.

The director's assistant was telling network master control, "We expect to break into the network with a bulletin. Please stand by."

The director inquired, "Is the special slide ready?"

A voice responded, "Here it is."

On another monitor bright red letters filled the screen:

CBA NEWS
SPECIAL BULLETIN

"Hold it there." The director turned in her chair to speak to Insen. "Chuck, we're ready as we'll ever be. Do we go or not?"

The executive producer told her, "I'm finding out now." He was calling the news-division president, who was in the main newsroom, where Crawford Sloane was pleading for delay.

WHEN the shattering national-desk announcement had begun, Crawford Sloane had been on his way to the newsroom. He stopped at the head of a stairway to listen; then, scarcely believing what he had heard, he stood dazed and in a state of shock.

His trance was interrupted by a Horseshoe secretary, who came running after him. "Mr. Sloane! The police want to talk to you."

He followed the woman back and took the call in his office.

"Mr. Sloane, this is Detective York. I'm at your home and have some unfortunate—"

"I just heard. Tell me what you know."

"Actually, sir, it's very little." The detective recited the known facts. Then he added, "I've been asked to tell you there's concern about your own safety. You'll receive police protection."

Sloane's mind was whirling. Consumed with anxiety, he asked, "Is there any idea who might have done this?"

"No, sir. It all happened suddenly. We're in the dark."

"Do many people know about this—what's happened?"

"As far as I know, not many." The detective added, "The longer we can keep it that way, the better because—"

Sloane interrupted. "Detective, I'll talk to you later." He raced for the stairs and descended them swiftly. Ahead he could see the towering figure of the CBA News president in hasty conference with several others around the national desk.

Leslie Chippingham, a thirty-year veteran of TV news, was six feet four and weighed a trim two hundred and five pounds. His face was more rugged than handsome, the eyes bright blue, and the hair a forest of tight curls, now mostly gray. He was saying, "Then I guess we should go with what we have."

Sloane broke into the circle. "No, no, no! Les, don't go with it. We need more time. Publicity could harm my family."

LaSalle said, "Crawf, we know what you're going through. But this is a big story and others have it. WNBC—"

Sloane shook his head. "I still say no!" He faced the news president directly. "Les, I beg of you—delay!"

There was an embarrassed silence. Everyone knew that in other circumstances Sloane would urge going ahead. Now no one had the heart to say, Crawf, you're not thinking coherently.

Chippingham glanced at the newsroom clock: eleven fifty-four.

LaSalle had taken over Insen's phone call. Now he reported, "Chuck says everyone's set to go. Are we breaking into the network or not?"

Chippingham said, "I'm still deciding." He debated: Should they wait until noon? On monitors overhead he could see the national feeds of all networks. On CBA a popular soap opera was in progress; commercials would follow. Cutting in now would be costly. Would another six minutes make much difference?

At that moment several newsroom computers beeped. On screens a bright B appeared—the signal for an urgent press wire bulletin. Someone called out, "AP has the story."

On the national desk another phone rang. LaSalle answered, listened, then said quietly, "Thank you for telling us." Hanging up, he informed the news president, "NBC called as a courtesy.

They're going with the story on the hour." The time was fifteen seconds short of eleven fifty-five.

Making a decision, Chippingham said, "We go now!" Then to LaSalle, "Tell Chuck to break the network."

IN THE CBA News headquarters building, two floors below street level in a small, plain room, a pair of technicians sat facing complex switching systems with a galaxy of colored lights and dials, computer terminals and television monitors.

This was network master control, technical command post for the entire CBA national network. Through here all network programming flowed—entertainment, news, sports, documentaries, Presidents' addresses, prerecordings and national commercials. Surprisingly, for all its importance as an electronic pulse center, master control's location and appearance were uninspiring.

At master control, each day of broadcasting advanced according to a meticulous plan. Execution was by computer, with the two technicians overseeing it—and occasionally interceding, when unexpected events required regular programming to be interrupted.

An interruption was occurring now.

Moments earlier, on a direct line from the news-division control room, Chuck Insen had instructed, "We have a news special. It's for the full network. We're taking air—*now!*"

As he spoke, the slide CBA NEWS SPECIAL BULLETIN, fed from the news control room, came up on a master-control monitor.

The master-control operator who received the call knew the command "now" meant exactly that: no delay, no holding. So, moving a switch, the operator cut the commercial being broadcast, thereby costing CBA some twenty-five thousand dollars in revenue. With another switch he put the SPECIAL BULLETIN slide on the network video feed. Instantly the words appeared on the screens of more than twelve million television sets.

Seconds later an announcer's voice was heard:

"We interrupt our regular programming to bring you a special report from CBA News. From New York, here is correspondent Don Kettering."

In the news control room, the director ordered, "Cue Don!"

Across the nation the face of CBA's business correspondent filled television screens.

His voice and expression serious, Kettering began:

"Police in Larchmont, New York, have reported the apparent kidnapping of the wife, young son and father of CBA News anchorman Crawford Sloane. . . ."

The time was eleven fifty-six a.m. Beating out its competitors, CBA News had broken the story first.

PART TWO

Chapter 5

THE aftereffects of CBA's special bulletin announcing the Sloane family kidnap were instantaneous and widespread.

NBC News, whose courteous gesture of informing CBA had robbed it of a possible lead, followed with its own bulletin barely a minute later—ahead of its original plan to break the story at noon. CBS, ABC and CNN, alerted by wire service reports, were all on the air with the news in minutes. So were independent TV stations across the country. Radio stations were even faster than television in spreading the story.

Shortly after the initial bulletins, the press and other media reporters reached Larchmont and interviewed—as an observer put it—"almost every breathing body in sight." The former schoolteacher Priscilla Rhea proved to be the favorite interviewee, with the police chief a close second.

A startling new development emerged when several people living near the Sloanes came forward with information that the Sloane house had been under observation for perhaps a month. A succession of vehicles had been seen near the house for long periods, the occupants remaining inside. The interviewers asked the obvious question: Why had no one reported the apparent surveillance to the police?

327

In each case the answer was the same: it was assumed that security protection was being provided for the famous Mr. Sloane, and why would neighbors interfere with that?

Now, belatedly, information about the various vehicles was being sought by police.

Overseas media, too, were showing keen interest in the kidnap story. While the face and voice of Crawford Sloane were not as familiar to foreigners as to North Americans, the involvement of a major TV personality seemed of international consequence in itself.

This overwhelming reaction was proof that the modern network anchorman had become a special breed, ranking in public idolization with kings and queens, movie and rock stars, popes, presidents and princes.

CRAWFORD Sloane's mind was a turmoil of emotions. He moved through the next several hours in a daze.

What troubled him greatly was the memory of his conversation the preceding evening with Jessica. It was he who had brought up the possibility of kidnap, but as he saw it now, his own selfishness and self-importance made him assume that only he could be a victim. Jessica had even asked, "What about families? Could they be targets too?" But he had dismissed the idea, not believing it could happen. His sense of guilt was overwhelming.

Sloane fretted impatiently, wanting to take some action yet knowing there was little he could do. Another reason for staying put was the arrival of three FBI field agents, who began a flurry of activity centering on him. They demanded of CBA that the entire building be secured immediately, then phoned the New York City Police Department to discuss police protection for him. With assurances that everything possible would be done, they questioned him at length.

"Mr. Sloane, is there anything you have reported on the news which could have caused special antagonism on the part of someone?" asked Special Agent Otis Havelock, senior in the trio.

Sloane said ruefully, "Once a day, at least."

The FBI man nodded. "Two of my colleagues will view tapes

of your broadcasts for the past two years to see if ideas suggest themselves. How about antagonistic mail? You must get some."

"I never see it. People in network news are shielded from it. It's a management decision."

Havelock's eyebrows went up as Sloane continued. "Everything we broadcast generates a phenomenal amount of mail. Reading all those letters would take too much time. Then we'd probably want to respond, which would take more time still. Something else management believes is that we're better able to keep our sense of perspective and fairness if protected from individual reactions to the news." He shrugged. "Some may disagree, but that's the way it is."

"So what happens to the mail?"

"It's handled by a department called audience services. All letters are answered, and anything judged important is sent to Mr. Chippingham, the news-division president."

Havelock made a note. "We'll go through that too."

During a pause Chuck Insen knocked on Sloane's office door.

The executive producer said, "If I can interrupt, Crawf, we all want to do the best we can—for you, for Jessica, Nicky . . ."

Sloane acknowledged, "Yes, I know."

"We feel you shouldn't do the news tonight. For one thing, it will be heavily about you. For another, what we're wondering is if you'd feel up to being interviewed—live."

Sloane considered, then said thoughtfully, "Do you think I should?"

"Now that the story's out," Insen said, "I think the wider attention it gets, the better. There's always a chance that someone watching might come through with information."

"Then I'll do it."

Insen nodded, then continued, "The other networks and the press want to interview you. How do you feel about a press conference this afternoon?"

Sloane gestured helplessly, then conceded. "All right."

Insen asked, "When you're through here, Crawf, can you join Les and me in my office? We'd like your views about some other plans."

Havelock interjected, "As much as possible, I'd like Mr. Sloane to stay in his office and be close to this telephone."

"I'll be close to it anyway," Sloane assured him.

LESLIE Chippingham was already seated in Insen's office when Sloane and Insen joined him. Chippingham had just telephoned Rita Abrams in Minnesota with the unhappy news that their planned lovers' weekend would have to be abandoned. There was no way, he explained, that in the midst of this breaking story he could leave New York.

Rita, while disappointed, understood. People in TV news were used to having their lives disrupted, even their illicit affairs.

Now Chippingham said, "Chuck, spell it out for Crawf."

"The fact is," Insen said, looking at Sloane directly, "we do not have confidence in government agencies and their ability to handle this situation. I don't want to depress you, but we all remember how long it took the FBI to find Patricia Hearst—more than a year and a half. And there's something else." From his desk he produced a copy of Sloane's book, *The Camera and the Truth*. Insen opened it to a page with a bookmark.

"You wrote, yourself, Crawf, 'We who live in the United States will not remain free from terrorism in our own backyard much longer. But neither are we prepared for this pervasive, ruthless kind of warfare.' " Insen closed the book. "Les and I agree with that. Totally."

A shocked silence followed. At length Sloane said, "Do you seriously think that terrorists—"

"At this point," Chippingham put in, "we've no idea who the people are or what they want. But we believe that we ourselves— an experienced news organization accustomed to investigative reporting—have a better-than-average chance to discover where your family has been taken."

For the first time that day, Sloane's spirits rose.

Chippingham continued, "So we've decided to set up our own CBA News investigative task force. Our effort will be nationwide at first, then, if necessary, worldwide. We'll use all our resources plus investigative techniques that have worked in the past. As for people, we'll throw in the best talent we have, starting now."

Sloane felt a surge of gratitude. He started to say, "Les, Chuck—"

Insen stopped him. "There's one thing we want to ask you at this point, Crawf. The task force needs to be headed by an experienced correspondent or producer, someone who can take charge, who's good at investigative reporting and in whom you have confidence. Is there anyone you'd like to name?"

Crawford Sloane hesitated for the briefest moment, weighing his personal feelings against what was at stake. Then he said firmly, "I want Harry Partridge."

THE Medellín group kidnappers, like foxes returning to a hidden burrow, had gone to ground in their temporary headquarters, the rented property south of Hackensack, New Jersey. It was a collection of old decaying structures—a main house and three outbuildings—which had been unused for several years until Miguel, not wishing to reveal that the place would be used for little more than a month, signed a one-year lease, with full payment in advance.

The property was ideal in numerous ways. The large house could accommodate all seven members of the gang, and the outbuildings made it possible to keep six vehicles out of sight. No other houses were close by, and privacy was aided by surrounding trees. A further advantage was that Teterboro Airport was not much more than a mile away. Teterboro, used mainly by private aircraft, figured largely in the kidnappers' plans.

The three prisoners, still drugged and unconscious, had been carried to a large room on the second floor of the main house. Two hospital cots with restraining side rails stood in the center of the room. Jessica was on one; the boy, Nicholas, on the other. Their arms and legs were secured by straps—a precaution in case they regained consciousness. Alongside the two cots was a narrow metal bed that had been hastily brought in to accommodate Angus. His limbs were secured with lengths of rope instead of straps.

The former doctor, Baudelio, was working around the three

recumbent forms, setting up intravenous stands. On a table covered with a green cotton cloth he had laid out instruments and drug packages. Assisting him was the woman, Socorro.

Socorro had raven-dark hair twisted into a bun behind her head, a slim, lithe body, olive skin, and features that might have been beautiful had she not worn a permanently sour expression. She seldom spoke and never revealed what went on within her mind. For these reasons Miguel had mentally labeled Socorro "the inscrutable one."

From a tilted-back chair on the far side of the room, Miguel said to Baudelio, "Tell me what it is you are doing."

"I am working quickly because midazolam, the sedative I administered, will very soon wear off. When it does, I shall begin injections of propofol, a longer-acting drug and more suitable for what is ahead. Propofol is a tricky drug to use."

Miguel asked, "Are you sure you can handle it?"

"If you have doubts," Baudelio said sarcastically, "you are free to get someone else." When Miguel failed to answer, he went on, "Because these people will be unconscious when we transport them, we must be certain there is no vomiting and aspiration into the lungs. Therefore, while we are waiting there will be a period of enforced starvation. In two days' time we shall be ready to put them into those." Baudelio gestured to the wall behind him.

Propped upright against the wall were two open funeral caskets, solidly constructed. One was smaller than the other. The caskets reminded Baudelio of a question. Pointing to Angus Sloane, he asked, "Do you want him prepared or not? If we take him, we'd need another." His eyes returned to the caskets.

Miguel said irritably, "I do not need to be told that."

Still, he wondered. If there had been some way to do so, Miguel would have asked his superiors. But to telephone would leave the record of a call. Miguel had been emphatic with everyone that the cellular phones were solely for vehicle-to-vehicle or vehicle-to-headquarters use. Positively no calls were to be made to other numbers.

Therefore, the decision was his alone. Obtaining an extra casket also meant taking additional risks. Was it worth it?

Miguel reasoned that it was. He told Baudelio, "Yes, the old man goes."

Baudelio nodded. Despite his outward assurance, he was nervous around Miguel today because the night before he had committed what he now recognized as a serious breach of security. While Baudelio was alone, in a moment of profound loneliness and dejection, he had used one of the cellular phones to call Peru. It was a woman he had spoken to, his slatternly living companion and only friend, whom he sorely missed.

It was because of Baudelio's continuing anxiety about that call that he was slow to react when suddenly, unexpectedly, a crisis confronted him.

JESSICA, during the struggle outside the supermarket, had had only a minute or two to grasp what was happening before blackness supervened and she fell into deep unconsciousness.

But now, without knowing how long it had lasted, she was reviving, her memory returning. She became aware, faintly at first, of sounds around her, of voices. She tried to move, to speak, but found she could do neither. Then, as more moments passed, the voices became clearer, the awful memory of events at Larchmont sharpened.

Jessica's eyes opened. At first she could not understand why her arms and legs wouldn't move. Then she saw that they were constricted by straps and realized she was on what looked like a hospital bed.

She turned her head slightly and froze in horror at what she saw. Nicky was on another bed, imprisoned like herself. Beyond him Angus, too, was tied down with ropes. And then—Oh, no! Oh, God!—she glimpsed the two open funeral caskets, one smaller than the other.

At once she began to scream and struggle wildly. Somehow in her demented terror she managed to get her left arm free.

Hearing the screams, Baudelio, Socorro and Miguel, who had been looking elsewhere, swung toward her. By then Jessica had seen them all. She reached out with her left hand, trying desperately to find something to use as a weapon to protect herself. The

333

table of instruments was beside her, and she seized what felt like a kitchen paring knife. It was a scalpel.

With Socorro's help Baudelio tried to refasten Jessica's free arm. But Jessica was faster. In her desperation she reached out with the scalpel, managing to gash Baudelio's face, then Socorro's hand. Thin red lines appeared on both; then blood gushed out.

Miguel, hurrying forward, hit Jessica savagely with his fist. He retrieved the scalpel, then helped Baudelio restrap Jessica's arm. Defeated and helpless, she broke down in tears.

Nicky's sedation was also wearing off. Becoming aware of the shouting and of his mother nearby, he, too, began screaming. But despite his struggles, he couldn't free himself from the straps. Angus, who had been sedated last, did not stir.

By now the noise and confusion were overwhelming, and both Baudelio and Socorro needed treatment for their wounds. Socorro, with the lesser injury, put an adhesive dressing on her cut hand, then turned to aid Baudelio. She taped gauze pads over his face. Nodding an acknowledgment, he pointed to the assembled equipment and murmured, "Help me."

Socorro tightened the strap above Jessica's left elbow. Then Baudelio inserted a hypodermic needle into a vein and injected the propofol he had prepared earlier. Jessica, watching and screaming, fought against the drug's effect until her eyes closed, and once more she was unconscious.

Baudelio and Socorro moved on to Nicky and repeated the process. Then, before he could regain consciousness and cause trouble, Angus was also given propofol.

Miguel had been glowering at Baudelio. Now he stormed at him, "You incompetent idiot! You could ruin everything!"

"I know." Despite the gauze pads, blood was streaming down Baudelio's face. "I made an error. It will not happen again."

His face flushed with anger, Miguel stalked out.

AT ELEVEN fifty a.m., in the apartment at Port Credit, Harry Partridge had switched the TV to a Buffalo, New York, station—a CBA affiliate. Vivien had gone out and would not be back until midafternoon.

Partridge hoped to learn from the noon news the latest developments following yesterday's airlines disaster. Consequently, when programming was interrupted by the CBA News special bulletin, Partridge was watching.

He was as shocked as everyone else. As he watched Don Kettering's face on the screen and heard the continuing report, he felt, more than anything, a personal concern for Jessica. And mixed with his emotions was a surge of camaraderie and pity for Crawford Sloane.

Partridge also knew that his vacation, which had scarcely begun, was already over. It was no surprise, then, to receive a phone call a while later asking him to come to headquarters in New York. What did surprise him was that it was a personal appeal from Crawford Sloane.

Sloane's voice was barely under control. "I desperately need you, Harry," he said. "Les and Chuck are setting up a special unit; it will work on two levels—daily reports on air and deep investigation. They asked me who I wanted in charge. I told them there's only one choice. You."

In all the years they had known each other, Partridge realized, they had never been closer than at this moment. He responded, "Hang in there, Crawf. I'll be on the next flight."

"Thank you, Harry. Anyone you especially want with you?"

"Yes. Find Rita Abrams, wherever she is—I heard in Minnesota somewhere—and bring her in. The same for Minh Van Canh." Thinking quickly, Partridge added, "And I want Teddy Cooper."

Teddy Cooper, CBA's London bureau researcher, was twenty-five years old and a cheerful cockney. He was also, in Partridge's opinion, a near genius at turning ordinary research into shrewd detective work.

"You've got him," Sloane replied. "He'll be on the next Concorde out of England."

After they hung up, Partridge resumed his own preparations. Even before Sloane's call he had begun packing a suitcase that only an hour earlier he had unpacked.

He telephoned Air Canada, making a reservation on a flight

335

leaving Toronto at two forty-five p.m. It was due into New York's
La Guardia Airport at four p.m. Next he called for a taxi to collect
him in twenty minutes.

After his packing was finished, Partridge scribbled a good-bye
note to Vivien. He knew she would be disappointed at his abrupt
departure, as he was himself. Along with the note he left a generous check to cover the apartment expenses.

As he looked around for a place to leave the note and check, a
buzzer sounded in the apartment. It was the intercom from the
lobby below. The taxi he ordered had arrived.

The last thing he saw before leaving was on a sideboard, the
tickets for the next day's Mozart concert. He reflected sadly that
those—as well as other unused tickets and invitations in the
past—represented, more than anything else, the uncertain pattern of a TV newsman's life.

THE Air Canada flight out of Toronto had a light passenger load,
and Partridge had a three-seat section to himself. While en route
to New York he sipped a vodka and tonic and allowed his
thoughts to drift.

He considered, on a personal level, Jessica and himself.

Over the years since Vietnam, he had grown accustomed to
regarding her as belonging only in the past, as someone he had
once loved but who was no longer relevant to him and in any case
far beyond his reach. To an extent, Partridge realized, his thinking had been an act of self-discipline, a safeguard against feeling
sorry for himself, self-pity being something he abhorred.

But now, because Jessica was in danger, he admitted to himself
that he cared as much about her as he ever had. Face it, you're
still in love with her. Yes, I am. And not with some shadowy
memory but with a person who is living, vital, real.

So whatever his role was to be in searching for Jessica, Harry
Partridge knew that his love for her would drive and sustain him,
even though he would hold that love secret, burning out of sight
within himself.

When the flight landed in New York, he was first off the airplane and strode quickly through La Guardia terminal. With only

hand baggage he was able to take a taxi to CBA News headquarters without delay.

As he headed for Chuck Insen's office a senior producer at the Horseshoe called, "Hi, Harry. Chuck's at a press conference that's been arranged for Crawf. The whole thing's being taped."

Then, as Partridge walked toward the Horseshoe, the producer added, "Oh, in case no one's told you, Crawf's on the sidelines tonight. You'll be anchoring the news."

THE press conference was well attended by print, television and radio reporters, along with camera and sound crews. It was held in another CBA building, a block away from news headquarters. On a soundstage folding chairs had been hastily set up; all were occupied, and many other participants were standing.

There were no formal introductions, and Crawford Sloane began with a brief statement. He expressed his shock and anxiety, then appealed to the news media and the public for any information that might help disclose where his wife, son and father had been taken, and by whom.

Twice during his statement he had to pause to control emotion in his voice. Each time there was a sympathetic silence. Then he announced he would answer questions.

At first the questioning was also sympathetic. Inevitably, though, the press corps weighed in with tougher queries.

An Associated Press reporter asked, "Do you think it's possible, as some are already speculating, that your family has been seized by foreign terrorists?"

Sloane shook his head. "It's too early even to think about that."

The AP woman objected. "You're ducking the question. Is it *possible?*"

Sloane conceded, "I suppose it's possible."

A gray-haired CNN correspondent held up a copy of Sloane's book. "Do you continue to believe, as you wrote here, that 'hostages should be regarded as expendable,' and are you still opposed to paying ransom—as you put it, 'directly or indirectly, ever'?"

Sloane had anticipated the question and answered, "I don't

believe that anyone as emotionally involved as I am at this moment can be objective about that."

The CNN man persisted. "I'll put it another way. Do you regret having written those words?"

"At this moment," Sloane said, "I find myself wishing they weren't being quoted against me."

Sloane was not enjoying what was happening. But he acknowledged mentally that at plenty of press conferences in the past he had played hardball as an interrogator himself.

An offbeat query came from a *Newsday* reporter. "I've been told that your son, Nicholas, is a talented musician and might become a concert pianist one day. Is that true?"

Sloane knew that in other circumstances Jessica would object to the question as an intrusion. At this moment, though, he didn't

see how he could avoid answering it. "Our son does love music, always has. As to his being a concert pianist, or anything else, only time will tell."

At length, when the questions seemed to be winding down, Leslie Chippingham stepped forward and declared the session at an end.

Sloanc was immediately surrounded by some who wanted to wish him well.

THAT EVENING, IN THE HIDEAWAY near Hackensack, Miguel watched a portable television, switching between news programs. The Sloane family kidnapping was the top item, though there were no reports of new leads. Watching CBA's *National Evening News*, Miguel was amused to see that Crawford Sloane was not in his usual anchor position; the substitute was someone named Partridge. Sloane, however, was interviewed on air and shown at a press conference.

Something of interest coming out of it was the description of the Sloane brat as a possible concert pianist. Without any clear notion of how he might use it, Miguel tucked the nugget of information away.

Early the next morning Miguel informed Luís that at eleven o'clock the two of them would be driving into Manhattan in the hearse. The hearse was the group's sixth vehicle, a secondhand Cadillac in good condition; it had stayed out of sight at the Hackensack house.

With Luís driving, they took a circuitous route from Hackensack, several times changing direction to be sure they were not followed. They entered the Lincoln Tunnel and emerged in Manhattan at eleven forty-five.

Both Miguel and Luís were wearing dark suits, appropriate to their presence in a hearse. Miguel told Luís, "We go now to the funeral place—the same one as before. You remember?"

Luís nodded and headed toward the Queensboro Bridge, which led to the New York City borough of Queens.

Chapter 6

AT TIMES when news was quiet, a network news organization was like a slumbering giant. It operated at considerably less than a hundred percent utilization, and a substantial number of its talented people had what was referred to in the trade as downtime—meaning they were not actively at work.

Which was why, when a major news event occurred, there were experienced hands who could be grabbed and fired up.

On Friday morning, one day after the Sloane family kidnapping, the firing-up process had begun as the special task force headed by Harry Partridge, with Rita Abrams as senior producer, began assembling within CBA News headquarters.

Rita, who had reached New York from Minnesota late the night before, came into the newly assigned task force offices at eight a.m. Harry, having spent the night in a hotel suite provided by the network, joined her soon after.

Wasting no time, he asked, "Any new developments?"

"Zilch on the kidnap," Rita answered. "But there's a mob scene outside Crawf's house."

The two were in the task force conference room. Despite the brevity of her vacation, Rita seemed refreshed, her usual vitality and drive restored. "These days everyone wants to touch the hem of an anchorman," she said. "Now that they've learned his address, Crawf's fans are pouring into Larchmont. Hundreds of them, maybe thousands. The police are having trouble coping."

"We have a camera crew on site?"

"Sure have. They camped out all night. I've told them to stay in place until Crawf leaves for work."

Partridge nodded his approval. "You know we've been given pretty much a blank check where talent is concerned?"

"So I was told. I've asked for three producers to begin—Iris Everly, Norman Jaeger and Karl Owens."

"Great choices." Partridge knew them well. They were among the best in CBA News. "What I'd like," he said, "is to have a meeting as soon as possible with everyone who'll be working with us. We can begin work on a spot for tonight's news."

"I'll set it up for ten o'clock," Rita said.

THE researcher from CBA's London bureau, Teddy Cooper, had been flown in, as promised, that morning. He came directly to the task force offices and reported to Harry and Rita. The three went to the conference room, where the group was assembling. On the way in, they met Crawford Sloane, who had arrived a few minutes earlier in an unmarked FBI car.

Cooper, a wiry slip of a man, radiated energy and confidence. His brown lank hair, worn long, made him seem even younger than his twenty-five years. Though a born-and-bred Londoner, he had been in the United States several times before and was familiar with New York.

Partridge said to him, "You'll be in charge of research here, with two assistants."

The assistant researchers, a young man and woman borrowed from another CBA project, were already in the conference room. While waiting for the meeting to begin, Partridge introduced them to Cooper, and the trio began discussing a Sequence of Events board already occupying an entire wall of the room. A standard procedure in task force reporting, it would record in sequence every known detail about the kidnapping. On another wall was a second board, headed Miscellaneous. This would contain incidental intelligence, some of it speculation or rumor.

The boards' purpose was twofold: first, to apprise everyone of available information; second, to focus progress reviews and brainstorming sessions, which often provoked new ideas.

At ten o'clock Rita Abrams opened the meeting. She was seated at the head of a long table, Harry Partridge beside her. Leslie Chippingham arrived and took his place at the table too. As he caught Rita's eye they exchanged discreet smiles.

Crawford Sloane seated himself at the far end. He did not expect to contribute to the discussion at this point and had confided to Partridge, "I feel helpless right now, like a loose nut."

Also at the table were the three producers Rita had recruited. Norman Jaeger, the oldest, was a CBA veteran. Soft-spoken, imaginative and scholarly, he was a producer for the network's highly acclaimed magazine program *Behind the Headlines*. Next to Jaeger was Iris Everly, petite, in her mid-twenties and a brightly shining star on the news-production scene. Karl Owens, the third producer, was a workhorse who had gained his reputation through tireless investigative work.

Others present were cameraman Minh Van Canh, a staff writer and a secretary.

"Okay, we all know why we're here," Rita said. "First I'll talk about organization. After that, Harry will direct us on the way we should march editorially."

Rita paused from her businesslike tone and looked down the table at Crawford Sloane. "Crawf, I want to tell you, very simply and from all of us—for your sake, your family's and our own because we care—we're going to do our *damnedest!*"

From the others' there was a sympathetic murmur.

Sloane managed to utter, "Thank you," his voice choked.

"From here in," Rita went on, "we shall operate on two levels—the long-term project and the daily breaking story. Norm," she continued, addressing the oldest producer, "you're to be in charge of long term."

"Right."

"Iris, you'll do the day-by-day, starting with a spot for the news tonight."

Iris Everly said crisply, "Got it."

To the third producer, Owens, Rita said, "Karl, you'll move between the two project sides as needed." Her attention turned to Cooper. "Teddy, you'll go to Larchmont."

Cooper looked up with a grin. "Yes, ma'am. I'll dig around and make like the famed Sherlock H."

"After this meeting," Rita advised him, "Minh will go to Larchmont, heading two fresh camera crews. You'll go with him, Teddy, and meet Bert Fisher, who's a stringer for our local affiliate station. He was first to break the story yesterday."

Minh Van Canh, his dark face impassive as usual, nodded.

"For now, that takes care of the nuts and bolts," Rita said. "More important, there's editorial direction. Harry, over to you."

"Our first objective," Partridge began, "is to find out more about the kidnappers. Who are they? Where are they from? What are they aiming for? Of course, very soon they may tell us that themselves; however, we won't wait for it to happen. Somewhere the kidnappers have left traces. Everybody leaves traces. The trick is to locate some." He said to Jaeger, "Concentrating on that will be your job, Norman."

Jaeger nodded.

"Iris, about our spot for tonight's news. How do you see the bones? Do you have a framework?"

She answered crisply, "If there's no fresh dramatic news, like

343

communication from the kidnappers, we'll go to the mob scene this morning outside Crawf's house. Then, as this is the first full day since the event, I'd like a recap of yesterday."

"What about reactions?" Jaeger asked. "As in Washington."

Partridge answered, "A short bite only, from the President, I think. Maybe some citizen interviews if we have time."

"But nothing from Capitol Hill?"

"Maybe tomorrow," Partridge said. "Maybe never. Everyone on the Hill will want to get in the act."

After another fifteen minutes of discussion Rita tapped the table. "That'll do," she announced. "The rap is over. The real work begins."

BACK in his office Harry Partridge began the procedure known to all journalists as working the phones.

Open in front of him was his private blue book—a catalogue of people he knew worldwide who had been useful to him and vice versa. The news business was full of debits and credits; at times like this, credits were called in. Also helpful was that most people were flattered to be sought after by TV news.

Partridge's list of those he would call included contacts in the Justice Department, White House, State Department, CIA, Immigration, Congress, several foreign embassies, New York City's police department, Mexico's judicial police, and a lawyer with organized-crime clients.

The ensuing phone conversations were low-key and began, "Hi, this is Harry Partridge. We haven't been in touch for a while." The personal mode continued with inquiries about wives, husbands, children—Partridge kept notes of those names too—then eased into the current scene. "I'm working on the Sloane kidnapping. I wonder if you've heard any rumbles, or have ideas of your own. . . . Will you ask around and call me back?"

It was standard practice, at times tedious and always requiring patience. Sometimes it produced results, occasionally delayed ones, often none. From today's telephoning nothing specific emerged, though the most interesting conversation was with the organized-crime lawyer.

A year ago the man's daughter, on a college trip to Venezuela, had been part of a drug orgy in which two students had died. Partridge, covering the story, had decided not to use the girl's name or picture in his report.

Today, after listening to Partridge's casual opener, the lawyer responded bluntly, "I owe you. But I haven't heard anything, except on TV. Sometimes my clients get to hear about things. I'll do some discreet asking around, and if I find out anything, I'll call you."

At the end of an hour, when he had covered half the names on his list, Partridge took a break and went to the conference room to pour himself coffee. Returning, he did what almost everyone in TV news did daily: went through *The New York Times* and the Washington *Post*. It always surprised visitors to TV news centers to see how many copies of those newspapers were around. The fact was, despite TV's own news achievements, a subtle ingrained attitude persisted that nothing was really news until printed in the *Times* or *Post*.

The strong voice of Chuck Insen broke into Partridge's reading.

"I bring tonight's lineup, Harry," the executive producer said, entering the office. "The word is, we'll do a split-anchor news. You're to be half the horse."

"Rear end or front?"

Insen smiled faintly. "Which of us ever knows? Anyway, from tonight on, you'll anchor anything to do with the kidnap, which—unless the President gets shot before airtime—will be our lead again. Crawf will anchor the rest of the news, as usual; we're damned if a bunch of thugs, whoever they are, are going to dictate how life goes on at CBA."

"Fine with me," Partridge said. "I presume it is with Crawf."

"Frankly, it was Crawf's idea. Like any king, he feels insecure if off his throne too long. Besides which, his staying invisible would achieve nothing. Oh, another thing—right at the end of the news Crawf will say a few spontaneous words thanking those who've sent messages about his family, or otherwise care."

"Spontaneous?"

"Of course. We have three writers toiling over them now."

ALMOST A MONTH AGO MIGUEL had bought funeral caskets from a small, shabby funeral home in Astoria for transporting his two intended kidnap victims to Peru.

The proprietor, Alberto Godoy, was obese, bald, with nicotine-stained fingers and bloated features. Miguel's meeting with him had begun in his tiny cluttered office.

"I have two elderly parents who wish certain planning for their eventual . . . er, passing." Miguel continued with his concocted story as Godoy listened with a mixture of boredom and disbelief.

At the end his only question was, "How will you pay?"

"Cash."

Godoy became a shade more friendly. "This way."

In the basement, Miguel had found two caskets that were suitable, one of average size, the other smaller. He paid fifty-five hundred dollars total for them, then took them by truck to the safe house in Little Colombia for later transfer to Hackensack.

Now, almost a month later, he returned to Alberto Godoy's establishment in search of one more casket.

Miguel instructed Luís to park their hearse a block from the Godoy Funeral Home. He then walked to the home, where a receptionist directed Miguel to the proprietor's office.

The fat man regarded Miguel warily. "So it's you again. What do you want?"

"I've been asked to do a favor for an elderly friend. He's seen the caskets I bought for my parents and asked if I would pick up one more casket. To be paid for as before."

Godoy peered forward through shifty eyes. It was clear he now had reservations about doing business with Miguel. "Mister, I run a business here. What I want to know is, Am I setting myself up for trouble?"

"There'll be no trouble. Not if you cooperate." Miguel let his own voice take on menace, and it had an effect.

"All right, you got it," Godoy said. "But since last time the price has gone up. For that same adult model, four thousand."

Without speaking, Miguel opened his wallet and began counting out the money. Then he told Godoy, "I have transportation outside. Get the casket to your loading dock."

On the dock, Godoy was surprised to see a hearse appear. The two previous caskets, he remembered, had been taken away in a truck. Still suspicious of his visitor, Godoy wrote down the hearse's license number as it drove away, though not really knowing why. Back in his office, he pushed the piece of paper into a drawer.

Godoy smiled as he put the four thousand dollars in an office safe, then decided to do what he often did—go to a nearby bar for a drink.

A short time later, mellowed by three whiskeys, he related to a group of cronies how some punk had bought two caskets and put them—so he said—in his parents' home, ready for the old folks to croak, and then come back for another casket, all of it like he was buying chairs or saucepans. As the others roared with laughter Godoy further confided that he'd charged the dumb punk three times the regular price.

At the bar was a former Colombian who wrote a column for an obscure Spanish-language weekly published in Queens. On the back of an envelope the man wrote the gist of Godoy's story. It would make a good item, he thought, for next week's column.

AT CBA News it had been a frantic day, especially for the Sloane kidnap task force.

The story had been allotted five and a half minutes of the *National Evening News,* an extraordinary duration in a business where fifteen-second segments were fiercely fought over. As a result, almost the entire effort of the task force was devoted to that day's production.

With Harry Partridge anchoring the opening portion of the news, the evening broadcast began.

"After more than thirty hours of agonized waiting there is no fresh news about the family of CBA anchorman Crawford Sloane, whose wife, young son and father were kidnapped yesterday morning in Larchmont, New York. The whereabouts of Jessica Sloane, eleven-year-old Nicholas and Angus Sloane remain unknown.

"Also unknown are the identities or objectives of the kidnappers. While the FBI, now in charge of the investigation, is withholding comment, privately FBI officials admit no progress has been made.

"Since yesterday an outpouring of concern and anger have come from the highest levels. . . ."

The broadcast continued with a statement from the President that "such evil" had no place in America. It was followed by equally strong comments from a black steelworker in Pittsburgh and a white housewife in Topeka.

Then the scene shifted to Larchmont, where viewers were shown the melee outside the Sloane house that morning. In an interview Priscilla Rhea, the elderly former schoolteacher, described yet again the struggle on the parking lot.

Minh Van Canh had used his camera creatively, going in for an extreme close-up of Miss Rhea's face. It showed the deep lines of age, with every wrinkle in sharp relief, but also brought out her intelligence and sturdy character. She said of the kidnappers, "They were brutal men, beasts, savages."

Next the Larchmont police chief confirmed that there had been no breakthrough in the case and the kidnappers had not been heard from.

A final statement in the special news segment was made by CBA's corporate president, Margot Lloyd-Mason.

CBA HAD been the last of the major broadcast networks to fall victim to what was known in the business as the "invasion of the Philistines." That was the takeover of the networks by industrial conglomerates whose insistence on constantly enlarging profits outweighed their sense of public duty.

Nine months ago the network had been swallowed by a corporate giant with worldwide holdings, Globanic Industries Inc. Like General Electric, which had earlier acquired NBC, Globanic was a major defense contractor. The transformation of CBA began with the arrival of Margot Lloyd-Mason as the network's corporate president and chief executive officer. Known to be efficient, ruthless and exceedingly ambitious, she was already a vice president of Globanic Industries. It was rumored that her move to CBA was a trial run for the eventual chairmanship of the parent company.

Leslie Chippingham first encountered his new chieftain when, a few days after her arrival, he received a peremptory message through a secretary to appear immediately at Stonehenge, the network's name for CBA's Third Avenue headquarters. He went there in a chauffeur-driven limousine.

Margot Lloyd-Mason was tall, with upswept blond hair, a high-cheekboned face and shrewdly appraising eyes. She wore an elegant taupe Chanel suit with a paler-toned silk blouse. Chippingham found her attractive but formidable, her manner both friendly and cool.

"You may use my first name," she told the news president, making it sound like an order. Then, without wasting time, she got down to business. "You came here in a chauffeured limo."

Chippingham was startled. "Yes, I did." The car and driver were one of the perks of his job, but the experience of being spied on—which had obviously happened—was new and unsettling.

"In future, use a taxi. I do. So can you. And something else. The news division's budget is to be cut by twenty percent immediately. You'll receive a memo from me tomorrow, and I shall expect a report within a week on how economies have been made."

Chippingham was too dazed for more than a polite leave-taking. He knew that from now on his job as news president was going to be monumentally more difficult.

The matter of budget cutting was an area where all networks were vulnerable and everyone knew it, including Leslie Chippingham. The news divisions in particular had become fat, over-staffed and ripe for pruning.

When it happened at CBA News—the result of the demanded economies—the process was painful, mainly because more than two hundred people lost their jobs. The firings produced cries of outrage from those left jobless, and the print press had a bonanza. That had all taken place many months before the Sloane family kidnap.

349

IT HAD BEEN LESLIE Chippingham's idea to include Margot Lloyd-Mason in this evening's special broadcast. Yesterday, after breaking into the network with the bulletin, Chippingham had reported to Margot by telephone and did so again this morning. Her reaction had, on the whole, been sympathetic, and after their first conversation she telephoned Crawford Sloane, expressing hope that his family would be recovered quickly.

While speaking with the news president, though, she added two caveats.

"Part of the reason something like this happens is that networks have misguidedly let anchorpeople become larger than life, so the public thinks of them as something extra special, almost gods." She did not elaborate on how a network could control public concepts, even if it wished, and for his part Chippingham saw no point in arguing the obvious.

The other proviso concerned the kidnap task force.

"I don't want you going wild about spending money," Margot Lloyd-Mason asserted. "You should be able to do whatever is necessary within the existing news budget."

Chippingham said, "Margot, I'll remind you that our ratings for the *National Evening News* shot up last night, and I expect that to continue while this crisis lasts."

"Which merely goes to show," she answered coolly, "that unfortunate events can be turned to profit."

While involving the corporate president in this evening's broadcast seemed appropriate, Chippingham also hoped it might soften her attitude toward some special expenditures that, in his view, would be needed.

On air, Margot spoke with authority, using words scripted for her but with revisions of her own.

"I am speaking for all the people of this network and our parent company, Globanic Industries, when I declare that our total resources are available in the search for the missing members of the Sloane family. We deplore what has happened, and we hope to see our friend and colleague Crawford Sloane united with his wife, son and father in the shortest possible time."

Chapter 7

THE lack of progress after a frantic first day for the task force did not surprise Harry Partridge. He knew it took members of any new team at least a day to orient themselves. Just the same, it was imperative they formulate more plans.

"Let's have a working dinner," he told Rita during the afternoon. She then arranged for the six principals in the task force— Partridge, Jaeger, Everly, Owens, Cooper and herself—to meet for Chinese food immediately after the *National Evening News*. Rita chose Shun Lee West, on West Sixty-fifth near Lincoln Center, a favorite with TV newsfolk.

Their table was in a quiet corner at the rear of the restaurant. Near the end of the first course—a steaming, delicately flavored winter melon soup—Partridge addressed Cooper. The young Englishman had spent most of the day in Larchmont talking with everyone who had knowledge of the kidnapping.

"Teddy, let's hear your impressions so far."

Cooper opened a well-worn exercise book. "Okay. Number one, it was a pro job all the way. The punks who planned it knew their business and didn't leave evidence behind. Number two, they had lotsa money."

Norman Jaeger asked, "How do you know?"

"Hopin' you'd ask." Cooper grinned as he looked around the table. "You've heard about the neighbors who now say they saw cars, and once or twice trucks, outside the Sloane house? Well, five people have reported that since yesterday; today I talked to four. They all said they saw those cars on and off for three weeks, maybe a month. And they described a regular fleet—all this year's models, and eight different colors. So I asked myself, Did the gang have eight different cars?"

"They could have," Iris Everly said, "if they were rentals."

Cooper shook his head. "Not the professional bunch we're tackling. I think they probably had three cars and repainted them, say once a week, hoping to lessen the chances of being noticed. Only thing was, in the repainting they made a dumb mistake."

While they were talking, fresh dishes had appeared—sautéed

shrimp with peppers, fried prawns, snow peas, fried rice. There was a pause to enjoy the hot food; then Cooper continued, addressing Partridge.

"This afternoon your stringer Bert Fisher phoned some car dealers for me. He learned that some of the colors people say they saw aren't available for those models. For instance, a Larchmont neighbor said he saw a yellow Ford Tempo, but there's no such color made. Same goes for a blue Plymouth Reliant. The mob we're looking for did the repaint jobs themselves."

Partridge said doubtfully, "That's a pretty big supposition."

"But is it?" Rita asked. "These people practically ran a fleet of vehicles—at least five we know of, including the Nissan van. Wherever they kept them would have to be sizable. So isn't it likely it would be big enough to include a paint shop?"

"An operating headquarters, you mean," Jaeger said. He turned to Teddy. "Isn't that what you're talking about?"

"Yep." Cooper beamed. "Sure am."

The group ate thoughtfully, concentrating on what had just been said.

"An operating center," Rita mused. "Where?"

"Number one, it would have to be well clear of Larchmont," Cooper said. "Staying anywhere in the area would be dangerous. But, number two, it shouldn't be too far. The snatchers would know that in minutes there'd be an alarm and police all over would be looking for them. Therefore they'd have calculated how much time they had. Guessing, I'd say half an hour."

Owens said slowly, "Translating that to miles, if I'm reading you right, and remembering the area—I'd say twenty-five."

"Just what I figured." Cooper produced a New York area map and opened it. Taking Larchmont as the center, he drew a circle with his finger. "Twenty-five-mile radius. I reckon the headquarters is somewhere inside here."

The kidnappers and their victims, he believed, were at that operating center now, the gang members lying low until the initial searching eased up. Then the gang and prisoners would move to some more distant location, perhaps in the United States, possibly elsewhere.

But Owens pointed out, "That's an enormous area you're talking about, densely populated, and there's no way of searching it effectively, even with an army." He added, needling Cooper, "That is, unless you have another brilliant idea."

"Not right now," Cooper had answered. "I need a good night's shut-eye first."

They ended the discussion there, and though the next day was Saturday, Partridge summoned a task force meeting for ten a.m.

LATER that night Partridge lay in bed. Sleep did not come easily. Too much had happened in the preceding thirty-six hours. His mind was full—a kaleidoscope of events, ideas, responsibilities, all of them intertwined with thoughts of Jessica, the past, the present . . . memories revived.

Where was she now? Was Teddy right about a twenty-five-mile radius? Was there a chance that somehow he, Harry, like a knight in shining armor, could successfully lead a crusade to find and free his former love?

Cut the whimsy! Save thoughts about Jessica for tomorrow.

In a New York hotel room, slowly, sadly, the image of Jessica faded. At last, exhausted, Harry Partridge slept.

IN THE Hackensack base Miguel received a message by telephone at seven thirty Saturday morning. Alert and waiting, he picked up the handset on the first ring and answered, *"Sí?"*

The caller then challenged him with a prearranged code word, *"Tiempo?"* to which Miguel responded, *"Relámpago."*

Miguel's answer to the query "Weather?" had been "Lightning." It conveyed, "We are ready to go. State place and time."

The crucial message followed: *"Sombrero,* twenty hundred."

Sombrero was Teterboro Airport, about a mile away. The words twenty hundred indicated the time—2000 hours or eight p.m.—when the kidnappers and their victims would board a Colombia-registered Learjet 55LR. The LR signified long range. It would fly them first to Opa-Locka Airport, Florida, and then directly to Peru.

The caller was a diplomat attached to the Colombian consulate general in New York. A Sendero Luminoso sympathizer, he had been a conduit for messages since Miguel's arrival in the United States more than a month ago.

After receiving the call, Miguel informed the others. Those to travel on the Learjet with the kidnap victims were Miguel, Baudelio, Socorro and Rafael. Julio would remain in the United States, becoming, once more, a Medellín cartel sleeping agent. Carlos and Luís would leave separately for Colombia within the next few days.

Julio, Carlos and Luís, though, would have a last duty after the Learjet had gone: to disperse and abandon the remaining vehicles.

Miguel told Rafael first. The burly handyman-mechanic, who was in the outbuilding they used as a paint shop, grunted and nodded, seeming more interested in the GMC Superbread truck, which had been transformed into a black one with the name SERENE FUNERAL HOMES in discreet gold lettering on both sides.

Miguel pointed to the truck's New Jersey license plates. "These are fresh ones?"

Rafael nodded. "From the last set. Ain't been used yet, an' I switched the others." Now all the remaining vehicles had license plates not seen during the surveillance.

Miguel went outside. Within a cluster of trees Julio and Luís were digging a deep hole in which to bury the cellular phones and some medical equipment that Baudelio would leave behind. Miguel told them of the plans, then found Carlos in another outbuilding burning surveillance records of the Sloane house in an iron stove. When Miguel told him about the evening departure, he seemed relieved.

A small pile of clothing was beside the stove. Miguel, Rafael and Baudelio would all wear dark suits during the departure, when they would pose as mourners, using a carefully designed cover story. Everything else would be left behind.

Miguel pointed to the clothes. "Don't burn those—too much smoke. Take everything out of the pockets and remove any labels. Then bury the rest." He gestured toward the digging.

After leaving Carlos, Miguel sought out Baudelio. He found him with Socorro in the large room where the captives were being held, which by this time resembled a hospital ward. Baudelio, the right side of his face covered with dressings, appeared like a patient himself. But he was continuing with preparations for departure, and after Miguel informed him of the time, he acknowledged, "We will be ready."

The former doctor confirmed that the three captives would achieve deep unconsciousness during the time they would spend in the sealed caskets. Also, the enforced starvation period for all three—which would be fifty-six hours by departure time—was satisfactory.

Miguel paused, looking down at the three bodies. They appeared peaceful, their faces untroubled. The woman had a certain beauty, he thought. The man looked dignified, like an old soldier at rest. The boy seemed frail, his face thin, which didn't matter as long as he was alive on arrival in Peru. All three were pale but were breathing evenly. Satisfied, Miguel turned away.

The funeral caskets were horizontal on trestles, a series of tiny vent holes drilled into each. Socorro had been watching, her face inscrutable as always, while Miguel examined the caskets. As part of the planned tableau, she would be a grieving mourner too.

He asked her, "When we need it, can you cry?"

Baudelio interjected, "I will place a grain of pepper beneath her lower eyelids. Same for mine. Our tears will be copious."

Despite earlier misgivings, Miguel felt satisfied that Baudelio knew what he was doing. Socorro too. Now it was simply a question of waiting through the day.

At CBA News headquarters the special task force meeting had assembled at ten a.m. on Saturday morning. Seated at the head of the conference table, Partridge had opened the discussion when a speakerphone broke in—an announcement from the main newsroom. He and the others listened.

"Assignment desk. Richardson. This just in from UPI. 'White Plains, New York. A passenger van believed to be the vehicle used in Thursday's kidnap of the Crawford Sloane family exploded violently a few minutes ago. At least three persons are dead, many others injured. Police were on their way to inspect the van when the explosion occurred in a parking building adjoining

Center City Mall. It happened as many weekend shoppers were arriving in their cars. . . . ' "

Even as the bulletin was continuing, chairs were being pushed back, people scrambling to their feet. Partridge was first out of the conference room, hurrying to the newsroom, Rita Abrams close behind.

Saturday morning in the main CBA newsroom was eerily quiet, with barely a third of the desks occupied. Today's assignment manager, Orv Richardson, was covering for the national desk when he saw Harry Partridge and Rita Abrams hurry his way.

While Partridge skimmed the UPI bulletin and read a follow-up story feeding in on a computer monitor, Rita told Richardson, "We should go on air immediately. Who has authority?"

"I have a number." He quickly tapped out digits for a CBA News vice president available at home. When the man answered, Richardson explained the situation and asked for authorization to take air with a special bulletin.

The vice president shot back, "You have it. Go!"

What followed was a near replay of Thursday's intrusion into the network when the kidnap news broke, though with a different cast. Partridge was in the flash facility studio occupying the correspondent's hot seat. Rita was acting executive producer, and in the control room a different director appeared.

CBA was on air within four minutes after receiving the UPI bulletin. There was no time to write a script. Harry Partridge, collected and articulate, simply memorized the contents of the wire reports and ad-libbed.

The special broadcast was over in two minutes. There were the bare facts only, few details and no on-scene pictures. A fuller report, Partridge promised viewers, would be aired later on CBA's Saturday *National Evening News*.

As soon as the red camera lights went out in the flash studio, Partridge phoned Rita in the control room. "I'm going to White Plains," he told her. "Will you set it up?"

"I have already. A camera crew is on the way. Iris, Teddy Cooper and I are going as well. Iris will produce a piece for tonight. There's a car and driver waiting."

DURING THE PRECEDING NIGHT an alert security guard in the Center City Mall parking building had noted the presence of a Nissan passenger van with New York plates. He wondered if it could be the one being sought in connection with the Sloane family kidnapping. He wrote a query to that effect on his report, and the maintenance supervisor, reading it next morning, promptly called the White Plains Police Department, who ordered a patrol car to investigate. The time, according to police records, was nine fifty a.m.

The maintenance supervisor, however, did not wait for the police arrival. Instead he went to the Nissan van, taking along a large bunch of car keys he had accumulated over the years. Quite quickly he found a key that fitted the van and opened the driver's door. It was his final act in the few remaining seconds of his life.

With a roar someone later described as "like fifty thunderstorms," the Nissan van disintegrated in an intense ball of flame. So did a substantial part of the building and several cars nearby. The Center City Mall itself sustained structural damage, and in the mall and beyond, windows and glass doors were shattered. Other debris descended on adjoining streets, traffic and people.

The shock effect was total. When the initial roar subsided, the screams began, followed by incoherent shouts and curses, hysterical pleas for help, unintelligible orders and, soon after, sirens approaching from all directions.

In the end it seemed extraordinary that the human toll was no greater than it was.

One thing became evident. The Nissan van had indeed been used by the kidnappers. The proximity to Larchmont and the fact that the van was booby-trapped pointed to that conclusion. And the owner's name, address and insurance data, when checked against motor vehicle records, were discovered to be phony.

One other conclusion was expressed by the White Plains police chief at the explosion scene. He told reporters grimly, "This was clearly the work of hardened terrorists."

When asked if, extending that reasoning, it was foreign terrorists who had abducted the Sloane family trio, the chief answered, "That didn't happen on my turf, but I would think so."

"LET'S MAKE THAT FOREIGN terrorist theory our main focus for this evening's news," Harry Partridge told Iris Everly and Rita when he heard about the police chief's comment.

The CBA contingent had arrived a few minutes ago in two vehicles—the camera crew aboard a Jeep Wagoneer; Partridge, Rita, Iris, and Teddy Cooper in a car driven by a network courier—both having covered the twenty-five miles from mid-Manhattan in a sizzling thirty minutes. As well as an assemblage of newspeople at the scene, a growing crowd of spectators was being herded behind police barriers. Minh Van Canh and sound man Ken O'Hara were already getting videotape and natural sound of the wrecked building, the injured who continued to be removed, and of piles of twisted, tortured vehicles, some still burning.

They had also joined an impromptu press conference in time to tape the police chief's statement.

After assessing the situation, Partridge summoned Canh and O'Hara and began conducting on-camera interviews with some of those involved in rescue efforts as well as witnesses to the explosion.

It was work that could have been performed by the camera crew alone or with a producer. But it gave Partridge a sense of involvement, being in action, of *touching* the story directly for the first time.

It also raised some questions: Now that a terrorist connection was virtually confirmed, were any civilized resources capable of tracking and outwitting so evil an enemy? And even if the answer happened to be yes, wasn't it an empty conceit to believe that an unarmed news-reporting cadre like CBA News could succeed where police, governments, intelligence and military so often failed?

Partridge wondered, Should I advise for pragmatic reasons the abandonment of active engagement by CBA, advocate our return to a standard role of news observing or, failing that, at least pass on responsibility to someone else?

Then he realized, We've never had one quite like this before, with so much depending not just on what we report, but on what we do.

PARTRIDGE, Rita, and Teddy Cooper rode back to Manhattan together—at a pace considerably less frantic than their drive out. Cooper appeared preoccupied. Partridge and Rita, too, at first seemed disinclined to talk. While they had witnessed many times the effects of terrorism overseas, to observe its invasion of American suburbia was traumatic.

After a while Partridge said, "So who the hell are they?" He pounded a fist into his palm. "That's what we must concentrate on. Who?"

Rita answered, "It's natural to think first of the Mideast—Iran, Lebanon, Libya . . . the religious lineup: Hezbollah, Amal, Shiites, Islamic Jihad, PLO, you name it."

Partridge nodded. "They may want to make an impression here." He looked at Cooper. "Any other thoughts?"

"Maybe you should be looking south, Harry."

"Latin America," Rita said. "It makes sense. Nicaragua's the most likely, Honduras or Mexico possibilities, even Colombia."

They continued to theorize; then Partridge said to Teddy, "What's at work in that convoluted mind of yours?"

Cooper considered, and began, "I'm guessing that the kidnappers have left this country. And taken Mr. S.'s family. What happened this morning was like a signature. To let us know the kind of people they are, how rough they play. It's a reminder for later on."

Rita asked, "If you're right, where does that leave us?"

"It leaves us having to decide if we want to make a big, expensive effort to find their hideaway if it's empty when we get there. Harry said yesterday, 'Everybody leaves traces.' "

Their car was nearing Manhattan. "Last night," Partridge reminded Cooper, "you told us you'd try for an idea to locate the gang's headquarters. Is that 'big, expensive effort' part of it?"

"It would be. It would also be a long shot. Let's figure what kind of a place the mob would need to park at least five vehicles, set up a paint shop, provide quarters for four people, probably more. Well, it would most likely be one of three things—a small disused factory, an empty warehouse, or a big house with outbuildings. But whichever it was, it would need to be somewhere isolated, lonely."

"The trouble is," Partridge objected, "even in our twenty-five-mile radius from Larchmont there could be thousands of places answering that description."

"I said it would be a long shot, but there might just be a way." As Partridge and Rita listened Cooper described his plan.

"Start by chewing over this. When those snatchers got here, they'd most likely pick a general area. After that they'd do what anyone else would—look through newspaper real estate advertising, study the classifieds in every newspaper, regional and local, inside that twenty-five-mile radius. Okay, what we should do is look for ads for the kinds of buildings we just talked about—especially any ad that ran for a while, then suddenly stopped."

Rita gasped. "Have you *any idea* how many papers, dailies and weeklies, and how many people . . . ?"

Cooper shrugged. "No, not exactly, except it's a hell of a lot. But what we'd do is hire people—bright young kids—to look through them all. It has to be done fast, before the trail gets cold."

There was a silence as Partridge and Rita weighed what they had heard. Then Partridge announced his judgment. "I salute you for an original idea, Teddy, but I think what you'd be trying to do is impossible. The amount of help you'd need would cost a fortune. Anyway, we're not making a decision here. Because of the money, Les Chippingham will do that."

THE two-and-a-half-minute spot produced by Iris Everly for the Saturday *National Evening News* was dramatic, shocking and video rich. At White Plains, Minh Van Canh had, as always, employed his camera creatively. Iris, back at CBA News headquarters and working with a videotape editor, had fashioned a small masterpiece of news theater.

The spot began with the pile of burning cars, then cut to the injured being carried out. Partridge had recorded an audio track over which pictures of the devastation were superimposed. He began:

"Today any remaining doubt that the kidnappers of the Sloane family are full-fledged terrorists was savagely dispelled. . . ."

The polished end result required hours of painstaking editing, a facet of TV news seldom understood by viewers. Partridge also recorded a final stand-up for the piece, facing a camera on the street outside the CBA News building.

Since returning from White Plains, he had agonized about what he would say. Some of the words he had considered using would, Partridge knew, bring anguish to Crawf. So should he soften them, or be the hard-nosed newsman with a single standard—objectivity? In the end the decision simply happened.

"The events in White Plains today—a monstrous tragedy for that city's innocent victims—is also the worst of news for my friend and colleague Crawford Sloane. It means that his wife, young son and father are in the hands of savage, merciless unknown outlaws.

"The nature and timing of the crime at White Plains also raise a question many are now asking: Have the kidnap victims by this time been removed from the United States and conveyed to some distant place, wherever that may be? Harry Partridge, CBA News, New York."

Chapter 8

THE kidnappers and their victims were just about ready to steal out of the country.

From the Hackensack hideaway Julio would drive the hearse to Teterboro Airport, Luís the Serene Funeral Homes truck. Both vehicles were loaded. The hearse contained a single casket in which Jessica lay, under deep sedation. Angus and Nicky, also unconscious and in closed caskets, were in the truck.

Strangely, the sight of the caskets subdued the conspirators, as if the roles they had rehearsed in their minds and were about to act out had somehow become easier to assume.

As the moment to leave approached, Socorro had appeared in a black linen dress with matching jacket. Her hair was tucked under a black cloche, and she wore gold earrings and a thin gold necklace. She was crying copiously, the result of Baudelio's prescription of a grain of pepper beneath each lower eyelid.

Rafael, Miguel and Baudelio, wearing their dark suits and ties, looked suitably cast as mourners. If questions were asked, Rafael and Socorro would pose as brother and sister of a dead Colombian woman, killed in a fiery auto accident while visiting the United States. Her remains were being flown home for burial with those of her young son, who—so the cover story went—was also killed in the accident. The third "dead" person, Angus, would be described as an older distant relative who had been traveling with the other two.

Baudelio would be a member of the bereaved family, Miguel a close family friend. A critical feature of the story was that all three bodies were so badly burned as to be unrecognizable. Miguel counted on that to deter any opening of the caskets.

Elaborate documentation corroborated the cover story—fake death certificates, and new passports for Miguel, Rafael, Socorro and Baudelio, all obtained through one of Miguel's Little Colombia contacts.

In the courtyard of the Hackensack house Miguel checked his watch. Seven forty p.m. He climbed into the front seat of the hearse, beside Socorro in the middle, and told Julio tersely, "Go."

The last traces of sunset had settled in as they headed for Teterboro, fifteen minutes away at most.

TETERBORO was a busy airport used exclusively by private planes. Along the northwest perimeter were the headquarters of several companies that provided operating services for all aircraft. Each company had a private entrance to the airport and handled its own security.

Of Teterboro's service companies the largest was Brunswick

Aviation, the one that the incoming Learjet 55LR from Colombia would use.

Approaching the brightly lit Brunswick building, the hearse was blocked by a gate. Beside it stood a uniformed security man. Next to him a tall man in civilian clothes was peering at the hearse. A police detective? Miguel felt a tightening of his gut.

The tall man stepped forward with authority. Julio lowered his window, and the man asked, "Do you have an uncommon shipment for Senor Pizarro?"

A wave of relief swept over Miguel. It was a coded question, prearranged. He used an answering code. "The consignment is ready for transfer, and all papers are in order."

The man nodded. "I'm your pilot. Denis Underhill." His accent was American. "Let's get going." As he went around to the passenger side Underhill motioned to the guard, and the gate swung open. Clearly there was to be no security check.

The pilot directed Julio as they moved onto a taxi strip between blue lights. The truck was behind.

Several aircraft loomed ahead. The pilot pointed to the largest, a Learjet 55LR. From its shadows a figure emerged.

Underhill said tersely, "Faulkner. Copilot."

On the Learjet's left side a clamshell door was open, the lower half filled with steps. The copilot had gone inside, and lights were coming on. Julio maneuvered the back of the hearse close to the Lear's steps for unloading. The truck had stopped, and from it Luís, Rafael and Baudelio jumped down.

At the Learjet's doorway Underhill said to Miguel, "I don't want to know anything about you or your business. We're providing a contract charter flight. Nothing else."

Miguel nodded. He knew both pilots would earn golden pay for this journey tonight.

With the copilot supervising, the first casket, containing Jessica, was transferred from the hearse to the jet. Inside, the right-side seats had been removed and straps provided to hold the caskets in place.

By the time the first casket was loaded, the hearse had been moved away and the truck backed in. The other two caskets followed speedily, after which Miguel, Baudelio, Socorro and Rafael boarded and the clamshell door was closed. As Miguel seated himself and looked through a window the lights of the two vehicles were already receding. The radio crackled as tower clearance was asked for and received.

Moments later the Learjet taxied and took off, climbing swiftly through the darkness and heading south for Florida.

IT WAS not until after the first-feed Saturday *National Evening News* that the special task force meeting resumed at CBA News headquarters. By then it was seven ten p.m.

Seated once more at the head of the conference-room table, Harry Partridge surveyed the others—Rita Abrams, Norman Jaeger, Iris Everly, Karl Owens, Teddy Cooper. Most looked tired. The room itself was messy, with waste containers overflowing, dirty coffee cups abounding, and discarded newspapers littering the floor.

The Sequence of Events and Miscellaneous boards had been added to considerably. The most recent contribution was a summary of this morning's White Plains havoc. Frustratingly, though, there was still nothing conclusive about the kidnappers' identities or their victims' whereabouts.

"Reports, anyone?" Partridge asked.

Jaeger raised a hand, then spoke in his quiet, scholarly fashion. "Today I've been telephoning Europe and the Middle East—our bureau chiefs, correspondents, stringers, fixers—asking about terrorist activity. Have any terrorists disappeared from sight recently? If they have, could they be in the United States? And so on."

Jaeger paused, shuffling notes. "There are some rumors and rumbles. No proof, though." He threw up his hands. "All these hoodlums are like slippery shadows."

Leslie Chippingham entered the conference room, followed by Crawford Sloane. Partridge observed Sloane and thought the anchorman looked ghastly, even more pale and gaunt than yesterday, though it was not surprising with the growing strain. As the meeting fell silent the news president urged, "Carry on, please."

Partridge thanked Norm Jaeger, then turned to Karl Owens. "I know you've been inquiring southward, Karl. Any results?"

"Nothing positive," the younger producer said. "I've talked with the same kind of contacts as Norm—mine in the major Latin American cities. Nothing fits a group movement of the kind we're looking for. I did stumble on one thing. It's from Colombia. About a guy called Ulises Rodríguez."

"A particularly nasty terrorist," Rita said. "I've heard him referred to as the Abu Nidal of Latin America."

"He's all of that," Owens agreed, "and he's also believed to have been involved in several Colombian kidnappings. Three months ago Rodríguez simply disappeared. Those who should know are convinced he's active somewhere. But wherever he is, he's stayed successfully out of sight."

"This gets interesting," Rita said. "Is there anything more?"

Owens nodded. "Rodríguez studied English at Berkeley and speaks it with an American accent. I called our San Francisco bureau and asked to have someone sent over to Berkeley to do some checking. They sent Fiona Gowan, who happens to be a Berkeley graduate. Fiona got lucky, and—if you'll believe it—located an English department faculty member who actually remembers Rodríguez from the class of '72."

Rita said, "We believe it." The others around the table were listening intently.

"Rodríguez was a loner, had no close friends. Also, it seems, he was camera shy. Eventually it got to be a joke, so a classmate who was a pretty good artist did a charcoal sketch of Rodríguez without his knowing. The artist made a dozen copies, which he doled out to his friends."

"Those copies—" Partridge began.

"We're on to it, Harry." Owens smiled. "Just before this meeting Fiona called me to say she's located one of the sketches and will have it to us by tomorrow."

There was an approving murmur around the table. "Nice staff work," Chippingham said.

"We should keep a sense of proportion," Owens pointed out. "It's only a guess Rodríguez is involved with our kidnap."

"What we can do is show the picture around Larchmont and ask if anyone remembers seeing him," Partridge said. "Anything else?"

"Washington bureau checked in," Rita said. "The FBI has nothing new. Their forensic people are working on what was left of the Nissan van at White Plains, but they're not hopeful. They're depending on the kidnappers making contact."

Partridge looked down the table toward Sloane. "I'm sorry, Crawf, but that seems to be all we have."

Rita reminded him, "Except for Teddy's idea."

Sloane said sharply, "What idea? I haven't heard it."

Partridge nodded to the young Englishman, and Cooper brightened as attention focused on him. "It's a possible way to find out where the snatchers had their hideout."

Cooper repeated the proposal made to Partridge and Rita earlier that day, to examine classified ads appearing over the past three months in newspapers within twenty-five miles of Larchmont. Objective: to match the kind of property he visualized as the kidnappers' headquarters. He ended, "It's a long shot, I admit."

"I wouldn't even put it that high," Chippingham said, frowning. "How many people would we need for the detail work?"

Rita said, "I estimate sixty people, plus some supervision."

Chippingham turned to Partridge. "Harry, are you seriously recommending this?"

Partridge hesitated. This morning, during the drive back from White Plains, he had mentally labeled Teddy's notion a harebrained scheme. Now he reasoned, Sometimes taking a stand was a good idea, even with a long shot.

"Yes, Les," he said. "In my opinion we ought to try it."

Chippingham was unhappy with the answer. Margot Lloyd-Mason's edict echoed in his mind: "I don't want you going wild about spending money. . . ."

"Harry, I'm going to veto that one," Chippingham said. "I simply don't think it has enough possibility to justify the effort."

Jaeger began, "I would have thought, Les—"

Before he could finish, Crawford Sloane said sharply, "Les, aren't you really saying you won't spend the money?"

"That's a factor; you know it always is."

Sloane said icily, "Then I have a question, and I'd like an answer. Has Margot Lloyd-Mason put on a spending freeze?"

Chippingham said uneasily, "We've discussed budget, that's all. For anything worthwhile I'll simply call Stonehenge—"

Sloane stormed, "And what *I'll* call is a press conference. To tell the world that while my family is suffering in some hellhole, this wealthy network is haggling over pennies."

The others could scarcely believe what they were hearing.

Eventually Norman Jaeger stood up. He said quietly, "Harry thinks we should give Teddy's idea a chance. So do I."

Karl Owens joined him. "Me too."

"Add me to the list," stated Iris Everly.

Rita, a touch reluctantly, caring about Chippingham, said, "I guess you'd better count me in."

"Okay, okay, let's cut the histrionics," Chippingham said. He knew that either way he was the loser, and silently cursed Margot. "Maybe I was wrong. Crawf, we'll go ahead." But he wouldn't, Chippingham decided, ask for Margot's approval; he knew too well what her response would be. He would authorize the expense and take his chances.

Rita, practical as always and seeking to defuse the scene, said, "If we're moving on this, we can't afford to lose time. We should have researchers working by Monday. So where do we begin?"

"We'll call in Uncle Arthur," Chippingham said. "I'll speak to him at home tonight and have him here tomorrow to begin recruiting."

Crawford Sloane brightened. "A good idea."

With tensions eased, Partridge said, "Les, there's something I think needs saying. At the best of times I wouldn't want your job. But especially right now, I'm certain that none of us here could juggle the priorities and people that you're having to—at least, not any better."

Chippingham looked at Partridge gratefully and nodded.

WITH the grace of a gull the Learjet 55LR descended through the night toward two parallel strands of lights, marking runway 18 of Opa-Locka Airport. Beyond the airport were the myriad lights of Greater Miami.

The time was just after eleven p.m. In the passenger cabin

Miguel turned toward Baudelio who, a few feet away, was monitoring the three caskets. Baudelio nodded, indicating all was well, and Miguel considered a potential problem.

His own and the Medellín cartel's intelligence about the rules and habits of U.S. customs was the reason Opa-Locka had been chosen as the airport of departure. Like Teterboro, Florida's Opa-Locka was used by private aircraft only. Because of incoming flights from overseas, it had a small U.S. customs office. Usually no more than two officers were on duty, and even then only until seven p.m. The present Learjet journey had been scheduled on the assumption that by this late hour customs would be closed.

But there was still the chance of occasional checks. Miguel knew that specific papers were required for each body. With careful foresight he had obtained all the documents; they were forgeries, but good ones. Yet a casket must be opened, its contents inspected by a customs officer.

Miguel felt himself tense as the Learjet landed smoothly and taxied toward hangar 1.

OPA-LOCKA Airport, though busy, had few buildings, and the area's overall dry flatness conveyed the impression of a desert.

Amid that desert hangar 1 was an oasis. It was an attractive modern building, only part of which was a hangar. The whole comprised a luxury passenger terminal catering to private aircraft and their passengers. Similar facilities existed for pilots, plus a comprehensive flight-planning area. It was in that area that Customs Inspector Wally Amsler approached the Learjet pilot, who was studying weather data.

"Good evening, Captain. You're scheduled out for Bogotá?"

The pilot, Underhill, looked up. "That's right."

In fact, both his answer and the flight plan were lies. The Learjet's destination was a dirt landing strip in the Andes, near Sion, in Peru, and the flight there would be nonstop. But Underhill's instructions specified that his departure data should show Bogotá.

"If you don't mind," Amsler said politely, "I'd like to inspect your ship and your people aboard."

Underhill did mind, but knew it would do no good to say so. He only hoped that his oddball quartet of passengers could satisfy this customs guy sufficiently to have him clear the airplane. He was uneasy about his own involvement with whatever was going on.

There was something unusual—possibly illegal—about those caskets, Denis Underhill suspected. Not for a moment did he believe the story told to him at the time the charter was arranged about accident victims and a grieving family. However, remembering his pay for the flight would be munificent, he decided to use the accident-victims yarn now, thereby putting himself on the record whatever else might happen.

"It's a sad situation," he told the customs man, and went on to describe the tale he had been told.

Amsler listened noncommittally, then said, "Let's go."

They walked from the hangar 1 main building to the Learjet, parked nearby. The Lear's door was open, and Underhill preceded Inspector Amsler up the steps into the cabin. He announced, "Lady and gentlemen, we have a friendly visit from United States customs."

AFTER the Learjet had landed, Miguel had talked seriously to the other three group members. He had warned them of the possibility of a customs inspection and that they must be prepared to play their rehearsed roles. All indicated they were ready. Socorro slipped a second grain of pepper beneath each lower eyelid, and almost at once her eyes filled with tears.

Miguel made clear he would be principal spokesman. Consequently, it was not a total shock when Underhill made his announcement and a customs officer appeared.

"Good evening, folks." Amsler looked around, taking in the caskets and the passengers—three seated, Miguel standing.

"Good evening, Officer." Miguel was holding a sheaf of documents and four passports. He proffered the passports first.

Amsler accepted them, but didn't look down. Instead he asked, "Where are you going and what is the purpose of this flight?"

"This is a tragic journey, Officer, and a once happy family is now overwhelmed with grief."

"And you, sir. What is your name?"

"I am Pedro Palacios, a close friend of the bereaved family." Miguel was using a new alias for which he had a matching Colombian passport. He added, "My friends have asked me to speak for them because they are not proficient in English."

Amsler looked at Miguel's passport and, glancing up, compared the photo with his face. "You speak English very well, senor."

Miguel answered with assurance, "Part of my education was at Berkeley. I love this country dearly."

Opening the remaining passports, Amsler compared the photos in them with the other three people, then, nodding, returned to Miguel. "Tell me about those." Amsler gestured to the caskets.

Miguel's voice became choked. "There was a terrible accident. This lady's sister, her sister's son, an older gentleman also of the family, were on vacation in America. They had reached Philadelphia and were driving . . . A truck, out of control, crossed the turnpike at great speed. It struck the family's car, killing everyone. A fire burned, and the bodies . . . Oh, my God, the bodies!"

At the mention of bodies Socorro wailed and sobbed. Rafael had his head down in his hands, his shoulders shaking.

Miguel thrust the remaining documents forward. "It is all here. Please, Officer, I ask you—read for yourself."

Amsler took the papers and leafed through them. The death certificates appeared to be in order; so did the body disposition permits and the entry permissions for Colombia. He read the words "bodies burned . . . mutilated beyond recognition," and his stomach turned at the thought of what he had to do next.

He told Miguel, "I'm truly sorry, but regulations require that the caskets be opened for inspection."

It was what Miguel had most feared. "Oh, please, Officer. I beg of you! There has been so much anguish, so much pain."

Amsler told Miguel, "I did not write the regulations. I suggest the caskets be taken from the airplane to somewhere private. Your pilot can arrange it."

Miguel knew he could not allow it. His hand slipped under his coat. He felt his Makarov 9-mm pistol and slid off the safety. Glancing at Rafael, he saw the big man nod.

Miguel shifted position slightly, placing himself between the customs man and the door. His fingers tightened on the gun. This was the moment. *Now!*

In that instant a voice spoke. "Echo one seven two. Sector."

It startled everyone except Amsler, who was used to hearing the walkie-talkie he carried on his belt. He lifted the radio to his lips. "Sector, this is Echo one seven two."

"Echo one seven two," the voice rasped back, "Lima two six eight requests you terminate present assignment and contact him immediately by landline."

Amsler transmitted the acknowledgment. He had received a clear order he could not disobey. Lima two six eight was the code number of his sector boss. He must get to a phone fast.

"I have been summoned away, Senor Palacios," he said. "Therefore I will clear your flight now, and you may leave."

Amsler was unaware of the suddenly lowered tension and relief.

A short time later the Learjet 55LR, clear of United States airspace and on course for Sion, Peru, climbed into the night.

Chapter 9

CBA EXECUTIVES used to find it a nuisance when asked by a succession of people—friends, relatives, business contacts—"Will you help my son/daughter/godchild/pupil/protégé get a job in television news?" But not anymore. Arthur Nalesworth saved his colleagues all of that trouble. Now a CBA big shot could say, "Certainly I'll help. We have a special vice president to deal with bright young people. Tell your candidate to call this number for an interview."

The interview was always given, because Arthur Nalesworth—urbane, dignified, and known to everyone as Uncle Arthur—interviewed *everybody*. And gradually certain young people employed at his urging moved quickly and successfully into the news department's mainstream.

Thus, on a Sunday morning in the third week of September, Uncle Arthur came to the task force conference room, where Partridge, Rita and Teddy Cooper were on hand to greet him.

Uncle Arthur was in his mid-sixties, with a cherubic face and a full head of silver hair.

He listened while Cooper described the attempts to identify the kidnappers and outlined his idea of searching through real estate ads in an attempt to locate the kidnappers' headquarters.

Partridge added, "At the moment it's the best we have."

"My experience," Arthur replied, "is that when you have nothing whatever to proceed on, long shots are the way to go."

Cooper then accompanied Uncle Arthur to his small office, where the older man spread files and index cards around until they covered the surface of his desk. Next he began telephoning—each call sounding as if a familiar friend were on the line.

He worked patiently through his files. By the end of the day Uncle Arthur made known that sixty of his "brightest and best" would be reporting to CBA News for duty on Monday morning.

EARLY on Sunday the Learjet 55LR entered airspace over San Martín province in the sparsely populated Selvas, a jungle region of Peru. On the dimly lit flight deck both pilots craned forward, their eyes searching the darkness ahead. Not far ahead were high mountain ranges. The local time was four fifteen a.m.

The copilot, Faulkner, was first to see the ground beacon. The white light flashed three times, then went out, but not before Faulkner, who was at the controls, had put the aircraft into a turn.

Captain Underhill was busy with a radio, using a special frequency and a prearranged call sign. A reply shot back with permission to land. The same beacon light came on again and continued flashing intermittently. Moments later, beyond it, three flares sprang into view along the hard dirt strip.

"I'll take us in," Underhill said, and assumed the controls. He made a pass over the area. He had been here before and knew they would need every foot of ground available—knew, too, there were trees and heavy foliage on both sides of the landing strip. Satisfied, he began an approach pattern.

The Lear's two bright landing lights sliced the darkness ahead. Now the strip was barely fifty feet distant. This was it! They touched the rough, uneven ground with a bump. Reverse thrust . . .

brakes. The end of the strip was disconcertingly close, but they made it—with nothing to spare.

The Learjet's engines fell silent, and Faulkner left his seat to open the door. Miguel and his crew filed out. In sudden contrast to the controlled temperature inside, the outside air was suffocatingly hot and humid.

The waiting force on the ground comprised eight men. Even in the darkness it was possible to see that all were sturdy peasant types, stockily built. The youngest-looking of the eight stepped forward, identified himself as Gustavo, and declared his willingness to accept Miguel's orders. Then he turned to Socorro with a bow of respect—because of her affiliation with Sendero Luminoso.

Miguel told Gustavo to have his men unload the caskets. Meanwhile, Captain Underhill, who had just emerged from the airplane, found himself looking into the barrels of six Kalashnikov rifles. Four of the Peruvians entered the airplane, and one by one the caskets were unloaded and carried into a small hut. Baudelio and Socorro followed inside.

AN HOUR and a half had passed since the Learjet's landing. The jet had been refueled, and Underhill was now looking for Miguel to inform him of their imminent departure.

The hut door was partially closed, and hearing voices inside, the pilot pushed it open. The next instant he stopped—shocked and horrified at what he saw.

Seated on the dirt floor were three figures, their backs to the wall, heads lolling, mouths open, comatose but certainly alive. Two of the caskets—now open and empty—had been placed on either side of the trio to help prop them up. A single oil lantern illuminated the scene.

Underhill knew immediately who the three were. He listened daily to radio news and read newspapers. It was impossible not to know about the kidnapped family of the famous U.S. anchorman.

Icy fear crept over Denis Underhill. Flying Latin American charters, he had skirted the borderlines of crime before. But he had never been involved in anything as felonious as this.

It was at that moment that a figure moved quickly toward

Underhill from the far side of the hut. It was Miguel. With a Makarov 9-mm pistol in his hand, he motioned. "Out!"

Underhill moved ahead of Miguel to the jungle outside. There, Miguel said menacingly, "You just *thought* you saw something. Maybe you didn't after all."

Underhill responded hastily, breathlessly, "That's right. Didn't see a damn thing."

"Get the airplane out of here," Miguel snarled, "and afterward keep your mouth shut."

Underhill nodded, trembling.

AFTER less than three full days of investigation an important success had been achieved by the CBA News special task force.

In Larchmont, New York, an infamous Colombian terrorist, Ulises Rodríguez, had been positively identified as one of the kidnappers of the Sloane family trio and, perhaps, the leader of the kidnap gang.

On Sunday morning, as promised, a copy of the charcoal sketch of Rodríguez, drawn twenty years earlier by a fellow student at Berkeley, had arrived at CBA News headquarters. At this point CBA had the information exclusively.

Late Sunday four task force members—Harry, Rita, Karl Owens and Iris Everly—discussed the breakthrough. Owens urged that it be included in Monday's edition of the *National Evening News*. When Partridge hesitated, Owens argued forcefully.

"Look, Harry, no one else has this yet. We're ahead of the whole pack. If we hold off, word about Rodríguez may get out and we'll lose our exclusive."

"I know," Partridge said. "I'd like to go with it. But there are reasons to wait. I'll make a decision tomorrow."

With that the others had to be content.

Partridge privately decided that Crawford Sloane must be informed. Crawf, he reasoned, was suffering such mental agony that any forward step would come as a relief. Late as it was—nearing ten p.m.—Partridge decided to visit Sloane himself.

He ordered a CBA car and driver to meet him at the news building's main entrance.

"I'M GRATEFUL YOU CAME OUT, Harry," Crawford Sloane said after Partridge made his report. "Will you go on air with this tomorrow?"

"I'm not sure," Partridge said. "I want to sleep on it."

The two newsmen were having drinks in the living room, where only four evenings earlier, Sloane thought sadly, he had sat with Jessica and Nicholas after his own return from work. An FBI agent regarded them from nearby.

"Whatever you decide," Sloane said, "I'll back your judgment. Either way, do you have enough reason to take off for Colombia?"

Partridge shook his head. "Not yet, because Rodríguez is a gun for hire. He's operated all over Latin America, Europe too. So I need to know more—specifically, where this operation is based. Tomorrow I'll work the phones again."

As Partridge was leaving, Sloane put a hand on his shoulder. "Harry, my friend," he said, his voice emotional, "I've come to believe that the only chance I have of getting Jessica, Nicky and my dad back is through you. There have been times when you and I weren't the closest companions, and for that, I'm sorry. But apart from that, I want you to know that most of what I have and care about in this world is riding on you."

Partridge tried to reply, but couldn't. Instead he nodded, touched Sloane on the shoulder too, and said, "Good night."

PART THREE

Chapter 10

JESSICA was trying desperately to hold on to awareness, to keep her mind functioning, and to understand what was going on around her. Mostly she was not succeeding. She would have moments of clarity in which she could see other people and feel pain. Then abruptly everything would ebb away, becoming a swirling, misty montage in which she could grasp nothing.

Now once more awareness had swirled in. There was a man leaning over her. . . . Wait! She had seen him before, recognized his cadaverous face. Yes! She had slashed his face with a knife because he had done something to Nicky! Wild anger sent adrenaline pumping, brought back movement to her limbs. She reached up, and her nails raked his bandaged face.

With a cry Baudelio leaped back. He put a hand to his cheek; it came away red with blood. That damn woman had messed up his face again! Enraged, he leaned forward and hit her hard.

An instant later he regretted having done it. He had wanted to see how far all three captives were advanced in consciousness—up to this point they had come out of sedation satisfactorily. But they should all be given water soon; he would attend to that.

Socorro appeared beside him, and he told her about the need for water. She nodded and went out into the damp jungle. Miguel, who had just entered the hut, called after her, "And get something to tie their hands behind their backs."

Turning to Baudelio, Miguel ordered, "Get the prisoners ready. First we go by truck. After that everyone will walk."

Jessica, now only feigning unconsciousness, heard it all. In hitting her, Baudelio had actually done her a favor. The jolt had brought her borderline awareness suddenly into focus. Everything was coming back: the Grand Union supermarket . . . then the parking lot, the brutal seizure of herself, Nicky and . . .

Nicky! Had he been harmed? Where was he now? And Angus. Oh, poor Angus! Barely opening her eyes, she shifted to see whether Nicky was with her. Oh, thank God! He was right alongside. His eyes were opening and closing; he was yawning.

And Angus? Yes! Angus was beyond Nicky, eyes closed, but she could see that he was breathing.

Which raised the question, Where were they? Jessica's glimpses of this place had shown her a small room, windowless and lit by an oil lantern. She was seated on what felt like a dirt floor, and it was hot and sticky here, which puzzled her. . . . Voices interrupted.

"The woman is faking," Miguel said.

"I know," Baudelio replied. "She's fully conscious."

Jessica lifted her head. She recognized both men looking down at her—the one whose face she had cut, the other whom she had caught sight of briefly in the van. Her voice was raspy, but she managed to say, "You'll be sorry for this."

"Silence!" Miguel said. He extended his right foot and shoved it into Jessica's ribs. "On your feet! We have places to go."

The savage kick made her wince. Then from beside her she heard Nicky stir and say, "What's happened? Where are we?"

It was Angus who answered softly, "It looks to me, old son, as if we've been kidnapped by some pretty nasty people. But keep your cool. Be strong! Your dad'll find us."

Jessica felt a hand on her arm and heard Nicky's voice say gently, "Mom, are you okay?"

Miguel shouted, "All of you! Keep silent!" He turned to Baudelio. "Get them ready to go."

Socorro had returned carrying a water jug and some rope.

"They should have water first," Baudelio said. He added with a hint of petulance, "That is, if you want them kept alive."

"First tie their hands," Miguel ordered. "I want no more trouble." Scowling, he left the hut as the sun ascended.

PHYSICALLY Jessica felt better for the water. Before leaving the hut, Nicky and Angus had been given water too, by a sour-faced woman whom Jessica also remembered seeing briefly before— she believed during her initial struggle with the man she had labeled Cutface.

Trying to appeal as one woman to another, Jessica had whispered between mouthfuls fed to her from a tin cup, "Thank you for the water. Please! Will you tell me where we are and why?"

The woman hissed, "You heard the order. *Silencio!* Speak again and you will go without water for a day."

After that Jessica had stayed silent. She, Nicky and Angus had been moved to the back portion of an open truck, along with a miscellaneous cargo of boxes and sacks. Then half a dozen motley-dressed men carrying guns had boarded also, followed by Cutface. The tailgate was raised, and the truck began to move, bouncing unevenly over rugged ground through dense woodland.

The heat was even more intense than in the hut. So where were they? Seeking clues, Jessica began listening to snatches of speech between the men with the guns, and recognized the language as Spanish.

Her thoughts were distracted by the sight of Nicky. Since the truck began moving he had had trouble keeping his body upright and, because of his tied hands, had slid down, so that with every bump his head was hitting the floor.

Jessica, frantic, now saw one of the gun-toting men take notice of Nicky's plight. The man moved Nicky back against a sack, his feet touching a box so that he wouldn't slip again. Jessica tried to thank the man with her eyes and a half smile. In return he gave the slightest of nods. The man mumbled some words that Nicky, having recently begun Spanish lessons at school, seemed to understand. As the journey continued, there were two more exchanges between the man and the boy.

After about twenty minutes the truck stopped, and Jessica, Nicky and Angus were shoved and lifted off it. Miguel came around from the front and announced curtly, "From here we walk." Gustavo and two other armed men led the way through thick foliage over a barely discernible trail. Though the trees overhead provided shade, the incredible heat persisted amid a constant buzz of insects.

At one point Nicky said in a low voice, "This leads to a river, Mom. The man on the truck said we're going in a boat."

At the next opportunity Jessica said, "I've been wondering about rescue, trying to guess where we are."

Nicky answered, "The man told me, Mom. We're in Peru."

IT WAS nine thirty a.m. Monday. Within the past half hour sixty bright young men and women had reported for temporary work at CBA News. All were now assembled on the soundstage of the CBA auxiliary building.

Among the group was a young black man named Jonathan Mony. "You may want to use Jonathan as a supervisor," Uncle Arthur told Teddy Cooper, adding, "He's a Columbia journalism grad who's been working as a waiter because he needs the money."

Mony had the build of a professional basketball player. His features were finely cut, with compelling eyes. After introducing himself to Cooper, he asked, "May I help you set this up?"

Cooper, who liked Mony instantly, responded, "Sure," and

within minutes Mony was showing fresh arrivals to seats and explaining the forms that the network required.

That was forty minutes ago. Now Teddy Cooper was concluding his introductory remarks. "So before leaving here, you'll be assigned to local newspaper offices or libraries, where you will read issues published during the past three months. Not just reading, though, but Sherlock Holmesing for clues to lead us to those body snatchers. You need not come back here at the end of each day, but you must report by telephone—and call immediately if you find anything important."

There was a hum of conversation, which quickly quieted as Cooper continued. "As well as looking for the kind of buildings I've described, I want you to be alert for anything unusual. Just possibly the kidnappers have left a trace behind. So look hard and look intelligently. You were hired because we think you're smart, so prove us right."

On arrival at CBA News that morning, Harry Partridge had telephoned his contact, the lawyer with organized-crime clients.

The response was less than cordial. "Oh, it's you. Well, I'm sure none of the people I represent were involved with the kidnapping. When you and I talked, I told you I would find out what I could. But I have to walk like I'm in a minefield."

Inwardly sighing, Partridge said, "I understand."

The lawyer's voice moderated. "Give me a few more days. And don't call me; I'll call you."

Hanging up, Partridge reflected that while contacts could be useful, you didn't necessarily have to like them.

Earlier that morning he had reached a decision on whether or not to reveal on the *National Evening News* that a known Colombian terrorist, Ulises Rodríguez, had been linked conclusively to the Sloane family kidnap. His decision was to withhold the information for the time being. If the only lead were broadcast, Rodríguez could hear of it and be driven further under cover. That would considerably lessen the chances of discovering his location and, of course, the Sloanes.

He also told himself, We should remember that this news thing we do is not some holy grail. When reporting endangers life and liberty, news has to take second place.

Because of its importance, Partridge told Les Chippingham and Chuck Insen of his decision. Both men agreed to trust his judgment, and Partridge settled down to resume telephoning.

Unlike last week, when his calls were mainly to U.S. sources, today he tried to reach contacts in Colombia and countries immediately adjoining it, including Peru. Something else different today was having the positive Rodríguez lead, which translated into a double-barreled question: Do you know of a terrorist named Ulises Rodríguez? If so, have you any idea where he is or what he's reputed to be doing?

Responses to the first part of the question were almost entirely yes, and to the second, no. An interesting point, though, emerged from a conversation with a longtime Colombian friend, a radio news reporter in Bogotá.

"Wherever he is," the broadcaster said, "I'd almost guarantee it isn't this country. He's a Colombian, after all, and he's too well known to be here for long without word getting around."

Then there was Peru. Partridge had made a call to that country that left him wondering. It was to another old acquaintance, Manuel Seminario, owner-editor of the weekly magazine *Escena*, published in Lima. After Partridge announced his reason for calling, Seminario had exclaimed, "My God! I should have realized you'd be involved. That kidnapping is a terrible thing. We'll have a full-page piece in this week's issue. Is there anything new we should include?"

"There *is* something new," Partridge said. "But for now we're keeping it under wraps, so I'd appreciate this being off the record. We believe Ulises Rodríguez is involved."

There was a silence before Seminario said softly, "You are speaking of bad company, Harry. That man is suspected of masterminding kidnappings, skulking in and out of Peru from Colombia for employment by others here. It is a way our criminal-revolutionary elements, such as Sendero Luminoso, work. As you know, in Peru nowadays kidnapping is almost a way of life."

"I did know that," Partridge said. "Have you heard any talk of

Rodríguez being in Peru, or recently working for anyone there?"

"Well . . . no."

"Did I sense some hesitation?"

"Not about Rodríguez. Everything here on what I call the criminal-revolutionary front has been strangely quiet for several weeks. I have seen the signs before, and it often means something big is about to happen. Usually unpleasant."

Seminario's voice changed tempo, became businesslike. "My dear Harry, it has been a pleasure talking to you. Do come to see me soon in Lima—a standing invitation."

Throughout the day the words kept coming back to Partridge: "It often means something big is about to happen."

COINCIDENTALLY, on the same day, Peru was discussed at an ultraprivate top-echelon meeting of CBA network's corporate owners, Globanic Industries Inc. The meeting was a twice yearly three-day policy workshop chaired by the conglomerate's chairman and chief executive officer, Theodore Elliott. Attendance was confined to other CEOs—those of Globanic's nine subsidiaries, all major companies themselves.

The locale of the meeting was the Fordly Cay Club, near Nassau, in the Bahamas, one of the world's most exclusive private clubs, with a resort facility including a yacht harbor, golf course, tennis courts and white sand beaches.

The first morning session was held in a small, comfortable library, with deep rattan chairs upholstered in beige leather. Theo Elliott, appropriately dressed in white slacks and a light blue polo shirt, was tall, lean and broad-shouldered, with a strong jaw and a full head of totally white hair. The hair was a reminder that in two years' time the chairman would reach retirement age and be succeeded, almost certainly, by one of those present today.

There were three strong candidates, of which Margot Lloyd-Mason was one. Margot was conscious of this as she reported on the state of CBA. Speaking precisely, she disclosed that since Globanic's acquisition of CBA, strict financial controls had been introduced. As a result, third-quarter profits would be up twenty-two percent over the year before.

"That's a fair beginning," Theodore Elliott commented, "though we'll expect even better in future."

Margot had dressed carefully today, not wanting to appear too feminine, yet not wishing to lose the advantage of her sex. At first she'd considered wearing a tailored suit, as she often did in her office at Stonehenge. In the end, this being the semitropics, she wore beige linen slacks and a cotton sweater in a soft peach shade. The outfit emphasized her well-proportioned body, a judgment confirmed by lingering glances from some of the men.

Continuing her report, Margot mentioned the recent kidnapping of the Crawford Sloane family.

The chairman of International Forest Products, a hard-driving Oregonian, injected, "That's too bad, and we all hope they catch those people. Just the same, your network's getting a lot of attention from it."

"So much attention," Margot informed him, "that our *National Evening News* ratings have soared almost three points within the past four days, which means an additional six million viewers and puts us strongly in front as number one. It's also raised the rating of our daily game show immediately after the news. And the same is true of our prime-time shows. The sponsors are all delighted." She added, "Networks know from experience that if viewers tune in to the evening news, the odds are they will stay with that network for the next ninety minutes, sometimes more."

"So it's an ill wind . . . as the old saying goes," the forest-products chief said, smiling.

Margot smiled back. "Since we're here in private, I'll agree, though please don't quote me."

Late in the morning it was the turn of "Fossie" Xenos, chairman of Globanic Financial Services, to address his fellow CEOs. A second-generation Greek American, Fossie retained a boyish manner, appearing much younger than his forty-one years. Since taking over Globanic Financial, he had created sparkling profits for the company, plus a dynamic reputation for himself. Margot viewed him as her most formidable rival for the chairmanship.

Today Fossie Xenos reported on a largely secret project expected to produce a multibillion-dollar bonanza for Globanic. It involved

so-called debt-to-equity swaps and a gigantic real estate invest-
ment fund, both relating to Peru, with Globanic working hand in
glove with that country's government.

Currently Peru had more than sixteen billion dollars of foreign
debt on which it had defaulted, and the international financial
community would lend it no more money. Suffering a desperate
economic crisis, the country was anxious to get back into reputa-
ble status and begin borrowing once more. At the same time,
Globanic had quietly bought up four and a half billion dollars of
Peru's outstanding debt, paying five cents on the dollar.

The government of Peru had been informed they could wipe
out that debt by buying it from Globanic for ten cents on the
dollar, but with all bookkeeping payments in Peru's own weak
currency. Two critical conditions were attached to Globanic's
acknowledgment of Peruvian currency. Globanic didn't want
cash but instead the debt-to-equity swap, giving it total ownership of two spectacular resort locations now owned by the Peruvian government. Along with those vast amounts of land would go
guarantees that Globanic was free to develop the resorts in its
own way.

Fossie's report ended with the information that agreement between the Peruvian government and Globanic Financial had
been reached a few days earlier, with all of Globanic's demands
accepted. As he sat down the audience applauded.

Theo Elliott, beaming, inquired, "Questions, anyone?"

Margot spoke up. "Tell us about Peru's stability, Fossie. Lately
there's been an increase in revolutionary activity, not just in the
usual Andes areas, but in Lima and elsewhere. Under those
circumstances, will vacationers want to go there?"

Fossie answered cheerfully, "All my information is that the
revolutionary outlook is short term and that Peru will survive with a
solid law-abiding democracy favorable to expanded tourism."

"If that's all the questioning," Theo Elliott pronounced, "let
me just say this. I don't want anything to damage our still delicate
relationship with the government of Peru and thereby spoil what
can evolve into the deal of the century." The chairman rose.
"Now that's understood, let's have lunch."

Chapter 11

JESSICA, Nicky and Angus, their hands tied behind them, were still walking, stumbling over the narrow trail hemmed in by dense trees and undergrowth. Some armed men were ahead, others behind, prodding with their rifles to urge the captives on.

And it was hot. Incredibly hot. Sweat poured from them all, and Jessica worried desperately about the other two. She herself was suffering an intense headache and nausea.

The ground beneath her feet had become soggy, making it increasingly difficult to walk. Suddenly, behind her, she heard a sharp cry and a thud. Angus had fallen. Gamely the old man struggled to get up, but failed because of his tied hands. Behind him the men with guns laughed.

From the front of the column Miguel now appeared, with Socorro and Baudelio behind him. Before anyone could speak, Jessica screamed, "We know we can't escape, and so do you. Why, then, tie our hands? All we want is to help ourselves, to keep from falling. I beg you, untie us!"

As Miguel hesitated Socorro told him softly, "If one of them breaks a leg or arm, or even has a cut, it could be infected. In Nueva Esperanza we'll have no means of dealing with it."

Beside her, Baudelio said, "She's right."

Miguel, with an impatient gesture, snapped an order in Spanish. The man who had helped Nicky in the truck stepped forward. With a knife he cut the rope binding Jessica's wrists. Nicky was next. Angus' bonds were severed too.

Amid shouted commands they again moved forward.

In the past few minutes Jessica had learned several things. First, their destination was Nueva Esperanza, though the name meant nothing to her. Second, the man who had befriended Nicky was Vicente—she had heard him called by name. Third, the woman who interceded with Miguel possessed some medical knowledge. So did Cutface. Possibly one or the other was a doctor.

Moments later, as the column rounded a bend in the trail, a wide river appeared ahead. As they drew nearer, Jessica could see two wooden workboats, each with twin outboard motors, moored close to the riverbank. Prodded by guns, she, Nicky and Angus waded knee-deep through water to board the first boat and, after climbing in, were ordered to sit on the damp bottom.

Some of the armed men who had been on the trail now climbed into the prisoners' boat. Miguel and the others boarded the second boat, and both boats started to move upriver. Jessica noticed that other men who had been in charge of the boats were also armed. The chances of getting away, even if there were somewhere to go, seemed nonexistent.

Nicky turned to Jessica. "Mom, I'm scared."

Jessica, holding him, admitted, "Darling, so am I."

SOME three hours later both boats slowed, their bows turning from the main river into a smaller stream, the banks on either side closing in.

Like everyone else, Jessica, Nicky and Angus were soaked in a deluge of rain shortly before landing at Nueva Esperanza. But as their boat made fast against a wooden jetty the rain stopped as suddenly as it had begun, and the spirits of all three sank as they saw the awful, forbidding place ahead.

Beyond a rough path from the riverbank was a series of dilapidated houses built from old packing cases and rusted corrugated iron. Most were windowless, though two had what appeared to be small storefronts. Thatched roofs showed disrepair, and some had gaping holes.

After being escorted by the armed men up the path, the prisoners were herded into the shack that stood farthest from the river. It took a few moments for their eyes to adjust to the semidarkness. When they did, Jessica screamed in anguish.

"Oh, my God, no! You can't shut us in those! Not in cages, like animals. *Please no!*"

Set against the far wall were three small partitioned cells made of thin but strong bamboo stalks. Between each cell, wire screening had been nailed so there could be no physical contact between occupants. The door of each cell was fitted with a sliding steel bar and a heavy padlock. Inside each was a low wooden bed with a thin soiled mattress, and a galvanized pail. The whole place stank.

While Jessica pleaded and protested she was seized and pushed into the enclosure farthest from the shack's outer door. Then the cell door closed, and she heard the padlock click. At the opposite end of the shack Angus was fighting and arguing too, but he was subdued, thrown in, and the padlock fastened. In the cell next to her own Jessica heard Nicky sobbing.

NINE days had passed since the sixty recruits had been turned loose by CBA News to make a study of the region's newspapers, searching for a headquarters that the kidnappers might have used.

The FBI, while not saying specifically it had reached a dead end, had nothing new to report. The CIA, now rumored to be involved, would make no statement.

Then, on a Wednesday morning, Harry Partridge looked up in his private office to see Teddy Cooper in the doorway and, behind him, Jonathan Mony. Partridge waved them in.

"We may have something, Harry," Cooper said. He motioned to the young black researcher. "Go ahead."

"Yesterday I went to a local newspaper in Astoria, Queens," Mony began. "Found nothing. Then, coming out, I saw the office of a Spanish-language weekly called *Semana*. It wasn't on the list, but I went in."

"You speak Spanish?"

Mony nodded. "Pretty well. Anyway, they let me check their latest issue. I took it home, looked through it last night."

"And brought it to me this morning." Cooper spread a tabloid-style newspaper on Partridge's desk. "Here's a column we think will interest you, and Jonathan's translation."

Partridge glanced at the paper, then read the translation.

You wouldn't think, would you, that some people buy funeral caskets the way you and me pick up cheese at the grocery. Happens, though.

Seems this guy came to Alberto Godoy, of the Godoy Funeral Home, and bought two caskets just like that off the shelf—one regular, one small. Said they were for his old Mom and Dad, the tiny one for Mom. Hey, how's that for a hint to the old folks?

Last week—that's six weeks later—this same guy comes back, wants another casket like before, regular size. He took it away, paid cash, same as he did for the other two. Didn't say who this one was for. Wonder if his wife's been cheating.

"A few minutes ago we phoned the *Semana* office," Cooper said. "Jonathan got lucky. The guy who wrote the column was there. And he said he wrote the piece a week ago last Friday. Which happened to be the day after the kidnap."

Stay calm, Partridge told himself. Don't get carried away.

He looked at the other two. "Do you think—"

"What I think," Cooper said, "is that we may have found how Mrs. Sloane and the others were taken out of the country."

"In caskets? Do you believe they were dead?"

Cooper shook his head. "Doped. It's been done before."

"As soon as I can, I'll interview Godoy," Partridge said.

"I'd like to come with you," Mony put in.

"I think he earned it, Harry," Cooper urged.

"So do I." Partridge smiled at Mony. "Nice going, Jonathan. Let's leave immediately."

As Cooper left, Partridge picked up a telephone and ordered a network car.

On the way out, passing through the main newsroom, he and Mony encountered Don Kettering, CBA's business correspondent. When news of the Sloane kidnap broke, it had been Kettering who went on the air with the special bulletin.

Now he asked, "Anything new, Harry?"

About to make a perfunctory answer, Partridge hesitated. He respected Kettering as a first-class reporter. "Something *has* come up, Don. What are you doing now?"

"Not much. Wall Street's quiet today. Need some help?"

"Could be. Come with us. I'll explain as we go."

Twenty minutes later Partridge, Don Kettering and Jonathan Mony faced Alberto Godoy in Godoy's cluttered funeral-home office in Queens. The undertaker regarded the visitors suspiciously.

"Mr. Godoy," Partridge said, "as I told your receptionist, we're all from CBA News."

"You been doin' all them Sloane kidnap bits."

"Yes, I have, and that's partly why we're here." Producing his copy of *Semana*, Partridge asked, "Have you seen this?"

The undertaker's features soured. "All that's my private business. And if you all don't mind, I've got work to do."

Don Kettering spoke, leaning forward over the undertaker's desk. "Listen to me carefully, Godoy. A network like ours has a lot of clout, and if we have to, we'll use it. We need answers to questions fast. And if we don't get honest answers, we'll bring in—here, today—the FBI, the New York City police, the sales tax force and the IRS to talk about those three caskets you sold. So take your choice. You can deal with us or them."

Godoy licked his lips. "I'll answer your questions, fellas."

"Mr. Godoy," Partridge said, "who bought those caskets?"

"He said his name was Novack. I didn't believe him."

"When I show you a picture, tell me your reaction." He held out a photocopy of the charcoal sketch of Rodríguez.

Without hesitation Godoy said, "That's him. That's Novack. Seen him twice. He's older than the picture—"

"Yes, we know." Partridge felt a surge of satisfaction. A positive connection between the caskets and the kidnap had been established.

During the questions and answers following, Partridge extracted as much from the undertaker as he could. In the end, however, it was not a lot, and it became clear that Ulises Rodríguez had been careful not to leave a trail behind him.

As Partridge, Kettering and Mony were about to leave, Godoy opened a drawer in his desk in which he kept a supply of cigarettes. He caught sight of a sheet of paper bearing his own handwriting. He had stuffed the paper in more than a week ago and forgotten it until now. He took it out.

"What is it?" Partridge asked sharply.

"I told you he had a Caddy hearse, with another guy driving." Godoy held out the paper. "This was the hearse license number."

"Thanks," Partridge said. "We'll check this out." He put the paper in a pocket, though he was not hopeful about the outcome. He remembered that the license number of the Nissan van in the

White Plains explosion had been phony and led nowhere. Still, any lead had to be pursued.

Partridge now reasoned that most of what they had uncovered would have to go on air within the next few days. There was a limit to how much information could remain dammed up at CBA; though luck had been with them so far, it could change at any moment. Also, they *were* in the news business. Partridge felt his excitement rise at the prospect of reporting progress.

He decided, too, that the time had come to begin his own search of Latin America. He intended to leave for Bogotá, Colombia, as soon as he could get away. Whether or not Ulises Rodríguez was in that country, Colombia was the obvious place to start.

PARTRIDGE dropped Kettering and Mony off, then went to a sporting goods store to buy some heavy socks, a pair of hiking boots and a flashlight. He suspected he might need all three quite soon. By the time he returned to CBA, it was midafternoon.

In the task force conference room, Rita waved him over. "A man's been trying to reach you since this morning. Wouldn't leave his name. I told him sooner or later you'd be back."

"Thanks. There's something I want to tell you. I've decided to go to Bogotá. I want to be there early tomorrow." Partridge described what he had learned.

"And how much do we broadcast, and when?" Rita said breathlessly, enjoying the promise of action.

"Everything we know, and soon. Exactly when, we'll discuss with Les and Chuck, but I'd like a clear twenty-four-hour lead. So starting right now, we'll work all night putting everything together. Call the task force in for a meeting"—Partridge glanced at his watch—"at five o'clock."

"Yessir!" Rita smiled.

At the same moment, the phone on the desk rang. After answering, she covered the mouthpiece and told Partridge, "It's the same man—the one who's been trying to get you all day."

He took the phone. "This is Harry Partridge."

"Don't use my name at any point in this conversation." The caller's words sounded muffled, but Partridge recognized the voice of his contact, the organized-crime lawyer. "I'm calling from a pay phone so the call's not traceable. And if you ever name me as the source of what I'm about to tell you, I shall swear you're a liar and deny it. When this call ends, my debt to you is paid in full. Understood?"

"Fully understood."

"Some clients I do business with have Latin American connections, so the information is solid. The people you are looking for were flown out of the United States and are now imprisoned in Peru. Got that?"

Partridge answered grimly, "I have it." Rita's eyes were fixed on him as he added, "I need a name. Who's holding them?"

"Good-bye."

"Wait! I'll speak a name, and if I'm wrong, give me a signal saying no. If I'm right, don't say anything. Will you do it?"

A pause, then, "Make it fast."

Partridge took a breath. "Sendero Luminoso."

At the other end, silence. Then a click as the caller hung up.

Partridge turned to Rita. "Cancel what I said about going to Bogotá. Now it's Lima."

Chapter 12

DURING those terrible first minutes when Jessica, Nicky and Angus were thrust into their separate cages and Jessica wept on hearing Nicky sobbing, there was a period of mental dislocation and misery to which Jessica, like the others, had succumbed.

But not for long. Before ten minutes had passed, Jessica called out softly, "Nicky, can you hear me?"

A subdued answer came back. "Yes, Mom." It was followed by movement as Nicky approached the screen between their cells. In the semidarkness they could just see each other.

Jessica asked, "Are you okay?"

"I think so." Nicky's voice quivered. "I don't like it here."

"Oh, darling, neither do I. But until we can do something, we have to hold on. Keep reminding yourself that your father and a lot of others are searching for us. Your father knows so many people—there isn't anyone he can't call on for help." Jessica hoped she sounded reassuring.

As she spoke a figure moved into view from the shadows beyond the cells. It was one of the gunmen, a heavyset man whom they would later identify as Ramón. He carried a Kalashnikov rifle and, aiming it at Jessica, ordered, *"Silencio!"*

About to protest, Jessica heard Angus advise softly, "Jessie, don't!" She curbed her impulse, and they all fell silent.

It was their first experience with a succession of armed guards, one of whom was always on duty in the hut. As they quickly discovered, the strictness of the guards varied. The most easygoing was Vicente, the man who, on Miguel's orders, had cut the ropes binding their wrists. Apart from motioning them to keep their voices lowered, Vicente allowed them to talk. Ramón was the strictest, permitting no talking at all.

As the first few days passed, a pattern of living—mainly miserable—took shape. Three times daily a monotonous diet of unappetizing food—principally cassava, rice and noodles—was brought to them. Drinking water was handed into each cell; occasionally there were bowls and water with which to wash. Every forty-eight hours the sanitary pails they'd been given were removed and emptied.

Nicky's morale, which was the most important to Jessica, at least remained stable. He also began attempting conversations with the guards. Nicky's Spanish was rudimentary, but he managed to achieve exchanges and gain information.

From Vicente they learned of the impending departure of the "doctor"—obviously Cutface—who, Vicente believed, was "going home to Lima." However, the "nurse" would stay on, and this was clearly the woman whose name they discovered was Socorro.

At Jessica's suggestion Nicky asked Vicente if the prisoners were to be allowed to go outside at all. To this question Vicente shook his head. Jessica, persisting, asked to have a message passed to Socorro that the prisoners would like to see her.

To their surprise, later that day Socorro came. She stood in the doorway, her slim, lithe body a distinctive silhouette, her nose wrinkling at the all-pervading smell of the cells.

Without waiting, Jessica spoke. "Unless we get out of here, into some fresh air for a while, we'll all be desperately ill."

"You have no right to ask for this," Socorro snapped.

Jessica slammed back, "I have a right to care about my son and my father-in-law, who is old and has been treated badly."

Socorro shrugged. "I will try to have more air let in here." Her lips twitched in the nearest thing to a smile. "It will be healthier for the guards."

Next day two men arrived with tools. They cut open several spaces in the walls facing the cells. Immediately the daytime semidarkness was replaced by light. As well, there was a flow of air through the building, occasionally a breeze.

But the light-and-air victory was minor, and as it proved, there were major agonies still to be endured.

Six days after the captives and their escorts arrived at Nueva Esperanza, Miguel received a series of written orders from Sendero Luminoso. Originating in Ayacucho, they were delivered by a messenger traveling in a truck that took two days to cover five hundred tortuous road miles over soggy jungle trails. Several items of specialized equipment were also delivered.

The most important instruction involved making a videotape of the woman prisoner. A script was supplied, and no deviation from it would be permitted. Another instruction confirmed that Baudelio's duties were at an end. He would accompany the messenger back to Ayacucho, from where he would fly to Lima.

Miguel turned his attention to the special recording equipment. It comprised a camcorder with cassettes, a tripod, a photoflood kit and a portable generator, gasoline powered. Suspecting that the woman would be difficult, he chose Gustavo and Ramón to help him with the recording session. Neither was likely to be squeamish, whatever punishment they were asked to inflict.

Soon after daylight the following morning Miguel, Gustavo and Ramón appeared in the prisoners' hut. All three were carrying equipment that Jessica recognized instantly. Taking his time, Miguel installed the camcorder on its tripod and arranged the photoflood lights, which he plugged into an extension cable.

Moments later the area in front of the three cells was brightly lit, the lights focused on an empty chair that the camcorder faced.

Miguel walked toward Jessica's cage. He held out three hand-written pages, and his voice was cold and hard. "This is what you will say, bitch—exactly that and no more."

Jessica took the pages, read them quickly, then tore them into pieces, which she threw through the bamboo bars. "I won't do it."

Miguel nodded to Gustavo, waiting nearby. "Get the boy."

Despite her determination, a shiver of apprehension ran through Jessica as she watched Gustavo open Nicky's cage. He seized Nicky by one arm, twisting it and propelling him outside.

Frantic now, Jessica demanded, "What are you going to do?"

No one answered. Instead Ramón brought the guards' chair from the other side of the hut. Gustavo pushed Nicky into it, and the two men tied him with rope. Before securing his arms, Gustavo loosened Nicky's shirt, exposing his small chest. Ramón, meanwhile, was lighting a cigarette.

Miguel signaled to Ramón, who inhaled, bringing the tip of his cigarette to a glowing red. Then, with a single swift movement, he removed the cigarette and pressed the burning end against Nicky's chest.

At first the boy was so surprised that no sound escaped him. Then, as he felt the searing agony, he screamed.

Jessica was screaming too—wildly, incoherently—tearfully pleading for the torture to cease, assuring Miguel she would do whatever he wanted. "Anything! But stop! Oh, stop!"

From the third cell Angus was banging against the screen of his cage and shouting, "You filthy bastards! You're animals."

Miguel waited until some of the noise had subsided, then informed Jessica, "You will sit in front of the camera and speak. I have written on cards what you are to say. The cards will be held up, and you will follow them exactly. Is that understood?"

"Yes," Jessica said dully, "it's understood."

She closed her eyes. To protect Nicky, she would concentrate on what had to be done, completing it without a mistake. But even then, a sudden thought occurred.

At home in Larchmont, the night before the kidnap, Crawf had described signals that a hostage making a video recording could transmit surreptitiously. Crawf had said, "Licking my lips would mean, 'I am doing this against my will. Do not believe anything I am saying.' Scratching or touching my right earlobe would mean, 'My captors are well organized and strongly armed.' Left earlobe would mean, 'Security here is sometimes lax; an attack from outside might succeed.'"

Jessica's cell was opened by Gustavo. Her impulse was to run to Nicky, but Miguel's face was glowering. Guided by Gustavo, she sat in the chair facing the photofloods and camcorder.

The message she would speak was written on two cards that Gustavo now held up. Miguel had moved to the camcorder. He ordered, "When I drop my hand, begin."

The signal came, and Jessica spoke, steeling herself to keep her voice even.

"We have all been treated well and fairly. Now that the reason we were taken has been explained to us, we understand why it was necessary. We also have been told how easy it will be for our American friends to ensure our safe return home. To have us released, you must simply follow—quickly and exactly—the instructions which accompany this recording."

Immediately after the word recording, Jessica moistened her lips with her tongue. She knew she was taking a risk, but the action passed unnoticed, and she felt a thrill of satisfaction as she continued reading from the cards.

"If you do not obey those instructions, you will not see any of us ever again. We beg of you, do not let that happen. . . ."

Meanwhile, she must make a choice about the next signal—left earlobe or right?

It was true the people here were armed and perhaps well organized, but security *was* lax at times, and often at night their guards fell asleep. Making her decision, Jessica casually scratched her left earlobe. She continued with the closing words.

"We will be waiting, counting on you, desperately hoping you will make the right decision and . . ."

Seconds later it was over. As Jessica closed her eyes in relief, Miguel switched off the floodlights, a smile on his face.

395

FROM THE MOMENT ON Wednesday afternoon when Harry Partridge announced his decision to leave for Peru, the CBA News special task force moved feverishly into high gear.

Immediately ahead, to be written and partially recorded overnight, was a report anchored by Partridge that would dominate the *National Evening News* on Friday, some thirty-six hours after his departure. This would contain all that was known concerning the kidnapping.

Partridge had called a task force meeting in the conference room for five o'clock, and it was well attended. Crawford Sloane, looking more gaunt than ever, and Leslie Chippingham were there. Partridge was at the head of the table, with Rita Abrams beside him. Iris Everly arrived several minutes late. Teddy Cooper was present, and Minh Van Canh came in, as did producers Norman Jaeger and Karl Owens.

Partridge began by announcing his intention to leave for Peru early the next morning, and the decision to broadcast everything they knew on Friday evening's news.

Les Chippingham cut in. "Harry, I think we should go one step further and do a one-hour news special, also on Friday night, covering the whole kidnap sequence at length."

From there other decisions flowed. Partridge announced that Minh Van Canh and Ken O'Hara would accompany him to Peru. Rita would remain in New York for overall supervision of the Friday-evening news report and one-hour special. Then, later that night, she would follow Partridge and the others.

Partridge, who had discussed the subject earlier with Chippingham, disclosed that after his own departure, Don Kettering would head the kidnap task force in New York. However, neither the *National Evening News* report of Friday nor the one-hour special later should convey any hint that Partridge had already left for Peru. In fact, if it could be made to appear at some point that he was broadcasting live—though without actually being deceptive—so much the better.

Nothing that would happen through that night and the next two days, Les Chippingham declared, must be discussed, even with others in the news division. The news president continued, "Let us not do or say *anything* that could release our news prematurely and deprive Harry of the twenty-four hours' lead time he so clearly needs."

IT WAS a few minutes before six a.m. when Harry Partridge, Minh Van Canh and Ken O'Hara took off from Teterboro Airport for Lima, Peru. Partridge and the other two had come directly from CBA News headquarters to the airport in a network car. During the busy night of composing and recording his co-anchor introductions, Partridge had managed to slip away for half an hour to his hotel and pack a bag.

In the airplane, on the right side of the passenger cabin, two facing seats had been lowered to become a bed, with a mattress, sheets and blankets invitingly in place. By the time they were in the air, Partridge was ready for sleep.

Foremost in his mind, though, was Jessica. No matter what the odds against him, he would find her and bring her back. Somehow, he would save her.

PART FOUR

Chapter 13

Partridge, Minh Van Canh and Ken O'Hara arrived in Peru's immense, sprawling capital city soon after one p.m. They had been met at the airport by Fernández Pabur, CBA's regular stringer in Peru and—when required—the network's fixer. Fernández was about thirty-five, heavyset and energetic. He whisked them through customs and arranged a suite for Partridge in the elegant five-star Cesar's hotel in Miraflores, with good rooms for the other two.

Before reaching Peru, Partridge had decided that the only way to go about locating the kidnap victims was to act as a TV-news correspondent normally would—meeting known contacts, seeking out new ones, searching for news, traveling where he could, questioning, questioning, and all the while hoping some clue would emerge, a lead to where the captives might be held.

397

After that, of course, would come the greater problem of how to rescue them. But that would have to be faced when the time arrived.

Using the TV-correspondent routine, first he visited Victor Velasco, the international manager of Entel Peru, the national telecommunications company with headquarters in downtown Lima. He made arrangements for Entel to be CBA's base for communication with New York, including satellite transmissions. When other U.S. network crews arrived, they would use the same facilities. Partridge discreetly handed over to Velasco a thousand dollars for his trouble.

Next Partridge phoned Manuel Seminario from the hotel and asked the *Escena* magazine owner-editor to dinner.

At eight fifteen they were sipping Pisco sours, the popular Peruvian cocktail, at La Pizzeria. Slightly built and dapper, with a neatly trimmed Vandyke beard, Seminario was wearing high-fashion spectacles and a Brioni suit.

Partridge reported why he was in Peru. He added, "I've been hearing that Sendero Luminoso is increasingly active in Lima."

"Exceedingly so," Seminario agreed. "Their people move around freely, and a recent bombing, which went wrong, was an exception. Most are successful."

Partridge asked, "Do you have any advice for me?"

"One thing you must realize is that Sendero Luminoso may already know of your presence here; their spies are everywhere. But even if not, they will learn of it shortly. So beginning at once, you must have a bodyguard accompany you, particularly if you go out at night."

Partridge smiled. "That seems to have happened already." Fernández Pabur, the stringer, had insisted on collecting Partridge from the hotel and bringing him here, and he was armed. He was waiting outside while Harry had dinner.

Seminario asked, "Are you carrying a gun?"

Partridge shook his head.

"You must. Many of us do."

When they had finished talking, most other diners were gone and the restaurant was preparing to close.

Shortly, Partridge returned to Cesar's hotel with Fernández. He asked him, "Can you get me a gun?"

"Of course. Do you have a preference?"

Partridge considered. The nature of his work had made him knowledgeable about guns and he had learned to use them. "I'd like a nine-millimeter Browning, also a silencer."

FRIDAY was a day of action at CBA, New York.

At six a.m., on the program *Sunrise Journal*, a CBA News promotion aired along with commercials. The promo was a recorded message spoken on-camera by Harry Partridge.

"Tonight . . . on CBA National Evening News . . . an exclusive report of startling new developments in the kidnapping of the Crawford Sloane family.

"And at nine p.m. eastern time . . . a one-hour news special— Network in Peril: The Sloane Kidnap."

Les Chippingham saw the promo while having an on-the-run breakfast in his Eighty-second Street apartment. The news president was in a hurry, knowing he must keep Margot Lloyd-Mason informed. He could see his CBA limo and driver already waiting outside. The limousine reminded him of Margot's instruction at their first meeting that he should use taxis instead, an order he had ignored. He must not ignore keeping Margot informed, however, and would call her as soon as he reached the office, since she was likely to have seen the promo too.

The decision was unnecessary. When he entered the car, the driver handed him a phone. Margot's voice barked, "What is all this about developments, and why haven't I been told?"

"It happened suddenly. I intended to call as soon as I got in."

"John Q. Public has been told. Why should I have to wait?"

"Margot, the public has not been told; they will be this evening. You, on the other hand, are going to be told as soon as I reach my desk."

There was a pause, then, "Do it as soon as you get in."

Some fifteen minutes later, connected again with the network

399

president and CEO, Chippingham began, "First, from your point of view the outlook is excellent. We've achieved several exclusive breakthroughs, which tonight may give CBA the largest news audience in our history, with matching ratings. Unfortunately, the news about the Sloane family is less than good for Crawf."

"Where are they?"

"In Peru. Held by Sendero Luminoso."

"Peru! Are you absolutely sure?" Margot's startled reaction at the mention of Peru surprised him.

"We've had experienced people on this, especially Harry Partridge, and what they've discovered is convincing. I've no doubts."

She said sharply, "I'd like to talk to Partridge."

"I'm afraid that isn't possible. He's already in Peru. We expect an update from him for Monday's news."

"Why are you moving so quickly?" she asked.

"This is the news business, Margot. We always work that way." The question amazed him. So did a hint of uncertainty, even nervousness, in Margot's voice. It prompted him to say, "You seem concerned about Peru. Why?"

There was hesitation before an answer. "At the moment Globanic Industries has a substantial business arrangement there. A great deal is at stake, and it's essential that our alliance with the Peruvian government remains good."

"May I point out that CBA News doesn't have an alliance with the Peruvian government—good or bad. We have to report the news the way it is. Also, I'll point out that as soon as our story breaks tonight, everyone else—networks, print press, you name it—will jump on the Peru story too."

Margot said impatiently, "CBA *is* Globanic. Globanic has an alliance with Peru; therefore so does CBA. Keep me informed. If there's any change, especially about Peru, I want to know immediately, not next day."

Chippingham heard a click as the connection was severed.

IN HER elegant office at Stonehenge, Margot Lloyd-Mason pondered. Should she call Theo Elliott or not? She recalled the Globanic chairman's cautioning words about Peru at the Fordly

Cay Club meeting: "I don't want anything to . . . spoil what can evolve into the deal of the century." In the end she decided that she must inform him.

To her surprise, he reacted calmly. "Well, if that Shining Path rabble did the kidnapping, I suppose there's no way it *cannot* be reported. But let's not forget that the Peruvian government is in no way involved, because they and the Shining Path are deadly enemies. Be sure your newspeople make that clear."

"I'll see that they do," Margot said.

"They can go even further," Theo Elliott continued. "Clearly the Peruvian government will do everything possible to find the kidnapped Americans—using Peru's military and police. So let's ensure they get proper credit, with upbeat pictures on our news."

Margot hesitated. "I'm not sure about going that far, Theo."

"Then *be* sure!" The chairman's voice rose. "We own the damn network, don't we? So once in a while let's put that ownership to our advantage. At the same time, remind your newspeople that this is a competitive, profit-oriented business that pays their fancy salaries, and they are a part of it, like it or not. If they don't like it, they've a clear choice—get out!"

"I hear you, Theo," Margot said.

FRIDAY, when the news broke on the *National Evening News* first feed at six thirty p.m., it was immediately copied and repeated throughout the world, with CBA News acknowledged as the source. At other TV networks, testy inquests would soon be held, asking, How did we miss out on this? Meanwhile, the networks hastily revised their second newscast feeds, using swiftly supplied videotape displaying "Courtesy CBA."

Amid the media rush a major new development occurred.

Don Kettering, now heading the CBA kidnap task force, heard about it shortly before ten p.m., as the one-hour news special was nearing its conclusion. Kettering was still at the anchor desk when Norman Jaeger telephoned during a commercial break. Jaeger was now senior producer, since Rita Abrams had left for her flight to Peru an hour ago.

"Don, there's to be a task force session after we've finished."

"Has something happened, Norm? Something hot?"

"Hot as hell! I've just had word from Les. Over at Stonehenge they've received the kidnappers' demands, along with a videotape of Jessica Sloane."

IT WAS ten thirty p.m. on Friday. In a private viewing room at CBA News ten people were assembled: Les Chippingham and Crawford Sloane; from the task force, Don Kettering, Norm Jaeger, Karl Owens and Iris Everly; from CBA corporate headquarters at Stonehenge, Margot Lloyd-Mason, Tom Nortandra—an executive vice president—and Irwin Bracebridge, president of CBA Broadcast Group; and from the FBI, Special Agent Otis Havelock.

Earlier in the evening a small, plain package had been delivered by messenger to Stonehenge, addressed "President, CBA Network." After a routine security check it was sent to Margot Lloyd-Mason's floor, where Nortandra, who happened to be working late, received the package and opened it. Realizing its importance, he telephoned Margot at dinner.

Margot hurried to Stonehenge, where she, Nortandra and Bracebridge, who had also been called in, screened the videotape and read an accompanying document. Immediately they arranged a meeting at CBA News headquarters.

Before the meeting Bracebridge, a former news president himself, took Sloane aside. "Crawf," he told him, "if you prefer to watch the video alone first, we'll understand."

Sloane had driven in from Larchmont with FBI Agent Havelock. He shook his head. "Thanks, but I'll see it with all of you."

It was Don Kettering who called to an operator behind the small audience, "Okay, let's go."

Lights in the viewing room dimmed. Almost at once a large elevated TV screen went to black with pinpoints of light, as was usual when running a blank tape without pictures. But sound was on the tape and was transmitted suddenly—a series of piercing screams. The group was transfixed. Sloane sat up straight, exclaiming in a broken voice, "Oh, God! That's Nicky!"

As abruptly as it had begun, the screaming was cut off.

A moment later a picture appeared—of Jessica's head and shoulders against a plain background. Her face was set and serious, and to those in the group who knew her, she appeared wan and under strain. But her voice was firm and controlled.

She began, "We have all been treated well and fairly. Now that the reason we were taken has been explained to us, we understand why it was necessary. We also have been told how easy it will be for our American friends to ensure our safe return home. To have us released, you must simply follow—quickly and exactly— the instructions which accompany this recording, but be sure of this . . ."

At the words "be sure of this," there was a sharp intake of breath by Sloane and a muted exclamation. The tape continued.

"If you do not obey these instructions, you will not see any of us ever again. We beg of you, do not let that happen. . . ."

Again a sudden sound from Crawford Sloane—a whispered exclamation, *"There!"*

"We will be waiting, counting on you, desperately hoping you will make the right decision and bring us safely home."

After Jessica concluded, there was a silence in which her face remained on-screen, her features expressionless. Then both sound and picture ended. In the viewing room the lights came on.

Les Chippingham asked gently, "Are you certain that first sound was Nicky, Crawf?"

Sloane said bleakly, "Positive." Then he added, "Jessica passed two signals."

"What kind of signals?" Chippingham sounded puzzled.

"The first was licking her lips, which means, 'I am doing this against my will. Don't believe anything I'm saying.' "

"Clever!" Bracebridge said. "Good for Jessica!" Others nodded approval.

Sloane went on, "We talked about signals the night before all this happened. I thought that one day I might need them myself. I guess Jessica remembered."

Before Sloane could explain the second signal, Iris Everly said impatiently, "Mrs. Sloane said something on the tape about instructions. Do we have them?"

Margot Lloyd-Mason answered by nodding to Nortandra. "You'd better read them aloud."

The executive vice president moved under a light. "The title of this document is 'The Shining Time Has Come.'"

"For Sendero Luminoso the time to advance along the Shining Path has come. We are ready to make ourselves better known and understood.

"For many years the lying capitalist-imperialist media has ignored or misrepresented the heroic struggle of Sendero Luminoso's people. That will now be changed. It is why capitalist captives have been taken and are held as hostages.

"The American CBA television network is hereby ordered to do the following:

"One: Commencing with the second Monday after receipt of this demand, CBA *National Evening News* will be canceled for five weekdays—one full week.

"Two: In its place another program, to be delivered to CBA in five tape cassettes, will be broadcast. The program's title is, 'World Revolution: Sendero Luminoso Shows the Way.'

"Three: Neither CBA nor any other agency will attempt to trace the source of the cassettes. Any such attempt will result in immediate execution of one of the three prisoners.

"Four: If there is full obedience of these orders, the three prisoners will be released four days after the fifth broadcast. But if the orders are not obeyed, the prisoners will not be seen again."

"There's something else," Nortandra said. "Copies of the tape cassette of Mrs. Sloane have been sent to other television networks and the press."

A silence followed. Several people glanced at Crawford Sloane, who was slumped in his chair, his face grimly set. The others shared his sense of hopelessness.

It was Les Chippingham who said finally, "Well, now we know. All along we've wondered what these people wanted. We'll put out a bulletin at midnight, which gives us an hour to consider how to handle the news and, more important, what our response will be."

"There is no way that we can accept those ridiculous terms,"

Margot declared. "We will certainly not put our network evening news out of business for one whole week."

"However, we don't have to say that," Nortandra pointed out. "We can say something like, The demands are being carefully considered."

"I doubt if that would deceive Sendero Luminoso," Jaeger told him. "Whatever else they may be, they aren't fools. This calls for finesse, not a blunderbuss approach."

"Finesse all you want," Margot snapped. "But what's involved here is a corporate matter requiring executive decision."

"No! Damn it, no!" The words were shouted. Heads turned. The speaker was Crawford Sloane, no longer seated and dejected, but standing, eyes fiery. "Keep corporate out of this! I *know* we can't close down CBA News for one week, Mrs. Lloyd-Mason. What we *can* do, here at news, is use our skills, our know-how, to play for time. That, and use Harry Partridge, who's the best hope we have—*my* best hope to get my family home."

Before anyone could react, Bracebridge tried a conciliatory tone. "A time like this is hard on everyone." He turned toward the network president. "Margot, I believe that what's been presented is worth considering, remembering that your end decision is understood and accepted."

Margot hesitated. "Very well." She informed Chippingham, "You may decide a temporary stratagem response."

Chapter 14

THROUGHOUT the weekend the news about Sendero Luminoso's demands and the videotape of Jessica Sloane stayed prominently in the news. Calls flooded into CBA requesting some comment from the network. In every case the response was the same: CBA had no comment.

Within CBA those who knew the story had promised Les Chippingham they'd keep secret the decision not to accept Sendero Luminoso's terms. They appeared to have kept their word. Unfortunately, the only one to break it was Margot Lloyd-Mason, who on Sunday advised Theodore Elliott of everything.

GLOBANIC INDUSTRIES WORLD Headquarters occupied a mansion-style office complex some thirty miles outside Manhattan. It was there, at ten a.m. on Monday, that Glen Dawson, a young reporter for the Baltimore *Star*, was waiting to interview Globanic's chief comptroller on the subject of palladium. Currently the precious metal was in the news, and Globanic owned mines in Brazil, where labor riots were threatening supplies.

Dawson waited outside the comptroller's office in an inconspicuous corner of an elegant circular lounge. He was sitting there when a door opened and two figures emerged. One was Theodore Elliott; the other was Alden Rhodes, under secretary for economic affairs. Continuing a conversation begun inside, Rhodes was saying, "Those threats from the Peru rebels put you in a difficult spot."

The Globanic chairman nodded. "In one way, yes. We've made a decision, though it hasn't been announced. What we're *not* going to do is let a bunch of crazy Commies push us around."

"So CBA won't cancel their evening news?"

"Absolutely not! As for running those Shining Path tapes, not a hope in hell. . . ." The voices faded as they walked on.

Dawson quickly scribbled the exact words he had heard on a notepad. His pulse was racing. He knew he had exclusive information that countless journalists had been seeking unsuccessfully since Saturday night.

"Mr. Dawson," a receptionist called, "you may go in now."

The interview with Globanic's comptroller seemed endless to Dawson; what he had stumbled onto seemed a ticket to a more exciting future. At length, pleading a deadline, he made his escape.

He could still make the paper's main afternoon edition.

GLEN Dawson's story, composed at a computer terminal at the Manhattan bureau office, led the Baltimore *Star*'s main afternoon edition. The banner headline read CBA SAYS NO TO SLOANE KIDNAPPERS.

Even before the Baltimore *Star* hit the streets, the wire services had the story, giving credit to the *Star*. Later that evening the *Star* was quoted on all network news broadcasts, including CBA's, where the news was received with near despair.

Next morning in Peru the media featured the disclosure with special emphasis on Theodore Elliott's "bunch of crazy Commies" description of Sendero Luminoso.

A RADIO report of Theodore Elliott's rejection of the kidnappers' demands and his low opinion of Sendero Luminoso reached the jungle hamlet of Nueva Esperanza and the terrorist Ulises Rodríguez, alias Miguel. Soon after, a telephone conversation took place between Miguel and a Sendero leader in Ayacucho. They talked in veiled references, though to both men the meaning was understood.

This was, something must be done to prove to the TV network CBA that they were dealing with neither fools nor weaklings. Killing one of the hostages was a possibility. Miguel, however, suggested another course of action, which—remembering something he had learned while at Hackensack—he believed would be devastating psychologically to those in New York.

This was promptly agreed to, and Miguel began his preparations by sending for Socorro.

JESSICA, Nicky and Angus looked up as a small procession filed into the shack. It consisted of Miguel, Socorro, Gustavo, Ramón and one of the guards. It was now six days since Jessica had made the videotape recording. Nicky's burn was sufficiently healed, so that he was no longer in pain. Jessica still felt guilty about his suffering, and was determined he would not be hurt again.

Consequently, when Nicky's cell was opened and the terrorists crowded in with him, Jessica cried anxiously, "What are you doing? I beg of you, don't hurt him! He's suffered enough."

It was Socorro who swung to face Jessica and shouted, "Shut up! There's no way you can stop what's going to happen."

Jessica screamed frantically, "What *is* happening?" Miguel, she saw, had brought a small wooden table into Nicky's cell while Gustavo and the fourth man were holding Nicky so he couldn't move. Jessica cried again, "For God's sake, let him go!"

Nicky, already frantic, screamed and struggled to free himself, but to no avail. His eyes moved wildly.

On the other side of Nicky's cell Angus was banging his screen and shouting.

While the boy continued to squirm, crying pitifully, Gustavo forced Nicky's right index finger on top of the table. Ramón produced a sheath knife, and with a single swift movement he severed the finger. The men exposed the little finger of the boy's right hand, and with another chop of Ramón's knife that finger, too, was separated from the hand.

Jessica emitted a piercing wail. "Oh, no! Not fingers! Please let me go to my son. Don't you understand? He plays the piano! It's his life."

"I know." Miguel smiled. "I heard your husband say so on television; he was answering a question. When he receives those fingers, he'll wish he hadn't."

Jessica covered her face with her hands, her body racked by sobbing.

By now Nicky—barely conscious, his features ashen—had fallen back on the narrow bed with agonized moans. As Miguel, Ramón and Gustavo left the cell, taking the table with them, Socorro cleansed Nicky's hand to forestall infection. Then, after covering both wounds with gauze pads, she bandaged the entire hand.

As THE hours passed and darkness advanced, the guard changed. Vicente came on duty, and Socorro arrived. She was carrying a bowl of warm soapy water, more gauze pads, a bandage, and a kerosene lamp, which she took into Nicky's cell. Gently she sat Nicky upright and began to change the dressing on his hand. Nicky seemed easier, less in pain.

After a while Jessica called out softly, "Socorro, please . . ."

Immediately Socorro signaled Jessica to be silent.

When the bandaging was done, Socorro left Nicky's cell but didn't lock it. Instead she came and opened Jessica's and waved her out. Then Socorro pointed to the open door of Nicky's cell.

"You must go back before daylight," Socorro whispered. She nodded in the direction of Vicente. "He will tell you when."

Moments later Jessica was holding Nicky. "Oh, Mom!" he said. As best they could, they hugged each other. Soon after, Nicky fell asleep.

AT TWO p.m. Tuesday, in the CBA News task force conference room, Teddy Cooper took a phone call from an excited Jonathan Mony. "I think we found it," Mony said.

"Found what, and where are you?"

"The place the kidnappers used, I'm almost sure. And I'm in Hackensack, New Jersey. There was an ad in the *Record*—that's the local paper—and we followed through. Seemed to fit what we were looking for."

One of the young women researchers had discovered the ad. On reading it, she had contacted Mony, who was in the area and now carried a CBA paging device. He had joined her at the newspaper's business office, then visited the property with her.

An hour later a CBA car pulled into the Hackensack property, bringing Kettering, Jaeger, Cooper and a two-man camera crew. Mony introduced the young woman researcher, Cokie Vale.

"The first thing you should see," Mony told them, "is on the second floor of the house." He led the way into the dilapidated main house and up a stairway. Near the head of the stairs he opened a door and stood back while the others filed in.

The room was clean, painted a hygienic white, and it had new floor covering. Overhead fluorescent lights revealed two hospital cots, both with side rails and straps. In contrast to the cots was a narrow, battered metal bed; it, too, had straps attached.

Kettering said, "The whole place looks like a first-aid station."

Jaeger nodded. "Or set up to handle three doped people, one of them unexpected."

They moved to an outbuilding. Inside, it was obvious it had been a paint shop. Cans of blue and yellow paint—some partially used—remained.

"This is the place," Jaeger said. "It has to be."

Kettering nodded. "I agree. We'll use this on the news tonight."

"There is one more thing," Mony said.

This time Cokie Vale took center stage. A petite redhead, she led the group to a cluster of trees away from the buildings and explained, "Somebody's been digging here—not long ago."

Among the group, eyes shifted back and forth. If something had been buried—what? A body, or bodies?

Kettering said, "I'd like to take a look at what's under that ground, if anything."

"There are some shovels in the furnace room," Mony said.

"Get them," Kettering told him. "Let's start digging."

A short time later it became evident that what they were opening was not a grave. It was a repository of items left by the property's recent occupants. Some things were innocuous—food supplies, clothing, toilet objects, newspapers. Others were more significant—medical supplies, maps, tools.

Mony was down in the excavated hole when he felt his foot touch something solid. A moment later he pulled out an object and called, "Hey, look at this!"

It was a cellular phone in a canvas outer cover. Passing it up to Cooper, Mony said, "I think there's another underneath."

Not only was there another but four more after that. Soon the six were laid out, side by side.

They called the local police, asking them to inform the FBI.

EVEN before the *National Evening News* went on the air, Kettering had telephoned a friend high in the New York and New Jersey telephone systems about the cellular phones. Kettering requested the name and address of the person to whom the six telephones were registered, plus a list of all calls made to or from those numbers during the past two months.

"There isn't a lot," his friend informed him. "The registered name and address look like a fake. Not that we ever had to send a bill. Right after numbers were issued for those phones, someone made a deposit of three thousand dollars. Less than a third of the money was used, and that's because, with one exception, all calls were solely among the six phones and not to other numbers."

"But you said there was an exception."

"Yes—on September thirteenth, a direct-dial call to Peru."

"That's the day before the kidnap. Do you have a number?"

"Of course."

Moments later, after consulting a notebook, Kettering made another call. When a voice answered, *"Buenas tardes, Cesar's,"* Kettering requested, "Mr. Partridge, *por favor."*

HARRY Partridge, Minh Van Canh and Ken O'Hara had been joined on Saturday by Rita Abrams and the videotape editor Bob Watson. Their first combined report had been transmitted by satellite from Lima on Monday and led CBA's *National Evening News* that night.

Partridge's editorial theme had been the drastically deteriorating situation in Peru—economically and in terms of law and order. Sound bites from Manuel Seminario, owner-editor of *Escena,* made those points, supplemented by pictures of an angry mob from the slums looting a food store and defying police. And Seminario had posed the unanswerable question: "What is it in us Latin Americans that makes us chronically incapable of stable government?"

Now it was Tuesday night, and in bed after a discouraging day, Partridge was brooding on Peru. The whole country was a paradox, a conflicting mixture of military despotism and free democracy. He had come close to that subject today during an interview with Cesar Acevedo, a lay leader of the Roman Catholic Church. They had met in a private office at the rear of the Archbishop's Palace on the Plaza de Armas, official center of the city.

"I believe," Partridge said early in their meeting, "that from time to time you have to deal with Sendero Luminoso."

Acevedo smiled. "Have to deal is correct. The church does not, of course, approve of Sendero."

The lay leader explained that Sendero Luminoso ordered priests and other church workers out of some areas when antigovernment action was intended so they could not witness it. If the orders were disobeyed, Sendero would not hesitate to kill.

A sudden thought occurred to Partridge. "Are there any such places now where your people have been told to leave?"

"There is one such area. Come! I will show you on the map."

Mounted on a wall was a large map of Peru. Acevedo pointed to a section of San Martín province ringed in red. "Until about three weeks ago we had a strong medical team in here, performing a vaccination program. Then Sendero Luminoso, which controls the area, insisted that our people leave."

Partridge studied the encircled section; it was depressingly large. He read place-names: Tocache, Uchiza, Sion, Nueva Esperanza, Pachiza. Without much hope he wrote them down. Even if the captives were at one of those places, it would do no good to enter the area without knowing which.

Effecting a rescue anywhere would be difficult, perhaps impossible. And time, he knew, was running out.

Now, in his hotel room, he had a sense of frustration at his lack of progress. Abruptly the bedside telephone rang.

"Harry?" Partridge recognized Don Kettering's voice. "Some things have happened that you ought to know about."

Rita, also in Cesar's hotel, answered her room phone.

"I've just had a call from New York," Partridge said. He repeated what Don Kettering had told him about the Hackensack house and the cellular phones, adding, "Don gave me a Lima number that was called. I want to find out whose it is and where."

"Give it to me," Rita said. "I'll try to get that Entel Peru manager Victor Velasco and start him working on it. Call you back if there's any news."

It was not until Wednesday afternoon that the Lima telephone number was identified. "It is, of course, restricted data," Velasco explained to Partridge and Rita, who were in CBA's Entel editing booth, where they had been working with videotape editor Bob Watson on another news spot for New York.

"I had trouble persuading one of my colleagues to release the information," Velasco continued, "but eventually I did." On a sheet torn from a memo pad were the words Calderón, G.—547 Huancavelica Street, 10F.

"We need Fernández," Partridge said.

"He's on his way here," Rita informed him.

The swarthy, energetic stringer-fixer arrived within the next few minutes. Told about the Huancavelica Street address, Fernández Pabur nodded briskly. "I know it. An old apartment building near the intersection with Avenida Tacna."

"I want to go there now," Partridge told him. He turned to Rita. "I'd like you, Minh and Ken to come along."

Avenida Tacna was a wide, heavily traveled thoroughfare, and Huancavelica Street crossed it at right angles. Number 547 was a large, drab building with peeling paint and chipped masonry. A group of men, standing idly around, watched with unfriendly expressions while Fernández and Partridge stepped out of the station wagon Fernández had hired, leaving Rita, Minh Van Canh and Ken O'Hara to wait with the driver.

Within the building an odor of dirt and general decay assaulted them. Apartment 10F was at the end of a gloomy corridor. At Partridge's knock the door opened two or three inches, halted by an inside chain. Simultaneously a woman's high-pitched voice let loose a tirade in Spanish.

Fernández spoke in reasonable, soothing tones. As he continued the voice from inside stopped; then the chain was released and the door opened.

The woman standing before them was probably around sixty. Long ago she might have been beautiful, but time and hard living had made her blowsy and coarse, her skin blotchy. Her eyes were red and swollen from crying. Fernández walked in past her, and Partridge followed.

Fernández talked briefly with the woman, then turned to Partridge. "It seems that a few hours ago the man she lived with here was murdered. She thought we were the killers."

Partridge said in English, "We are truly sorry to hear of your friend's death. Have you any idea who killed him?"

When Fernández had translated for her, the woman mouthed a stream of words ending with "Sendero Luminoso."

It confirmed what Partridge had feared. The person they had hoped to see—whoever he was—had connections to Sendero but was now beyond reach. He said to Fernández, "Tell her I would be grateful if she will answer some questions."

Fernández repeated the request and translated the reply. "She says yes, if she can. And, by the way, her name is Dolores."

Partridge continued, with Fernández translating. "Your man friend who was killed—what kind of work did he do?"

"He was a doctor. He put people to sleep."

"An anesthesiologist?"

Dolores shook her head, not understanding. Then she went to a cupboard and produced a file containing papers. She passed them to Partridge; he saw they were medical diplomas.

The first declared that Hartley Harold Gossage, a graduate of Boston University School of Medicine, was entitled to practice medicine. The second diploma certified that he was a qualified specialist in anesthesiology.

Among the other papers was a letter on stationery of the Massachusetts Board of Registration in Medicine. It began, "You are hereby notified that your license to practice medicine has been revoked for life."

Partridge put the letter down. A picture was becoming clearer. The man who had lived here was a former American anesthesiologist who had some connection with Sendero Luminoso. The kidnap victims had been spirited out of the United States, presumably drugged or sedated at the time. It seemed likely that Gossage had done the sedating.

With Fernández's help Partridge resumed the questioning of Dolores. "Why do you believe that Sendero Luminoso murdered your doctor friend?"

"Because he worked for those *bastardos*." A pause, then a recollection. "Sendero had a name for him—Baudelio."

"Was Baudelio away from Lima recently?"

A vigorous series of nods. "For a long time. I missed him. He phoned me from America."

Everything was fitting together, Partridge thought. But there was one important question left. "After Baudelio was in America and before returning here, was he somewhere in Peru?"

Dolores nodded affirmatively. "Yes. Nueva Esperanza."

Partridge could scarcely believe what so unexpectedly had come his way. His hands shook as he turned pages in his notebook to the list of places where Sendero had ordered the Catholic medical teams out. A name leaped at him: Nueva Esperanza.

HE WAS STILL FIRST AND foremost a TV-news correspondent, Partridge reminded himself as he went downstairs to discuss with Rita, Canh and O'Hara the video shots they needed—of Dolores, the apartment and the building's exterior. Partridge wanted close-ups, too, of the medical diplomas and the letter consigning Gossage/Baudelio to the medical profession's garbage heap.

However, even though Baudelio's role in the kidnapping was important to the full news story, Partridge knew that releasing it would be a mistake, alerting Sendero to the information his CBA group possessed exclusively. But he wanted the Baudelio segment prepackaged, ready for use when the time came.

Now Partridge was free to move on to essentials—planning a rescue expedition to Nueva Esperanza. At the thought of it his excitement rose, the old addiction to danger stirring within him.

Chapter 15

ON THURSDAY morning Crawford Sloane went to CBA News headquarters knowing nothing of the breakthrough in Lima the day before. He arrived slightly later than usual, at ten fifty-five; a young FBI agent named Ivan Ungar accompanied him. The FBI was still guarding against a possible attempt to kidnap him.

Sloane took an elevator to the fourth floor, then walked to his office adjoining the Horseshoe. He left the door of his office open. Ungar seated himself on a chair outside.

As Sloane hung up his raincoat he noticed on his desk a white Styrofoam package of the kind used by take-out restaurants. To his surprise, the package was neatly tied with white string and had "C. Sloane" written on it. Without much interest he snipped the string with scissors, then eased the package open.

After staring at the contents in dazed disbelief, Crawford Sloane screamed—a tortured, earsplitting scream. Heads shot up among those working nearby. FBI agent Ungar leaped from his chair and raced in, drawing a gun. But Sloane was alone, staring down at the package, his eyes wide and crazed, his face ashen. Agent Ungar examined the box, saw two human fingers, and, swallowing his revulsion, swiftly took charge. He shouted to those beginning to crowd into the office, "Everyone out, please!" Picking up a phone, he pressed the OPERATOR button and demanded, "Security—fast!" When there was an answer, he rapped out, "This is FBI Special Agent Ungar. Advise all guards that no one is to leave this building. After that, call the police for help."

While Ungar had been speaking Sloane collapsed into his chair. The executive producer, Chuck Insen, elbowed his way in through the growing throng and asked, "What's all this about?"

Recognizing him, Ungar gestured to the white box, then instructed, "Nothing in here must be touched. I suggest you take Mr. Sloane somewhere else and lock the door until I come back."

Insen nodded. He eased the anchorman from the room and took him to his own office, firing orders on the way. He told a secretary, "Talk to the switchboard; there's a doctor on call—get him here." To a producer, "Get Don Kettering up here; we'll need something for the news tonight."

Inside his office, Insen helped Sloane into a chair. Sloane leaned forward, his head in his hands. Speaking half to himself, he agonized, "Those people knew about Nicky and the piano. And how did they know? *I let it out! It was me!* At that press conference after the kidnap."

Insen said gently, "I remember, Crawf. But you were answering a question. Anyway, who could have foreseen . . ." He stopped, knowing that reasoning at this moment would do no good.

THE temporary ban on people leaving the building was lifted when everyone inside was identified and their presence accounted for. It seemed likely that the package had been left much earlier, and no one had seen anything unusual.

In the midst of the general gloom another small package was delivered. This one found its way to Margot Lloyd-Mason's Stonehenge office suite early Thursday afternoon. Inside was a videotape cassette sent by Sendero Luminoso. Margot sent it immediately to the CBA News president, Les Chippingham. He called in Don Kettering and Norman Jaeger, and the trio viewed the tape in Chippingham's office.

All three noted at once the recording's high quality, both technically and in presentation. The opening titles, beginning with "World Revolution: Sendero Luminoso Shows the Way," were superimposed over some of Peru's most breathtaking scenery. The majestic music of Beethoven's Third Symphony, "Eroica," accompanied the opening.

"Sendero hired production people who know their business," Kettering murmured. "I'd expected something cruder."

The extremist message that followed was delivered over scenes of rioting in Lima, of industrial strikes, of the grisly aftermath of attacks on Andes villages by government forces. "We are the world," an unseen commentator expounded, "and the world is ready for a revolutionary explosion."

What followed was predictable. "Revolution is justified because of imperialist exploitation of all poor people in the world. . . . Sendero is more humane than the superpowers, who are willing to destroy mankind with nuclear arsenals. . . ."

"If we were running this instead of the evening news," Chippingham commented, "the ratings would be in the cellar."

The half-hour tape ended with additional Beethoven, more scenic beauty and a rallying cry from the commentator, "Long life to Marxism-Leninism-Maoism, our guiding doctrine!"

"All right," Chippingham said at the end. "Only the three of us have viewed this tape. I suggest we don't discuss it with anyone."

The news president glanced at a clock: three fifty-three. "At four o'clock, Don, break into the network with a bulletin. Say that we've received a tape from the kidnappers, but it's defective. Getting a replacement tape to us is now up to Sendero Luminoso."

"Right."

The misinformation issued by CBA News was circulated promptly and widely. It was available in Lima for evening radio and TV news as well as the following day's newspapers.

Also in the day's news was a report of the discovery of Nicky's severed fingers by his distraught father.

In Ayacucho, Sendero leaders noted both reports. As to the one about a damaged tape, they did not believe it. What was needed, they reasoned, was some more compelling action.

JESSICA HAD A SENSE OF foreboding as soon as she awoke that morning in the half-light of dawn. Over the past three days her earlier confidence that rescue would come had ebbed away, though she tried to conceal it from Angus and Nicky.

Today was Friday. Yesterday Nicky had been in less pain, but he was silent and brooding, unresponsive to Jessica's attempts to lift him from his deep despair.

With the arrival of full daylight Jessica heard activity outside and footsteps approaching the prisoners' shack. The first person to enter was Gustavo, leader of the guards, who went directly to Angus' cell, opened it, and entered.

Miguel was immediately behind. He was scowling as he, too, moved toward Angus, carrying something Jessica had not seen him with before—an automatic rifle. At the sight of the powerful weapon her heart beat faster. Oh, no! Not Angus!

Nicky was on his feet. He, too, had grasped the significance of the automatic rifle.

Gustavo had roughly pulled the old man to his feet. Now Angus' hands were being tied behind him.

Jessica called out, "Listen to me! What are you doing? Why?"

Angus turned his head toward her. "Jessie dear, don't be distressed. There's nothing you can do. These people are barbarians. They don't understand decency or honor. . . ." He straightened his body and squared his shoulders. "We haven't much time," he added. "Both of you—stay strong and keep believing! Remember, Crawford is doing everything he can. Help is coming!"

Tears were streaming down Jessica's face. Her voice choked, she managed to call, "Dearest Angus, we love you so much!"

"I love you too, Jessie . . . Nicky!"

Gustavo was pushing Angus forward, propelling him from the cell.

Then Angus was outside the shack, beyond their sight. Seconds passed, and the silence was broken by gunfire—four shots.

OUTSIDE, Miguel stood over the body of Angus Sloane.

The four shots he fired had killed the old man instantly. Miguel had fulfilled the instructions received from Sendero Luminoso last night. Gustavo would now begin a distasteful chore that was expected of him. Soon a boat from Nueva Esperanza would leave for a nearby jungle airstrip, after which the airplane would transport to Lima the result of Gustavo's work.

LATER that same morning a car skidded to a halt outside the American embassy in Lima. A man carrying a large cardboard box jumped out. He deposited the box outside the embassy's protective railings, then ran back to the car, which sped away.

A U.S. marine guard sounded an alarm, and a bomb-disposal squad was summoned. When the box proved to contain no explosives, it was opened carefully—revealing the bloodstained head of an elderly man. Alongside was a wallet containing a U.S. Social Security card, a Florida driver's license and other documents belonging to Angus Sloane.

THE plan to attempt a rescue at Nueva Esperanza was complete. At dawn on Saturday, Partridge and his crew would fly from Lima.

But since Wednesday, on learning of the prisoners' location, Partridge had fretted impatiently. His first inclination had been to leave at once, but Fernández Pabur's arguments plus his own experience had persuaded him to delay. "We need at least two days to prepare," Fernández had pointed out.

The "we" made clear that the resourceful stringer-fixer intended to be part of the expedition. "You will need me," he'd stated simply. "I have been in the Selvas many times. The jungle can be a friend; it can also be an enemy. I know its ways."

Air transport was their principal concern. On Thursday morning Fernández collected Partridge and Rita and took them to a one-story office building not far from Lima's airport. They entered a small office, and Fernández introduced his companions to Oswaldo Zileri, the owner of AeroLibertad, a charter flight service, and also its chief pilot.

Zileri, in his thirties, was good-looking, with a trim, athletic build. His attitude was businesslike and direct. He told Partridge, "I understand you intend to pay a surprise visit to Nueva Esperanza. The airplane you are chartering is a Cheyenne Two. There will be two pilots and room for seven passengers. How you fill those seven seats is your affair. Now, may we talk money?"

They talked about a six-thousand-dollar cash deposit; then Zileri led them to a chart table, where a large-scale map of San Martín province was spread open. "I recommend landing here." With a pencil Zileri indicated a point on the map.

"Isn't that a roadway?" Partridge asked.

"Yes, but there is little traffic, often none. At several points like this one it's been widened and resurfaced by drug shippers so that planes can land. From that point a rough trail goes close to Nueva Esperanza."

Fernández put in, "I have a good map of the trail."

"Now, about your return," Zileri said. "Fernández and I have discussed this and have a suggested plan."

Two possible pickup points existed for the return journey. First, the highway where the initial landing was intended. Second, Sion airstrip, which could be reached by river, plus a three-mile overland journey. The reason for options was, as Fernández explained, "We do not know what will happen at Nueva Esperanza, or which way will be clear, or best, for us to leave by."

The airplane making the pickup could easily pass over both places and respond to a signal from the ground. Partridge's group would carry a flare gun with green and red flares. A green flare would mean, "Land normally, everything is clear." A red flare, "Land as quickly as possible, we are in danger." The plane would fly over the area on Sunday morning at eight a.m. and, failing any contact between ground and air, again on Monday at the same time.

The discussion continued, decisions and salient facts emerging.

Afterward, looking at Partridge directly, the pilot said, "We shall keep our part of the agreement and do our best for you."

Back at the hotel, Partridge held a meeting with all the CBA group members to decide who would make the journey. Three selections were Partridge; Minh Van Canh, since some visual record was essential; and Fernández Pabur. Allowing for three extra passengers returning, this left a fourth place open. Partridge chose the sound man, Ken O'Hara. Rita would remain in Lima.

SINCE WEDNESDAY, WHEN HE had learned that Nueva Esperanza was the target, Partridge had asked himself, Should I inform the Peruvian authorities, specifically the antiterrorism police? On Thursday afternoon he went for advice to Sergio Hurtado, a radio broadcaster who had warned him earlier not to seek help from the armed forces or the police.

Speaking in mutually agreed confidence, Partridge informed Sergio of the latest developments and asked if the advice was still the same.

"In exactly the kind of situation you are looking at," Sergio answered, "the government forces are notorious for going in with maximum firepower. They wipe out everyone, innocent as well as guilty, and ask questions after."

Sergio had been fidgeting with a paper on his desk. Now he said, "Before you came here, had you received any bad news?"

Partridge shook his head.

"Then I'm sorry to give you some, Harry." Picking up the paper, Sergio passed it across. "This just came in."

It was a Reuters dispatch about the receipt of Nicholas Sloane's fingers at CBA and his father's brokenhearted grief.

"Oh, God!" Partridge was suddenly overwhelmed by anguish and self-reproach. Why, he grieved, had his own planned action not been undertaken sooner?

"Harry," Sergio was saying, "there's something else. Isn't your company, CBA, owned by Globanic Industries?"

"Yes, it is."

The broadcaster slid open a desk drawer and removed several clipped sheets. "I obtain my information from many sources, and it may surprise you that one is Sendero Luminoso. They sent this recently, hoping I would broadcast it."

Partridge accepted the sheets and began reading.

"As you can see," Sergio said, "it purports to be an agreement between Globanic Financial Services and the Peruvian government. Globanic will receive enormous amounts of land, including two major resort locations, for what can only be called a giveaway price. In return some of Peru's international debt will be reduced. It's known financially as a debt-to-equity swap. It's an exceedingly rich deal for Globanic, a poor one for Peruvians."

Partridge waved the pages. "Can I have a copy?"

"Keep that one. I have another."

DURING the next day, Friday, the CBA group learned through Peru radio the tragic news of Angus Sloane's death. Partridge was quickly on the scene at the American embassy with Minh Van Canh and sent a report via satellite for the *National Evening News* that evening. By that time, too, other network crews and print press reporters had arrived.

Later, after doing what was needed, Partridge went back to his hotel and spent the evening lying on his bed, awake, lonely and dejected.

Next morning he was up before dawn, his intention to complete two tasks. One was to compose a simple handwritten will, the other to draft a telegram. Soon after, on the way to the airport in the station wagon, he had Rita witness the will and left it with her. He also asked her to send the telegram, which was addressed to Oakland, California.

They also discussed the Globanic-Peru agreement. Partridge told Rita, "When you've read it, let Les Chippingham have this copy. But it has nothing to do with why we're here, and I don't plan to use the information." He smiled. "I suppose that's the least we can do for Globanic, since they butter our bread."

THE Cheyenne II took off from Lima in the still, pre-dawn air without incident. Seventy minutes later the plane reached the portion of jungle highway where Partridge, Canh, O'Hara and Fernández were to disembark.

By now there was ample light to see below. The highway was deserted. On either side miles of jungle stretched like a vast green quilt. Turning briefly from the controls, Oswaldo Zileri called back, "We're going in. Be ready to get out fast. I don't want to stay on the ground a second longer than necessary."

Then, with a steep, fast-descending turn, he lined up over the highway, touched down, and stopped after a surprisingly short landing run. As quickly as they could, the four passengers tumbled out, taking backpacks and equipment. Moments later the aircraft taxied into position and took off.

"Let's get under cover fast," Partridge urged the others, and they headed for the jungle trail.

Chapter 16

UNKNOWN to Harry Partridge during his crowded day on Friday, a crisis concerning him had erupted in New York.

While breakfasting at home that morning, Margot Lloyd-Mason received a telephone message that Theodore Elliott wished to see her immediately at Globanic's main headquarters.

When Margot entered the chairman's office, Elliott demanded, "Why the hell aren't you keeping better control of your newspeople in Peru? Last night I received a call from President Castañeda, in Lima. He claims everything CBA has been putting out about Peru is negative and damaging."

They were both standing. Elliott, glowering, had not asked her to sit down. She asked, "Is there anything specific, Theo?"

The Globanic chairman pointed to some videocassettes on his desk. "I sent for the tapes of this week's evening news programs. They're full of doom and gloom! Nothing saying Peru has a great future or that it's a wonderful place to visit or that those lousy Shining Path rebels will be beaten soon. I warned you about this."

"Perhaps we can do something to improve what's happening." Margot was thinking quickly. Her future in Globanic, she realized, could be at stake.

"I'll tell you *exactly* what you'll do." Elliott's voice had become steely. "I want that meddling reporter—Partridge is his name—brought back on the next airplane and fired. I want him out of CBA so that I can call the president of Peru and say, 'Look! We threw the troublemaker out. We're sorry we sent him to your country.'"

Margot said, "Theo, I have to point out that Partridge has been with the network a long time and has a good record."

Elliott permitted himself a sly smile. "Then give him a gold watch. Just get rid of him, so I can make that phone call Monday. And I'll warn you about something else, Margot. Don't think that

I'm not aware how you're hoping one day to sit where I am now." The chairman waved a hand. "That's all. Call me later today, when the Peru thing is all wrapped up."

IT WAS late morning when Margot, back in her office at Stone-henge, sent for Leslie Chippingham.

When he appeared, she came speedily to the point. "I'm giving you an order. The employment of Harry Partridge is to be terminated at once. I want him out of CBA by tomorrow. I'm aware he has a contract, and you'll do whatever we have to under it. He's to be out of Peru, preferably tomorrow, but no later than Sunday."

Chippingham stared at her, unbelieving. "You can't be serious!"

Margot told him firmly, "I *am* serious."

"The hell with that!" Chippingham's voice was raised emotionally. "I'm not standing by seeing one of our best correspondents thrown out without any reason. Margot, what's Harry done?"

"If you must know, it's a question of his type of coverage."

"Which is the absolute best! Ask anybody."

"I don't need to. In any case, not everyone agrees with you."

Chippingham regarded her suspiciously. Intuition came to him. "This is Globanic's work, isn't it? And Theodore Elliott's?"

"Be careful," she warned him. "I don't plan to do any more explaining, but I'll tell you this: if my order has not been carried out by the end of the day, I'll appoint someone else acting news president and have them do it."

He looked at her with a mixture of wonder and hatred.

"If you decide to stay employed," Margot went on coldly, "report to me this afternoon that what I wanted has been done."

BACK at CBA News headquarters, Chippingham instructed his secretary that he was not to be disturbed. He needed time to think.

He knew he had reached a crisis in his life. If he did as Margot ordered and fired Harry Partridge, he would forfeit his self-respect. He would have done something shameful and unjust to a decent, highly skilled and respected human being, a friend and colleague, merely to satisfy another person's whim. On the other hand, if he didn't do it, someone else would. And Margot would

425

have no trouble finding someone. There were too many ambitious people around CBA News.

So Partridge was going down the drain anyway—at least at CBA. But when word got around that he was leaving CBA, other networks would fall over themselves vying for him.

But what about a fired and fallen news president? That was a totally different story. Chippingham knew he would not be sought out by other networks. They wanted news presidents who were successes, not someone dismissed in doubtful circumstances.

The prospect was daunting.

Unless—*unless* he did what Margot wanted.

Fifteen minutes later Chippingham read over the letter he had typed personally. It began:

> Dear Harry:
> It is with great regret I have to inform you that your employment by CBA News is terminated, effective immediately.
> Under the terms of your contract with CBA . . .

He intended to fax the letter to Lima. He was about to sign it when he heard a knock at his office door. Instinctively Chippingham turned the letter face down.

Crawford Sloane entered. He was holding a press wire printout. When he spoke, his voice was choked. "Les," he said, "I had to see you. This just came in."

Chippingham read the printout. It repeated a Chicago *Tribune* report from Lima about the tragic death of Angus Sloane.

"Oh, God! Crawf, I'm . . ." Unable to finish the words, Chippingham shook his head.

Sloane said, "Don't say anything more. I can't do the news tonight. I told them outside to call—"

"Forget everything, Crawf. We'll take care of it."

"No! There's something I must do. I want to go to Lima. While there's still a chance for Jessica and Nicky. I must be there."

Chippingham said doubtfully, "Are you sure, Crawf?"

"I'm going, Les," Sloane said. "Don't try to stop me. If CBA won't pay for the trip, I will."

"That won't be necessary," Chippingham said.

IT WAS LATE THAT AFTERNOON before Chippingham's letter to Partridge was signed and faxed to Entel Peru, in Lima, where it would be delivered to the CBA booth in the same building. Chippingham added a note asking for the letter to be placed in an envelope addressed to Mr. Harry Partridge and marked PERSONAL.

At six fifteen p.m. Chippingham telephoned Margot Lloyd-Mason, who was still in her office. He told her, "I have done what you asked," then gave her the news about Sloane's father.

"I heard," she said, "and I'm sorry. About the other, you cut it fine and I was beginning to think you wouldn't call. But thank you."

AWAY from the highway where the Cheyenne II had landed, the trek through the jungle for Partridge and the other three men was difficult and slow.

The trail—if it could be called that—was often overgrown and frequently disappeared entirely. They had to hack a way through dense vegetation using machetes. Bamboos, ferns, lianas and parasitic plants were everywhere intertwined. Tall trees formed a canopy above their heads, under an overcast sky that hinted of rain to come.

Fernández's large-scale contour map showed several hills near Nueva Esperanza, one of which might work as an observation post. From there, hidden by the jungle, they could observe the hamlet. Nueva Esperanza itself was about nine miles from their present position—a formidable distance under these conditions.

Partridge had been encouraged by the second message Jessica had conveyed during her videotape recording, as reported to him by Sloane. She had scratched her left earlobe to mean, "Security here is sometimes lax; an attack from outside might succeed." Soon that information would be put to the test.

Meanwhile, they labored on through the jungle.

It was well into the steamy afternoon when Fernández warned them that Nueva Esperanza was near. "We must not be seen," he said. "If we hear anyone coming, we must melt into the jungle."

Soon after, the going became easier, and several other trails crisscrossed their own. After another hour they entered a clearing and, beyond it, could see a hut amid jungle trees.

Fernández inspected the clearing, including the hut, satisfying himself that no one was there. Then he led the others a little way into the jungle again. Halting, he parted a cluster of ferns and motioned them to look. About half a mile away and two hundred feet below were two dozen or so shacks located on a riverbank. A muddy path led from the buildings to a rough wooden jetty, where a motley collection of boats was moored.

Partridge said softly, "I guess we found Nueva Esperanza."

The sun was already near the horizon, the journey having taken far longer than expected. "I want to observe as much as possible before dark," Harry now told the others. "Minh, bring the other binoculars and join me forward. Fernández and Ken, pick a sentry post and make sure we're not approached from behind."

Partridge dropped to his belly and wriggled forward, carrying the binoculars he had brought. Canh, beside him, did the same. Moving the binoculars slowly, they studied the scene below.

At the jetty two men were working on a boat. A woman left one shack, emptied a pail of slops behind it, and returned inside. Garbage littered the area. Viewed over all, Nueva Esperanza appeared to be a jungle slum.

Partridge began studying the buildings individually. Presumably, the prisoners were being held in one of them. A full day's observation would be needed, and there could be no question of a rescue attempt tonight and departure by air tomorrow morning. He settled down, simply to wait and watch.

As always in the tropics, darkness fell quickly. In the houses a few dim lights had come on. Partridge lowered his binoculars after more than an hour of concentration.

At that moment Canh touched his arm, gesturing toward the huts. Partridge picked up his binoculars and peered again. At once he saw movement in the now dim light—a man walking down the path between two groups of houses. In contrast to the others they had seen, this man was different: he had a rifle slung over his shoulder.

The man reached a shack and disappeared inside. For a few minutes nothing happened. Then, from the same shack, a different man emerged and walked away. He, too, was carrying a gun.

Could it be, Partridge wondered excitedly, a changing of the prisoners' guard? And could that shack hold Jessica and Nicky Sloane?

AT PARTRIDGE's request Canh stayed another hour alone at the observation point, and later Ken O'Hara relieved him.

"Everyone get as much rest as you can," Partridge ordered. Earlier Fernández had rigged hammocks with mosquito netting inside the hut they had found on arrival. "But we should man the observation point and the sentry post all the time," he went on. "Which means only two people can sleep at once." After discussion it was decided they would work two-hour shifts.

Their routine continued through the next day. During this time, at the sentry post there had been no alarms. The observation point, however, had produced specific information.

There was a regular change of an armed person, suggesting that prisoners were indeed housed in that building. But the casualness of the changeover, Partridge believed, confirmed the message conveyed by Jessica: security here is sometimes lax.

Since morning, what appeared to be food in containers had been delivered twice by a woman entering the building. And during the day all comings and goings to and from Nueva Esperanza were by boat. No road vehicle was seen. The people being observed were almost totally relaxed and did not seem to expect any aggressive incursion from outside.

At dusk Partridge called the others together and told them, "We've watched long enough. We go down tonight."

He told Fernández, "You'll guide us from here. I want to arrive at that hut at two a.m. Everyone must be silent all the way."

Canh asked, "Is there an order of battle, Harry?"

"Yes," Partridge answered. "I'll enter first. I'd like you right behind me, Minh, covering my back. Fernández will hang behind, watch the other houses for anyone appearing, but join us if we need help." He turned to O'Hara. "Ken, you'll go directly to the jetty. I've decided we'll leave by boat. Jessica and Nicholas may not be up to the journey we had coming here."

O'Hara said, "I assume you want me to grab a boat."

"Yes, and disable some of the others. But no noise!"

A mixture of excitement and apprehension gripped them all.

And for Harry, beyond all other thoughts, was Jessica. Jessica, who was now close at hand, somewhere inside that hut.

BACK in Lima on Saturday morning, after watching the Cheyenne II depart, Rita Abrams had been taken by surprise twice.

First, a message awaiting her at CBA's Entel Peru booth announced that Crawford Sloane would be in Lima by early that morning. She promptly called Cesar's hotel, where he would be staying. She left a request that he phone.

Second, and even more surprising, was the faxed letter from Les Chippingham, sent the previous evening to Harry Partridge. The instruction to place the letter in an envelope marked PERSONAL had clearly not been noticed, and it arrived open, so that anyone could read it. Rita did, and was incredulous.

Harry had been fired, dismissed by CBA! The more Rita thought about it, the more ridiculous and outrageous it seemed, especially now. Meanwhile, there was no way she could communicate the letter's contents to Partridge, since he was already on his way to Nueva Esperanza.

SLOANE didn't telephone. After arriving at the hotel and receiving Rita's message, he took a taxi immediately to Entel. His first question to Rita was, "Where's Harry?"

"In the jungle," she answered. She took in the extra lines of strain on his face, the anguish in his eyes. Swallowing hard, she described the expedition to Nueva Esperanza, explaining what Harry and the others were trying to do.

At length she said, "Let's go have breakfast. There's a cafeteria in the building."

Over coffee and croissants Rita said gently, "Crawf, we were all shocked and saddened by the news about your father. Harry blamed himself for not moving faster, but we didn't have—"

Sloane stopped her with a gesture. "Harry's my friend. I'll never blame him for anything—whatever happens. No one could have done more."

"I agree," Rita said, "which is what makes this so unbelievable." She produced Les Chippingham's faxed letter.

Sloane took the letter, read it twice, then shook his head. "This is a mistake. It has to be."

"This is no mistake, Crawf. This was intended. There's something behind it you and I don't know. Yesterday at CBA—did anything happen out of the ordinary?"

Sloane considered. "Well, Les was at Stonehenge."

A sudden thought struck Rita. "Could it have been something to do with this?" Opening her purse, she took out the clipped sheets of paper Partridge had given her this morning.

Sloane took the sheets and read them. "Interesting. A huge debt-to-equity swap between Globanic and the Peruvian government. Really big money! Where did you get this?"

"From Harry." She explained how Partridge had received the document from a radio commentator, Sergio Hurtado. Rita added, "Harry didn't plan to use the story. Said it was the least we could do for Globanic, since they butter our bread."

"There *could* be a linkage between this and Harry's firing," Sloane said thoughtfully. "I see a possibility."

"What are you thinking of?" Rita asked.

"Calling Margot Lloyd-Mason. Let's go upstairs."

At the CBA Entel Peru booth, he picked up the phone and tapped out the U.S. overseas code and the number of Stonehenge.

An operator soon told him, "Mrs. Lloyd-Mason is not in her office today."

"This is Crawford Sloane. Will you give me her home number, please." He wrote it down as she read it out.

This time the phone was answered by a butler. Sloane identified himself and asked for Mrs. Lloyd-Mason.

He waited several minutes; then Margot's voice said, "Yes?"

"This is Crawf. I'm calling from Lima."

"So I was told, Mr. Sloane. I'm curious to know why you are calling me at home. First, though, I'd like to offer my sympathy about your father's death."

"Thank you."

Sloane, despite his stature, had never been on a first-name

basis with the CBA president, and clearly she intended to keep it that way. He guessed from her tone that he would get nowhere with questions. He decided to try a timeworn journalist's trick.

"Mrs. Lloyd-Mason, yesterday when you decided to fire Harry Partridge, I wonder if you realized how much he's accomplished in the effort to find and free my wife, son and father."

The reply was explosive. "Who *told* you it was my decision?"

He was tempted to answer, You just did! But restraining himself, he said, "In the TV news business almost nothing is secret."

Margot snapped, "I do not wish to discuss this now."

"That's a pity," Sloane said, "since I thought we might talk about the connection between Harry's firing and that big debt-to-equity swap Globanic is arranging with Peru. Did Harry's honest reporting offend someone with a stake in that deal?"

At the other end of the line there was a long silence. Then, her voice subdued, Margot asked, "Where did you hear that?"

"Well," Sloane said, "the fact is, Harry Partridge learned about it. He's a first-class reporter, you know, one of the best in our business. Anyway, Harry decided not to use the information. His words were, 'That's the least we can do for Globanic, since they butter our bread.'"

Margot didn't respond. He asked, "Are you wishing, by chance, that you hadn't done what you did to Harry Partridge?"

"No." The answer seemed disembodied, as if Margot's mind were far away. "No, I was thinking of other things."

"Mrs. Lloyd-Mason"—Sloane employed the cutting tone he used occasionally for repulsive items in the news—"has anyone told you lately that you're a coldhearted bitch?"

He replaced the phone.

THE AeroLibertad owner and pilot, Oswaldo Zileri, had heard of Crawford Sloane and was appropriately respectful. "I wish you and your friends well, Mr. Sloane."

"Thank you," Sloane said. He and Rita were in Zileri's modest office near Lima's airport.

"I have heard the sad news about your father." The pilot shook his head. "Are you wondering if there might be room for you and Miss Abrams to go on the trips to bring the people back?"

"Yes," Sloane replied.

"It will be okay. You must be here before dawn tomorrow—and the next day if we go."

"We will be," Rita said.

Chapter 17

IT WAS two ten a.m. in Nueva Esperanza. Jessica had been drifting in and out of sleep, dreaming at times—the dreams becoming nightmares merging with reality.

Moments earlier, certain she was awake, Jessica had peered through the roughly cut opening facing her cell, and what she thought she saw in the dim light was the face of Harry Partridge. Then the face disappeared. Was she still dreaming?

The face appeared again, rising slowly above the window level, and this time it stayed. *Could it be?* Her heart leaped as she decided. *Yes, it could!* It was Harry Partridge.

The face was mouthing something silently. She managed to grasp the words "the guard." Where was the guard?

Vicente had come on duty an hour ago—apparently drunk. Jessica could see him now. He was seated in the guards' chair, out of sight of the window. His eyes seemed closed; his automatic rifle was propped against the wall alongside him. Nearby a kerosene lamp hung from a beam.

Being careful, Jessica answered Harry by inclining her head toward where Vicente was seated.

At once Harry began to form words again. Once more she understood the message: call him!

Jessica nodded slightly. Her heart was pounding. It could only mean that the rescue she had hoped for was finally happening, although she had no idea what Harry had in mind.

"Vicente!" she called, then tried again. "Vicente!"

He stirred; his eyes opened and met Jessica's.

She beckoned him. Vicente stood, started to come toward her, then quickly turned back to collect his rifle. He held it in a businesslike way, she noticed, clearly ready to use it if required.

CROUCHED LOW BENEATH THE window, Partridge gripped his 9-mm Browning pistol, the silencer extending from the barrel. So far tonight everything had gone as planned, but he knew the most crucial part of the action was about to begin.

One thing was working in his favor: Jessica was resourceful, quick to think and understand—exactly as he remembered her.

He listened to her call twice, heard noises from somewhere out of sight, then footsteps as the guard walked over. Now the man faced Jessica. Harry recognized that he was carrying a Kalashnikov automatic rifle. Compared with the Kalashnikov, Partridge's Browning was a peashooter.

The conclusion was inescapable: he would have to kill the guard and get his shot in first. But there was an obstacle. Jessica was exactly in line with the guard. A shot aimed at him could hit her too.

Partridge had to gamble. There was no other choice.

Taking a breath, he called out loudly, clearly, "Jessica, drop to the floor—now!"

Instantly the guard spun around, his rifle raised. But Partridge already had the Browning sighted; he squeezed the trigger, and the Browning fired with a near silent *pfft*. For an instant the man looked surprised, then fell where he was.

Partridge turned toward the outside doorway, but a swiftly moving shadow was ahead of him. It was Minh Van Canh, who now came forward, his own gun at the ready. Canh went swiftly to the guard, then confirmed with a nod that the man was dead. Next Canh moved to Jessica's cell, inspected the padlock, and asked, "Where is the key?"

Jessica was scrambling to her feet. She told him, "Over where the guard was sitting. Nicky's too."

In the adjoining cell Nicky stirred from sleep. He took in the new arrivals—Partridge, approaching and holding the Kalashnikov rifle he had just picked up, and Canh, collecting keys that were hanging from a nail. "Who are they, Mom?"

"Friends, dear. Very good friends."

Nicky, still sleepy, brightened. Then, with a flash of recognition, he said, "You're Mr. Partridge."

Jessica said emotionally, "Oh, bless you, Harry! Dear Harry!"

Speaking softly, Partridge cautioned, "We're not out of this yet, and we've a way to go. We all have to move quickly."

Canh had returned with the keys and was trying them one by one in the padlock of Jessica's cell. Suddenly the lock opened, and Jessica walked out. Within seconds Nicky was free too.

"Help me," Partridge told Canh. Together they dragged the body of the guard toward Nicky's cell and lifted it onto the low wooden bed. Partridge also lowered the light in the kerosene lamp so it was merely a glimmer.

"Let's go," he said.

In his free hand he kept the Kalashnikov. He had also pocketed two spare magazines he found on the guard's body.

Canh was ahead of them at the doorway. He had retrieved his camera from outside and, using a special night lens, was recording their departure, with the cells as background. He would have passable pictures, even in this dimmest light.

Encountering no one, the group moved through the darkened hamlet. Fernández, who had been watching the other buildings, eventually caught up with them.

At the jetty, O'Hara said, "Thought you'd never get here."

"We had problems," Partridge told him. "Which boat?"

"This one." It was an open wooden workboat about thirty feet long, with twin outboard motors. Two lines secured it.

"Everybody aboard," Partridge ordered.

Fernández helped Jessica and Nicky into the boat. Jessica was shaking uncontrollably. Canh jumped in last, as O'Hara, casting off, used an oar to push out from shore. Fernández grabbed a second oar. Together he and O'Hara rowed toward midstream, and Nueva Esperanza began to fade in the moonlight.

When Partridge considered the boat was well out of earshot, he told Ken O'Hara to start the engines. They fired immediately, and the boat surged forward. Bright moonlight, reflected on the water, made navigation relatively easy along the river's winding course.

"We aim for the Sion airstrip," Partridge told the others. "When we leave the river, we'll have to push hard and fast through the jungle, so get whatever rest you can."

436

As the time passed, Jessica became more composed; her involuntary shaking ceased. And Nicky was safe—at least for the moment—and that was what mattered most.

She had been watching him, aware that ever since they left the prison shack he had stayed close to Harry. Even now he had settled beside him in the boat. In fact, Harry had put his arm around Nicky, and the two at this moment seemed as one.

Jessica liked that. She had once loved Harry—in a way still did, especially now, when gratitude and love mingled. It was not strange at all that her son instinctively shared that feeling.

Partridge, too, had been thinking of the past—what he and Jessica had once meant to each other. And even in this short time he could see that all the things he'd most admired—her quick mind, strong spirit, warmth, resourcefulness—were still in place. He asked her now, "Back there, did you ever give up hope?"

"There were times I came close to it, though never entirely," Jessica said. She smiled. "Of course, if I'd known you were in charge of the rescue, that would have made a difference."

"We were a team," he told her. "Crawf was part of it. He's gone through hell, but then so have you. When we get back, you'll both need each other."

He sensed she knew what he was saying too: though he had returned briefly to her life, he would shortly disappear.

"That's a sweet thought, Harry. And what will you do?"

He shrugged. "Go on reporting. There'll be other wars."

"And in between wars?"

Some questions had no answers. He changed the subject. "Your Nicky's fine—the kind of boy I would have liked to have."

It could have happened, Jessica thought. For both of us, all those years ago. Then she reached out and put her hand on his.

"Thank you, Harry," she said. "Thank you for everything—the past, the present . . . my dearest love."

Miguel fired three shots into the air, shattering the silence. He knew it was the quickest way to sound an alarm.

It was three fifteen a.m., precisely forty minutes since the boat containing Partridge and the others had left the jetty.

A minute ago he had discovered Vicente's body and realized the prisoners were gone. His anger was savage and explosive. In the hut he had broken the guards' chair against a wall. Now he wanted to bludgeon those responsible for the escape.

Unfortunately, Miguel was painfully aware that he also must share the blame. He had never taken seriously the possibility of a rescue attempt; Nueva Esperanza, so deep in Sendero territory, had seemed remote and safe.

Miguel thought bitterly, when Sendero Luminoso got word of this, he would pay with his life, especially if the prisoners were not recaptured. His priority was to recapture them—at any cost.

Now alerted by his shots, with Gustavo in the lead, the other guards were running toward him.

He flailed them with his tongue. "You useless morons! Strangers came here while you slept, and you ignored them! Find out how they left. There must be traces."

Gustavo was back within moments. "They left by the river."

Miguel hurried to the jetty. He told Gustavo, "I want the two best boats, with two motors on each. Use everybody. Work fast, fast, fast! Then I want everyone assembled on the dock, with guns and ammunition."

He decided that whoever engineered the prisoners' release almost certainly had come by air into the area. Therefore they would leave the same way. Miguel instructed one armed boatload to go to the nearer jungle strip, a second to Sion. He decided to go with the Sion-destined boat.

A few minutes before four a.m. both boats were under way. Miguel's boat was substantially faster and pulled ahead soon after leaving the jetty. Gustavo was at the helm.

Chapter 18

THE Cheyenne II lifted off from Lima airport at dawn.

Rita was beside Sloane in the aircraft's second row of seats. Ahead of them were the pilot, Oswaldo Zileri, and a young co-pilot, Felipe Guerra.

Yesterday, Sunday, they had flown over the prearranged points but without result. Sloane had had difficulty distinguishing one from another, so impenetrable did the Selvas seem when viewed from above. "It's like parts of Vietnam," he told Rita.

Today, as dawn changed to daylight, the Cheyenne II began a slow descent toward the Selvas.

PARTRIDGE knew he had miscalculated. They were late.

What he had not allowed for in choosing Sion over the nearer airstrip was a problem with their boat. It happened about two hours after leaving Nueva Esperanza. Both outboard motors had been running smoothly when a strident horn abruptly sounded on the port-side motor. Ken O'Hara stopped the engine; as he did, the horn went silent. With the starboard engine alone operating, the boat was moving at a seriously slower speed.

O'Hara examined the engine. "It's overheated. Almost certainly the coolant pump has gone. Even if I had tools . . ." He let the words trail off.

"Run it," Partridge said. "Let's get the most out of it."

"You're the skipper, Harry," acknowledged O'Hara.

The engine ran for a few minutes, then stopped and would not start again. With the boat's speed reduced by half, the remainder of their river journey, instead of taking an hour, would take two.

In fact, it took two and a quarter hours, and now, shortly before seven a.m., their landing point was in sight. They would have to cover in an hour the three miles of jungle trail to the Sion airstrip.

"We have to do it," Partridge said, explaining their problem to Jessica and Nicky. "It may be exhausting, but there's no time to rest. Fernández will lead. I'll be in the rear."

Minutes later the keel scraped on a sandy beach, and they walked ashore through shallow water. They were about to enter an opening in the jungle wall when Fernández halted, motioning everyone to silence. Cocking his head to one side, he asked Partridge softly, "Do you hear?"

Partridge thought he could hear a distant murmuring sound.

"Another boat," Fernández said. "From the direction we've just come. Still a good distance away, but coming fast."

Without further delay they moved into the jungle. The trail was not as difficult as the one the rescue team had traversed two days earlier, because it was only slightly overgrown. Just the same, it was treacherous underfoot. Fernández set a fast, forced pace.

Partridge wondered how long Jessica and Nicky would last in the sweltering heat and under this grueling pressure. After a while he decided Jessica would make it; she had the determination and stamina. Nicky, though, showed signs of flagging.

Partridge insisted that the boy and Jessica be up forward, immediately behind Fernández. Assuming the boat they had heard was carrying their pursuers, any assault would come from behind. If that happened, Harry would do his best to fight off the attack while the others continued on. He had already checked his Kalashnikov rifle and had the two spare magazines handy.

He checked his watch: seven thirty-five. Remembering the eight-o'clock rendezvous with AeroLibertad, he hoped they had covered three quarters of the way.

Moments later they were forced to stop. Fernández had fallen heavily, and his foot was trapped in a muddy mess of roots.

As Partridge hurried toward him, the man grimaced with pain.

"I appear to have done some damage," he told Partridge. "I am sorry. I have let you down."

When the foot was free, Fernández was unable to walk without excruciating pain. Clearly his ankle was broken or sprained.

"We'll make a litter and carry you," Partridge said.

Fernández shook his head. "There is not time, Harry. They are following, and not far away. You must go on and leave me."

Jessica told Harry, "We *can't* leave him here."

But Partridge knew Fernández was right; there could be no other choice than leaving him.

"I need to say something quickly, Harry," Fernández said now. Partridge knelt beside him; Jessica joined them.

"I have a wife and four children," Fernández continued. "I would like to think someone will take care of them."

"You work for CBA," Partridge said, "and CBA will do it. I give you my solemn word, an official promise."

Fernández nodded, then motioned to an M-16 rifle he had been carrying. "Take this—you may need it as well as what you have.

But I do not intend to be taken alive. I would like a pistol."

Partridge gave him the Browning.

"Oh, Fernández!" Jessica's eyes filled with tears. "Nicky and I owe you so much." She leaned forward and kissed him.

"Go," Fernández urged. "Do not waste more time."

As Jessica rose, Partridge leaned forward and held Fernández tightly. Then he rose and moved forward. He did not look back.

WHEN Miguel saw a boat beached at the entrance to the jungle, he was glad he had joined the Sion airstrip sortie.

He was even more pleased when Ramón, leaping quickly from their own boat to the shore, ran to the other boat and announced that their quarry's engine had burned out.

Besides Miguel, the Sendero group comprised seven well-armed men. They filed quickly into the jungle.

"WE'RE early," Rita Abrams told the pilot Zileri as they approached the Sion airstrip—first point of call on their itinerary. She had just checked her watch: seven fifty-five.

"We'll circle and watch," he said. "In any case, this is the least likely place for your friends to be."

As they had yesterday, all four in the plane—Rita, Sloane, Zileri and the copilot Felipe—peered down at the short, tree-lined airstrip. Like yesterday, there was no visible activity at all.

ALONG the jungle trail Nicky was finding it increasingly difficult to maintain the punishing pace. Jessica and Minh Van Canh were helping him, each grabbing an arm and partially lifting him over difficult patches. It was about ten minutes since they had left Fernández.

Above their heads the trees appeared to be thinning; also, the trail had widened. Partridge hoped they were nearing the airstrip.

At that moment, from behind, came a short, sharp crack—unmistakably a single shot. It had to be Fernández, Partridge reasoned. And even in using the Browning, the stringer-fixer provided a final service—a warning that pursuit was close. As if in confirmation, several other shots followed.

441

Partridge himself was near exhaustion. Through the past fifty hours he had pushed himself to the limit. Mentally meandering, he decided what he wanted most was relief from action. When this adventure ended, he would resume the vacation he had barely started, and simply disappear. And wherever he went, he would take Vivien—the woman who loved him. Jessica had been the past; Vivien could be the future. . . .

Suddenly the airstrip was in view. Overhead an airplane was circling—it was a Cheyenne! Ken O'Hara, reliable to the end, Partridge thought, was loading a green cartridge into the flare gun. Green for "Land normally, everything is clear."

With equal suddenness, from behind came the sound of two more shots, this time much closer.

"Send up a red flare, not a green!" Partridge yelled at O'Hara. Red for "Land as quickly as possible, we are in danger."

O'Hara fired a red flare and then another. The airplane had already turned toward them.

"They've seen us!" Partridge said. When he knew which way the plane was going to land, he would pick a position to fight off the pursuers, while the others boarded first. The answer quickly became evident. The Cheyenne II was in a tight descending turn; it would land facing away from the jungle trail from where the shooting had been coming.

Partridge told O'Hara, "Get Jessica and Nicky down by the landing strip fast! When the plane gets to the far end, they'll swing around and taxi back. All of you get aboard. Did you hear that, Minh?"

"I heard." Canh, with an eye glued to his camera, was imperturbably taking pictures, as he had whenever possible throughout the journey.

Jessica asked anxiously, "What about you, Harry?"

He told her, "I'm going to cover you by firing down the trail. As soon as you're aboard, I'll join you. Now get going!"

O'Hara put an arm around Jessica, who was holding Nicky, and hurried them away.

Partridge could now see several figures in the jungle, advancing on the airstrip, guns pointed. He dropped behind a hillock.

Lying on his belly, he rested the Kalashnikov in front of him, the sights directed at the moving figures. He squeezed the trigger and, amid a burst of fire, saw one figure fall, the others dive for cover. At the same time he heard the Cheyenne II swoop in low above his head.

"THERE they are!" Crawford Sloane shouted. "I see them! It's Jessica and Nicky!" The airplane was still on its landing run, traveling fast on an uneven dirt surface.

As the end of the short strip was looming nearer, Zileri braked hard and swung the plane around. Then, accelerating both engines, he taxied back down the strip.

The Cheyenne II stopped at the point where Jessica, Nicky and O'Hara were waiting. The copilot Felipe had already opened the door. Nicky first, then Jessica and O'Hara climbed aboard, outstretched hands helping pull them in. Canh appeared and scrambled in behind the others.

As Sloane, Jessica and Nicky hugged each other O'Hara called out breathlessly, "Harry's up ahead. We have to get him."

"I see him," Zileri said. "Hold on!" He opened the throttles again, and the airplane shot forward, taxiing fast.

At the runway's far end he turned the airplane around again, ready for takeoff. Gunfire was heard through the open doorway.

"Your friend will have to make a run for it." Zileri's voice was urgent. "I want to get the hell out of here."

PARTRIDGE had both seen and heard the airplane; it was about a hundred yards away. He would make it at a fast run, keeping low. First, though, he had to spray fire back into the jungle trail.

Squeezing the trigger, he poured a deadly hail of bullets along both sides of the jungle path. When the magazine had emptied, he dropped the rifle, sprang to his feet, and ran.

Partridge was a third of the way to the plane when a bullet struck his leg. He fell instantly.

The bullet had impacted at the back of his right knee, shattering the joint. A terrible pain, more pain than he had ever felt, swept over him. He knew at that moment that he would never reach the airplane. He knew, too, that there was no time left. The plane must go. Summoning all his strength, he raised himself, waving the Cheyenne forward. All that mattered now was that his intention should be clear.

CANH was in the airplane doorway, shooting pictures.

Sloane cried out, "Harry's hit! He's waving for us to go, but we have to get him!"

Jessica cried out, "Yes! Oh, yes!"

"We can't," Zileri said. "There isn't time." Just then several bullets hit the plane.

Zileri pushed the throttles forward. The copilot Felipe secured the door. As airspeed built, Zileri eased back on the control column. The Cheyenne II left the airstrip and climbed.

Jessica and Nicky were holding each other, weeping. Sloane, his eyes partially closed, was shaking his head slowly, as if not believing what he had just seen.

ON THE ground Partridge saw the plane go, and tears long held back began to flow. Then more bullets hit him, and he died.

ABOARD the Cheyenne II several minutes passed before anyone felt capable of speech. Crawford Sloane was holding Jessica and Nicky close to him, the three oblivious to all else.

At length Sloane raised his head and asked Minh Van Canh, "About Harry . . . did you see anything more?"

Canh nodded sadly. "I was focused on him. He was hit again, several times. There isn't any doubt."

It was Rita, the professional with responsibilities, who asked Canh, "May I see some of your pictures?"

Canh did some rewinding, then passed his camcorder to Rita. Squinting through the viewfinder, she watched the stark, moving shots of Harry wounded, then falling to the fatal bullets. As she handed the camera back Rita's eyes were moist.

Sloane asked, "Did Harry have anybody—a girlfriend?"

"There was—is someone," Rita said. "Her name's Vivien. She's a nurse and lives in Port Credit, outside Toronto."

"We should call. I'll talk to her if you like."

"Yes, and when you do, tell her Harry made a will before he left, and I have it. He told me he was leaving everything to her."

Reaching into a briefcase, Rita produced a Teletype message received through Entel Peru.

"Before Harry left," she told the others, "he asked me to send a cable to a friend—a surgeon in Oakland, California. It seems he is among the world's ranking experts on injured hands. The cable asked questions about Nicholas. This is the reply."

She passed the typed sheet to Sloane, who read it aloud.

"Have read info you sent, also details in newspapers about your young friend's hand. Prostheses not recommended. He should learn to rotate hand downward until what remains of index and little fingers comes in contact with piano keys. Will take patience, perseverance. Being young helps."

There was a silence as Sloane finished reading; then he said, "I guess there will never be a time when there isn't something we'll have reason to thank Harry for."

"Fernández too," Jessica said to him. She now told Crawford and Rita of the promise Harry had made in the jungle about providing for Fernández's wife and four children.

"If Harry said that," Sloane said, "he was speaking for CBA, and it's binding, like a legal document."

"There's one snag," Rita pointed out. "Harry was fired before that, even though he didn't know it."

Minh Van Canh, who overheard, looked startled.

"It makes no difference," Sloane said. "Harry's promise will be honored. I'll see it's put into effect."

The Cheyenne II droned on, still climbing, gaining altitude to pass over the peaks of the Andes, after which they would descend toward Lima. The flight would take another forty minutes.

WHAT was necessary now, Rita realized, was to put a report together for the *National Evening News* tonight. It would be a long, dramatic one and use most of Canh's best pictures. Crawf

445

would do the narration and stand-ups. He was a professional, like Rita and the rest.

But there must first be a bulletin to say Nicky and Jessica were safe. When CBA News received it in New York, they would break instantly into network programming. Rita would send just a few pictures, transmitting quick and dirty—the way she had from Dallas–Fort Worth Airport for the airbus crash story she, Harry, Minh and Ken O'Hara had worked on less than a month ago.

Rita tapped Zileri on the shoulder, pointing to the aircraft radio. "Can you patch a phone call through to New York?" She scribbled a number and passed it forward.

In a surprisingly short time a voice said, "CBA foreign desk." Zileri passed back a microphone. "Go ahead," he told her.

She held the TRANSMIT button down. "This is Rita Abrams. Get me a bird out of Lima for a bulletin at ten thirty Lima time. Make sure the Horseshoe knows."

A voice replied laconically, "You got it. Will do."

"Thanks. Good-bye." She handed the microphone back.

A script would be needed for the bulletin. Rita scribbled a few phrases, then decided Crawf would find the right words. He always did. He would probably ad-lib in part. He was good at that too.

In what was left of the flight she and Crawf must work together. Unfortunately, it meant pulling him away from the arms of Jessica and Nicky. But he would accept the need and so would they. Like everyone else in the business, they all understood that the news came first.

"Crawf," Rita said gently, "you and I have work to do. It's time we started."

When Arthur Hailey brings out a new novel, it is more than just another book. It is a publishing event. *The Evening News* is Hailey's tenth blockbuster in a string of successes that includes *Hotel, Airport, Wheels,* and *Strong Medicine* (all Condensed Books selections). And, like the others, this one plumbs the depths of a large and complex industry.

Why television news this time? "I'm a newsaholic," Hailey explains. "When I was a boy growing up in Britain, I was fascinated by the news, whether it came in the newspaper my father brought home or on the wireless." As a television dramatist in Canada in the 1950s, he also gained an insider's understanding of the TV world.

Arthur Hailey

Still, when he began his research for *The Evening News,* he undertook it with the same intensity that has become his trademark. He traveled extensively from network boardrooms to small newsrooms, and spoke with everyone from news executives to studio technicians. He also journeyed twice into the jungles of Peru to seek background on the Sendero Luminoso guerrillas. Peruvian authorities warned him, however, against meeting directly with the terrorists. "It's unlikely I would have lived long enough to write up my research notes," Hailey comments wryly. In all, his research for the book absorbed him for a year and a half; the writing took two years more.

Now, as Arthur Hailey approaches the age of seventy, he is circumspect about his future plans. He may write a few short novels, he suggests. But for the present he is content to enjoy his home in Lyford Cay, the Bahamas, with his wife of thirty-nine years, Sheila. "I won't stop writing," he says. "But I won't let my life be taken over for years at a time as those other books demanded. It's a promise I made to my wife," he adds with a smile. "And she'll make sure I keep it."

THE
COURTSHIP OF
PEGGY
McCOY

by
RAY SIPHERD

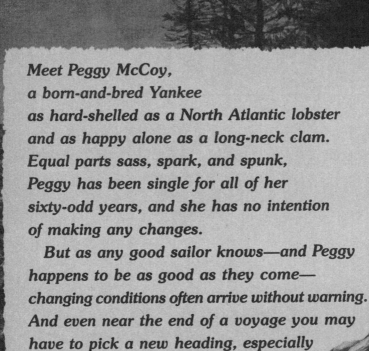

Meet Peggy McCoy,
a born-and-bred Yankee
as hard-shelled as a North Atlantic lobster
and as happy alone as a long-neck clam.
Equal parts sass, spark, and spunk,
Peggy has been single for all of her
sixty-odd years, and she has no intention
of making any changes.

  But as any good sailor knows—and Peggy
happens to be as good as they come—
changing conditions often arrive without warning.
And even near the end of a voyage you may
have to pick a new heading, especially
when love is in the wind.

1

F REE SPIRIT.
The words, in bold black letters across the stern, were plainly visible as the sailboat approached the narrow channel out of Hasty Harbor. The boat cut smoothly through the blue-gray water. But even in the sanctuary of the cove there was a slight chop to the waves. The telltale of red ribbon that showed the wind direction fluttered outward from the rigging. Fifty yards ahead a conical red buoy bobbed, listing lazily with the incoming tide. The sailboat was of the Thistle class, seventeen feet long, white with dark blue trim. The mainsail curved forward in a wide arc that took full advantage of the steady northwest breeze. The jib lay crumpled on the foredeck, ready to be raised.

The boat's lone occupant, seated well down inside the open cockpit, was almost completely hidden. What could be seen was a tan bare arm hooked over the tiller, and an old worn sailor hat pulled down over a head of curly gray hair.

As the sailboat drew nearer to the red buoy she tacked abruptly, the sail swinging over to the starboard side. The bow now pointed toward the slender opening between steep granite rocks that rose to a height of thirty feet and were topped by weathered firs. Tidal currents surging through the channel began to pitch the boat from bow to stern. As if apprehensive of what lay ahead, the boat shuddered momentarily, and sailed on.

Among the hundreds of small coves, inlets, islands, and peninsulas that made up the mid-coastal region of Maine, there were special words—a few unprintable—for the passage that connected Hasty Harbor with the broad estuary of the Kerrenac River beyond. It was not so much the channel's narrowness nor its fast-moving currents. Rather, it was the huge ragged boulders at its mouth that reached into the river in the shape of a haphazard jetty. The rocks were called the Sawteeth. Dark and continually washed by the sea, they had a malevolent majesty that commanded awe.

At twelve thirty on an afternoon in mid-July, *Free Spirit* sailed out of Hasty Harbor and began to pass the Sawteeth rocks.

The skipper of the boat remained low, avoiding the spray that was thrown up against the bow. One hand operated the line leading the mainsail; the other hand now gripped the tiller, deftly playing it against the wind and tide.

Then simultaneously two things happened: a downdraft whipped the sail in the opposite direction, and a huge wave hit the far side of the Sawteeth, spilling over them and slamming down on the boat. Suddenly adrift and helpless, the boat was swept broadside toward the rocks.

The next moment, incredibly, the figure in the boat stood up, grabbed at the outermost rock, and with both hands gave a mighty shove. The sailboat shot by the Sawteeth, missing them by inches, and now drifted out into the open water. The figure sat down and regained control of the tiller and sail. The mainsail caught the wind and billowed, and *Free Spirit* began reaching for the sea.

"Too close for comfort," Peggy McCoy said aloud. She took a slow, deep breath, then patted the boat's deck. "Good work, old girl. Another couple seconds, and you and I would have become flotsam for the Gulf of Maine."

The woman played out the sail gradually and looked around. No other water traffic was within a mile of her and *Free Spirit* to witness their near collision with the rocks. If so, the witnesses might have been surprised to see that *Free Spirit*'s sailor was, in fact, a trim woman in her sixties. They would have also seen that she was dressed in what she called her summer finery—old sneakers without socks, a pair of khaki shorts, and a man's faded blue shirt, the sleeves cut off above the elbows.

Peggy McCoy moved forward and began to raise the jib. The wind filled it immediately, and the boat sprang forward. Peggy returned to the tiller, checked the telltale, and made a slight correction in her course.

She pushed the sailor hat down firmly on her head, tucking in a curl as she did. To those who knew her, the graying sailor hat was Peggy's trademark; she wore it every time she sailed. She'd had the hat for more than forty years, she once told a friend. It had been a gift from a young navy flier she had known during World War II. The face below the hat was round, with deep-set eyes, a turned-up nose, and a mouth that appeared perpetually pursed.

The jib started to flap noisily, and Peggy noticed that the wind was lessening. The whitecaps of foam were fewer, and in the distance, patches of smooth water rose and fell.

Peggy studied the horizon. Far to the east, in the summer sunlight, was the jagged line of trees and tidal marshes she had known since childhood. Nowhereland, her father said it was—and as she still preferred to think of it. How often had he driven the family there in the old Ford coupe to picnic or to walk the rock-strewn shore. Today it was a state park, named after some forgotten former governor. Campers, six-packs, and portable radios the size of small suitcases had replaced the world of silent green that she remembered now with melancholy wistfulness.

Looking west, Peggy saw that she was passing Stiles Head, a massive outcropping of rock that had claimed more than a dozen ships over the years. Soon, surrounded by majestic pines, would emerge the twin turrets of Elysia-by-the-Sea, the venerable gray clapboard mansion that was built by a lumber baron in the 1920s and that now served as a hotel. Half a mile farther would be a cluster of newly built leisure condominiums, each with a cantilevered deck that jutted arrogantly out over the water's edge. One good winter storm, thought Peggy, and those decks—and maybe houses, too—would be reduced to hunks of refuse drifting in the North Atlantic.

A mile beyond them, where scrub pine met the shore, Peggy

453

knew what she would see—the small white saltbox with the tall flagpole in front of it. Every day two flags flew from that flagpole: the American flag and, below it, the blue-and-white flag of the U.S. Navy. The house was Peggy's. Past it there was no one, no house, nothing but the barren stretch of sand called Lonely Point.

Peggy brought the sailboat about on a new tack, and as she did, she scanned the water for other boats. Nearest to her was an inbound lobster boat. Beyond it she saw the high superstructure of the Portland–Nova Scotia ferry outward bound. Also heading up the coast were two large sailboats. Rich summer people on their way to Camden or Boothbay Harbor, Peggy guessed.

The lobster boat continued toward her, with gulls wheeling overhead and dipping low into the wake. Drawing closer, it decreased its speed, and Peggy recognized the green hull of the *Mary G.* In the wheelhouse she could see the lean figure of Link Mallott, wearing his ancient Windbreaker, which still bore the emblem of the Boston Braves. On the open deck Link's son and nephew were busy stacking lobster crates, the shiny darkish claws of the wet lobsters reaching out between the slats.

"Ahoy, Link!" called Peggy as the two boats came abreast.

Without altering his forward gaze, the lobsterman lifted one hand from the wheel in a faint gesture of acknowledgment.

"You're all personality! You know that, Link!" Peggy shouted after the lobster boat as it resumed its speed.

Peggy swung the tiller over, and the sail followed. On this new tack her course would take her toward the lighthouse on Kidds Rock, the tiny steep-sided island that lay offshore.

Suddenly something caught her eye. Well out to sea, on a course perpendicular to hers, was a large ship moving at great speed. Judging by its wake, the vessel was probably traveling at close to thirty knots.

There were several miles of open water separating the ship from *Free Spirit.* But the silhouette soon became apparent—slim lines, a narrow pointed bow, and a tall communications mast above the bridge. Undoubtedly a cruiser, Peggy thought, the kind the Whitby Shipworks had been building for the navy recently. Peggy assumed that the ship was undergoing sea trials.

Transfixed, she watched the ship move through the water, waves exploding at her bow, the wake roiling up into a rooster tail of white foam behind the stern. The navy men aboard are giving this ship all she's got, Peggy thought. But she knew that soon the ship would cut her speed, turn, and head inland toward Kidds Rock and eventually the Whitby Shipworks, the huge shipbuilding complex on the Newell River in the town of Whitby.

By now the wind had calmed to a modest breeze. Peggy checked her wristwatch: it was one o'clock.

"Mess time, mates," she said.

She reached down near her feet and found a plastic food bag. Unzipping it, she took out a sandwich wrapped in wax paper and a carton of fruit juice, and began to eat.

"You make a terrific tuna sandwich," Peggy went on.

"You bet I do," she answered herself.

She opened the juice carton and drank from it, her free hand remaining on the tiller. When she was done eating, she crumpled the wax paper into a ball, carefully put it inside the empty juice carton, and returned them to the food bag. Peggy now took out a jar of peanuts. She unscrewed the lid, tossed a handful of peanuts into her mouth, and placed the open jar upright in the bag.

The day had warmed considerably. Peggy stretched out her legs across the cockpit floor, turned her face full to the sun, and shut her eyes. This ritual was part of every summer sail. The wind touched her face fleetingly, and the sun felt warm and kind. She felt herself a spirit buoyed by the sea, something gossamer and airborne, carried effortlessly upward toward the sun itself.

FIRST came the sounds—the deep reverberations of engines and the tumbling of water. Peggy opened her eyes. She wanted to shout, but couldn't.

Less than half a mile from her, squarely in *Free Spirit*'s path, the navy ship was bearing down. For an instant Peggy remained frozen, watching as the ship came on, sending waves cascading past the large white number 37 at her bow.

The next moment Peggy leaped forward to strike down the jib but, in reaching for it, slipped and fell sharply on her left knee.

Without rising, she grabbed the boom with one hand, and with the other swung the tiller out as far as it would go.

For a moment the sailboat hung in the water, motionless. Then slowly she turned parallel to the cruiser's heading. At the same time the cruiser abruptly altered course and slowed.

Peggy took a breath. She looked down at the red streak across her palm where the boom line had bitten into it, and for the first time she was conscious of a painful throbbing in her knee.

Raising her head again, she saw a new danger approaching her. The wake thrown up by the cruiser's stern spread outward in a rolling wall of water. *Free Spirit* had no way of escaping it.

Quickly Peggy reset the mainsail, pointing the bow of the sailboat directly at the tumbling wake. Then, sitting down inside the cockpit, she shoved a cushion under her and put another at her back. She took the tiller with both hands, shut her eyes, and waited.

A moment, two . . . and nothing. Suddenly she felt *Free Spirit*'s bow thrust upward as the water rose. A second later the wave struck, crashing over the foredeck, bounding past the cockpit, and striking Peggy's head and pinning her against the cockpit wall. Ice-cold water doused her legs.

Then there was silence. Calm.

Peggy opened her eyes and looked around. The jib was drenched, as was a good part of the mainsail. But the mast and rigging were intact. Slowly Peggy unbent her legs. Pain seized her injured knee. She raised herself, and as she moved, the water in the cockpit lapped at her sneakers and around the cushion where she had sat. Beside her, also partially submerged, was the food bag. But still standing upright in it was the open peanut jar.

With effort she stood up. She grabbed the jar, turned, and with all her strength threw it in the direction of the navy ship.

"Nuts to you!" she shouted.

She turned back and began to sail up the river as quickly as her boat would carry her.

THE four men stood on the deck of the cruiser saying nothing, watching as the large ship was edged into its berth under the gentle prodding of the tugs. Three of the men—a lieutenant commander and two young ensigns—were in white summer uniforms.

The fourth man was considerably older, in his seventies, and taller than the others. He was dressed in green slacks and a yellow sport shirt. But just as they did, he wore black navy dress shoes that were polished to a high sheen.

As the cruiser drew closer to the dock the older man leaned forward at the rail, his jaw set and his brow tightened below a full head of white hair, as if he were docking the ship himself.

"What's her name again?" the man asked no one in particular.

The lieutenant commander stepped forward. "The *Corregidor*, sir," he said patiently. "It's a guided-missile cruiser, as you know. They're named for great battles."

The man grunted. There was a sudden bump, a whirr of the ship's propellers, and the rattle of chains as gangplanks were swung out. When the forward gangplank was positioned and secured in place, the four men moved toward it, the three uniformed officers walking deferentially behind the older man.

Without acknowledging them, he started briskly down the gangplank, ignoring the guide rope, which the younger officers instinctively grasped on the steep decline. Once he reached the pier, the man turned to the ship and watched as a hawser was thrown down past the white number 37 near the bow and was made fast to the dock. He strode ahead again. With crisp assurance he followed the arrows that directed him toward the main gate and through the labyrinth of passageways and vast gray metal structures that made up the Whitby Shipworks.

Passing a hangar-size building, the man abruptly stopped to peer in at the large sections of still-to-be-assembled ships. He watched as shipyard workers swarmed among the scaffolding and as welders' torches sprayed down pyrotechnic showers. Then he lowered his head, thrust out his chin, and moved on.

As the four men reached the main gate of the yard a car bearing the navy emblem on its front doors drove in and stopped. The four officers approached the car, but short of it, the older man halted and turned to the lieutenant commander behind him.

"It was a good run, Commander," he said with a firm handshake. "Thank you. Thank all the men."

"It was our pleasure. We were honored, sir."

The lieutenant commander saluted, and the ensigns did also.

The older man returned the salutes. "And thank you for that short turn at the helm. My apologies for giving everyone a little problem out there. I guess I don't quite have my sea legs back. Still," he went on, "if I'd had an officer of the bridge perform that way, I'd have sent him back to basic piloting class." He chuckled mildly. The younger officers did likewise.

"It was no real problem, sir," the lieutenant commander said. "During the summer we have a great number of pleasure craft in the area."

"All's well that ends well, anyway. Nobody sank." The older man chuckled again. He gave another salute, which the other officers returned. He then stepped into the car and settled with a sigh into the back seat. The car made a quick U-turn and headed out the gate.

THE distance between the small city of Whitby, Maine, and the village of Hasty Harbor is twenty miles by water, fifteen by land. Along the highway and amid the timeless stands of firs and hemlocks are souvenir booths, often with folding chairs set by the roadside for the display of everything from garish seascapes painted on black velvet to T-shirts boasting I'M A MAINE-IAC.

At one point along the highway is a faded green sign that states simply HASTY HARBOR (POP. 423). The sign was put up in the early '50s, and no one has bothered to update it since.

But the likelihood is that the number has changed little in the years the sign has stood. The road leading from the highway onto the peninsula is called River Road, a strip of patched and re-patched asphalt that meanders through woods and marshes with no indication of a river nearby. Then, when one least expects it, over the last curving rise Hasty Harbor suddenly appears below.

A Maine summer guidebook describes Hasty Harbor as "a small, picturesque harbor community typical of many along the mid-coastal region of the state." It says nothing about the freshly painted white clapboard houses next to others with darkened unstained wooden shingles. Nor does it mention the tidy gardens of primroses and hydrangeas clustering at the picket fences that enclose each yard.

Beyond the village is the harbor itself, dotted with boats of all sorts—cabin cruisers, sailboats, lobster boats, and trawlers. Totally protected except for the narrow opening to the Kerrenac River beyond, the harbor has been considered a snug anchorage to coastal mariners for centuries.

River Road continues downward, ending at the water's edge. Here, at one side of a dusty turnaround, is T. C. Dabney's General Store, which also serves as a post office. Opposite the general store is a sign reading DODGE'S BOATYARD, and a narrow dirt road. At the end of the road is a pier and a small white wooden building that is the boatyard office.

On this summer afternoon Noah Dodge stood watching the activity. Tall, with a fringe beard and faded flannel shirt, he was a familiar sight. Between mid-May and mid-September, Dodge's Boatyard was a busy place. Aside from the local lobstermen and fishermen and scallopers, who used the yard throughout the year, there were the out-of-state vacationers and the day-trippers from Portland and Portsmouth and as far away as Boston. Add to their numbers those who came down from the mountains and the woods of inland Maine itself, and it was like a manic rush of lemmings to the sea.

For the other eight months of the year Noah managed reasonably well. But in the summer he had to hire several teenage boys to take care of routine maintenance. In the boatyard office his wife, Addie, handled the paperwork. Worse luck, now that a bout of sciatica was keeping her housebound. But at least their daughter, Sarah, had returned from college and had volunteered to help him run the office for the next few weeks.

The activity was light today, so Noah was enjoying the sight of the two children on the floating dock below the pier. The boy, about eight, was demonstrating for his younger sister the subtleties of baiting a crab trap with a fresh fish head. And kneeling beside them was Sarah, talking to the children in her soft, sure voice.

Noah realized how much of a woman she had become in the

last year. In her white shorts and T-shirt, she was as lean and lanky as any girl her age. But that age was twenty-one now, as she continued to remind him, adding that she was quite capable of independence in whatever form it took.

Sarah wished the children luck and turned back in the direction of the ramp that led up to the pier. Noah watched her brush away the straight blond hair that fell around her shoulders. It had the look and color of pale silk.

She came up the ramp, smiling. "I hope those two catch something," she said. "They're from Nebraska, and they've never seen a crab before. In fact, this is the first time they've seen the ocean. They're really sweet. Look how excited they are."

But her father was now watching something else. "Strange," he said. "Did you see Peg when she went out this morning?"

"Yes. Why?"

"Take a look." He pointed out into the harbor. Fifty yards from where they stood, *Free Spirit* was coming at great speed.

"There she is now," Sarah said, and waved. "Hi, Peggy!"

"Something's wrong," Noah said. "She's moving like the dickens, and at this distance she'd be waving back at us."

Without slowing, the sailboat headed directly at the floating dock. The jib and the mainsail were both raised, and at the stern sat Peggy, guiding the boat's course.

"Something *is* wrong," Sarah said. She raced down the ramp to the dock.

Sails flapping, *Free Spirit* did a sudden about-face and came to rest against the dock with a loud thud.

Sarah was waiting. "Peggy . . ."

"That's me," Peggy called. "Have one of the boys moor *Spirit* for me, will you, Sarah?" She let go of the tiller but remained seated.

The girl grabbed the side of the sailboat with one hand and held it. Peggy stood, adjusted her sailor hat, picked up her food bag, and stepped out of the boat.

"Are you all right, Peg?"

"I'm tired, wet, and mad. That's just for starters. First I almost smashed up on the Sawteeth. Then some hotshot navy type decided to play chicken near the lighthouse."

460

Peggy limped up the ramp to find Noah standing at the head of it. He reached down to help her. "Peg, how are you?"

"Alive, at least."

"You're limping."

"No kidding."

"Come into the office and sit down. I'll fix you something."

"Good," the woman said. "What can you give a person who today fought the battle of Kidds Rock? On second thought, I just want to go home."

"Peg, do you need a doctor?" Noah asked her.

"What I need is answers," Peggy told him. "I want to know who almost ran me down out there."

"What kind of boat was it?"

"It wasn't a boat. It was a big damn ship. A navy cruiser."

"Did you get the number?"

"I'll never forget it. Number thirty-seven," Peggy said.

"Why don't you let Sarah drive you home?"

"No." Peggy shook her head. "I've still got one good leg to drive. And I'm going to use it to start kicking a few butts."

Peggy began limping toward her blue Ford Pinto, carrying her food bag. Noah moved again to help her, but she shook the bag briefly, waving him away.

"I'm okay, I'm okay," she told him. "As you know, Commander McCoy can take care of herself."

"I know she can," said Noah as he walked beside her.

2

UNTIL the telephone call it had been a fine day for Captain Robert Carnes. Arriving promptly at eight that morning, he had attended to his duties as navy supervisor of shipbuilding, Whitby Division. He'd prepared his monthly report for his Pentagon superiors, advising them of the sixteen ships the Whitby Shipworks was constructing for the navy, all on budget and on schedule. At noon there'd been a splendid lunch of broiled fresh swordfish with a former navy colleague.

Then, just before the afternoon shift change, Captain Carnes had observed his lieutenant commander and two ensigns accompanying Rear Admiral Charles Deering to the front gate. So far the old man's visit had been going very well. And he would be on his way in two days' time.

It was late afternoon when the intercom buzzed on the captain's desk. He responded with a brisk "Carnes here."

"Excuse me, sir, but there's a lady on the phone who wants to talk to you," the captain's aide announced. "Except she doesn't sound much like a lady. Her name is Miss McCoy, sir. She says you know her."

"Everyone knows Miss McCoy. Thank you." Captain Carnes took a deep breath and patted his crew cut, as if to make even his telephone appearance as presentable as possible. The phone clicked, and he said casually, "How are you, Peggy?"

"I'll tell you how I am," she said. "But first you tell me—was it one of their men or one of yours?"

"Sorry, but you've lost me. Who was what?"

"Who was at the wheel of the ship that nearly ran me down this afternoon when I was sailing? There was a cruiser out there, probably on sea trials, making thirty knots. The ship was number thirty-seven, by the way."

The captain had a sudden disquieting feeling, which he disallowed at once. Keeping his voice affable, he said, "We did have a cruiser out there on sea trials today."

"Well, I want to know who was at the helm. I'm going to hang him up with my navy flag."

"First of all, are you all right?" Captain Carnes asked.

"Forgetting my knee, which I fell on just before it happened, I'm terrific. I'm also ready to declare war on the U.S. Navy. Another couple yards, and me and my sailboat would have been at the bottom of the Gulf of Maine by now." Sitting at her kitchen table, Peggy took a swallow of coffee from the mug in front of her.

The disquieting thought Carnes had just had refused to go away. "I'll check it out," he said after a moment. "I mean, we can't have a navy man in a big ship running down a navy woman in a little one, now can we?" He laughed easily, or hoped it would sound so. The reaction from the other end was total silence.

"Oh, while I think of it," he said, seeking to change the subject, "did you get my invitation to the launching?"

"Yes."

"It's tomorrow afternoon, you know." He pressed on. "I hadn't heard from you, and I really hope you'll be there. I have a seat saved for you."

There was another pause. Then Peggy said, "Robert, you're a nice young man to send me invitations to your launchings just because I'm an old blue."

"But you're a naval *officer*."

"*Ex*-officer."

"An ex-*commander*."

"Even so, I'm going to pass on this one," the woman said. "My knee's killing me, and I'm sure whatever ship you launch will glide into the river without my help."

"The ship is a destroyer, in fact," Captain Carnes said. "She'll be christened the *Willoughby*. It's the first time a ship is being named for a navy man from Maine. Willoughby was killed during the battle of the Coral Sea. Didn't you do your first tour of duty as a navy nurse down that way?"

"Yes. So?"

"Well, the guest speaker at the launching is an ex–navy man who was in the same fleet command as Willoughby back then: Rear Admiral Charles Deering."

"Again, so?"

"He received some sort of citation from the White House last year calling him the father of modern naval communications."

"What should I do? Whistle 'Anchors Aweigh'?"

"And . . . uh . . . there's one more reason I'd like you to be there," the captain went on. "As you know, the military services in general are perceived as being male oriented and male dominated."

"They are. What's the big surprise?"

"Well, if people could see you at the launching, they might think differently. If you're in uniform, I mean."

"You want me to wear my old WAVE uniform?"

"Yes. My thought is that some young women might see you and decide to make the navy a career."

"You make me sound like a walking recruiting poster." Peggy drained her coffee mug. "Okay. I will attend your launching. And I'll wear my uniform if I can find it. And if I can get into it."

"Thank you. I'd appreciate it," Captain Carnes said.

"But I'm still going to file a complaint about that ship today."

"I understand."

"Good," Peggy answered, and hung up the phone.

PEGGY sat for several moments, then raised herself from the table and walked to the other side of the kitchen. Slowly, favoring her injured knee, she began to climb the stairs to the attic.

After half an hour of searching she found what she was looking for. It smelled musty, and the brass buttons no longer had the luster she remembered. But the uniform was still neatly folded, and the three service stripes on the sleeves remained a deep and solid blue against the white. Carefully carrying the uniform in both arms, she went down the steps again and into her bedroom.

There, standing in front of the mirror that hung above her bedroom bureau, Peggy unfolded the uniform. The waist appeared so narrow she wondered how she ever fit into it.

She decided she would try it on right now. Yet as she turned to lay the uniform across the bed before undressing, she saw the photograph. It was a small black-and-white snapshot set inside a thin gilt frame that rested on her bedside table. The picture showed a young man and a young woman smiling and squinting slightly into the bright sun. Above them hung the tip of a palm frond; behind them was a stretch of sand and water. The man, one arm casually around the girl's slender waist, was tall and sandy-haired and dressed in the fatigues of a navy flier. The girl was wearing a white dress and sandals. On her head, above her short dark curls, was a sailor hat.

Her expression was one of complete happiness. Mixed with it also was a look of wonderment at how anyone who had known only the harsh granite hills of Maine could now be on an island in the South Seas and be this much in love.

Peggy picked up the uniform and held it in front of her again. To the photograph she said gently, "You never saw this uniform,

Tom. Would you believe your little Pegs made it to commander? But you were never much for ranks or uniforms. Whatever I wore, you always said I was the prettiest girl on Toku. That's what you told me, Tom. Long ago."

THE blue Ford Pinto waited in the line of cars outside the main gate of the shipyard. From where she sat behind the wheel, Peggy watched the flow of people pressing around her. There were naval officers and sailors in their summer whites, plus townspeople, tourists, and shipyard workers in a variety of outfits: suits and party dresses, jeans and T-shirts. All had come to watch the launching ceremony.

A policeman waved Peggy through the main gate, and she found a space in the parking lot. She got out of her car and straightened the skirt of her WAVE uniform. From the occasional curious looks she became aware of, she realized that she was the only woman in the crowd who wore a military outfit.

"Yoo-hoo!" The shrill voice came from behind her, and she knew at once who the caller was. "Oh, yoo-hoo, Pegg-eee!"

With all the other noises surrounding them, Peggy was tempted to quicken her step and lose herself among the crowd. But her knee made such a swift escape impossible, and after a few moments the caller finally appeared beside her, puffing.

"My dear, I *knew* it must be you," the woman gasped.

"Hello, Ernestine," said Peggy.

Mrs. Ernestine Doberman, widow of the founder of the Whitby Seafood Cannery, was perspiring and breathing like a boated fish. She was also staring in surprise and curiosity at Peggy's uniform.

"Don't you look *unique* in that attire!" she said.

Peggy looked at Mrs. Doberman and thought of saying the same thing. As Mrs. Doberman frequently did at local functions in summertime, she was wearing that ridiculous pink frilly dress that was two sizes too small for her excessive girth.

"I'd like to talk to you about the summer festival," the woman said. "It's just two weeks away, you know."

They were interrupted by a loud cheer from the crowd. Suddenly

465

a group of children carrying balloons pushed in between Peggy and Mrs. Doberman, and Peggy seized the moment to escape.

"Sorry, Ernestine," Peggy shouted, and permitted herself to be swept off with the crowd. She moved past the shipyard's administrative offices and assembly buildings and emerged onto the broad tarmac of the dock area, where the ship was to be launched.

She halted—and remembered with a chill that she'd been even closer to another ship the day before. Yet this one sat immobile in the giant wood-and-steel cradle, mute to the increasing activity surrounding her. Swaths of red, white, and blue bunting trailed down her prow, and flags and pennants fluttered from her halyards and mast.

Near the ship's bow a raised platform held a lectern and a dozen chairs. Members of the crowd who, like Peggy, had received invitations were now filling the folding chairs that faced the platform and the ship. There were still a few seats in the front row of chairs, and although Peggy did not wish to be that close, she had no choice. She found a seat and sat down.

Peggy looked at her watch: it was five minutes to four. Better get this show on the road, she thought. She knew that any ship launched into the Newell River had to hit the water at slack tide, a period of just ten minutes. Otherwise there was the real possibility that the strong tidal currents would carry the new billion-dollar destroyer away before the tugs could get their lines on her.

At that moment twelve people appeared, mounted the platform, and took seats. The nine men in the group included Captain Carnes and other naval officers, a navy chaplain, shipworks executives, and a Congressman. Peggy guessed that the three women in the group were related to the young sailor for whom the ship was being named.

After several minutes the chaplain rose from his chair and approached the lectern. The crowd quieted.

"Let us recall the words of psalm one hundred seven," said the chaplain as many people bowed their heads. *"They that go down to the sea in ships, that do business in great waters . . ."* The launching of the United States Navy ship *Willoughby* was under way.

Peggy knew the routine by heart. After the chaplain there were the welcoming remarks of Arne Knudsen, the shipyard president. And the speaker after that was a smooth Commander Somebody-or-other from the office of the Chief of Naval Operations, in Washington.

"Now, it is with considerable pride," she heard him say, "that I present to you our distinguished guest this afternoon . . ."

Peggy saw a white-haired older man in an admiral's full-dress uniform look toward the speaker at the lectern. He unfurled some papers in his hand and gave them a quick glance. She wondered if his speech had been written for him by some public-information hack in the Department of Defense so that he could say something appropriate and totally forgettable.

"Rear Admiral Charles T. Deering."

As if a light had swept across him, the admiral stood up, nodded to the speaker, acknowledged the applause of the crowd, and strode quickly to the lectern.

"Give 'em hell, Admiral!" somebody shouted from the crowd. The admiral looked up and smiled.

"Young man, I compliment your spirit and your lung power. I wanted to say the same thing to *my* admiral before the battle of Leyte Gulf. I didn't, but we won the battle anyway."

The crowd laughed, and applauded again. As the man waited for the crowd to quiet, Peggy studied him and realized she was smiling. He was tall, well over six feet. In fact, he looked like some aging character actor cast in the role of a World War II admiral—the great mane of hair, the crisp white uniform, the colorful display of service ribbons. Even the forthright jaw bespoke indomitable character.

"Honored guests, former comrades-in-arms, ladies, and gentlemen," he began. "First let me comment briefly on this splendid ship we see before us. She represents the best in modern military technology. And," he added parenthetically, "if I am to believe the press, that also includes seven-hundred-dollar hammers that are all shaft and no head."

The crowd roared, and Peggy knew at once that no Pentagon press officer had written *this* speech.

467

"This ship," the man continued, "is equipped with the most up-to-date computer guidance and weapons systems. She can communicate to any point on the globe by means of satellites hundreds of miles out in space. The fact is that in a few minutes the U.S.S. *Willoughby* will join the fleet of what the press also delights in calling the *new* navy. Still, there are some of us who remember the *old* navy. By old I mean the ships, equipment, procedures. Definitely not the people. If some of us don't look exactly new, it's only because we've spent a little time in dry dock."

More laughter from the audience, including Peggy. The admiral smiled broadly and grasped the sides of the lectern as he leaned forward.

"And yet," he went on, "the old and the new navies have much in common. In short . . ."

In short, Peggy realized, she liked the man. She liked his vigor, his openness, and his rough, wry humor.

"There are some things that have not changed as the present navy has come into its own," the admiral continued. "One is the devotion to duty of its men and women and their heroism in the defense of freedom everywhere. Although I never had the honor of serving with Henry Willoughby, I have known many like him—heroes all—to whom courage was inborn and the defense of freedom as natural as life itself. Henry Willoughby of Waldoboro, Maine, sacrificed *his* young life so that all of *you* might live and breathe the air of freedom here today!"

As the applause began to swell, the admiral raised both hands, acknowledging it. More cheers and whistles followed, and to her surprise Peggy found that she was cheering, too.

Admiral Deering extended a hand in the direction of a handsome gray-haired woman seated on the platform. "Now, it is with great pleasure that I present Mrs. Everett Hodges, sister of the seaman whose name this valiant vessel bears."

The woman nodded. At the same time Captain Carnes rose and guided her to the rear of the platform, where the bow of the ship stood only a few feet away. A large bottle, festooned with red-white-and-blue crepe paper, hung down in front of it. The captain offered the woman the bottle.

She grasped it, and in a strong voice with a distinct Maine accent she called out, "I christen you the U.S.S. *Willoughby!*"

She swung the bottle, smashing it squarely on the thick metal plate that had been welded to the ship's bow for the occasion.

The crowd roared, the whistles of the Whitby Shipworks shrieked, and the Whitby Fireman's Band struck up a rousing version of "Anchors Aweigh." Then, as banners streamed down from her halyards and her bow, the thirty-six-hundred-ton ship retreated slowly and gracefully away from the platform.

Peggy felt a surge of pride and patriotic fervor.

"*Anchors aweigh, my boys, anchors aweigh. . . .*" She sang as loudly and applauded as enthusiastically as any person there.

The ship hit the river stern first, and great waves of spray and water exploded up around the hull.

On the platform many were shaking hands and patting others on the back. Only one person stood facing away from the crowd, hands on his hips, watching as the tugs secured lines to the ship and began guiding her to her first berth. It was the admiral.

Is he recalling old commands of years ago? Peggy wondered as she looked at him. Or is he thinking wistfully that he will not command this ship or any other ship again? She wondered what sort of a man he was.

Whatever he was, Peggy admitted to herself, no one had so stirred her curiosity and interest in a long, long time.

ON ALL days of the year parking lot 6 contained an assortment of cars and motorcycles. Except on launch days. On those days the lot was cordoned off, and in the center of the empty asphalt rectangle a huge red-white-and-blue canopy was raised. Long tables were set up and covered with white linen tablecloths. Trays of hot and cold hors d'oeuvres were placed on them.

When the ceremony was concluded, the crowd dispersed, and Peggy walked alone to lot 6, where she displayed her invitation and joined those already gathered under the canopy.

There was a scattering of Whitby notables: Oren Bellweather, the undertaker; the new chamber of commerce president, his bald pate gleaming in the afternoon sun; the head of the local

VFW chapter, wearing his bemedaled overseas cap; and, of course, the relentlessly social and still panting Mrs. Doberman.

Near the far end of the bar tables Peggy saw a crowd of naval officers, with some local men and women among them. There was a burst of laughter from the group, and Peggy caught sight of Admiral Deering himself standing in the center. She ordered a ginger ale and made her way to the edge of the circle of people. At first she could hear only snatches of the conversation the admiral was having with a short, fat man in a seersucker suit.

"One thing I don't have on my boat," the seersuckered man was saying, "is a torpedo launcher. If I did, I'd blow some of those summer sailors straight out of the water."

"Ah, yes. Why is it," the admiral asked, "that in the summer months would-be sailors attempt to navigate a boat when most of them don't know their keel from their fantail?"

There were chortles from the group, and the admiral went on. "For instance, yesterday I had the privilege of being given the helm of a cruiser out on a sea trial. But wouldn't you know, as we were heading in, our path was blocked by some little woman in a sailboat. Now I know what's meant by the phrase dames at sea."

More laughter followed. Peggy stared at the man and felt a sudden sharp pain course through her knee.

"And no offense to you ladies," the admiral said, "but as far as I could tell yesterday, the woman sailor we encountered was somebody's grandmother who had no idea how to sail."

Peggy went numb. Her next reaction was a flush of anger and embarrassment, as if she had been struck across the face.

A man moved to the side, and Peggy found herself facing the admiral. Someone began speaking, but Peggy cut through, her own words sounding in her ears as if someone else were saying them.

"I would have thought, Admiral," she said, "that a large ship like a cruiser, with all its sophisticated equipment, could have seen that little woman in the sailboat much sooner. Unless the cruiser was going too fast and in the wrong direction."

The admiral looked down at her and was nonplussed for a moment. Then he saw Peggy's uniform. "I recognize the service ribbons of the South Pacific theater, Lieutenant."

"The rank is commander."

The admiral smiled. "Well, Commander, the fact is, as I understand it, that area is reserved for naval operations."

"The fact is," Peggy McCoy told him, "that's an ocean out there, and it's not reserved for anybody."

The man was silent. The group was silent as well.

"The fact is," Peggy went on, "power craft, including navy cruisers, are supposed to give the right-of-way to sailboats. Or have you forgotten your rules of the road?"

After several moments the admiral recovered, waved his glass expansively, and thrust his smile down upon her.

"Quite right, Commander. Forgive me if that woman in the sailboat was a friend of yours." He chuckled briefly, as if to break the chill.

"The woman in the sailboat is someone I know," Peggy said.

"I see. Well—"

"No. You don't see well. If you had, you might have seen *me* yesterday before you nearly ran me down."

This time it was the admiral who looked as if he'd been struck. Of the dozen or so people in the circle, no one spoke or moved.

Then suddenly, in a gesture she had not at all intended, Peggy snapped her right hand to her forehead in a sharp salute.

"Good day, Admiral. And go to hell."

Instinctively the admiral's own hand half lifted, returning the salute. But the short gray-haired woman in the WAVE commander's uniform had turned abruptly and disappeared into the crowd.

3

AT DAWN a low sea fog enshrouded Lonely Point. For some minutes Peggy lay in bed and listened to the foghorns. It was only by the time she'd fixed her breakfast that the fog showed any sign of burning off. She ate breakfast; then she poured herself a second mug of coffee and went to the glass doors that faced the deck and slid them open.

Generally her habit was to perch on the deck's wooden railing while she sipped her coffee. But this morning she chose to sit in the single piece of furniture the deck possessed: an old sling chair. It had a wrought-iron frame that looked like a giant misshapen paper clip. Years of sun and rain had bleached its yellow canvas seat to a dull buff tone. Still, it was comfortable. At her age, Peggy felt, familiarity and comfort counted more than fashion.

The deck faced eastward, toward the water. It always gave Peggy a sense of peace to sit outside on summer mornings. Maybe later she'd call Miriam and they would . . .

Peggy caught herself. Dear Miriam. How difficult it was to realize that she was gone. Until that day three weeks ago, Miriam had never had a sick day in her life. All her friends had remarked on that at the funeral. A widow, almost Peggy's age, Miriam had been her best friend for years. Now she was gone. Dear Miriam.

Yes, thought Peggy. With the possible exception of young Sarah Dodge, good friends were decidedly in short supply this year.

Her reverie was broken by the beat of wings. She looked around to see a large gray-and-white herring gull descend on the deck. It landed squarely, tucked back its wings, and stared up at Peggy, its beak open. Because of the bird's gross underbelly and short spindly legs, she had named him Captain Bligh.

"Well, I'm glad to see I still have my old feathered friend, at least," Peggy said. "Good morning, Bligh. Wait here." She went to the kitchen, grabbed two slices of bread, and returned.

The sea gull opened his beak wide again, watching her with his unblinking yellow eyes. She tore apart a slice and offered a small piece. The gull seized it directly from her hand.

"So where have you been keeping yourself?" Peggy asked, tossing more pieces of bread onto the deck. "I haven't seen you in a week. Don't tell me you've been hanging around with those gulls at the town dump again. You shouldn't be influenced by them for the sake of company, Bligh. Be your own bird. Independent. Self-reliant. Free to go where the wind carries you."

She tore off pieces of the second slice of bread, and the sea gull gobbled them up. Finally Peggy held her palms up. "See? All gone. No more."

The gull looked up at her and burped as the outline of the last piece of bread moved down his crop.

"Sorry, Captain. But that's breakfast for today. Oh, by the way, this morning I'm going to start repainting this house. The west wall first. Therefore, if you fly over it, be careful."

The sea gull took several steps backward on the deck.

"One more thing," Peggy added. "Yesterday I met a man. I liked him—until he got my feathers ruffled. So what is your advice? Forget him?" Peggy thought, then nodded. "Yes, I guess I should."

She waved her hands and started for the sliding doors. The sea gull gave a farewell cry and lifted from the deck. Peggy turned and watched the bird as he flew off above the trees.

"But I liked him," she said. "I liked the man."

CAPTAIN Carnes was certain he was lost. Twenty minutes ago he had turned off the main highway, following a faint sign for Kare Free Kabins. After a circuitous two miles the road had given way to a graveled surface and, finally, to a pair of tire tracks.

Abruptly the tracks ended, and Captain Carnes found himself in a clearing studded with tall pines. Among the pines stood a dozen wooden cabins. The captain parked and got out of the car. As he walked past the cabins he noticed that each had a wooden plaque nailed above the door bearing the name of a fish. He continued past SWORDFISH, BASS, and STURGEON before he found PIKE. He approached the door, took a deep breath, and knocked.

"Admiral? It's Captain Carnes," he called out.

The door opened, and the admiral looked out, his hair uncombed. "Carnes, well, this *is* a surprise. Come in before the mosquitoes take all the blood you've got. I'm just doing my breakfast dishes."

The old man disappeared from view, and the captain stepped into the cabin. Although small, the main room had a rustic homeyness. There was a maplewood couch and an armchair with floral chintz covering and a knotty-pine table. Two doors led off the room—to a bathroom and a bedroom. A lobster trap set on end served as a small table for the telephone. Diagonally opposite it was a kitchenette unit.

The admiral stood at the sink barefoot, wearing a turquoise golf shirt and an apron over a pair of red Bermuda shorts.

"Have a seat, Captain. Be with you in a minute." The admiral scrubbed vigorously at a grease-encrusted skillet. "Ever had fresh fish for breakfast, Captain?"

"No, sir."

"Try it."

The admiral now picked with his fingernails at the baked-on carbon of the skillet. "So to what do I owe this unexpected visit?" he asked. "Don't tell me the ship we launched yesterday sank."

"No, sir. But as you know, you have a noon flight out of Portland. And I thought I'd drive you to the airport myself."

The admiral looked surprised. "You didn't get my message, then? You must have left your office before I called. I'm staying. A week or so, anyway." The admiral returned to the skillet, now hacking with a fork at the black residue. "This place brings back some happy memories. That's why I'm glad you booked me in here and not in some fancy-pants motel. My wife and I visited this same neck of the woods nearly forty years ago. We had a cabin just like this. It was wonderful—picking wildflowers, walking hand in hand along the beach. Grace loved it. So did I. Oh, and boating. We did lots of boating. Sailing mostly. I thought I'd take time to relive those memories."

He turned off the water and held up the skillet for inspection. "Only thing that'll get this pan clean is barnacle remover. Hell with it." He tossed it in the trash.

"Sir," Captain Carnes began, "another purpose of my coming here personally was to apologize for the incident yesterday."

"What incident?" Admiral Deering looked surprised. "Oh, you mean that woman? Forget it. I have." He chuckled. "Still, I'm not used to being chewed out by a junior officer."

"Well, Miss McCoy—"

"*Commander* McCoy. I learned that much about her yesterday. Did she ask you to apologize?"

"No, sir."

"Good," the admiral said. "Because I was the one at fault. First when I nearly ran her down at sea and yesterday when I made a joke of it. She had a right to be upset. I was a jackass." He untied his apron. "Peggy McCoy . . ." He pondered the name. "I'll say this for her: she has sass and substance. Spunk. And besides that, she's old navy. What else do you know about her?"

"She's in her sixties, born not far from here. She became a navy nurse early in the war and was sent to the South Pacific. She continued in the nursing service after the war ended."

The admiral nodded. "I'll bet no sailor malingered in sick bay if *she* had anything to say about it. Is she married?"

"No, sir. Never has been that I know of."

"Well, that's neither here nor there," the admiral said. "You're on your way back to the shipyard, I presume."

"Yessir," Captain Carnes said.

"Then you wouldn't mind dropping me off at the car-rental place in Whitby. Today I thought I'd get to know the area."

The admiral disappeared into the bedroom and emerged a moment later wearing the same shirt but white duck slacks and black shoes. He started toward the front door, then stopped.

"I just can't tell you how I'm looking forward to these days here, Carnes. I mean, I could be home wandering around a golf course with all the rest of the old dinosaurs, but this should be something different. Special."

"Yessir. I'm sure it will be, sir." Captain Carnes opened the door for the admiral. But the man continued to regard him.

"Does Commander McCoy live around here?"

"Yessir. Down past Hasty Harbor."

"One thing I'll say for her: she's the real McCoy, all right." The admiral grunted and walked out the door.

THE staccato of typewriter keys greeted Peggy as she approached Dodge's Boatyard office early in the afternoon. She opened the screen door and saw Sarah hammering intently at a vintage Smith Corona.

"Hi, Peg," Sarah said. She stopped typing to consult a dictionary on the desk. "Sometimes I totally forget how to spell pelecypod," the girl said, and resumed typing.

Peggy sat on the edge of the table opposite. "Just what is a pelecypod? In case I should run into one on a dark night."

Sarah looked up briefly. "Any of a class of bivalve mollusks with bilateral symmetry, compressed body, and connected shell."

"It doesn't sound like you're typing boatyard bills."

"They're notes for my senior thesis. Since my major is marine biology, I've decided to write my thesis about clams indigenous to the mid-Maine coast. There hasn't been a good study of them in fifteen years."

"A pity. It all sounds very scientific. But a pretty girl like you should be going out on dates."

Sarah shrugged. "I'm very busy. Besides, there's nobody here I *want* to date. Most of the boys work on their fathers' boats. Who likes going on a date surrounded by the smell of fish?"

Peggy stood up and glanced out the office window. "I see they've got *Free Spirit* at the dock. I better go."

"Oh, by the way, how was the launching at the shipworks yesterday?" Sarah asked her. "The newspaper said the admiral's speech was one of the best they'd heard in a long time."

"I thought the speaker was terrific, too. Until I talked to him in person. Turned out he was at the wheel of that ship that almost ran me down. And at the reception he treated it as a joke."

"What did you do?"

"I told him to go to hell."

"You *said* that?"

"And meant it." Peggy started for the door but stopped. "The newspaper was right. It was a terrific speech."

She turned again and headed out the door.

AN HOUR later Sarah stood on the floating dock helping a girl attach a jibstay to the bow of a Lightning-class sailboat. When Sarah was done, she turned back toward the pier and saw a tall elderly man in a turquoise shirt and white slacks, obviously in need of assistance.

Sarah went up the ramp to the pier. "May I help you?" she asked as she approached the man. "I'm Sarah Dodge."

"Miss Dodge, how do you do," he said. "I'm Charles Deering."

"*Admiral* Deering?"

"Yes, ma'am. I was told I could rent a sailboat here."

She gave him an uncertain smile. "We rent them, yes. What kind of sailboat did you have in mind?"

"Something adequate. Twenty-five or thirty feet." He chuckled. "It needn't be a windjammer."

She glanced toward the far end of the floating dock. "Well, a boat did come back a while ago. But I don't think it's exactly what you had in mind."

"What sort of boat is it?"

"A twelve-foot Cape Cod baby knockabout."

The man peered at her. "Good God, it sounds like it belongs in a wading pond."

"I'm sorry. It's all we've got right now," Sarah said doggedly.

The man shrugged. "In that case, I'll try it."

"If you come with me, I'll write out the form."

They headed toward the office. When the form was completed, the admiral signed it and paid the deposit. Then Sarah led him down to the dock, where two young boys were attaching brightly colored plugs and lures to their fishing poles. Opposite them a small blue sailboat with yellow trim bobbed gently in the water.

The admiral examined the tiny boat. "It looks like one of those boats I used to make out of a walnut shell and a toothpick when I was a boy." He stepped into it, then pointed out across the harbor. "I presume there is a channel out there that leads somewhere."

"To the Kerrenac River," Sarah said. "And the Gulf of Maine. Just be careful of the rocks outside the channel entrance. But the wind is light. You should be okay. Happy sailing." She gave the bow of the sailboat a gentle nudge to point it out into the harbor.

The breeze was steady, and it carried the admiral across the water more quickly than he had expected. Still, he felt confident. The boat handled easily, he assured himself.

The admiral's first tactical sailing challenge came as he drew nearer to the channel out of Hasty Harbor. From a distance it had looked reasonably navigable. But closer to it, he discovered how narrow the opening actually was. Even so, he decided he could probably sail through it without having to tack again.

He looked back briefly toward the harbor and took a long, deep breath. The admiral was pleased at how quickly he'd picked up his sailing skills. It was then he remembered he had forgotten to put on the orange life vest that lay at his feet. He probably should, he thought. But to do so now would mean trying to do it with one hand while at the same time managing the tiller and the sail.

The formidable size of the jagged rocks beyond the harbor entrance startled him the moment he saw them. But he sailed past them without incident. He eased the tiller over and played out the sail. The boat bounded forward as her sail sought the wind.

Well out in the river now, he chose a downwind course that would give him an opportunity to observe the rugged beauty of the Maine coastline. Directly ahead was a high promontory. Beyond it emerged a large gray mansion with turrets at each end. Along the sandy shore he saw a young couple making their way across some driftwood. He remembered how he and his young wife had taken just such a walk many years ago.

The admiral continued out for some minutes, tacking back and forth with ease. Despite his earlier misgivings about the boat's size and seaworthiness, she handled well. Still, he was farther from the shoreline than he really wished to be, and he angled the sailboat back toward it.

It was when the admiral looked seaward again that he saw an object straight ahead, dark and glistening, barely visible above the water and waiting for his boat to strike.

He rammed the tiller over. The boat veered, the sails suddenly ballooned, and before he knew it, Admiral Deering was lifted up and flung overboard as the boat capsized.

He came up in the water sputtering and gasping; his arms flailed. He felt his hand hit something flat, and clung to it. When he looked, he saw he was clutching the edge of the boat's centerboard. The hull lay sideways on the surface of the water.

His naval training almost led him to shout, Man overboard! But he settled for a bellowed "Help!"

He wondered if the young couple on the shore had seen the accident and rushed for aid.

"Help me!" he called louder, then realized dishearteningly that he and his small boat were drifting slowly out to sea.

"Help! Can anybody hear me? Help!"

"Take it easy! I can hear you. Keep holding on."

The voice came from behind him, from a distance of a hundred feet or so. He tried to turn around to face his rescuer, but he couldn't without letting go.

The voice continued, drawing closer, calling to him frequently. "I'm coming. Just hang on."

The man did as he was told. Soon he saw a white sailboat approaching. Abruptly a life vest splashed down next to him.

"Don't try to put it on now," a woman said. "Hold on to it and let go of the boat. I'm going to try to right it."

Again he followed orders, and pressed the life vest to his chest. A short time later the hull of his sailboat turned upright. The next moment his rescuer's own sailboat appeared beside him, and he grabbed at a line flung down to him.

Peggy stood in the cockpit of *Free Spirit*. She looked at the man's face and the wet mass of white hair that fell across his forehead. She said nothing.

At the same time he raised his head and looked at her. "How do you do, Commander," he said.

"A lot better than you," Peggy answered. "Do you think you can get into my boat?"

"I don't know. I'll try." He struggled to get over the splash rail. Head down and arms reaching, he tumbled into her boat.

He sat up quickly. "I'm in," he said. "Thank you for rescuing me. I mean, I'm glad you were out sailing today."

"I'm out sailing every day," Peggy said. She attached a line to his sailboat and put it in tow.

"Now sit amidships to starboard," she told him. "I'll have to tack to get upriver. By the way, to tack means to bring your sails over and start on a new heading. To change course."

"I know what the word tack means," the admiral said somewhat defensively. "I know how to sail."

Peggy looked at him.

"What happened back there was an accident," he went on. "I turned to avoid a submerged rock and tipped over."

"There aren't any rocks in that part of the river," Peggy said matter-of-factly. "What you probably saw was a floating log."

"The fact is, in my younger days I did a fair amount of sailing. But I guess I've forgotten a few things," he admitted.

He was grateful she said nothing in response. Instead, Peggy checked the sails. "Anyway, I think it's time we came about."

"You're the captain. Tell me what I can do."

"When I call ready about, crouch down in the cockpit so the boom can swing across you. All right," she said. "Ready about."

He lowered himself onto the cockpit floor and kept his head down. Peggy pulled the tiller toward her and also bowed her head as the boom swung across them. At once the mainsail and the jib billowed out, and *Free Spirit* altered course. The admiral raised himself again and sat on the opposite side of the cockpit.

He leaned back on the rail and felt the warmth of the sun on his face. But his clothing was sodden, and the wind made him shiver. Inside his shoes, his feet squished. He untied the laces and slipped off his shoes, emptying the water over the side of the boat. He set them down on the cockpit floor to dry. When he turned back, he found Peggy staring at him. Suddenly she laughed.

"I'm sorry," she apologized. "But you're really a sight."

"I'm sure I am. At least the local press took their pictures of me yesterday and not today. Speaking of which . . ." He paused, then went on. "I owe you an apology. I was wrong to say the things I did at the reception. And you were right to put me in my place."

"Thank you," Peggy said.

They remained looking at each other in an awkward silence. It was Peggy who finally spoke. "Listen, do you mind taking the helm? I want to fix the jib."

"Certainly." He moved into her place beside the tiller, while she edged toward *Free Spirit*'s bow.

As she knelt down to wrestle with the jib he had the opportunity to study her. It was the old sailor hat that caught his interest. He wondered if there was a story connected with the hat.

"Damn it!" She sat up abruptly. "Sorry, but that jib has been a problem all week."

She edged back along the deck and resumed her place beside the tiller. He slid around her to the cockpit rail.

"What seems to be the matter?" he inquired.

"Too much slack. The turnbuckle on the jibstay needs replacing."

He leaned out also to inspect the jib, then nodded to her. "Maybe. But when you're running with the wind, you could at least use a whisker pole and wing out the jib."

Peggy gave the admiral a brief but unanticipated smile. "I guess you do know something about sailboats," she said.

"One or two things," he answered. And returned the smile.

IT WAS well past four o'clock when *Free Spirit* and the smaller boat in tow were finally in the harbor and moving in the direction of the boatyard dock.

"Miss McCoy?" The admiral decided he would ask about the hat, after all. "Your hat—the sailor hat—it looks like the genuine article, the kind the navy issued in the war."

"It is," she said. "I got it from a navy friend."

"Was he also in the South Pacific theater?"

Peggy nodded. "It's a long story."

After a while they neared the floating dock. Peggy came around in a wide C and slowly eased up against it. With the admiral holding on to a mooring cleat, Peggy jumped out and secured *Free Spirit*'s forward mooring line.

The admiral then retrieved his shoes from *Free Spirit*'s cockpit and went back to his own boat. He noticed that the tackle box and the pair of fishing poles had been left unattended at the far end of the dock by the two boys who had been there earlier.

The admiral tied his boat to a cleat, then knelt down and joined Peggy as she removed the towline between her boat and his.

"Thank you again for rescuing me," he said to her.

Peggy shrugged. "I couldn't let you drown."

"You know," he said, "I've decided to stay in Maine awhile. Perhaps I could call you and we could get together."

Peggy stood up quickly. "I don't know." She was flustered by the invitation. "I guess if you're around, I'll see you anyway." As she spoke, she backed away from him. "I'm pretty busy. I—"

Too late he saw the tackle box behind her. He tried to call out. But the heel of her left foot hit the box, her right foot struck the fishing poles, and with a small gasp, arms outflung, she pitched backward off the dock.

He sprang forward just as Peggy's head and arms emerged from the water a short distance from the dock.

"Help!" she shouted. "Throw me something!"

He grabbed the towline and tossed the end of it in her direction. Her hands reached for it but missed.

"The water's freezing! Help me!"

Suddenly he realized she couldn't swim.

"Hold on!" he shouted down. "I'm coming!"

And he plunged into the water after her.

4

"CARNES? Deering here. . . ."

Captain Carnes had arrived at his office early and wasn't prepared for the abruptness of the greeting. The clarion voice on the phone boomed out from someone who had held a flag command.

"Carnes, is that you?"

"Yes. . . . Yes, Admiral." Captain Carnes had recovered sufficiently to ease back in his chair. "How are you enjoying your stay in Maine so far?"

"Very much. Except yesterday I nearly drowned. Not really drowned, you understand. But I went into the drink. I took a small sailboat out of Hasty Harbor and proceeded to capsize."

Images of the admiral splashing about helplessly swept through the captain's mind.

"And can you guess who rescued me?" the admiral asked. "None other than Commander McCoy."

"Peggy McCoy?" Captain Carnes sat upright in his chair.

"I had a very wet tail between my legs, I'll tell you that. But never mind. I've decided I'd like to take some sailing lessons."

"Under the circumstances that sounds"— Carnes searched for the word—"appropriate."

"I'm still a damn good sailor, mind you. But I could use brushing up. Is there anyone on your staff who knows how to sail?"

"I'm sure there is," Carnes said. "I'll check the roster." Just then his eye caught the request for transfer from Ensign Joseph M. Marino at the corner of his desk. Good man, Marino, thought the captain. He recalled that Marino had once mentioned something about being on the sailing team at the Naval Academy.

"Admiral," the captain said, "I think I have a young man who can help you."

"Who is he? Not some old boatswain's mate, I hope, who's never sailed anything larger than an inner tube."

"No, sir. This is an ensign here. His name is Marino."

"Marino . . . Means 'of the sea,' doesn't it? I can't go wrong with that. When can he give me my first lesson?"

"I don't know, I'll—"

"How's two o'clock this afternoon?"

The captain flipped through his assignment book. "He's not due for sea duty anytime soon," he said. "I can let you have him. Where shall he meet you? At your cabin?"

"No. Let's say the boatyard. Dodge's. It's in Hasty Harbor," the admiral added, and hung up.

PEGGY MADE UP HER MIND that she would drive to Whitby early in the day. By nine the temperature was in the seventies and climbing rapidly. By nine fifteen she was driving north to Whitby, giving little notice to the line of cars and campers headed toward the beaches to escape the heat.

As she drove, Peggy tried not to think about what had happened yesterday. After being pulled out of the water by the admiral, she'd mumbled her embarrassed thanks and hurried home.

The truth was, since her near encounter with the navy ship three days ago, her life had lost the careful order that she prized. She acknowledged to herself she was confused—about the admiral, about what sort of man he really was, about his casual suggestion that they meet again. But mostly Peggy was confused about herself. Did she want to put in jeopardy her carefully structured and protected life as a single woman?

Arriving finally in Whitby, she found a parking space on Maine Street, formerly Main Street. Nearest to her was the Whitby Chandlery—"Provisions to the Seafarer since 1848"—and, beyond it, Crofut's Drugstore. A sign blinked the time and temperature from the corner of the First National Bank. The time was 10:16; the temperature, 84°.

The repeated flashing of that temperature made Peggy feel warm. Across the street the Mr. Igloo Ice-cream Shop was already doing a brisk business. She crossed the street, bought an ice-cream soda, and sipped it on the bench outside the store.

As she sat, she watched the passersby. Eventually she saw a young man and woman. The girl was in her early twenties, dressed in a nurse's uniform. The man was a few years older, sandy-haired, and wearing tan chinos and a white short-sleeved shirt. They had been walking hand in hand when suddenly they stopped and, oblivious to everyone, embraced and kissed a deep, impassioned kiss. The act was so incongruous to the surroundings that Peggy gave a little gasp. After a long moment the young couple took up each other's hands again and continued on.

Perhaps it was their age, the girl's nurse's uniform, the boy's sandy hair. Whatever it was, the comparison with her and Tom was inescapable. She and Tom—they had also been very much in love. Suppose there'd been no war. Suppose Tom had been a local boy. Suppose . . . Suppose . . . But there *had* been a war, and only she had lived to see it end.

And today, she told herself, I am sitting here alone, a woman in her sixties, watching my life and the world pass me by.

There was the grinding scrape of brakes. A jitney bus pulled in and stopped next to the curb. Every morning the bus brought elderly men and women from the Whitby Senior Center to the stores in town. As Peggy watched, the dozen occupants of the bus began to file slowly out onto the sidewalk.

Two passengers caught Peggy's attention. Moving slowly was a couple well into their eighties. The man walked with a cane but otherwise looked spry. The woman, short and round, with a cherubic face, wore dark glasses and a wide-brimmed hat. She walked with her head down, and after every four or five steps she stopped. Each time the man would stop as well. Each time he would take her arm, squeeze it, and whisper something gentle. Then they would set off again for four or five more steps.

Again, suppose. Suppose Tom and I had married as we had promised one another. Suppose after the war we had come here to Whitby to live our lives together—raising children, sleeping side by side in the big four-poster bed we'd talked about, in summer flying kites along the beach, in winter waking together to a snowfall—until one day we too were in our eighties. Might we also walk those four or five steps just as they did now, limbs unsteady—but together? Just suppose . . .

Peggy finished the last of her soda and hurried to her car.

AT PRECISELY two p.m. the admiral stood on the far end of the pier in front of Dodge's Boatyard studying the water traffic. He assumed that the officer assigned to help him sail would probably be some young patrician-looking ROTC lieutenant out of Yale, who, when his service stint was over, would be on his way to Wall Street and the New York Yacht Club.

Thus he was not prepared for the officer who stepped out of the black navy car that stopped near the office. He was young, all right. He was also about five feet five (didn't the service have a height requirement?), with an aureole of black curly hair and a face as round and ruddy as the Neapolitan sun.

When the admiral saw the look of recognition and the wave in his direction, he knew this was the man Carnes had sent. The ensign was dressed in his summer white trousers and shirt. As he approached the admiral he stopped and saluted.

"Admiral Deering, I'm Ensign Marino, sir. Joseph Marino. Captain Carnes suggested I might be of some assistance, sir."

The admiral returned the salute, and the two shook hands.

"Yes. Well, I sailed some years ago," he assured the ensign, "but I'd like to brush up a bit now. Not that I need a lot of help."

"Yessir."

"I assume you're a fairly good sailor yourself."

Joe smiled pleasantly. "Yessir. I was captain of the sailing team at the United States Naval Academy."

"You're an Annapolis man?"

"Yessir." Joe smiled again. "Just as you are, sir. You're still remembered there with fondness. I heard you were called Daring Deering. But I never learned the reason why."

The admiral shrugged. "I'll tell you the story sometime. Right now let's limber up our sea legs and get out there on the water."

"Fine. Should I rent us a boat?"

"No," the admiral said over his shoulder as he started down the ramp. "I've got the boat I rented yesterday."

Joe approached the ramp—and came to a sudden halt. Standing on the dock was a tall blond girl with the most captivating back view he could remember in a long, long time. Her hair hung halfway to her waist, and her tan legs were long, slender, and exquisitely shaped.

She turned, and it was then that Joe saw her profile and decided this girl was better than good—she was fantastic. She had great lines fore and aft. And my, oh my, the way she trimmed her sails.

At that moment the admiral approached her. Joe started down the ramp in broad strides to join them.

"Miss Dodge"—the admiral gestured as Joe came up—"this is Ensign Marino."

Sarah looked at Joe. She gave a neutral nod, but neither spoke. She was a full two inches taller, but Joe was used to that and it didn't bother him. He smiled and returned the nod.

"And this is Miss Dodge," the admiral went on. "She was very helpful to me yesterday when I rented my sailboat."

"Oh?" Joe asked pleasantly. "What kind of boat was it?"

The admiral pointed to the small blue sailboat tied up at the dock nearby. "It's that one."

Joe looked down at the boat and frowned. "I'm sure you can handle something bigger," he said. "Am I right, sir?"

"Yes. Well, yes, of course." The admiral cleared his throat.

"I'll see what else we have." Now it was Sarah who frowned. She turned abruptly and walked toward the ramp.

"I hope that's all right with you, sir," Joe said. "I mean, you could capsize in a little boat like that."

"Exactly. A bigger boat is better. Safer. Good idea." The admiral was beginning to think that Captain Carnes had made the right decision sending this young fellow, after all.

Sarah reappeared at the top of the ramp. "There's a Lightning available." She looked directly at Joe and asked him, "Will that be acceptable to you, Ensign Marino?"

Joe smiled up at her ingenuously. "Yeah. Sure. A Lightning is fine. Thank you very much, Miss Dodge."

A few minutes later a blue nineteen-foot Lightning-class sailboat was delivered to the dock by a teenage boy. Joe looked over the boat, pulling at this line and that.

"Is she seaworthy?" the admiral asked, watching him.

"Shipshape," Joe declared. "How about a cruise?"

"Let's go."

As the admiral stepped into the center of the boat and moved to the stern, Joe climbed aboard, reached under the foredeck, and brought out two life vests.

"Better put this on," Joe said, offering one to the admiral. "Can you imagine what the navy would do to me if I lost one of their admirals at sea? I'd be in the brig for a hundred years."

The other man shook his head. "For losing a retired admiral it's only fifty years."

They donned the vests, and the boy, who had been standing by, helped them cast off.

"We'll practice some maneuvers out on the river," the young man said. "So let's take a port tack toward that shed." Joe pointed to an abandoned fishing shed on the far side of the harbor.

The admiral disagreed. "I'd say a starboard tack—"

"Sir," Joe interrupted him, "you requested lessons. I have been given that assignment. You also know there can be only one captain of a ship. I don't outrank you, but right now, with all due respect, sir, I *am* your instructor." Joe felt awkward suddenly, addressing the much older man as if he were a plebe. Joe hesitated, then went on. "So I'd like a port tack in the direction of that shed."

"Yessir." The admiral's answer was immediate, spontaneous, and natural. And it surprised them both. They stared at one another for an instant; in the next, they laughed.

IT WAS the window trim that took the time. Throughout the afternoon Peggy had maintained a steady pace, spreading the white paint across the long, wide clapboard siding of the west wall of her house. But it was when she started on the trim around the bedroom windows that her efforts slowed. The day had remained hot, and several times she'd wished she had spent it on the water.

Peggy stepped down from the ladder and examined all she had done. She saw a spot she'd missed. It would have to wait. Already clouds were building, and rain, in fact, would probably arrive tonight.

Peggy hurried to the kitchen and scrubbed vigorously at the paint spots on her hands. Looking out the window, she saw for the first time the wall of fog several miles out to sea, fusing seamlessly with the gray water. There was nothing left to do, Peggy thought, but have an early dinner, get a book, and go to bed.

She turned to the refrigerator and took out a packaged frozen dinner from the freezer. The contents were some sort of boil-in-bag beef concoction in a glutinous brown sauce.

Peggy tossed the box back into the freezer, went to the telephone, and dialed.

After a few rings Sarah's voice came on the line. "Hello. Dodge's Boatyard."

"Sarah, it's me—Peggy." She pulled up the kitchen stool and sat on it. "Listen, how about dinner tonight? Here at my house."

"Peg—"

"It's spur of the moment, I know. But I've got some spaghetti I can do up, and I'll fix a salad. I thought—"

"I can't," Sarah interrupted. "Peg, is something wrong?"

The question surprised Peggy. "Wrong? Why should anything be wrong? I just get bored sometimes with eating by myself and talking back to TV anchormen. Nothing's wrong," she said.

"I'm really sorry, Peg. But tonight I have to go to Portland to hear a marine biologist speak about kelp," Sarah said. "He spent a year in the Sargasso Sea."

Peggy sighed. "Sounds like a million laughs."

"Really, Peggy, I'm sorry. Maybe I can stop by tomorrow night if you're home."

"*If* I'm home? Nights I'm always home. I don't even have a good kelp man to keep me company."

"I better go. Talk to you tomorrow. Thanks for the invitation."

"You bet."

Peggy heard the phone click off.

In the living room the wall clock chimed four bells—six o'clock—and went on ticking, louder than she had ever heard.

THAT afternoon on an impulse the admiral had bought himself a small club steak in Hasty Harbor. Now it smoked and sizzled in the frying pan. To one side of the sink a lettuce-and-tomato salad lay heaped in a red plastic bowl. He added oil and a touch of vinegar to the salad, then checked the oven timer. Another few minutes, and the baked potato would be done.

As he waited, he looked out the window and saw the fog. Before he'd left the boatyard, he had heard talk of rain tonight. The admiral hoped not; he had enjoyed his first sail with young Marino. He liked the ensign's sharp intelligence, and the fellow was good with sailboats. The admiral hoped they could sail in the morning as planned.

The oven timer rang. The admiral speared the club steak with a fork, then opened the oven door and grabbed up the baked potato, which he put beside the steak on a plate. He carried both the plate and salad bowl to the small table in the living room.

It was at that moment that memories came flooding back of the last anniversary—the forty-fifth—that he and Grace had shared. She had insisted on preparing the dinner herself and had set the table with their finest china and silver service, plus two Baccarat crystal goblets from the set they had received on their wedding day. The wine that night had been red, an exquisite cabernet. With the candles lit, he had proposed a toast: "To the most wonderful woman in my life, the one who *is* my life."

Well, her life had reached its end four years ago. Since then, he had gone on alone for all the days and nights that followed. How many mornings had he wakened with the knowledge that the pillow next to his was empty and unmarked? How many more meals like this one would he eat alone? At least at home, in Maryland, he could divert his mind while he ate by watching television or skimming the newspaper or feeding table scraps to his pet bulldog, Halsey. But the cabin was without a television set, he had no newspaper, and Halsey was spending his own vacation in a kennel.

Enough of memories, the admiral thought. He ate his dinner quickly and looked out the window again. Darkness had come quickly, and he could see almost nothing now.

Here I am, a man in his seventies, he thought. Is that what I await—facing the dark alone? After Grace had died, his grief at first had been ameliorated by relief—relief that her pain no longer drained the spirit from her life. But there had been relief also for himself. No longer did he have to constantly display a dogged optimism in her company when they both knew the truth with hopeless certainty.

Yet after she had died, he'd found companionship in solitude. He had rediscovered a streak of independence he had not known since his teens. He could sleep as late as he wanted, see just those few friends he wished to see, and travel wherever and whenever the mood struck him. Still, at times like this his life seemed threadbare, even pitiable. Was what he chose to call solitude a euphemism for his loneliness?

Some people could deal with their loneliness, he decided, like that McCoy woman. But, of course, she'd never married. Marriage changed things. She had never loved and lost the way he had. Oh, maybe there had been a few romances in her life, but that was not the same as being married almost fifty years.

The admiral stood up and shook his head. What the devil was he thinking about *her* for, anyway? Maybe it was really just curiosity about her. Or was it glands, even at his age?

He walked over to the sink, carrying the empty dishes and utensils. All right, he would probably see her at the boatyard sometime. Maybe they could have a lobster roll and a soda on the pier. That would be fine. The next time he saw her, he'd be cautious, circumspect. In a week he'd be gone from here.

And yet. And yet. She had affected him as no other woman in his life had done since Grace.

In a flash he realized it. That was the word he associated with her—life. Sass and substance, he had called it. Spunk.

As he sat in the living room he saw the upended lobster trap. On it were a dog-eared phone book and the telephone. He opened the book and thumbed through the pages.

McClanahan . . . McCormack . . . McCourt . . .

THE ringing of the bedside telephone cut slowly into Peggy's sleep. When she was finally awake enough to comprehend the sound, she reached for the phone and mumbled a hello.

"Commander McCoy?" said the male voice at the other end.

"Who is this?"

"Charles Deering."

"Who?"

"Charles Deering. Did I wake you?"

"Do you know what time—"

"It's nine o'clock. And I *did* wake you. I apologize."

Peggy lay back on her pillow. "What do you want?" she asked.

"Well, it occurred to me I really didn't thank you enough for rescuing me yesterday at sea."

"Oh, that. But you also rescued me. Listen, I'd like to go back to sleep, if you don't mind. I spent most of the afternoon painting my house."

"If you'd like help, I'll get paint in Whitby and come down."

Peggy was about to tell him he could help her most by hanging up the phone. But she did not. For a reason she did not understand, she was glad their conversation had continued.

"That's okay," she told him. "But thanks, anyway."

"Dinner, then?"

"What?"

"I would very much enjoy taking you to dinner. There's a place in Whitby I've heard recommended. Galahad's. I gather it's a favorite of the navy personnel. So I trust they could probably handle a couple of old salts like us. Tomorrow night?"

"No," Peggy said at once. "I can't."

"Day after tomorrow, then?"

Maybe she was sleepier than she had realized, but for whatever reason, Peggy paused, then answered, "Yes."

"That's splendid!" His voice was ebullient. "How's seven?"

"Fine."

"Lonely Point Road. Is that right?"

"Yes," she said again.

"I'll see you then. Good night."

"Good night," she said. She put the phone down into its cradle. But she did not let go of the receiver. And in the darkness of the room she repeated, "Yes."

5

THE rain began at midnight and continued on throughout the day—a cool, soaking rain with gusty winds that gave a feeling more of late September than of July.

Denied an opportunity to sail, the admiral amused himself by finishing a paperback detective novel he'd brought to Maine.

As for Peggy, she stocked up with a week's supply of groceries. In the afternoon she cleaned and dusted her house thoroughly and wrote a letter to a friend in Florida. Dinner she ate alone.

Before dawn of the next day the rain ended, promising a dry and brighter morning and a brisk breeze from the north. The admiral and Joe Marino had rescheduled their sail for nine thirty and this time out were going to concentrate on short tacking work.

They spent several hours practicing in the harbor.

It was just after noon when the Lightning made a sharp tack to starboard, slowed, and gently glided in against the fenders of the floating dock. The admiral released his grip on the tiller and allowed the sail to go slack.

"Neat and clean," Joe said. He leaped out of the sailboat and secured a line to a mooring cleat. "You were good out there."

"Better than you would have thought for an old man?" the admiral asked Joe, an eyebrow raised.

"Age has nothing to do with it. People in their seventies still circumnavigate the globe." Joe stood and removed his life vest. "But there is something I would like you to do. Keep a log."

The admiral started to remove his life vest. "A ship's log?"

"Sort of. After every sail write down the date, weather, and sea conditions. Then add what you did well and what you think you need to work on. It's for your benefit."

"Sounds like a good idea. I'll start it this afternoon." The admiral stepped out of the boat gingerly and began securing the stern line to a piling. When that was done, he looked down at the boat for several minutes.

"I just realized something," he said finally. "This boat doesn't have a name. A ship without a name is like a person without a name. A name gives personality and character."

"Then let's find one. We'll hold a christening ceremony." Joe seemed amused at the idea.

"Just what I was thinking. Wait here." The admiral crossed the dock and started up the ramp. He spotted Sarah on the pier and called to her. "Miss Dodge, I'd like to give my boat—that is, your boat—a name. I'd like to hold a christening. Is that all right?"

The girl looked at him uncertainly. "I guess so."

The admiral nodded his gratitude and returned down the ramp. As Sarah followed, the half a dozen people on the pier moved closer, their curiosity aroused.

494

Admiral Deering approached the sailboat and took up a position opposite the bow. He beckoned to Joe and Sarah. "You two, step up, please." Sarah looked nonplussed, but dutifully she and Joe moved nearer to each other.

The admiral lifted his hands. "Ladies and gentlemen, just as every child is provided with a name at baptism, so should every ship be given one to sanctify her and protect her. Therefore," he went on, "I christen this ship—"

"Wait a second!" a voice among the spectators called down. "Aren't you gonna break a bottle of champagne over the bow?"

"I've got a wine cooler," a young woman offered.

The admiral considered. "Yes. Wine will be acceptable."

The woman opened the picnic hamper she was carrying and took out a small green bottle, which she tossed to the admiral.

He caught it and extended it to Sarah. "Miss Dodge, will you do the honors? Just pour the contents on the bow."

Sarah stepped forward and poured. As she did, the admiral intoned, "I christen this ship the—let's see—the *Invincible*. May fair winds forever fill her sails."

The applause was immediate and enthusiastic.

"Thank you. Thanks to you all," the admiral said to the spectators. The people now began to drift off, and the admiral turned to Joe and Sarah.

"Until tomorrow, then," he said, and started up the ramp.

"He's a great guy," Joe said to Sarah as the admiral disappeared across the pier.

"And a real gentleman," she added.

They strode up the ramp together. "Listen, sailors are great, " Joe said. "Especially on dates. You should find out for yourself."

Sarah looked at him evenly. "What does that mean?"

"That we go out tonight. Us—you and me."

"You get right to the point, don't you, Ensign?"

"Yep. *Carpe diem*," Joe said. "It's an old Italian saying."

"Sorry," Sarah told him. "Tonight I'm writing about clams."

"I beg your pardon?"

"I'm studying clams for my senior thesis in marine biology. At a clam bed in the mud flats past Lonely Point, where I do research."

"You mean you dig them up?" he asked her.

"Sometimes."

"Hey, I dig clams, too. Especially deep-fried, with tartar sauce." He saw at once the joke fell flat. "I only meant—"

"Excuse me, Ensign, but today's a busy day. Bye." Sarah turned and walked away.

Joe headed slowly to the navy car and got in. Clams, he repeated to himself as he drove up the boatyard road. Hunks of rocks pretending to be animals. Who wants to study *clams?*

He paused before the stop sign at the turnaround and looked around. Granted, Hasty Harbor had a quaint provincial charm, he thought. But what sort of life did it offer anyone like Sarah? What did she want to do with her life, anyway?

Joe admitted he didn't know the answers to those questions. But at that moment he decided he would make it his business to find out.

PEGGY had sailed early in the afternoon, leaving several hours to continue painting the house. By five o'clock she had completed a major portion of the south wall. She went to the kitchen and poured herself a large glass of iced tea, and had just begun to drink it when something caught her eye.

Pulling into her driveway was a lengthy yellow Cadillac. Peggy sighed. Only one person on the peninsula had a car like that. As she watched, the door on the driver's side opened slowly. Lower legs the size of Presto logs emerged, and after some effort, so did the rest of Mrs. Ernestine Doberman.

Peggy thought of fleeing to her bedroom and pretending she wasn't home. But she was sure Mrs. Doberman would search for her. After adjusting her foundation garments, Mrs. Doberman walked up the path to the house. She paused to catch her breath, then opened the screen door, planted one foot squarely in the living room, and burbled, "Yoo-hoo!" in a singsong voice.

"I'm here, Ernestine." Peggy stepped out from the kitchen.

"You *are* here!" Mrs. Doberman enthused. She was wearing a lavender sundress that hugged her figure like a sausage casing. She moved into the room. "You know, it's been *so* long since I've been inside your little house," she added. Before Peggy could reply, Mrs. Doberman had sunk into the sofa.

"I'll get us iced tea," Peggy said, and hurried to the kitchen. When she returned, Mrs. Doberman was scrutinizing the room.

"So quaint," the woman said. "And that little toy boat there." She pointed to a model of a World War II aircraft carrier that sat on the windowsill.

"It's a ship, Ernestine. It was sunk during the battle of Leyte Gulf." She handed an iced tea to Mrs. Doberman.

"You know, what this room could use are some flowers, Peggy. Flowers do add such a touch."

"You're right," Peggy said. "I'll remember to steal some the next time I go past the cemetery."

Mrs. Doberman regarded her, then smiled uncertainly. "Oh, Peggy. Always the tease."

"That's me. What brings you here, Ernestine?"

Mrs. Doberman drank half the contents of her glass. "As you know, our annual summer festival will be occurring soon. Of course, I'm on the planning board again."

Peggy nodded. The Hasty Harbor Summer Festival was a glorified clambake intended to lure dedicated locals and unsuspecting tourists and subject them to homemade dishes perpetrated by the ladies of the town.

"The order of events will be the same this year. The grand parade and auction in the morning. In the afternoon the sailing race. In the evening, as always, there will be the covered-dish supper and the clambake on the beach. And after dark the *pièce de nonrésistance*—the fireworks."

"Who's in the race this year? The usual boys?" Peggy asked. The "boys" who competed in the ragtag sailing competition were always men from the peninsula who had blind faith in their own seamanship but who, in fact, sailed as if they were blind or blind drunk.

Mrs. Doberman was continuing. "I understand the race committee will soon release the names. Be that as it may, I myself am in charge of the committee for the gathering of *objets* for the auction. This year nearly everyone has given something."

497

"Such as?" Peggy asked her.

"Daisy Williams has contributed a needlework tea cozy. And Miles Robinhill is offering free snowmobile lessons."

"In July?"

"And I have come to ask you if there's something you will donate to the auction." The woman finished her iced tea and smiled.

"I'm not sure," Peggy said. "Maybe I still have that matching pair of porcelain chamber pots my grandmother and grandfather used. They should make great *objets*."

Mrs. Doberman blinked, then nodded. "Yes. Well, whatever you contribute will be most appreciated, dear." The woman slowly pushed her way up out of the sofa. "I'll stop by in a few days."

Peggy took the iced-tea glass from her hand.

Mrs. Doberman walked backward toward the door. "Well, till then, bye-bye, dear." She waved, wiggling her fingertips, then opened the screen door and stepped out.

"Bye, Ernestine," said Peggy. "And close the screen on your way out . . . dear. You're letting in the bugs."

DRIVING to Whitby after his sailing lesson, the admiral had stopped at a stationery store and picked up a tide table for mid-coastal Maine, as well as a spiral notebook and a ballpoint pen.

Back in his cabin, he went to the table, opened the notebook, and wrote on the first page:

The Log of the Sailboat "Invincible"
By Her Captain, C. T. Deering

Wednesday, July 20—Fine weather to be on the sea. Steady N. wind, approx. 12-15 knots. Practiced tacking and really had a feel for it. Approach to dock was "neat and clean," according to Ensign Marino. Nice young man, Ensign Marino. Or Joe, as he wants me to call him.

The admiral paused. Then he wrote:

As for tonight . . . ???

EARLY EVENING SUNLIGHT SLANTED through the trees as the admiral turned off the main highway onto the peninsula road. Dressed now in a blue blazer and white linen slacks, he was reminded of some of the outlandish outfits he had worn on dates during his college years. But that was more than fifty years ago. Thank heaven fashions had changed a good deal since then.

The digital clock on the car's dashboard showed 6:28 when he reached Lonely Point Road. He was much too early for his seven-o'clock date with Peggy. A mile or so short of her house, he pulled his car over on the beach and stopped.

The admiral stepped out onto the sand and surveyed the water. He realized there was a tension growing in him about tonight, and he took a deep breath to relieve it. As he began to walk he noticed movement in a cluster of bulrushes at the far end of the beach. Then he caught sight of two pairs of tan young legs, and a moment later a girl's bathing suit came flying upward.

The admiral turned away and walked back quickly toward his car. The couple's presence and their unselfconscious passion made him feel old suddenly. Perhaps it was their first date, too, and this was how they chose to get acquainted.

He and Peggy, on the other hand, born in another time and to a different set of standards, would probably spend their own first date in conversation and nostalgia. While that young couple were absorbed in matters of the moment, he and Miss McCoy would live tonight as if it were twenty, forty, even fifty years ago. At their age the past was what they had the most of. They knew that pleasures of the present—if they came at all—were transitory. The future was increasingly finite; the shadows stretched and deepened with each passing year.

The admiral got back into the car, swung onto the road, and drove until he saw the small white house with the two flags flying from the flagpole.

Peggy was standing at the door, wearing a blue dress that made her look younger and more feminine than he had somehow expected. In her hands she clutched a small white purse.

"Seven o'clock on the button," she called to him as he opened the door of the car and started up the walk.

For a moment they stood face to face, neither of them quite sure what to say next.

"Well, it turned out to be a nice day," Peggy said.

"And a perfect summer evening, yessiree."

There was another silence, broken only by the admiral's unconscious juggling of coins in his pocket.

Peggy asked him, "Would you like a drink?"

"If you would."

She shrugged. "I'm not much of a drinker. But I think I have some sherry. Is sherry okay with you?"

"Fine," he said agreeably. "Just fine." If there was one drink he hated, it was sherry.

They moved into the living room, and Peggy went to the kitchen. The admiral remained standing near the door and looked around the room. It had the neatness of crew quarters, he thought. There was a sofa covered with a plaid slipcover, several armchairs, and a heavy mahogany table pushed up against the wall. He noticed nautical memorabilia. On the windowsill, near a brass clock, was a wooden model of a World War II ship. There were a few pictures on the wall, most of them seascapes, and a metal plaque that said ABOARD THIS SHIP THE CAPTAIN'S WORD IS LAW. But what interested him most was a short embroidered prayer.

He was reading it as Peggy returned from the kitchen empty-handed. "Sorry," she said. "But I'm out of sherry, after all."

"Then what do you say we have something at the restaurant? Our reservation is for eight. I'm sure if we arrive a little early, they'll accept us."

For the first time since his arrival Peggy smiled. "Sure. To-night's the night they set aside for senior citizens."

The drive to Whitby took them half an hour and was accomplished mostly in silence. When they arrived, the admiral found a parking space directly opposite the restaurant, which he considered a good omen. He said so to Peggy. She looked at him with an expression that seemed to answer, We'll see.

Galahad's was crowded, but the maître d' led them to a table in the corner, apart from the other diners. Soon after, a young waiter with flowing blond-white hair and a gold earring in his left ear hovered at their table. He lit the stubby candle planted in the Perrier bottle, and was off again before the admiral could speak.

The admiral frowned briefly. "How about a drink?" he asked Peggy. "Sherry for you?"

"No. I'll have white wine."

"Would you mind if I had a bourbon?" the admiral inquired.

"Not at all."

"You know, living down south among the gentry, bourbon and branch is the drink of choice. A branch is what they call a stream."

"I see."

"Well, what do they call a stream up here in Maine?"

"They call it a stream."

"That figures." The admiral shifted in his chair. "Tell it like it is. Good old Yankee plain speaking, eh?"

Peggy looked at him, and he said nothing more. Fortunately, the waiter reappeared. He wrote down their drink orders and slipped away again. Simultaneously Peggy and the admiral took out their eyeglasses, picked up their menus, and began to study them.

Finally he asked her, "Anything you recommend?"

"I hear the fish is good."

Their conversation was going absolutely nowhere, he thought. Their date had been doomed from the start.

The waiter returned and set down their drinks. The admiral picked up his glass. "What say we have a toast?"

"Fine." Peggy raised her wineglass.

"Let's see. There's an old navy toast that goes something like 'To friends, ships, and—' " He stopped abruptly. "On the other hand," he muttered, "that may not be appropriate."

Peggy smiled for the second time that night. "I know that toast. 'To friends, ships, and women. May all of them be fast.' "

He smiled back. "It is more imaginative than cheers."

They sipped their drinks, and Peggy said, "You're okay, you know. If I didn't say much on the ride here, I was just nervous. I still feel a little bit like a schoolgirl on a first date."

"Frankly, so was I. Nervous, I mean," the admiral said, easing back in his chair.

Peggy went on. "I'll also admit I'm not all that used to trusting people. I've lived most of my life by myself and for myself. I wasn't sure about your motives either. First, I thought you were just lonely. Second, that you wanted another old navy swab to reminisce with. And third—"

"May I tell you tonight's specials?" cooed the waiter, who appeared at tableside. "There's monkfish jardiniere—"

"We're not ready," the admiral snapped back.

The waiter gave a breathy oops, and backed away. The admiral turned to Peggy. "And what was my third motive?"

"For right now, let's stick with the second," Peggy told him. "Navy reminiscences. Why did you want to join the navy?"

"I was encouraged by the example of Themistocles."

"Who?"

"Themistocles, the Greek naval hero of the Persian Wars. That's what my middle initial, T, stands for. It was my father's idea. He loved literature and the classics. As a boy, I can recall him reading aloud to me the exploits of men like Lord Nelson and John Paul Jones. I was born about as far from the sea as you can get—Grand River, Iowa. Yet I became so fascinated by the *idea* of the sea that when I graduated from high school, my father asked our local Congressman to write a letter to Annapolis on my behalf. And to everybody's great surprise I was accepted."

"So how was it you got into communications?"

"I loved to fool around with telegraph keys and crystal-radio sets. But my first assignment in the navy was as signal officer. It meant standing out on deck, even in the damnedest weather, whipping those semaphore flags back and forth. Anyway, I started out with semaphore and ended up with satellites."

"Moral of story: keep your flags flying," Peggy said, "and there's no telling where you'll end up."

The admiral laughed and took a deep sip of his drink. "In fact, I still remember the semaphore alphabet. Give me your napkin, and I'll spell out your name."

As he took up his own napkin Peggy handed hers to him. He held them open in each hand. He thrust out his right hand so that it was horizontal with his shoulder, and lifted his left hand into the air above his head.

"That's the letter P." With sharp rapid motions he began snapping the napkins up and down. "E . . . G . . . G . . . Y!"

With a flourish he executed the last letter, flinging his left arm outward and at the same time sending his drink flying to the floor in a great crash. Every diner in the room turned at the sound. The blond-haired waiter rushed toward them with a towel. A busboy followed with a brush and dustpan and began sweeping up the broken glass.

In the midst of the commotion the admiral slowly folded Peggy's napkin on the tabletop and handed it back to her.

"If you don't mind," he said, "I won't spell your last name."

"Maybe we should order," Peggy said.

They picked up their menus and scanned them again.

"The sole sounds good," she said after a moment.

"I'm tempted by the lobster," he said. "Yes, the lobster. But I guess that will mark me as a tourist, won't it? Do the sons and daughters of Maine ever order lobsters in a restaurant?"

Peggy shook her head. "Not much in the summer. Right now they mostly get young lobsters that have shed their shells. I prefer the big old boys, with their hard shells and crafty ways. They haven't lived that long for nothing."

The waiter wafted casually in their direction and lingered long enough for Peggy and the admiral to place their orders.

Then the admiral looked around the dining room. "I don't see anybody who looks like a native," he said.

"What about me?" Peggy asked.

"What about you? You haven't told me anything about yourself."

"There isn't much to tell." She shrugged. "I was born in Gaffney, about forty miles north of here. No brothers, no sisters. Only a pet dog named Woof. My father ran the local hardware store. I went to the state college near Augusta without any idea of what I wanted to be. Except married, maybe. In those days if you got married, the future took care of itself one way or another. After college I thought I might become a nurse. My mother was ill and I did a lot of taking care of her. So when she died, I enlisted in the Navy Nurse Corps."

"And you were sent to the South Pacific."

Peggy nodded. "They needed nurses, and I couldn't wait to see another part of the world. Oh, I was a regular Nellie Forbush in those days. You know, the nurse in *South Pacific*."

"Except you didn't marry a French planter."

"No. . . . I didn't marry anyone." There was a brief silence. "When the war was over, I came back to the States and worked in several navy hospitals. I got my commander's stripes, retired in '68, and moved back to Gaffney to live with my father. He died two years later, and I moved here." She added, "Pretty boring story, isn't it?"

"Not at all."

"You're just being polite. It's not the sort of life story Hollywood makes into a movie. Unlike yours. I bet they already had John Wayne cast to play you in some patriotic naval epic."

"Hardly likely," the admiral said, although it flattered him a bit that Peggy thought so. He went on. "Except for seeing action in the South Pacific, I've had a career that's been a series of naval bases, with a few years spent at the Pentagon."

A moment later their dinners arrived. The waiter set them down and tied the paper lobster bib around the admiral's neck.

"How's your sole?" the admiral asked Peggy as she sampled her fish.

"Good. Your lobster looks good, too."

He nodded, struggling to break the claw. The shell finally gave way, and the admiral began picking at the meat inside.

"So when did you become the father of modern naval communications?" Peggy asked.

"Oh, after I retired. The media was fascinated by the paternity thing. Rickover became the father of the nuclear navy, and I sired modern communications. I think they even found a father of the flushless head."

Peggy laughed.

Galahad's continued to flow with people arriving and departing, but the older couple did not seem to notice. As the remaining daylight faded to a deep lapis hue the admiral and Peggy reminisced easily about the war years in the South Pacific, recalling the names and places—Halsey and Kinkaid; Mindoro, Samar, and the Coral Sea. The candle in their Perrier bottle sputtered and went out, but neither noticed it.

At last the admiral pushed aside his plate, the lobster's carapace stripped clean. He patted his midsection.

"You did very well," Peggy assured him. "For a tourist."

"I take that as a compliment, coming from you."

By the time they had decaffeinated coffee and left the restaurant, it was dark. They drove in silence.

But now it was a different sort of silence than it had been on the drive earlier. At one point the admiral switched on the car radio, then abruptly turned it off. "Automatic reaction," he said. "I guess I listen to the radio a lot. Sometimes it's the only company I have."

"Listen to it if you want."

"I don't want. I have very pleasant company right here, right now." He added, "Besides, this radio only gets one station, and all it plays is rock and roll. In fact, it's been years since I've heard a good melody. Why don't they write songs like 'Star Dust' and 'Sweet Lorraine' anymore?"

"One of my favorites is 'Long Ago and Far Away,' " Peggy said. "I haven't heard that in years, though."

He nodded. "I remember. It was 1944. Let's see." He thought for several moments, then sang in a rough but rich baritone as Peggy joined in:

> *"Long ago and far away,*
> *I dreamed a dream one day,*
> *And now that dream is here beside me."*

Both appeared somewhat embarrassed and sang no more.

They approached Peggy's house at last, and the admiral pulled into the driveway.

"Thank you for tonight," Peggy said, reaching for the door.

"May I call you tomorrow?" he asked her suddenly.

The question caught her off guard. "I guess so. Why not?"

"Why not, indeed. I will!"

Peggy opened the car door.

"Another question," the admiral said quickly. "In the restaurant you mentioned I might have had a third motive for asking you out tonight. But you didn't tell me what you thought it was. Can you tell me?"

Peggy took a breath. "I hoped it was because you liked me."

"I do. I—"

He wanted to continue, but had no idea what to say.

It didn't matter. The next moment she was out of his car and hurrying up the path to the front steps of her house.

6

THE navy car approached the dirt road that led to Dodge's Boatyard. When it continued on and was out of sight, the two men sitting on the wooden bench in front of T. C. Dabney's Store exchanged looks. One man bit into an orange and spit out a pit.

The other man pointed in the direction the navy car had taken. "What's the navy doing at the boatyard at this hour of the morning?" Jimmy Smiley wondered.

"Beats me," Able Fenstermacher said.

Jimmy Smiley and Able Fenstermacher were in their late fifties. Able was a retired road-crew foreman, now on a pension from the state. He was also the fish-and-game warden in town. He had a short gray beard, which he trimmed weekly with a fish knife. Able's appearance was what tourist brochures liked to describe as the archetypal Yankee. In fact, tourists now and then asked him to pose for snapshots, for which Able genially obliged.

Jimmy Smiley, on the other hand, was seldom asked to pose for anything, perhaps because of his unconscious habit of continually digging wax out of his ears. Jimmy and his two sons ran Smiley's Garbage Service, crisscrossing the peninsula in an open truck.

At that moment a battered green Dodge Dart drove up and parked beside the store. The driver, a large, round man wearing yellow rubber waders, got out and waddled toward the two men.

His name was Cabot Lodge. Although he made his living as a scalloper, he was, he assured anyone who asked, very distantly related to the Boston Lodges. But it was the waders that gave him his celebrity. Local gossip had it that he ate in them and slept in

them, the latter being all the more remarkable since he had sired seven daughters in ten years.

Cabot sat on the bench. By order of the Hasty Harbor first selectman, together the three men made up the race committee for this year's Hasty Harbor Summer Festival.

"Wait till you hear the news I got," Cabot told them. "The Rexford fella's out."

"What do you mean?" Jimmy asked.

"I mean, out of our race. Remember, it was you and Able who voted for a two-man race this year. So you picked Rexford and the Commodore to be your only racers. And now you just got one: the Commodore. I always told you Rexford drinks too much."

"So what happened to him?" Able asked.

"Last night Rexford laid one on and tried to sail under South Yarmouth Bridge. Right now Rexford's boat has got a busted mast and a hole where the deck was. And the man himself has got a compound fracture of the arm."

Able Fenstermacher sighed and leaned back against the bench. "At least we got the Commodore," he said.

The Commodore, as he was known to everyone on the peninsula, was Hugh Fitzroy Pugh, a man of ample wealth and size. Although his age remained a mystery, it was rumored that he had crewed for Sir Thomas Lipton in a transatlantic sailing race in 1923. His beautiful old sailboat, the *Wind Song*, had a lapstrake mahogany hull, original canvas sails, and brass fittings.

"Thank God we got the Commodore," said Cabot.

"Thank God," echoed Jimmy Smiley.

"What is this? A prayer meeting?" The voice came from the doorway of T. C. Dabney's Store. The three men turned. At the door stood the store owner himself.

Able spoke up. "Seems we lost Rexford for our sailing race. We were just saying that at least we got the Commodore."

"Guess you didn't hear the news," Dabney said. "He went last night. Heart attack while in the act of love, they say."

"What a man," said Able. Everyone agreed.

"Rest in peace," said Cabot.

Dabney turned and went back inside his store. For a long while none of the men spoke.

"What do we do now?" asked Jimmy at last.

"Beats me," Able said. And the three men remained sitting on the bench, thinking in silence.

IT WAS seven thirty in the morning when Joe arrived at the boatyard. Today's sailing lesson with the admiral was scheduled for eight.

As he walked across the pier he looked down. The *Invincible* was moored at the dock. Joe glanced at the office. The door was ajar, and he could see Sarah inside.

Crossing to the office, he knocked briefly on the door, then stepped inside. "Hi," he said.

Sarah turned from the table where she had been standing. "Hi. Can I do something for you?"

"I just wanted to thank you for readying the boat."

"The boys must have done it. They get here at seven."

"You're here on the early side yourself."

"It's a good time to get my other work done."

"Other work? Oh, you mean 'The Life Story of the Clam from Birth to Bouillabaisse.' "

"You might find the subject funny," Sarah said, "but I don't."

"Sorry. It was a flip remark. To be honest with you, I don't know much at all about clams. Maybe you could fill me in."

Sarah looked at him, unsure if he was serious or not. Finally she stepped back and pointed to two open clams. She held up a dissecting knife and indicated the globular body of the clam.

"This section consists of the visceral mass, the foot for digging in the sand, and a pair of siphons: one to bring food, oxygen, and water in and the other to pump waste matter out."

Joe peered down at the slimy whitish blob. At that hour of the morning it was not a particularly appetizing sight.

"And how do you tell Mr. Clam from Mrs. Clam?" he asked.

Sarah's pale blue eyes were impassive. Her attention shifted past him, out the open door. "The admiral is here," she told Joe.

"One more question, and I'll go. Do clams have feelings, the way people do?"

"I don't know, Ensign," the girl said. "But I'd guess so."

He smiled and went out the door. "See you."

Joe walked across the pier and caught up with the admiral at the top of the ramp. He greeted him.

"Good morning, Joe," the admiral said cheerily. "A fine day for sailing. What's our lesson going to be today?"

"I thought maybe some jib work. In the river."

"Splendid," the admiral said ebulliently.

"We've got a good wind from the west." Joe followed him down to the dock. "You're certainly in a good mood," he added.

The admiral beamed. "And do you know why? Because I spent the evening with a most interesting woman."

"Really?" Somehow the man's statement startled Joe. He found it hard to think of anybody the admiral's age having dates.

The admiral had already set about raising the sail, thrusting in the battens as he did.

For the next hour and a half they sailed up and down and back

509

and forth across the river, tacking again and again while the admiral reset the jib for what seemed to him innumerable times.

Once, on a cross-river heading, the admiral thought he saw Peggy's boat in the distance. He raised a hand above his eyes to shade them. Yes, it *was* her. He was certain of it.

Suddenly he heard the sound of flapping sails and Joe shouting, "Yo! You're in stays. Head her up!"

The admiral realized his boat was drifting aimlessly. He quickly came about and regained control of the boat. "Sorry," he mumbled to Joe. "I lost my concentration for a moment."

Joe made a wry face. "That's what the lookout on the *Titanic* said after he was pulled into the lifeboat."

For Peggy the conditions for sailing had been almost perfect— a brisk, steady breeze from the west and a moderate outgoing tide. The sun was bright but filtered just enough by haze to make it seem benevolent.

For three hours her attention was directed to the nautical details the boat required. So it was not until she reentered Hasty Harbor shortly before noon that she thought about the admiral.

The admiral. Rear admiral actually. "Rear Admiral Charles T. Deering, U.S.N.," she said aloud, and smiled.

From the time he'd brought her home last night until sleep finally overtook her, she had lain awake replaying every moment of the evening in her mind. During dinner they had joked about behaving like teenagers on a date. But for Peggy that *was* how she felt.

Peggy headed toward her car and drove quickly up the boatyard road. She remembered that she needed to get a few groceries and drove straight to T. C. Dabney's Store. As she stepped from her car she saw the three men sitting on the bench in front.

"Ahoy, Commander," Able Fenstermacher said. The others also greeted her.

"Ahoy, yourselves," Peggy said. "Why is it every time I see you three, you're always sitting on this bench?"

"Oh, we do work," Cabot Lodge corrected her.

"We work hard," Jimmy Smiley said.

"Maybe that's why the Hasty Harbor first selectman made us

into a committee," Able added. "Fact is, right now we're holding a race-committee meeting for this year's summer festival."

"Well, what's the committee committed itself to?"

"First off, we've decided this year it's going to be a two-man race," said Able. "Except we're having trouble finding two men."

"We had 'em," Cabot told her, "but we lost 'em."

"Good luck," Peggy offered, and went into the store.

Able leaned back on the bench, his hands behind his head. "Frankly," he said, "whatever two men we *do* choose, that woman could probably whip either one of 'em hands down."

It was almost a full minute before Able looked at Jimmy. "Are you thinking what I'm thinking?" he asked him.

"I'm definitely thinking it," said Jimmy. He turned his head and looked at Cabot.

Cabot nodded. "That makes three of us who have been thinking what we're thinking."

All three men then simultaneously turned and looked in through the open door of T. C. Dabney's Store.

THE telephone did not ring as Peggy ate her lunch. Nor did it ring as she retrieved the paint and paintbrush from the storage cabinet beneath the deck. The day had become hot and hazy. Thunderstorms had been predicted for that evening, but Peggy guessed she would have the afternoon to paint her house before the weather changed. She would paint at ground level, nearest to the door, just in case the telephone should ring.

The paint spread easily across the lower clapboards of the wall, and Peggy's mind wandered. As they often did, such thoughts included memories of Tom. Had he lived, he would be seventy years old. His sandy hair would probably be white, but still those hazel eyes would dance. Those loving eyes.

She thrust the brush into the can of paint and in bold strokes wrote TOM across a board she was about to paint. She looked at it for several moments, the fresh white glistening against the weathered dullness of the wall. Then she painted over it.

Those times with Tom were long ago and far away. After him there had been no one in her life to take his place. She had gradually accepted the belief that Mr. Right was not to be and increasingly, as the years went on, embraced solitude. Her cozy singularity she wore like protective armor, which, though heavy at times, fit her better every year.

Then, uninvited, the admiral had come into her life. And had broken through the armor that protected her.

The more she thought about the man, the more she wanted to be with him. How he felt about her, Peggy wasn't sure. But from his behavior last night . . . Peggy smiled to herself and went on with her painting.

By five thirty, thunderheads had gathered in such number that the sun was obscured. And still the telephone did not ring.

PEGGY had just switched on the television set in the living room to watch the six-o'clock news when the lights flickered. The sky had darkened rapidly. There were rumblings of thunder in the distance, and the wind had increased, blowing fitfully in gusts. Peggy went from room to room closing the windows.

She returned to the living room. It was even darker than before, illuminated only by the chattering face of the television news reporter on the screen. Peggy moved around the room turning on lights. From her experience with summer storms she guessed that loss of her electric power was a certainty. Better fix a sandwich, she thought.

Rain was falling furiously now, flung against the windows by the wind. Peggy was in the process of unwrapping cold cuts from the refrigerator when the lights flickered and went out. She swore softly to herself and got a flashlight from a kitchen drawer. She then lit two candles in the living room.

It was then she heard the sound.

At first she thought it was the wind. But as she listened, she knew that it was someone knocking. It was coming from the front door, and it made her shudder. She picked up the flashlight.

Louder knocking. It was followed by a muffled male voice calling above the wind, "Hello! Anybody home?"

She edged along the shadows and heard the screen door open. In the candlelight she saw the knob of the front door begin to turn. She caught her breath and shined the flashlight at the door. "Who is it?"

"Me! It's Charles. Charles Deering. May I come in?"

Peggy flung open the door. Outside stood the admiral. His sport shirt, madras shorts, and all other visible parts of him were completely soaked.

She stared at him. "For God's sake, what are you doing out in the rain?"

"Getting wetter." He stepped inside, dripping water on the rug. "Get me a towel, and I'll explain," he said apologetically.

Peggy went to the linen closet in the bathroom, grabbed a large bath towel, and brought it to him.

"Thank you. Thank you very much." He began to dry his face and hair. "I'm glad you're home, believe me."

Peggy continued to stare at him. She said finally, "I have some of my father's old clothes in my closet. You can try them on." As she headed to her bedroom she pointed to the bathroom. He went toward it dutifully, water squeaking in his loafers.

Peggy found a pair of trousers and a shirt and returned with them. She knocked on the bathroom door, and when he opened it a crack, she handed him the clothes.

"I found these things in the attic last week. I was going to give them to the Salvation Army," she said.

"Tonight they're a salvation to me, I'll tell you," he called out.

"Would you like a drink?" she asked him. "I bought some bourbon today and some wine."

"Splendid. Bourbon on the rocks with water, if I may."

"Bourbon with branch?" she asked.

"You remembered. Good for you!"

Peggy went into the kitchen. She added ice cubes to a glass and filled the rest with bourbon. In the candlelight the glass had an inviting amber glow. Peggy put it to her lips and sampled the drink. The taste was sharp but tingling. Why spoil it with water?

She started back into the living room carrying his drink—and stopped. Across the room, the admiral stood dressed in her father's clothes, the trousers ending halfway to the ankles, the shirtsleeves well above the wrists.

The admiral held up a hand. "I know, I know. I look ridiculous. But at least these clothes are dry."

Peggy handed him his drink and sat in an armchair. He moved to the sofa and sat as well. "So," he said, "I told you I'd explain my unorthodox arrival. Simply put, I wanted to surprise you."

"You did."

"No. I mean, I told you last night I'd call. But then today I thought, Why not just show up at her door? But without keeping my weather eye well peeled, I sailed down here in my sailboat. Unforgivable for an old navy man like me." The admiral paused, picked up his bourbon, sipped it—and expelled a gasp of air. "Dear lady!" He put down the glass at once. "If you poured medicine as a nurse the way you pour your drinks, you would have taken care of the wounded in no time at all. They'd be either dead or cured."

"Charles . . ." Peggy said. "I like that."

He looked puzzled. "You like what?"

"I like your name. Tonight, when you arrived, you said, 'It's Charles.' It's much easier than calling you Admiral."

He seemed pleased. "I'd be delighted if you would," he said.

A lightning bolt struck suddenly somewhere in the nearby woods, and the accompanying bang of thunder shook the house.

"Where's your boat?" Peggy asked.

"Pulled up on the beach about a quarter mile down, along with a very soggy picnic hamper and a ukulele."

"A *ukulele?*"

"I rented it. I'll admit, I don't sound like Rudy Vallee. But I thought, well, tonight I might surprise you with a moonlight sail."

"While you serenaded me with golden oldies?"

"Corny, isn't it? I'm a corny sort of man sometimes."

"I think you're a very nice man," Peggy told him. She came to him and sat down on the sofa next to him.

"Thank you," he said. He held out his hand and placed it over hers. "I think you're quite a woman, too."

She looked at him, the candlelight illuminating her face. He lifted his hand to her cheek. "A wonderful woman," he said.

At that, the lights went on.

He pulled his hand away abruptly. "Lights! How could they restore power in the middle of a storm?"

With the blaze of lamplight, Peggy retreated to the far end of the sofa. She motioned vaguely in the direction of the kitchen. "How about some dinner while we still have the electricity? How is spaghetti?"

"Sounds good to me."

She turned and headed toward the kitchen. As he watched, she quickly filled a pot with water and set it on the stove. She reached up to the cabinet to get the package of spaghetti.

"I've also got a can of clam sauce," she said. "Would you like that on the spaghetti?"

"Fine. And why don't I make some salad for us?"

"It's a deal," Peggy said. From the refrigerator she took out a head of lettuce, a tomato, and a cucumber.

While he fixed the salad, Peggy waited for the water to boil. Rain still pelted at the windows; several times the lights flickered, but remained lit. As the spaghetti began roiling in the pot Peggy set two places at a small table in the living room. She took the wine from the refrigerator and handed it to the admiral.

"Okay," Peggy said at last. "I guess we're ready."

She served up the spaghetti, and they took seats at the table. He poured the wine, and they began to eat.

"Good pasta," he said after a few bites. He took a drink from his wineglass. "And the wine, too. What kind is it?"

Peggy shrugged. "A local product. Château de Kennebunkport."

He laughed. "You know, I like your sense of humor. Grace always—" He stopped, and his face clouded. "I'm sorry. Even after four years I still talk about my wife as if she were alive."

She looked at him impassively for several moments. "Would you like to talk about her?" she asked. "Can you?"

"Yes to both questions," he said finally. "For a long time I couldn't. Talk about her, that is. Now I can."

"How long were you married?"

"Forty-five years. A long time."

The admiral picked at a loose strand of spaghetti that was edging off his plate. "I was a young lieutenant stationed at the

Norfolk base. She was from one of those first families of Virginia. Fine-boned, upswept hair, a classic profile. Not that she was snobbish. Quite the opposite. We met in June 1941, and six months later we were married. By that time the U.S. was at war, and a week later I was on a cruiser bound for the Panama Canal."

He anticipated her next question. "We had one son. Called him Chip. A chip off the old block. He died during the Vietnam War."

"I'm sorry."

The admiral took a swallow of his wine. "So these days I'm just another retired salt who makes port in Maryland, on Chesapeake Bay. A good deal of the time I play golf or poker, and now and then I'm asked to speak at a launching ceremony. End of story."

There was a flash of lightning, a thunderclap, and once again the lights went out.

Peggy relit the candles, and the two of them resumed their dinner, talking generally about the storm, tomorrow's weather, and her love of sailing. It was her sole passion, Peggy said. From May through October, every day the weather and the sea were good, she sailed. And she was the best sailor around Hasty Harbor, she added modestly but with complete assurance.

When they had finished dinner, Peggy asked, "So what shall we do now? After I do the dishes, I mean."

"Beg your pardon?"

"I mean, we can't watch television with the power out, and I don't play cards. So I think the best thing is to go to bed." She looked at him across the table. "What do you say?"

The admiral looked back at her, saying nothing. She took up the plates and went into the kitchen.

He sat. He thought, Good heavens, did she mean exactly what she said? It may not have been romantic, but it *was* direct. And if anything, this woman was direct. Still, for her to make such a suggestion . . . Well, nowadays young people were encouraged to be candid in such matters. Why not older people, too?

The more he sat and thought, the more it made sense. She *has* been lonely for many years. And in out of a raging storm he comes. Not exactly a Prince Charming, he admitted to himself. But not bad either. For his age he had vigor. He also had a certain craggy handsomeness, he knew. Sailing was her single passion, she'd told him. He wondered.

He picked up the empty wineglasses and went into the kitchen. As Peggy washed the plates he moved behind her. He put one wineglass on the countertop to her left side, the other to her right, so that his arms almost encircled her. "Yes," he said softly. "I think getting into bed would be a wonderful idea."

"Okay," Peggy said over her shoulder, and dumped the left-over spaghetti in the garbage can below the sink.

"There's extra sheets and blankets in the hall closet," she announced. "You make up the sofa for yourself. I'll finish here."

Suddenly confused, he backed out of the kitchen and found the linens. He quickly made up the sofa.

As he finished, Peggy stepped out of the kitchen, carrying a candle. "Ready to bunk down?" she asked him.

He nodded. "Ready. And thanks for dinner. And the bunk."

"I'm glad you were here tonight," she said, and paused. "It's been . . . a very long time since I was close to anyone."

"May I ask you a question before you go?" He pointed to the windowsill nearby that held the model ship. "That replica—the aircraft carrier—is that the *Princeton?*"

Peggy looked surprised. "How did you know?"

"I recognize her lines. Did you know someone aboard?"

She nodded. "Tom was a pilot. We were to be married, but a Japanese plane broke through the overcast and dropped a bomb on the flight deck. There were explosions. Hundreds of her crew got off, but Tom stayed to help the wounded, I was told."

She went on. "Some ships did try to help—the *Gatling* and the *Irwin*. And the *Birmingham*. The *Birmingham* came along the *Princeton's* starboard side to fight the fire."

"Port side. We were on the *Princeton's* port side."

In the candlelight her face looked stricken. "Then you saw?"

"I was a communications officer aboard the *Birmingham.* I was one of the lucky ones. When the *Princeton* blew up, more than two hundred of our own crew were killed."

"Oh, Charles." Suddenly her arms were holding him. "I didn't know. I'm sorry. I'm so sorry."

Tenderly he put his arms around her, but said nothing.

Distant thunder, as from long-forgotten battles, echoed as the storm moved out to sea, away from them.

But holding one another, neither of them heard.

7

WHEN he opened his eyes, the admiral discovered bright sunlight streaming in the space between the living-room curtains. Turning his head, he found a mug of freshly made coffee sitting on the low table near the sofa.

He saw folded over the end of the couch a man's wool plaid bathrobe. He stood up and put it on quickly. From the kitchen he heard sounds of dishes being moved around the countertop.

He called out, "Peggy?"

"Good morning, Charles," she said, stepping into the living room. "I see you found your coffee."

"Yes, thank you." He picked up the coffee and sipped it.

"Your shirt and shorts are in the bathroom. They're mostly dry, considering how wet they were last night. I'll fix us breakfast while you change. Would you like cereal?"

"Oh, no, thank you. Toast and coffee's plenty."

He headed for the bathroom and reemerged a short time later dressed in his own clothes and carrying his shoes. He glanced out the window. The sky was a bright summer blue, cloudless and benign. The only hints of last night's storm were some scattered leaves and a few broken branches strewn around the lawn.

"It looks like a nice day," he said to Peggy.

"A good breeze from the northwest. Perfect for sailing."

"My boat!" he remembered. "It's still down on the beach."

"It may, or it may not be," Peggy said. "Earlier, while you were asleep, I called the boatyard. I told them I was out walking this morning and found a boat from Dodge's Boatyard pulled up on the sand. Noah said he'd send one of the boys down to tow it back."

The admiral still looked concerned. "I'd better call them myself. When they discover it's my boat, they might think I was lost at sea during the storm. I also have a sailing lesson in an hour."

"Then I'll drive you to your cabin," Peggy said. "But have some breakfast first."

She refilled the coffee mugs, and they sat down at the table. He found a jar of beach-plum jam and began spreading great gobs of it on his toast.

"About last night," she said. "A lot of memories are locked up in the *Princeton*. And until last night I thought that, like the ship, they were sunk too deep to ever surface after all these years. I guess I'm just vulnerable."

"To be vulnerable to memories is not a vice."

"I know. But I was brought up to be strong. People have expected me to be."

"Who, for instance?"

"The patients I took care of as a nurse. Other people."

"Including you?"

"I guess. . . . How are your sailing lessons coming?" she asked him, changing the subject.

"Very well." He took a swallow of coffee. "I'm surprised—pleased, really—that I still remember as much about sailing as I do. I guess it's like a lot of things you enjoy. Even if you haven't done them in a while, it doesn't take long to pick up the technique again. But I'll confess, I'm still uncertain of when to change my heading. There are moments when I think I'm getting nowhere fast."

"You know the basic rule of sailing," Peggy said. "If you're going nowhere, put some wind behind you, reset your sails, and change course."

"Maybe you should write a sailing book," he said lightly. "Something simple and direct, like *Peggy's Book of Sailing*."

"If I did, I'd include a special chapter entitled 'Be Aware of Changing Conditions.' "

"Such as?"

"Wind, tide, currents—anything that can affect your boat. You know nothing stays the same as when you started out."

"I'd like to read it. And I should take you with me the next time I go sailing. Seriously, would you like to go?"

"Sure. Sometime."

"Tonight? The weather is more promising than last night's was," he reassured her. "The only thing I won't promise you is ukulele music. How about it? Will you sail with me?"

"Yes, Charles. I think that would be very nice."

"Wonderful!" He lifted up his coffee mug, saluting her.

A few minutes later they were headed north along Lonely Point Road, Peggy's small car careening back and forth around the curves. The road was a single lane of aging asphalt, with shoulders of sand and beach grass.

"Down!" said Peggy suddenly as she turned a curve.

It was too late. Approaching them from the center of the road was the large yellow Cadillac of Mrs. Ernestine Doberman.

Peggy wrenched the Pinto's steering wheel and shot past the Cadillac. She glanced up at the rearview mirror as she sped on. Mrs. Doberman had come to a dead stop, turned her head, and was staring after Peggy and the admiral, her mouth agape.

SEATED at the office desk, Sarah put a piece of boatyard stationery in the typewriter and began typing.

"Hi," said a falsetto voice.

Sarah stopped typing. Leaning just inside the office door was a large clam with round eyes painted on its upper shell. In fact, measuring two feet across, it was the largest clam Sarah had ever seen. It also appeared to be made of Styrofoam.

"Hi," the clam repeated, flapping its shells up and down.

Sarah didn't know whether to be annoyed or amused. The clam went on. "My name is Clementine Clam. And I am here for three reasons. First, to assure you, Sarah Dodge, that you're considered a true friend of the clam. Therefore, on behalf of all clams everywhere, I wish to thank you for your attention and support."

Joe's forearm appeared briefly between the clam and the doorframe, then withdrew.

"The second reason I am here," the clam said, "is to apologize for my friend, Joe Marino."

"I didn't know he was a friend of yours," said Sarah.

"Oh, yes." The clam bobbed up and down in a vigorous nod.

"For years he's taken pleasure in our company in a variety of forms—raw, fried, and casino. And he wants to apologize to you if what he said the other day sounded like anything less than total admiration for our species."

"Why didn't he come and apologize himself?"

"Because he's shy. Very shy," the clam anwered.

"And what's the third reason you're here?" Sarah asked.

"That's the best part," Clementine Clam said. "Joe and I would like to invite you to—excuse the expression—a clambake."

"A clambake?"

"Shh," the clam cautioned. "Among us clams the word is almost never mentioned. Tomorrow evening, Saturday, sixty Bismarck Street, in Whitby. How does seven o'clock sound?"

"I'd like to think about it," Sarah said. "But thank you."

"My pleasure," the clam answered, opening as wide as possible. "I await your response with baited shell."

Sarah thought a moment. "There are two messages you can give Ensign Marino when you see him."

"Really? What?" The clam opened wide again.

"You can tell him that he's a terrible ventriloquist."

"He knows that. What's the other message?"

"The admiral's sailboat was found this morning down near Lonely Point. Empty."

"*What!*" Joe stepped into the office, the clam hanging from his hand.

"Don't worry," Sarah said. "He got caught in the storm and beached the boat, and somebody gave him a lift home. But he did leave some things in the boat."

"Like what?"

"A picnic hamper . . . and a ukulele." Sarah reached under the desk and brought out the instrument, its strings limp from exposure to the water.

"Where's the boat now?"

"At the floating dock. The boys towed it back."

Joe started out the door. "Sailing in a gale with a picnic hamper and a ukulele. Unbelievable!" He raised his arms, the clam still dangling from one of them.

It took Joe half an hour to bail the water from the admiral's sailboat. When he finally finished, he saw the admiral striding rapidly across the pier.

"Sorry I'm late," the admiral said as he came down the ramp.

Joe looked visibly annoyed. "Let me ask you something. Did you listen to any marine weather forecasts yesterday?"

"Well, yes. But the storm came sooner than I thought. I was prepared. I had my life vest—"

"And a ukulele. Did you plan to use it as a paddle if the sea got rough?"

"Oh, that. Well, that's another story."

"Come on," Joe said. "Let's hit the water. You take the helm."

The admiral stepped into the boat and began raising the sail as Joe prepared to cast off from the dock.

"By the way," Joe said after he had settled into the cockpit. "It seems there are three gentlemen observing us, who are very interested in how you sail." He pointed to a sandy area near the boathouse, a large corrugated-metal structure beyond the pier. Three men sat on an overturned dinghy. One was bearded, one wore yellow waders, and the third man had a finger in his ear.

"They came down to the dock while I was bailing water," Joe said. "They asked about you, said they heard you were staying in the area and doing lots of sailing here."

"I never saw them before," the admiral said.

"Okay. If they want a show, we'll give 'em one," Joe said. He pushed the boat away from the dock. The mainsail swung out and billowed, and the boat responded smartly to the wind.

Still seated on the upturned dinghy, the three men watched until the *Invincible* was well into the harbor. Then, as one, they turned and shared a nod.

PEGGY had never been that high before, at least not on her own house. She straddled the peak of her roof. In one hand she held a large screwdriver; in the other, a shiny copper weather vane of an angel holding a long trumpet out before him as he flew.

The view afforded her was breathtaking. The expanse of water was vaster than she'd ever been aware of closer to ground level. In the river and out into the Gulf of Maine, boats were everywhere.

She heard a car, and looking to her left, she saw Sarah's red VW hurrying down Lonely Point Road. It pulled into the driveway, and the girl got out of the car and went to the front door.

"Peggy?" Sarah called in through the screen.

"I'm here!" Peggy shouted down. "Up here! On the roof!"

Sarah stepped onto the lawn and looked up, shading her eyes against the sun. "What are you doing on the roof?"

"Putting up a weather vane." Peggy held it aloft. "I was painting yesterday and realized this house had never had a weather vane. So when I was in town this morning, I saw the angel Gabriel, and here he is, announcing a new life for one and all."

"He must have started with you first," Sarah said.

"You're right. Today I'm on top of the world."

"When I talked to you the other night, you sounded really down."

"I was," admitted Peggy. "But that's changed."

"Well, I'm on my way to the mud flats to see my clams. I can stop by on my way back. We can have dinner."

"Sorry, Sarah. But tonight I've got a date."

"A *date*? Who is he? *Tell* me."

Peggy shook her head. "I can't. Not yet."

"Then have a good time with your man of mystery!" Sarah called up. She waved and started toward her car. Peggy watched as she backed out of the driveway and drove out of sight.

"Gabriel," she said, "a whole new day has dawned."

When she finally came down from the roof, it was past four o'clock. She showered and dressed quickly, and still had ample time to prepare a picnic for tonight.

As she packed paper cups, napkins, and plastic forks she saw Smiley's garbage truck. It pulled into her driveway and stopped. This isn't trash-collection day, she told herself. What's Smiley doing here? She also noticed two other figures in the truck. It surprised her when she saw Able Fenstermacher emerge, followed by Cabot Lodge and Jimmy Smiley.

Peggy went into the living room as the men started up the steps.

"Hi, Peggy!" Able called from outside the screen door. "Got a minute?"

"Only a minute," Peggy said. She did not open the screen.

"As you well know," Able began, "we are the race committee for this year's summer festival, which is eight days off."

"I know," said Peggy.

"Being a longtime resident of Hasty Harbor," Jimmy said, "you'll agree the race is the highlight of the festival."

"I thought Emma Wilmott's covered-dish baked-bean surprise was," Peggy said.

Able made a face. "The food committee is asking Emma to try something less surprising this year."

"As you know also," Cabot said, "we decided on a two-person race this year. And you're the best sailor around."

"And we want you to be one of the racers," Jimmy said.

"No."

"Peg," Able said, "think of the advantages."

"The answer is still no," she told them. "The race may be the high point of the festival, but it's a joke. And even if I did accept, you might not find another racer to compete against me."

"Maybe last year's race was a joke," Able acknowledged. "But we want to change that. We want to show everyone that Hasty Harbor is a little town that can make a big splash in the yachting world. As for competition—"

"We got the other racer lined up," Cabot blurted.

"He's from Maryland," Able said. "Ex-navy, like yourself."

A queasy feeling started in the pit of Peggy's stomach.

"It's that admiral who spoke at last week's launching," Able added. "For an old man he's pretty handy with a sailboat."

Peggy stared at the three men, her face a blank. The three men looked back at Peggy, hopeful and expectant.

It was Able, finally, who filled the silence. "We talked to him this afternoon. We did tell him one little fib, though. We said you'd already agreed to be the other racer. When he heard that, he said he'd race, too."

She said softly, "Get your truck out of my driveway, Jimmy. There's somebody I've got to talk to. Now."

ON THE BOATYARD PIER, NOAH had heard the sudden squeak of brakes, then seen Peggy spring out of her car and hurry over. Now she stood before him, hands on her hips.

"Has the admiral been here yet?" she demanded.

"He's here now," Noah said. He pointed to the boathouse. "Peg," he said, "you seem upset."

"I am. Those three stooges who call themselves the race committee may have just ruined my life."

She ran in the direction of the boathouse and went to the building's huge sliding doors, which stood open. At first all Peggy could make out inside were sailboats. Then, to one side, she saw a mane of white hair moving in the labyrinth of rigging. She threaded her way through the hulls toward the admiral.

Suddenly he saw her. "Peggy!"

"I thought you might be here. Charles, we have to talk. You've got to tell that so-called race committee that you've changed your mind. Tell them that we can't."

"Can't what?" he asked. "You mean the race?"

"Of course the race!"

"But those three men told me you'd agreed, so naturally—"

"What they told you was a trick to get you to say yes."

"Now, Peggy." He made an open-handed gesture. "The race sounds like fun. I mean, this morning you said you'd sail with me."

"*With* you," Peggy told him. "Not *against* you. Do you know what people are going to call us out there? The old fogies' flotilla. Two gray-haired sailors trying to prove they're not ready for a nursing home."

The admiral looked at her. "My age doesn't bother me. I'm proud of it. And I didn't think it bothered you."

"It doesn't. But the publicity, the newspapers. When word gets out you're one of the contestants—"

"Peggy, I told you, I'm an old retired salt the world passed by long ago. I don't anticipate what you call publicity."

It struck Peggy that her hands were in constant motion, and she grabbed the rigging of a nearby sailboat to quiet them. "But can't you see? It's more than that to me. I mean, whatever was beginning, was beginning just between us. I thought maybe in time—"

She stopped and looked at him, her eyes wet. "That's ended now."

"It's not."

"It is. You and I are about to become a public spectacle."

"Peg." He reached to hold her shoulders, but she backed away. "Peggy," he said, "I gave my word I'd race."

"Your word," she repeated. "Thus spake the admiral, whose words can nevermore be changed."

"Sarcasm does not become you," he said gently.

"Well, I'm so sorry, sir. *So* sorry."

"Peg, it's just a little local race. In a week or so, all this will be over. You and I sail for a couple of hours on race day, and the whole thing will be forgotten by the time the clambake starts."

"And after that?" she asked him.

"We'll pick up where we left off."

"No."

"Peggy, please." He took her arms in both his hands.

"Don't say anything," she said. "You gave your word you'd race. Then so will I. I may be an old retired sailor, too. But I will race against you, and I'll beat you."

She twisted from his grasp and fought her way out of the boathouse through the maze of boats.

8

SAILBOAT RACE IS HIGHLIGHT OF FESTIVAL WEEK

THE headline leaped out at Peggy as she opened the newspaper at her doorstep the next morning. The *Peninsula Pilot* was a local weekly serving the small communities of the peninsula. Peggy carried the paper into her kitchen and read it as she ate her breakfast. Below the headline it said:

FAMOUS ADMIRAL AND LOCAL LADY TO SQUARE OFF AT SEA

All the peninsula is agog with anticipation of the impending sailboat race that will be the featured event of this year's Hasty Harbor Summer Festival. Mr. James G. Smiley, spokesman for the race committee, said, "We're proud as h--- to have our Peg pitted against Admiral Charles T. Deering, the father of modern navel communications."

Peggy had just taken a mouthful of coffee, and choked briefly when she caught the misspelling of the word naval.

She went on reading. The story was mostly a profile of the admiral and his career. When she thumbed through the rest of the paper, she saw that much of it was devoted to the festival.

There was a diagram of the race course, with a brief piece about "The Hazards Confronting Our Two Stalwart Competitors," mentioning the Sawteeth rocks and the dangerous rock known as Big Momma, submerged during high tide. Another column announced that Emma Wilmott's memorable baked-bean surprise would not be offered at the clambake and supper this year.

Enough of this, thought Peggy. It was then that the telephone began to ring. Peggy started for it and then stopped. It could be Sarah. On the other hand, it could be Mrs. Doberman or someone else who'd seen the story in the paper.

The telephone continued ringing. Or could it be him? She looked at the phone and let it ring until it stopped.

Then she opened the front door and hurried out as the telephone began to ring again.

NOAH Dodge couldn't understand it. Every morning when he went to collect his mail at the post office in T. C. Dabney's Store, there were never more than two or three people in line at the grille window. Yet this morning Noah had to stop abruptly to avoid knocking over old Hetty Joy, leaning patiently on her cane and counting out the contents of her change purse. Ahead of her were eight other Hasty Harbor residents.

It wasn't until Noah was within four people of the window that he noticed that everyone was handing money through the grille. Dabney would accept the money, make a quick note on a postal slip, and wish the person a good-day. No one received stamps or envelopes or money orders. Nothing.

Finally Noah himself stood before the grille. "T.C., what's going on here?"

"Taking stamp orders, that's all," Dabney said. "As of this morning, the navy-hero stamps are selling for six cents and the lady suffragettes for two. But, of course, that's subject to change."

"I want a roll of one hundred regular first-class stamps with the American flag on 'em," Noah told the man. "That's it."

"Okay. But you're missing a bet." Dabney chuckled and reached into the drawer below the counter.

Noah was ready to ask what was so special about navy-hero and lady-suffragette stamps when the answer became clear. He leaned toward the grille. "T.C.," he asked, "are you bookmaking on the sailing race next week? Six to two odds for the admiral?"

Dabney put a finger to his lips. "Careful, Noah. You never know when there might be a postal inspector behind you. Let's just say a lot of folks have certain . . . feelings about the race. And if they want to place a wager on it, I'm happy to oblige."

Noah frowned as his roll of stamps was pushed toward him. "Will that be all?" T.C. said, winking.

Noah sighed, and reached for his wallet. "All right. Here's for the roll of first-class stamps. And put me down for ten dollars' worth on the lady suffragette."

T. C. Dabney smiled a weasel smile. "I figured that's how you'd go, being a friend of Peggy's, and all."

"I still don't like the idea," Noah told him.

Dabney shrugged. "Lots of your friends around here don't agree with you. Just look behind you."

Noah turned. He saw that the line behind him now stretched out the door of T. C. Dabney's Store.

THE navigational chart lay spread out across the table in the admiral's cabin. It was held down at the corners by the cans of beer that Joe and the admiral were drinking and by one of the admiral's books on sailing. Drawn in pencil on the face of the chart were three straight lines forming an irregular triangle. The northernmost part of the triangle was a buoy with a flashing signal, near the Hasty Harbor entrance and the Sawteeth rocks. One line extended in a southwesterly direction from the buoy to a gray-shaded object referred to as Big Momma. From there another line went east to a gong buoy marked 4-CL. The final line ran northwest, back to Hasty Harbor.

Joe took a sip of his beer. "What do you think?" he asked the admiral. "Can you sail the ten-mile course fast enough to win?"

"Yes," the man said simply. "If I go faster than the other boat."

"And that's what we're going to spend the next week working on." Joe rose from the table. "Now that we've sailed it on paper, let's see how you are on the water."

Several hours later, as the *Invincible* struggled to make headway against a swift incoming tide, the admiral had the answer to Joe's question: he was not doing well at all. Joe said little while they sailed. As they approached their first mark, Big Momma, the admiral made a wide cautious turn around it, keeping at least fifty feet away.

He glanced at Joe. "I know I should have gotten closer."

"Timidity does not win races," Joe said. "I'm guessing your competitor will get a *lot* closer. I've seen her sail."

"So have I," the admiral admitted. "But one thing just occurred to me: now that we *are* competitors, what's to prevent us from practicing out here at the same time?"

"Don't worry. I've worked out a schedule with her second."

"Her second? Who is it?"

"Miss Dodge."

The admiral nodded with approval. "She seems very nice. And very pretty. You should make her acquaintance."

"Uh-huh" was all Joe said. He was about to add more, but didn't. Instead, he looked eastward, toward the second mark.

They continued running with the wind behind them toward gong buoy 4-CL. Occasionally Joe would check his watch and write some things on the clipboard that he carried. At first the admiral wondered if they were critiques of his performance at the helm. But that wasn't Joe's style. If he had any remarks to make, good or bad, he would make them. The admiral liked that quality in the young man.

In fact, the more time he spent with Joe, the more he liked him. He'll be a fine naval officer, the admiral thought. He would command respect because of the qualities he possessed: intelligence, assurance, competence, and that intangible instinct that marked a born sailor—a true feeling for the sea.

The *Invincible*'s speed increased. As they approached the gong buoy the admiral felt as if he were at the throttle of a power launch. Now twenty-five feet from the buoy, he kept coming straight for it. Twenty feet, then ten, then seven, and he tacked around it in a neat, sharp turn.

Joe looked at the admiral. "Clean and close. No wonder you were called Daring Deering."

On the final leg of the course now, the admiral gazed across the water. He recalled his own days as a young naval officer, recalled how at the beginning of the war he and his fellow officers, comrades-in-arms all, had been filled with patriotic fever. Proudly, almost passionately, they had gone off to fight. For some, all that their passion got them was a plot at Arlington. The admiral had come to detest war. War had taken him from his new bride only days after their wedding. War had killed his only son.

Chip . . .

Sometimes the recollections of his son came flooding back. He'd had his mother's light blond hair and clear blue eyes. Full of youthful spirit and an honors graduate of the Academy, he had opportunities ahead of him that seemed endless.

Instead, the end came in the instant it took the mine to detonate against the hull of Chip's patrol boat off the Vietnamese coast. Now, when the admiral was in Washington, D.C., he often visited the long black marble wall that bore the names of those killed in the tragic war. Each time he would stand for a few moments and read the name—Charles T. Deering, Jr.—and see his own reflection mirrored in the wall. Then his eyes would begin to mist.

Looking forward in the sailboat now, he prayed that Joe would never have to fight and die, as Chip had.

At last the *Invincible* reached the flashing buoy near the Sawteeth rocks. The admiral lowered the jib and started through the channel into Hasty Harbor. He approached the boatyard, came about, and let the *Invincible* be carried broadside up against the dock. After securing the sailboat to the mooring cleats, he and Joe walked toward the ramp.

As they stepped onto it Joe said, "After a slow start you really put the pedal to the metal. Maybe you'll win, after all."

The admiral grinned. "I told you, I intend to."

"Well, we have seven days to practice, barring weather problems. But if you sail then as you did today, you should be shooting through the water like a loose torpedo."

NEVER a sailor.

Sarah had said that to herself for as long as she could remember. Some of them might seem gentlemanly at the start, but they had one thing in mind only. She recalled how schoolgirl friends would giggle when the stories were exchanged.

So what was she doing now? Why had she decided suddenly to accept Joe's invitation to his cookout? Maybe it was curiosity. He seemed nicer than a lot of the navy men she'd met. And he had a sense of humor. But he was still a sailor. And if he thought she was just another of the Whitby girls who chased the fleet, he was in for a rude shock.

Driving across the Newell River into Whitby, Sarah took the first exit past the bridge and zigzagged through the local streets until she came to Bismarck Street.

Sixty Bismarck Street was a large, solid structure of brown-painted wood, with a porch running the width of the front and curving gracefully around the side. A walkway led up to the house.

Sarah took a breath and got out of her car. She stood for a moment smoothing her rose-colored summer dress. As she started up the walk she heard voices and laughter coming from behind the house. She turned and followed a narrow flagstone path toward the sound. She arrived in the backyard and stopped.

At the far end of the yard a metal barbecue on wheels was sending up a column of white smoke. Near it stood two young men dressed in shorts and sport shirts, a tall thin girl in a white sleeveless blouse and white slacks, and a short blond girl in a low-cut dress with orange polka dots that displayed more than enough of her ample bosom. Joe was also near the grill, occasionally poking at it with a pair of cooking tongs.

Joe saw Sarah, grinned, and waved the tongs. He came toward her. "Hi," he said. "I wasn't sure you'd come."

"I wasn't either," Sarah said.

"Well, I want you to meet the two jokers I room with, and their dates." Joe started back across the yard as Sarah followed.

"Sarah, this is Ensign Sandy Whittemore." Joe indicated the tall young man who stood beside the girl in white. "And this is Gayle Holyoke." They nodded and smiled.

Joe turned to the other young man, who had his arm around the polka-dotted girl's waist. "This clown is Ensign Billy Buxon, and the young lady is his friend Corky Canty. Everybody, this is Sarah Dodge."

There were some murmured greetings. Meanwhile, the tall ensign had picked up a gallon jug of wine, filled a paper cup, and presented it to Sarah as Joe went to check the kitchen.

"Joe says you live down on the peninsula," the ensign said.

"Yes. Hasty Harbor," Sarah said.

The girl in white said, "I find that part of the peninsula quite charming."

"Dodge . . . Dodge," Corky Canty chimed. "How come I know that name from down around there?"

"My father has a boatyard there," Sarah answered.

"*Attenzione!*" Joe called, returning. "In five minutes I start barbecuing the lobsters." Then he smiled at Sarah. "You'll be glad to hear I decided against serving clams."

She smiled back. "I'm glad to hear."

AN HOUR and twenty minutes later, with the dinner guests seated in a circle on a variety of chairs, the cookout wound toward its conclusion. Throughout the dinner Joe had talked engagingly and easily. Sarah had remained generally mute.

When dinner ended, Joe, Sandy, and Billy cleared the plates. Billy then thrust a tape into a huge Walkman tape player. Sarah watched as the other couples sprang up and began gyrating, feet stomping, elbows pumping, heads bobbing in the air.

"Care to dance?" Joe asked. When Sarah turned, he stood before her with his hand outstretched.

"I— No, thank you."

"Come on. I bet you're a fantastic dancer."

"I'm used to other kinds of dancing, really," Sarah told him.

"I understand. I haven't seen a single new-age club in Hasty Harbor. But it's time you broadened your horizons." With that, he took hold of both her hands and pulled her to her feet. "Now kick off your shoes."

Sarah did so.

"That's it," Joe said. "Do your thing."

Sarah tried a few steps. After a few minutes, though, she felt ridiculous, and stopped. "If you don't mind, I'll sit and watch."

Joe also stopped. "No problem. I'll sit with you."

In the growing darkness the manic actions of the dancers made them look like the subjects of some tribal rite. Finally the tape ended, and the dancers staggered to the chairs.

Before long the other couples announced that they were going to take a drive. Joe saw them off, then returned and sat down across from Sarah.

"Thanks for coming tonight," he said.

"I should be going soon myself," she told him.

"But not yet. Since you did make the decision to come to my

soiree, tell me about Sarah Dodge. You'll be in your senior year of college where?"

"Orono. That's where the state university is."

"And you're studying marine biology. Then, after college, what?"

"Graduate school, I hope. How did you get into the Naval Academy?" she asked, hoping to turn the questioning in his direction.

"Since both my parents worked, I spent a lot of time at my grandparents' apartment, in Brooklyn, New York," Joe answered. "My grandfather had a shoe-repair shop, and the cousin of a local Congressman always had his shoes fixed at the shop. One day my grandfather told the man he wouldn't give him back his shoes until the Congressman wrote a letter to the Academy on my behalf. After that I was a shoe-in, you could say."

Joe drew out his wallet. "I've got a picture of them both, my grandfather and my grandmother. They were immigrants from Napoli—Naples—and they took a great chance coming to America. 'We dared to live!' my grandfather used to say."

He picked up one of the candles he'd lit and moved next to Sarah. She looked at the aging snapshot of a young couple wearing very formal clothes. Joe pointed to the woman. "She was the artistic talent in the family. She had reproductions of old paintings on the walls of the apartment."

"Were they by anybody famous?" Sarah asked him.

Joe laughed. "Leo D. Vinci and Mike L. Angelo did a few."

The girl smiled. "I've seen their work."

"Once, I thought I would become an artist. When I was in fourth grade, I sat for an hour outside our building and drew a picture of the fireplug beside the curb. I will modestly admit that that picture won me first prize in the elementary-school art exhibit."

"I'm impressed," said Sarah.

As the candle flickered, Joe moved closer to her. "There's something else I'd like to impress on you," he told her. "How much do you know about *il bacio?*"

"*Il bacio?* Is he an Italian painter, too?"

As Sarah waited for his explanation, Joe kissed her softly.

"That is what *il bacio* is," he said.

535

VERY EARLY IN THE MORNING T. C. Dabney stepped onto the porch of his store carrying a felt eraser. Still chalked on the blackboard next to the front door were Saturday's grocery specials. Dabney wiped the blackboard clean and wrote: *Six Days to Festival Day*.

He underlined six for emphasis. He then added, in parentheses, 6–2.

Since yesterday, when Dabney had decided on them, the odds on the race had remained 6–2 in favor of the admiral. The disparity was not based on any feeling that the admiral was the better sailor; in fact, throughout the area Peggy's skill was acknowledged and respected. The reason was that almost all of the initial bettors had been men—those same men who were absolutely certain that a man could beat a woman at any time, at anything. What's more, the rank of admiral itself led them to assume that Charles Deering had mastered every vessel from a dinghy to a battleship.

But Dabney had assured his clientele those odds were certain to change. He had already enlisted half a dozen of the local lobstermen and fishermen to report what they observed of the competitors' practice sessions. He studied the numbers: 6–2. Finally he erased the 2. He picked up the piece of chalk that hung down on a string beside the blackboard, and in place of the number 2 he wrote a 3.

THE admiral stood morosely at the window of his cabin looking at the rain that had begun to fall. At last he turned back to the table. He sat down, opened the logbook, and began to write:

Sunday, July 24 (3:30 p.m.)—The weather is a bust—steady drizzle in the morning; rain this afternoon. I can't afford many such days this week. Peggy may not need the sailing practice, but I do.

I confess I still vacillate about whether I did the right thing in agreeing to this race. I want to win—and yet I don't if winning means I will lose seeing her again. But I'm committed to go through with it. Even my neighbors in the other cabins are asking me about it.

THE phone had begun ringing at six thirty in the morning. Now, two hours and four unanswered phone calls later, Peggy finished her final coffee for the morning. She had just begun to wash her breakfast dishes when she heard a familiar squawk coming from the deck. The squawk was followed by a staccato tapping on the sliding doors. Captain Bligh had obviously arrived.

Peggy turned off the faucet. She took a box of cornflakes from the kitchen cabinet and headed for the deck. The gull saw her and flapped its wings briefly as she slid open the door.

She stepped out. "Sorry, Captain, but there's no more bread. How about cornflakes? Very healthy for a growing bird."

She scattered some flakes in Captain Bligh's direction. The bird leaped forward as they fell, devouring several in midair.

"So did you finally hear about the race and come to wish me luck?" she said. "You know, I'll consider you my good-luck bird."

The sea gull gave an impatient squawk, and Peggy tossed more flakes in his direction.

"Now tell me. Have you and the other gulls made any bets on who is going to win the race? Because, I'll admit, I'm nervous. More than that—I'm scared. Not about losing, but because I feel trapped. The race is suddenly a great big deal. Everybody's taking sides, and when the admiral and I head out onto the river Saturday, it'll be worse. People will be cheering us as if we were two gladiators in a struggle to the death.

"But do you know what's died already? Something nice. Something the admiral and I had just begun to find. It made me happy.... And it's over now. This stupid race has made us public adversaries. It's our bad luck."

Peggy knelt. The sea gull didn't move; it simply stared at her as if it understood and sympathized with all she'd said.

"Even so, I'm going to win, Bligh. No, I *have* to win. So bring me luck. Will you do that?"

THE digital clock on the dashboard of Joe's car showed 9:29. He was due to meet the admiral at the boatyard at ten. With five days' practice left before the race, the lone objective was winning.

Except, Joe had to admit, his mind was also occupied with something other than the race. Some*one*. Sarah Dodge.

Since the cookout two nights earlier, she had been on his mind constantly. Seated beside each other in the darkness of the summer night, they had talked until almost midnight. And in that time he had discovered a young woman who was bright as well as beautiful. The other night confirmed what Joe felt when he'd first seen her—this girl was different. This girl had class.

Still deep in thought, Joe slowed the car and turned onto the boatyard road. At the pier he stopped the car and looked around. The admiral was nowhere to be seen. Joe adjusted his officer's cap, stepped out, and marched in the direction of the boatyard office.

Inside, seated at the desk, was a large woman with a flat, round face and dark hair pinned up in a bun. She smiled at Joe. "You must be Ensign Marino. I'm Mrs. Dodge, Sarah's mother."

Joe hoped his disappointment was not too obvious. "Hello. Pleased to meet you, ma'am. By any chance, is Sarah—"

"She's in Portland for the day. Is there something I can do?"

"I'd like to rent another sailboat. A Lightning."

Mrs. Dodge seemed puzzled. "Aren't you and the admiral sailing together?"

"Yes. But I want him to get the feel of the boat without me."

Mrs. Dodge gave Joe another friendly round-faced smile and began flipping through the card file on the desk.

"It should be quite a race on Saturday," the woman said. "We even got a call from *Yachting* magazine about it."

"Is that so?" Joe said.

At last Mrs. Dodge drew a card out of the file. "Here it is, another Lightning. It's probably at the dock already."

"Good. Thank you." Joe started out, then hesitated. "By the way, would you please tell Sarah I said hello?" He touched the brim of his hat and closed the door behind him.

SHORTLY after dawn on Tuesday morning, T. C. Dabney went to the blackboard next to the front door. He erased what had been there and wrote: *Four Days to Festival Day.*

What he had not erased, he realized, were yesterday's odds on the race, still listed as 6–3.

T. C. Dabney pondered. Then he picked up the piece of chalk, and where the 3 had been, he made a 4.

PEGGY regretted she had sailed in the morning. By afternoon the heat had begun to build, and she would have preferred to be on the water now, enjoying a sea breeze, rather than where she was—up on a ladder painting the north wall of her house.

She had just begun painting under the rain gutter when she heard a faint and fitful sort of crying. The sound ended, then resumed, then stopped. Peggy stood on the ladder listening. When it began again, she realized it was coming from the roof.

She had the answer—it was the weather vane she had put up several days before. She hadn't oiled any of the moving parts, and the vane was squeaking as it turned.

Peggy descended the ladder for a can of lubricating oil, then climbed up to the weather vane and squirted oil down into the shaft holding the supporting rod. She spun the weather vane around. The squeak was gone.

At that moment she saw the yellow Cadillac of Mrs. Doberman glide imperiously toward the house. Since last week, Peggy had succeeded in avoiding the woman. But now she was a captive audience, trapped on her own roof.

As the Cadillac approached, Peggy devised a plan. The ladder was behind the house. If she could press herself down flat enough against the roof, the woman might not even think of looking up.

Peggy waited. She heard a car door close.

"Yoo-hoo!" she heard Mrs. Doberman call out. "Pegg-eee! Are you home? I tried phoning you *so* many times, my dear, but you were never here."

There was a silence, then Peggy heard the screen door open. There followed a series of yoo-hoos. Obviously Mrs. Doberman had taken it upon herself to search the house.

At last the screen door could be heard opening again.

"Well," Mrs. Doberman said, addressing the absent Peggy,

"you could be here and not here. I mean, you could be walking on the beach or somewhere in the area.

"What I wished to tell you," she went on, "is that there is no need for you to make a contribution to the auction for the festival. The contribution you're making just by being in the race is more than any of the rest of us could give. Some people may think I'm a silly woman. But I *am* a woman. And a single one, like you. And I know the courage it took to accept the challenge of that race. I'm very proud of you, my dear. I *know* you're going to win."

Once more there was silence. Peggy heard footsteps descending the walk and the car door closing, then the engine starting and the car backing out. It was only after the sound of the car faded off that Peggy raised her head.

She looked in the direction the car had gone. From this day on, thought Peggy, I will have a very different attitude toward Mrs. Doberman.

9

Three Days to Festival Day (6–5)

"IT STILL seems odd with you in another boat," the admiral called over at Joe. The *Invincible* and the sailboat that Joe had rented were drifting side by side. Ahead was the flashing buoy near the Sawteeth rocks, which marked the start and finish of the race.

"That's the rule," Joe called back. "One sailor to a boat."

"But suppose I capsize. What then?" the admiral asked.

"Don't worry," Joe said. "I'm sure a member of the spectator fleet will rescue you. Don't think of anything except the race. Just keep repeating to yourself, I'm going to win, I'm going to win."

"I'm going to win, I'm going to win," echoed the admiral. "I sound like the little sailboat that could."

"Okay. Enough of ship-to-ship communications," Joe told him. "Come on. *Avanti!* Let's get sailing!"

And for the next three hours, sail they did. The day was even hotter than the day before had been, and the wind was steady from the west. For half an hour they practiced crossing the imaginary starting line beside the flashing buoy. Each time Joe would call out a warning, each time both men would put their sailboats in readiness to make the starting run, and each time they would turn and race toward the buoy, maneuvering to gain an advantage over the other and be first across the line.

When Joe signaled with a wave of his hand, they continued down the opening leg of the course. Approaching the first mark, Joe led by two boat lengths. Suddenly the admiral jibed, swinging in behind Joe's boat. The move caught Joe by surprise—literally taking the wind out of his sails—and the admiral shot past him, making a hairbreadth turn around the rock.

The admiral looked back at Joe and beamed.

"Well done!" Joe shouted to him.

Spinnakers set, both sailboats now pointed eastward, toward the second mark—gong buoy 4-CL. Joe knew there wasn't much point in attempting any fancy sail handling: both boats would travel at approximately the same speed no matter what. So he just sat beside the tiller and let his sailboat run free. Now and then the admiral gave Joe a backward glance from his position several lengths ahead. At last the admiral tacked around the gong buoy, dropped the spinnaker, and began sailing toward the Sawteeth rocks. Gradually, in a series of small but frequent tacks, Joe began to gain on the admiral.

Abruptly Joe swung his boat sharply away from the line the two were sailing. Immediately the wind billowed his mainsail and jib. Joe tacked again at once, aiming his boat squarely in the direction of the admiral's.

The admiral saw Joe's boat coming for him at great speed and was dumbfounded. Instinctively he tacked off to avoid a collision as Joe came about again and took the lead.

Joe held it till he crossed the finish line, four boat lengths ahead of the *Invincible*.

The admiral shouted over to him, "What was that trick you just used to get by me?"

"It's part of what I call the Marino maneuver!" Joe shouted back. "I'll give you the details later."

The admiral tacked sharply to the starting line with a flourish, ready for another duel.

541

By THAT AFTERNOON, TEMPERATURES were in the nineties. Tourists had taken to the beaches. Even the stray dogs that scavenged at the dumpster behind T. C. Dabney's Store sought the shady side of buildings.

When Peggy drove onto the boatyard road, she was not surprised to see more parked cars than usual, and she guessed that Noah was doing a brisk business in boat rentals. What did surprise her, after she had parked, was that several of the cars bore the names of area newspapers: the Portland *Herald,* the Augusta *Sentinel,* the Rockport *News.* Although Peggy had stopped answering her telephone, she assumed that some of the calls, at least, came from newspeople inquisitive about the race.

As Peggy crossed the pier she saw some men and women holding notepads, while others focused cameras. Most were engaging Noah Dodge in earnest conversation.

She gave Noah a small wave and saw him look in her direction without acknowledging her. She realized his inattentiveness was meant to spare her. The press people buttonholing Noah now had had no idea who she was when she'd walked past them. And she hoped they never would.

Free Spirit was waiting for her when she reached the floating dock. Peggy stepped into the boat, cast off, and quickly raised the sails. The wind was light today, and she knew it would take her longer to complete a circuit of the course.

Peggy sailed out across the harbor, through the channel, and past the Sawteeth. When she was well past the flashing buoy, she reached into the pocket of her shorts, took out a stopwatch, set it running, and headed toward Big Momma.

Arriving there soon after high tide, Peggy rounded it, then started eastward, toward gong buoy 4-CL. She checked her time and discovered that her first leg had been faster than she'd anticipated. But now the wind was squarely at *Free Spirit*'s stern, and with the spinnaker raised, it would be an easy, even boring, run to the next mark.

Peggy rounded gong buoy 4-CL and set her heading toward the finish line. Unless her boat or the admiral's had an unchallengeable lead on Saturday, this would be the leg in which the race was won or lost. Spurred on by the thought, she trimmed *Free Spirit's* sails and reset her heading, seeking every bit of speed her sailboat could give.

"CLAMS?" Joe asked.

"Deep-fried, with tartar sauce," the girl said. "The way you like them. I also brought some french fries."

Joe raised himself on his elbows and blinked. The heat had so fatigued him that after his practice session he had come back to his apartment and fallen asleep on the living-room couch. He had awakened to the sound of the screen door swinging back. When he opened his eyes, Sarah was standing in the doorway. She was dressed in a blue halter top and a short white skirt.

As Joe stared, she went on standing there, the sun at her back, a grease-stained paper bag and a bottle of rosé in her hands.

Joe moved to sit up on the couch. "What time is it?"

"Six o'clock. May I come in?"

"Of course."

Sarah stepped in and at once disappeared into the kitchen. Joe could hear the sound of a wine opener at work. When Sarah returned to the living room, she was carrying a glass of rosé in each hand. She handed one to Joe, then sat down beside him on the couch.

"Thanks," he said.

"I think it's the hottest day so far this summer," Sarah said. "That's why I got us chilled wine." She sipped from her glass.

"Listen, let me see if there's an electric fan around."

Sarah shook her head. "I'm fine. After the frigid winters we have, real Mainers never complain about spending a day or two in the heat."

Joe was amused at her choice of words, but didn't say so. "Well," he said, "did you pick up any further tidbits in Portland about clams that I should know?"

"Nothing, unless you plan to become a marine biologist. But I did come across some research about their hearts."

"Really? You mean clams have hearts, too?"

"Why shouldn't they?"

"Oh, they should, by all means. Especially if they have feelings, like you said. In fact, it makes them seem almost romantic. I can picture their tiny hearts going pitter-patter whenever they touch shells."

Sarah smiled. "You're teasing me again. But I don't mind."

"A couple of days ago you took offense at my clam jokes. Is this a whole new Sarah Dodge I'm seeing now?"

Her blue eyes were fixed on him. "Maybe," she answered.

"I tried to call you several times the last few days," Joe said. "You never returned the calls."

"Yes, I know. I guess I needed time to think," she said.

"And now you've thought?" he asked her.

"Yes." She sipped her wine. "So how did the sailing go today?"

"Very well. The old man's really getting into it."

"He's quite a person, isn't he? I mean, besides being sort of famous and all. Does he have a family?"

"Nope. He had one son, who was killed during the Vietnam War. His wife died of cancer a couple years ago. But you wouldn't know all that just to talk to him. Most of the time he seems on top of the world. And he's a good sailor. Still, I'm doing everything I can to help him win. Today I showed him a racing technique I developed at the Academy—the Marino maneuver. But I shouldn't be telling you this. Aren't you on the side of the opposition?"

"Peggy's a friend. But I'm trying to stay impartial."

Joe leaned forward on the couch. "Let me ask you another question. Why did you bring fried clams?"

"I thought you might be hungry. It's almost suppertime."

"But why clams? I got the idea you considered it a sacrilege to appreciate clams in anything but their natural state."

"Maybe I'm broadening my horizons," Sarah said, "and trying to understand the attitudes of other people, as you told me I should do."

"True. Well, why don't we have something to eat now."

Sarah stood up. "All right. I'll fix a plate of clams and french fries for you. But I'll just have the french fries. I haven't reached the point where I can eat the subject of my year's research. *Especially* deep-fried, with tartar sauce."

She turned and walked quickly to the kitchen.

Joe leaned back on the couch and closed his eyes. For the first time in a long time he realized that he was greatly puzzled. All this week Sarah had been absent from the boatyard. Yesterday he had been prepared to write off any hope of making headway with this girl.

And yet now, tonight, she'd shown up at his apartment unannounced and bearing *clams*. That proved she wasn't giving him the brush-off, as he'd thought.

Joe smiled to himself. In fact, she *likes* me.

Several minutes later they were sitting side by side again, Joe dabbing the fried clams into a small paper cup of tartar sauce and Sarah nibbling her french fries.

"I've got to hand it to you," Joe said finally. "You deserve a lot of credit."

"Why?"

"Because these clams are terrific."

Sarah turned, her blue eyes fixed on him once more. "Do you know why I came here tonight?" she asked him.

"Why?"

"Because the other night you told me that in order for anyone to make their life complete, they had to dare to live."

The blue eyes that still regarded him remained serene. Joe put his plate on a side table.

"All my life I've been afraid to take a chance on anything," Sarah said. "Until now."

Joe stretched an arm behind her, feeling her long blond hair. He gently began to stroke the nape of her neck.

"Is this also a Marino maneuver?" she asked quietly.

"One of many," Joe said. "One of many."

Two Days to Festival Day (6–5)

ON THURSDAY morning the admiral rose promptly at dawn. He had always been an early riser, but as the race approached, the less relaxed and confident he felt and the more fitful sleep became. Last night was no different. Until midnight he had tossed in bed with only a sheet over him.

He began to fix his breakfast, then found that he was out of coffee. The single egg remaining in the carton broke as he removed it. Even so, today he wasn't scheduled to meet Joe at the boatyard until the afternoon. He could get breakfast at a diner.

Thus half an hour later he slid onto a counter stool at Rocky's Roadside Rest, between two truckers on his right and a state trooper on his left. A mug of steaming coffee suddenly appeared before him. From the counterman the admiral requested two eggs scrambled, with sausages and toast.

The order seemed to come almost at once, and the admiral began to eat. It was not until he'd started on his second sausage that he became aware of voices rising from a booth behind him. "That's him. I'm sure it is."

Several moments later the admiral felt a large hand come down on his shoulder. When he turned, he found a squat man in his fifties grinning at him. The man was dressed in an orange sweatshirt.

"Hubert Wiggim," the man said. "Put her there." He grasped the admiral's hand and pumped it. "I know you. You're that admiral. Am I right, or am I right?"

"I'm Admiral Deering. Yes."

The man turned back to his booth. "It's him, Dot!" he shouted to a woman sitting there. "I'm right." He looked at the admiral again. "Come join us for a minute. I told my grandsons you was a navy hero. A damn living legend. They won't leave this place until they meet you."

With that, Hubert Wiggim picked up the admiral's coffee mug and carried it toward his booth. The admiral had no choice but to follow him. As he sat, he found himself face to face with a woman who looked like a female clone of Hubert Wiggim himself. She also wore an orange sweatshirt. Next to her were two small boys, both with prominent front teeth. Both were staring at him.

Hubert Wiggim made the introductions. "This is my wife, Dot. And these are our grandsons, Rod and Tod." He gestured to the admiral. "And this here is the famous admiral."

"Salute the admiral, boys," Mrs. Wiggim said. At once both boys attempted a salute. The admiral returned it.

Hubert Wiggim then stood up. "Dot, kids, atten*shun* and fall

546

out!" On command, his wife and grandsons stood and stepped into the aisle. "Now 'bout-face and forward march!"

The woman and the boys turned and headed toward the door. Wiggim remained standing at the booth. He looked down at the admiral and placed his hand over his heart. "Admiral, I just want to say, God bless America, God bless the U.S. Navy, and God bless you on Saturday!"

Several patrons turned and stared at them. "Thank you," muttered the admiral. Hubert Wiggim then marched toward the door.

The admiral checked his watch. Time flies, he thought. Back at his stool, he finished his breakfast, then signaled for his check.

One Day to Festival Day (6–6)

T. C. DABNEY had debated with himself before posting the day's odds. On Wednesday he had made them 6–5 in favor of the admiral. Now that it was Friday, Dabney felt he had no choice but to make them even. Those who'd observed the practice sessions of both racers had come back with stories of Peggy's skill and speed around the course. But the admiral looked just as good, they added. It was even-steven, the observers said.

To match the odds made sense for other reasons, too. It made the outcome of the race seem more uncertain, spurring increased betting. Also, it should put an end to the complaints of the women of Hasty Harbor, who throughout the week had scolded Dabney for siding with the admiral. So 6–6 it would be.

Yessiree, he told himself with satisfaction. Today the Hasty Harbor post office would be busier than it had ever been.

AT ABOUT nine that morning neither the admiral nor Joe was aware of the new odds. As they headed from the admiral's cabin to the boatyard the admiral spoke up. "I could have driven myself to the boatyard, you know."

"After what happened yesterday," Joe answered, "you need me to run interference for you."

The admiral grunted, and said nothing.

Early in the week only one or two reporters from small-town newspapers in the area had been waiting at the boatyard when the admiral arrived. Being gregarious, he had enjoyed chatting with them; he was even a bit flattered they had sought him out.

Then, yesterday, he'd been surrounded by a pack of noisy reporters and photographers, assaulting him with questions that were becoming more and more trivial and personal. When Joe had appeared several minutes later, it was all the two of them could do to get free, reach the safety of their boats, and sail to the river. So finally, last night, the admiral had decided he would do nothing more than wave and smile at the reporters and photographers, then get away from them as quickly as he could.

For most of the ride Joe had been silent. When he looked over at the admiral and began to speak at last, his face was serious.

"Sir, do you mind if I ask you a question?" he said.

The admiral looked curious. "No. Go ahead."

"Yesterday, when I got home after our practice, I found a letter from the navy telling me my request for a transfer to San Diego had been approved."

"Congratulations. San Diego is a fine facility. It shows the navy has its eye on you. You've accepted, I'm sure."

"No." Joe shook his head. "I mean, not yet."

The admiral studied him. "There's no problem, is there?"

"Not really, but—"

"Something personal, is that it? A young lady?"

"Yessir."

"Local?"

"Yes. We got together . . . several nights ago."

The admiral thought a moment. "You may believe you love this girl. But if you want to make the navy your career, just be aware of how difficult it's going to be if you *should* marry her *and* have to support a child."

Joe kept his focus on the road.

The admiral leaned his head back on the headrest and was silent, thinking. He said finally, "Of course, if I'd taken my own advice, I'd never have married the wonderful woman I did." He turned to Joe. "You're a bright young man, and any girl who loves you—and whom you choose to love—must be quite special."

"She is," Joe said, still looking at the road. "She is."

They drove on in silence. When they reached the junction of the state highway and River Road, the admiral saw for the first time the banner that hung across the intersection. It read:

HASTY HARBOR SUMMER FESTIVAL
SATURDAY, JULY 30
WELCOME ONE AND ALL!

For the first time the admiral felt his stomach tighten with anxiety in anticipation of the race.

SHORTLY after noon Peggy left her house, went down to the shore, and walked northward half a mile to a small protected cove. Extending into the cove was an unused dilapidated dock. For Peggy and *Free Spirit* the cove was perfect—a safe harbor in which to moor the sailboat, away from the press or the merely curious who had descended on the boatyard in the last few days. She stepped out cautiously onto the dock, boarded *Free Spirit*, and raised the sails. Maneuvering the boat, she made her way into the river.

As *Free Spirit* found the open water and her sails billowed out, Peggy studied the horizon. A mile off the starboard bow the jagged outline of Big Momma could be seen. Peggy and Sarah had agreed to meet there and begin their practice runs. In the two days that Sarah had raced against her in a second sailboat, Peggy had been glad to have the competition. And the girl was a proficient sailor. Several times she'd even beaten Peggy's time between the marks. Peggy knew her own mistakes had been the reason each time—an errant turn, a jib line that had fouled, a heading that had cost her time.

Even so, the rapport between them had been good. Each challenged the other as they sparred tack for tack, stealing one another's wind, then losing it, then stealing it again.

Tomorrow at this hour Peggy and the admiral would be battling each other on the first leg of the course. Until tomorrow, no other thoughts, no personal concerns should be permitted to distract her. Until tomorrow, all her concentration, all her efforts would be fused into a single goal: winning the race.

FRIDAY, JULY 29 (9 P.M.)—FINAL log entry of the sailboat *Invincible*. The lessons and the practice runs are over. Tomorrow is the race. I should probably say the BIG race. Unfortunately, what began as a small community event has become a so-called human-interest story that the media has magnified beyond all bounds. Shows how little real news there is in the summertime.

As for this morning's practice, Joe was very pleased. He says I've learned more about the art of sail racing in a week than most people do in a year's time. It just shows that you can teach an old dog new tricks.

The marine weather forecast for the race is perfect—wind from the west, about 15–20 knots, with an incoming tide. Tonight my head is full of all the racing techniques I've learned from Joe, plus some special tricks I might use to outfox my opponent, Miss Mc—

The admiral stopped writing.

My opponent. Just over a week ago she was someone whom I thought I might even be in love with, he admitted to himself. Now she is Miss McCoy, my opponent.

Looking out the window above the sink, he could see lights shining in the other cabins. Next door he could hear a man and woman laughing. The laughter gently quieted. The admiral took a sip of coffee, picked up the pen, and completed the name McCoy on the page.

He paused and then continued writing:

Since this is my last entry, I will add a word or two about myself and why I am participating in this race. Of course, once committed, I was too determined—or stubborn—to back out. But there's another reason.

I am in my seventies. With my seniority I should be content to settle for old age. But old age is something that happens to my friends, not me. It's always been five years ahead of me. And this I know about myself: I still have too much zest for life, but nobody to share it with. I have too much love to give, but nobody to give it to. Last week I thought—I still think—Peggy might have been that person. Now she is Miss McCoy. My opponent.

The admiral set aside the pen and slowly closed the logbook.

*F*ESTIVAL *DAY!* T. C. Dabney wrote the words across the black-board of his store at dawn.

Precisely at nine o'clock, in front of the Hasty Harbor Fire Station #1, the drum major of the Peninsula Regional High School marching band blew his whistle, and the festival parade began. Behind was the twenty-member band—in their blue-and-gold uniforms—flanked by two majorettes twirling red-white-and-blue batons. They were followed by the community's lone fire engine. Behind it came a white Rambler convertible, driven by the president of the Hasty Harbor Lobstermen's Association. At the top of the back seat sat the two other officers of the association, jovially waving live lobsters at the crowd. Walking gamely in their wake were the dozen women of the Ladies Auxiliary and a smattering of legionnaires, Boy Scouts, and Girl Scouts. Bringing up the rear came Jimmy Smiley's garbage truck, festooned with multicolored crepe paper.

Along the parade route to T. C. Dabney's Store and back, dozens of people stood or sat in camp chairs watching the paraders.

Peggy McCoy herself was not among the celebrants. She had awakened early, tossed some bread to Captain Bligh, then fixed her breakfast while she listened to the marine weather forecast. The day was blue and bright; already a breeze was building from the west and was expected to reach twenty knots by race time.

As for the race committee's recommendation that the competitors "affect attire suitable to the event," Peggy had already chosen her outfit: a pair of navy blue shorts and a simple white T-shirt. But certainly she'd bring along her sailor hat.

She gazed out the kitchen window. Sunlight sparkled off the surface of the water, and a few boats were visible. Last night she had given *Free Spirit's* sails a good rinsing, and the large white Dacron triangles now lay stretched out across the lawn, drying in the sun. They would be filled with wind several hours from now. And depending on how skillfully she played them, they would carry her and *Free Spirit* to victory or—

No, she would not even think the other word.

AT EXACTLY THE SAME MOMENT the admiral peered at the navigational chart spread out across the table in his cabin. The experience reminded him of the days when he had played football at Annapolis. Before each game he would pore over the playbook, studying the diagrams and running them in his imagination.

The admiral quickly reviewed the basic sailing tactics that he planned to use, plus several tricks that Joe had taught him. Finally he made a fist and banged it squarely at the center of the chart. "All right, Deering!" He remembered the words of his football coach so many years ago: "Get out there! And let's see if you have the stuff it takes to win!"

PEGGY gripped the door handle of the police cruiser as it turned onto River Road. The whole thing was silly and unnecessary, she thought—a waste of public money. Shortly before she was to leave her house, a state police car had appeared in her driveway. The pleasant young officer who drove it had informed her he'd been sent to escort her into Hasty Harbor. Peggy had protested. If there were crowds—and he insisted that there were—she'd simply ignore them and go on her way.

But as the car started downward toward the village and the pier, Peggy understood the officer's concern. Parked next to T. C. Dabney's Store was the trailer of an Augusta television station. Other cars identified by press signs on their dashboards were parked on both sides of the turnaround. But it was the number of spectators that surprised her most. Already some people along the road had spotted her, and they now cheered and waved as she passed.

The officer stopped the car at the entrance to the pier. Another officer, standing nearby, stepped forward and opened Peggy's door.

"Morning, ma'am," he told her.

Peggy stepped out of the car, and the applause and shouts ignited, rising to a roar. She took a deep breath, pushed her hat down firmly on her head, and walked slowly to the pier.

Less than a minute later two dark blue sedans, both bearing the insignia of the U.S. Navy, also approached. In the lead car were four young naval officers. In the second car, with Ensign Joe Marino at the wheel, came Rear Admiral Charles Deering.

As the two navy cars drew up to the pier's entrance the crowds again broke into applause and cheers.

The admiral looked over at Joe. "I guess this is the moment of truth, isn't it?" He gave the young man a nervous smile.

Joe reached out a hand. "Good luck."

The admiral grasped Joe's hand. "Thank you. Thank you for a lot of things." He stepped out of the car.

Escorted by a policeman and the four naval officers, the admiral walked onto the pier.

As SHE stood before them, Peggy thought the three men of the race committee looked ridiculous. It was the only time she could remember seeing Cabot Lodge dressed in a jacket or, for that matter, a clean shirt and tie. But, like the other two, he was outfitted today in white linen slacks and a blue blazer. The sight of the three men helped relieve some of the tension she felt.

Able Fenstermacher greeted her. "Hi, Peggy. See you made it through the crowds." He looked past her at the entrance to the pier. "Appears the admiral himself has just arrived."

Peggy heard an ovation for the admiral, but didn't turn around. Instead, she put her hands together and looked down. She had the sense of panic a bride must feel after she has been escorted to the altar and is left standing alone waiting for the groom.

At least her wait wasn't long. The admiral appeared beside her. She nodded to him briefly and saw that he was dressed in white slacks and a simple white short-sleeved shirt. He returned the nod, then shook hands with the members of the race committee as cameras clicked around them.

"First off," Able said, "we'll have a little prayer from Reverend Clapp so as to bless this race we are about to have."

Reverend Clapp stepped forward from a gathering of townspeople on the pier. He opened his Bible and read from it in brisk, dramatic bursts. Then he stepped back into the crowd.

"Okay, now," Able said to Peggy and the admiral. "Us three committeemen will get into Cabot's scalloper *Persephone,* and you two follow us into the river in your sailboats. And may the best man—the best sailor—win."

"How about a handshake between racers?" someone shouted from the crowd.

"Guess we ought to. How about it?" Able asked them.

The admiral took Peggy's hand. He looked down at her and smiled. "Good luck, Peggy."

She felt her hand tremble slightly. "Good luck to you."

The crowd broke into sustained applause.

"Enough," Able whispered to them. "Let's get going."

WITH *Free Spirit* and the *Invincible* astern of the committee boat and with a flotilla of boats in their wake, the passage to the starting line began.

As Peggy crossed the harbor she cast her eyes over the spectator fleet that was accompanying them. Some of the larger runabouts were obviously occupied by members of the press. As *Free Spirit* moved into the river, Peggy could see more boats—many more, in fact.

But it was not until she passed the Sawteeth that their numbers were apparent. There were small rowboats and huge windjammers, canoes and cabin cruisers, windsurfers and catboats. Even Link Mallott, the lobsterman, hard-shelled as he was, had relinquished half a day of work to watch the race.

Peggy's watch showed six minutes to twelve. She swung the tiller and began to sail toward the area where she could begin her opening run at the starting line. Fifty yards beyond the flashing buoy bobbed an orange float. It had been placed there yesterday, and between it and the buoy was the imaginary line that marked the start and finish of the race.

A short time later there was a loud bang. Peggy looked at the committee boat and saw Able with the starter's pistol held in the air. The five-minute warning had been given.

Because the starting line was reasonably broad, both boats could cross it without one blanketing the other's wind. In any case, Peggy chose to sail closer to the flashing buoy than to the orange float. In a stretch of open water, with a stiff breeze blowing from the west, Peggy put *Free Spirit* through some practice tacks and jibes. As she did, she watched the sails and pulled them taut—any slackness could cost her dearly once the race began.

She looked over in the direction of the *Invincible*. The admiral was also making small adjustments in his sails. He had obviously decided to put his boat nearer to the float for the start.

Another pistol shot rang out. One minute.

Peggy took a deep breath. Then she swung *Free Spirit*'s bow around and headed toward the starting line.

She gave the hull a pat. "Come on, old girl. Let's show everyone what we can do."

The starting line was rushing toward her now.

The pistol fired.

The horns and whistles of the spectator boats erupted with a din that filled the river and surrounding hills.

The race was under way.

IN THE wheelhouses of several commercial fishing boats—the *Bluebonnet, Jumping Jack, Porpoiser*, and *Kathy's Pride*—the radios crackled. Their skippers were providing continuous reports on the race for a Brunswick radio station.

"*Jumping Jack*, this is *Bluebonnet*. Looks like the admiral's out front. What'd you see? Over."

"Looks like he is, *Blue*. He caught a wind gust as he crossed the line."

THE admiral grinned broadly. He hoped Joe had seen the way the *Invincible* had hit the starting line. Those hours of practice had paid off. He didn't lead by much, he guessed—only a few seconds. But it gave him confidence that he *was* a skillful sailor.

"DAMN!" Peggy swore. The admiral had crossed the line first and was ahead.

She told herself, Don't panic. Take it easy. It's a long race. What's a couple of seconds at the starting line?

Peggy gave *Free Spirit* another pat of confidence and pointed the boat closer to the wind. Pulling on the tiller hard, she tacked, but in the opposite direction from the one the admiral was expecting, and at once found a burst of speed. The move surprised the admiral. Reacting, he abruptly tacked in an attempt to cover her.

He was too late. Increasing her speed further, Peggy pulled ahead of him and seized the lead.

What followed for exactly half an hour was a tacking duel. Several times the *Invincible* attempted to outtack *Free Spirit*, and failed. For every move the admiral made, Peggy countered it.

After tacking for what seemed the hundredth time, the admiral looked seaward. Ahead he saw Big Momma. Although Peggy had increased her lead to two boat lengths, the admiral suspected she would have to change her heading soon if she intended sailing close around the rock. His angle of approach was better. He could probably even catch her as she went around. It was worth a try.

He aimed almost directly for the rock.

"PORPOISER, this is *Jumping Jack*. What do you see? Over."

"This is *Porpoiser, Jack*. I can see both sailboats closin' on Big Momma fast. *Free Spirit*'s still ahead, but the *Invincible* is comin'! Peggy sees him! He's still comin'! . . . He's inside! . . . He's caught her now. The *Invincible* has got the lead!"

I DID it! The admiral wiped his eyes and looked back at *Free Spirit*. It had been a daring move: he'd cut inside of Peggy at Big Momma, skirting the rock so closely that the *Invincible* and he were drenched as a wave broke over the rock.

Forget the self-congratulations, he immediately told himself. Astern of him, Peggy had begun to raise her spinnaker for the second leg. He'd do the same. He set the tiller and mainsail, and scrambled forward to raise his own large red-white-and-blue sail.

With both huge spinnakers now ballooning out in front of them, the two sailboats sped toward gong buoy 4-CL.

WELL, well, he certainly surprised you at Big Momma, didn't he? Peggy admitted to herself that his bravado at the rock was a gutsy move. A sudden wind shift, and he'd have grazed the rock, doing damage to his boat, or worse.

For some minutes *Free Spirit* and the *Invincible* sailed parallel to one another, Peggy's boat a length behind the admiral's and about twenty feet off to his right.

Peggy adjusted her position at the cockpit rail. She heard a small burst of applause from the spectator boats she was now passing. When she looked over, she saw a pair of six-meter sailboats at anchor. What surprised her was that the anemometers atop their masts were spinning furiously. It meant one thing: a stronger breeze was blowing along the outside of the course.

At once Peggy eased *Free Spirit* farther to the outside—and felt the extra push the wind had given her. Ahead, the admiral seemed ignorant of what she'd done.

Ignorance is bliss, thought Peggy.

"*Kathy's Pride*, this is *Porpoiser*. Looks like they're comin' up on the gong buoy. Over to you, *K.P.*"

"*Porpoiser*, this is *K.P.* I can't see who's leadin', though. The admiral, I think. Now Peggy's comin' up on the outside. They're comin' closer! . . . Closer! . . . Peggy's pulled up! They're dead even as they go around the mark! . . . They're in the home stretch now! Their spinnakers are droppin' like old maids' bloomers!"

Peggy looked across her shoulder and allowed herself a smile. Soon after both sailboats had rounded the gong buoy, *Free Spirit* had begun to edge ahead. At first her lead was imperceptible, in part because the *Invincible* had gone far to the outside of the course to keep from being caught in her wind shadow. But by the time the two of them were halfway down the final leg, Peggy knew it would be difficult to take the lead away from her. And if his constant glances in the direction of her boat meant anything, the admiral knew it, too.

The admiral's situation was grim. He had attempted a variety of tacks and other actions to increase his speed or at least to prevent *Free Spirit* from making it a runaway. But with two miles remaining in the race, Peggy held the lead now by as much as twenty feet, and she was not about to give it up.

Faintly, in the distance, he could see what he assumed to be the finish line. Boats were clustered around it, and in one of them, awaiting his return, he knew would be Joe Marino.

Joe! It came to him. Of course! Why hadn't he thought of it before? The trick Joe used on him in practice—the Marino maneuver. If there was a time to try it, it was now.

Peggy, he observed, was concentrating on the run for home. Trailing her as closely as he could, he waited for sufficient leeway on the inside of the course. He found it.

Now! He pulled the tiller fiercely. At once the *Invincible* swung away sharply from the line both were sailing, passing just behind *Free Spirit*'s stern, and rocketed toward the spectator boats beside the course. As skippers and their passengers gasped and scrambled to avoid a collision, the admiral jibed now and headed straight for Peggy's boat.

558

The crowd shrieked. Peggy turned and saw him coming, and instinctively fell off to keep from being hit.

The *Invincible*, however, cut back in the opposite direction and resumed her course, leading by a boat length on the windward side. A roar from the crowd followed.

The admiral finally allowed himself a breath—and looked ahead.

Three hundred yards away was the finish line.

"*BLUEBONNET* to *Jumping Jack*. They're coming!"

"That they are, *Blue!* Two hundred yards, and the *Invincible* is leadin' by a length! *Free Spirit's* tryin'! Peggy's pullin' up her centerboard and pointin' sharper to the wind. And she's gettin' speed! . . . A hundred yards to go! Both boats are bow to bow! . . . Seventy-five yards! . . . Sixty yards! . . ."

THE noise that surrounded them was rising to a crescendo. For a moment sea spray clouded Peggy's vision. The boats around the finish line were no more than a blurry mass.

Above the shouting of the crowd the admiral heard nothing, but he felt the thud—the tiller jolted in his hand. He saw it suddenly: a fragment of a fishnet that was held fast to his rudder. Frantically he reached down to remove it, but the object disappeared as mysteriously as it had come.

"SHE's done it!"

THERE was a pistol shot and a tumultuous reaction from the crowd. *Free Spirit* had won the Hasty Harbor Cup.

As Peggy crossed the finish line she saw the committee boat swing toward the harbor entrance. At the same time Able Fenstermacher beckoned to her. Obediently Peggy came about and slipped in behind the committee boat.

A chorus of horns, whistles, cheers, and applause continued as *Free Spirit* slowly made her way past the spectator fleet. Occasionally Peggy raised her hand in brief acknowledgment.

But what appeared as diffidence or modesty on her part masked the exuberance she felt. She had won.

Peggy turned around. The admiral was at the tiller of the *Invincible,* trailing in her wake by thirty yards. She waved; he nodded, and waved as well. Above the noise of the crowd he called, "Congratulations."

"Thank you," Peggy answered.

WHEN the shuffle of photographers on the pier had ended and the crowd had quieted sufficiently, Able stepped forward. "On behalf of the race committee of the Hasty Harbor Summer Festival," he announced, "I hereby present this cup to the winner of this year's sailing race—Miss Peggy McCoy."

He thrust the cup at Peggy as the crowd broke into applause.

"Speech! Speech!" someone called.

"I . . . " Peggy started, then stopped.

"Louder!" people shouted.

"I—I just want to say thanks to everybody who believed in me and who thought I could win. I had a good boat and a good friend who helped me." Briefly she saw Sarah beaming in the crowd. "And thanks, too, to Admiral Deering. He gave me a good run." She looked at the admiral, then looked away. "Anyway, I'm not used to making speeches. So I guess that's it."

There was polite applause.

"Admiral?" said Able. "Anything you'd like to say?"

The admiral nodded. "While I was out there, a quotation came to mind: 'The race is to the swift.' Well, I also had a good boat, and a good friend to help me." He surveyed the crowd, but Joe was nowhere to be seen. He went on. "But neither I nor my boat was swift enough. I congratulate a fine sailor—Miss McCoy."

He extended a hand toward Peggy; she accepted it, and they shook hands as cameras clicked.

"Aren't you going to kiss her?" someone shouted.

"May I?" he asked Peggy.

"Yes!" the crowd shouted in a body.

"I guess so," Peggy answered.

Gently he took both her hands in his. Then he kissed her lightly on the cheek.

There were hoots and whistles from the crowd, and Able clapped his hands. "Okay. The ceremony's over," he said firmly.

As THE admiral made his way through the crowd and approached the navy car, he saw Joe, his arms folded on his chest. Joe opened the door for him, then went around and slipped in on the driver's side.

He started the car. "What *happened?*" He looked at the admiral. "I was watching. You slowed down when you could've won! Something happened out there. Tell me what it was."

Joe put the car in gear and pulled out.

The admiral said, "Several things. Principal among them is that Miss McCoy *is* an excellent sailor."

"Agreed. But so are you," Joe said.

The admiral suddenly felt weary. He leaned back against the headrest of the seat and watched the scenery pass by.

"Joe," he began again, "both of us are navy men. Officers and gentlemen. What I am about to tell you goes no further than this car. I fouled on a fishnet. It caught the rudder."

"What? We'll file a protest! You should have won!"

"We'll do nothing of the sort. The race is over. Done."

Joe drove along the road in silence.

"I'm sorry," he said finally. "I'm sorry I got mad."

The admiral looked over. "As my coach and trainer, you're right to be upset."

"Sir, this may sound funny, but you're one of the best men I've ever met."

The admiral shrugged and gave a little sign as if to dismiss the remark. "I tried my best, at least." He thought for several moments. "As it is, the race was only the first of today's challenges. The second comes tonight. And it may be a lot tougher for me than the race was."

11

WHAT the residents of Hasty Harbor called a beach was not what someone other than a native of Maine would think of as a beach at all. Along the water's edge there was a narrow margin of sand. But it gave way almost at once to long horizontal slabs of granite that rose tierlike to a crumbling macadam parking lot.

For the purposes of the clambake and supper, nonetheless, the smooth flat rocks nearest to the sand provided secure footing for the tables of food that had been set up and around which fussed a dozen or so members of the Ladies Auxiliary. Some members' husbands had also been pressed into service, tending to the steaming caldrons that contained the lobsters and to the barbecues that were now roasting open clams and ears of corn.

Peggy arrived at the beach parking lot about six thirty, parked her Pinto, and, carrying her boat cushion, got in line with those already moving toward the stairway leading to the beach. Among the townspeople who noticed her, most waved or called out their congratulations. Peggy did her best to thank them, and smiled.

At the top of the stairway, Peggy suddenly felt someone touch her elbow. She turned and saw it was the admiral.

"Good evening," he said. "Looks like quite a little shindig they've got going. Is it like this for every summer festival?"

"I don't know," Peggy said. "I haven't been to one of these in years."

There was an awkward pause, as if neither of them quite knew what to say next.

"Yoo-hoo, my dear! Congratulations!" a voice from behind now called out.

It was Mrs. Doberman. Beside her, randy octogenarian Mr. Fogerty beamed happily and carried a beach blanket. As she passed Peggy and the admiral Mrs. Doberman gave Peggy a broad wink that said, You found your man; I've found mine, before she seized Mr. Fogerty's free hand and started down the stairs.

After a moment the admiral said to Peggy, "Do you plan to be with your friends?"

"No. I'm alone."

"Good," he said. "I mean, it's not good you're alone. It's good you're here. But I'm alone, too. Shall we dine together?"

"Yes, I guess. That's fine."

"Fine," he hastened to say. "You get us a place to sit, and I'll report to the chow line. Any idea where you'd like to sit?"

Peggy pointed to a spot high on the rocks. "How about there?"

"In the box seats. All right. I'll look for you there."

Peggy turned and began making her way to the spot she had suggested. Arriving there, she placed her cushion on the flat expanse of rock and sat. She looked at the activity below her. The admiral was right. It was like being in the box seats of a theater— she, a witness to the drama, watching with interest but avoiding participation. That's the story of my life, she thought.

The declining sun had begun to cast long shadows over the rocks. The tables of food and the long line of people near them were bathed in an amber glow.

Peggy watched as the admiral, bearing two large paper plates, stepped up to the tables and was served something from that caldron, this salad bowl, that breadbasket.

563

Soon he was out of the line and making his way up again.

Puffing, he came to her and handed her a plate. He reached into his shirt pocket and withdrew some plastic forks and knives, then pulled out a wad of paper napkins from a trouser pocket. He gave several to Peggy. "I brought plenty of these for the lobster."

Peggy smiled, then pointed to a flat space on the rock beside her. As the admiral sat down, she took a fork and began eating from her plate. "This is good potato salad," she said.

"Good." The admiral looked from her to his own plate. "So," he said, "how do you feel now that the race is over?"

"Relieved," she answered. "Once more I'm a totally anonymous person, I'm glad to say."

"Then, the Hasty Harbor Cup is the last award your trophy case will hold?"

"Hardly," Peggy said. "I'll probably plant petunias in it."

They returned to their dinners. The sunlight was continuing to fade as Peggy looked over at him. "May I ask you something?"

"Certainly. What is it?"

"At the end of the race, before you crossed the finish line, you slowed down. Why?"

"One of those freakish things," he said. "I lost the wind."

"But you were windward. I was close, and I didn't lose it."

He gave an open-handed gesture. "Things like that can happen when you sail. It just happened to me at the wrong time."

"I mean, you didn't let me win deliberately?"

He shook his head. "You won the race on your abilities. And believe me, I am not about to seek a rematch."

"Good," Peggy said. "I don't think I could go through it again."

JOE did not want to be here. Not sitting in the middle of a hundred or more Hasty Harbor citizens as they watched fireworks. Tonight Joe wanted to avoid fireworks of any kind.

Where would he prefer to be? He wasn't sure. Maybe at an out-of-the-way local restaurant, where the two of them could talk.

But it was Sarah who had wanted to come here.

She led the way. Under her arm she carried a blanket. They approached the food tables, and each took a plate.

"I'm not really hungry," Sarah told him. "What about you?"

"I'll admit I am," Joe said. "I couldn't eat before the race."

"Maybe I'll just have the shortcake," Sarah said.

Joe took her plate. "Why don't I grab the food for us."

Afterward they started along the beach, with Sarah several steps ahead. For the first hundred yards they passed crowds of people, some standing in groups and some seated on the sand. But as they continued, the number of spectators thinned rapidly.

Finally Sarah turned away from the water and led them into a small protected area among high boulders. She spread the blanket out on the sand and sat down. As Joe approached, she patted a space next to her, and he sat and handed her a plate.

They began to eat, with little conversation between them. When she was done, Sarah put aside her plate and stared in the direction of the water. By now the afterglow of the sunset had disappeared, and only the sliver of a waning moon was reflected on the surface of the sea. Beyond them, in the darkness, the waves tumbled against the shore.

"When do you go back to college?" Joe asked.

"In a month. I plan to do a lot of things my senior year."

"That's the spirit," Joe said cheerfully. "Seize the day. Live life to the fullest. Gather rosebuds while you can."

Sarah lay back on the blanket and put her hands behind her head. "There are so many stars tonight," she said, looking up to where the boulders parted to display a star-filled sky.

Joe sat forward. "You're right. Look at them. There's the constellation Andromeda. And the Dippers, of course." Joe felt Sarah's hand touching his. "That's Cassiopeia."

He paused, then turned to her. "Sarah," he said, "something happened that I was going to tell you about. A couple of months ago, before we met, I asked the navy for a transfer. It came through the other day. It's to San Diego, and I accepted it. It's a great chance for advancement."

Sarah sat up. "When do you leave?" she asked him quietly.

"Soon. In a few days."

"I understand." She stood up slowly and began walking away from him in the direction of the beach.

Joe also stood. He wanted to go after her to tell her that he had changed his mind, that he would stay.

But he did not.

RED, white, and blue Roman candles burst one after another, and skyrockets showered down. The spectators applauded.

The admiral was staring up. "They certainly bring back some memories, these fireworks," he said to Peggy.

"The big displays are in Portland, generally," Peggy said. "Or in Old Orchard Beach."

"You love Maine, don't you?" he asked.

"Yes. I can't think of living anywhere else."

"What about Maryland?"

She looked at him. "I don't know. I've never lived there."

"Would you like to?"

"I—I don't know," she stammered.

"The race is over," the admiral said. "But we're still the people we were before the race. Let's begin again. Peggy, when my wife died, I thought that all that Grace and I had shared could never be replaced. And it can't. I know that. But I've learned since then that my own life *isn't* over and that I can begin with someone else. Someone such as you."

He paused, expecting a reaction from her. There was none. Peggy sat rigidly beside him looking toward the sky. Now an orange flare arced upward. Around them the crowd gasped at the bright foliating light that rained down in golden sparks.

"Damn it, Peggy. I won't beat around the bush." He thrust a hand into his trouser pocket and produced a small object, which he held out in her direction. "I want you to have this," he said. "It's my class ring from the Academy. I gave it to Grace the night we were engaged. I want you to have it now."

She spoke softly, without discernible emotion. "Are you asking me to marry you?"

"Yes, I guess I am. Will you?"

"No." Peggy shook her head.

Her response flustered him. "Well, I know it comes as a surprise, but think about it."

"I've thought about it, Charles. Since the day we met, I've thought about it. You're the most wonderful man I've known in years. If I were to marry anyone, it would be you. But you, this— it's all so sudden. Maybe if we'd had more time."

"Yes, true. But at my age I can't afford the luxury of time."

In the darkness Peggy took his hand. "I can't marry you."

"Why can't you?"

"Ghosts. That's one reason."

"You mean that flier you were engaged to years ago?"

"Yes."

"Ghosts can be exorcised. Sometimes they have to be, or else they'll hold you captive."

Peggy said, "I'm comfortable with my life. Call it habit. The fact is that I've lived alone so long I'm used to it. I am a single woman. I've made a virtue of my singularity. And at my age I'm not about to change."

"People can change their lives at any age," he said. "If they want to. Is it that you can't? Or are you afraid to try?"

She thought for several moments. "Maybe that, too. Maybe I'm afraid to change a lot of things."

"When I visited your house the first time," the admiral said, "I saw a little prayer you had hanging in a frame on the wall."

" 'Dear Lord,' " she recited, " 'watch over me. The sea is so vast and my boat is so small.' "

"That says it, doesn't it? You've always sailed within sight of shore, afraid of facing those vast seas. Because out there, beyond the beacons and the buoys, it's uncharted waters. Out there, wind and storms and God knows what may await you and your little boat. But you know as well as I do that the sea can also be calm and bright and beautiful, its horizons limitless. Peggy, I am asking you to marry me."

He was about to go on when a kaleidoscope of brilliant colors filled the heavens, and the rocks beneath them shook. One after another the filaments of light from the fireworks fell seaward, until the last spark was extinguished, the last echo gone.

There was a moment's silence. Then, as one, the crowd erupted in a roar of cheers and applause.

Soon lights from flashlights began winking across the rocks. Around them people were dispersing quickly.

Peggy said at last, "We better go."

She picked up her boat cushion. Then, without a word, they followed the departing crowd.

When they reached the parking lot, it was nearly empty.

He was about to ask her again to marry him. He knew, however, it would do no good.

"Well," he began finally, "circumstances being what they are, I'll probably leave tomorrow for Maryland. Good-bye, Peggy."

He embraced her gently and felt her arms encircle him. Then he touched her wet face and kissed her lips.

"Peggy—"

"Please, don't say any more. Good-bye, Charles."

"Good-bye."

Slowly he released her.

12

THE sea gull stood thoughtfully on the planks of the deck. He lowered his head and poked at a scrap of blackened toast.

"Sorry about the burned toast, Bligh," Peggy said. "I'm not functioning too well this morning."

As if in answer, the bird uttered a loud squawk.

"Go easy, Bligh. I could use a little quiet. And some tender loving care."

The bird pecked at some large crumbs.

"I have a confession to make, Bligh," she said. "I may have lost my best chance at something that will never come my way again. From now on you'll be the only one who I'll share my breakfast with. Just two old birds together."

Captain Bligh observed her pensively.

"Now that the race is history," she said, "I can show my face in Hasty Harbor. I might even buy some things at Dabney's Store. I wonder how much the old crook pocketed on me and the admiral. You never met the admiral, Bligh. He was a nice man. A wonderful man. And I have a feeling that I made a terrible mistake." She drew a breath. "In any case, this afternoon I'll go sailing. This afternoon it will be just me and my little boat."

Peggy tossed the last of the toast pieces onto the deck.

"That's it for breakfast, Captain. But come back for supper tonight. I thought I'd do a frozen pizza. It's a brand you like. Now shoo. Scram. I've got work to do."

She clapped her hands. The sea gull blinked and, with a beat of wings, lifted from the deck and headed seaward, toward the sun.

AT TEN thirty that morning Sarah Dodge crossed the mud flats of Lonely Point carrying a short clam rake, a bucket, and a metal scoop. She stepped around some isolated pools of seawater and knelt down on the wet sand. She was about to begin digging when she heard a sound.

Her back was to the path she had just traveled, and along it she could hear dry rushes snapping underfoot.

She turned. Joe stood at the edge of the flats.

"How are you?" he asked.

"Okay."

Joe started toward her but stopped several feet away. "Last night after you left, I walked up and down the beach looking for you. I still had something to tell you."

"I thought you told me everything before I left."

"Not quite," Joe said, shifting awkwardly. "Sarah, I want us to be together. So, having said that, I guess I ought to go. I promised the admiral I'd drive him to the airport."

He hesitated, then turned and started toward the path among the reeds, his footprints leaving soft impressions in the sand.

"Joe?"

He stopped and looked back at her.

"When you get to San Diego, will you send me your address?"

"Sure. If you'd like."

"Good-bye." Sarah raised her hand to wave. But he had disappeared through the reeds.

When she later returned to her car, she found Clementine Clam lying on the driver's seat. Between the Styrofoam shells of the toy was a note:

Dear Sarah,
    I hope you will take care of me now that Joe is gone.
                                        Love,
                                            Clementine
P.S. I know that clams have hearts. But I wish I didn't, because
my heart is as sad as Joe's is now.

Sarah picked up the clam and held it close to her. "So is mine,
Clementine," she whispered. "So is mine."

THE admiral was waiting outside the car-rental office in Whitby.
Joe parked the car, walked around to the trunk, and unlocked it.
    The admiral lifted his suitcases one by one and placed them
inside. "Would you believe," he told Joe, "that when I arrived
several weeks ago, I had only one suitcase? After I decided to
stay, I bought more things and needed more suitcases."
    Once they were both in the car, they drove through the streets
of Whitby, neither man speaking. At last Joe turned onto the ramp
to the main highway and eased into the traffic.
    They had not traveled far when the admiral noticed a sign atop
a gray commercial building: SPEND TIME IN WHITBY, MAINE, AND
YOU'LL HAVE MEMORIES TO LAST A LIFETIME! The admiral grunted.
'He stared out his window at the occasional small lakes and at
the surrounding stands of firs and hemlocks. He realized that this
was very likely the last time in his life he would see Maine.
    "Nice day, isn't it?" Joe asked to break the silence.
    "What? Oh, yes, lovely," the admiral answered.
    Joe looked at him a moment. "It's too bad you're not staying
one more day. It looks like a great day for a sail."
    "I can think of someone who will be out there."
    They drove on, once again in silence. As they were approach-
ing Freeport, Joe said, "I hope it's okay with you if I don't stay at
the airport to see you off. I'm due back at the shipyard at two."
    "Not at all. I appreciate your taking me."
    "There's a cruiser going out on a sea trial this afternoon," Joe
added as an explanation. "And I've been asked to go along."
    Traffic had increased substantially. But the admiral didn't notice.
Instead, he smiled. "I remember a story," he began. "It con-

cerns a PT boat during the Battle of Midway, one of the fiercest battles of the war. This navy torpedo boat was zipping around firing everything it had. The battle went on for three days, and as darkness fell on the third day the PT boat captain found himself less than a mile from a Japanese battleship. He also discovered he had only one torpedo left."

"So what happened?"

"Ah, that's the best part of the story. The captain knew the wisest thing to do would be to turn around and run back to the safety of the U.S. fleet. Instead, he faced that battleship and let go his last torpedo. It struck the ship directly in her powder magazine, and she exploded. Later, when they acclaimed him as a hero, the skipper simply said, 'I did what any navy man would do. I had one shot left, and I took it.'"

"That's quite a story," Joe agreed.

"Turn the car around," the admiral requested.

"I beg your pardon?"

"Turn around and take me to the shipworks. I have one shot left," the admiral announced, "and I am going to take it."

AT TWO thirty in the afternoon on the last day of July, *Free Spirit* sailed out of Hasty Harbor. When the sailboat was clear of the Sawteeth rocks, Peggy came about and set her heading south in the direction of Big Momma. Her course, she realized, was much the same as it had been yesterday.

But, unlike yesterday, there were no sounds of boat horns and cheers—only the keening cries of gulls and the lapping of the waves against *Free Spirit*'s hull.

Peggy pushed her sailor hat down firmly on her head.

A mile or so farther on, the flagpole and the flags in front of her house gradually emerged. It was all familiar. The sea, the sky, the outline of the shore—they were exactly as they had always been. Since that day when she had had the confrontation with the navy ship, a great deal had happened. But how much had changed? Nothing, really. Today, as she'd done for countless summers past, she'd set her course and trimmed her sails, and they were once more carrying her on the heading she had sought.

But when Peggy tried to make a small adjustment, she discovered that the line was slack. *Free Spirit* had begun to slow. Peggy glanced around her. A hundred yards ahead she could see waves scalloping the surface; small patches of spume rose and fell. But where *Free Spirit* drifted helplessly, the sea was smooth as glass.

Peggy was becalmed.

She went forward and found the small paddle she had stowed near the bow. She peered down at the surface of the sea, and with a start she saw her own reflection staring back at her. It was at that moment that Peggy realized the truth. Something had changed.

She had.

What she saw mirrored in her face was fear.

He had asked her last night if she was afraid. Peggy knew she was. Afraid of time. Afraid of age. Afraid to change. Afraid to try.

Peggy thrust the paddle down into the water and paddled rapidly. She could not sail anymore today.

Slowly the sailboat began to turn. She paddled harder. The boat continued turning. Finally, her arms aching, she paused. Unsure of what direction she was pointed in, Peggy raised her head—and could not believe the sight she saw.

Less than a mile from her was a large navy ship—a cruiser—moving slowly but relentlessly in her direction.

Her alarm grew as the ship came toward her, the noise of the engines growing louder, waves arcing upward at the prow. Peggy paddled furiously, but it did little good. The cruiser was a hundred yards away.

Then suddenly the cruiser slowed. "Commander McCoy! Now hear this!" The words rang out.

In shock, Peggy realized it was the voice of the admiral, standing at the cruiser's bow, bullhorn in his hand. Other naval officers surrounded him. Once more the bullhorn blared out across the water. "Miss McCoy! A few weeks ago in these same waters you and I met. I suspected I would find you here today."

Peggy stood up. At the same time she felt a breeze begin to stir. Slowly it was carrying *Free Spirit* in the direction of the ship.

"In a minute," the admiral went on, "the steps will be lowered on the starboard side. I will come down those steps."

He handed the bullhorn to the young ensign beside him. A short time later a set of portable steps swung out from the cruiser and lowered toward the water. As soon as they were in place, the admiral started down. When he reached the bottom step, he stopped and looked out at Peggy's boat.

Free Spirit was now near enough to the cruiser that the shadow of the large ship fell across the sailboat. Then a gentle swell lifted her and eased her broadside toward the admiral.

"Commander McCoy," he called down to her, "I request permission to board."

Peggy reached out and caught hold of the bottom step. She continued to regard the admiral with a look of incredulity.

"To repeat, Commander, I request—"

"Permission granted," Peggy said in a thin voice.

"Thank you," the admiral said. He stepped gingerly into the sailboat. "To begin with—"

"To begin with," Peggy said, "we'd better sit down, or your navy friends will have to rescue both of us."

He sat at once opposite the mast, while Peggy took her place astern beside the tiller.

Neither noticed as the steps were drawn up and the cruiser gradually withdrew. The wind began to fill out *Free Spirit*'s sails.

Peggy spoke first. "I didn't think I'd ever see you again."

"You almost didn't. But the fact is, there were many things I hoped to say last night and never got the chance. Blame it on the fireworks. It's virtually impossible to propose to a woman with skyrockets bursting overhead. Therefore, I've decided to stay in Maine for as long as it takes to get those things said. Perhaps we can sail together. I could even help you with your book."

"What book?"

"*Peggy's Book of Sailing.* Wasn't that the title?"

"I think that's what you called it," Peggy told him.

"What *we* called it," he corrected her. "We—you and I. You're still not used to any other form except the singular."

"I guess that's true."

"There was also a chapter in the book entitled 'Be Aware of Changing Conditions.' Do you remember?"

"Yes."

He leaned back on the cockpit railing and spread both his hands outward on the deck. "Be aware, Peggy," he repeated. "The conditions now are changing—*have* changed. Be aware."

Peggy realized she had held such a tight grip on the tiller that her hand was numb. She shifted it.

"Charles," she said to him at last, "you are, without a doubt, the most persistent man I have ever known."

"And *you* are the most stubborn woman *I* have ever known," he told her. "Excuse me. Strong-minded is a better term. And where in God's name were you going when the cruiser spotted you? You were paddling around in circles."

"I was becalmed."

"You looked it."

"I wanted to get back to Hasty Harbor."

"On that heading it would have taken you all day. By the way, there was another basic rule of sailing you pointed out to me the morning we had breakfast."

"Oh?"

"If you're going nowhere, you said, put some wind behind you, reset your sails, and change course." He leaned forward toward her. "Do you think you can do that, Peggy? Change your course?"

For a few moments Peggy held fast to the sail lines. Then she nodded. "Yes, I think I can. I'd like to try."

He took hold of the lines as well and helped to play them out. "Then let's try together, shall we? Ready about, Commander?"

"Ready about," Peggy said.

She eased the tiller over. The sails billowed forward, and *Free Spirit* began running with the wind toward home.

ABOUT THE AUTHOR

Ray Sipherd got an early start bringing characters to life. As a boy growing up in New York, he created a marionette troupe, wrote all the scripts, then toured the troupe on the local Cub Scout–library circuit, where he was even paid for his efforts. "Although payment then meant a piece of cake or whatever they were serving at the library," he says.

Ray Sipherd

Yet that first experience creating characters was a hint of things to come. In 1962, after graduating from Yale and working as a story editor at CBS Television in New York City, Sipherd became one of the original writers of the acclaimed children's television series *Sesame Street*. He wrote for the series for seventeen years, winning three Emmy awards along the way. He has also penned many children's books for the publishing division of *Sesame Street*, their titles as colorful as the personalities he's helped shape. *Down on the Farm with Grover* and *Big Bird's Animal Alphabet* are two examples. Says Sipherd, "People have often asked me how I've gotten my ideas for *Sesame Street*. I've told them, by knowing they're due Tuesday!"

The author's long list of writing credits includes more than thirty other television programs, among them an award-winning documentary, *Years Without Harvest*, which chronicled the plight of the farmer during the Depression. *The Courtship of Peggy McCoy* is his first novel, and, says Sipherd, he found it much different from the collaborative nature of television work. "Writing a novel is a lot like sailing a boat alone—you have to select your own course and destination."

As for that pleasant pastime, sailing, Sipherd has spent many a happy afternoon in a sailboat, like his own Peggy McCoy. He and his wife, Anne Marie, live in western Connecticut but frequently vacation on the New England coast. True to form, the author is already experimenting with several new writing projects.

ILLUSTRATORS

John Beswick: *Straight*

Bill Farnsworth: *No Roof But Heaven*

Dan Gonzalez: *The Evening News*

Guy Deel: *The Courtship of Peggy McCoy*

ACKNOWLEDGMENTS

Page 2: © 1989 by William A. Bake.
Page 505, lines 25–27: from "Long Ago (and Far
Away)," music by Jerome Kern and lyrics by
Ira Gershwin. Copyright © 1944 PolyGram
International Publishing, Inc. Copyright renewed.
International copyright secured. All rights
reserved. Used by permission.

Reader's Digest Fund for the Blind is publisher of the Large-Type Edition of *Reader's Digest*.
For subscription information about this magazine, please contact Reader's Digest Fund for
the Blind, Inc., Dept. 250, Pleasantville, N.Y. 10570.